THE BODLEY HEAD

HENRY JAMES

VOLUME X

THE PRINCESS CASAMASSIMA

WITH THE AUTHOR'S PREFACE AND
AN INTRODUCTION BY
LEON EDEL

THE BODLEY HEAD

LONDON   SYDNEY
TORONTO

Introduction © Leon Edel 1972
ISBN 0 370 10237 1
Printed and bound in Great Britain for
The Bodley Head Ltd
9 Bow Street, London, WC2E 7AL
by William Clowes & Sons Ltd, Beccles
Set in Linotype Plantin
First published 1886
This text is taken from the
New York Edition
This edition 1972

INTRODUCTION

The Princess Casamassima was written by Henry James during a season of unrest and riot in Europe, of dynamite and assassination. Its atmosphere is conspiratorial, its theme is revolution, its voice is a strange mixture of anguish and aestheticism. Critics have tried to show that James documented himself thoroughly in anarchism; others have called him politically naive; still others have attempted to show that he followed the headlines in *The Times*—for newspapers always see conspiracy very large. The facts are less complicated or controversial. Few in England in 1880 knew much about anarchism, 'scientific' revolution or trade union strategy, and James was as ignorant as the rest. He simply described what he observed; he made a virtue of his ignorance by writing of the plight of the working class out of his own sentience and empathy; and when he needed material he followed Emile Zola and 'got it up' after the manner of the French naturalists. He visited Millbank Prison in order to write the novel's first scene; he sat in working-class pubs listening to the voices of the jobless. And he recorded with accuracy the faltering impotence of men who wanted to act against their misery and didn't know how. If his book had originality it was in his refusal to use Dickensian pathos and sentimentality in dealing with the slum-dwellers. His novel was 'topical', and therefore unusual for the discoverer of the 'American girl' and her life abroad; and it survives many other works of this kind because of his transfiguring touch—perhaps too because he was among the first to understand, as he watched the turmoil around him, the psychology of 'power'.

James could hardly have imagined that his novel would be topical in our time. Yet we can draw a straight line from Joseph Conrad's use of the Greenwich Observatory bomb plot of 1894 in *The Secret Agent* to the recent 'Weatherman' explosion in Greenwich Village in New York, in which new-style activists, working out of their ignorance, blew themselves up. Perhaps some novelist at this moment is writing a fiction about that eerie episode. James gave us in his novel a certain archetype—the enraged young who seek to overthrow 'the system' but deep in their hearts would like to embrace it. Recent history is filled with leftists of the 1930s who now are writing their apologias.

That Henry James had looked closely at London poverty about which he wrote, and did not altogether draw on his Victorian predecessors, we know from his travel sketches first published in *Portraits of Places*. In them we find descriptions of the ragged slum children in the London parks, gin mills, prostitutes, an old woman 'lying prone in a puddle of whisky'. The English upper classes, the observant stranger from America wrote, were too refined, the lower classes were too miserable. In one article he told how he pushed his way into the Abbey for an Easter service amid an odour that was 'not that of incense', and mused on the population explosion of the time which made human life seem 'cheap'. It created 'pallid, stunted, misbegotten and in every way miserable figures' born of degradation and brutality in 'the slums and purlieus of this duskiest of modern Babylons'. Aware that he could not be witness to the activities of the would-be revolutionaries, he confined himself to the unhappiness of the workers. They were sufficiently visible, and audible if one listened; and he wrote down in his notebook the words he heard muttered over a pint of bitter, such as, 'What the hell am I to do with half a quid?' Trade unionism, as we know it, had not yet taken form. H. M. Hyndman founded the Social Democratic Federation in 1881; the Fabian Society was founded in 1884, the Independent Labour Party in 1893. James began his novel in 1884, and it was serialised during 1885. Prince Kropotkin, ideologist of anarchism, coming to London in 1881, felt there was 'no atmosphere to breathe in' among British workers. Returning in 1886, he was astonished at the 'animated' socialist movement that had begun to flourish. The five-year interval mentioned by Kropotkin fits the actual and fictional boundaries of *The Princess Casamassima* whose events were set in 1881. The novel, then, is only peripherally about revolutionary plotting; its substance is the 'general muddle' in England before socialism, particularly among the workers, their disaffection, their despair, their helplessness.

Hyacinth Robinson, James's young hero, a modest, small, earnest product of the slums, is, like many of the anarchists of the time, an artisan—a bookbinder. He is filled with hesitancies and bewilderment, with romantic revolutionary ardour and much aesthetic feeling. As in all naturalist novels —and James had talked with Zola about this—Hyacinth's fate is determined by heredity and environment. He is the bastard son of a French seamstress who had killed her lover, an English lord. It had been a *crime passionel*, and she had died in prison. Hyacinth joins the anarchists, and ultimately is ordered to assassinate a duke—in effect to re-enact his mother's crime on the level of social theory and class hatred rather than of passion. However he has been taken up by the Princess Casamassima (a kind of premature Lady Ottoline Morell) and has had a vision of the spacious life, but also 'idle, trifling, luxurious, yet at the same time pretentious leisure, the sort of thing that led people to invent false, humbugging duties because they had no real ones'. Then, inheriting a small sum of money from the dressmaker who had reared him, he goes to Paris and to Venice. Musing before palace fronts, frescoes, mosaics, churches, the artefacts of the ages, he finds his revolutionary ardour has evaporated. The natural son of a lord and a seamstress rejects the rebel in himself. 'What was supreme in his mind today was not the idea of how the society that surrounded him should be destroyed; it was, much more, the sense of the wonderful and precious things it had produced, of the fabric of beauty and power it had raised.' William Morris had written, 'What business have we with art at all, unless we all can share it?' Hyacinth's answer is that the arts cannot be democratised, the revolutionist 'wouldn't have the least feeling for this incomparable, abominable old Venice. He would cut up the ceilings of the Veronese in strips, so that everyone might have a little piece.' He adds, 'I don't want every one to have a little piece of anything and I have a great horror of that kind of invidious jealousy which is at the bottom of the idea of a redistribution.' James could not foresee that the process would be less simple: that revolutions would destroy art by bureaucracy and by harnessing it to the state.

This is the conflict James sets before us; above all he invites us to understand the loneliness of Hyacinth in his dilemma, and his discovery that so long as he is militant and aggressive he can be 'used', but that the moment he entertains doubt he is alone. No part of this novel is more perceptive and painful than the vision we have of the young bookbinder wandering about in London without a confessional; his friends do not want to listen. The great Princess, a 'parlour Bolshevik' before her time, is absorbed by her 'radicalism' and the characters she meets from the periphery of conspiracy; she is now interested in Hyacinth's friend, Paul Muniment, a calculating, cold, secretive young man, the sort who ends up as a labour strategist. Millicent Henning, the cockney girl of his childhood, is busy with the shoddy Captain Sholto, in her desire to rise above her station. Hyacinth has nowhere to turn. He senses at this point that idealists can also be egotists, that revolutionaries can be more concerned with winning power than reforming the world. He ends up a kind of water-colour Hamlet, too aesthetic to be a convincing rebel, possessed of too much feeling to be ruthless.

Hyacinth's fate is at the centre of the novel; and we might properly ask why Henry James named the book instead after the Princess Casamassima. The answer belongs to the mysteries of art—the predicament of an author in search of his characters. James himself wondered why he had felt a compelling need to revive the Princess who had appeared in his first novel, *Roderick Hudson*, as Christina Light. He speculated that perhaps he had not 'completely recorded' her and needed to finish the job. At any rate she is now ten years older, world-weary and filled with a *nostalgie de la boue*; she seems to like 'revolutionary politics of a hole-in-corner-sort', having sincere melioristic feeling, but also a need to skirt danger, to flirt with the odd and idiosyncratic; in a word she is a very bored woman who also enjoys the sense of power, vicarious to be sure, which radicals, dreaming their utopias, give her. James had loved Christina when he created her, and he had tried to make her a creature of impetuosity and will, of caprice and passion and indifference. She is not able to like men who fall in love with her; she pursues men indifferent to her: they offer her a sense of conquest. She seems the opposite of Hyacinth, but is really quite as anxious and restless. Both crave worlds not their own. Both reach out to one another with the recognition that they are displaced spirits—both natural children, both nursing old grievances. Hyacinth is simply not passionate enough, nor independent enough, for so passionate and indifferent a woman. Christina wants men of tougher fibre.

The Princess Casamassima is filled with an uncommon amount of rhetoric for a Henry James novel, quite as much as its predecessor, The Bostonians, which also dealt with reformers. James believes that the world's iniquities cannot be abolished by abolishing the civilisation which has harboured them. Shaw and Wells would make art didactic—the playwright on behalf of socialism, the novelist on behalf of the utopias of his mind. Yet James's novel on a social theme seems less dated than some of their works, perhaps because he preached the supremacy of human awareness rather than of specific dogmas, and like Proust believed in the survival of art. To those who would scoff at James, so involved in upper-class life, trying to understand the nature of poverty, he had his answer. Hyacinth is 'aware the people were direfully wretched—more aware, it often seemed to him, than they themselves were'. Poverty can brutalise its victims into insensibility. This James understood. It would be left to writers like Gissing or Wells to picture lower-class life from the 'inside'. And yet there is a value in James's detachment —he writes out of a genuine love for his people, whereas the

victims of the class structure wrote often out of old in-
dignities and indignations, and with a strong animus.

In its rhetoric, its form, its variety and number of small
characters, its sketches of 'low life', *The Princess Casamassima* is James's most Victorian novel. He is closer in it
to Dickens and Thackeray than in any of his other works.
Miss Pynsent (Pinnie), the dressmaker who rears Hyacinth,
Rosy Muniment, the sharp-tongued little cripple (whose
brother is regarded as a future labour leader) who knows all
London from her bed of invalidism, Eustache Poupin and
the émigrés from European revolutions, Mr Vetch, the
fiddler, the strange and unpleasant social dilettante, Sholto,
the sturdy Millicent 'enning, most lovable of James's cock-
neys, Lady Aurora, who emits the light of charity whereas
Christina Light pierces and destroys—these characters are
seen through kind and affectionate eyes, as human beings,
not as caricatures or social 'types' designed to illustrate a
thesis. We move in this novel in a series of perpetual Sundays, in the era of the 70-hour week—the one day the
workers could go to the parks. And then, in the background,
there are the gregariousness and loneliness of London, the
damp smell of clothes and of beer in the 'Sun and Moon',
the conspiratorial pub, the crepuscular ambiance of dirt and
dinginess.

Few naturalist novels have survived their time. They are
too prosaic, wedded too closely to crusade and theory and to
propaganda; and they tend to be excessively 'documentary'.
The Princess was saved by James's infusion of the poetry of
suffering and of longing, his sense of 'caring' for people
rather than for doctrine, and his understanding of how even
the downtrodden use their fellows to climb to power. This
will explain why a sympathetic reader may want to place it

on the shelf of fiction beside *Le Rouge et le Noir*, *Virgin Soil*, *L'Education Sentimentale*, *The Secret Agent*, *Under Western Eyes* or *The Heart of the Matter*. It belongs with these reports of the human condition.

LEON EDEL

PREFACE

THE SIMPLEST account of the origin of *The Princess Casamassima* is, I think, that this fiction proceeded quite directly, during the first year of a long residence in London, from the habit and the interest of walking the streets. I walked a great deal—for exercise, for amusement, for acquisition, and above all I always walked home at the evening's end, when the evening had been spent elsewhere, as happened more often than not; and as to do this was to receive many impressions, so the impressions worked and sought an issue, so the book after a time was born. It is a fact that, as I look back, the attentive exploration of London, the assault directly made by the great city upon an imagination quick to react, fully explains a large part of it. There is a minor element that refers itself to another source, of which I shall presently speak; but the prime idea was unmistakeably the ripe round fruit of perambulation. One walked of course with one's eyes greatly open, and I hasten to declare that such a practice, carried on for a long time and over a considerable space, positively provokes, all round, a mystic solicitation, the urgent appeal, on the part of everything, to be interpreted and, so far as may be, reproduced. 'Subjects' and situations, character and history, the tragedy and comedy of life, are things of which the common air, in such conditions, seems pungently to taste; and to a mind curious, before the human scene, of meanings and revelations the great grey Babylon easily becomes, on its face, a garden bristling with an immense illustrative flora. Possible stories, presentable figures, rise from the thick jungle as the observer moves, fluttering up like startled game, and before he knows it indeed he has fairly to guard himself against the brush of importunate wings. He goes on as with his head in a cloud of humming presences—especially during the younger, the initiatory time, the fresh, the sharply-apprehensive months or years, more or less numerous. We use our material up, we use up even the thick tribute of the London streets—if perception and attention but sufficiently light our steps. But I think of them as lasting, for myself, quite sufficiently long; I think of them as even still—dreadfully changed for the worse in respect to any romantic idea as I find them—breaking out on occasion into eloquence, throwing out deep notes from their vast vague murmur.

There was a moment at any rate when they offered me no image more vivid than that of some individual sensitive nature of fine mind, some small obscure intelligent creature whose education should have been almost wholly derived from them, capable of profiting by all the civilisation, all the accumulations to which they testify, yet condemned to see these things only from outside—in mere quickened consideration, mere wistfulness and envy and despair. It seemed to me I had only to imagine such a spirit intent enough and troubled enough, and to place it in presence of the comings and goings, the great gregarious company, of the more fortunate than himself—all on the scale on which London could show them—to get possession of an interesting theme. I arrived so at the history of little Hyacinth Robinson—he sprang up for me out of the London pavement. To find his possible adventure interesting I had only to conceive his watching the same public show, the same innumerable appearances, I had watched myself, and of his watching very much as I had watched; save indeed for one little difference. This difference would be that so far as all the swarming facts should speak of freedom and ease, knowledge and power, money, opportunity and satiety, he should be able to revolve round them but at the most respectful of distances and with every door of approach shut in his face. For one's self, all conveniently, there had been doors that opened—opened into light and warmth and cheer, into good and charming relations; and if the place as a whole lay heavy on one's consciousness there was yet always for relief this implication of one's own lucky share of the freedom and ease, lucky acquaintance with the number of lurking springs

at light pressure of which particular vistas would begin to
recede, great lighted, furnished, peopled galleries, sending
forth gusts of agreeable sound.

That main happy sense of the picture was always there
and that retreat from the general grimness never forbidden;
whereby one's own relation to the mere formidable mass and
weight of things was eased off and adjusted. One learned
from an early period what it might be to know London in
such a way as that—an immense and interesting discipline,
an education on terms mostly convenient and delightful.
But what would be the effect of the other way, of having so
many precious things perpetually in one's eyes, yet of missing them all for any closer knowledge, and of the confine-
ment of closer knowledge entirely to matters with which a
connexion, however intimate, couldn't possibly pass for a
privilege? Truly, of course, there are London mysteries
(dense categories of dark arcana) for every spectator, and
it's in a degree an exclusion and a state of weakness to be
without experience of the meaner conditions, the lower manners and types, the general sordid struggle, the weight of
the burden of labour, the ignorance, the misery and the vice.
With such matters as those my tormented young man would
have had contact—they would have formed, fundamentally,
from the first, his natural and immediate London. But the
reward of a romantic curiosity would be the question of
what the total assault, that of the world of his work-a-day
life and the world of his divination and his envy together,
would have made of him, and what in especial he would
have made of them. As tormented, I say, I thought of him,
and that would be the point—if one could only see him feel
enough to be interesting without his feeling so much as not
to be natural.

This in fact I have ever found rather terribly the point—
that the figures in any picture, the agents in any drama, are
interesting only in proportion as they feel their respective
situations; since the consciousness, on their part, of the
complication exhibited forms for us their link of connexion
with it. But there are degrees of feeling—the muffled, the

faint, the just sufficient, the barely intelligent, as we may say; and the acute, the intense, the complete, in a word—the power to be finely aware and richly responsible. It is those moved in this latter fashion who 'get most' out of all that happens to them and who in so doing enable us, as readers of their record, as participators by a fond attention, also to get most. Their being finely aware—as Hamlet and Lear, say, are finely aware—*makes* absolutely the intensity of their adventure, gives the maximum of sense to what befalls them. We care, our curiosity and our sympathy care, comparatively little for what happens to the stupid, the coarse and the blind; care for it, and for the effects of it, at the most as helping to precipitate what happens to the more deeply wondering, to the really sentient. Hamlet and Lear are surrounded, amid their complications, by the stupid and the blind, who minister in all sorts of ways to their recorded fate. Persons of markedly limited sense would, on such a principle as that, play a part in the career of my tormented youth; but he wouldn't be of markedly limited sense himself—he would note as many things and vibrate to as many occasions as I might venture to make him.

There wouldn't moreover simply be the question of his suffering—of which we might soon get enough; there would be the question of what, all beset and all perceptive, he should thus adventurously do, thus dream and hazard and attempt. The interest of the attitude and the act would be the actor's imagination and vision of them, together with the nature and degree of their felt return upon him. So the intelligent creature would be required and so some picture of his intelligence involved. The picture of an intelligence appears for the most part, it is true, a dead weight for the reader of the English novel to carry, this reader having so often the wondrous property of caring for the displayed tangle of human relation without caring for its intelligibility. The teller of a story is primarily, none the less, the listener to it, the reader of it, too; and, having needed thus to make it out, distinctly, on the crabbed page of life, to disengage it from the rude human character and the more or less gothic text in which it has been packed away, the very essence of his affair has been the *imputing* of intelligence. The basis of his attention has been that such and such an imbroglio has got started—on the page of life—because of something that some one has felt and more or less understood.

I recognise at the same time, and in planning *The Princess Casamassima* felt it highly important to recognise, the danger of filling too full any supposed and above all any obviously limited vessel of consciousness. If persons either tragically or comically embroiled with life allow us the comic or tragic value of their embroilment in proportion as their struggle is a measured and directed one, it is strangely true, none the less, that beyond a certain point they are spoiled for us by this carrying of a due light. They may carry too much of it for our credence, for our compassion, for our derision. They may be shown as knowing too much and feeling too much— not certainly for their remaining remarkable, but for their remaining 'natural' and typical, for their having the needful communities with our own precious liability to fall into traps and be bewildered. It seems probable that if we were never bewildered there would never be a story to tell about us; we should partake of the superior nature of the all-knowing immortals whose annals are dreadfully dull so long as flurried humans are not, for the positive relief of bored Olympians, mixed up with them. Therefore it is that the wary reader for the most part warns the novelist against making his characters too *interpretative* of the muddle of fate, or in other words too divinely, too priggishly clever. 'Give us plenty of bewilderment,' this monitor seems to say, 'so long as there is plenty of slashing out in the bewilderment too. But don't, we beseech you, give us too much intelligence! for intelligence—well, *endangers*; endangers not perhaps the slasher himself, but the very slashing, the subject-matter of any self-respecting story. It opens up too many considerations, possibilities, issues; it *may* lead the slasher into dreary realms where slashing somehow fails and falls to the ground.'

That is well reasoned on the part of the reader, who can

in spite of it never have an idea—or his earnest discriminations would come to him less easily—of the extreme difficulty, for the painter of the human mixture, of reproducing
that mixture aright. 'Give us in the persons represented, the
subjects of the bewilderment (that bewilderment without
which there would be no question of an issue or of the fact
of suspense, prime implications in any story) as much experience as possible, but keep down the terms in which you
report that experience, because we only understand the very
simplest': such in effect are the words in which the novelist
constantly hears himself addressed, such the plea made him
by the would-be victims of his spell on behalf of that
sovereign principle the economy of interest, a principle as to
which their instinct is justly strong. He listens anxiously to
the charge—nothing can exceed his own solicitude for an
economy of interest; but feels himself all in presence of an
abyss of ambiguities, the mutual accommodations in which
the reader wholly leaves to him. Experience, as I see it, is
our apprehension and our measure of what happens to us as
social creatures—any intelligent report of which has to be
based on that apprehension. The picture of the exposed and
entangled state is what is required, and there are certainly
always plenty of grounds for keeping down the complexities
of a picture. A picture it still has to be, however, and by
that condition has to deal effectually with its subject, so that
the simple device of more and more keeping down may well
not see us quite to our end or even quite to our middle. One
suggested way of keeping down, for instance, is not to attribute feeling, or feelings, to persons who wouldn't in all
probability have had any to speak of. The less space, within
the frame of the picture, their feelings take up the more
space is left for their doings—a fact that may at first seem
to make for a refinement of economy.

All of which is charming—yet would be infinitely more
so if here at once ambiguity didn't yawn; the unreality of the
sharp distinction, where the interest of observation is at
stake, between doing and feeling. In the immediate field of
life, for action, for application, for getting through a job,

nothing may so much matter perhaps as the descent of a suspended weight on this, that or the other spot, with all its subjective concomitants quite secondary and irrelevant. But the affair of the painter is not the immediate, it is the reflected field of life, the realm not of application, but of *appreciation*—a truth that makes our measure of effect altogether different. My report of people's experience—my report as a 'story-teller'—is essentially my appreciation of it, and there is no 'interest' for me in what my hero, my heroine or any one else does save through that admirable process. As soon as I begin to appreciate simplification is imperilled: the sharply distinguished parts of any adventure, any case of endurance and performance, melt together as an appeal. I then see their 'doing', that of the persons just mentioned, as, immensely, their feeling, their feeling as their doing; since I can have none of the conveyed sense and taste of their situation without becoming intimate with them. I can't be intimate without that sense and taste, and I can't appreciate save by intimacy, any more than I can report save by a projected light. Intimacy with a man's specific behaviour, with his given case, is desperately certain to make us see it as a whole—in which event arbitrary limitations of our vision lose whatever beauty they may on occasion have pretended to. What a man thinks and what he feels are the history and the character of what he does; on all of which things the logic of intensity rests. Without intensity where is vividness, and without vividness where is presentability? If I have called the most general state of one's most exposed and assaulted figures the state of bewilderment—the condition for instance on which Thackeray so much insists in the interest of *his* exhibited careers, the condition of a humble heart, a bowed head, a patient wonder, a suspended judgement, before the 'awful will' and the mysterious decrees of Providence—so it is rather witless to talk of merely getting rid of that displayed mode of reaction, one of the oft-encountered, one of the highly recommended, categories of feeling.

The whole thing comes to depend thus on the *quality* of

bewilderment characteristic of one's creature, the quality involved in the given case or supplied by one's data. There are doubtless many such qualities, ranging from vague and crepuscular to sharpest and most critical; and we have but to imagine one of these latter to see how easily—from the moment it gets its head at all—it may insist on playing a part. There we have then at once a case of feeling, of ever so many possible feelings, stretched across the scene like an attached thread on which the pearls of interest are strung. There are threads shorter and less tense, and I am far from implying that the minor, the coarser and less fruitful forms and degrees of moral reaction, as we may conveniently call it, may not yield lively results. They have their subordinate, comparative, illustrative human value—that appeal of the witless which is often so penetrating. Verily even, I think, no 'story' is possible without its fools—as most of the fine painters of life, Shakespeare, Cervantes and Balzac, Fielding, Scott, Thackeray, Dickens, George Meredith, George Eliot, Jane Austen, have abundantly felt. At the same time I confess I never see the *leading* interest of any human hazard but in a consciousness (on the part of the moved and moving creature) subject to fine intensification and wide enlargement. It is as mirrored in that consciousness that the gross fools, the headlong fools, the fatal fools play their part for us—they have much less to show us in themselves. The troubled life mostly at the centre of our subject—whatever our subject, for the artistic hour, happens to be—embraces them and deals with them for its amusement and its anguish: they are apt largely indeed, on a near view, to be all the cause of its trouble. This means, exactly, that the person capable of feeling in the given case more than another of what is to be felt for it, and so serving in the highest degree to *record* it dramatically and objectively, is the only sort of person on whom we can count not to betray, to cheapen or, as we say, give away, the value and beauty of the thing. By so much as the affair matters *for* some such individual, by so much do we get the best there is of it, and by so much as it falls within the scope of a denser and duller, a more vulgar and more shallow capacity, do we get a picture dim and meagre.

The great chroniclers have clearly always been aware of this; they have at least always either placed a mind of some sort—in the sense of a reflecting and colouring medium—in possession of the general adventure (when the latter has not been purely epic, as with Scott, say, as with old Dumas and with Zola); or else paid signally, as to the interest created, for their failure to do so. We may note moreover in passing that this failure is in almost no case intentional or part of a plan, but has sprung from their limited curiosity, their short conception of the particular sensibility projected. Edgar of Ravenswood for instance, visited by the tragic tempest of *The Bride of Lammermoor*, has a black cloak and hat and feathers more than he has a mind; just as Hamlet, while equally sabled and draped and plumed, while at least equally romantic, has yet a mind still more than he has a costume. The situation represented is that Ravenswood loves Lucy Ashton through dire difficulty and danger, and that she in the same way loves him; but the relation so created between them is by this neglect of the 'feeling' question never shown us as primarily taking place. It is shown only in its secondary, its confused and disfigured aspects—where, however, luckily, it is presented with great romantic good faith. The thing has nevertheless paid for its deviation, as I say, by a sacrifice of intensity; the centre of the subject is empty and the development pushed off, all round, toward the frame—which is, so to speak, beautifully rich and curious. But I mention that relation to each other of the appearances in a particular work only as a striking negative case; there are in the connexion I have glanced at plenty of striking positive ones. It is very true that Fielding's hero in *Tom Jones* is but as 'finely', that is but as intimately, bewildered as a young man of great health and spirits may be when he hasn't a grain of imagination: the point to be made is, at all events, that his sense of bewilderment obtains altogether on the comic, never on the tragic plane. He has so much 'life' that it amounts, for the effect of comedy and application of satire, almost to his having a mind, that is to his having reactions and a full consciousness; besides which his author—*he* handsomely possessed of a mind—has such an amplitude of reflection for him and round him that we see him through the mellow air of Fielding's fine old moralism, fine old humour and fine old style, which somehow really enlarge, make every one and every thing important.

All of which furthers my remarking how much I have been interested, on reading *The Princess Casamassima* over, to recognise my sense, sharp from far back, that clearness and concreteness constantly depend, for any pictorial whole, on some *concentrated* individual notation of them. That notation goes forward here in the mind of little Hyacinth, immensely quickened by the fact of its so mattering to his very life what he does make of things: which passion of intelligence is, as I have already hinted, precisely his highest value for our curiosity and our sympathy. Yet if his highest it is not at all his only one, since the truth for 'a young man in a book' by no means entirely resides in his being either exquisitely sensitive or shiningly clever. It resides in some such measure of these things as may consort with the fine measure of other things too—with that of the other faces of his situation and character. If he's too sensitive and too clever for *them*, if he knows more than is likely or natural—for *him*—it's as if he weren't at all, as if he were false and impossible. Extreme and attaching always the difficulty of fixing at a hundred points the place where one's impelled *bonhomme* may feel enough and 'know' enough— or be in the way of learning enough—for his maximum dramatic value without feeling and knowing too much for his minimum verisimilitude, his proper fusion with the fable. This is the charming, the tormenting, the eternal little matter *to be made right*, in all the weaving of silver threads and tapping on golden nails; and I should take perhaps too fantastic a comfort—I mean were not the comforts of the artist just of the raw essence of fantasy—in any glimpse of such achieved rightnesses, whether in my own work or that of others. In no work whatever, doubtless, are they the felicities the most frequent; but they have so inherent a price that even the traceable attempt at them, wherever met, sheds, I think, a fine influence about.

I have for example a weakness of sympathy with that constant effort of George Eliot's which plays through Adam Bede and Felix Holt and Tito Melema, through Daniel Deronda and through Lydgate in *Middlemarch*, through Maggie Tulliver, through Romola, though Dorothea Brooke and Gwendolen Harleth; the effort to show their adventures and their history—the author's subject-matter all—as determined by their feelings and the nature of their minds. Their emotions, their stirred intelligence, their moral consciousness, become thus, by sufficiently charmed perusal, our own very adventure. The creator of Deronda and of Romola is charged, I know, with having on occasion—as in dealing with those very celebrities themselves—left the figure, the concrete man and woman, too abstract by reason of the quantity of soul employed; but such mischances, where imagination and humour still keep them company, often have an interest that is wanting to agitations of the mere surface or to those that may be only taken for granted. I should even like to give myself the pleasure of retracing from one of my own productions to another the play of a like instinctive disposition, of catching in the fact, at one point after another, from *Roderick Hudson* to *The Golden Bowl*, that provision for interest which consists in placing advantageously, placing right in the middle of the light, the most polished of possible mirrors of the subject. Rowland Mallet, in *Roderick Hudson*, is exactly such a mirror, not a bit autobiographic or formally 'first person' though he be, and I might exemplify the case through a long list, through the nature of such a 'mind' even as the all-objective Newman in *The American*, through the thickly-peopled imagination of Isabel Archer in *The Portrait of a Lady* (her imagination positively the deepest depth of her imbroglio) down to such unmistakeable examples as that of Merton Densher in *The Wings of the Dove*, that of Lambert Strether in *The Ambassadors* (*he* a mirror verily of miracu-

lous silver and quite pre-eminent, I think, for the connexion)
and that of the Prince in the first half and that of the Princess in the second half of *The Golden Bowl*. I should note
the extent to which these persons are, so far as their other
passions permit, intense *perceivers*, all, of their respective
predicaments, and I should go on from them to fifty other
examples; even to the divided Vanderbank of *The Awkward
Age*, the extreme pinch of whose romance is the vivacity
in him, to his positive sorrow and loss, of the state of being
aware; even to scanted Fleda Vetch in *The Spoils of Poyn-
ton*, through whose own delicate vision of everything so
little of the human value of her situation is wasted for us;
even to the small recording governess confronted with the
horrors of *The Turn of the Screw* and to the innocent child
patching together all ineffectually those of *What Maisie
Knew*; even in short, since I may name so few cases, to the
disaffected guardian of an overgrown legend in *The Birth-
place*, to the luckless fine artist of *The Next Time*, trying to
despoil himself, for a 'hit' and bread and butter, of his fatal
fineness, to blunt the tips of his intellectual fingers, and to
the hapless butler Brooksmith, ruined by good talk, disquali-
fied for common domestic service by the beautiful growth
of his habit of quiet attention, his faculty of appreciation.
But though this demonstration of a rooted vice—since a
vice it would appear mainly accounted—might yield amusement, the examples referred to must await their turn.

I had had for a long time well before me, at any rate, my
small obscure but ardent observer of the 'London world', saw
him roam and wonder and yearn, saw all the unanswered
questions and baffled passions that might ferment in him
—once he should be made both sufficiently thoughtful and
sufficiently 'disinherited'; but this image, however interesting, was of course not by itself a progression, an action,
didn't by itself make a drama. I got my action however—
failing which one has nothing—under the prompt sense
that the state of feeling I was concerned with might develop
and beget another state, might return at a given moment,
and with the greatest vivacity, on itself. To see this was

really to feel one's subject swim into one's ken, especially
after a certain other ingenious connexion had been made for
it. I find myself again recalling, and with the possible 'fun'
of it reviving too, how I recognised, as revealed and prescribed, the particular complexion, profession and other
conditions of my little presumptuous adventurer, with his
combination of intrinsic fineness and fortuitous adversity,
his small cluster of 'dingy' London associations and the
swelling spirit in him which was to be the field of his strange
experience. Accessible through his imagination, as I have
hinted, to a thousand provocations and intimations, he
would become most acquainted with destiny in the form of
a lively inward revolution. His being jealous of all the ease
of life of which he tastes so little, and, bitten, under this
exasperation, with an aggressive, vindictive, destructive
social faith, his turning to 'treasons, stratagems and spoils'
might be as vivid a picture as one chose, but would move to
pity and terror only by the aid of some deeper complication,
some imposed and formidable issue.

The complication most interesting then would be that he
should fall in love with the beauty of the world, actual order
and all, at the moment of his most feeling and most hating
the famous 'iniquity of its social arrangements'; so that his
position as an irreconcilable pledged enemy to it, thus rendered false by something more personal than his opinions
and his vows, becomes the sharpest of his torments. To make
it a torment that really matters, however, he must have got
practically involved, specifically committed to the stand he
has, under the pressure of more knowledge, found impossible; out of which has come for him the deep dilemma of
the disillusioned and repentant conspirator. He has thrown
himself into the more than 'shady' underworld of militant
socialism, he has undertaken to play a part—a part that with
the drop of his exasperation and the growth, simply expressed, of his taste, is out of all tune with his passion, at
any cost, for life itself, the life, whatever it be, that surrounds
him. Dabbling deeply in revolutionary politics of a hole-and-
corner sort, he would be 'in' up to his neck, and with that

precarious part of him particularly involved, so that his tergiversation is the climax of his adventure. What was essential with this was that he should have a social—not less than a socialist—connexion, find a door somehow open to him in the appeased and civilised state, into that warmer glow of things he is precisely to help to undermine. To look for this necessary connexion was for me to meet it suddenly in the form of that extremely *disponible* figure of Christina Light whom I had ten years before found left on my hands at the conclusion of *Roderick Hudson*. She had for so long, in the vague limbo of those ghosts we have conjured but not exorcised, been looking for a situation, awaiting a niche and a function.

I shall not pretend to trace the steps and stages by which the imputability of a future to that young woman—which was like the act of clothing her chilled and patient nakedness —had for its prime effect to plant her in my little book-binder's path. Nothing would doubtless beckon us on further, with a large leisure, than such a chance to study the obscure law under which certain of a novelist's characters, more or less honourably buried, revive for him by a force or a whim of their own and 'walk' round his house of art like haunting ghosts, feeling for the old doors they knew, fumbling at stiff latches and pressing their pale faces, in the outer dark, to lighted windows. I mistrust them, I confess, in general; my sense of a really expressed character is that it shall have originally so tasted of the ordeal of service as to feel no disposition to yield again to the strain. Why should the Princess of the climax of *Roderick Hudson* still have made her desire felt, unless in fact to testify that she had not been—for what she was—completely recorded? To continue in evidence, that had struck me from far back as her natural passion; in evidence at any price, not consenting to be laid away with folded hands in the pasteboard tomb, the doll's box, to which we usually relegate the spent puppet after the fashion of a recumbent worthy on the slab of a sepulchral monument. I was to see this, after all, in the event, as the fruit of a restless vanity: Christina had felt herself, known herself, striking, in the earlier connexion, and couldn't resign herself not to strike again. Her pressure then was not to be resisted—sharply as the question might come up of why she should pretend to strike just *there*. I shall not attempt to answer it with reasons (one can never tell everything); it was enough that I could recognise her claim to have travelled far—far from where I had last left her: that, one felt, was in character—that was what she naturally *would* have done. Her prime note had been an aversion to the *banal*, and nothing could be of an effect less *banal*, I judged, than her intervention in the life of a dingy little London bookbinder whose sensibility, whose flow of opinions on 'public questions' in especial, should have been poisoned at the source.

She would be world-weary—that was another of her notes; and the extravagance of her attitude in these new relations would have its root and its apparent logic in her need to feel freshly about something or other—it might scarce matter what. She can, or she believes she can, feel freshly about the 'people' and their wrongs and their sorrows and their perpetual smothered ferment; for these things are furthest removed from those others among which she has hitherto tried to make her life. That was to a certainty where I was to have looked for her—quite *off* and away (once granted the wisdom of listening to her anew at all): therefore Hyacinth's encounter with her could pass for natural, and it was fortunately to be noted that she was to serve for his experience in quite another and a more 'leading' sense than any in which he was to serve for hers. I confess I was not averse—such are the possible weaknesses of the artist in face of high difficulties—to feeling that if his appearance of consistency were obtained I might at least try to remain comparatively at my ease about hers. I may add moreover that the resuscitation of Christina (and, on the minor scale, of the Prince and of Madame Grandoni) put in a strong light for me the whole question, for the romancer, of 'going on with a character': as Balzac first of all systematically went on, as Thackeray, as Trollope, as Zola all more or less ingeniously went on. I was to find no small savour in the reflexions so precipitated; though I may treat myself here only to this remark about them—that the revivalist impulse on the fond writer's part strikes me as one thing, a charmingly conceivable thing, but the effect of a free indulgence in it (effect, that is, on the nerves of the reader) is, for twenty rather ineffable reasons, quite another.

I remember at any rate feeling myself all in possession of little Hyacinth's consistency, as I have called it, down at Dover during certain weeks that were none too remotely precedent to the autumn of 1885 and the appearance, in the 'Atlantic Monthly' again, of the first chapters of the story. There were certain sunny, breezy balconied rooms at the quieter end of the Esplanade of that cheerful castle-crested little town—now infinitely perturbed by gigantic 'harbour works', but then only faded and over-soldiered and all pleasantly and humbly submissive to the law that snubs in due course the presumption of flourishing resorts—to which I had already more than once had recourse in hours of quickened industry and which, though much else has been swept away, still archaically exist. To have lately noted this again from the old benched and asphalted walk by the sea, the twinkling Channel beyond which on occasion the opposite coast of France used to gleam as an incident of the charming tendency of the whole prospect (immediate picture and fond design alike) amusingly to *shine*, was somehow to taste afresh, and with a certain surprise, the odd quality of that original confidence that the parts of my plan *would* somehow hang together. I may wonder at my confidence now—given the extreme, the very particular truth and 'authority' required at so many points; but to wonder is to live back gratefully into the finer reasons of things, with all the detail of harsh application and friction (that there must have been) quite happily blurred and dim. The finest of reasons—I mean for the sublime confidence I speak of— was that I felt in full *personal* possession of my matter; this really seemed the fruit of direct experience. My scheme called for the suggested nearness (to all our apparently ordered life) of some sinister anarchic underworld, heaving in its pain, its power and its hate; a presentation not of sharp particulars, but of loose appearances, vague motions and sounds and symptoms, just perceptible presences and general looming possibilities. To have adopted the scheme was to have had to meet the question of one's 'notes', over the whole ground, the question of what, in such directions, one had 'gone into' and how far one had gone; and to have answered that question—to one's own satisfaction at least— was truly to see one's way.

My notes then, on the much-mixed world of my hero's both overt and covert consciousness, were exactly my gath- ered impressions and stirred perceptions, the deposit in my working imagination of all my visual and all my constructive sense of London. The very plan of my book had in fact directly confronted me with the rich principle of the Note, and was to do much to clear up, once for all, my practical view of it. If one was to undertake to tell tales and to report with truth on the human scene, it could be but because 'notes' had been from the cradle the ineluctable consequence of one's greatest inward energy: to take them was as natural as to look, to think, to feel, to recognise, to remember, as to perform any act of understanding. The play of the energy had been continuous and couldn't change; what changed was only the objects and situations pressing the spring of it. Notes had been in other words the things one couldn't *not* take, and the prime result of all fresh experience was to remind one of that. I have endeavoured to characterise the peremptory fashion in which my fresh experience of London —the London of the habitual observer, the preoccupied painter, the pedestrian prowler—reminded me; an admoni- tion that represented, I think, the sum of my investigations. I recall pulling no wires, knocking at no closed doors, apply- ing for no 'authentic' information; but I recall also on the other hand the practice of never missing an opportunity to add a drop, however small, to the bucket of my impressions or to renew my sense of being able to dip into it. To haunt the great city and by this habit to penetrate it, imaginatively, in as many places as possible—*that* was to be informed, *that* was to pull wires, *that* was to open doors, *that* positively was to groan at times under the weight of one's accumulations.

Face to face with the idea of Hyacinth's subterraneous politics and occult affiliations, I recollect feeling, in short, that I might well be ashamed if, with my advantages—and there wasn't a street, a corner, an hour, of London that was not an advantage—I shouldn't be able to piece together a proper semblance of all the odd parts of his life. There was always of course the chance that the propriety might be challenged—challenged by readers of a knowledge greater than mine. Yet knowledge, after all, of what? My vision of the aspects I more or less fortunately rendered *was*, exactly, my knowledge. If I made my appearances live, what was this but the utmost one could do with them? Let me at the same time not deny that, in answer to probable ironic reflexions on the full licence for sketchiness and vagueness and dimness taken indeed by my picture, I had to bethink myself in advance of a defence of my 'artistic position'. Shouldn't I find it in the happy contention that the value I wished most to render and the effect I wished most to produce were precisely those of our not knowing, of society's not knowing, but only guessing and suspecting and trying to ignore, what 'goes on' irreconcileably, subversively, beneath the vast smug surface? I couldn't deal with that positive quantity for itself—my subject had another too exacting side; but I might perhaps show the social ear as on occasion applied to the ground, or catch some gust of the hot breath that I had at many an hour seemed to see escape and hover. What it all came back to was, no doubt, something like *this* wisdom—that if you haven't, for fiction, the root of the matter in you, haven't the sense of life and the penetrating imagination, you are a fool in the very presence of the revealed and assured; but that if you *are* so armed you are not really helpless, not without your resource, even before mysteries abysmal.

HENRY JAMES

BOOK FIRST

THE PRINCESS CASAMASSIMA

I

'Oh yes, I dare say I can find the child, if you would like to see him,' Miss Pynsent said; she had a fluttered wish to assent to every suggestion made by her visitor, whom she regarded as a high and rather terrible personage. To look for the little boy she came out of her small parlour, which she had been ashamed to exhibit in so untidy a state, with paper 'patterns' lying about on the furniture and snippings of stuff scattered over the carpet—she came out of this somewhat stuffy sanctuary, dedicated at once to social inter-course and to the ingenious art to which her life had been devoted, and, opening the house-door, turned her eyes up and down the little street. It would presently be tea-time, and she knew that at that solemn hour Hyacinth narrowed the circle of his wanderings. She was anxious and impatient and in a fever of excitement and complacency, not wanting to keep Mrs Bowerbank waiting, though she sat there, heavily and consideringly, as if she meant to stay; and won-dering not a little whether the object of her quest would have a dirty face. Mrs Bowerbank had intimated so defi-nitely that she thought it remarkable on Miss Pynsent's part to have taken care of him gratuitously for so many years, that the humble dressmaker, whose imagination took flights about every one but herself and who had never been con-scious of an exemplary benevolence, suddenly aspired to appear, throughout, as devoted to the child as she had struck her large, grave guest as being, and felt how much she should like him to come in fresh and frank and looking as pretty as he sometimes did. Miss Pynsent, who blinked con-fusedly as she surveyed the outer prospect, was very much flushed, partly with the agitation of what Mrs Bowerbank had told her and partly because, when she offered that lady a drop of refreshment at the end of so long an expedition, she had said she couldn't think of touching anything unless Miss Pynsent would keep her company. The 'cheffoneer', as Amanda was always careful to call it, yielded up a small bottle which, formerly containing eau-de-cologne, now exhibited half a pint of a rich gold-coloured liquid. Miss Pynsent was very delicate; she lived on tea and watercress and kept the little bottle in the cheffoneer only for great emergencies. She didn't like hot brandy and water with a lump or two of sugar, but she partook of half a tumbler on the present occasion, which was of a highly exceptional kind. At this time of day the boy was often planted in front of the little sweet-shop on the other side of the street, an establishment where periodical literature, as well as tough toffy and hard lollipops, was dispensed and where song-books and pictorial sheets were attractively exhibited in the small-paned dirty window. He used to stand there for half an hour at a time and spell out the first page of the romances in the *Family Herald* and the *London Journal*, where he particularly admired the obligatory illustration in which the noble characters (they were always of the highest birth) were presented to the carnal eye. When he had a penny he spent only a fraction of it on stale sugar-candy; for the remaining halfpenny he always bought a ballad with a vivid woodcut at the top. Now, however, he was not at his post of contemplation, nor was he visible anywhere to Miss Pynsent's impatient glance.

'Millicent 'Enning, tell me quickly, have you seen my child?' These words were addressed by Miss Pynsent to a little girl who sat on the doorstep of the adjacent house nursing a dingy doll and whose extraordinary luxuriance of dark brown hair was surmounted by a torn straw hat.

The child looked up from her dandling and patting and, after a stare of which the blankness was visibly overdone, replied: 'Law no, Miss Pynsent, I never see him.'

'Aren't you always messing about with him, you naughty little girl?' the dressmaker returned with sharpness. 'Isn't he

round the corner, playing marbles or—or some jumping game?' Miss Pynsent went on, trying to be suggestive.

'I assure *you* he never plays nothing,' said Millicent Henning with a mature manner which she bore out by adding: 'And I don't know why I should be called naughty, neither.'

'Well, if you want to be called good please go find him and tell him there's a lady come here on purpose to see him this very instant.' Miss Pynsent waited a moment to see if her injunction would be obeyed, but she got no satisfaction beyond another gaze of deliberation, which made her feel that the child's perversity was as great as the beauty, somewhat soiled and dimmed, of her insolent little face. She turned back into the house with an exclamation of despair, and as soon as she had disappeared Millicent Henning sprang erect and began to race down the street in the direction of another, which crossed it. I take no unfair advantage of the innocence of childhood in saying that the motive of this young lady's flight was not a desire to be agreeable to Miss Pynsent, but an extreme curiosity on the subject of the visitor who wanted to see Hyacinth Robinson. She wished to participate, if only in imagination, in the interview that might take place, and she was moved also by a quick revival of friendly feeling for the boy, from whom she had parted only half an hour before with considerable asperity. She was not a very clinging little creature, and there was no one in her own domestic circle to whom she was much attached; but she liked to kiss Hyacinth when he didn't push her away and tell her she was hateful. It was in this action and epithet he had indulged half an hour ago; but she had reflected rapidly (while she made play with Miss Pynsent) that it was the worst he had ever done. Millicent Henning was only eight years of age, but she knew there was worse in the world than that.

Mrs Bowerbank, in a leisurely, roundabout way, wandered off to her sister, Mrs Chipperfield, whom she had come into that part of the world to see, and the whole history of the dropsical tendencies of whose husband, an undertaker with a business that had been a blessing because you could always count on it, she unfolded to Miss Pynsent between the sips of a second glass. She was a high-shouldered, towering woman, and suggested squareness as well as a pervasion of the upper air, so that Amanda reflected that she must be very difficult to fit, and had a sinking at the idea of the number of pins she would take. Her sister had nine children and she herself had seven, the eldest of whom she left in charge of the others when she went to her service. She was on duty at the prison only during the day; she had to be there at seven in the morning, but she got her evenings at home, quite regular and comfortable. Miss Pynsent thought it wonderful she could talk of comfort in such a life as that, but could easily imagine she should be glad to get away at night, for at that time the place must be much more terrible.

'And aren't you frightened of them—ever?' she enquired, looking up at her visitor with her little heated face.

Mrs Bowerbank, who was very slow, considered her so long before replying that she felt herself to be, to an alarming degree, in the eye of the law; for who could be more closely connected with the administration of justice than a female turnkey, especially so big and majestic a one? 'I expect they're more frightened of me,' she declared at last; and it was an idea into which Miss Pynsent could easily enter.

'And at night I suppose they rave quite awful,' the little dressmaker suggested, feeling vaguely that prisons and mad-houses came very much to the same.

'Well, if they do we hush 'em up,' Mrs Bowerbank re-marked rather portentously; while Miss Pynsent fidgeted to the door again, without results, to see if the child had be-come visible. She observed to her guest that she couldn't call it anything but contrary that he shouldn't turn up when he knew so well, most days in the week, when his tea was ready. To which Mrs Bowerbank rejoined, fixing her com-panion again with the steady orb of justice: 'And do he have his tea that way by himself, like a real little gentleman?'

'Well, I try to give it to him tidy-like, at a suitable hour,' said Miss Pynsent guiltily. 'And there might be some who would say that, for the matter of that, he *is* a real little gentleman,' she added with an effort at mitigation which, as she immediately became conscious, only involved her more deeply.

'There are people silly enough to say anything. If it's your parents that settle your station the child hasn't much to be thankful for,' Mrs Bowerbank went on in the manner of a woman accustomed to looking facts in the face.

Miss Pynsent was very timid, but she adored the aristocracy, and there were elements in the boy's life which she was not prepared to sacrifice even to a person who represented such a possibility of grating bolts and clanking chains. 'I suppose we oughtn't to forget that his father was very high,' she suggested appealingly and with a tight clasp of her hands in her lap.

'His father? Who knows who *he* was? He doesn't set up for having a father, does he?'

'But surely, wasn't it proved that Lord Frederick——?'

'My dear woman, nothing was proved except that she stabbed his lordship in the back with a very long knife, that he died of the blow, and that she got the full sentence. What does such a piece as that know about fathers? The less said about the poor child's ancestors the better!'

This view of the case caused Miss Pynsent fairly to gasp, for it pushed over with a touch a tall fond fantastic structure that she had been piling up for years. Even as she heard it crash around her she couldn't forbear the attempt to save at least some of the material. 'Really—really,' she panted, 'she never had to do with any one but the nobility!'

Mrs Bowerbank surveyed her hostess with an expressionless eye. 'My dear young lady, what does a respectable little body like you, that sits all day with her needle and scissors, know about the doings of a wicked low foreigner of the sort that carries a knife? I was there when she came in and I know to what she had sunk. Her conversation was choice, I assure you.'

'Oh, it's very dreadful, and of course I know nothing in particular,' Miss Pynsent quavered. 'But she wasn't low when I worked at the same place with her, and she often told me she would do nothing for any one that wasn't at the very top.'

'She might have talked to you of something that would have done you both more good,' Mrs Bowerbank remarked, while the dressmaker felt rebuked in the past as well as in the present. 'At the very top, poor thing! Well, she's at the very bottom now. If she wasn't low when she worked, it's a pity she didn't stick to her work; and as for pride of birth, that's an article I recommend your young friend to leave to others. You had better believe what I say, because I'm a woman of the world.'

Indeed she was, as Miss Pynsent felt, to whom all this was very terrible, letting in the cold light of the penal system on a dear, dim little theory. She had cared for the child because maternity was in her nature and this was the only manner in which fortune had put it in her path to become a mother. She had had herself as few belongings as the desolate baby, and it had seemed to her he would add to her importance in the little world of Lomax Place (if she kept it a secret how she came by him) quite in the proportion in which she should contribute to his maintenance. Her own isolation went out to his, and in the course of time their associated solitude was peopled by the dressmaker's romantic mind with a hundred consoling evocations. The boy proved neither a dunce nor a reprobate; but what endeared him to her most was her conviction that he belonged, 'by the left hand', as she had read in a novel, to a proud and ancient race, the list of whose representatives and the record of whose alliances she had once (when she took home some work and was made to wait, alone, in a lady's boudoir) had the opportunity of reading in a fat red book, eagerly and tremblingly consulted. She bent her head before Mrs Bowerbank's overwhelming logic, but she felt in her heart that she shouldn't give the child up for mere words she couldn't answer—of course she couldn't answer them—that she believed in him still, and that she recognised as distinctly as she revered the quality of her betters. To believe in Hyacinth, for Miss Pynsent, was to believe that he *was* the son of the extremely immoral Lord Frederick. She had from his earliest age made him feel that there was a grandeur in his past, and as Mrs Bowerbank would be sure not to approve of such aberrations she prayed she might not be questioned on that part of the business. It was not that when it was necessary the little dressmaker had any scruple about using the arts of prevarication; she was a kind and innocent creature, but she told fibs as freely as she applied trimmings. She had, however, not yet been questioned by an emissary of the law, and her heart beat faster when Mrs Bowerbank said to her in deep tones, with an effect of abruptness: 'And pray, Miss Pynsent, does the innocent child know it?'

'Know about Lord Frederick?' Miss Pynsent palpitated.

'Bother Lord Frederick! Know about his mother.'

'Oh, I can't say that. I've never told him.'

'But has any one else told him?'

To this enquiry Miss Pynsent's answer was more prompt and more proud; it was with an agreeable sense of having conducted herself with extraordinary wisdom and propriety that she replied: 'How could any one know? I've never breathed it to a creature!'

Mrs Bowerbank gave utterance to no commendation; she only put down her empty glass and wiped her large mouth with much thoroughness and judgement. Then she said, as if it were as cheerful an idea as, in the premises, she was capable of expressing: 'Ah, well, there'll be plenty later on to give him all information!'

'I pray God he may live and die without knowing it!' Miss Pynsent cried with intensity.

Her companion gazed at her with a kind of professional patience. 'You don't keep your ideas together. How can he go to her then, if he's never to know?'

'Oh, did you mean she'd tell him?' Miss Pynsent plaintively gasped.

'Tell him! He won't need to be told, once she gets hold of him and gives him—what she mentioned to me.'

'What she mentioned——?' Miss Pynsent repeated, open-eyed.

'The kiss her lips have been famished for all these years.'

'Ah, poor desolate woman!' the little dressmaker murmured while her pity gushed up again. 'Of course he'll see she's fond of him,' she pursued simply. Then she added with an inspiration more brilliant: 'We might tell him she's his aunt!'

'You may tell him she's his grandmother if you like. But it's all in the family.'

'Yes, on that side,' said Miss Pynsent musingly and irrepressibly. 'And will she speak that fluent French?' she enquired as from a full mind. 'In that case he won't understand.'

'Oh, a child will understand its own mother, whatever she speaks,' Mrs Bowerbank returned, declining to administer a superficial comfort. But she subjoined, opening the door for escape from a prospect which bristled with danger: 'Of course it's just according to your own idea. You needn't bring the child at all unless you like. There's many a one that wouldn't. There's no compulsion.'

'And would nothing be done to me if I didn't?' poor Miss Pynsent asked, unable to rid herself of the impression that it was somehow the arm of the law that was stretched out to touch her.

'The only thing that could happen to you would be that *he* might throw it up against you later,' the lady from the prison observed with a gloomy breadth of view.

'Yes indeed, if he were to know that I had kept him back.'

'Oh, he'd be sure to know, one of these days. We see a great deal of that—the way things come out,' said Mrs Bowerbank, whose outlook appeared to abound in cheerless contingencies. 'You must remember that it's her dying wish and that you may have it on your conscience.'

'That's a thing I *never* could abide!' the little dressmaker exclaimed with great emphasis and a visible shiver; after which she picked up various scattered remnants of muslin and cut paper and began to roll them together with a desperate and mechanical haste. 'It's quite awful, to know what to do—if you're very sure she *is* dying.'

'Do you mean she's shamming? We've plenty of that—but we know how to treat 'em.'

'Lord, I suppose so,' murmured Miss Pynsent; while her visitor went on to say that the unfortunate person on whose behalf she had undertaken this solemn pilgrimage might live a week and might live a fortnight, but if she lived a month would violate (as Mrs Bowerbank might express herself) every established law of nature, being reduced to skin and bone and with nothing left of her but the main desire to see her child.

'If you're afraid of her talking, it isn't much she'd be able to say. And we shouldn't allow you more than about eight minutes,' Mrs Bowerbank pursued in a tone that seemed to refer itself to an iron discipline.

'I'm sure I shouldn't want more; that would be enough to last me many a year,' said Miss Pynsent accommodatingly. And then she added with another illumination: 'Don't you think he might throw it up against me that I *did* take him? People might tell him about her in later years; but if he hadn't seen her he wouldn't be obliged to believe them.'

Mrs Bowerbank considered this a moment as if it were rather an intricate argument, and then answered quite in the spirit of her official pessimism. 'There's one thing you may be sure of: whatever you decide to do, as soon as ever he grows up he'll make you wish you had done the opposite.' Mrs Bowerbank called it oppo*site*.

'Oh dear then, I'm glad it will be a long time.'

'It will be ever so long, if once he gets it into his head! At any rate you must do as you think best. Only if you come you mustn't come when it's all over.'

'It's too impossible to decide.'

'It is indeed,' said Mrs Bowerbank with superior consistency. And she seemed more placidly grim than ever when she remarked, gathering up her loosened shawl, that she was much obliged to Miss Pynsent for her civility and had been quite freshened up: her visit had so completely deprived her hostess of that sort of calm. Miss Pynsent gave the fullest expression to her perplexity in the supreme exclamation:

'If you could only wait and see the child I'm sure it would help you to judge!'

'My dear woman, I don't want to judge—it's none of our business!' Mrs Bowerbank exclaimed; and she had no sooner uttered the words than the door of the room creaked open and a small boy stood there gazing at her. Her eyes rested on him a moment, and then, most unexpectedly, she gave an inconsequent cry. 'Is that the child? Oh, Lord o' mercy, don't take *him!*'

'Now *ain't* he shrinking and sensitive?' demanded Miss Pynsent, who had pounced upon him and, holding him an instant at arm's length, appealed eagerly to her visitor. 'Ain't he delicate and high-bred, and wouldn't he be thrown into a state?' Delicate as he might be the little dressmaker shook him smartly for his naughtiness in being out of the way when he was wanted, and brought him to the big square-faced, deep-voiced lady who took up, as it were, all that side of the room. But Mrs Bowerbank laid no hand upon him; she only dropped her gaze from a tremendous height, and her forbearance seemed a tribute to that fragility of constitution on which Miss Pynsent desired to insist, just as her continued gravity was an implication that this scrupulous woman might well not know what to do. 'Speak to the lady nicely and tell her you're very sorry to have kept her waiting.'

The child hesitated while he repaid with interest Mrs Bowerbank's inspection, and then he said with a cool, conscious indifference which Miss Pynsent instantly recognised as his aristocratic manner: 'I don't think she can have been in a very great hurry.'

There was irony in the words, for it is a remarkable fact that even at the age of ten Hyacinth Robinson was ironic; but the subject of his allusion, who was not nimble withal, appeared not to interpret it; so that she met it only by remarking over his head to Miss Pynsent: 'It's the very face of her again—only for the complexion!'

'Of *her*? But what do you say to Lord Frederick?'

'I *have* seen lords that wasn't so dainty!'

Miss Pynsent had seen very few lords, but she entered with a passionate thrill into this generalisation; controlling herself, however, for she remembered the child was tremendously sharp, sufficiently to declare in an edifying tone that he would look more like what he ought to if his face were a little cleaner.

'It was probably Millicent Henning dirtied my face when she kissed me,' the boy announced with slow gravity, looking all the while at Mrs Bowerbank. He exhibited not a symptom of shyness.

'Millicent 'Enning's a very bad little girl; she'll come to no good,' said Miss Pynsent with familiar decision and also, considering the young lady in question had been her effective messenger, with marked ingratitude.

Against this qualification the child instantly protested. 'Why is she bad? I don't think she's bad; I like her awfully.' It came over him that he had too hastily shifted to her shoulders the responsibility of his unseemly appearance, and he wished to make up to her for this betrayal. He dimly felt that nothing but that particular accusation could have pushed him to it, for he hated people with too few fair interspaces, too many smutches and streaks. Millicent Henning generally had two or three of these at least, which she borrowed from her doll, into whom she was always rubbing her nose and whose dinginess was contagious. It was quite inevitable she should have left her mark under his own nose when she claimed her reward for coming to tell him about the lady who wanted him.

Miss Pynsent held the boy against her knee, trying to present him so that Mrs Bowerbank should agree with her about his having the air of race. He was exceedingly diminutive, even for his years, and though his appearance was not so sickly as to excite remark, it seemed written in his attenuated little person that he would never be either tall or positively hard. His dark blue eyes were separated by a wide interval, which increased the fairness and sweetness of his face, and his abundant curly hair, which grew thick and long, had the golden brownness predestined to elicit exclamations of delight from ladies when they take the inventory of a child. His features were formed and distributed; his head was set on a slim, straight neck; his expression, grave and clear, showed a quick perception as well as a great credulity; and he was altogether, in his tender fineness, an interesting, an appealing little person.

'Yes, he's one that would be sure to remember,' said Mrs Bowerbank, mentally contrasting him with the undeveloped members of her own brood, who had never been retentive of anything but the halfpence which they occasionally contrived to filch from her. Her eyes descended to the details of his dress: the careful mending of his short breeches and his long, coloured stockings, which she was in a position to appreciate, as well as the knot of bright ribbon which the dressmaker had passed into his collar, slightly crumpled by Miss Henning's embrace. Of course Miss Pynsent had only one to look after, but her visitor was obliged to recognise that she had the highest standard in respect to buttons. 'And you *do* turn him out so it's a pleasure,' she went on, noting the ingenious patches in the child's shoes, which, to her mind, were repaired for all the world like those of a little nobleman.

'I'm sure you're very civil,' said Miss Pynsent, in a state of severe exaltation. 'There's never a needle but mine has come near him. That's exactly what I think: the impression would go so deep.'

'Do you want to see me only to look at me?' Hyacinth enquired with a candour which, though unstudied, had again much satiric force.

'I'm sure it's very kind of the lady to notice you at all!' cried his protectress, giving him an ineffectual jerk. 'You're no bigger than a flea; there are many that wouldn't know you from one, and not one of them "performing" ones either.'

'You'll find he's big enough, I expect, when he begins to go,' Mrs Bowerbank remarked tranquilly; and she added that now she saw how he was done for she couldn't but feel the other side was to be considered. In her effort to be discreet by reason of his being present (and so precociously attentive) she became slightly enigmatical; but Miss Pynsent gathered her meaning, which was that it was very true the child would take everything in and keep it, yet that at the same time it was precisely his being so attractive that made it a kind of sin not to gratify the poor woman, who, if she knew what he looked like today, wouldn't forgive the person who had stepped into her place for not producing him. 'Certainly, in her position, I should go off easier if I had seen them curls,' Mrs Bowerbank declared with a flight of maternal imagination which brought her to her feet; while Miss Pynsent felt she was leaving her dreadfully ploughed up and without any really fertilising seed sown. The little dressmaker packed the child upstairs to tidy himself for his tea, and as she accompanied her visitor to the door pleaded that if the latter would have a little more patience she would think a day or two longer what was best and write when she should have decided. Mrs Bowerbank continued to move in a realm superior to poor Miss Pynsent's vacillations and timidities, and her detachment gave her hostess a high idea of her respectability; but the way was a little smoothed when, after Amanda had moaned once more, on the threshold, helplessly and irrelevantly, 'Ain't it a pity she's so bad?' the ponderous lady from the prison rejoined in those tones which seemed meant to resound through corridors of stone: 'I assure you there's a many that's ever so much worse!'

II

MISS PYNSENT, when she found herself alone, felt she was really quite upside down; for this lurid crisis had never entered into her calculations: the very nature of the case had seemed to preclude it. All she had known or had wished to know was that in one of the dreadful establishments constructed for such purposes her quondam comrade was serving out the sentence that had been substituted for the other (the unspeakable horror) almost when the halter was already round her neck. As there had been no question of *that* concession's being stretched any further, poor Florentine had seemed only a little more dead than other people, having no decent tombstone to mark the place where she lay. Miss Pynsent had therefore never thought of her dying again; she had had no idea to what prison she was committed on removal from Newgate (she had wished to keep her mind a blank about the matter in the interest of the child), and it couldn't occur to her that out of such silence and darkness a second voice would reach her, especially a voice she should really have to listen to. Miss Pynsent would have said, before Mrs Bowerbank's visit, that she had no account to render to any one; that she had taken up the child (who might have starved in the gutter) out of charity, and had brought him on, poor and precarious though her own subsistence, without a penny's help from another source; that the mother had forfeited every right and title; and that this had been understood between them—if anything in so dreadful an hour could have been said to be understood—when she had gone to see her at Newgate (that terrible episode, nine years before, still overshadowed all Miss Pynsent's other memories): had gone to see her because Florentine had sent for her (a name, face and address coming up out of the still recent but sharply separated past of their working-girl years) as the one friend to whom she could appeal with some chance of a pitying answer. The effect of violent emotion with Miss Pynsent was not to make her sit with idle hands or fidget about to no purpose; under its influence, on the contrary, she threw herself into little jobs as a fugitive takes to by-paths, and clipped and cut and stitched and basted as if to run a race with hysterics. And while her hands, her scissors, her needle flew an infinite succession of fantastic possibilities trotted through her confused little head: she had a furious imagination, and the act of reflexion, in her mind, was always a panorama of figures and scenes. She had had her picture of the future, painted in rather rosy hues, hung up before her now for a good many years; but it struck her that Mrs Bowerbank's heavy hand had suddenly punched a hole in the canvas. It must be added, however, that if Amanda's thoughts were apt to be bewildering visions they sometimes led her to make up her mind, and on this particular September evening she arrived at a momentous decision. What she made up her mind to was to take advice, and in pursuance of this view she rushed downstairs and, jerking Hyacinth away from his simple but unfinished repast, packed him across the street to tell Mr Vetch (if he had not yet started for the theatre) that she begged he would come in to see her when he came home that night, as she had something very particular indeed to say to him. It didn't matter if he should be very late, he could come in at any hour—he would see her light in the window—and he would do her no end of good. Miss Pynsent knew it was no use for her to go to bed; she felt as if she should never close her eyes again. Mr Vetch was her most distinguished friend; she had an immense appreciation of his cleverness and knowledge of the world, as well as of the purity of his taste in matters of conduct and opinion; and she had already consulted him about Hyacinth's education. The boy needed no urging to go on such an errand, for he too had his ideas about the little fiddler, the second violin in the orchestra of the Bloomsbury Theatre. Mr Vetch had on a great occasion, within the year, obtained for the pair an order for two seats at a pantomime, and to Hyacinth the impression of that ecstatic evening had consecrated him, placed him for ever in the golden glow of the footlights. There were things in life of which, even at the age of ten, it was a conviction of the boy's that it would be his fate never to see enough, and one of these was the wonder-world illuminated by those playhouse lamps. But there would be chances perhaps if one didn't lose sight of

Mr Vetch: he might open the door again—he was a privileged, magical mortal who went to the play every night.

He came in to see Miss Pynsent about midnight; as soon as she heard the lame tinkle of the bell she went to the door and let him in. He was an original, in the fullest sense of the word: a lonely, disappointed, embittered, cynical little man, whose musical organisation had been sterile, who had the nerves and sensibilities of a gentleman, yet whose fate had condemned him for the last ten years to play a fiddle at a second-rate establishment for a few shillings a week. He had ideas of his own about everything, and they were not always very improving. For Amanda Pynsent he represented art, literature (the literature of the play-bill) and philosophy, so that she always felt about him as if he belonged to a higher social sphere, though his earnings were hardly greater than her own and he occupied a single back room in a house where she had never seen a window washed. He had for her the glamour of reduced gentility and fallen fortunes; she was conscious that he spoke a different language (though she couldn't have said in what, unless in more wicked words as well as more grand ones, the difference consisted) from the other members of her humble, almost suburban circle; and the shape of his hands was distinctly aristocratic. (Miss Pynsent, as I have intimated, was immensely preoccupied with that element in life.) Mr Vetch displeased her only by one of the aspects of his character—his blasphemous republican, radical views and the licentious manner in which he expressed himself about the nobility. On that ground he worried her extremely, though he never seemed to her so probably well-connected, like Hyacinth himself, as when he horrified her most. These dreadful theories (expressed so brilliantly that really they might have been dangerous if Miss Pynsent had not been so grounded in the Christian faith and known thereby her own place so well) constituted no presumption against his refined origin; they were explained rather to a certain extent by a just resentment at finding himself excluded from his proper position. Mr Vetch was short, fat and bald, though he was not much older than Miss Pynsent, who was not much older than some people who called themselves forty-five; he always went to the theatre in evening dress, with a flower in his buttonhole, and wore a glass in one eye. He looked placid and genial and as if he would fidget at the most about the 'get up' of his linen; you would have thought him finical but superficial, and never have suspected that he was a revolutionist, or even an at all bold critic of life. Sometimes when he could get away from the theatre early enough he went with a pianist, a friend of his, to play dance-music at small parties; and after such expeditions he was particularly cynical and startling; he indulged in diatribes against the British middle-class, its Philistinism, its absurdity, its snobbery. He seldom had much conversation with Miss Pynsent without telling her that she had the intellectual outlook of a caterpillar; but this was his privilege after a friendship now of seven years' standing, which had begun (the year after he came to live in Lomax Place) with her going over to nurse him on learning from the milk-woman that he was alone at number 17—laid up there with an attack of gastritis. He always compared her to an insect or a bird, and she didn't mind, because she knew he liked her, and she herself liked all winged creatures. How indeed could she complain after hearing him call the Queen a superannuated form and the Archbishop of Canterbury a grotesque superstition?

He laid his violin-case on the table, which was covered with a confusion of fashion-plates and pin-cushions, and glanced toward the fire where a kettle was gently hissing. Miss Pynsent, who had put it on half an hour before, read his glance and reflected with complacency that Mrs Bower-bank had not absolutely drained the little bottle in the cheffoneer. She placed it on the table again, this time with a single glass, and told her visitor that, as a great exception, he might light his pipe. In fact she always made the exception, and he always replied to the gracious speech by enquiring whether she supposed the greengrocers' wives, the butchers' daughters, for whom she worked had fine enough noses to smell in the garments she sent home the fumes of his tobacco. He knew her 'connexion' was confined to small shopkeepers, but she didn't wish others to know it and would have liked them to believe it important the poor little stuffs she made up (into very queer fashions I am afraid) should not surprise the feminine nostril. But it had always been impossible to impose on Mr Vetch; he guessed the truth, the treacherous untrimmed truth, about everything in a moment. She was sure he would do so now in regard to this solemn question that had come up for Hyacinth; he would see that, though agreeably flurried at finding herself whirled in the last eddies of a case that had been so celebrated in its day, her secret wish was to shirk her duty—if it *was* a duty; to keep the child from ever knowing his mother's unmentionable history, the shame that attached to his origin, the opportunity she had had of letting him see the wretched woman before it was too late. She knew Mr Vetch would read her troubled thoughts, but she hoped he would say they were natural and just: she reflected that as he took an interest in Hyacinth he wouldn't desire him to be subjected to a mortification that might rankle for ever and perhaps even crush him to the earth. She related Mrs Bowerbank's visit while he sat on the sofa in the very place where that majestic woman had reposed and puffed his smoke-wreaths into the dusky little room. He knew the story of the child's birth, had known it years before, so that she had no startling revelation to make. He was not in the least agitated to hear of Florentine's approaching end in prison and of her having managed to get a message conveyed to Amanda; he thought this so much in the usual course that he said to Miss Pynsent: 'Did you expect her to live on there for ever, working out her terrible sentence, just to spare you the annoyance of a dilemma, to save you a reminder of her miserable existence, which you have preferred to forget?' That was just the sort of question Mr Vetch was sure to ask, and he enquired further of his dismayed hostess if she were sure her friend's message (he called the unhappy creature her friend) had come to her in the regular way. The warders surely had no authority to introduce visitors to their captives, and was it a question of her going off to the prison on the sole authority of Mrs Bowerbank? The little dressmaker explained that this lady had merely come to sound her: Florentine had begged so hard. She had been in Mrs Bowerbank's ward before her removal to the infirmary, where she now lay ebbing away, and she had communicated her desire to the Catholic chaplain, who had undertaken that some satisfaction—of enquiry, at least—should be given her. He had thought it best to ascertain first whether the person in charge of the child would be willing to bring him, such a course being perfectly optional, and he had had some talk with Mrs Bowerbank on the subject, in which it was agreed between them that if she would approach Miss Pynsent and explain to her the situation, leaving her to do what she thought best, he would answer for it that the consent of the governor of the prison should be given to the interview. Miss Pynsent had lived for fourteen years in Lomax Place, and Florentine had never forgotten that this was her address at the time she came to her at Newgate (before her dreadful sentence had been commuted) and promised, in an outgush of pity for one whom she had known in the days of her honesty and brightness, that she would save the child, rescue it from the workhouse and the streets, keep it from the fate that had swallowed up the mother. Mrs Bowerbank had had a half-holiday, and she also rejoiced in a sister living in the north of London, to whom she had been for some time intending a visit; so that after her domestic duty had been performed it had been possible for her to drop in on Miss Pynsent in an informal, natural way and put the case before her. It would be just as she might be disposed to view it. She was to think it over a day or two, but not long, because the woman was so ill, and then write to Mrs Bowerbank at the prison. If she should consent Mrs Bowerbank would tell the chaplain, and the chaplain would obtain the order from the governor and send it to Lomax Place; after which Amanda would immediately set out with her unconscious victim. But should she—*must* she—consent? That was the terrible, the heart-shaking question, with which Miss Pynsent's unaided wisdom had been unable to grapple.

'After all, he isn't hers any more—he's mine, mine only and mine always. I should like to know if all I've done for him doesn't make him so!' It was in this manner that Amanda Pynsent delivered herself while she plied her needle faster than ever in a piece of stuff that was pinned to her knee.

Mr Vetch watched her a while, blowing silently at his pipe, his head thrown back on the high, stiff, old-fashioned sofa and his little legs crossed under him like a Turk's. 'It's true you've done a good deal for him. You're a good little woman, my dear Pinnie, after all.' He said 'after all' because that was a part of his tone. In reality he had never had a moment's doubt that she was the best little woman in the north of London.

'I've done what I could, and I don't put myself forward above others. Only it does make a difference when you come to look at it—about taking him off to see another woman. And *such* another woman—and in such a place! I think it's hardly right to take an innocent child.'

'I don't know about that; there are people who would tell you it would do him good. If he didn't like the place as a child he'd take more care to keep out of it later.'

'Lord, Mr Vetch, how can you think? And him such a perfect little gentleman!' Miss Pynsent cried.

'Is it you that have made him one?' the fiddler asked. 'It doesn't run in the family, you'd say.'

'Family? what do you know about that?' she returned quickly, catching at her dearest, her only hobby.

'Yes indeed, what does any one know? what did she know herself?' And then Miss Pynsent's visitor added irrelevantly: 'Why should you have taken him on your back? Why did you want to be so extra good? No one else thinks it necessary.'

'I didn't want to be extra good. That is I do want to, of course, in a general way: but that wasn't the reason then.

You see I had nothing of my own—I had nothing in the world but my thimble.'

'That would have seemed to most people a reason for not adopting a prostitute's bastard.'

'Well, I went to see him at the place where he was (just where she had left him, with the woman of the house) and I saw what kind of a shop *that* was, and felt it a shame an unspotted child should grow up in such a place.' Miss Pynsent defended herself as earnestly as if her inconsistency had been of a criminal cast. 'And he wouldn't have grown up neither. *They* wouldn't have troubled themselves long with a helpless baby. *They'd* have played some bad trick on him, if it was only to send him to the workhouse. Besides, I always was fond of tiny creatures and I've been fond of this one,' she went on, speaking as if with a consciousness, on her own part, of almost heroic proportions. 'He was in my way the first two or three years, and it was a good deal of a pull to look after the business and him together. But now he's like the business—he seems to go of himself.'

'Oh, if he flourishes as the business flourishes you can just enjoy your peace of mind,' said the fiddler, still with his manner of making a small dry joke of everything.

'That's all very well, but it doesn't close my eyes to that poor woman lying there and moaning just for the touch of his little 'and before she passes away. Mrs Bowerbank says she believes I'll bring him.'

'Who believes? Mrs Bowerbank?'

'I wonder if there's anything in life holy enough for you to take it seriously,' Miss Pynsent rejoined, snapping off a thread with temper. 'The day you stop laughing I should like to be there.'

'So long as you're there I shall never stop. What is it you want me to advise you? to take the child, or to leave the mother to wail herself away?'

'I want you to tell me if he'll curse me when he grows older.'

'That depends on what you do. However, he'll probably curse you in either case.'

'You don't believe that, because you like him, you love him,' said Amanda with acuteness.

'Precisely; and he'll curse me too. He'll curse every one. Much good will our love do us! He won't be happy.'

'I don't know how you think I bring him up,' the little dressmaker remarked with dignity.

'You don't bring him up at all. He brings you up.'

'That's what you've always said; but you don't know. If you mean that he does as he likes, then he ought to be happy. It ain't kind of you to say he won't be,' Miss Pynsent added reproachfully.

'I'd say anything you like if what I say would help the matter. He's a thin-skinned, morbid, mooning, introspective little beggar, with a good deal of imagination and not much perseverance, who'll expect a good deal more of life than he'll find in it. That's why he won't be happy.'

Miss Pynsent listened to this description of her *protégé* with an appearance of criticising it mentally; but in reality she didn't know what 'introspective' meant and didn't like to ask. 'He's the cleverest person I know except yourself,' she said in a moment; for Mr Vetch's words had been in the key of what she thought most remarkable in him. What that was she would have been unable to say.

'Thank you very much for putting me first,' the fiddler returned after a series of puffs. 'The youngster's interesting; one sees he has a mind and even a soul, and in that respect he's—I won't say unique, but peculiar. I shall watch with curiosity to see what he grows into. But I shall always be glad that I'm a selfish brute of a decent bachelor—that I never invested in that class of goods.'

'Well, you *are* comforting. You'd spoil him more than I do,' said Amanda.

'Possibly, but it would be in a different way. I wouldn't tell him every three minutes that his father was a duke.'

'A duke I never mentioned!' the little dressmaker cried with eagerness. 'I never specified any rank nor said a word about any one in particular. I never so much as insinuated the name of his lordship. But I may have said that if the truth was to be found out he might be proved to be connected—in the way of cousinship, or something of the kind —with the highest in the land. I should have thought myself wanting if I hadn't given him a glimpse of that. But there's one thing I've always added—that the truth never *is* found out.'

'You're still more comforting than I!' Mr Vetch exclaimed. He continued to watch her with his charitable, round-faced smile, and then he said: 'You won't do what I say; so what's the use of my telling you?'

'I assure you I will, if you say you believe it's the only right.'

'Do I often say anything so asinine? Right—right? what have you to do with that? If you want the only right you're very particular.'

'Please then what am I to go by?' the dressmaker asked bewildered.

'You're to go by this, by what will take the youngster down.'

'Take him down, my poor little pet?'

'Your poor little pet thinks himself the flower of creation. I don't say there's any harm in that: a fine, blooming, odoriferous conceit is a natural appendage of youth and intelligence. I don't say there's any great harm in it, but if you want a guide as to how you're to treat the boy, that's as good a guide as any other.'

'You want me to arrange the interview then?'

'I don't want you to do anything but give me another *leetle* swig—thanks. I just say this: that I think it's a great gain, early in life, to know the worst; then we don't live in a rank fools' paradise. I did that till I was nearly forty; then I woke up and found I was in Lomax Place.' Whenever Mr Vetch said anything that could be construed as a reference to a former position that had had elements of distinction Miss Pynsent observed a respectful, a tasteful silence and that is why she didn't challenge him now, though she wanted very much to say that Hyacinth was no more 'presumptious' (that was the term she would have used) than he had reason to be, with his genteel appearance and his acknowledged powers; and that as for thinking himself a 'flower' of any kind he knew but too well that he lived in a small black-faced house miles away from any good family, rented by a poor little woman who took lodgers and who, as they were of such a class that they were not always to be depended upon to settle her weekly account, had a strain to make two ends meet, for all the sign between her windows—

MISS AMANDA PYNSENT
Modes et Robes
DRESSMAKING IN ALL ITS BRANCHES: COURT-DRESSES: MANTLES AND FASHIONABLE BONNETS

Singularly enough, her companion, before she had permitted herself to interpose, took up her own thought (in one of its parts) and remarked that perhaps she would say of the child that he was, so far as his actual circumstances were concerned, low enough down in the world without one's wanting him to be any lower. 'But by the time he's twenty he'll persuade himself that Lomax Place was a bad dream, that your lodgers and your dressmaking were as imaginary as they are vulgar, and that when an old friend came to see you late at night it was not your amiable practice to make him a glass of brandy and water. He'll teach himself to forget all this: he'll have a way.'

'Do you mean he'll forget *me*, he'll deny me?' cried Miss Pynsent, stopping the movement of her needle short off for the first time.

'As the person designated in that attractive blazonry on the outside of your house decidedly he will; and me, equally, as a bald-headed, pot-bellied fiddler who regarded you as the most perfect lady of his acquaintance. I don't mean he'll disown you and pretend he never knew you: I don't think he'll ever be such an odious little cad as that; he probably won't be a sneak, and he strikes me as having some affection, and possibly even some gratitude, in him. But his imagination (which will always give him his cue about everything) shall subject you to some extraordinary metamorphosis. He'll dress you up.'

'He'll dress me up?' Amanda ejaculated, quite ceasing to follow the train of Mr Vetch's demonstration. 'Do you mean he'll have the property—that his relations will take him up?'

'My dear, delightful, idiotic Pinnie, I'm speaking in a figurative manner. I don't pretend to say what his precise position will be when we're relegated; but I'm sure relegation will be our fate. Therefore don't stuff him with any more false notions and fine illusions than are necessary to keep him alive; he'll be sure to pick up enough on the way. On the contrary, give him a good stiff dose of the truth at the start.'

'Dear me, of course you see much further into it than I could ever do,' Pinnie murmured as she threaded a needle.

Mr Vetch paused a minute, but apparently not out of deference to this amiable interruption. He went on suddenly with a ring of feeling in his voice. 'Let him know, because it will be useful to him later, the state of the account between society and himself; he can then conduct himself accordingly. If he's the illegitimate child of a French impropriety who murdered one of her numerous lovers, don't shuffle out of sight so important a fact. I regard that as a most valuable origin.'

'Lord, Mr Vetch, how you *can* talk!' cried Miss Pynsent with her ever-fresh faculty of vain protest. 'I don't know what one would think, to hear you.'

'Surely, my dear lady, and for this reason: that those are the people with whom society has to count. It hasn't with you and me.' Miss Pynsent gave a sigh which might have meant either that she was well aware of that or that Mr Vetch had a terrible way of enlarging a subject, especially when it was already too big for her; and her philosophic visitor went on: 'Poor little devil, let him see her, take him straight.'

'And if later, when he's twenty, he says to me that if I

hadn't meddled in it he need never have known, need never have had that shame, pray what am I to say to him then? That's what I can't get out of my head.'

'You can say to him that a young man who's sorry for having gone to his mother when, in her last hours, she lay crying for him on a pallet in a penitentiary, deserves more than the sharpest pang he can possibly feel.' And the little fiddler, getting up, went over to the fireplace and shook out the ashes of his pipe.

'Well, I'm sure it's natural he should feel badly,' said Miss Pynsent, folding up her work with the same desperate quickness that had animated her through the evening.

'I haven't the least objection to his feeling badly; that's not the worst thing in the world! If a few more people felt badly, in this sodden, stolid, stupid race of ours, the world would wake up to an idea or two and we should see the beginning of the dance. It's the dull acceptance, the absence of reflection, the impenetrable density.' Here Mr Vetch stopped short; his hostess stood before him with eyes of entreaty, with clasped hands.

'Now, Anastasius Vetch, don't go off into them dreadful wild theories!' she cried, always ungrammatical when she was strongly moved. 'You always fly away over the house-tops. I thought you liked him better—the dear little unfortunate.'

Anastasius Vetch had pocketed his pipe; he put on his hat with the freedom of old acquaintance and of Lomax Place, and took up his small coffin-like fiddle-case. 'My good Pinnie, I don't think you understand a word I say. It's no use talking—do as you like!'

'Well, I must say I don't think it was worth your coming in at midnight only to tell me that. I don't like anything—I hate the whole dreadful business!'

He bent over, for all his figure, to kiss her hand with the flourish of a troubadour and as he had seen people do on the stage. 'My dear friend, we've different ideas, and I never shall succeed in driving mine into your head. It's because I *am* fond of him, poor little devil; but you'll never understand that. I want him to know everything, and especially the worst—the very worst, as I've said. If I were in his position I shouldn't thank you for trying to make a fool of me.'

'A fool of you?—as if I thought of anything but his 'appiness!' Amanda Pynsent exclaimed. She stood looking at him but following her own reflexions; she had given up the attempt to enter into his whims. She remembered what she had noticed in other occurrences, that his reasons were always more extraordinary than his behaviour itself. If you only considered his life you wouldn't have thought him so immoral. 'Very likely I think too much of that,' she added. 'She wants him and cries for him; that's what keeps coming back to me.' She took up her lamp to light Mr Vetch to the door (for the dim luminary in the passage had long since been extinguished) and before he left the house he turned suddenly, stopping short and with his composed face taking a strange expression from the quizzical glimmer of his little round eyes.

'What does it matter after all, and why do you worry? What difference can it make what happens—on either side —to such low people?'

III

MRS BOWERBANK had let her know she would meet her almost at the threshold of the dreadful place; and this thought had sustained Miss Pynsent in her long and devious journey, performed partly on foot, partly in a succession of omnibuses. She had had ideas about a cab, but she decided to reserve the cab for the return, as then, very likely, she should be so prostrate with emotion, so overpoweringly affected, that it would be a comfort to escape from observation. She had no confidence that if once she passed the door of the prison she should ever be restored to liberty and her customers; it seemed to her an adventure as dangerous as it was dismal, and she was immensely touched by the clear-

faced eagerness of the child at her side, who strained forward as brightly as he had done on another occasion, still
celebrated in Miss Pynsent's industrious annals, a certain
sultry Saturday in August when she had taken him to the
Tower. It had been a terrible question with her, once she
had made up her mind, what she should tell him about the
nature of their errand. She determined to tell him as little
as possible, to say only that she was going to see a poor
woman who was in prison on account of a crime committed
many years before, and who had sent for her and caused her
to be told at the same time that if there was any child she
could see—as children (if they were good) were bright and
cheering—it would make her very happy that such a little
visitor should come as well. It was very difficult, with
Hyacinth, to make reservations or mysteries; he wanted to
know everything about everything and he projected the
fierce light of his questions on Miss Pynsent's incarcerated
friend. She had to admit that she had been her friend (since
where else was the obligation to go to see her?) but she
spoke of the acquaintance as if it were of the slightest (it had
survived in the memory of the prisoner only because every
one else—the world was so very severe!—had turned away
from her) and she congratulated herself on a happy inspiration when she represented the crime for which such a
penalty had been exacted as the theft of a gold watch in a
moment of cruel want. The woman had had a wicked husband who maltreated and deserted her; she had been very
poor, almost starving, dreadfully pressed. Hyacinth listened
to her history with absorbed attention and then said:

'And hadn't she any children—hadn't she a little boy?'

This enquiry seemed to Miss Pynsent an omen of future
embarrassments, but she met it as bravely as she could,
replying that she believed the wretched victim of the law
had had (once upon a time) a very small baby, but was afraid
she had completely lost sight of it. He must know they
didn't allow babies in prisons. To this Hyacinth rejoined
that of course they would allow him, because of his size.
Miss Pynsent fortified herself with the memory of her other

pilgrimage, the visit to Newgate upwards of ten years before; she had escaped from *that* ordeal and had even had the comfort of knowing that in its fruits the interview had been beneficent. The responsibility, however, was much greater now, and, after all, it was not on her own account she faltered and feared, but on that of the tender sensibility over which the shadow of the house of shame might cast itself.

They made the last part of their approach on foot, having got themselves deposited as near as possible to the river and keeping beside it (according to advice elicited by Miss Pynsent, on the way, in a dozen confidential interviews with policemen, conductors of omnibuses and small shopkeepers) till they came to a big dark-towered building which they would know as soon as they looked at it. They knew it in fact soon enough when they saw it lift its dusky mass from the bank of the Thames, lying there and sprawling over the whole neighbourhood with brown, bare, windowless walls, ugly, truncated pinnacles and a character unspeakably sad and stern. It looked very sinister and wicked, to Miss Pynsent's eyes, and she wondered why a prison should have such an evil air if it was erected in the interest of justice and order—a builded protest, precisely, against vice and villainy. This particular penitentiary struck her as about as bad and wrong as those who were in it; it threw a blight on the face of day, making the river seem foul and poisonous and the opposite bank, with a protrusion of long-necked chimneys, unsightly gasometers and deposits of rubbish, wear the aspect of a region at whose expense the jail had been populated. She looked up at the dull, closed gates, tightening her grasp of Hyacinth's small hand; and if it was hard to believe anything so barred and blind and deaf would relax itself to let her in, there was a dreadful premonitory sinking of the heart attached to the idea of its taking the same trouble to let her out. As she hung back, murmuring vague ejaculations, at the very goal of her journey, an incident occurred which fanned all her scruples and reluctances into life again. The child suddenly jerked away his hand and, placing it behind him in the clutch of the other, said to her respectfully but resolutely, while he planted himself at a considerable distance:

'I don't like this place.'

'Neither do I like it, my darling,' cried the dressmaker pitifully. 'Oh, if you knew how little!'

'Then we'll go away. I won't go in.'

She would have embraced this proposition with alacrity if it had not become very vivid to her while she stood there, in the midst of her shrinking, that behind those sullen walls the mother who bore him was even then counting the minutes. She was alive in that huge dark tomb, and Miss Pynsent could feel that they had already entered into relation with her. They were near her and she was aware; in a few minutes she would taste the cup of the only mercy (except the reprieve from hanging) she had known since her fall. A few, a very few minutes would do it, and it seemed to our pilgrim that if she should fail of her charity now the watches of the night in Lomax Place would be haunted with remorse—perhaps even with something worse. There was something inside that waited and listened, something that would burst, with an awful sound, a shriek or a curse, were she to lead the boy away. She looked into his pale face, perfectly conscious it would be vain for her to take the tone of command; besides, that would have seemed to her shocking. She had another inspiration, and she said to him in a manner in which she had had occasion to speak before:

'The reason why we've come is only to be kind. If we're kind we shan't mind its being disagreeable.'

'Why should we be so kind if she's a bad woman?' Hyacinth demanded. 'She must be very low; I don't want to know her.'

'Hush, hush,' groaned poor Amanda, edging toward him with clasped hands. 'She's not bad now; it has all been washed away—it has been expiated.'

'What's "expiated"?' asked the child while she almost knelt down in the dust to catch him to her bosom.

'It's when you've suffered terribly—suffered so much that it has made you good again.'

'Has *she* suffered very much?'

'For years and years. And now she's dying. It proves she's very good now—that she should want to see us.'

'Do you mean because *we* are good?' Hyacinth went on, probing the matter in a way that made his companion quiver and gazing away from her, very seriously, across the river, at the dreary waste of Battersea.

'We shall be good if we're compassionate, if we make an effort,' said the dressmaker, seeming to look up at him rather than down.

'But if she's dying? I don't want to see any one die.'

Miss Pynsent was bewildered, but her desperation helped. 'If we go to her perhaps she won't. Maybe we shall save her.'

He transferred his remarkable little eyes—eyes which always appeared to her to belong to a person older and stronger than herself—to her face; and then he put to her: 'Why should I save such a creature if I don't like her?'

'If she likes you, that will be enough.'

At this Miss Pynsent began to see that he was moved. 'Will she like me very much?'

'More, much more, than any one—ever.'

'More than you, now?'

'Oh,' said Amanda quickly, 'I mean more than she likes any one.'

Hyacinth had slipped his hands into the pockets of his scanty knickerbockers and, with his legs slightly apart, looked from his companion back to the immense dreary jail. A great deal, to her sense, depended on that moment. 'Oh well,' he said at last, 'I'll just step in.'

'Deary, deary!' the dressmaker murmured to herself as they crossed the bare semicircle which separated the gateway from the unfrequented street. She exerted herself to pull the bell, which seemed to her terribly big and stiff, and while she waited again for the consequences of this effort the boy broke out abruptly:

'How can she like me so much if she has never seen me?'

Miss Pynsent wished the gate would open before an answer to this question should become imperative, but the people within were a long time arriving, and their delay gave Hyacinth an opportunity to repeat it. So she replied, seizing the first pretext that came into her head: 'It's because the little baby she had of old was also named Hyacinth.'

'That's a rummy reason,' the boy murmured, still staring across at the Battersea shore.

A moment later they found themselves in a vast interior dimness, while a grinding of keys and bolts went on behind them. Hereupon Miss Pynsent gave herself up to an over-ruling providence, and she remembered afterwards no circumstance of what happened to her till the great person of Mrs Bowerbank loomed up in the narrowness of a strange, dark corridor. She had only had meanwhile a confused impression of being surrounded with high black walls, whose inner face was more dreadful than the other, the one that overlooked the river; of passing through grey, stony courts, in some of which dreadful figures, scarcely female, in hideous brown misfitting uniforms and perfect frights of hoods, were marching round in a circle; of squeezing up steep unlighted staircases at the heels of a woman who had taken possession of her at the first stage and who made incomprehensible remarks to other women, of lumpish aspect, as she saw them erect themselves, suddenly and spectrally, with dowdy untied bonnets, in uncanny corners and recesses of the draughty labyrinth. If the place had seemed cruel to the poor little dressmaker outside, it may be trusted not to have struck her as an abode of mercy while she pursued her tortuous way into the circular shafts of cells where she had an opportunity of looking at captives through grated peepholes and of edging past others who had temporarily been turned into the corridors—silent women, with fixed eyes, who flattened themselves against the stone walls at the brush of the visitor's dress and whom Miss Pynsent was afraid to glance at. She never had felt so immured, so made sure of; there were walls within walls and galleries on top of galleries; even the daylight lost its colour and you couldn't imagine what o'clock it was. Mrs Bowerbank appeared to have failed her, and that made her feel worse; a panic seized her, as she went, in regard to the child. On him too the horror of the scene would have fallen, and she had a sickening prevision that he would have convulsions after they got home. It was a most improper place to have brought him to, no matter who had sent for him and no matter who was dying. The stillness would terrify him, she was sure—the penitential dumbness of the clustered or isolated women. She clasped his hand more tightly and felt him keep close to her without speaking a word. At last in an open doorway darkened by her ample person Mrs Bowerbank revealed herself, and Miss Pynsent thought it subsequently a sign of her place and power that she should not condescend to apologise for not having appeared till that moment, or to explain why she had not met the bewildered pilgrims near the principal entrance according to her promise. Miss Pynsent couldn't embrace the state of mind of people who didn't apologise, though she vaguely envied and admired it, she herself spending much of her time making excuses for obnoxious acts she had not committed. Mrs Bowerbank, however, was not arrogant, she was only massive and muscular; and after she had taken her timorous friends in tow the dressmaker was able to comfort herself with the reflexion that even so masterful a woman couldn't inflict anything gratuitously disagreeable on a person who had made her visit in Lomax Place pass off so pleasantly.

It was on the outskirts of the infirmary she had been hovering, and it was into certain dismal chambers dedicated to sick criminals she presently ushered her guests. These chambers were naked and grated, like all the rest of the place, and caused Miss Pynsent to say to herself that it must be a blessing to be ill in such a hole, because you couldn't possibly pick up again, whereby your case was simple. Such simplification, nevertheless, had for the moment been offered to very few of Florentine's fellow-sufferers, for only three of the small stiff beds were occupied—occupied by white-faced women in tight, sordid caps, on whom, in the stale ugly room, the sallow light itself seemed to rest without pity. Mrs Bowerbank discreetly paid no attention whatever to Hyacinth; she only said to Miss Pynsent with her hoarse distinctness: 'You'll find her very low; she wouldn't have waited another day.' And she guided them, through a still further door, to the smallest room of all, where there were but three beds placed in a row. Miss Pynsent's frightened eyes rather faltered than enquired, but she became aware that a woman was lying on the middle bed and that her face was turned toward the door. Mrs Bowerbank led the way straight up to her and, giving a businesslike pat to her pillow, signed invitation and encouragement to the visitors, who clung together not far within the threshold. Their conductress reminded them that very few minutes were allowed them and that they had better not dawdle them away; whereupon, as the boy still hung back, the little dressmaker advanced alone, looking at the sick woman with what courage she could muster. It seemed to her she was approaching a perfect stranger, so completely had nine years of prison transformed Florentine. She felt it immediately to have been a mercy she hadn't told Hyacinth she was pretty (as she used to be) since there was no beauty left in the hollow bloodless mask that presented itself without a movement. She *had* told him the poor woman was good, but she didn't look so, nor evidently was he struck with it as he returned her gaze across the interval he declined to traverse, though kept at the same time from retreating by this appeal of her strange, fixed eyes, the only part of all her wasted person in which was still any appearance of life. She looked unnatural to Amanda Pynsent, and terribly old; a speechless, motionless creature, dazed and stupid, whereas Florentine Vivier, in the obliterated past, had been her idea of personal as distinguished from social brilliancy. Above all she seemed disfigured and ugly, cruelly misrepresented by her coarse cap and short rough hair. Amanda, as she stood beside her, thought with a degree of scared elation that Hyacinth would never guess that a person in whom there was so little trace of smartness, or of cleverness of any kind, was his mother, which would be quite another matter. At the very most it might occur to him, as Mrs Bowerbank had suggested, that she was his grandmother. Mrs Bowerbank seated herself on the further bed with folded hands, a monumental time-keeper, and remarked, in the manner of one speaking from a sense of duty, that the poor thing wouldn't get much good of the child unless he showed more confidence. This observation was evidently lost on the boy; he was too intensely absorbed in watching the prisoner. A chair had been placed near her pillow, and Miss Pynsent sat down without her appearing to notice it. In a moment, however, she lifted her hand a little, pushing it out from under the coverlet, and the dressmaker laid her own hand softly on it. This gesture elicited no response, but after a little, still gazing at the boy, Florentine murmured in words no one present was in a position to understand—

'*Dieu de Dieu, qu'il est donc beau!*'

'She won't speak nothing but French since she has been so bad—you can't get a natural word out of her,' Mrs Bowerbank said.

'It used to be so pretty when she spoke her odd English—and so very amusing,' Miss Pynsent ventured to mention with a feeble attempt to brighten up the scene. 'I suppose she has forgotten it all.'

'She may well have forgotten it—she never gave her tongue much exercise. There was little enough trouble to keep *her* from chattering,' Mrs Bowerbank rejoined, giving a twitch to the prisoner's counterpane. Miss Pynsent settled it a little on the other side and considered, in the same train, that this separation of language was indeed a mercy; for how could it ever come into her small companion's head that he was the offspring of a person who couldn't so much as say good-morning to him? She felt at the same time that the scene might have been somewhat less painful if they had been able to communicate with the object of their compassion. As it was they had too much the air of having been brought together simply to look at each other, and there was a gruesome awkwardness in that, considering the delicacy of

Florentine's position. Not indeed that she looked much at her old comrade; it was as if she were conscious of Miss Pynsent's being there and would have been glad to thank her for it—glad even to examine her for her own sake and see what change for her too the horrible years had brought, yet felt, more than this, how she had but the thinnest pulse of energy left and how not a moment that could still be of use to her was too much to take in her child. She took him in with all the glazed entreaty of her eyes, quite giving up his substituted guardian, who evidently would have to take her gratitude for granted. Hyacinth, on his side, after some moments of embarrassing silence—there was nothing audible but Mrs Bowerbank's breathing—had satisfied himself, and he turned about to look for a place of patience while Miss Pynsent should finish her business, which as yet made so little show. He appeared to wish not to leave the room altogether, as that would be the confession of a broken spirit, but to take some attitude that should express his complete disapproval of the unpleasant situation. He was not in sympathy, and he could not have made it more clear than by the way he presently went and placed himself on a low stool in a corner near the door by which they had entered.

'*Est-il possible, mon Dieu, qu'il soit gentil comme ça?*' his mother moaned just above her breath.

'We're very glad you should have cared—that they look after you so well,' said Miss Pynsent confusedly and at random; feeling first that Hyacinth's coldness was perhaps excessive and his scepticism too marked, and then that allusions to the way the poor woman was looked after were not exactly happy. These didn't matter, however, for she evidently heard nothing, giving no sign of interest even when Mrs Bowerbank, in a tone between a desire to make the interview more lively and an idea of showing she knew how to treat the young, referred herself to the little boy.

'Is there nothing the little gentleman would like to say, now, to the unfortunate? Hasn't he any pleasant remark to make to her about his coming so far to see her when she's so sunk? It isn't often that children are shown over the place

(as the little man has been) and there's many that'd think
themselves lucky if they could see what he has seen.'

'*Mon pauvre joujou, mon pauvre chéri,*' the prisoner went
on in her tender, tragic whisper.

'He only wants to be very good; he always sits that way at
home,' said Miss Pynsent, alarmed at Mrs Bowerbank's address and hoping there wouldn't be a scene.

'He might have stayed at home then—with this wretched
person taking on so over him,' Mrs Bowerbank remarked
with some sternness. She plainly felt the occasion threaten
to be wanting in brilliancy, and wished to intimate that
though she was to be trusted for discipline she thought they
were all getting off too easily.

'I came because Pinnie brought me,' Hyacinth spoke up
from his low perch. 'I thought at first it would be pleasant.
But it ain't pleasant—I don't like prisons.' And he placed
his little feet on the crosspiece of the stool as if to touch the
institution at as few points as possible.

The woman in bed continued her strange, almost whining
plaint. '*Il ne veut pas s'approcher, il a honte de moi.*'

'There's a many who begin like that!' laughed Mrs Bowerbank, irritated by the boy's contempt for one of Her
Majesty's finest establishments.

Hyacinth's little white face exhibited no confusion; he
only turned it to the prisoner again, and Miss Pynsent felt
that some extraordinary dumb exchange of meanings was
taking place between them. 'She used to be so elegant: she
was a fine woman,' she observed gently and helplessly.

'*Il a honte de moi—il a honte, Dieu le pardonne!*' Florentine Vivier went on, never moving her eyes.

'She's asking for something, in her language. I used to
know a few words,' said Miss Pynsent, stroking down the
bed very nervously.

'Who is that woman? what does she want?' Hyacinth
broke out again, his small, clear voice ringing over the dreary
room.

'She wants you to come near her, she wants to kiss you,

sir,' said Mrs Bowerbank, as if it were more than he deserved.

'I won't kiss her; Pinnie says she stole a watch!' the child answered with resolution.

'Oh, you dreadful—how could you ever?' cried Pinnie, blushing all over and starting out of her chair.

It was partly Amanda's agitation perhaps, which by the jolt it administered gave an impulse to the sick woman, and partly the penetrating and expressive tone in which Hyacinth announced his repugnance: at any rate Florentine, in the most unexpected and violent manner, jerked herself up from her pillow and, with dilated eyes and protesting hands, shrieked out, '*Ah quelle infamie!* I never stole a watch, I never stole anything—anything! *Ah par exemple!*' Then she fell back sobbing with the passion that had given her a moment's strength.

'I'm sure you needn't put more on her than she has by rights,' said Mrs Bowerbank with dignity to the dressmaker, and laid a large red hand on the patient to keep her in her place.

'Mercy, more? I thought it so much less!' cried Miss Pynsent, convulsed with confusion and jerking herself in a wild tremor from the mother to the child, as if she wished to fling herself on the one for contrition and the other for revenge.

'*Il a honte de moi—il a honte de moi!*' Florentine repeated in the misery of her sobs. '*Dieu de bonté, quelle horreur!*'

Miss Pynsent dropped on her knees beside the bed and, trying to possess herself of the unfortunate's hand again, protested with an almost equal passion (she felt that her nerves had been screwed up to the snapping-point, and now they were all in shreds) that she hadn't meant what she had told the child, that he hadn't understood, that Florentine herself hadn't understood, that she had only said she had been accused and meant that no one had ever believed it. The Frenchwoman paid no attention to her whatever, and Amanda buried her face and her embarrassment in the side of the hard little prison-bed, while, above the sound of their

common lamentation, she heard the judicial tones of Mrs
Bowerbank.

'The child's delicate—you might well say! I'm disappointed in the effect—I was in hopes you'd hearten her up.
The doctor'll be down on *me* of course for putting her in
such a state, so we'll just pass out again.'

'I'm very sorry I made you cry. And you must pardon
Pinnie—I asked her so many questions.'

These words came from close beside the prostrate dressmaker, who, lifting herself quickly, found the little boy had
advanced to her elbow and was taking a nearer view of the
mysterious captive. They produced on the latter an effect
even more powerful than his misguided speech of a moment
before; for she found strength partly to raise herself in her
bed again and to hold out her arms to him with the same
thrilling sobs. She was talking still, but had become quite
inarticulate, and Miss Pynsent had but a glimpse of her
white ravaged face and the hollows of its eyes and the rude
crop of her hair. Amanda caught the child with an eagerness
almost as great as Florentine's and, drawing him to the head
of the bed, pushed him into his mother's arms. 'Kiss her—
kiss her well, and we'll go home!' she whispered desperately
while they closed about him and the poor dishonoured head
pressed itself against his young cheek. It was a terrible, irresistible embrace, to which Hyacinth submitted with instant
patience. Mrs Bowerbank had tried at first to keep her sad
charge from rising, evidently wishing to abbreviate the
scene; then as the child was enfolded she accepted the situation and gave judicious support from behind, with an eye
to clearing the room as soon as this effort should have spent
itself. She propped up her patient with a vigorous arm; Miss
Pynsent rose from her knees and turned away, and there was
a minute's stillness during which the boy accommodated
himself as he might to his strange ordeal. What thoughts
were begotten at that moment in his wondering little mind
his protectress was destined to learn at another time. Before
she had faced round to the bed again she was swept out of
the room by Mrs Bowerbank, who had lowered the prisoner,

exhausted and with closed eyes, to her pillow and given Hyacinth a businesslike little push which sent him on in advance. Miss Pynsent went home in a cab—she was so shaken; though she reflected very nervously, getting into it, on the opportunities it would give Hyacinth for the exercise of inquisitorial rights. To her surprise, however, he completely neglected them; he sat looking out of the window in silence till they re-entered Lomax Place.

IV

'WELL, YOU'LL have to guess my name before I tell you,' the girl said with a free laugh, pushing her way into the narrow hall and leaning against the tattered wall-paper which, representing blocks of marble with bevelled edges, in streaks and speckles of black and grey, had not been renewed for years and came back to her out of the past. As Miss Pynsent closed the door, seeing her visitor so resolute, the light filtered in from the street through the narrow dusty glass above, and then the very smell and sense of the place returned to Millicent: the impression of a musty dimness with a small steep staircase at the end, covered with the very strip of oilcloth she could recognise and made a little less dark by a window in the turn (you could see it from the hall) where you might almost bump your head against the house behind. Nothing was changed but Miss Pynsent and of course the girl herself. She had noticed outside how the sign between the windows had not even been touched up; there was still the same preposterous announcement of 'fashionable bonnets'—as if the poor little dressmaker had the slightest acquaintance with that style of head-dress, of which Miss Henning's own knowledge was now so complete. She could see this artist was looking at her hat, a wonderful composition of flowers and ribbons; her eyes had travelled up and down Millicent's whole person, but they rested in fascination on that grandest ornament. The girl had forgotten how small the dressmaker was; she barely came up to her shoulder. She had lost her hair and wore a cap which Millicent noticed in return, wondering if it were a specimen of what she thought the fashion. Miss Pynsent stared up at her as if she had been six foot high; but she was used to that sort of surprised admiration, being perfectly conscious she was a magnificent young woman.

'Won't you take me into your shop?' she asked. 'I don't want to order anything; I only came to enquire after your 'ealth. Isn't this rather an awkward place to talk?' She made her way further in without waiting for permission, seeing that her startled hostess had not yet guessed.

'The show-room's on the right hand,' said Miss Pynsent with her professional manner, which was intended evidently to mark a difference. She spoke as if on the other side, where the horizon was bounded by the partition of the next house, there were labyrinths of apartments. Passing in after her guest she found the young lady already spread out upon the sofa, the everlasting sofa in the right-hand corner as you faced the window, a piece of furniture covered with a tight shrunken shroud of strange yellow stuff, the tinge of which revealed years of washing, and surmounted by a coloured print of Rebekah at the Well, balancing, in the opposite quarter, against a portrait of the Empress of the French taken from an illustrated newspaper and framed and glazed in the manner of 1853. Millicent looked about, asking herself what Miss Pynsent had to show and acting perfectly the part of the most brilliant figure the place had ever contained. The old implements were there on the table: the pincushions and needle-books, the pink measuring-tape with which, as children, she and Hyacinth used to take each other's height; and the same collection of fashion-plates (she could see in a minute) crumpled, sallow and fly-blown. The little dressmaker bristled, as she used to do, with needles and pins stuck all over the front of her dress—they might almost have figured the stiff sparse fur of a sick animal; but there were no rustling fabrics tossed in heaps over the room—nothing but the skirt of a shabby dress (it might have been her own) which she was evidently repairing and had flung upon the table when she came to the door. Miss Henning speedily arrived at the conclusion that her old friend's business had not increased, and felt some safe luxurious scorn of a person who knew so little what was to be got out of London. It was Millicent's belief that she herself was already perfectly acquainted with the resources of the capital.

'Now tell me, how's old Hyacinth? I should like so much to see him,' she remarked while she extended a pair of large protrusive feet and supported herself on the sofa by her hands.

'Old Hyacinth?' Miss Pynsent repeated with majestic blankness and as if she had never heard of such a person. She felt the girl to be cruelly, scathingly well dressed and couldn't imagine who she was nor with what design she might have presented herself.

'Perhaps you call him Mr Robinson today—you always wanted him to hold himself so high. But to his face at any rate I'll call him as I used to: you just see if I don't!'

'Bless my soul, you must be the awful little 'Enning!' Miss Pynsent exclaimed, planted before her and going now into every detail.

'Well, I'm glad you've made up your mind. I thought you'd know me directly and I dare say I *was* awful. But I ain't so bad now, hey?' the young woman went on with confidence. 'I had a call to make in this part, and it came into my 'ead to look you up. I don't like to lose sight of old friends.'

'I never knew you—you've improved as I couldn't have believed,' Miss Pynsent returned with a candour justified by her age and her consciousness of respectability.

'Well, *you* haven't changed; you were always calling me something horrid.'

'I dare say it doesn't matter to you now, does it?' said the dressmaker, seating herself but quite unable to take up her work, blank as she was before the greatness of her visitor.

'Oh, I'm all right now,' Miss Henning declared with the air of one who had nothing to fear from human judgements.

'You were a pretty child—I never said the contrary to that; but I had no idea you'd turn out like this. You're too tall for a woman,' Miss Pynsent added, much divided between an old prejudice and a new appreciation.

'Well, I enjoy beautiful 'ealth,' said the young lady; 'every one thinks I'm at least twenty-two.' She spoke with a certain artless pride in her bigness and her bloom and as if, to show her development, she would have taken off her jacket or let you feel her upper arm. She was certainly handsome, with a shining, bold, good-natured eye, a fine, free, physiognomic oval, an abundance of brown hair and a smile that fairly flaunted the whiteness of her teeth. Her head was set on a fair strong neck and her robust young figure was rich in feminine curves. Her gloves, covering her wrists insufficiently, showed the redness of those parts in the interstices of the numerous silver bracelets that encircled them, and Miss Pynsent made the observation that her hands were not more delicate than her feet. She was not graceful, and even the little dressmaker, whose preference for distinguished forms never deserted her, indulged in the mental reflection that she was common, despite her magnificence; but there was something about her indescribably fresh, successful and satisfying. She was to her blunt, expanded finger-tips a daughter of London, of the crowded streets and bustling traffic of the great city; she had drawn her health and strength from its dingy courts and foggy thoroughfares and peopled its parks and squares and crescents with her ambitions; it had entered into her blood and her bone, the sound of her voice and the carriage of her head; she understood it by instinct and loved it with passion; she represented its immense vulgarities and curiosities, its brutality and its knowingness, its good-nature and its impudence, and might have figured, in an allegorical procession, as a kind of glorified townswoman, a nymph of the wilderness of Middlesex, a flower of the clustered parishes, the genius of urban civilisation, the muse of cockneyism. The restrictions under which Miss Pynsent regarded her would have cost the dressmaker some fewer scruples if she had guessed the impression she herself made on Millicent, and how the whole place seemed to that prosperous young lady to smell of poverty and failure. Her childish image of its mistress had shown her as neat, fine, superior, with round loops of hair fastened on the temples by combs and associations of brilliancy arising from the constant manipulation of precious stuffs —tissues at least that Millicent regarded with envy. But the little woman before her was bald and white and pinched; she looked shrunken and sickly and insufficiently nourished; her small eyes were sharp and suspicious and her hideous cap didn't disguise the way everything had gone. Miss Henning thanked her stars, as she had often done before, that she hadn't been obliged to get *her* living by drudging over needlework year after year in that undiscoverable street, in a dismal little room where nothing had been changed for ages; the absence of change had such an exasperating effect upon her vigorous young nature. She reflected with complacency on her good fortune in being attached to a more exciting, a more dramatic department of the great drapery interest, and noticed that though it was already November there was no fire in the neatly-kept grate beneath the chimney-piece, on which a design, partly architectural, partly botanical, executed in the hair of Miss Pynsent's parents, was flanked by a pair of vases, under glass, containing muslin flowers.

If she thought that lady's eyes suspicious it must be confessed that her hostess felt much on her guard in presence of so unexpected and undesired a reminder of one of the least honourable episodes in the annals of Lomax Place. Miss Pynsent esteemed people in proportion to their success in constituting a family circle—in cases, that is, when the materials were under their hand. This success, among the various members of the house of Henning, had been of the scantiest, and the domestic broils in the establishment adjacent to her own, the vicissitudes of which she was able to follow, as she sat near her window at work, by simply inclining an ear to the thin partition behind her—these scenes, rendering the crash of crockery and the imprecations of the wounded frequently and peculiarly audible, had long been the scandal of a humble but harmonious neighbourhood. Mr Henning was supposed to fill a place of confidence in a brush factory, while his wife, at home, occupied herself with the washing and mending of a considerable brood, mainly of sons. But economy and sobriety and indeed a virtue more important still had never presided at their councils. The freedom and frequency of Mrs Henning's relations with a stove-polisher off the Euston Road were at least not a secret to a person who lived next door and looked up from her work so often that it was a wonder it was always finished so quickly. The little Hennings, unwashed and unchidden, spent most of their time either in pushing each other into the gutter or in running to the public-house at the corner for a pennyworth of gin, and the borrowing propensities of their elders were a theme for exclamation. There was no object of personal or domestic use which Mrs Henning had not at one time or another endeavoured to elicit from the dressmaker; beginning with a mattress, on an occasion when she was about to take to her bed for a considerable period, and ending with a flannel petticoat and a pewter teapot. Lomax Place had eventually, from its over-peeping windows and doorways, been present at the seizure, by a long-suffering landlord, of the chattels of this interesting race and at the ejectment of the whole insolvent group, who departed in a straggling, jeering, unabashed, cynical manner, carrying with them but little of the sympathy of the street. Millicent, whose childish intimacy with Hyacinth Robinson Miss Pynsent had always viewed with vague anxiety—she thought the girl a nasty little thing and was afraid she would teach the innocent orphan low ways—Millicent, with her luxuriant tresses, her precocious beauty, her staring, mocking manner on the doorstep, was at this time twelve years of age. She vanished with her vanishing companions; Lomax Place saw them double the cape, that is turn the corner, and returned to its occupations with a conviction that they would make shipwreck on the outer reefs. But neither spar nor splinter floated back to their former haunts, and they were engulfed

altogether in the fathomless deeps of the town. Miss Pynsent drew a long breath; it was her judgement that none of
them would come to any good whatever, and Millicent least
of all.

When therefore this young lady reappeared with all the
signs of accomplished survival she couldn't fail to ask herself
whether, under a specious seeming, the phenomenon didn't
simply represent the triumph of vice. She was alarmed, but
she would have given her silver thimble to know the girl's
history, and between her shock and her curiosity she passed
an uncomfortable half-hour. She felt the familiar mysterious
creature to be playing with her; revenging herself for former
animadversions, for having been snubbed and miscalled by
a prying little spinster who could now make no figure beside
her. If it was not the triumph of vice it was at least the
triumph of impertinence, as well as of youth, health and a
greater acquaintance with the art of dress than Miss Pynsent
could boast, for all her ridiculous signboards. She perceived,
or she believed she perceived, that Millicent wanted to scare
her, to make her think she had come after Hyacinth, that she
wished to get hold of him and somehow mislead and tempt
him. I should be sorry to impute to Miss Henning any
motive more complicated than the desire to amuse herself,
of a Saturday afternoon, by a ramble her vigorous legs had
no occasion to deprecate; but it must be confessed that with
her shrewd guess of this estimate of her as a ravening wolf
and of her early playmate as an unspotted lamb she laughed
out, in Miss Pynsent's anxious face, irrelevantly and good-
humouredly and without deigning to explain. But what indeed
had she come for if she hadn't come for Hyacinth? It was
not for the love of the dressmaker's pretty ways. She remembered the boy and some of their tender passages, and in
the wantonness of her full-blown freedom—her attachment
also to any tolerable pretext for wandering through the
streets of London and gazing into shop-windows—had said
to herself she might dedicate an afternoon to the pleasures
of memory, might revisit the scenes of her childhood. She
considered that her childhood had ended with the departure

of her family from Lomax Place. If the tenants of that scarce-dissimulated slum had never learned what their banished fellows were to go through she herself had at least retained a deep impression of those horrible intermediate years. The family, as a family, had gone downhill, to the very bottom; and in her humbler moments Millicent sometimes wondered what lucky star had checked her own descent and indeed enabled her to mount the slope again. In her humbler moments, I say, for as a general thing she was provided with an explanation of any good fortune that might befall her. What was more natural than that a girl should achieve miracles when she was at once so handsome and so clever? Millicent thought with compassion of the young persons whom a niggardly fate had endowed with only one of these advantages. She was good-natured, but she had no idea of gratifying Miss Pynsent's curiosity: it seemed to her quite a sufficient kindness to stimulate it.

She told the dressmaker she had a high position at a great haberdasher's in the neighbourhood of Buckingham Palace; she was in the department for jackets and mantles; she put on all these articles to show them off to the customers, and on her person they appeared to such advantage that nothing she took up ever failed to go off. Miss Pynsent could imagine from this how highly her services were prized. She had had a splendid offer from another establishment, an immense one in Oxford Street, and was just thinking if she should accept it. 'We have to be beautifully dressed, but I don't care, because I like to look nice,' she remarked to her hostess, who at the end of half an hour, very grave behind the clumsy glasses she had been obliged to wear of late years, seemed still not to know what to make of her. On the subject of her parents, of her history during the interval that was to be accounted for, the girl was large and vague, and Miss Pynsent saw that the domestic circle had not even a shadow of sanctity for her. She stood on her own feet—stood very firm. Her staying so long, her remaining over the half-hour, proved she had come for Hyacinth, since poor Amanda gave her as little information as was decent, told her nothing that would encourage or attract. She simply mentioned that Mr Robinson (she was careful to speak of him in that manner) had given his attention to bookbinding and had served an apprenticeship in a house where they turned out the best work of that kind that was to be found in London.

'A bookbindery? Laws!' said Miss Henning. 'Do you mean they get them up for the shops? Well, I always thought he would have something to do with books.' Then she added: 'But I didn't think he would ever follow a trade.'

'A trade?' cried Miss Pynsent. 'You should hear Mr Robinson speak of it. He considers it too lovely, quite one of the fine arts.'

Millicent smiled as if she knew how people often considered things, and remarked that very likely it was tidy comfortable work, but she couldn't believe there was much to be seen in it. 'Perhaps you'll say there's more than there is here,' she went on, finding at last an effect of irritation, of reprehension, an implication of aggressive respectability, in the image of the patient dressmaker's sitting for so many years in her close brown little den with the foggy familiarities of Lomax Place on the other side of the pane. Millicent liked to think she herself was strong, yet she was not strong enough for that.

This allusion to her shrunken industry seemed to Miss Pynsent very cruel; but she reflected it was natural one should be insulted if one talked to a vulgar girl. She judged this young lady in the manner of a person who was not vulgar herself, and if there was a difference between them she was right in feeling it to be in her favour. Miss Pynsent's 'cut', as I have intimated, was not truly fashionable, and in the application of gimp and the matching of colours she was not absolutely to be trusted; but morally she had the best taste in the world. 'I haven't so much work as I used to have, if that's what you mean. My eyes are not so good and my health has failed with advancing years.'

I know not to what extent Millicent was touched by the dignity of this admission, but she replied without embarrassment that what Miss Pynsent wanted was a smart young

assistant, some nice girl of a 'tasty' turn who would brighten
up the business and give her new ideas. 'I can see you've
got the same old ones, always: I can tell that by the way
you've stuck the braid on that dress'; and she directed a
poke of her neat little umbrella at the drapery in the dressmaker's lap. She continued to patronise and exasperate her,
and to offer her consolation and encouragement with the
heaviest hand that had ever been applied to Miss Pynsent's
sensitive surface. Poor Amanda ended by gazing at her as if
she had been a public performer of some kind, a ballad-
singer or a conjurer, and went so far as to ask herself
whether the creature could be (in her own mind) the 'nice
girl' who was to regild the tarnished sign. Miss Pynsent had
had assistants in the past—she had even once, for a few
months, had a 'forewoman'; and some of these damsels had
been precious specimens, whose misdemeanours lived vividly
in her memory. Never, all the same, in her worst hour of
delusion, had she trusted her interests to such an exponent
of the latest thing as this. She was quickly reassured as to
Millicent's own views, perceiving more and more that she
was a tremendous highflyer, who required a much larger
field of action than the musty bower she now honoured,
goodness only knew why, with her presence. Miss Pynsent
held her tongue as she always did when the sorrow of her
life had been touched, the thought of the slow, inexorable
decline on which she had entered that day, nearly ten years
before, when her hesitations and scruples resolved themselves into a hideous mistake. The deep conviction of error
on this unspeakably important occasion had ached and
throbbed within her ever since like an incurable disease. She
had sown in her boy's mind the seeds of shame and rancour;
she had made him conscious of his stigma, of his exquisitely
vulnerable spot, and condemned him to know that for him
the sun would never shine as it shone for most others. By the
time he was sixteen years old she had learned—or believed
she had learned—the judgement he had passed on her, and
at that period she had lived through a series of horrible
months, an ordeal in which every element of her old pros-

perity perished. She cried her eyes out, on coming to a sense of her blunder, so blinded and weakened herself with weeping that she might for a while have believed she should never be able to touch a needle again. She lost all interest in her work, and that play of invention which had always been her pride deserted her, together with the reputation of keeping the tidiest lodgings in Lomax Place. A couple of commercial gentlemen and a Welsh plumber of religious tendencies who for several years had made her establishment their home withdrew their patronage on the ground that the airing of her beds was not what it used to be, and disseminated cruelly this injurious legend. She ceased to notice or to care how sleeves were worn, and on the question of flounces and gores her mind was a blank. She fell into a grievous debility and then into a long, low, languid fever, during which Hyacinth tended her with a devotion that only made the wrong she had done him seem sharper, and that determined in Mr Vetch, so soon as she was able to hold up her head a little, the impulse to come and sit with her through the dull hours of convalescence. She re-established to a certain extent, after a time, her connection, so far as the letting of her rooms was concerned (from the other department of her activity the tide had ebbed apparently for ever); but nothing was the same again, and she knew it was the beginning of the end. So it had gone on, and she watched the end approach; she felt it very near indeed when a child she had seen playing in the gutters came to flaunt it over her in silk and lace. She gave a low, inaudible sigh of relief as Millicent at last got up and stood there, smoothing the glossy cylinder of her umbrella.

'Mind you give my love to Hyacinth,' the girl said with an assurance which showed all her insensibility to tacit protests. 'I don't care if you do guess that if I've stopped so long it was in the hope he would be dropping in to his tea. You can tell him I sat an hour, on purpose, if you like; there's no shame in my wanting to see my childhood's sweetheart. He may know I call him that!' Millicent continued with her show-room laugh, as Miss Pynsent judged it to be; conferring these permissions, successively, as if they were great indulgences. 'Do give him my best love and tell him I hope he'll come and see me. I see you won't tell him anything. I don't know what you're afraid of; but I'll leave my card for him, all the same.' She drew forth a little bright-coloured pocket-book, and it was with amazement that Miss Pynsent saw her extract from it a morsel of engraved pasteboard—so monstrous did it seem that one of the squalid little Hennings should have lived to display this emblem of social consideration. Millicent enjoyed the effect she produced as she laid the card on the table, and gave another ringing peal of mirth at the sight of her hostess's half-hungry, half astonished look. 'What *do* you think I want to do with him? I could swallow him at a single bite!' she cried.

Poor Amanda gave no second glance at the document on the table, though she had perceived it contained, in the corner, her visitor's address, which Millicent had amused herself ingeniously with not mentioning: she only got up, laying down her work with an agitated hand, so that she should be able to see Miss Henning well out of the house. 'You needn't think I shall put myself out to keep him in the dark. I shall certainly tell him you've been here, and exactly how you strike me.'

'Of course you'll say something nasty—like you used to when I was a child. You usually let me 'ave it then, you know!'

'Ah well,' said Miss Pynsent, nettled at this reminder of an acerbity which the girl's present development caused to appear absurdly ineffectual, 'you're very different now, when I think what you've come from.'

'What I've come from?' Millicent threw back her head and opened her eyes very wide, while all her feathers and ribbons nodded. 'Did you want me to stick fast in this low place for the rest of my days? You've had to stay in it yourself, so you might speak civilly of it.' She coloured and raised her voice and looked magnificent in her scorn. 'And pray what have you come from yourself, and what has *he* come from—the mysterious "Mr Robinson" who used to be such a puzzle to the whole Plice? I thought perhaps I might clear it up, but you haven't told me that yet!'

Miss Pynsent turned straight away, covering her ears with her hands. 'I've nothing to tell you! Leave my room—leave my house!' she cried with a trembling voice.

V

IT WAS in this way she failed either to see or to hear the opening of the door of the room, which obeyed a slow, apparently cautious impulse given it from the hall and revealed the figure of a young man standing there with a short pipe in his teeth. There was something in his face which immediately told Millicent Henning he had heard her last tones resound into the passage. He entered as if, young as he was, he knew that when women were squabbling men were not called upon to be headlong, and now evidently wondered who the dressmaker's evident 'match' might be. She recognised on the instant her old playmate, and without reflexion, confusion or diplomacy, in the fulness of her vulgarity and sociability, exclaimed at no lower pitch: 'Gracious, Hyacinth Robinson, is *that* your form?'

Miss Pynsent turned round in a flash, but kept silent; then, very white and shaken, took up her work again and seated herself in her window. Hyacinth on his side stood staring—he blushed all over. He knew who she was but didn't say so; he only asked in a voice which struck the girl as quite different from the old one—the one in which he used to tell her she was beastly tiresome—'Is it of me you were speaking just now?'

'When I asked where you had come from? That was because we 'eard you in the 'all,' said Millicent smiling. 'I suppose you've come from your work.'

'You used to live in the Place—you always wanted to kiss me,' the young man remarked with an effort not to show all the surprise and satisfaction he felt. 'Didn't she live in the Place, Pinnie?'

Pinnie, for all answer, fixed a pair of strange pleading eyes upon him, and Millicent broke out, with her recurrent laugh, in which the dressmaker had been right in discovering the note of affectation, 'Do you want to know what you look like? You look for all the world like a little plastered-up Frenchman! Don't he look like a funny little Frenchman, Miss Pynsent?' she went on as if she were on the best possible terms with the mistress of the establishment.

Hyacinth caught a light from that afflicted woman; he saw something in her face that he knew very well by this time and in the sight of which he always found an odd, perverse, unholy relish. It seemed to say that she prostrated herself, that she did penance in the dust, that she was his to trample upon, to spit upon. He did neither of these things, but she was constantly offering herself, and her permanent humility, her perpetual abjection, was a vague counter-irritant to the soreness lodged in his own heart for ever and which had often at night made him cry with rage in his little room under the roof. Pinnie meant this today as a matter of course, and could only especially mean it in the presence of Miss Henning's remark about his looking like a Frenchman. He knew he looked like a Frenchman, he had often been told so before, and a large part of the time, often quite grandly, he felt like one—like one of those he had read about in Michelet and Carlyle. He had picked up their language with the most extraordinary facility, by the aid of one of his mates, a refugee from Paris, in the workroom, and of a second-hand dog's-eared dictionary bought for a shilling in the Brompton Road during one of his interminable, restless, melancholy, moody, yet all-observant strolls through London. He spoke it, he believed, by a natural impulse, caught the accent, the gesture, the movement of eyebrow and shoulder; so that on any occasion of his having to pass for a foreigner—there was no telling what might happen—he should certainly be able to do so to admiration, especially if he could borrow a blouse. He had never seen a blouse in his life, but he knew exactly the form and colour of such a garment and how it was worn. What the complications might be which should compel him to assume the disguise of a person of a social station lower still than his own he would not for the world have mentioned to you; but as they were very present to the mind of our imaginative, ingenious youth we shall catch a glimpse of them in the course of a further acquaintance with him. Actually, when there was no question of masquerading, it made him blush again that such a note should be struck by a loud, laughing, handsome girl who came back out of his past. There was more in Pinnie's weak eyes now than her usual rueful profession; there was a dumb intimation, almost as pathetic as the other, that if he cared to let her off easily he wouldn't detain their terrible visitor very long. He had no wish to do that; he kept the door open on purpose; he didn't enjoy talking to girls under Pinnie's eyes and could see that this one had every disposition to talk. So without responding to her observation about his appearance he said, not knowing exactly what to say: 'Have you come back to live in the Place?'

'Heaven forbid I should ever do that!' cried Miss Henning with genuine emotion. 'I must live near the establishment in which I'm employed.'

'And what establishment is that now?' the young man asked, gaining confidence and perceiving in detail how handsome she was. He hadn't roamed about London for nothing, and he knew that when a girl had such looks a jocular tone of address, a pleasing freedom, was *de rigueur*; so he added: 'Is it the Bull and Gate or the Elephant and Castle?'

'A public-house? Well, you haven't got the politeness of a Frenchman at all events!' Her good-nature had come back to her perfectly, and her resentment of his imputation of her looking like a barmaid—a blowsy beauty who handled pewter—was tempered by her more and more curious consideration of Hyacinth's form. He was exceedingly 'rum', but he had a stamp as sharp for her as that of a new coin and which also agreeably suggested value. Since he remem-

bered so well that she had been fond of kissing him in their
early days she would have liked to show herself prepared to
repeat this graceful attention. But she reminded herself in
time that her line should be religiously the ladylike, and she
was content to exclaim simply: 'I don't care what a man
looks like so long as he knows a lot. That's the form *I* like!'

Miss Pynsent had promised herself the satisfaction of
taking no further notice of her brilliant invader; but the
temptation was great to expose her to Hyacinth, in mitigation of her brilliancy, by remarking sarcastically, according
to opportunity, 'Miss 'Enning wouldn't live in Lomax Plice
for the world. She thinks it too dreadfully low.'

'So it is; it's a beastly hole,' said the young man.

The poor dressmaker's little dart fell to the ground and
Millicent exclaimed jovially 'Right you are!' while she
directed to the object of her childhood's admiration an
expression of face that put him more and more at his ease.

'Don't you suppose I know something?' he asked, planted
before her with his little legs slightly apart and, with his
hands behind him, making the open door waver to and fro.

'You? Oh, I don't care a straw what you know!' she said;
and he had at any rate a mind sufficiently enriched to see
what she meant by that. If she meant he was so good-look-
ing that he might pass on this score alone her judgement
was conceivable, though many women would strongly have
dissented from it. He was as small as he had announced
from the first—he had never got his growth—and she could
easily see that he was not what she at least would call
strong. His bones were small, his chest was narrow, his
complexion pale, his whole figure almost childishly slight;
and Millicent noted afterwards that he had a very delicate
hand—the hand, as she said to herself, of a gentleman.
What she liked was his face and something jaunty and
romantic, almost theatrical, in his whole little person. Miss
Henning was not acquainted with any member of the
dramatic profession, but she supposed vaguely that that was
the way an actor would look in private life. Hyacinth's
features were perfect; his eyes, large and much divided, had

as their usual expression a kind of witty, almost an impertinent, candour, and a small, soft, fair moustache disposed
itself upon his upper lip in a way that made him appear to
smile even when his heart was heavy. The waves of his dense
fine hair clustered round a forehead which was high enough
to suggest remarkable things, and Miss Henning had
observed that when he first appeared he wore his little soft
circular hat in a way that left these frontal locks very
visible. He was dressed in an old brown velveteen jacket and
wore exactly the bright-coloured necktie which Miss Pynsent's quick fingers used of old to shape out of hoarded
remnants of silk and muslin. He was shabby and work-
stained, but an observant eye would have caught the hint
of an 'arrangement' in his dress (his appearance being
plainly not a matter of indifference to himself) while a
painter (not of the heroic) would have liked to make a
sketch of him. There was something exotic in him, and yet,
with his sharp young face, destitute of bloom but not of
sweetness, and a certain conscious cockneyism that pervaded him, he was as strikingly as Millicent, in her own
degree, a product of the London streets and the London air.
He looked both ingenuous and slightly wasted, amused,
amusing and indefinably sad. Women had always found him
touching, but he made them—so they had repeatedly
assured him—die of laughing.

'I think you had better shut the door,' said Miss Pynsent,
meaning that he had better shut their departing visitor out.

'Did you come here on purpose to see us?' he went on,
not heeding this injunction, of which he divined the spirit,
and wishing the girl would take her leave so that he might
go out again with her. He should like talking with her
much better away from Pinnie, who evidently was ready to
stick a bodkin into her for reasons he perfectly understood.
He had seen plenty of them before, Pinnie's reasons, even
where girls were concerned who were not nearly so good-
looking as this one. She was always in a fearful 'funk' about
their getting hold of him and persuading him to make a
marriage beneath his station. His station!—poor Hyacinth

had often asked himself and enquired of Miss Pynsent what it could possibly be. He had thought of it bitterly enough, wondering how in the world he could marry 'beneath' it. He would never marry at all—to that his mind was absolutely made up; he would never hand on to another the burden that had made his own young spirit so intolerably sore, the inheritance that had darkened the whole threshold of his manhood. All the more reason why he should have his compensation; why, if the soft society of women was to be enjoyed on other terms, he should cultivate it with a bold free mind.

'I thought I'd just give a look at the old shop; I had an engagement not far off,' Millicent said. 'But I wouldn't have believed any one who had told me I should find you just where I left you.'

'We needed you to look after us!' Miss Pynsent irrepressibly exclaimed.

'Oh, you're such a rattling swell yourself!' Hyacinth observed without heeding the dressmaker.

'None of *your* "rattling" impudence! I'm as good a girl as there is in London.' And to corroborate this Miss Henning went on: 'If you were to offer to see me a part of the way home I'd tell you I don't knock about that way with gentlemen.'

'I'll go with you as far as you like,' Hyacinth replied simply, as if he knew how to treat that sort of speech.

'Well, it's only because I knew you as a baby!' And they went out together, Hyacinth careful not to look at poor Pinnie at all (he felt her glaring whitely and tearfully at him out of her dim corner—it had by this time grown too dusky to work without a lamp) and his companion giving her a cruelly familiar nod of farewell over her shoulder.

It was a long walk from Lomax Place to the quarter of the town in which (to be near the haberdashers of the Buckingham Palace Road) Miss Henning occupied a modest back room; but the influences of the hour were such as to make the excursion very agreeable to our young man, who liked the streets at all times, but especially at nightfall in the autumn, of a Saturday, when in the vulgar districts the smaller shops and open-air industries were doubly active, and big clumsy torches flared and smoked over hand-carts and costermongers' barrows drawn up in the gutters. Hyacinth had roamed through the great city since he was an urchin, but his imagination had never ceased to be stirred by the preparations for Sunday that went on in the evening among the toilers and spinners, his brothers and sisters, and he lost himself in all the quickened crowding and pushing and staring at lighted windows and chaffering at the stalls of fishmongers and hucksters. He liked the people who looked as if they had got their week's wage and were prepared to lay it out discreetly; and even those whose use of it would plainly be extravagant and intemperate; and, best of all, those who evidently hadn't received it at all and who wandered about disinterestedly and vaguely, their hands in empty pockets, watching others make their bargains and fill their satchels, or staring at the striated sides of bacon, at the golden cubes and triangles of cheese, at the graceful festoons of sausage, in the most brilliant of the windows. He liked the reflexion of the lamps on the wet pavements, the feeling and smell of the carboniferous London damp; the way the winter fog blurred and suffused the whole place, made it seem bigger and more crowded, produced halos and dim radiations, trickles and evaporations on the plates of glass. He moved in the midst of these impressions this evening, but he enjoyed them in silence, with an attention taken up mainly by his companion, and pleased to be already so intimate with a young lady whom people turned round to look at. She herself affected to speak of the rush and crush of the week's end with disgust: she said she liked the streets, but liked the respectable ones; she couldn't abide the smell of fish, which the whole place seemed full of, so that she hoped they would soon get into the Edgware Road, toward which they tended and which was a proper street for a lady. To Hyacinth she appeared to have no connexion with the long-haired little girl who, in Lomax Place, years before, was always hugging a smutty doll and courting his society; she was a stranger, a new acquaintance, and he observed her in suspense, wondering by what transitions she had reached her present pitch.

She enlightened him but little on this point, though she talked a great deal on a variety of subjects and mentioned to him her habits, her aspirations, her likes and dislikes—which last were as emphatic as the giggles of a person tickled. She was tremendously particular, difficult to please, he could see that; and she assured him she never put up with anything a moment after she had ceased to care for it. Especially was she particular about gentlemen's society, and she made it plain that a young fellow who wanted to have anything to say to her must be in receipt of wages amounting at the least to fifty shillings a week. Hyacinth assured her he didn't earn that as yet, and she remarked again that she made an exception for him because she knew all about him (or if not all at least a great deal) and he could see that her good-nature was equal to her beauty. She made such an exception that when, after they were moving down the Edgware Road (which had still the brightness of late closing, but with more nobleness) he proposed she should enter a coffee-house with him and 'take something' (he could hardly tell himself afterwards what brought him to this point) she acceded without a demur—without a demur even on the ground of his slender earnings. Slender as they were he had them in his pocket (they had been destined in some degree for Pinnie) and therefore felt equal to the occasion. Millicent partook profusely of tea and bread and butter, with a relish of raspberry jam, and thought the place most comfortable, though he himself, after finding himself ensconced, was visited by doubts of its propriety, suggested, among several things, by photographs, on the walls, of young ladies in tights. He himself was hungry, he had not yet had his tea, but he was too excited, too preoccupied to eat; the situation made him restless and gave him thrills; it seemed the beginning of something new and rare. He had never yet 'stood' even a glass of beer to a girl of Millicent's stamp—a girl who rustled and glittered and smelt of musk

—and if she should turn out as jolly a specimen of the sex as she seemed it might make a great difference in his leisure hours, in his evenings, in which he had often felt a likeness to great square blackboards uninscribed with a stroke of chalk. That it would also make a difference in his savings (he was under a pledge to Pinnie and to Mr Vetch to put by something every week) it didn't concern him for the moment to reflect; and indeed, though he thought it odious and insufferable to be poor, the ways and means of ceasing to be so had hitherto left his fancy unstirred. He knew what Millicent's age must be, but felt her nevertheless older, much older, than himself—she seemed to know so much about London and about life; and this made it still more of a sensation to be entertaining her like a young swell. He thought of it too in connexion with the question of the character of the establishment; if this character was what it easily might be she would perceive it as soon as he, and very likely it would be a part of the general initiation she had given him an impression of that she wouldn't mind so long as the tea was strong and the bread and butter thick. She described to him what had passed between Miss Pynsent and herself (she didn't call her Pinnie, and he was glad, for he wouldn't have liked it) before he came in, and let him know that she should never dare to come to the place again, as his mother would tear her eyes out. Then she checked herself. 'But of course she ain't your mother! How stupid I am! I keep forgetting.'

Hyacinth had, as he supposed, from far back cultivated a manner with which he could meet allusions of this kind: he had had first and last so many opportunities to practise it. Therefore he looked at his companion very steadily while he said: 'My mother died many years ago; she was a great invalid. But Pinnie has been awfully good to me.'

'My mother's dead too'—Miss Henning was prompt, as if 'capping' it. 'She died very suddenly. I dare say you remember her in the Plice.' Then, while Hyacinth disengaged from the past the obscure figure of Mrs Henning, of whom he mainly remembered that she used to strike him

as cross and dirty, the girl added, smiling, but with more
sentiment, 'But I've had no Pinnie.'

'You look as if you could take care of yourself.'

'Well, I'm very confiding,' said Millicent Henning. Then
she asked what had become of Mr Vetch. 'We used to say
that if Miss Pynsent was your mamma he was your papa.
In our family we used to call him Miss Pynsent's young
man.'

'He's her young man still,' Hyacinth returned. 'He's our
best friend—or supposed to be. He got me the place I'm in
now. He lives by his fiddle, as he used to do.'

Millicent looked a little at her companion, after which
she observed, 'I should have thought he would have got you
a place at his theatre.'

'At his theatre? That would have been no use. I don't
play any instrument.'

'I don't mean in the orchestra, you gaby! You'd look very
nice in a fancy costume.' She had her elbows on the table
and her shoulders lifted, an attitude of extreme familiarity.
He was on the point of replying that he didn't care for
fancy costumes, he wished to go through life in his own
character; but he checked himself with the reflexion that
this was exactly what he was apparently destined not to do.
His own character? He was to cover that up as carefully as
possible; he was to go through life in a mask, in a borrowed
mantle; he was to be every day and every hour an actor.
Suddenly and with the utmost irrelevance Miss Henning
enquired: 'Is Miss Pynsent some relation? What gave her
any right over you?'

Hyacinth had an answer ready for this question; he had
determined to say as he had several times said before: 'Miss
Pynsent's an old friend of my family. My mother was very
fond of her and she was very fond of my mother.' He
repeated the formula now, looking at the girl with the same
inscrutable calmness, as he fancied; though a remark more
to his taste would have been that his mother was none of her
business. But she was too handsome for such risks, and she
presented her large fair face to him across the table with an

air of solicitation to be cosy and comfortable. There were things in his heart and a torment and a hidden passion in his life which he should be glad enough to lay open to some woman. He believed that perhaps this would be the cure ultimately; that in return for something he might drop, syllable by syllable, into some listening ear that would be attached to some kissable cheek, certain other words would be spoken to him which would make his pain for ever less sharp. But what woman could he trust, what ear would be both safe and happily enough attached? How much didn't he already ask? The answer was not in this loud fresh laughing creature, whose sympathy couldn't have the fineness he was looking for, since her curiosity was vulgar. Hyacinth objected to the vulgar as much as Miss Pynsent herself; in this respect she had long since discovered that he was after her own heart. He had not at any rate now taken up the subject of Mrs Henning's death; he felt himself incapable of researches into that lady and had no desire for knowledge of Millicent's relationships. Moreover he always suffered, to sickness, when people began to hover about the question of his origin, the reasons why Pinnie had had the care of him from a baby. Mrs Henning had been repulsive, but at least her daughter could speak of her. 'Mr Vetch has changed his lodgings: he moved out of 17 three years ago,' he said, to vary the topic. 'He couldn't stand the other people in the house; there was a man who played the accordeon.'

Millicent, however, was but moderately interested in this anecdote, though wanting to know why people should like Mr Vetch's fiddle any better. Then she added: 'And I think that while he was about it he might have put you into something better than a bookbinder's.'

'He wasn't obliged to put me into anything. It's a very good place.'

'All the same, it isn't where I should have looked to find you,' the girl declared, not so much in the tone of wishing to offer him tribute as of resentment at having miscalculated.

'Where should you have looked to find me? In the House

of Commons? It's a pity you couldn't have told me in advance what you would have liked me to be.'

She faced him over her cup while she drank in ladylike sips. 'Do you know what they used to say in the Plice? That your father was a lord.'

'Very likely. That's the kind of rot they talk in that precious hole,' the young man said without blenching.

'Well, perhaps he was,' Millicent ventured.

'He may have been a prime-minister for all the good it has done me.'

'Fancy your talking as if you didn't know!' said Millicent.

'Finish your tea—don't mind how I talk.'

'Well, you 'ave got a temper!' she archly retorted. 'I should have thought you'd be a clerk at a banker's.'

'Do they select them for their tempers?'

'You know what I mean. You used to be too clever to follow a trade.'

'Well, I'm not clever enough to live on air.'

'You might be, really, for all the tea you drink! Why didn't you go in for some high profession?'

'How was I to go in? Who the devil was to help me?' Hyacinth asked with a certain vibration.

'Haven't you got any relations?' said Millicent after a moment.

'What are you doing? Are you trying to make me swagger?'

When he spoke sharply she only laughed, not in the least ruffled, and by the way she looked at him seemed to like the effect. 'Well, I'm sorry you're only a journeyman,' she went on as she pushed away her cup.

'So am I,' Hyacinth answered; but he called for the bill as if he had been an employer of labour. Then while they waited he remarked to his companion that he didn't believe she had an idea of what his work was and how charming it could be. 'Yes, I get up books for the shops,' he said when she had asserted that she perfectly understood. 'But the art of the binder's an exquisite art.'

'So Miss Pynsent told me. She said you had some samples at home. I should like to see them.'

'You wouldn't know how good they are,' he finely smiled.

He expected she would exclaim in answer that he was an impudent wretch, and for a moment she seemed on the point of doing so. But the words changed on her lips and she replied almost tenderly: 'That's just the way you used to speak to me years ago in the Plice.'

'I don't care about that. I hate all that time.'

'Oh, so do I, if you come to that,' said Millicent as if she could rise to any breadth of view. With which she returned to her idea that he had not done himself justice. 'You used always to have your nose in something or other. I never thought you'd work with your 'ands.'

This seemed to irritate him, and, having paid the bill and given threepence, ostentatiously, to the young woman with a languid manner and hair of an unnatural yellow who had waited on them, he said: 'You may depend upon it I shan't do it an hour longer than I can help.'

'What will you do then?'

'Oh, you'll see some day.' In the street, after they had begun to walk again, he went on: 'You speak as if I could have my pick. What was an obscure little beggar to do, buried in a squalid corner of London under a million of idiots? I had no help, no influence, no acquaintance of any kind with professional people, and no means of getting at them. I had to do something; I couldn't go on living on Pinnie. Thank God I help her now a little. I took what I could get.' He spoke as if he had been touched by the imputation of having derogated.

Millicent seemed to imply that he defended himself successfully when she said: 'You express yourself like a reg'lar gentleman'—a speech to which he made no response. But he began to talk again afterwards, and, the evening having definitely set in, his companion took his arm for the rest of the way home. By the time he reached her door he had confided to her that in secret he wrote—quite as for publication; he was haunted with the dream of literary distinction. This appeared to impress her, and she branched off to remark, with the agreeable incoherence that characterised her, that she didn't care anything for a man's family if she liked the man himself; she thought families and that sort of rot were about played out. Hyacinth wished she would leave his origin alone; and while they lingered in front of her house before she went in he broke out:

'I've no doubt you're a jolly girl, and I'm very happy to have seen you again. But you've awfully little tact.'

'*I* have little tact? You should see me work off an old jacket!'

He was silent a little, standing before her with his hands in his pockets. 'It's a good job you're so lovely.'

Millicent didn't blush at this compliment, and probably didn't understand all it conveyed, but she looked into his eyes a while, with all the smile that showed her teeth, and then came back more inconsequently than ever. 'Come now, who are you?'

'Who am I? I'm a wretched little "forwarder" in the shop.'

'I didn't think I ever could fancy any one in that line!' she competently cried. Then she let him know she couldn't ask him in, as she made it a point not to receive gentlemen, but she didn't mind if she took another walk with him and she didn't care if she met him somewhere—if it were handy enough. As she lived so far from Lomax Place she didn't care if she met him half-way. So in the dusky by-street in Pimlico, before separating, they took a casual tryst; the most interesting, the young man felt, that had yet been—he could scarcely call it granted him.

VI

ONE DAY shortly after this, at the bindery, his friend Poupin, absent, had failed to send the explanation customary in case of illness or domestic accident. There were two or three men employed in the place whose non-appearance, usually following close upon pay-day, was better unexplained, was in fact an implication of moral feebleness; but as a general thing Mr Crookenden's establishment was a haunt of punctuality and sobriety. Least of all had Eustache Poupin been in the habit of asking for a margin. Hyacinth knew how little indulgence he had ever craved, and this was part of his admiration for the extraordinary Frenchman, an ardent stoic, a cold conspirator and an exquisite artist, who was by far the most interesting person in the ranks of his acquaintance and whose conversation, in the workshop, helped him sometimes to forget the smell of leather and glue. His conversation! Hyacinth had had plenty of that and had endeared himself to the passionate refugee by the solemnity and candour of his attention. Poupin had come to England after the Commune of 1871, to escape the reprisals of the government of M. Thiers, and had remained there in spite of amnesties and rehabilitations. He was a Republican of the old-fashioned sort, of the note of 1848, humanitary and idealistic, infinitely addicted to fraternity and equality and inexhaustibly surprised and exasperated at finding so little enthusiasm for them in the land of his exile. He had a marked claim upon Hyacinth's esteem and gratitude, for he had been his *parrain*, his protector at the bindery. When Anastasius Vetch found something for Miss Pynsent's young charge to do, it was through the Frenchman, with whom he had accidentally made acquaintance, that he found it.

When the boy was about fifteen years of age Mr Vetch made him a present of the essays of Lord Bacon, and the purchase of this volume had important consequences for Hyacinth. Anastasius Vetch was a poor man, and the luxury of giving was for the most part denied him; but when once in a way he tasted it he liked the sensation to be pure. No man knew better the difference between the common and the rare, or was more capable of appreciating a book which opened well—of which the margin was not hideously chopped and of which the lettering on the back was sharp. It was only such a book that he could bring himself to offer even to a poor little devil whom a fifth-rate dressmaker (he knew Pinnie was fifth-rate) had rescued from the workhouse. So when it became a question of fitting the great Elizabethan with a new coat—a coat of full morocco discreetly, delicately gilt—he went with his little cloth-bound volume, a Pickering, straight to Mr Crookenden, whom every one who knew anything about the matter knew to be a prince of binders, though they also knew that his work, limited in quantity, was mainly done for a particular bookseller and only through the latter's agency. Anastasius Vetch had no idea of paying the bookseller's commission, and though he could be lavish (for him) when he made a present, he was capable of taking an immense deal of trouble to save sixpence. He made his way into Mr Crookenden's workshop, which was situated in a small superannuated square in Soho and where the proposal of so slender a job was received at first with chilling calm. Mr Vetch, however, insisted; he explained with irresistible frankness the motive of his errand: the desire to obtain the best possible binding for the least possible money. He made his conception of the best possible binding so vivid, so exemplary, that the master of the shop at last confessed to that disinterested sympathy which, in favouring conditions, establishes itself between the artist and the connoisseur. Mr Vetch's little book was put in hand as a particular service to an eccentric gentleman whose visit had been a smile-stirring interlude (for the circle of listening workmen) in a merely mechanical day; and when he went back three weeks later to see if the job were done he had the pleasure of finding that his injunctions, punctually complied with, had even been bettered. The work had been accomplished with a perfection of skill which made him ask whom he was to thank for it (he had been told that one man should do the whole of it) and in this manner he made the acquaintance of the most brilliant craftsman in the establishment, the incorruptible, the imaginative, the unerring Eustache Poupin.

In response to an appreciation which he felt not to be
banal M. Poupin remarked that he had at home a small
collection of experiments in morocco, russia, parchment, of
fanciful specimens with which, for the love of the thing
itself, he had amused his leisure hours and which he should
be happy to show his interlocutor if the latter would do
him the honour to call upon him at his lodgings in Lisson
Grove. Mr Vetch made a note of the address and, for the
love of the thing itself, went one Sunday afternoon to see
the binder's esoteric studies. On this occasion he made the
acquaintance of Madame Poupin, a small, fat lady with a
bristling moustache, the white cap of an *ouvrière*, a knowledge of her husband's craft that was equal to his own, and
not a syllable of English save the words 'What you think,
what you think?' which she introduced with indefatigable
frequency. He also discovered that his new acquaintance had
been a political proscript and that he regarded the iniquitous
fabric of Church and State with an eye scarcely more
reverent than the fiddler's own. M. Poupin was an aggressive
socialist, which Anastasius Vetch was not, and a constructive
democrat (instead of being a mere scoffer at effete things)
and a theorist and an optimist and a collectivist and a per-
fectionist and a visionary; he believed the day was to come
when all the nations of the earth would abolish their
frontiers and armies and custom-houses, and embrace on
both cheeks and cover the globe with boulevards, radiating
from Paris, where the human family would sit in groups at
little tables, according to affinities, drinking coffee (not tea,
par exemple!) and listening to the music of the spheres.
Mr Vetch neither prefigured nor desired this organised
beatitude; he was fond of his cup of tea and only wanted to
see the British constitution a good deal simplified; he
thought it a much overrated system, but his heresies rubbed
shoulders sociably with those of the little bookbinder, and
his friend in Lisson Grove became for him the type of the
intelligent foreigner whose conversation gives wings to our
heavy-footed culture. Poupin's humanitary zeal was as unlimited as his English vocabulary was the reverse, and the

new friends agreed with each other enough, and not too much, to discuss, which was much better than an unspeakable harmony. On several other Sunday afternoons the fiddler went back to Lisson Grove, and having, at his theatre, as a veteran, a faithful servant, an occasional privilege, he was able to carry thither, one day in the autumn, an order for two seats in the second balcony. Madame Poupin and her husband passed a lugubrious evening at the English comedy, where they didn't understand a word that was spoken and consoled themselves by hanging on the agitated fiddle-stick of their friend in the orchestra. But this adventure failed to arrest the development of a friendship into which, eventually, Amanda Pynsent was drawn. Madame Poupin, among the cold insularies, lacked female society, and Mr Vetch proposed to his amiable friend in Lomax Place to call upon her. The little dressmaker, who in the course of her life had known no Frenchwoman but the unhappy Florentine (so favourable a specimen till she began to go wrong) adopted his suggestion in the hope that she should get a few ideas from a lady whose appearance would doubtless exemplify (as Florentine's originally had done) the fine taste of her nation; but she found the bookbinder and his wife a bewildering mixture of the brilliant and the relaxed, and was haunted long afterwards by the memory of the lady's camisole in some hideous print, her uncorseted overflow and her carpet slippers.

The acquaintance, none the less, was sealed three months later by a supper, one Sunday night, in Lisson Grove, to which Mr Vetch brought his fiddle, at which Amanda presented to her hosts her adoptive son, and which also revealed to her that Madame Poupin could dress a Michaelmas goose if she couldn't dress a fat Frenchwoman. This lady confided to the fiddler that she thought Miss Pynsent exceedingly *comme il faut—dans le genre anglais*; and neither Amanda nor Hyacinth had ever passed an evening of such splendour. It took its place, in the boy's recollection, beside the visit, years before, to Mr Vetch's theatre. He drank in the remarks exchanged between that gentleman and M. Poupin. M. Poupin showed him his bindings, the most precious trophies of his skill, and it seemed to Hyacinth that on the spot he was initiated into a fascinating mystery. He handled the books for half an hour; Anastasius Vetch watched him without giving any particular sign. When therefore presently, Miss Pynsent consulted her friend for the twentieth time on the subject of Hyacinth's 'career'—she spoke as if she were hesitating between the diplomatic service, the army and the church—the fiddler replied with promptitude: 'Make him, if you can, what the Frenchman is.' At the mention of a handicraft poor Pinnie always looked very solemn, yet when Mr Vetch asked her if she were prepared to send the boy to one of the universities, or to pay the premium required for his being articled to a solicitor, or to make favour on his behalf with a bank director or a merchant prince, or, yet again, to provide him with a comfortable home while he should woo the muse and await the laurels of literature—when, I say, he put the case before her with this cynical, ironical lucidity she only sighed and said that all the money she had ever saved was ninety pounds, which, as he knew perfectly well, it would cost her his acquaintance for evermore to take out of the bank. The fiddler had in fact declared to her in a manner not to be mistaken that if she should divest herself, on the boy's account, of this sole nest-egg of her old age, he would wash his hands of her and her affairs. Her standard of success for Hyacinth was vague save on one point, as regards which she was passionately, fiercely firm: she was perfectly determined he should never go into a small shop. She would rather see him a bricklayer or a costermonger than dedicated to a retail business, tying up candles at a grocer's or giving change for a shilling across a counter. She would rather, she declared on one occasion, see him articled to a shoemaker or a tailor.

A stationer in a neighbouring street had affixed to his window a written notice that he was in want of a smart errand-boy, and Pinnie, on hearing of it, had presented Hyacinth to his consideration. The stationer was a dreadful bullying man with a patch over his eye, who seemed to think the boy would be richly remunerated with three shillings a week; a contemptible measure, as it seemed to the dressmaker, of his rare abilities and acquirements. His schooling had been desultory, precarious, and had had a certain continuity mainly in his early years, while he was under the care of an old lady who combined with the functions of pew-opener at a neighbouring church the manipulation, in the Place itself, where she resided with her sister, a monthly nurse, of such pupils as could be spared (in their families) from the more urgent exercise of holding the baby and fetching the beer. Later, for a twelvemonth, Pinnie had paid five shillings a week for him at an 'Academy' in a genteel part of Islington, where there was an 'instructor in the foreign languages', a platform for oratory and a high social standard, but where Hyacinth suffered from the fact that almost all his mates were the sons of dealers in edible articles—pastry-cooks, grocers and fishmongers—and in this capacity subjected him to pangs and ignominious contrasts by bringing to school, for their exclusive consumption or for exchange and barter, various buns, oranges, spices and marine animals, which the boy, with his hands in his empty pockets and the sense of a savourless home in heart, was obliged to see devoured without his participation. Miss Pynsent would not have pretended he was highly educated in the technical sense of the word, but she believed that at fifteen he had read almost every book in the world. The limits of his reading had been in fact only the limits of his opportunity. Mr Vetch, who talked with him more and more as he grew older, knew this, and lent him every volume he possessed or could pick up for the purpose. Reading was his extravagance, while the absence of any direct contact with a library represented for him mainly the hard shock of the real; the shock, that is, he could most easily complain of. Mr Vetch believed him subtly intelligent, and therefore thought it a woeful pity that he couldn't have furtherance in some liberal walk; but he would have thought it a greater pity still that a youth with that expression in his eyes should be condemned to measure tape or cut slices of cheese. He himself had no influence he could bring into play, no connexion with the great world of capital or the market of labour. That is he touched these mighty institutions at but one very small point—a point which, such as it was, he kept well in mind.

When Pinnie replied to the stationer round the corner, after he had mentioned the 'terms' on which he was prepared to receive applications from errand-boys, that, thank her stars, she hadn't sunk so low as that—so low as to sell her darling into slavery for three shillings a week—he felt that she only gave more florid expression to his own sentiment. Of course if Hyacinth didn't begin by carrying parcels he couldn't hope to be promoted, through the more refined nimbleness of tying them up, to a position as accountant or manager; but both the fiddler and his friend—Miss Pynsent indeed only in the last resort—resigned themselves to the forfeiture of this prospect. Mr Vetch saw clearly that a charming handicraft was a finer thing than a vulgar 'business', and one day after his acquaintance with Eustache Poupin had gone a considerable length he enquired of the fervid Frenchman if there were a chance of the lad's obtaining a footing, under his own wing, in Mr Crookenden's workshop. There could be no better place for him to acquire a knowledge of the most elegant of the mechanical arts; and to be received into such an establishment and at the instance of such an artist would be a real start in life. M. Poupin meditated, and that evening confided his meditations to the companion who reduplicated all his thoughts and understood him better even than he understood himself. The pair had no children and had felt the deficiency; moreover they had heard from Mr Vetch the dolorous tale of the boy's entrance into life. He was one of the disinherited, one of the expropriated, one of the exceptionally interesting; and moreover he was one of themselves, a child, as it were, of the inexhaustible France, an offshoot of the sacred race. It is not the most authenticated point in this veracious history, but there is strong reason to believe that tears were shed that night, in Lisson Grove, over poor Hyacinth Robinson. In a day or two M. Poupin replied to the fiddler that he had now been several years in *le vieux* 'Crook's' employ; that during that time he had done work for him which he would have had *bien du mal* to get done by another, and had never asked for an indulgence, an allowance, a remission, an augmentation. It was time, if only for the dignity of the thing, he should ask for something, and he would make their little friend the subject of his demand. '*La société lui doit bien cela*,' he remarked afterwards, when, Mr Crookenden proving dryly hospitable and the arrangement being formally complete, Mr Vetch thanked him in his kindly, casual, bashful English way. He was paternal when Hyacinth began to occupy a place in the malodorous chambers in Soho; he took him in hand, made him a disciple, the recipient of a precious tradition, discovered in him a susceptibility to philosophic, to cosmic, as well as to technic truth. He taught him French and socialism, encouraged him to spend his evenings in Lisson Grove, invited him to regard Madame Poupin as a second, or rather as a third, mother, and in short made a very considerable mark on the boy's mind. He fostered and drew out the latent Gallicism of his nature, and by the time he was twenty Hyacinth, who had completely assimilated his influence, regarded him with a mixture of veneration and amusement. M. Poupin was the person who consoled him most when he was miserable; and he was very often miserable.

His staying away from his work was so rare that, in the afternoon, before he went home, Hyacinth walked to Lisson Grove to see what ailed him. He found his friend in bed with a plaster on his chest and Madame Poupin making *tisane* over the fire. The Frenchman took his indisposition solemnly but resignedly, like a man who believed that all illness was owing to the imperfect organisation of society, and lay covered up to his chin with a red cotton handkerchief bound round his head. Near his bed sat a visitor, a young man unknown to Hyacinth. Hyacinth naturally had never been to Paris, but he always supposed that the *in-*

térieur of his friends in Lisson Grove gave rather a vivid idea of that city. The two small rooms constituting their establishment contained a great many mirrors as well as little portraits (old-fashioned prints) of revolutionary heroes. The chimney-piece in the bedroom was muffled in some red drapery which appeared to Hyacinth extraordinarily magnificent; the principal ornament of the salon was a group of small and highly-decorated cups, on a tray, accompanied by gilt bottles and glasses, the latter still more diminutive—the whole intended for black coffee and liqueurs. There was no carpet on the floor, but rugs and mats of various shapes and sizes disposed themselves at the feet of the chairs and sofas; and in the sitting-room, where stood a wonderful gilt clock of the Empire, surmounted with a 'subject' representing Virtue receiving a crown of laurel from the hands of Faith, Madame Poupin, with the aid of a tiny stove, a handful of charcoal and two or three saucepans, carried on a triumphant *cuisine*. In the windows were curtains of white muslin much fluted and frilled and tied with pink ribbon.

VII

'I'M SUFFERING extremely, but we must all suffer so long as the social question is so abominably, so iniquitously neglected,' Poupin remarked, speaking French and rolling toward Hyacinth his salient, excited-looking eyes, which always had the same declamatory, reclamatory, proclamatory, the same universally inaugurative expression, whatever his occupation or his topic. Hyacinth had seated himself near his friend's pillow, opposite the strange young man, who had been accommodated with a chair at the foot of the bed.

'Ah yes; with their filthy politics the situation of the *pauvre monde* is the last thing they ever think of!' his wife exclaimed from the fire. 'There are times when I ask myself how long it will go on.'

'It will go on till the measure of their imbecility, their infamy, is full. It will go on till the day of justice, till the
reintegration of the despoiled and disinherited, is ushered
in with a force that will shake the globe.'

'Oh, we always see things go on; we never see them
change,' said Madame Poupin, making a very cheerful clatter with a big spoon in a saucepan.

'We may not see it, but *they'll* see it,' her husband returned. 'But what do I say, my children? I do see it,' he
pursued. 'It's before my eyes in its radiant reality, especially
as I lie here—the revendication, the rehabilitation, the rectification.'

Hyacinth ceased to pay attention, not because he had a
differing opinion about what M. Poupin called the *avène-
ment* of the disinherited, but, on the contrary, precisely on
account of his familiarity with that prospect. It was the
constant theme of his French friends, whom he had long
since perceived to be in a state of chronic spiritual inflammation. For them the social question was always in order,
the political question always abhorrent, the disinherited
always present. He wondered at their zeal, their continuity,
their vivacity, their incorruptibility; at the abundant supply
of conviction and prophecy they always had on hand. He
believed that at bottom he was sorer than they, yet he had
deviations and lapses, moments when the social question
bored him and he forgot not only his own wrongs, which
would have been pardonable, but those of the people at
large, of his brothers and sisters in misery. They, however,
were perpetually in the breach, and perpetually consistent
with themselves and, what is more, with each other. Hyacinth had heard that the institution of marriage in France
was lightly considered, but he was struck with the closeness
and intimacy of the union in Lisson Grove, the passionate
identity of interest: especially on the day when M. Poupin
informed him, in a moment of extreme but not indiscreet
expansion, that the lady was his wife only in a spiritual,
affectional sense. There were hypocritical concessions and
debasing superstitions of which this exalted pair had wholly

disapproved. Hyacinth knew their vocabulary by heart and could have said everything, in the same words, that on any given occasion M. Poupin was likely to say. He knew that 'they', in their phraseology, was a comprehensive allusion to every one in the world but the people—though who, exactly, in their length and breadth, the people were was less definitely established. He himself was of this sacred body, for which the future was to have such compensations; and so of course were his French friends, and so was Pinnie, and so were most of the inhabitants of Lomax Place and the workmen in old Crook's shop. But was old Crook himself, who wore an apron rather dirtier than the rest of them and was a master-hand at 'forwarding', yet who, on the other side, was the occupant of a villa all but detached, at Putney, with a wife known to have secret aspirations toward a page in buttons? Above all was Mr Vetch, who earned a weekly wage, and not a large one, with his fiddle, but who had mysterious affinities of another sort, reminiscences of a phase in which he smoked cigars, had a hat-box and used cabs—besides visiting Boulogne? Anastasius Vetch had interfered in his life, atrociously, at a terrible crisis; but Hyacinth, who strove to cultivate justice in his own conduct, believed he had acted conscientiously, and tried to esteem him, the more so as the fiddler evidently felt he had something to make up to him for and had ever treated him with marked benevolence. He believed in short that Mr. Vetch took a sincere interest in him and if he should meddle again would meddle in a different way: he used to see him sometimes look at him with the kindest eyes. It would make a difference therefore if he were of the people or not, inasmuch as on the day of the great revenge it would only be the people who should be saved. It was for the people the world was made: whoever was not of them was against them; and all others were cumberers, usurpers, exploiters, *accapareurs*, as M. Poupin used to say. Hyacinth had once put the question directly to Mr Vetch, who looked at him a while through the fumes of his eternal pipe and then said: 'Do you think I'm an aristocrat?'

'I didn't know but you were a bourgeois,' the young man answered.

'No, I'm neither. I'm a Bohemian.'

'With your evening dress, every night?'

'My dear boy,' said the fiddler, 'those are the most confirmed.'

Hyacinth was only half satisfied with this, for it was by no means definite to him that Bohemians were also to be saved; if he could be sure perhaps he would become one himself. Yet he never suspected Mr Vetch of being a governmental agent, though Eustache Poupin had told him that there were a great many who looked a good deal like that: not of course with any purpose of incriminating the fiddler, whom he had trusted from the first and continued to trust. The governmental agent in extraordinary disguises, the wondrous *mouchard* of M. Poupin's view, became a very familiar type to Hyacinth, and though he had never caught one of the infamous brotherhood in the act there were plenty of persons to whom, on the very face of the matter, he had no hesitation in attributing the character. There was nothing of the Bohemian, at any rate, about the Poupins, whom Hyacinth had now known long enough not to be surprised at the way they combined the socialistic passion, a red-hot impatience for the general rectification, with an extraordinary decency of life and a worship of proper work. The Frenchman spoke habitually as if the great swindle practised upon the people were too impudent to be endured a moment longer, and yet he found patience for the most exquisite 'tooling' and took a book in hand with the deliberation of one who should believe that everything was immutably constituted. Hyacinth knew what he thought of priests and theologies, but he had the religion of conscientious craftsmanship and he reduced the boy, on his side, to a kind of prostration before his delicate wonder-working fingers. 'What will you have? *J'ai la main parisienne*,' M. Poupin would reply modestly when Hyacinth's admiration broke out; and he was good enough, after he had seen a few specimens of what our hero could do, to inform him that *he* had the same happy conformation. 'There's no reason why you shouldn't be a good workman, *il n'y a que ça*'; and his own life was practically governed by this conviction. He delighted in the use of his hands and his tools and the exercise of his taste, which was faultless, and Hyacinth could easily imagine how it must torment him to spend a day on his back. He ended by perceiving, however, that consolation was on this occasion in some degree conveyed by the presence of the young man who sat at the foot of the bed and with whom M. Poupin exhibited such signs of acquaintance as to make our hero wonder why he had not seen him before, nor even heard of him.

'What do you mean by force that will shake the globe?' the young man enquired, leaning back in his chair with raised arms and his interlocked hands, behind him, support- ing his head. M. Poupin had spoken French, which he always preferred to do, the insular tongue being an immense tribu- lation to him; but his visitor spoke English, and Hyacinth immediately took in that there was nothing French about *him*—M. Poupin could never tell him he had *la main parisienne*.

'I mean a force that will make the bourgeois go down into their cellars and hide, pale with fear, behind their barrels of wine and their heaps of gold!' cried M. Poupin, rolling ter- rible eyes.

'And in this country, I hope, in their coal-bins. *La-la*, we shall find them even there,' his wife remarked.

' '89 was an irresistible force,' said M. Poupin. 'I believe you would have thought so if you had been there.'

'And so was the entrance of the Versaillais, which sent you over here ten years ago,' the young man returned. He saw Hyacinth was watching him and he met his eyes, smil- ing a little, in a way that added to our hero's interest.

'*Pardon, pardon*, I resist!' cried Eustache Poupin, glaring, in his improvised nightcap, out of his sheets; and Madame repeated that they resisted—she believed well that they resisted! The young man burst out laughing; whereupon his host declared with a dignity which even his recumbent position didn't abate that it was really frivolous of him to ask such questions as that, knowing as he did—what he did know.

'Yes, I know—I know,' said the young man good-naturedly, lowering his arms and thrusting his hands into his pockets while he stretched his long legs a little. 'But everything is yet to be tried.'

'Oh the trial will be on a great scale—*soyez tranquille!* It will be one of those experiments that constitute a proof.'

Hyacinth wondered what they were talking about, and perceived that it must be something important, for the stranger was not a man who would take an interest in anything else. Hyacinth was immensely struck with him, could see he was remarkable, and felt slightly aggrieved that he should be a stranger: that is that he should be apparently a familiar of Lisson Grove and yet that M. Poupin should not have thought his young friend from Lomax Place worthy up to this time to be made acquainted with him. I know not to what degree the visitor in the other chair discovered these reflexions in Hyacinth's face, but after a moment, looking across at him, he said in a friendly yet just slightly diffident way, a way our hero liked: 'And do you know too?'

'Do I know what?' asked Hyacinth in wonder.

'Oh, if you did you would!' the young man exclaimed and laughed again. Such a rejoinder from any one else would have irritated our sensitive hero, but it only made him more curious about his interlocutor, whose laugh was loud and extraordinarily gay.

'*Mon ami*, you ought to present *ces messieurs*,' Madame Poupin remarked.

'*Ah ça*, is that the way you trifle with state secrets?' her husband cried without heeding her. Then he went on in a different tone: 'M. Hyacinthe is a gifted child, *un enfant très-doué*, in whom I take a tender interest—a child who has an account to settle. Oh, a thumping big one! Isn't it so, *mon petit*?'

This was very well meant, but it made Hyacinth blush,

and, without knowing exactly what to say, he murmured shyly: 'Oh, I only want them to let me alone!'

'He's very young,' said Eustache Poupin.

'He's the person we have seen in this country whom we like best,' his wife added.

'Perhaps you're French,' suggested the strange young man.

The trio seemed to Hyacinth to be waiting for his answer to this; it was as if a listening stillness had fallen. He found it a difficult pass, partly because there was something exciting and embarrassing in the attention of the other visitor, and partly because he had never yet had to decide that important question. He didn't really know if he were French or were English, or which of the two he should prefer to be. His mother's blood, her suffering in an alien land, the unspeakable, irremediable misery that consumed her in a place and among a people she must have execrated—all this made him French; yet he was conscious at the same time of qualities that didn't mix with it. He had spun to the last fineness, long ago, a legend about his mother, built it up slowly, adding piece to piece, in passionate musings and broodings, when his cheeks burned and his eyes filled; but there were times when it wavered and faded, when it ceased to console him and he ceased to trust it. He had had a father too, and his father had suffered as well, and had fallen under a blow, and had paid with his life; and him also he felt in his spirit and his senses, when the effort to think it out didn't simply end in darkness and confusion, challenging still even while they baffled, and inevitable freezing horror. At any rate he seemed rooted in the place where his wretched parents had expiated, and he knew nothing of any other. Moreover when old Poupin said 'M. Hyacinthe', as he had often done before, he didn't altogether enjoy it; he thought it made his name, which he liked well enough in English, sound like the name of a hairdresser. Our young friend was under a cloud and a stigma, but he was not yet prepared to admit he was ridiculous. 'Oh, I dare say I ain't anything,' he replied in a moment.

'En v'là des bêtises!' cried Madame Poupin. 'Do you mean

to say you're not as good as any one in the world? I should like to see!'

'We all have an account to settle, don't you know?' said the strange young man.

He evidently meant this to be encouraging to Hyacinth, whose quick desire to avert M. Poupin's allusions had not been lost on him; but our hero could see that he himself would be sure to be one of the first to be paid. He would make society bankrupt, but he would be paid. He was tall and fair and good-natured looking, but you couldn't tell—or at least Hyacinth couldn't—if he were handsome or ugly, with his large head and square forehead, his thick, straight hair, his heavy mouth and rather vulgar nose, his admirably clear steady eyes, light-coloured and set very deep; for despite a want of fineness in some of its parts his face had a marked expression of intelligence and resolution, spoke somehow, as if it had showed you his soul drawing deep and even breaths, of a state of moral health. He was dressed as a workman in his Sunday toggery, having evidently put on his best to call in Lisson Grove, where he was to meet a lady, and wearing in particular a necktie which was both cheap and pretentious and of which Hyacinth, who noticed everything of that kind, observed the crude false blue. He had very big shoes—the shoes almost of a country labourer —and spoke with a provincial accent which Hyacinth believed to be that of Lancashire. This didn't suggest cleverness, but it didn't prevent Hyacinth from feeling sure he was the reverse of stupid, that he probably indeed had a large easy brain quite as some people had big strong fists. Our little hero had a great desire to know superior persons, and he interested himself on the spot in this quiet stranger whose gravity, by any fine balance, showed, like that of a precious metal, in the small piece as well as in the big. He had the complexion of a ploughboy and the glance of a commander-in-chief, and might have been a distinguished young *savant* in the disguise of an artisan. The disguise would have been very complete, for he had several brown stains on his fingers. Hyacinth's curiosity on this occasion was both excited and gratified; for after two or three allusions, which he didn't understand, had been made to a certain place where Poupin and their friend had met and expected to meet again, Madame Poupin exclaimed that it was a shame not to take in M. Hyacinthe, who, she would answer for it, had in him the making of one of the pure.

'All in good time, in good time, *ma bonne*,' the worthy invalid replied. 'M. Hyacinthe knows I count on him, whether or no I make him an *interne* to-day or only wait a little longer.'

'What do you mean by an *interne*?' Hyacinth asked.

'*Mon Dieu*, what shall I say!'—and Eustache Poupin stared at him solemnly from his pillow. 'You're very sympathetic, but I'm afraid you're too young.'

'One is never too young to contribute one's *obole*,' said Madame Poupin.

'Can you keep a secret?' asked the other guest, but not as if he thought it probable.

'Is it a plot—a conspiracy?' Hyacinth broke out.

'He asks that as if he were asking if it's a plum-pudding,' said M. Poupin. 'It isn't good to eat, and we don't do it for our amusement. It's terribly serious, my child.'

'It's a group of workers to which he and I and a good many others belong. There's no harm in telling him that,' the young man went on.

'I advise you not to tell it to Mademoiselle; she's quite in the old ideas,' Madam Poupin suggested to Hyacinth, tasting her *tisane*.

Hyacinth sat baffled and wondering, looking from his fellow-labourer in Soho to his new acquaintance opposite. 'If you've some plan, something to which one can give one's self, I think you might have told me,' he remarked in a moment to Poupin.

The latter merely viewed him a little as if he were a pleasing object and then said to the strange young man: 'He's a little jealous of you. But there's no harm in that; it's of his age. You must know him, you must like him. We'll tell you his history some other day; it will make you feel that he belongs to us of necessity. It's an accident that he hasn't met you here before.'

'How could *ces messieurs* have met when M. Paul never comes? He doesn't spoil us!' Madame Poupin cried.

'Well, you see I've my little sister at home to take care of when I ain't at the works,' M. Paul explained. 'This afternoon it was just a chance; there was a lady we know came in to sit with her.'

'A lady—a real lady?'

'Oh yes, every inch,' smiled M. Paul.

'Do you like them to thrust themselves into your apartment like that because you've the *désagrément* of being poor? It seems to be the custom in this country, but it wouldn't suit me at all,' Madame Poupin continued. 'I should like to see one of *ces dames*—the real ones—coming in to sit with me!'

'Oh, you're not a cripple; you've got the use of your legs!'

'Yes, and of my arms!' cried the Frenchwoman.

'This lady looks after several others in our court and she reads to my sister.'

'Oh, well, you're patient, you other English.'

'We shall never do anything without that,' said M. Paul with undisturbed good-humour.

'You're perfectly right; you can't say that too often. It will be a tremendous job and only the strong will prevail,' his host murmured a little wearily, turning his eyes to Madame Poupin, who approached slowly, holding the *tisane* in rather a full bowl and tasting it again and yet again as she came.

Hyacinth had been watching his fellow-visitor with deepening interest; a fact of which M. Paul apparently became aware, for he volunteered presently, giving a little nod in the direction of the bed, 'He says we ought to know each other. I'm sure I've nothing against it. I like to know folk if they're likely to be worth it.'

Hyacinth was too pleased with this even to take it up; it seemed to him for a moment that he couldn't touch it gracefully enough. But he said with sufficient eagerness: 'Will you tell me all about your plot?'

'Oh, it's no plot. I don't think I care much for plots.' And with his mild, steady, light-blue English eye, M. Paul certainly had not much the appearance of a conspirator.

'Isn't it a new era?' asked Hyacinth, rather disappointed.

'Well, I don't know; it's just a taking of a stand on two or three points.'

'*Ah bien, voilà du propre*; between us we've thrown him into a fever!' cried Madame Poupin, who had put down her bowl on a table near her husband's bed and was bending over him with her hand on his forehead. Her patient was flushed, he had closed his eyes, and it was evident there had been more than enough conversation. Madame Poupin announced as much, with the addition that if the young men wished to make acquaintance they must do it outside; their friend must be perfectly quiet. They accordingly withdrew with apologies and promises to return for further news on the morrow, and two minutes later Hyacinth found himself standing face to face with his companion on the pavement in front of M. Poupin's residence, under a street-lamp which struggled ineffectually with the brown winter dusk.

'Is that your name, M. Paul?' he asked as he looked up at him.

'Oh bless you, no; that's only her Frenchified way of putting it. My name *is* Paul, though—Paul Muniment.'

'And what's your trade?' Hyacinth demanded with a jump into familiarity; for his friend seemed to have told him a great deal more than was usually conveyed in that item of information.

Paul Muniment looked down at him from above broad shoulders. 'I work for a firm of wholesale chemists at Lambeth.'

'And where do you live?'

'I live over the water too; in the far south of London.'

'And are you going home now?'

'Oh yes, I'm going to toddle.'

'And may I toddle with you?'

Mr Muniment considered him further and then gave a laugh. 'I'll carry you if you like.'

'Thank you; I expect I can walk as far as you,' said Hyacinth.

'Well, I admire your spirit and I dare say I shall like your company.'

There was something in his face, taken in connexion with the idea that he was concerned in the taking of a stand—it offered our quick youth the image of a rank of bristling bayonets—which made Hyacinth feel the desire to go with him till he dropped; and in a moment they started away together and took the direction Muniment had mentioned. They discoursed as they went, exchanging a great many opinions and anecdotes; but they reached the south-westerly court in which the young chemist lived with his infirm sister before he had told Hyacinth anything definite about the 'points' of his reference or Hyacinth, on his side, had detailed the circumstances involved in his being, according to M. Poupin, one of the disinherited. Hyacinth didn't wish to press, wouldn't for the world have appeared indiscreet, and moreover, though he had taken so great a fancy to Muniment, was not quite prepared as yet to be pressed himself. Therefore it failed to become very clear how his companion had made Poupin's acquaintance and how long he had enjoyed it. Paul Muniment nevertheless was to a certain extent communicative, especially on the question of his living in a very poor little corner. He had his sister to keep—she could do nothing for herself; and he paid a low rent because she had to have doctors and doses and all sorts of little comforts. He spent a bob a week for her on flowers. It was better too when you got upstairs, and from the back windows you could see the dome of Saint Paul's. Audley Court, with its pretty name, which reminded Hyacinth of Tennyson, proved to be a still dingier nook than Lomax Place; and it had the further drawback that you had to penetrate a narrow alley, a passage between high black walls, to enter it. At the door of one of the houses the young men paused, lingering a little, and then Muniment said: 'I say, why shouldn't you come

up? I like you well enough for that, and you can see my
sister; her name's Rosy.' He spoke as if this would be a
great privilege and added, for the joke, that Rosy enjoyed a
call from a gentleman of all things. Hyacinth needed no urging, and he groped his way at his companion's heels up a
dark staircase which appeared to him—for they stopped only
when they could go no further—the longest and steepest he
had ever ascended. At the top Paul Muniment pushed open
a door, but exclaimed 'Hullo, have you gone to roost?' on
perceiving the room on the threshold of which they stood
to be unlighted.

'Oh dear, no; we're sitting in the dark,' a small bright
voice instantly replied. 'Lady Aurora's so kind; she's here
still.'

The voice came out of a corner so pervaded by gloom
that the speaker was indistinguishable. 'Well now, that's
beautiful!' Paul Muniment rejoined. 'You'll have a party
then, for I've brought some one else. We're poor, you know,
but honest, and not afraid of showing up, and I dare say we
can manage a candle.'

At this, in the dim firelight, Hyacinth saw a tall figure
erect itself—a figure angular and slim, crowned with a large
vague hat and a flowing umbrageous veil. This unknown
person gave a singular laugh and said: 'Oh I brought some
candles; we could have had a light if we had wished.' Both
the tone and the purport of the words announced to Hyacinth that they proceeded from Lady Aurora.

VIII

PAUL MUNIMENT took a match out of his pocket and
lighted it on the sole of his shoe; after which he applied it
to a tallow candle which stood in a tin receptacle on the
low mantel-shelf. This enabled Hyacinth to perceive a narrow bed in a corner and a small object stretched upon it—an
object revealed to him mainly by the bright fixedness of a

pair of large eyes, of which the whites were sharply contrasted with the dark pupil and which gazed at him across a counterpane of gaudy patchwork. The brown room seemed crowded with heterogeneous objects and presented moreover, thanks to a multitude of small prints, both plain and coloured, fastened all over the walls, a highly-decorated appearance. The little person in the corner had the air of having gone to bed in a picture-gallery, and as soon as Hyacinth became aware of this his impression deepened that Paul Muniment and his sister were very wonderful people. Lady Aurora hovered before him with an odd drooping, swaying erectness, and she laughed a good deal, vaguely and shyly, as for the awkwardness of her being found still on the premises. 'Rosy, girl, I've brought you a visitor,' Hyacinth's guide soon said. 'This young man has walked all the way from Lisson Grove to make your acquaintance.' Rosy continued to look at the visitor from over her counterpane, and he felt slightly embarrassed, for he had never yet been presented to a young lady in her position. 'You mustn't mind her being in bed—she's always in bed,' her brother went on. 'She's in bed just the same as a little slippery trout's in the water.'

'Dear me, if I didn't receive company because I was in bed, there wouldn't be much use, would there, Lady Aurora?'

Rosy put this question in a light, gay tone, with a dart of shining eyes at her companion, who replied at once with still greater hilarity and in a voice which struck Hyacinth as strange and affected: 'Oh mercy, no; it seems quite the natural place!' Then she added: 'And it's such a lovely bed, such a comfortable bed!'

'Indeed it is, when your ladyship makes it up,' said Rosy; while Hyacinth wondered at this strange phenomenon of a peer's daughter (for he knew she must be that) performing the functions of a housemaid.

'I say now, you haven't been doing that again today?' Muniment asked, punching the mattress of the invalid with a vigorous hand.

'Pray, who would if I didn't?' Lady Aurora enquired. 'It only takes a minute if one knows how.' Her manner was jocosely apologetic and she seemed to plead guilty to having been absurd; in the dim light Hyacinth thought he saw her blush as if she were much embarrassed. In spite of her blushing her appearance and manner suggested to him a personage in a comedy. She sounded the letter *r* as a *w*.

'I can do it beautifully. I often do it, when Mrs Major doesn't come up,' Paul Muniment said, continuing to thump his sister's couch in an appreciative but somewhat subversive manner.

'Oh, I've no doubt whatever!' Lady Aurora exclaimed quickly. 'Mrs Major must have so very much to do.'

'Not in the making-up of beds, I'm afraid; there are only two or three, down there, for so many,' the young man returned loudly and with a kind of inconsequent cheerfulness.

'Yes, I've thought a great deal about that. But there wouldn't be room for more, you know,' said Lady Aurora, this time with all gravity.

'There's not much room for a family of that sort anywhere—thirteen people of all ages and sizes,' her host observed. 'The world's pretty big, but there doesn't seem room.'

'We're also thirteen at home,' Lady Aurora hastened to mention. 'We're also rather crowded.'

'Surely you don't mean at Inglefield?' Rosy demanded from her dusky nook.

'I don't know about Inglefield. I'm so much in town.' Hyacinth could see that Inglefield was a subject she wished to turn off, and to do so she added: 'We too are of all ages and sizes.'

'Well, it's fortunate you're not all *your* size!' Paul Muniment declared with a freedom at which Hyacinth was rather shocked and which led him to suspect that though his new friend was a very fine fellow a delicate tact was not his main characteristic. Later he explained this by the fact that he was rural and provincial and had not had, like himself, the benefit of the life of a capital; and later still he wished to know what, after all, such a character as that had to do with tact or compliments, and why its work in the world was not most properly performed by the simple exercise of a rude manly strength.

At this familiar allusion to her stature Lady Aurora turned hither and thither a little confusedly; Hyacinth saw her high, lean figure almost rock in the dim little room. Her commotion carried her to the door, and with ejaculations of which it was difficult to guess the meaning she was about to depart when Rosy detained her, having evidently much more social art than Paul. 'Don't you see it's only because her ladyship's standing up that she's so, you gawk? *We're* not thirteen at any rate, and we've got all the furniture we want, so there's a chair for every one. Do be seated again, Lady Aurora, and help me to entertain this gentleman. I don't know your name, sir; perhaps my brother will mention it when he has collected his wits. I'm very glad to see you, though I don't see you very well. Why shouldn't we light one of her ladyship's candles? It's very different to that common thing.'

Hyacinth thought Miss Muniment very charming; he had begun to make her out better by this time, and he watched her small wan, pointed face, framed on the pillow by thick black hair. She was a diminutive dark person, pale and wasted with a lifelong infirmity; Hyacinth thought her manner denoted high accomplishment—he judged it impossible to tell her age. Lady Aurora pleaded that she ought to have gone, long since; but she seated herself nevertheless on the chair that Paul pushed toward her.

'Here's a go!' this young man exclaimed to the other guest. 'You told me your name, but I've clean forgotten it.' Then when Hyacinth had pronounced it again he said to his sister: 'That won't tell you much; there are bushels of Robinsons in the north. But you'll like him, he's all right; I met him at the Poupins.' 'Puppin' would represent the sound by which he designated the French bookbinder, and that was the name by which Hyacinth always heard him called at Crookenden's. Hyacinth knew how much nearer to the right thing he himself came.

'Your name, like mine, represents a flower,' said the little woman in the bed. 'Mine is Rose Muniment and her ladyship's is Aurora Langrish. That means the morning or the dawn; it's the most beautiful of all, don't you think?' Rose Muniment addressed this question to Hyacinth while Lady Aurora gazed at her shyly and mutely and as if admiring her manner, her self-possession and flow of conversation. Her brother lighted one of the visitor's candles and the girl went on without waiting for Hyacinth's response. 'Isn't it right she should be called the dawn when she brings light where she goes? The Puppins are the charming foreigners I've told you about,' she explained to her friend.

'Oh, it's so pleasant knowing a few foreigners!' Lady Aurora exclaimed with a spasm of expression. 'They're often so very fresh.'

'Mr Robinson's a sort of foreigner and he's very fresh,' said Paul Muniment. 'He meets Mr Puppin quite on his own ground. If I had his gift of tongues it would bring me on.'

'I'm sure I should be very happy to help you with your French. I feel the advantage of knowing it,' Hyacinth remarked finely, becoming conscious that his declaration drew the attention of Lady Aurora toward him; so that he wondered what he could go on to say to keep at that level. This was the first time he had encountered socially a member of that aristocracy to which he had now for a good while known it was Miss Pynsent's theory that he belonged; and the occasion was interesting in spite of the lady's appearing to have so few of the qualities of her caste. She was about thirty years of age; her nose was large and, in spite of the sudden retreat of her chin, her face long and lean. She had the manner of extreme near-sightedness; her front teeth projected from her upper gums, which she revealed when she smiled, and her fair hair, in tangled silky skeins (Rose Muniment thought it too lovely) drooped over her pink cheeks. Her clothes looked as if she had worn them a good deal in the rain, and the note of a certain disrepair in her apparel

was given by a hole in one of her black gloves, through
which a white finger gleamed. She was plain and diffident
and she might have been poor; but in the fine grain and
sloping, shrinking slimness of her whole person, the delicacy
of her curious features and a kind of cultivated quality in her
sweet, vague, civil expression, there was a suggestion of race,
of long transmission, of an organism that had resulted from
fortunate touch after touch. She was not a common woman;
she was one of the caprices of an aristocracy. Hyacinth
didn't define her in this manner to himself, but he received
from her the impression that if she was a simple creature
(which he learned later she was not) aristocracies were yet
complicated things. Lady Aurora remarked that there were
many delightful books in French, and he proclaimed it a
torment to know that (as he did very well) when you saw no
way to getting hold of them. This led Lady Aurora to say
after a moment's hesitation that she had a good lot of her
own and that if he liked she should be most happy to lend
them to him. Hyacinth thanked her—thanked her even too
much, and felt both the kindness and the brilliant promise
of the offer (he knew the exasperation of having volumes in
his hands, for external treatment, which he couldn't take
home at night, having tried that method surreptitiously
during his first weeks at old Crook's and come very near
being sacked in consequence) while he wondered how such
a system could be put into practice; whether she would
expect him to call at her house and wait in the hall till the
books were sent out to him. Rose Muniment exclaimed that
that was her ladyship all over—always wanting to make up
to people for being less lucky than herself: she would take
the shoes off her feet for any one that might take a fancy
to them. At this the visitor declared that she would stop
coming to see her if the girl caught her up that way for
everything; and Rosy, without heeding the remonstrance,
explained to Hyacinth that she thought it the least she could
do to give what she had. She was so ashamed of being rich
that she wondered the lower classes didn't break into Inglefield and take possession of all the treasures in the Italian

room. She was a tremendous socialist; she was worse than any one—she was worse even than Paul.

'I wonder if she's worse than me,' Hyacinth returned at a venture, not understanding the allusions to Inglefield and the Italian room, which Miss Muniment made as if she knew all about these places. After learning more of the world he remembered this tone of Muniment's sister—he was to have plenty of observation of it on other occasions—as that of a person in the habit of visiting the nobility at their country-seats; she talked about Inglefield as if she had stayed there.

'Hullo, I didn't know you were so advanced!' exclaimed the master of the scene, who had been sitting silent and sidewise in a chair that was too narrow for him, his big arm hugging the back. 'Have we been entertaining an angel unawares?'

Hyacinth made out he was chaffing him, but he knew the way to face that sort of thing was to exaggerate one's meaning. 'You didn't know I was advanced? Why, I thought that was the principal thing about me. I think I go about as far as any one.'

'I thought the principal thing about you was that you knew French,' Paul Muniment said with an air of derision which showed him he wouldn't put that ridicule upon him unless he liked him, at the same time that it revealed to him how he had come within an ace of posturing.

'Well, I don't know it for nothing. I'll say something that will take your head off if you don't look out—just the sort of thing they say so well in French.'

'Oh, do say something of that kind; we should enjoy it so much!' cried Rosy in perfect good faith and clasping her hands for expectation.

The appeal was embarrassing, but Hyacinth was saved from the consequences of it by a remark from Lady Aurora, who quavered out the words after two or three false starts, appearing to address him, now that she spoke to him directly, with a sort of overdone consideration. 'I should like so very much to know—it would be so interesting—if you don't mind—how far exactly you do go.' She threw back her head very far and thrust her shoulders forward, and if her chin had been more adapted to such a purpose would have appeared to point it at him.

This challenge was hardly less alarming than the other, for he was far from being ready with an impressive formula. He replied, however, with a candour in which he tried as far as possible to sink his vagueness: 'Well, I'm very strong indeed. I think I see my way to conclusions from which even Monsieur and Madame Poupin would shrink. Poupin, at any rate; I'm not so sure about his wife.'

'I should like so much to know Madame,' Lady Aurora murmured as if politeness demanded that she should content herself with this answer.

'Oh, Puppin isn't strong,' said Muniment; 'you can easily look over his head! He has a sweet assortment of phrases—they're really pretty things to hear, some of them; but he hasn't had a new idea these thirty years. It's the old stock that has been withering in the window. All the same he warms one up; he has a spark of the sacred fire. The principal conclusion Mr Robinson sees his way to,' he added to Lady Aurora, 'is that your father ought to have his head chopped off and carried on a pike.'

'Ah yes, the French Revolution.'

'Lord, I don't know anything about your father, my lady!' Hyacinth interposed.

'Didn't you ever hear of the Earl of Inglefield?' cried Rose Muniment.

'He's one of the best,' said Lady Aurora as if she were pleading for him.

'Very likely, but he's a landlord, and he has an hereditary seat and a park of five thousand acres all to himself, while we're bundled together into this sort of kennel.' Hyacinth admired the young man's consistency till he saw he was amusing himself; after which he still admired the way he could mix that up with the tremendous opinions it must have been certain he entertained. In his own imagination he associated bitterness with the revolutionary passion; but the young chemical expert, at the same time that he was planning far ahead, seemed capable of turning revolutionists themselves into ridicule even for the entertainment of the revolutionised.

'Well, I've told you often enough that I don't go with you at all,' said Rose Muniment, whose recumbency appeared not in the least to interfere with her universal participation. 'You'll make a tremendous mistake if you try to turn everything round. There ought to be differences, and high and low, and there always will be, true as ever I lie here. I think it's against everything, pulling down them that's above.'

'Everything points to great changes in this country, but if once our Rosy's against them how can you be sure? That's the only thing that makes me doubt,' her brother went on, looking at her with a placidity which showed the habit of indulgence.

'Well, I may be ill, but I ain't buried, and if I'm content with my position—such a position as it is—surely other folk might be with theirs. Her ladyship may think I'm as good as her if she takes that notion; but she'll have a deal to do to make *me* believe it.'

'I think you're much better than I, and I know very few people so good as you,' Lady Aurora brought out, blushing not for her opinions but for her timidity. It was easy to see that though she was original she would have liked to be even more original than she was. She was conscious, however, that such a declaration might appear rather gross to persons who didn't see exactly how she meant it; so she added, as quickly as her hesitating manner permitted, to cover it up: 'You know there's one thing you ought to remember, *à propos* of revolutions and changes and all that sort of thing; I just mention it because we were talking of some of the dreadful things that were done in France. If there were to be a great disturbance in this country—and of course one hopes there won't—it would be my impression that the people would behave in a different way altogether.'

'What people do you mean?' Hyacinth allowed himself to enquire.

'Oh, the upper class, the people who've got all the things.'

'We don't call them the *people*,' observed Hyacinth, reflecting the next instant that his remark was a little primitive.

'I suppose you call them the wretches, the scoundrels!' Rose Muniment suggested, laughing merrily.

'All the things, but not all the brains,' her brother said.

'No indeed, aren't they stupid?' exclaimed her ladyship. 'All the same, I don't think they'd all go abroad.'

'Go abroad?'

'I mean like the French nobles who emigrated so much. They'd stay at home and resist; they'd make more of a fight. I think they'd fight very hard.'

'I'm delighted to hear it, and I'm sure they'd win!' cried Rosy.

'They wouldn't collapse, don't you know,' Lady Aurora continued. 'They'd struggle till they were beaten.'

'And you think they'd be beaten in the end?' Hyacinth asked.

'Oh dear, yes,' she replied with a familiar confidence at which he was greatly surprised. 'But of course one hopes it won't happen.'

'I infer from what you say that they talk it over a good deal among themselves, to settle the line they'll take,' said Paul Muniment.

But Rosy intruded before Lady Aurora could answer. 'I think it's wicked to talk it over, and I'm sure we haven't any business to talk it over here! When her ladyship says the aristocracy will make a fine stand I like to hear her say it and I think she speaks in a manner that becomes her own position. But there's something else in her tone which, if I may be allowed to say so, I think a great mistake. If her ladyship expects, in case of the lower classes coming up in that odious manner, to be let off easily, for the sake of the concessions she may have made in advance, I'd just advise her to save herself the disappointment and the trouble.

They won't be a bit the wiser and they won't either know or care. If they're going to trample over their betters it isn't on account of her having seemed to give up everything to us here that they'll let *her* off. They'll trample on her just the same as on the others, and they'll say she has got to pay for her title and her grand relations and her fine appearance. Therefore I advise her not to waste her good-nature in trying to let herself down. When you're up so high as that you've got to stay there; and if the powers above have made you a lady the best thing you can do is to hold up your head. I can promise your ladyship *I* would!'

The close logic of this speech and the quaint self-possession with which the little bedridden speaker delivered it struck Hyacinth as amazing and confirmed his idea that the brother and sister were a most extraordinary pair. It had a terrible effect on poor Lady Aurora, by whom so stern a lesson from so humble a quarter had evidently not been expected and who sought refuge from her confusion in a series of pleading gasps, while Paul Muniment, with his humorous density, which was deliberate, and acute too, not seeing, or at any rate not heeding, that she had been sufficiently snubbed by his sister, inflicted a fresh humiliation in saying, 'Rosy's right, my lady. It's no use trying to buy yourself off. You can't do enough; your sacrifices don't count. You spoil your fun now and you don't get it made up to you later. To all you people nothing will ever be made up. Eat your pudding while you have it; you mayn't have it long.'

Lady Aurora listened to him with her eyes on his face, and as they rested there Hyacinth scarcely knew what to make of her expression. Afterwards he thought he could attach a meaning to it. She got up quickly when Muniment had ceased speaking; the movement suggested she had taken offence and he would have liked to show her he thought she had been rather roughly used. But she gave him no chance, not glancing at him for a moment. Then he saw he was mistaken and that if she had flushed considerably it was only with the excitement of pleasure, the enjoyment of such original talk and of seeing her friends at last as free and familiar as she wished them to be. 'You're the most delightful people—I wish every one could know you!' she broke out. 'But I must really be going.' She went to the bed and bent over Rosy and kissed her.

'Paul will see you as far as you like on your way home,' this young woman remarked.

Lady Aurora protested, but Paul, without protesting in return, only took up his hat and smiled at her as if he knew his duty. On this her ladyship said: 'Well, you may see me downstairs; I forgot it was so dark.'

'You must take her ladyship's own candle and you must call a cab,' Rosy directed.

'Oh, I don't go in cabs, I walk.'

'Well, you may go on the top of a 'bus if you like; you can't help being superb,' Miss Muniment declared, watching her sympathetically.

'Superb? Oh mercy!' cried the poor devoted, grotesque lady, leaving the room with Paul, who told Hyacinth to wait for him a little. She neglected to take leave of our young man, and he asked himself what was to be hoped from that sort of people when even the best of them—those that wished to be agreeable to the *demos*—reverted inevitably to the supercilious. She had said no more about lending him her books.

IX

'SHE LIVES in Belgrave Square; she has ever so many brothers and sisters; one of her sisters is married to Lord Warmington,' Rose Muniment instantly began, not apparently in the least discomposed at being left alone with a strange young man in a room which was now half dark again, thanks to her brother's having carried off the second and more brilliant candle. She was so interested for the time in telling Hyacinth the history of Lady Aurora that she appeared not to remember how little she knew about himself. Her ladyship had declared her life and her pocket-money to the poor and sick; she cared nothing for parties and races and dances and picnics and cards and life in great houses, the usual amusements of the aristocracy: she was like one of the saints of old come to life again out of a legend. She had made their acquaintance, Paul's and hers, about a year before, through a friend of theirs, such a fine brave young woman, who was in Saint Thomas's Hospital for a surgical operation. She had been laid up there for weeks during which Lady Aurora, always looking out for those who couldn't help themselves, used to come and talk to her and read to her, till the end of her time in the ward, when the poor girl, parting with her kind friend, told her how she knew of another unfortunate creature (for whom there was no place there, because she was incurable) who would be mighty thankful for any little attention of that sort. She had given Lady Aurora the address in Audley Court and the very next day her ladyship had knocked at their door. It wasn't because she was poor—though in all con-science they were pinched enough—but because she had so little satisfaction in her limbs. Lady Aurora came very often, for several months, without meeting Paul, because he was always at his work; but one day he came home early on purpose to find her, to thank her for her goodness, and also to see (Miss Muniment rather shyly intimated) if she were really so good as his extravagant little sister made her out. Rosy had a triumph after that: Paul had to admit that her ladyship was beyond anything that any one in his wak-ing senses would believe. She seemed to want to give up everything to those who were below her and never to expect any thanks at all. And she wasn't always preaching and showing you your duty; she wanted to talk to you sociable-like, as if you were just her own sister. And *her* own sisters were the highest in the land, and you might see her name in the newspapers the day they were presented to the Queen. Lady Aurora had been presented too, with feathers in her head and a long tail to her gown; but she had turned her back on it all with a kind of terror—a sort of shivering sinking state which she had often described to Miss Muniment. The day she had first seen Paul was the day they became so intimate, the three of them together—if she might apply such a word as that to such a peculiar connexion. The little woman, the little girl, as she lay there (Hyacinth scarce knew how to characterise her) told our young man a very great secret, in which he found himself too much interested to think of criticising so precipitate a confidence. The secret was that, of all the people she had ever seen in the world, her ladyship thought Rosy's Paul the very cleverest. And she had seen the greatest, the most famous, the brightest of every kind, for they all came to stay at Inglefield, thirty and forty of them at once. She had talked with them all and heard them say their best (and you could fancy how they would try to give it out at such a place as that, where there was nearly a mile of conservatories and a hundred wax candles were lighted at a time) and at the end of it all she had made the remark to herself—and she had made it to Rosy too—that there was none of them had such a head on his shoulders as the young man in Audley Court. Rosy wouldn't spread such a rumour as that in the court itself, but she wanted every friend of her brother's (and she could see Hyacinth was a real one by the way he listened) to know what was thought of him by them that had an experience of intellect. She didn't wish to give it out that her ladyship had lowered herself in any manner to a person that earned his bread in a dirty shop (clever as he *might* be) but it was easy to see she minded what he said as if he had been a bishop—or more indeed, for she didn't think much of bishops, any more than Paul himself, and that was an idea she had got from him. Oh, she took it none so ill if he came back from his work before she had gone, and tonight Hyacinth could see for himself how she had lingered. This evening, she was sure, her ladyship would let him walk home with her half the way. This announcement gave Hyacinth the prospect of a considerable session with his communicative hostess; but he was very glad to wait, for

he was vaguely, strangely excited by her talk, fascinated by
the little queer-smelling, high-perched interior, encumbered
with relics, treasured and polished, of a poor north-country
home, bedecked with penny ornaments and related in so
unexpected a manner to Belgrave Square and the great
landed estates. He spent half an hour with Paul Muniment's
small, odd, sharp, crippled, chattering sister, who gave him
an impression of education and native wit (she expressed
herself far better than Pinnie or than Milly Henning) and
who startled, puzzled and at the same time rather distressed
him by the manner in which she referred herself to the
most abject class—the class that prostrated itself, that was
in a fever and flutter, in the presence of its betters. That
was Pinnie's attitude of course, but Hyacinth had long ago
perceived that his adoptive mother had generations of
plebeian patience in her blood, and that though she had a
tender soul she had not a truly high spirit. He was more
entertained than afflicted, however, by Miss Muniment's
tone, and he was thrilled by the frequency and familiarity of
her allusions to a kind of life he had often wondered about;
this was the first time he had heard it described with that
degree of authority. By the nature of his mind he was
perpetually, almost morbidly conscious that the circle in
which he lived was an infinitesimally small shallow eddy
in the roaring vortex of London, and his imagination
plunged again and again into the flood that whirled past it
and round it, in the hope of being carried to some brighter,
happier vision—the vision of societies where, in splendid
rooms, with smiles and soft voices, distinguished men, with
women who were both proud and gentle, talked of art,
literature and history. When Rosy had delivered herself to
her complete satisfaction on the subject of Lady Aurora she
became more quiet, asking as yet, however, no straight
questions of her guest, whom she seemed to take very much
for granted. He presently remarked that she must let him
come very soon again, and he added, to explain this wish:
'You know you seem to me very curious people.'

Miss Muniment didn't in the least repudiate the imputation. 'Oh yes, I dare say we seem very curious. I think we're generally thought so; especially me, being so miserable and yet so lively.' And she laughed till her bed creaked again.

'Perhaps it's lucky you're ill; perhaps if you had your health you'd be all over the place,' Hyacinth suggested. And he went on candidly: 'I can't make it out, your being so up in everything.'

'I don't see why you need make it out! But you would, perhaps, if you had known my father and mother.'

'Were they such a rare lot?'

'I think you'd say so if you had ever been in the mines. Yes, in the mines, where the filthy coal's dug out. That's where my father came from—he was working in the pit when he was a child of ten. He never had a day's schooling in his life, but he climbed up out of his black hole into day-light and air, and he invented a machine, and he married my mother, who came out of Durham, and (by her people) out of the pits and the awfulness too. My father had no great figure, but *she* was magnificent—the finest woman in the country and the bravest and the best. She's in her grave now, and I couldn't go to look at it even if it were in the nearest churchyard. My father was as black as the coal he worked in: I know I'm just his pattern, barring that *he* did have his legs, when the liquor hadn't got into them. Yet between him and my mother, for grand high intelligence, there wasn't much to choose. But what's the use of brains if you haven't got a backbone? My poor father had even less of that than I, for with me it's only the body that can't stand up, and with him it was the very nature. He invented, for use in machine-shops, a mechanical improvement—a new kind of beam-fixing, whatever that is—and he sold it at Bradford for fifteen pounds: I mean the whole right and profit of it and every hope and comfort of his family. He was always straying and my mother was always bringing him back. She had plenty to do, with me a puny ailing brat from the moment I opened my eyes. Well, one night he strayed so far that he never came home, or only came a loose bloody bundle of clothes. He had fallen into a gravel-pit, he didn't know where he was going. That's the reason my brother won't ever touch so much as you could wet your finger with, and that I've only a drop once a week or so in the way of a strengthener. I take what her ladyship brings me, but I take no more. If she could but have come to us before my mother went—that would have been a saving! I was only nine when my father died, and I'm three years older than Paul. My mother did for us with all her might, and she kept us decent—if such a useless little mess as me can be said to be decent. At any rate she kept me alive, and that's a proof she was handy. She went to the wash-tub, and she might have been a queen as she stood there with her bare arms in the foul linen and her long hair braided on her head. She was terrible handsome, but he'd have been a bold man that had taken on himself to tell her so. And it was from her we got our education—she was determined we should rise above the common. You might have thought, in her position, that she couldn't go into such things, but she was a rare one for keeping you at your book. She could hold to her idea when my poor father couldn't, and her idea for us was that Paul should get learning and should look after me. You can see for yourself that that's what has come of it. How he got it's more than I can say, as we never had a penny to pay for it; and of course my mother's head wouldn't have been of much use if he hadn't had a head himself. Well, it was all in the family. Paul was a boy that would learn more from a yellow poster on a wall or a time-table at a railway station than many a young fellow from a year at college. That was his only college, poor lad—picking up what he could. Mother was taken when she was still needed, nearly five years ago. There was an epidemic of typhoid, and of course it must pass me over, the goose of a thing—only that I'd have made a poor feast—and just lay that really grand character on her back. Well, she never again made it ache over her soapsuds, straight and broad as it was. Not having seen her, you wouldn't believe,' said Rose Muniment in conclusion; 'but I just wanted you to understand that our parents had jolly good brains at least to give us.'

Hyacinth listened to this eloquence—the clearest statement of anything he had ever heard made by a woman—with the deepest interest, and without being in the least moved to allow for filial exaggeration; inasmuch as his impression of the brother and sister was such as it would have taken a much more marvellous tale to account for. The very way Rose Muniment talked of brains made him feel this; she pronounced the word as if she were distributing prizes for intellectual eminence from off a platform. No doubt the weak inventor and the strong worker had been fine specimens, but that didn't diminish the merit of their highly original offspring. The girl's insistence on her mother's virtues (even now that her age had become more definite to him he thought of her as a girl) touched in his heart a chord that was always ready to throb—the chord of melancholy aimless wonder as to the difference it would have made for his life to have had some rich warm presence like that in it.

'Are you very fond of your brother?' he enquired after a little.

The eyes of his hostess glittered at him. 'If you ever quarrel with him you'll see whose side I shall take.'

'Ah, before that I shall make you like *me*.'

'That's very possible, and you'll see how I shall fling you over!'

'Why then do you object so to his views—his ideas about the way the people are to come up?'

'Because I think he'll get over them.'

'Never—never!' cried Hyacinth. 'I've only known him an hour or two, but I deny that with all my strength.'

'Is that the way you're going to make me like you—contradicting me so?' Miss Muniment asked with familiar archness.

'What's the use, when you tell me I shall be sacrificed? One might as well perish for a lamb as for a sheep.'

'I don't believe you're a lamb at all. Certainly you're not

if you want all the great people pulled down and the most dreadful scenes enacted.'

'Don't you believe in human equality? Don't you want anything done for the groaning, toiling millions—those who have been cheated and crushed and bamboozled from the beginning of time?'

Hyacinth asked this question with considerable heat, but the effect of it was to send his companion off into a new ring of laughter. 'You say that just like a man my brother described to me three days ago, a little man at some club whose hair stood up—Paul imitated the way he raved and stamped. I don't mean that you do either, but you use almost the same words as him.' Hyacinth scarce knew what to make of this allusion or of the picture offered him of Paul Muniment casting ridicule on those who spoke in the name of the down-trodden. But Rosy went on before he had time to do more than reflect that there would evidently be great things to learn about her brother: 'I haven't the least objection to seeing the people improved, but I don't want to see the aristocracy lowered an inch. I like so much to look at it up there.'

'You ought to know my Aunt Pinnie—she's just such another benighted idolater!' Hyacinth returned.

'Oh, you're making me like you very fast! And pray who's your Aunt Pinnie?'

'She's a dressmaker and a charming little woman. I should like her to come and see you.'

'I'm afraid I'm not in her line—I never had on a dress in my life. But, as a charming woman, I should be delighted to see her,' Miss Muniment hastened to add.

'I'll bring her some day,' he said; and then he went on rather incongruously, for he was irritated by the girl's optimism, thinking it a shame her sharpness should be enlisted on the wrong side. 'Don't you want, for yourself, a better place to live in?'

She jerked herself up and for a moment he thought she would jump out of her bed at him. 'A better place than this? Pray how could there be a better place? Every one thinks it's lovely; you should see our view by daylight—you should see everything I've got. Perhaps you're used to something very fine, but Lady Aurora says that in all Belgrave Square there isn't such a cosy little room. If you think I'm not perfectly content you're very much mistaken!'

Such an attitude could only exasperate him, and his exasperation made him indifferent to the mistake of his having appeared to sniff at Miss Muniment's quarters. Pinnie herself, submissive as she was, had spared him that sort of displeasure; she groaned over the dinginess of Lomax Place sufficiently to remind him that she had not been absolutely stultified by misery. 'Don't you sometimes make your brother very cross?' he asked, smiling, of his present entertainer.

'Cross? I don't know what you take us for! I never saw him lose his temper in his life.'

'He must be a rum customer! Doesn't he really care for —for what we were talking about?'

For a space Rosy was silent; then she replied: 'What my brother really cares for—well, one of these days, when you know, you'll tell me.'

Hyacinth stared. 'But isn't he tremendously deep in——' What should he call the mystery?

'Deep in what?'

'Well, in what's going on beneath the surface. Doesn't he belong to important things?'

'I'm sure I don't know what he belongs to—you may ask him!' cried Rosy, who laughed gaily again as the opening door re-admitted the subject of their conversation. 'You must have crossed the water with her ladyship,' she pursued. 'I wonder who enjoyed their walk most.'

'She's a handy old girl and she has a goodish stride,' said the young man.

'I think she's in love with you simply, Mr Muniment.'

'Really, my dear, for an admirer of the aristocracy you allow yourself a licence,' Paul scoffed, smiling at Hyacinth.

Hyacinth got up, feeling that really he had paid a long visit; his curiosity was far from satisfied, but there was a limit to the time one should spend in a young lady's sleeping apartment. 'Perhaps she is; why not?' he struck out.

'Perhaps she is then, she's daft enough for anything.'

'There have been fine folks before who have patted the people on the back and pretended to enter into their life,' Hyacinth said. 'Is she only playing with that idea or is she in earnest?'

'In earnest—in terrible deadly earnest, my dear fellow! I think she must be rather crowded out at home.'

'Crowded out of Inglefield? Why, there's room for three hundred!' Rosy broke in.

'Well, if that's the kind of mob that's in possession, no wonder she prefers Camberwell. We must be kind to the poor lady,' Paul added in a tone that Hyacinth noticed. He attributed a remarkable meaning to it; it seemed to say that people such as he were now so sure of their game that they could afford to be magnanimous; or else it expressed a prevision of the doom that hung over her ladyship's head. Muniment asked if Hyacinth and Rosy had got on together, and the girl replied that Mr Robinson had made himself most agreeable. 'Then you must tell me all about him after he goes, for you know I don't know him much myself,' said her brother.

'Oh yes, I'll tell you everything—you know how I like describing.'

Hyacinth found himself amused at the young lady's account of his efforts to please her, the fact being that he had only listened to her own eager discourse without opening his mouth; but Paul, whether or no guessing the truth, said to him all pertinently: 'It's very wonderful—she can describe things she has never seen. And they're just like the reality.'

'There's nothing I've never seen,' Rosy declared. 'That's the advantage of my lying here in such a manner. I see everything in the world.'

'You don't seem to see your brother's meetings—his secret societies and his revolutionary clubs. You put that aside when I asked you.'

'Oh, you mustn't ask her that sort of thing,' said Paul, lowering at Hyacinth with a fierce frown—an expression he perceived in a moment to be facetiously assumed.

'What am I to do then, since you won't tell me anything definite yourself?'

'It will be definite enough when you get hanged for it!' Rosy exclaimed mockingly.

'Why do you want to poke your head into ugly black holes?' Muniment asked, laying his hand on Hyacinth's shoulder and shaking it gently.

'Don't you belong to the party of action?' our young man gravely demanded.

'Look at the way he has picked up all the silly bits of catchwords!' Paul cried in not unkindly derision to his sister. 'You must have got that precious phrase out of the newspapers, out of some drivelling leader. Is that the party you want to belong to?' he went on with his clear eyes ranging over his diminutive friend.

'If you'll show me the thing itself I shall have no more occasion to mind the newspapers,' Hyacinth candidly pleaded, rejoicing all the while to feel himself in such a relation. It was his view of himself, and not an unfair one, that his was a character that would never sue for a favour; but now he felt that in any connexion with Paul Muniment such a law would be suspended. This rare man he could go on his knees to without a sense of humiliation.

'What thing do you mean, infatuated, deluded youth?' Paul pursued, refusing to be serious.

'Well, you know you do go to places you had far better keep out of, and that often when I lie here and listen to steps on the stairs I'm sure they are coming in to make a search for your papers,' Miss Muniment lucidly interposed.

'The day they find my papers, my dear, will be the day you'll get up and dance.'

'What did you ask me to come home with you for?' Hyacinth demanded as he twirled his hat. It was an effort for a moment to keep the tears from his eyes; he saw himself forced to put such a different construction on his new friend's hospitality. He had had a happy impression that Muniment had divined in him a possible associate of a high type in a subterranean crusade against the existing order of things, whereas it now came over him that the real use he had been put to was to beguile an hour for a pert invalid. That was all very well, and he would sit by Miss Rosy's bedside, were it a part of his service, every day in the week; only in such a case it should be his reward to enjoy the confidence of her brother. This young man justified at the present juncture the high estimate Lady Aurora Langrish had formed of his intelligence: whatever his natural reply to Hyacinth's question would have been he invented straight off a better one and said at random, smiling and not knowing exactly what his visitor had meant—

'What did I ask you to come with me for? To see if you'd be afraid.'

What there was to be afraid of was to Hyacinth a quantity equally vague; but he answered quickly enough: 'I think you've only to try me to see.'

'I'm sure that if you introduce him to some of your low wicked friends he'll be quite satisfied after he has looked round a bit,' Miss Muniment remarked irrepressibly.

'Those are just the kind of people I want to know,' Hyacinth rang out.

His sincerity appeared to touch his friend. 'Well, I see you're a good 'un. Just meet me some night.'

'Where, where?' asked Hyacinth eagerly.

'Oh, I'll tell you where when we get away from *her*.' And Muniment led him good-humouredly out.

X

SEVERAL MONTHS after Hyacinth had made his acquaintance Millicent Henning remarked that it was high time our hero should take her to some first-class place of amusement. He proposed hereupon the Canterbury Music Hall; at which she tossed her head and affirmed that when a young lady had done for a young man what she had done for him the least he could do was to give her an evening at some theatre in the Strand. Hyacinth would have been a good deal at a loss to say exactly what she had done for him, but it was familiar to him by this time that she regarded him as under great obligations. From the day she had come to look him up in Lomax Place she had taken a position, largely, in his life, and he had seen poor Pinnie's wan countenance grow several degrees more blank. Amanda Pynsent's forebodings had been answered to the letter; the flaring cometary creature had become a fixed star. She had never spoken to him of Millicent but once, several weeks after her interview with the girl; and this had not been in a tone of rebuke, for she had divested herself for ever of any maternal prerogative. Tearful, tremulous, deferential enquiry was now her only weapon, and nothing could be more humble and circumspect than the manner in which she made use of it. He was never at home of an evening, at present, and he had mysterious ways of spending his Sundays, with which church-going had nothing to do. The time had been when often, after tea, he sat near the lamp with the dressmaker and, while her fingers flew, read out to her the works of Dickens and of Scott; happy hours of vain semblance that he had forgotten the wrong she had done him, so that she could almost forget it herself. But now he gulped down his tea so fast that he hardly took off his hat while he sat there, and Pinnie, with her quick eye for all matters of costume, noticed that he wore it still more gracefully askew than usual, cocking it with a victorious exalted air. He hummed to himself; he fingered his moustache; he looked out of the window when there was nothing to look at; he seemed preoccupied, launched in intellectual excursions, half anxious and half in spirits. During the whole winter Miss Pynsent explained everything by four words murmured beneath her breath: 'That beastly forward jade!' On the single occasion, however, on which she had sought relief from her agitation in an appeal to Hyacinth she didn't trust herself to designate the girl by epithet or title.

'There's only one thing I want to know,' she said to him in a manner which might have seemed casual if in her silence, knowing her as well as he did, he had not already perceived the implication of her thought. 'Does she expect you to marry her, dearest?'

'Does who expect me? I should like to see the woman who does!'

'Of course you know who I mean. The one that came after you—and picked you right up—from the other end of London.' And at the remembrance of that insufferable scene poor Pinnie flamed for a moment. 'Aren't there plenty of vulgar fellows in that low part where she lives without her ravaging over here? Why can't she stick to her own beat, I should like to know?' Hyacinth had flushed at the question, and she had seen something in his face to make her change her tone. 'Just promise me this, my precious child: that if you get into any sort of mess with that piece you'll immediately confide it to your poor old Pinnie.'

'My poor old Pinnie sometimes makes me quite sick,' he remarked for answer. 'What sort of a mess do you suppose I shall get into?'

'Well, suppose she does come it over you that you promised to marry her?'

'You don't know what you're talking about. She doesn't want to marry any one—the way she sees it.'

'Then how the dickens does she see it?'

'Do you imagine I'd tell a lady's secrets?' the young man returned.

'Oh laws, if she was a lady I shouldn't be afraid!' said Pinnie.

'Every woman's a lady when she has placed herself under one's protection,' Hyacinth declared with his little manner of a man of the great world.

'Under your protection? Oh I say!' cried Pinnie, staring. 'And pray who's to protect *you*?'

As soon as she had said this she repented, because it

seemed just the sort of exclamation that would have made Hyacinth bite her head off. One of the things she loved him for, however, was that he gave you touching surprises in this line, had sudden inconsistencies of temper that were all for your advantage. He was by no means always mild when he ought to have been, but he was sometimes heavenly when he needn't have been at all. At such moments Pinnie wanted to kiss him and had often tried to make Mr Vetch understand what fascinating traits of character she was always noting in their young friend. This particular one was rather difficult to describe, and Mr Vetch never would admit that he understood, or that he had observed anything that seemed to correspond to the dressmaker's somewhat confused psychological sketch. It was a comfort to her in these days, and almost the only one she had, that she was sure Anastasius Vetch understood a good deal more than he felt bound to acknowledge. He was always up to his old game of being a great deal cleverer than cleverness itself required; and it consoled her present weak, pinched feeling to know that, though he still talked of the boy as if it would be a pity to take him too seriously, that wasn't the way he thought of him. He also took him seriously and had even a certain sense of duty in regard to him. Miss Pynsent went so far as to say to herself that the fiddler probably had savings and that no one had ever known of any one else belonging to him. She wouldn't have mentioned it to Hyacinth for the world, for fear of leading up to a disappointment; but she had visions of a foolscap sheet folded away in some queer little bachelor's box (she couldn't fancy what men kept in such places) on which the youth's name would have been written down in very big letters before a solicitor.

'Oh, I'm unprotected in the nature of things,' he replied, smiling at his too scrupulous companion. Then he added: 'At any rate, it isn't from that girl any danger will come to me.'

'I can't think why you like her,' Pinnie remarked as if she had spent on the question treasures of impartiality.

'It's jolly to hear one woman on the subject of another,' Hyacinth said. 'You're kind and good and yet you're ready——!' He gave a sigh as for long experience.

'Well, what am I ready to do? I'm not ready to see you gobbled up before my eyes!'

'You needn't be afraid. She won't drag me to the altar.'

'And pray doesn't she think you good enough—for one of the beautiful 'Ennings?'

'You don't understand, my poor Pinnie,' he wearily pleaded. 'I sometimes think there isn't a single thing in life that you understand. One of these days she'll marry an alderman.'

'An alderman—that creature?'

'An alderman or a banker or a bishop or some of that bloated kind. She doesn't want to end her career today—she wants to begin it.'

'Well, I wish she'd take you later!' the dressmaker returned.

Hyacinth said nothing for a little, but then broke out: 'What are you afraid of? Look here, we had better clear this up once for all. Are you afraid of my marrying a girl out of a shop?'

'Oh, you wouldn't, would you?' cried Pinnie with conciliatory eagerness. 'That's the way I like to hear you talk!'

'Do you think I'd marry any one who would marry *me*?' Hyacinth went on. 'The kind of girl who'd look at me is the kind of girl I'd never look at.' He struck Pinnie as having thought it all out; which didn't surprise her, as she had been familiar from his youth with his way of following things up. But she was always delighted when he made a remark that showed he was conscious of being of fine clay—flashed out an allusion to his not being what he seemed. He was not what he seemed, but even with Pinnie's valuable assistance he had not succeeded in representing to himself very definitely what he was. She had placed at his disposal for this purpose a passionate idealism which, employed in some case where it could have consequences, might have been termed profligate and which yet never cost her a scruple or a compunction.

'I'm sure a princess might look at you and be none the worse!' she declared in her delight at this assurance, more positive than any she had yet received, that he was safe from the worse danger. This the dressmaker considered to be the chance of his marrying some person of her own base order. Still it came over her that his taste might be lowered, and before the subject was dropped, on the present occasion, she said that of course he must be quite aware of all that was wanting to such a girl as Millicent 'Enning—who visibly wasn't worth any struggle for her aspirate.

'Oh, I don't bother about what's wanting to her. I'm content with what she has.'

'Content, dearest—how do you mean?' the little dressmaker quavered. 'Content to make an intimate friend of her?'

'It's impossible I should discuss these matters with you,' Hyacinth grandly enough replied.

'Of course I see that. But I should think she'd bore you sometimes,' Miss Pynsent threw off cunningly.

'She does, I assure you, to extinction!'

'Then why do you spend every evening with her?'

'Where should you like me to spend my evenings? At some beastly public-house—or at the Italian opera?' His association with Miss Henning was not so close as that, but nevertheless he wouldn't take the trouble to prove to poor Pinnie that he enjoyed her society only two or three times a week; that on other evenings he simply strolled about the streets (this boyish habit clung to him) and that he had even occasionally the resource of going to the Poupins' or of gossiping and smoking a pipe at some open house-door, when the night was not cold, with a fellow-mechanic. Later in the winter, after he had made Paul Muniment's acquaintance, the aspect of his life changed considerably, though Millicent continued to be exceedingly mixed up with it. He hated the taste of liquor and still more the taste of the places where it was sold; besides which the types of misery and vice that one was liable to see collected in them frightened and harrowed him, made him ask himself questions that pierced the deeper because they were met by no answer. It was both a blessing and a drawback to him that the delicate, charming character of the work he did at old Crook's, under Eustache Poupin's influence, was a kind of education of the taste, trained him in the finest discriminations, in the recognition of the rare and the hatred of the cheap. This made the brutal, garish, stodgy decoration of public-houses, with their deluge of gaslight, their glittering brass and pewter, their lumpish woodwork and false colours, detestable to him. He had been still very young when the 'gin-palace' ceased to convey to him an idea of the palatial.

For this unfortunate but remarkably-organised youth every displeasure or gratification of the visual sense coloured his whole mind, and though he lived in Pentonville and worked in Soho, though he was poor and obscure and cramped and full of unattainable desires, nothing in life had such an interest or such a price for him as his impressions and reflexions. They came from everything he touched, they made him vibrate, kept him thrilled and throbbing, for most of his waking consciousness, and they constituted as yet the principal events and stages of his career. Fortunately they were often an immense amusement. Everything in the field of observation suggested this or that; everything struck him, penetrated, stirred; he had in a word more news of life, as he might have called it, than he knew what to do with—felt sometimes as he could have imagined an overwhelmed man of business to whom the post brought too many letters. The man of business indeed could keep a secretary, but what secretary could have cleared up for Hyacinth some of the strange communications of life? He liked to talk about these things, but it was only a few here and there he could discuss with Milly. He allowed Miss Pynsent to imagine that his hours of leisure were almost exclusively dedicated to this young lady, because, as he said to himself, if he were to account to her

for every evening in the week it would make no difference—
she would stick to her suspicion; and he referred this perversity to the general weight of misconception under which
he at this crude period of his growth held it was his lot to
languish. It didn't matter if one was a little more or a little
less misunderstood. He might indeed have remembered it
mattered to Pinnie, who, after her first relief at hearing him
express himself so properly on the subject of a matrimonial
connexion with Miss Henning, allowed her faded, kind,
weak face little by little to lengthen out to its old solemnity.
This came back as the days went on, for it wasn't much
comfort that he didn't want to marry the young woman in
Pimlico when he allowed himself to be held as tight as if
he did. For the present, however, she simply said, 'Oh well,
if you see her as she is I don't care what you do'—a sentiment implying a certain moral recklessness on the part of
the good little dressmaker. She was irreproachable herself,
but she had lived more than fifty years in a world of wickedness; like so many London women of her class and kind
she had little sentimental softness for her own sex, whose
general 'paying' seemed the simplest and most natural
arrangement; and she judged it quite a minor evil that
Millicent should be left lamenting if only Hyacinth might
get out of the scrape. Between a young person who had
taken a gross risk and a premature, lowering marriage for
her beloved little boy she very well knew which she preferred. It should be added that her view of Millicent's
power to look after herself was such as to make it absurd to
pity her in advance. Pinnie thought Hyacinth the cleverest
young man in the, or at least in their, world, but her state
of mind implied that the young lady in Pimlico was cleverer.
Her ability, at any rate, was of a kind that precluded the
knowledge of suffering, whereas Hyacinth's was somehow
fairly founded on it.

By the time he had enjoyed for three months the acquaintance of the brother and sister in Audley Court the whole
complexion of his life seemed changed; it was pervaded by
an element of romance which overshadowed, though by no

means eclipsing, the brilliant figure of Miss Henning. It was pitched in a higher key altogether and appeared to command a view of horizons equally fresh and vast. Millicent therefore shared her dominion without knowing exactly what it was that drew her old playfellow off and without indeed demanding of him an account she was not on her own side prepared to give. Hyacinth was, in the language of the circle in which she moved, her personal fancy, and she was content to fill as regards himself the same eminent and somewhat irresponsible position. She had the assurance that she was a beneficent friend: fond of him and careful of him as an elder sister might be; warning him as no one else could do against the dangers of the town; putting that stiff common sense, of which she was convinced that she possessed an extraordinary supply, at the service of his incurable verdancy; looking after him generally as no one, poor child, had ever done. Millicent made light of the dingy dressmaker in this view of her friend's meagre little past (she thought Pinnie no better than a starved cat) and enjoyed herself immensely in the character of guide and philosopher. She felt that character never so high as when she pushed the young man with a robust elbow or said to him, 'Well, you *are* a sharp 'un, you are!' Her theory of herself, as we know, was that she was the 'best sort' in the world, as well as one of the greatest beauties and quickest wits, and there could be no better proof of her kindness of heart than her disinterested affection for a snippet of a bookbinder. Her sociability was certainly immense, and so were her vanity, her grossness, her presumption, her appetite for beer, for buns, for entertainment of every kind. She represented for Hyacinth during this period the eternal feminine, and his taste, considering he was fastidious, will be wondered at; the judgement will be that she didn't represent it very favourably.

It may easily be believed that he criticised his inclination even while he gave himself up to it, and that he often wondered he should find so much to attract in a girl in whom he found so much to condemn. She was vulgar, clumsy and grotesquely ignorant; her conceit was proportionate and she hadn't a grain of tact or of quick perception. And yet there was something so elementally free in her, by his loose measure, she carried with such an air the advantages she did possess, that her figure constantly mingled itself even with those bright visions hovering before him after Paul Muniment had opened a queerly-placed but far-reaching window. She was bold and generous and incalculable, and if she was coarse she was neither false nor cruel. She laughed with the laugh of the people and if you hit her hard enough would cry with their tears. When he himself was not letting his imagination wander among the haunts of the aristocracy and stretching it in the shadow of an ancestral beech to read the last number of the *Revue des Deux Mondes* he was occupied with contemplations of a very different kind; he was absorbed in the struggles and sufferings of the millions whose life flowed in the same current as his and who, though they constantly excited his disgust and made him shrink and turn away, had the power to chain his sympathy, to raise it to passion, to convince him for the time at least that real success in the world would be to do something with them and for them. All this, strange to say, was never so vivid as in Millicent's company —which is a proof of his fantastic, erratic way of seeing things. She had no such ideas about herself; they were almost the only ideas she didn't have. She had no theories about redeeming or uplifting the people; she simply loathed them, for being so dirty, with the outspoken violence of one who had known poverty and the strange bedfellows it makes in a very different degree from Hyacinth, brought up (with Pinnie to put sugar in his tea and let him never want for neckties) like a regular little swell.

Millicent, to hear her talk, only asked to keep her skirts clear and marry some respectable tea-merchant. But for our hero she was magnificently plebeian, in the sense that implied loud recklessness of danger and the qualities that shine forth in a row. She summed up the sociable humourous ignorant chatter of the masses, their capacity for offensive and defensive passion, their instinctive perception of their strength on the day they should really exercise it; and as much as any of this their ideal of something smug and prosperous, where washed hands and oiled hair and plates in rows on dressers and stuffed birds under glass and family photographs of a quite similar effect would symbolise success. She was none the less plucky for being at bottom a shameless Philistine, ambitious of a front garden with rockwork; and she presented the plebeian character in none the less plastic a form. Having the history of the French Revolution at his fingers' ends, Hyacinth could easily see her (if there should ever be barricades in the streets of London) with a red cap of liberty on her head and her white throat bared so that she should be able to shout the louder the Marseillaise of that hour, whatever it might be. If the festival of the Goddess of Reason should ever be enacted in the British Capital—and Hyacinth could consider such possibilities without a smile, so much was it a part of the little religion he had to remember always that there was no knowing what might happen—if this solemnity, I say, should be revived in Hyde Park, who was better designated than Miss Henning to figure in a grand statuesque manner as the heroine of the occasion? It was plain she had laid her inconsequent admirer under a peculiar spell, since he could associate her with such scenes as that while she consumed beer and buns at his expense. If she had a weakness it was for prawns; and she had, all winter, a plan for his taking her down to Gravesend, where this luxury was cheap and abundant, when the fine long days should arrive. She was never so frank and facetious as when she dwelt on the details of a project of this kind; and then Hyacinth was reminded afresh that it was an immense good fortune for him she was so handsome. If she had been ugly he couldn't have listened to her; but the rare bloom and grand style of her person glorified even her accent, interfused her cockney genius with prismatic hues, gave her a large and constant impunity.

XI

SHE DESIRED at last to raise their common experience to a loftier level, to enjoy what she called a high-class treat. Their commerce had been condemned for the most part to go forward in the streets, the wintry, dusky, foggy streets, which looked bigger and more numerous in their perpetual obscurity and in which everything was covered with damp, gritty smut, an odour extremely agreeable to Miss Henning. Happily she shared Hyacinth's relish of vague perambulation and was still more addicted than he to looking into the windows of shops, before which, in long, contemplative halts, she picked out freely the articles she shouldn't mind having put up for her. He invariably pronounced the objects of her selection hideous and made no scruple to assure her she had the worst taste of any girl in the place. Nothing he could say to her affronted her so much, for her pretensions in the way of a cultivated judgement were boundless. Had not indeed her natural aptitude been fortified, in the neighbourhood of Buckingham Palace (there was scarcely anything they didn't sell in the great shop of which she was an ornament) by daily contact with the freshest products of modern industry? Hyacinth laughed this establishment to scorn and made the point that there was nothing in it from top to bottom that a real artist would look at. She enquired with answering derision if this were a description of his own few inches; but in reality she was fascinated as much as she was provoked by his attitude of being difficult to please, of seeing indescribable differences among the smartest things. She had given herself out originally as very knowing, but he could make her gape with doubts. When once in a while he pointed out a commodity that he condescended to like (this didn't happen often, because the only shops in which there was a chance of his making such a discovery were closed at nightfall) she stared and bruised him with her elbow, declaring that if any one should give her such a piece of rubbish she would sell it for fourpence. Once or twice she asked him to be so good as to explain to her in what its superiority consisted—she couldn't rid herself of a suspicion that there might be something in his judgement and was angry at not finding herself as positive as any one. Then he would reply that it was no use attempting to tell her; she wouldn't understand and had better continue to admire the insipid productions of an age that had lost the sense of fineness—a phrase she remembered, proposing to herself even to make use of it on some future occasion, but was quite unable to interpret.

When her companion demeaned himself in this manner it was not with a view of strengthening the tie that united him to his childhood's friend; but the effect followed on Millicent's side and the girl was proud to think herself in possession of a young man whose knowledge was of so high an order that it was inexpressible. In spite of her vanity she was not so convinced of her perfection as not to be full of ungratified aspirations; she had an idea it might be to her advantage some day to exhibit a sample of that learning; and at the same time, when, in consideration for instance of a jeweller's gas-lighted display in Great Portland Street, Hyacinth lingered for five minutes in perfect silence and she delivered herself according to her wont at such junctures, she was a thousand miles from guessing the perverse sentiments that made it impossible for him to speak. She could long for things she was not likely to have; envy other people for possessing them and say it was a 'regular shime'; draw brilliant pictures of what she should do with them if she did have them; and pass immediately, with a mind un-encumbered by superfluous inductions, to some other topic equally intimate and personal. The sense of privation with her was often extremely acute; but she could always put her finger on the remedy. With her fellow-sufferer the case was very different; the remedy for him was terribly vague and inaccessible. He was liable to moods in which the sense of exclusion from all he would have liked most to enjoy in life settled on him like a pall. They had a bitterness, but they were not invidious—they were not moods of vengeance, of imaginary spoliation: they were simply states of paralysing melancholy, of infinite sad reflexion, in which he felt how in this world of effort and suffering life was endurable, the spirit able to expand, only in the best conditions, and how a sordid struggle in which one should go down to the grave without having tasted them was not worth the misery it would cost, the dull demoralisation it would involve.

In such hours the great roaring indifferent world of London seemed to him a huge organisation for mocking at his poverty, at his inanition; and then its vulgarest ornaments, the windows of third-rate jewellers, the young man in a white tie and a crush-hat who dandled by on his way to a dinner-party in a hansom that nearly ran over one—these familiar phenomena became symbolic, insolent, defiant, took on themselves to make him smart with the sense that *he* was above all out of it. He felt moreover that there was neither consolation nor refutation in saying to himself that the immense majority of mankind were out of it with him and appeared to put up well enough with the annoyance. That was their own affair; he knew nothing of their reasons or their resignation, and if they chose neither to rebel nor to compare he at least, among the disinherited, would keep up the standard. When these fits were on our young man his brothers of the people fared, collectively, very ill at his hands; their function then was to represent in massive shape precisely the grovelling interests which attracted one's contempt, and the only acknowledgement one owed them was for the completeness of the illustration. Everything which in a great city could touch the sentient faculty of a youth on whom nothing was lost ministered to his conviction that there was no possible good fortune in life of too 'quiet' an order for him to appreciate—no privilege, no opportunity, no luxury to which he mightn't do full justice. It was not so much that he wanted to enjoy as that he wanted to know; his desire wasn't to be pampered but to be initiated. Sometimes of a Saturday in the long evenings of June and July he made his way into Hyde Park at the hour when the throng of carriages, of riders, of brilliant pedestrians was thickest; and though lately, on two or three of these occasions, he had been accompanied by Miss Henning, whose criticism of the scene was rich and distinct, a tremendous little drama had taken place privately on the stage of his inner consciousness. He wanted to drive in every carriage, to mount on every horse, to feel on his arm the hand of every pretty woman in the place. In the midst of this his sense was vivid that he belonged to the class whom the 'bloated' as they passed didn't so much as rest their eyes on for a quarter of a second. They looked at Millicent, who was safe to be looked at anywhere and was one of the handsomest girls in any company, but they only reminded him of the high human walls, the deep gulfs of tradition, the steep embankments of privilege and dense layers of stupidity fencing the 'likes' of him off from social recognition.

And this was not the fruit of a morbid vanity on his part, or of a jealousy that couldn't be intelligent; his personal discomfort was the result of an intense admiration for what he had missed. There were individuals whom he followed with his eyes, with his thoughts, sometimes even with his steps; they seemed to tell him what it was to be the flower of a high civilisation. At moments he was aghast when he reflected that the cause he had secretly espoused, the cause from which M. Poupin and Paul Muniment (especially the latter) had within the last few months drawn aside the curtain, proposed to itself to bring about a state of things in which that particular scene would be impossible. It made him even rather faint to think that he must choose; that he couldn't (with any respect for his own consistency) work underground for the enthronement of the democracy and yet continue to enjoy in however platonic a manner a spectacle which rested on a hideous social inequality. He must either suffer with the people as he had suffered before, or he must apologise to others, as he sometimes came so near doing to himself, for the rich; inasmuch as the day

was certainly near when these two mighty forces would
come to a death-grapple. Hyacinth thought himself obliged
at present to have reasons for his feelings; his intimacy with
Paul Muniment, which had now grown very great, laid a
good deal of that sort of responsibility upon him. Muniment laughed at his reasons whenever he produced them,
but appeared to expect him nevertheless to have them ready
on demand, and Hyacinth had ever a desire to do what he
expected. There were times when he said to himself that it
might very well be his fate to be divided to the point of
torture, to be split open by sympathies that pulled him in
different ways; for hadn't he an extraordinarily mingled
current in his blood, and from the time he could remember
wasn't there one half of him always either playing tricks
on the other or getting snubs and pinches from it?

That dim, dreadful, confused legend of his mother's
history, as regards which what Pinnie had been able to tell
him when he first began to question her was at once too
much and too little—this stupefying explanation had supplied him first and last with a hundred different theories of
his identity. What he knew, what he guessed had sickened
and what he didn't know tormented him; but in his illuminated ignorance he had fashioned forth an article of faith.
This had gradually emerged from the depths of darkness
in which he found himself plunged as a consequence of
the challenge he had addressed to Pinnie—while he was
still only a child—on the memorable day that had transformed the whole face of his future. It was one January
afternoon when he had come in from a walk. She was seated
at her lamp, as usual, with her work, and had begun to tell
him of a letter one of the lodgers had got describing the
manner in which his brother-in-law's shop at Nottingham
had been rifled by burglars. He had listened to her story,
standing in front of her, and then by way of response had
suddenly said to her: 'Who was that awful woman you took
me to see ever so long ago?' The expression of her white
face as she looked up at him, her fear of such an attack all
dormant after so many years—this strange, scared, sick

glance was a thing he could never forget, any more than the
tone, with her breath failing her, in which she had repeated,
'That awful woman?'

'That woman in the prison years ago—how old was I?—
who was dying and who kissed me so, as I've never been
kissed, as I never shall be again! Who *was* she, who WAS
she?' Poor Pinnie, to do her justice, had made, after she
recovered her breath, a gallant fight: it had lasted a week;
it was to leave her spent and sore for ever after, and before
it was over Anastasius Vetch had been called in. At his instance she had retracted the falsehoods with which she had
previously tried to put the boy off, and had made at last a
confession and a report which he was satisfied to believe as
complete as her knowledge. Hyacinth could never have told
you why the crisis had occurred on such a day, why his
question had broken out at that particular moment. The
strangeness of the matter to himself was that the germ of
his curiosity should have developed so slowly; that the
haunting wonder which now, as he looked back, appeared
to fill his whole childhood, should only after so long an
interval have crept up to the air. It was only of course little
by little that he had recovered his bearings in his new and
more poignant consciousness; little by little that he had re-
constructed his antecedents, taken the measure, so far as was
possible, of his heredity. His having the courage to disinter
from the *Times* in the reading-room of the British Museum
a report of his mother's trial for the murder of Lord Frederick Purvis, which was very copious, the affair having been
quite a *cause célèbre*; his resolution in sitting under that
splendid dome and, with his head bent to hide his hot eyes,
going through every syllable of the ghastly record had been
an achievement of comparatively recent years. There were
certain things Pinnie knew that appalled him; and there
were others, as to which he would have given his hand to
have some light, that it made his heart ache supremely to
find she was honestly ignorant of. He scarce understood
what sort of favour Mr Vetch wished to make with him (as
a compensation for the precious part he had played in the

business years before) when the fiddler permitted himself to pass judgement on the family of the wretched young nobleman for not having provided in some manner for the infant child of his assassin. Why should they have provided when it was evident they had refused absolutely to recognise his lordship's responsibility? Pinnie had to admit this under Hyacinth's terrible cross-questioning; she couldn't pretend with any show of evidence that Lord Whiteroy and the other brothers (there had been no less than seven, most of them still living) had at the time of the trial given any symptom of believing Florentine Vivier's asseverations. That was their affair; he had long since made up his mind that his own was very different. One couldn't believe at will, and fortunately, in the case, he had no effort to make; for from the moment he began to consider the established facts (few as they were and poor and hideous) he regarded himself immutably as the son of the recreant and sacrificed Lord Frederick.

He had no need to reason about it; all his nerves and pulses pleaded and testified. His mother had been a daughter of the wild French people—all Pinnie could tell him of her parentage was that Florentine had once mentioned that in her extreme childhood her father, his gun in his hand, had fallen in the blood-stained streets of Paris on a barricade; but on the other side it took an English aristocrat to account for him, though a poor specimen apparently had to suffice. This, with its further implications, became Hyacinth's article of faith; the reflexion that he was a bastard involved in a remarkable manner the reflexion that he was a gentleman. He was conscious he didn't hate the image of his father as he might have been expected to do; and he supposed this was because Lord Frederick had paid so tremendous a penalty. It was in the exaction of that penalty that the moral proof for him resided; his mother wouldn't have armed herself on account of any injury less cruel than the passage of which her miserable baby was the living sign. She had avenged herself because she had been thrown over, and the bitterness of that wrong had been in the fact that he, hopeless brat, lay there in her lap. *He* was the one properly to have been sacrificed: that remark our young man often made to himself. That his judgement of the whole question was passionate and personal and took little account of any disturbing conflict of evidence is proved by the importance he attached for instance to the name by which his mother had told poor Pinnie (when this excellent creature consented to take him) that she wished him to be called. Hyacinth had been the name of her father, a republican clockmaker, the martyr of his opinions, whose memory she professed to worship; and when Lord Frederick had insinuated himself into her confidence he had had reasons for preferring to be known as plain Mr Robinson—reasons, however, into which, in spite of the light thrown upon them at the trial, it was difficult after so many years to enter.

Hyacinth had never known of Mr Vetch's saying more than once to Pinnie, 'If her contention as regards that dissolute young swell was true why didn't she make the child bear his real name instead of his false one?'—an enquiry which the dressmaker had answered, with some ingenuity, by remarking that she couldn't call him after a man she had murdered, as one must suppose her unwilling to publish to every one his connexion with a crime that had been so much talked about. If Hyacinth had assisted at this little discussion it is needless to say that he would have sided with Miss Pynsent; though that his judgement was independently formed is proved by the fact that Pinnie's fearfully indiscreet attempts at condolence should not have made him throw up his version in disgust. It was after the complete revelation that he understood the romantic innuendoes with which his childhood had been surrounded and of which he had never caught the meaning; they having seemed but a feature of the general fact of the poor woman's professional life—so much cutting and trimming and shaping and embroidering, so much turning and altering and doing-up. When it came over him that she had for years made a fool of him to himself and to others he could have beaten her for grief and shame; and yet before he administered this rebuke he had to remember that she only chattered (though she professed to have been extraordinarily dumb) about a matter over which he spent nine tenths of his own time in all gloomily brooding. When she tried to console him for the horror of his mother's history by descanting on the glory of the Purvises and reminding him that he was related through them to half the aristocracy of England he felt her to be turning the tragedy of his life into a monstrous farce; and yet he none the less continued to cherish the belief that he was a gentleman born. He allowed her to tell him nothing about the family in question, and his impracticability on this subject was one of the reasons of the deep dejection of her later years. If he had only let her idealise him a little to himself she would have felt she was making up by so much for her grand mistake. He sometimes saw the name of his father's kin in the newspaper, but he then always cast the sheet away. He had nothing to ask of them and wished to prove to himself that he could ignore them (who had been willing to let him die like a rat) as completely as they ignored him. A thousand times yes, he was with the people and every possible vengeance of the people as against such shameless egoism as that; but all the same he was happy to feel he had blood in his veins that would account for the finest sensibilities.

He had no money to pay for places at a theatre in the Strand, Millicent Henning having made it clear to him that on this occasion she expected something better than the pit. 'Should you like the royal box or a couple of stalls at ten bob apiece?' he asked of her on a note of that too uniform irony which formed the basis of almost all their talk. She had replied that she would content herself with a seat in the second balcony, in the very front; and as such a position involved an expenditure still beyond his compass he waited one night on Mr Vetch, to whom he had already more than once had recourse in moments of pecuniary embarrassment. His relations with the caustic fiddler were of the oddest and much easier when put to the proof than in theory. Mr Vetch had let him know—long before this and with the purpose of

covering Pinnie to the utmost—the part he had played at
the crisis of that question of her captive's being taken to call
on Mrs Bowerbank; and Hyacinth, in the face of this information, had asked with some sublimity what the devil the
fiddler had had to do with his private affairs. Their neighbour had replied that it was not as an affair of his but as an
affair of Pinnie's he had considered the matter; and our hero
had afterwards let it drop, though he had never been formally reconciled to so officious a critic. Of course his feeling
on this head had been immensely modified by the trouble
Mr Vetch had taken to get him a place with old Crook; and
at the period of which I write it had long been familiar to
him that the author of that benefit didn't care a straw what
he thought of his advice at the dark hour and in fact took a
perverse pleasure in 'following' the career of a youth put together of such queer pieces. It was impossible to Hyacinth
not to be conscious that this projected attention was kindly;
and to-day, at any rate, he would have declared that nothing
could have made up to him for not knowing the truth, horrible as it might be. His miserable mother's embrace seemed
to furnish him with an inexhaustible fund of motive, and in
the conditions that was a support. What he chiefly objected
to in Mr Vetch was the betrayed habit of still regarding him
as extremely juvenile; he would have got on much better
with a better recognition of his being already a man of the
world. The obscure virtuoso knew an immense deal about
society and seemed to know the more because he never
swaggered—it was only little by little you discovered it; but
that was no reason for his looking as if his chief boon in life
was a private diverting commentary on the conversation of
his young friend. Hyacinth felt that he gave considerable
evidence of patience with this when he occasionally asked
his fellow-resident in Lomax Place to lend him half-a-crown.
Somehow circumstances had of old tied them together, and
though this partly vexed the little bookbinder it also touched
him; he had more than once solved the problem of deciding
how to behave (when the fiddler exasperated him) by simply
asking of him some substantial service. Mr Vetch had never

once refused. It was satisfactory to Hyacinth to remember as much when knocking at his door late, after allowing him time to come home from the theatre. He knew his habits: he never went straight to bed, but sat by his fire an hour, smoking his pipe, mixing a grog and reading some old book. Hyacinth could tell when to go up by the light in his window, which he could see from a court behind.

'Oh, I know I haven't been to see you for a long time,' he said in response to the remark with which his neighbour greeted him; 'and I may as well tell you immediately what has brought me at present—in addition to the desire to ask after your health. I want to take a young lady to the theatre.'

Mr Vetch was habited in a tattered dressing-gown; his apartment smelt strongly of the liquor he was consuming. Divested of his evening-gear he looked to our hero so plucked and blighted as on the spot to settle his claims in the event of a social liquidation; he too was unmistakeably a creditor. 'I'm afraid you find your young lady rather expensive.'

'I find everything expensive,' said Hyacinth as if to finish that subject.

'Especially, I suppose, your secret societies.'

'What do you mean by that?' the young man asked with a fine stare.

'Why, you told me in the autumn that you were just about to join a few.'

'A few? How many do you suppose?' But our friend checked himself. 'Do you suppose if I had been serious I'd tell?'

'Oh dear, oh dear!' sighed Mr Vetch. Then he went on: 'You want to take her to my shop, eh?'

'I'm sorry to say she won't go there. She wants something in the Strand: that's a great point. She wants very much to see *The Pearl of Paraguay*. I don't wish to pay anything, if possible; I'm sorry to say I haven't a penny. But as you know people at the other theatres and I've heard you say that you do each other little favours from place to place, *à charge de revanche*, it occurred to me you might be able to get me an order. The piece has been running a long time and most people (except poor devils like me) must have seen it: therefore there probably isn't a rush.'

Mr Vetch listened in silence and presently said: 'Do you want a box?'

'Oh no; something more modest.'

'Why not a box?' asked the fiddler in a tone the youth knew.

'Because I haven't the clothes people wear in that sort of place—if you must have such a definite reason.'

'And your young lady—has *she* the clothes?'

'Oh, I dare say; she seems to have everything.'

'Where does she get 'em?'

'Oh, I don't know. She belongs to a big shop; she has to be fine.'

'Won't you have a pipe?' Mr Vetch asked, pushing an old tobacco-pouch across the table; and while the young man helped himself he puffed a while in silence. 'What will she do with you?' he finally asked.

'What will who do with me?'

'Your big beauty—Miss Henning. I know all about her from Pinnie.'

'Then you know what she'll do with me!' Hyacinth returned with rather a scornful laugh.

'Yes, but, after all, it doesn't very much matter.'

'I don't know what you're talking about,' said Hyacinth.

'Well, now the other thing—what do they call it? the Subterranean?—are you very deep in that?' the fiddler went on as if he had not heard him.

'Did Pinnie tell you also about that?'

'No, our friend Puppin has told me a good deal. He knows you've put your head into something. Besides, I see it,' said Mr Vetch.

'How do you see it, pray?'

'You've got such a speaking eye. Any one can tell, to look at you, that you've taken some oath on bloody bones, that you belong to some terrible gang. You seem to say to every one "Slow torture won't induce me to tell where it meets!"'

'You won't get me an order then?' Hyacinth said in a moment.

'My dear boy, I offer you a box. I take the greatest interest in you.'

They smoked together a while and at last Hyacinth remarked: 'It has nothing to do with the Subterranean.'

'Is it more terrible, more deadly secret?' his companion asked with extreme seriousness.

'I thought you pretended to be a radical,' Hyacinth returned.

'Well, so I am—of the old-fashioned, constitutional, milk-and-water, jog-trot sort. I'm not an exterminator.'

'We don't know what we may be when the time comes,' Hyacinth observed more sententiously than he intended.

'Is the time coming then, my dear young friend?'

'I don't think I've a right to give you any more of a warning than that,' smiled our hero.

'It's very kind of you to do so much, I'm sure, and to rush in here at the small hours for the purpose. Meanwhile, in a few weeks or months or years, or whatever they are, that are left, you wish to crowd in all possible enjoyment with the young ladies: that's a very natural inclination.' To which Mr Vetch irrelevantly added: 'Do you see many foreigners?'

'Yes, a good many.'

'And what do you think of them?'

'Oh, all sorts of things. I rather like Englishmen best.'

'Mr Muniment for example?'

'I say, what do you know about *him*?' Hyacinth asked.

'I've seen him at the Puppins'. I know you and he are as thick as thieves.'

'He'll distinguish himself some day very much,' said Hyacinth, who was perfectly willing and indeed very proud to be thought a close ally of a highly original man.

'Very likely—very likely. And what will *he* do with you?' the fiddler enquired.

Hyacinth got up; they looked at each other hard. 'Do get me two good places in the second balcony.'

Mr Vetch replied that he would do what he could, and three days afterwards he handed his young friend the coveted order. He accompanied it with the injunction, 'You had better put in all the fun you can, you know!'

BOOK SECOND

XII

HYACINTH AND his companion took their seats with extreme promptitude before the curtain rose on *The Pearl of Paraguay*. Thanks to Millicent's eagerness not to be late they encountered the discomfort which had constituted her main objection to going into the pit: they waited for twenty minutes at the door of the theatre, in a tight, stolid crowd, before the official hour of opening. Millicent, bareheaded and powerfully laced, presented a splendid appearance and, on Hyacinth's part, gratified a youthful, ingenuous pride of possession in every respect save a tendency, while ingress was denied them, to make her neighbours feel her elbows and to comment loudly and sarcastically on the situation. It was more clear to him even than it had been before that she was a young lady who in public places might easily need a champion or an apologist. Hyacinth knew there was only one way to apologise for a 'female' when the female was attached very closely and heavily to one's arm, and was reminded afresh of how little constitutional aversion Miss Henning had to a row. He had an idea she might think his own taste ran even too little in that direction, and entertained visions of violent confused scenes in which he should in some way distinguish himself: he scarcely knew in what way and imagined himself more easily routing some hulking adversary by an exquisite application of the retort courteous than by flying at him with a pair of very small fists.

By the time they had reached their places in the balcony she was rather flushed and a good deal ruffled; but she had composed herself in season for the rising of the curtain on the farce preceding the melodrama and which the pair had no intention of losing. At this stage a more genial agitation took possession of her and she surrendered her sympathies to the horse-play of the traditional prelude. Hyacinth found it less amusing, but the theatre, in any conditions, was full of sweet deception for him. His imagination projected itself lovingly across the footlights, gilded and coloured the shabby canvas and battered accessories, losing itself so effectually in the fictive world that the end of the piece, however long or however short, brought with it something of the alarm of a stoppage of his personal life. It was impossible to be more friendly to the dramatic illusion. Millicent, as the audience thickened, rejoiced more largely and loudly, held herself as a lady, surveyed the place as if she knew all about it, leaned back and leaned forward, fanned herself with majesty, gave her opinion upon the appearance and coiffure of every woman within sight, abounded in question and conjecture and produced from her pocket a little paper of peppermint-drops of which under cruel threats she compelled Hyacinth to partake. She followed with attention, though not always with success, the complicated adventures of the Pearl of Paraguay through scenes luxuriantly tropical, in which the male characters wore sombreros and stilettos and the ladies either danced the cachucha or fled from licentious pursuit; but her eyes wandered intermittently to the occupants of the boxes and stalls, concerning several of whom she had theories which she imparted to Hyacinth, while the play went on, greatly to his discomfiture, he being unable to conceive of such levity. She had the pretension of knowing who every one was; not individually and by name, but as regards their exact social station, the quarter of London in which they lived and the amount of money they were prepared to spend in the neighbourhood of Buckingham Palace. She had seen the whole town pass through her establishment there, and though Hyacinth, from his infancy, had been watching it at his own point of view, his companion made him feel all the characteristic points he had missed. Her interpretations differed from his largely in being so very bold and irreverent. Miss Henning's observation of the London world had not been of a nature to impress her with its high moral tone, and she had a free off-hand cynicism which imposed itself. She thought most ladies hypocrites and had in all ways a low opinion of her own sex, which more than once before this she had justified to Hyacinth by narrating observations of a surprising kind gathered during her career as a shop-girl. There was a pleasing inconsequence therefore in her being moved to tears in the third act of the play, when the Pearl of Paraguay, dishevelled and distracted, dragging herself on her knees, implored the stern hidalgo her father to believe in her innocence in spite of circumstances appearing to condemn her—a midnight meeting with the wicked hero in the grove of cocoanuts. It was at this crisis none the less that she asked Hyacinth who his friends were in the principal box on the left of the stage and let him know that a gentleman seated there had been watching him at intervals for the past half-hour.

'Watching *me*! I like that! When I want to be watched I take you with me.'

'Of course he has looked at me,' Millicent answered as if she had no interest in denying that. 'But you're the one he wants to get hold of.'

'To get hold of!'

'Yes, you ninny: don't hang back. He may make your fortune.'

'Well, if you'd like him to come and sit by you I'll go and take a walk in the Strand,' said Hyacinth, entering into the humour of the occasion but not seeing from where he was placed any gentleman in the box. Millicent explained that the mysterious observer had just altered his position; he had gone to the back, which must have had considerable depth. There were other persons there, out of sight; she and Hyacinth were too much on the same side. One of them was a lady concealed by the curtain; her arm, bare save for its bracelets, was visible at moments on the cushioned ledge. Hyacinth saw it in effect reappear there, and even while the piece proceeded regarded it with a certain interest; but till the curtain fell at the end of the act there was no further symptom that a gentleman wished to get hold of him.

'Now do you say it's me he's after?' Millicent asked abruptly, giving him a sidelong dig while the fiddlers in the orchestra began to scrape their instruments for the interlude.

'Of course! I'm only the pretext,' Hyacinth replied, after
he had looked a moment, in a manner which he flattered
himself was a proof of quick self-possession. The gentleman
designated by his friend was once more at the front and
leaning forward with his arms on the ledge. Hyacinth saw
he was looking straight at him, and our young man returned
his gaze—an effort not rendered the more easy by the fact
that after an instant he recognised him.

'Well, if he knows us he might give some sign, and if he
doesn't he might leave us alone,' Millicent declared, aban-
doning the distinction she had made between herself and her
companion. She had no sooner spoken than the gentleman
complied with the first-mentioned of these conditions; he
smiled at Hyacinth across the house—he nodded to him
with unmistakeable friendliness. Millicent, perceiving this,
glanced at the young man from Lomax Place and saw that
the demonstration had brought a deep colour to his cheek.
He was blushing, flushing; whether with pleasure or embarrassment didn't immediately appear. 'I say, I say—is it one
of your grand relations?' she promptly asked. 'Well, I can
stare as well as him'; and she told Hyacinth it was 'a shime'
to bring a young lady to the play when you hadn't so much
as an opera-glass for her to look at the company. 'Is he one
of those lords your aunt was always talking about in the
Plice? Is he your uncle or your grandfather or your first or
second cousin? No, he's too young for your grandfather.
What a pity I can't see if he looks like you!'

At any other time Hyacinth would have thought these
enquiries in the worst possible taste, but now he was too
much given up to other reflexions. It pleased him that the
gentleman in the box should recognise and notice him, because even so small a fact as this was an extension of his
social existence; but it no less surprised and puzzled him,
producing altogether, in his easily-excited organism, an agitation of which, in spite of his attempted self-control, the
air he had for Millicent was the sign. They had met three
times, he and his fellow-spectator; but they had met in
quarters that, to Hyacinth's mind, would have made a fur-

tive wink, a mere tremor of the eyelid, a more judicious
reference to the fact than so public a salutation. Our friend
would never have permitted himself to greet him first, and
this was not because the gentleman in the box belonged—
conspicuously as he did so—to a different walk of society.
He was apparently a man of forty, tall, lean and loose-
jointed; he fell into lounging, dawdling attitudes and even at
a distance looked lazy. He had a long, amused, contented
face, unadorned with moustache or whisker, and his brown
hair, parted at the side, came forward on either temple in
a rich, well-brushed lock, after the fashion of the portraits
of 1820. Millicent had a glance of such range and keenness
that she was able to make out the details of his evening-
dress, of which she appreciated the 'form'; to observe the
character of his large hands; and to note that he continually
smiled at something, that his eyes were extraordinarily light
in colour and that in spite of the dark, well-marked brows
arching over them his fine skin never had produced and never
would produce a beard of any strength. Our young lady pronounced him mentally a 'swell' of the first magnitude and
wondered more than ever where he had picked up Hyacinth.
Her companion seemed to echo her thought when he exclaimed with a little surprised sigh, almost an exhalation of
awe: 'Well, I had no idea he was one of that lot!'

'You might at least tell me his name, so that I shall know
what to call him when he comes round to speak to us,' the
girl said, provoked at her companion's reserve.

'Comes round to speak to us—a chap like that!' Hyacinth
echoed.

'Well, I'm sure if he had been your own brother he
couldn't have grinned at you more! He may want to make
my acquaintance after all; he won't be the first.'

The gentleman had once more retreated from sight, and
there was that amount of evidence of the intention she imputed to him. 'I don't think I'm at all clear that I've a right
to tell his name.' Hyacinth spoke responsibly, yet with all
disposition to magnify an incident which deepened the brilliancy of the entertainment he had been able to offer Miss

Henning. 'I met him in a place where he may not like to
have it known he goes.'

'Do you go to places that people are ashamed of? Is it one
of your political clubs, as you call them, where that dirty
young man from Camberwell, Mr Monument (what do you
call him?), fills your head with ideas that'll bring you to no
good? I'm sure your friend over there doesn't look as if he'd
be on *your* side.'

Hyacinth had indulged in this reflexion himself; but the
only answer he made to Millicent was: 'Well then, perhaps
he'll be on yours!'

'Laws, I hope *she* ain't one of the aristocracy!' Millicent
exclaimed with apparent irrelevance; and following the
direction of her eyes Hyacinth saw that the chair his mysterious acquaintance had quitted in the stage-box was now
occupied by a lady hitherto invisible—not the one who had
given them a glimpse of her shoulder and bare arm. This
was an ancient personage muffled in a voluminous and
crumpled white shawl—a stout, odd, foreign-looking woman
with a fair, nodding, wiggy head. She had a placid, patient
air and a round wrinkled face in which, however, a pair of
small bright eyes moved quickly enough. Her rather soiled
white gloves were too large for her, and round her head,
horizontally arranged as if to keep her wig in its place, she
wore a narrow band of tinsel decorated in the middle of the
forehead by a jewel which the rest of her appearance would
lead the spectator to suppose false. 'Is the old woman his
mother? Where did she dig up her clothes? They look as if
she had hired them for the evening. Does *she* come to your
wonderful club too? I dare say she cuts it fine, don't she?'
Millicent went on; and when Hyacinth suggested sportively
that the old lady might be not the gentleman's mother but
his wife or his fancy of the moment she declared that in that
case, were he to come to see them, she shouldn't fear for
herself. No wonder he wanted to get out of *that* box! The
party in the wig—and what a wig!—was sitting there on
purpose to look at them, but she couldn't say she was particularly honoured by the notice of such an old guy. Hya-

cinth pretended he quite liked her appearance and admired in her a charm of her own; he offered to bet another paper of peppermints that if they could find out she would be some tremendous dowager, some one with a handle to her name. To this Millicent replied with an air of experience that she had never thought the greatest beauty was in the upper class; and her companion could see she was covertly looking over her shoulder to watch for his strange clubmate and that she would be disappointed if he didn't come. This idea didn't make Hyacinth jealous, for his mind was occupied with another side of the business; and if he offered sportive suggestions it was because he was really excited, was dazzled, by an incident of which the reader will have failed as yet to perceive the larger relations. What moved him was not the pleasure of being patronised by a rich man; it was simply the prospect of new experience—a sensation for which he was always ready to exchange any present boon; and he was convinced that if the gentleman with whom he had conversed in a small occult back room in Bloomsbury as Captain Godfrey Sholto—the Captain had given him his card—had in more positive fashion than by Millicent's supposing it come out of the stage-box to see him, he would bring with him rare influences. His view of this possibility made suspense akin to preparation; therefore when at the end of a few minutes he became aware that his young woman, with her head turned, was taking the measure of some one who had come in behind them, he felt fate to be doing for him by way of a change as much as could be expected. He got up in his place, but not too soon to see that Captain Sholto had been standing there a moment in contemplation of Millicent and that she on her side had performed with deliberation the ceremony of appraising him. The Captain had his hands in his pockets and wore his crush-hat pushed a good deal back. He laughed to the young couple in the balcony in the friendliest way, as if he had known them both for years, and Millicent could see on a nearer view that he was a fine distinguished easy genial gentleman, at least six feet high in spite of a habit or an affectation of carrying himself in a casual relaxed familiar manner. Hyacinth felt a little, after the first, as if he were treating them rather too much as a pair of children on whom he had stolen to startle them; but this impression was speedily removed by the air with which he said, laying his hand on our hero's shoulder as he stood in the little passage at the end of the bench where the holders of Mr Vetch's order occupied the first seats: 'My dear fellow, I really thought I must come round and speak to you. My spirits are all gone with this brute of a play. And those boxes are fearfully stuffy, you know,' he added—quite as if Hyacinth had had at least an equal experience of that part of the theatre.

'It's hot enough here too,' Millicent's companion returned. He had suddenly become much more conscious of the high temperature, of his proximity to the fierce chandelier, and he mentioned that the plot of the play certainly was unnatural, though he thought the piece rather well acted.

'Oh, it's the good old stodgy British tradition. This is the only place where you find it still, and even here it can't last much longer; it can't survive old Baskerville and Mrs Ruffler. 'Gad, how old they are! I remember her, long past her prime, when I used to be taken to the play, as a boy, in the Christmas holidays. Between them they must be something like a hundred and eighty, eh? I believe one's supposed to cry a good deal about the middle,' Captain Sholto continued in the same friendly familiar encouraging way, addressing himself to Millicent, upon whom indeed his eyes had rested almost uninterruptedly from the start. She sustained his glance with composure, but with just enough of emphasised reserve to intimate (what was perfectly true) that she was not in the habit of conversing with gentlemen with whom she was unacquainted. She turned away her face at this (she had already given the visitor the benefit of a good deal of it) and left him, as in the little passage he leaned against the parapet of the balcony with his back to the stage, facing toward Hyacinth, who was now wondering, with rather more vivid a sense of the relation of things, what he had come for. He wanted to do him honour in return for his civility, but didn't know what one could talk of at such short notice to a person whom he immediately perceived to be, and the more finely that it was all unaggressively, a man of the world. He instantly saw Captain Sholto didn't take the play seriously, so that he felt himself warned off that topic, on which otherwise he might have had much to say. On the other hand he couldn't in the presence of a third person allude to the matters they had discussed at the 'Sun and Moon'; nor might he suppose his visitor would expect this, though indeed he impressed him as a man of humours and whims, disposed to amuse himself with everything, including esoteric socialism and a little bookbinder who had so much more of the gentleman about him than one would expect. Captain Sholto may have been slightly embarrassed, now that he was completely launched in his attempt at fraternisation, especially after failing to elicit a smile from Millicent's rare respectability; but he left to Hyacinth the burden of no initiative and went on to say that it was just this prospect of the dying-out of the old British tradition that had brought him to-night. He was with a friend, a lady who had lived much abroad, who had never seen anything of the kind and who liked everything that was characteristic. 'You know the foreign school of acting's a very different affair,' he said again to Millicent, who this time replied 'Oh yes, of course,' and, considering afresh the old woman in the box, reflected that she looked as if there were nothing in the world that she at least hadn't seen.

'We've never been abroad,' Hyacinth candidly said while he looked into his friend's curious light-coloured eyes, the palest in tint he had ever encountered.

'Oh well, there's a lot of nonsense talked about that!' Captain Sholto replied; on which Hyacinth remained uncertain of his reference and Millicent decided to volunteer a remark.

'They're making a tremendous row on the stage. I should think it would be very bad in those boxes.' There was a banging and thumping behind the curtain, the sound of heavy scenery pushed about.

'Oh yes, it's much better here in every way. I think you've the best seats in the house,' said their visitor. 'I should like very much to finish my evening beside you. The trouble is I've ladies—a pair of them,' he pursued as if he were seriously considering this possibility. Then laying his hand again on Hyacinth's shoulder he smiled at him a moment and indulged in a still greater burst of frankness. 'My dear fellow, that's just what, as a partial reason, has brought me up here to see you. One of my ladies has a great desire to make your acquaintance!'

'To make my acquaintance?' Hyacinth felt himself turn pale; the first impulse he could have in connexion with such an announcement as that—and it lay far down in the depths of the unspeakable—was a conjecture that it had something to do with his parentage on his father's side. Captain Sholto's smooth bright face, irradiating such unexpected advances, seemed for an instant to swim before him. The Captain went on to say that he had told the lady of the talks they had had, that she was immensely interested in such matters—'You know what I mean, she really is'—and that as a consequence of what he had said she had begged him to come and ask—a—his young friend (Hyacinth saw in a moment that the Captain had forgotten his name) to look in at her if he didn't mind.

'She has a tremendous desire to meet some one who looks at the whole business from your standpoint, don't you see? And in her position she scarcely ever has a chance, she doesn't come across them—to her great annoyance. So when I spotted you tonight she immediately declared I must introduce you at any cost. I hope you won't mind just for a quarter of an hour. I ought perhaps to tell you that she's a person used to having nothing refused her. "Go up and bring him down," you know, as if it were the simplest thing in the world. She's really very much in earnest: I don't mean about wishing to see you—that goes without saying—but about our whole job, yours and mine. Then I should add —it doesn't spoil anything—that she's the most charming woman in the world, simply! Honestly, my dear boy, she's perhaps the most remarkable woman in Europe.'

So Captain Sholto delivered himself, with the highest naturalness and plausibility, and Hyacinth, listening, felt that he himself ought perhaps to resent the idea of being served up for the entertainment of capricious not to say presumptuous triflers, but that somehow he didn't, and that it was more worthy of the part he aspired to play in life to meet such occasions calmly and urbanely than to take the trouble of avoidance. Of course the lady in the box couldn't be sincere; she might think she was, though even that was questionable; but you didn't really care for the cause exemplified in the guarded back room in Bloomsbury when you came to the theatre in that style. It was Captain Sholto's style as well, but it had been by no means clear to Hyacinth hitherto that *he* really cared. All the same this was no time for going into the question of the lady's sincerity, and at the end of sixty seconds our young man had made up his mind that he could afford to indulge her. None the less, I must add, the whole proposal continued to make things dance, to appear fictive and phantasmagoric; so that it sounded in comparison like a note of reality when Millicent, who had been turning from one of the men to the other, exclaimed—

'That's all very well, but who's to look after *me*?' Her assumption of the majestic had broken down and this was the cry of nature.

Nothing could have been pleasanter and more charitable to her alarm than the manner in which Captain Sholto reassured her. 'My dear young lady, can you suppose I've been unmindful of that? I've been hoping that after I've taken down our friend and introduced him you might allow me to come back and in his absence occupy his seat.'

Hyacinth was preoccupied with the idea of meeting the most remarkable woman in Europe; but at this juncture he looked at Millicent Henning with some curiosity. She rose grandly to the occasion. 'I'm much obliged to you, but I don't know who you are.'

'Oh, I'll tell you all about that!' the Captain benevolently cried.

'Of course I should introduce you,' said Hyacinth, and he mentioned to Miss Henning the name of his distinguished acquaintance.

'In the army?' the young lady enquired as if she must have every guarantee of social position.

'Yes—not in the navy! I've left the army, but it always sticks to one.'

'Mr Robinson, is it your intention to leave me?' Millicent asked in a tone of the highest propriety.

Hyacinth's imagination had taken such a flight that the idea of what he owed to the beautiful girl who had placed herself under his care for the evening had somehow effaced itself. Her words put it before him in a manner that threw him quickly and consciously back on his honour; yet there was something in the way she uttered them that made him look at her harder still before he replied: 'Oh dear, no—of course it would never do. I must put off to some other opportunity the honour of making the acquaintance of your friend,' he added to their visitor.

'Ah, my dear fellow, we might manage it so easily now,' this gentleman murmured with evident disappointment. 'It's not as if Miss—a—Miss—a—were to be alone.'

It flashed upon Hyacinth that the root of the project might be a desire of Captain Sholto to insinuate himself into Millicent's good graces; then he wondered why the most remarkable woman in Europe should lend herself to that design, consenting even to receive a visit from a little book-binder for the sake of furthering it. Perhaps after all she was not the most remarkable; still, even at a lower estimate, of what advantage could such a complication be to her? To Hyacinth's surprise Millicent's face made acknowledgement of his implied renunciation; and she said to Captain Sholto as if she were considering the matter very impartially: 'Might one know the name of the lady who sent you?'

'The Princess Casamassima.'

'Laws!' cried Millicent Henning. And then quickly, as if

to cover up this crudity: 'And might one also know what it is, as you say, that she wants to talk to him about?'

'About the lower orders, the rising democracy, the spread of ideas and all that.'

'The lower orders? Does she think we belong to them?' the girl demanded with a strange provoking laugh.

Captain Sholto was certainly the readiest of men. 'If she could see you she'd think you one of the first ladies in the land.'

'She'll never see me!' Millicent replied in a manner which made it plain that she at least was not to be whistled for.

Being whistled for by a princess presented itself to Hyacinth as an indignity endured gracefully enough by the heroes of several French novels in which he had found a thrilling interest; nevertheless he said incorruptibly to the Captain, who hovered there like a Mephistopheles converted to inscrutable good: 'Having been in the army you'll know that one can't desert one's post.'

The Captain, for the third time, laid his hands on his young friend's shoulder, and for a minute his smile rested in silence on Millicent Henning. 'If I tell you simply I want to talk with this young lady, that certainly won't help me particularly, and there's no reason why it should. Therefore I'll tell you the whole truth: I want to talk with her about *you*!' And he patted Hyacinth in a way which conveyed at once that this idea must surely commend him to the young man's companion and that he himself liked him infinitely.

Hyacinth was conscious of the endearment, but he put before Millicent that he would do just as she liked; he was determined not to let a member of a justly-doomed patriciate suppose he held any daughter of the people cheap. 'Oh, I don't care if you go,' said Miss Henning. 'You had better hurry—the curtain's going to rise.'

'That's charming of you! I'll rejoin you in three minutes!' Captain Sholto exclaimed.

He passed his hand into Hyacinth's arm, and as our hero lingered still, a little uneasy and questioning Millicent

always with his eyes, the girl spoke with her bright boldness: 'That kind of princess—I should like to hear all about
her.'

'Oh, I'll tell you that too,' the Captain returned with his
perfect ease as he led his young friend away. It must be
confessed that Hyacinth also rather wondered what kind of
princess she was, and his suspense on this point made his
heart beat fast when, after traversing steep staircases and
winding corridors, they reached the small door of the stage-
box.

XIII

HIS FIRST consciousness after his companion had opened
it was of his proximity to the stage, on which the curtain
had now again risen. The play was in progress, the actors'
voices came straight into the box, and it was impossible to
speak without disturbing them. This at least was his inference from the noiseless way his conductor drew him in and,
without announcing or introducing him, simply pointed to a
chair and whispered: 'Just drop into that; you'll see and
hear beautifully.' He heard the door close behind him and
became aware that Captain Sholto had already retreated.
Millicent would at any rate not be left long to languish in
solitude. Two ladies were seated in the front of the box,
which was so large that there was a considerable space between them; and as he stood there, where Captain Sholto
had planted him—they appeared not to have noticed the
opening of the door—they turned their heads and looked at
him. The one on whom his eyes first rested was the odd
party he had already viewed at a distance; she looked
queerer still on a close view and gave him a little friendly
gratified nod. The other was partly overshadowed by the
curtain of the box, drawn forward with the intention of
shielding her from the observation of the house; she had
still the air of youth, and the simplest way to express the
instant effect upon Hyacinth of her fair face of welcome is

to say that she dazzled him. He remained as Sholto had left him, staring rather confusedly and not moving an inch; whereupon the younger lady put out her hand—it was her left, the other rested on the ledge of the box—with the expectation, as he perceived, to his extreme mortification, too late, that he would give her his own. She converted the gesture into a sign of invitation and beckoned him silently but graciously to move his chair forward. He did so and seated himself between the two; then for ten minutes he stared straight before him at the stage, not turning his eyes sufficiently even to glance up at Millicent in the balcony. He looked at the play, but was far from seeing it; he had no sense of anything but the woman who sat there, close to him, on his right, with a fragrance in her garments and a light about her which he seemed to see even while his head was averted. The vision had been only of a moment, but it hung before him, threw a vague white mist over the proceedings on the stage. He was consciously embarrassed, overturned and bewildered; he made a great effort to collect himself, to consider the situation lucidly. He wondered if he ought to speak, to look at her again, to behave differently in some way; if she would take him for a clown, for an idiot; if she were really as beautiful as she had seemed or it were only a superficial glamour which a renewed inspection would dissipate. While he so pondered the minutes lapsed and neither of his hostesses spoke; they watched the play in perfect stillness, so that he divined this to be the proper thing and that he himself must remain dumb until a word should be addressed him. Little by little he recovered himself, took possession of his predicament and at last transferred his eyes to the Princess. She immediately perceived this and returned his glance with a bright benevolence. She might well be a princess—it was impossible to conform more to the finest evocations of that romantic word. She was fair, shining, slender, with an effortless majesty. Her beauty had an air of perfection; it astonished and lifted one up, the sight of it seemed a privilege, a reward. If the first impression it had given Hyacinth was to make him feel strangely transported he need still not have set that down to his simplicity, for this was the effect the Princess Casamassima produced on persons of a wider experience and greater pretensions. Her dark eyes, blue or grey, something that was not brown, were as kind as they were splendid, and there was an extraordinary light nobleness in the way she held her head. That head, where two or three diamond stars glittered in the thick, delicate hair which defined its shape, suggested to Hyacinth something antique and celebrated, something he had admired of old—the memory was vague—in a statue, in a picture, in a museum. Purity of line and form, of cheek and chin and lip and brow, a colour that seemed to live and glow, a radiance of grace and eminence and success—these things were seated in triumph in the face of the Princess, and her visitor, as he held himself in his chair trembling with the revelation, questioned if she were really of the same substance with the humanity he had hitherto known. She might be divine, but he could see she understood human needs—that she wished him to be at his ease and happy; there was something familiar in her benignity, as if she had seen him many times before. Her dress was dark and rich; she had pearls round her neck and an old rococo fan in her hand. He took in all these things and finally said to himself that if she wanted nothing more of him he was content, he would like it to go on; so pleasant was it to be enthroned with fine ladies in a dusky, spacious receptacle which framed the bright picture of the stage and made one's own situation seem a play within the play. The act was a long one, and the repose in which his companions left him might have been a calculated charity, to enable him to get used to them, to see how harmless they were. He looked at Millicent in the course of time and saw that Captain Sholto, seated beside her, had not the same standard of propriety, inasmuch as he made a remark to her every few minutes. Like himself the young lady in the balcony was losing the play, thanks to her so keeping her eyes on her friend from Lomax Place, whose position she thus endeavoured to gauge. He had quite given up the

Paraguayan complications; by the end of the half-hour his attention might have come back to them had he not then been engaged in wondering what the Princess would say to him after the descent of the curtain—or if she would say anything. The consideration of this problem as the moment of the solution drew nearer made his heart again beat fast. He watched the old lady on his left and supposed it was natural a princess should have an attendant—he took for granted she was an attendant—as different as possible from herself. This ancient dame was without majesty or grace; huddled together with her hands folded on her stomach and her lips protruding, she solemnly followed the performance. Several times, however, she turned her head to Hyacinth, and then her expression changed; she repeated the jovial, encouraging, almost motherly nod with which she had greeted him on his making his bow and by which she appeared to wish to intimate that, better than the serene beauty on the other side, she could enter into the full anomaly of his situation. She seemed to argue that he must keep his head and that if the worst should come to the worst she was there to look after him. Even when at last the curtain descended it was some moments before the Princess spoke, though she rested her smile on her guest as if she were considering what he would best like her to say. He might at that instant have guessed what he discovered later —that among this lady's faults (he was destined to learn they were numerous) not the least eminent was an exaggerated fear of the commonplace. He expected she would make some remark about the play, but what she said was, very gently and kindly, 'I like to know all sorts of people.'

'I shouldn't think you'd find the least difficulty in that,' Hyacinth replied.

'Oh, if one wants anything very much it's sure to be difficult. Every one isn't so obliging as you.'

Hyacinth could think immediately of no proper answer to this, but the old lady saved him the trouble by declaring with a foreign accent: 'I think you were most extraordinarily good-natured. I had no idea you'd come—to two strange women.'

'Yes, we're strange women,' said the Princess musingly.

'It's not true she finds things difficult; she makes every one do everything,' her companion went on.

The Princess glanced at her and then remarked to Hyacinth: 'Her name is Madame Grandoni.' The tone was not familiar, but there was a happy shade in it, as if he had really taken so much trouble for them that it was but just he should be entertained a little at their expense. It seemed to imply also that Madame Grandoni's fitness for supplying such entertainment was obvious.

'But I'm not Italian—ah no!' the old lady cried. 'In spite of my name I'm an honest, ugly, unfortunate German. But *cela n'a pas d'importance*. She also, with such a name, isn't Italian either. It's an accident; the world's full of accidents. But she isn't German, poor lady, any more.' Madame Grandoni appeared to have entered into the Princess's view, and Hyacinth thought her exceedingly droll. In a moment she added: 'That was a very charming person you were with.'

'Yes, she's very charming,' Hyacinth replied, not sorry to have a chance to say it.

The Princess made no remark on this subject, and Hyacinth saw not only that from her position in the box she could have had no glimpse of Millicent, but that she would never take up such an allusion as that. It was as if she had not heard it that she asked: 'Do you find the play very interesting?'

He hesitated, then told the simple truth. 'I must confess I've lost the whole of this last act.'

'Ah, poor bothered young man!' cried Madame Grandoni. 'You see—you see!'

'What do I see?' the Princess enquired. 'If you're annoyed at being here now you'll like us later; probably at least. We take a great interest in the things you care for. We take a great interest in the people,' the Princess went on.

'Oh, allow me, allow me, and speak only for yourself!'

the elder lady interposed. 'I take no interest whatever in the people; I don't understand them and I know nothing about them. An honourable nature, of any class, I always respect; but I won't pretend to a passion for the ignorant masses, because I have it not. Moreover that doesn't touch the gentleman.'

The Princess Casamassima had a clear faculty of completely ignoring things of which she wished to take no account; it was not in the least the air of contempt, but thoughtful, tranquil, convenient absence, after which she came back to the point where she wished to be. She made no protest against her companion's speech, but said to Hyacinth, as if vaguely conscious she had been committing herself in some absurd way: 'She lives with me; she's everything to me; she's the best woman in the world.'

'Yes, fortunately, with many superficial defects I'm as good as good bread,' Madame Grandoni conceded.

Hyacinth was by this time less embarrassed than when he had presented himself, but he was not less mystified; he wondered afresh if he were not being practised on for some inconceivable end; so strangely did it strike him that two such products of another world than his own should of their own movement take the trouble to explain each other to a dire little bookbinder. This idea made him flush; it might have come over him that he had fallen into a trap. He was conscious he looked frightened, and he was conscious the moment afterwards that the Princess noticed it. This was apparently what made her say: 'If you've lost so much of the play I ought to tell you what has happened.'

'Do you think he would follow that any more?' Madame Grandoni asked.

'If you would tell me—if you would tell me——!' And then Hyacinth stopped. He had been going to say 'If you would tell me what all this means and what you want of me it would be more to the point!' but the words died on his lips and he sat staring, for the woman at his right hand was simply too beautiful. She was too beautiful to question, to judge by common logic; and how could he

know moreover what was natural to a person in that exaltation of grace and splendour? Perhaps it was her habit to
send out every evening for some witless stranger to amuse
her; perhaps that was the way the foreign aristocracy lived.
There was no sharpness in her face—for the present hour
at least: there was nothing but luminous charity, yet she
looked as if she knew what was going on in his mind. She
made no eager attempt to reassure him, but there was a
world almost of direct tenderness in the tone in which she
said: 'Do you know I'm afraid I've already forgotten what
they have been doing——? It's terribly complicated; some
one or other was hurled over a precipice.'

'Ah, you're a brilliant pair,' Madame Grandoni declared
with a laugh of long experience. 'I could describe everything. The person who was hurled over the precipice was
the virtuous hero, and you'll see him in the next act all the
better for it.'

'Don't describe anything; I've so much to ask.' Hyacinth
had looked away in tacit deprecation at hearing himself
'paired' with the Princess, and he felt she was watching
him. 'What do you think of Captain Sholto?' she went on
suddenly, to his surprise, if anything in his position could
excite surprise more than anything else; and as he hesitated,
not knowing what to say, she added: 'Isn't he a very
curious type?'

'I know him very little.' But he had no sooner uttered the
words than it struck him they were far from brilliant, were
poor and flat and very little calculated to satisfy the
Princess. Indeed he had said nothing at all that could place
him in a favourable light; so he continued at a venture:
'I mean I've never seen him at home.' That sounded still
more silly.

'At home? Oh, he's never at home; he's all over the
world. Tonight he was as likely to have been in Paraguay
for instance—though what a place to be!' she smiled—'as
here. He is what they call a cosmopolite. I don't know if
you know that species; very modern, more and more frequent and exceedingly tiresome. I prefer the Chinese. He

had told me he had had a lot of very interesting talk with you. That was what made me say: "Oh, do ask him to come in and see me. A little interesting talk, that would be a change!"'

'She's very complimentary to me!' said Madame Grandoni.

'Ah my dear, you and I, you know, we never talk: we understand each other without that!' Then the Princess pursued, addressing herself to Hyacinth: 'Do you never admit women?'

'Admit women——?'

'Into those seances—what do you call them?—those little meetings that Captain Sholto describes to me. I should like so much to be present. Why not?'

'I haven't seen any ladies,' Hyacinth said. 'I don't know if it's a rule, but I've seen nothing but men'; and he sub-joined, smiling, though he thought the dereliction rather serious and couldn't understand the part Captain Sholto was playing, nor, considering the grand company he kept, how he had originally secured admittance into the subversive little circle in Bloomsbury: 'You know I'm not sure he ought to go about reporting our proceedings.'

'I see. Perhaps you think he's a spy, an *agent provocateur* or something of that sort.'

'No,' said Hyacinth after a moment. 'I think a spy would be more careful—would disguise himself more. Besides, after all, he has heard very little.' He spoke as with mild amusement.

'You mean he hasn't really been behind the scenes?' the Princess asked, bending forward a little and now covering the young man steadily with her beautiful deep eyes, as if by this time he must have got used to her and wouldn't flinch from such attention. 'Of course he hasn't,' she said of herself, however, 'and he never will be. He knows that, and that it's quite out of his power to tell any real secrets. What he repeated to me was interesting, but of course I could see there was nothing the authorities anywhere could put their hand on. It was mainly the talk he had had with you which struck him so very much, and which struck me, as I tell you. Perhaps you didn't know how he was drawing you out.'

'I'm afraid that's rather easy,' said Hyacinth with perfect candour; for it came over him that he *had* chattered with a vengeance in Bloomsbury and had thought it natural enough there that his sociable fellow-visitor should offer him cigars and attach importance to the views of a clever and original young artisan.

'I'm not sure that I find it so! However, I ought to tell you that you needn't have the least fear of Captain Sholto. He's a perfectly honest man, so far as he goes; and even if you had trusted him much more than you appear to have done he'd be incapable of betraying you. However, don't trust him: not because he's not safe, but because——!' She took herself up. 'No matter, you'll see for yourself. He has gone into that sort of thing simply to please me. I should tell you, merely to make you understand, that he would do anything for that. That's his own affair. I wanted to know something, to learn something, to ascertain what really is going on; and for a woman everything of that sort's so difficult, especially for a woman in my position, who's tiresomely known and to whom every sort of bad faith is sure to be imputed. So Sholto said he would look into the subject for me. Poor man, he has had to look into so many subjects! What I particularly wanted was that he should make friends with some of the leading spirits, really characteristic types.' The Princess's voice was low and rather deep, but her tone perfectly natural and easy, with a charming assumption— for you could call it nothing else—of more wonderful things than he could count. Her manner of speaking was in fact altogether new to her listener, for whom the pronunciation of her words and the very punctuation of her sentences were the revelation of what he supposed to be society—the very Society to the destruction of which he was dedicated.

'Surely Captain Sholto doesn't suppose *I'm* a leading spirit!' he exclaimed with the resolve not to be laughed at any more than he could help.

'He told me you were very original.'

'He doesn't know, and—if you'll allow me to say so—I don't think *you* know. How should you? I'm one of many thousands of young men of my class—you know, I suppose, what *that* is—in whose brains certain ideas are fermenting. There's nothing original about me at all. I'm very young and very ignorant; it's only a few months since I began to talk of the possibility of a social revolution with men who have considered the whole ground much more than I could possibly do. I'm a mere particle,' Hyacinth wound up, 'in the grey immensity of the people. All I pretend to is my good faith and a great desire that justice shall be done.'

The Princess listened to him intently and her attitude made him feel how little *he*, in comparison, expressed himself like a person who had the habit of conversation; he seemed to himself to betray ridiculous effort, to stammer and emit vulgar sounds. For a moment she said nothing, only looking at him with her exquisite smile. 'I do draw you out!' she exclaimed at last. 'You're much more interesting to me than if you were an exception.' At these last words Hyacinth flinched a hair's breadth; the movement was shown by his dropping his eyes. We know to what extent he really regarded himself as of the stuff of the common herd. The Princess doubtless guessed it as well, for she quickly added: 'At the same time I can see you're remarkable enough.'

'What do you think I'm remarkable for?'

'Well, you've general ideas.'

'Every one has them today. They have them in Bloomsbury to a terrible degree. I've a friend (who understands the matter much better than I) who has no patience with them: he declares they're our folly, our danger and our bane. A few very special ideas—if they're the right ones—are what we want.'

'Who's your friend?' the Princess asked abruptly.

'Ah, Christina, Christina!' Madame Grandoni murmured from the other side of the box.

Christina took no notice of her, and Hyacinth, not understanding the warning and only remembering how personal women always are, replied: 'A young man who lives in Camberwell and who's in the employ of a big wholesale chemist.'

If he had designed in this description of his friend a stronger dose than his hostess would be able to digest he was greatly mistaken. She seemed to gaze tenderly at the picture suggested by his words, and she immediately enquired if the young man were also clever and if she mightn't hope to know him. Hadn't Captain Sholto seen him, and if so why hadn't he spoken of him too? When Hyacinth had replied that Captain Sholto had probably seen him, but, as he believed, had had no particular conversation with him, the Princess asked with startling frankness if her visitor wouldn't bring the person so vividly described some day to see her.

Hyacinth glanced at Madame Grandoni, but that worthy woman was engaged in a survey of the house through an old-fashioned eyeglass with a long gilt handle. He had perceived much before this that the Princess Casamassima had no desire for vain phrases, and he had the good taste to feel that from himself to such a great lady compliments, even had he wished to pay them, would have had no suitability. 'I don't know whether he would be willing to come. He's the sort of man that in such a case you can't answer for.'

'That makes me want to know him all the more. But you'll come yourself at all events, eh?'

Poor Hyacinth murmured something about the unexpected honour; after all he had a French heredity and it wasn't so easy for him to say things as ill as his other idiom mainly required. But Madame Grandoni, laying down her eyeglass, almost took the words out of his mouth with the cheerful exhortation: 'Go and see her—go and see her once or twice. She'll treat you like an angel.'

'You must think me very peculiar,' the Princess remarked sadly.

'I don't know what I think. It will take a good while.'

'I wish I could make you trust me—inspire you with

confidence,' she went on. 'I don't mean only you personally, but others who think as you do. You'd find I'd go with you —pretty far. I was answering just now for Captain Sholto; but who in the world's to answer for *me*?' And her sadness merged itself in a smile that affected Hyacinth as indescribably magnanimous and touching.

'Not I, my dear, I promise you!' her ancient companion ejaculated with a laugh which made the people in the stalls look up at the box.

Her spirit was contagious; it gave Hyacinth the audacity to say to her 'I'd trust *you*, if you did!' though he felt the next minute that this was even a more familiar speech than if he had expressed a want of confidence.

'It comes then to the same thing,' said the Princess. 'She wouldn't show herself with me in public if I weren't respectable. If you knew more about me you'd understand what has led me to turn my attention to the great social question. It's a long story and the details wouldn't interest you; but perhaps some day, if we have more talk, you'll put yourself a little in my place. I'm very serious, you know; I'm not amusing myself with peeping and running away. I'm convinced that we're living in a fool's paradise, that the ground's heaving under our feet.'

'It's not the ground, my dear; it's you who are turning somersaults,' Madame Grandoni interposed.

'Ah you, my friend, you've the happy faculty of believing what you like to believe. I have to believe what I see.'

'She wishes to throw herself into the revolution, to guide it, to enlighten it,' Madame Grandoni said to Hyacinth, speaking now with imperturbable gravity.

'I'm sure she could direct it in any sense she would wish!' the young man responded in his glow. The pure, high dignity with which the Princess had just spoken and which appeared to cover a suppressed tremor of passion set his pulses throbbing, and though he scarcely saw what she meant—her aspirations appearing as yet so vague—her tone, her voice, her wonderful face showed she had a generous soul.

She answered his eager declaration with a serious smile and a melancholy head-shake. 'I've no such pretensions and my good old friend's laughing at me. Of course that's very easy; for what in fact can be more absurd on the face of it than for a woman with a title, with diamonds, with a carriage, with servants, with a position, as they call it, to sympathise with the upward struggles of those who are below? "Give all that up and we'll believe you," you've a right to say. I'm ready to give them up the moment it will help the cause; I assure you that's the least difficulty. I don't want to teach, I want to learn; and above all I want to know *à quoi m'en tenir*. Are we on the eve of great changes or are we not? Is everything that's gathering force underground, in the dark, in the night, in little hidden rooms, out of sight of governments and policemen and idiotic "statesmen"—heaven save them!—is all this going to burst forth some fine morning and set the world on fire? Or is it to sputter out and spend itself in vain conspiracies, be dissipated in sterile heroisms and abortive isolated movements? I want to know *à quoi m'en tenir*,' she repeated, fixing her visitor with more brilliant eyes and almost as if he could tell her on the spot. Then suddenly she added in quite a different tone: 'Pardon me, I've an idea you know French. Didn't Captain Sholto tell me so?'

'I've some little acquaintance with it,' Hyacinth replied. 'I've French blood in my veins.'

She considered him as if he had proposed to her some attaching problem. 'Yes, I can see you're not *le premier venu*. Now your friend, of whom you were speaking, is a chemist; and you yourself—what's your occupation?'

'I'm just a bookbinder.'

'That must be delightful. I wonder if you'd bind me some books.'

'You'd have to bring them to our shop, and I can do there only the work that's given out to me. I might manage it by myself at home,' Hyacinth freely professed.

'I should like that better. And what do you call home?'

'The place I live in, in the north of London: a little street you certainly never heard of.'

'What is it called?'

'Lomax Place, at your service,' he laughed.

She seemed to reflect his innocent gaiety; she wasn't a bit afraid to let him see she liked him. 'No, I don't think I've heard of it. I don't know London very well; I haven't lived here long. I've spent most of my life abroad. My husband's a foreigner, a South Italian. We don't live always together. I haven't the manners of this country—not of any class, have I, eh? Oh this country—there's a great deal to be said about it and a great deal to be done, as you of course understand better than any one. But I want to know London; it interests me more than I can say—the huge, swarming, smoky, human city. I mean real London, the people and all their sufferings and passions; not Park Lane and Bond Street. Perhaps you can help me—it would be a great kindness: that's what I want to know men like you for. You see it isn't idle, my having given you so much trouble tonight.'

'I shall be very glad to show you all I know. But it isn't much and above all it isn't pretty,' said Hyacinth.

'Whom do you live with in Lomax Place?' she asked, a little oddly, by way of allowance for this.

'Captain's Sholto's leaving the young lady—he's coming back here,' Madame Grandoni announced, inspecting the balcony with her instrument. The orchestra had been for some time playing the overture to the following act.

Hyacinth had just hesitated. 'I live with a dressmaker.'

'With a dressmaker? Do you mean—do you mean——?' But the Princess paused.

'Do you mean she's your wife?' asked Madame Grandoni more bravely.

'Perhaps she gives you rooms,' the Princess suggested.

'How many do you think I have? She gives me everything, or has done so in the past. She brought me up; she's the best little woman in the world.'

'You had better command a dress of her,' Madame Grandoni threw off.

'And your family, where are they?' the Princess continued.

'I have no family.'

'None at all?'

'None at all. I never had.'

'But the French blood you speak of and which I see perfectly in your face—you haven't the English expression or want of expression—that must have come to you through some one.'

'Yes, through my mother.'

'And she's dead?'

'Long ago.'

'That's a great loss, because French mothers are usually so much to their sons.' The Princess looked at her painted fan as she opened and closed it; after which she said: 'Well then, you'll come some day. We'll arrange it.' Hyacinth felt the answer to this could be only a silent inclination of his utmost stature, and to make it he rose from his chair. As he stood there, conscious he had stayed long enough and yet not knowing exactly how to withdraw, the Princess, with her fan closed, resting upright on her knee, and her hands clasped on the end of it, turned up her strangely lovely eyes at him and said: 'Do you think anything will occur soon?'

'Will occur——?'

'That there'll be a crisis—that you'll make yourselves felt?'

In this beautiful woman's face there was to his bewildered perception something at once inspiring, tempting and mocking; and the effect of her expression was to make him say rather clumsily 'I'll try and ascertain——' as if she had asked him whether her carriage were at the door.

'I don't quite know what you're talking about; but please don't have it for another hour or two. I want to see what becomes of the Pearl!' Madame Grandoni interposed.

'Remember what I told you: I'd give up everything—everything!' And the Princess kept looking up at him. Then she held out her hand, and this time he knew sufficiently what he was about to take it.

When he bade good-night to Madame Grandoni the old lady sounded at him with a comical sigh 'Well, she *is* respectable!' and out in the lobby when he had closed the door of the box behind him he found himself echoing these words and repeating mechanically 'She *is* respectable!' They were on his lips as he stood suddenly face to face with Captain Sholto, who grasped his shoulder once more and shook him in that free yet insinuating manner for which this officer appeared remarkable.

'My dear fellow, you were born under a lucky star.'

'I never supposed it,' said Hyacinth, changing colour.

'Why what in the world would you have? You've the faculty, the precious faculty, of inspiring women with an interest—but an interest!'

'Yes, ask them in the box there! I behaved like an awful muff,' Hyacinth declared, overwhelmed now with a sense of opportunities missed.

'They won't tell me that. And the lady upstairs?'

'Well,' said Hyacinth gravely, 'what about her?'

'She wouldn't talk to me of anything but you. You may imagine how I liked it!'

'I don't like it either. But I must go up.'

'Oh yes, she counts the minutes. Such a charming person!' Captain Sholto added with more propriety of tone. As Hyacinth left him he called out: 'Don't be afraid—you'll go far.'

When the young man took his place in the balcony beside Millicent she gave him no greeting nor asked any question about his adventures in the most privileged part of the house. She only turned her fine complexion upon him for some minutes, and as he himself was not in the mood to begin to chatter the silence continued—continued till after the curtain had risen on the last act of the play. Millicent's attention was now evidently not at her disposal for the stage, and in the midst of a violent scene which included pistol-shots and shrieks she said at last to her companion: 'She's a tidy lot, your Princess, by what I learn.'

'Pray what do you know about her?'

'I know what that fellow told me.'

'And what may that have been?'

'Well, she's a bad 'un as ever was. Her own husband has had to turn her out of the house.'

Hyacinth remembered the allusion the lady herself had made to her matrimonial situation; in spite of which he would have liked to be able to reply to Miss Henning that he didn't believe a word of it. He withheld the doubt and after a moment simply remarked: 'Well, I don't care.'

'You don't care? Well, I do then!' Millicent cried. And as it was impossible in view of the performance and the jealous attention of their neighbours to continue the conversation at this pitch, she contented herself with ejaculating in a somewhat lower key at the end of five minutes during which she had been watching the stage: 'Gracious, what dreadful common stuff!' Hyacinth then wondered if Captain Sholto had given her this formula.

XIV

HE DIDN'T mention to Pinnie or Mr Vetch that he had been taken up by a great lady; but he mentioned it to Paul Muniment, to whom he now confided a great many things. He had at first been in considerable fear of his straight loud north-country friend, who showed signs of cultivating logic and criticism in a degree that was hostile to fine loose talk; but he discovered in him later a man to whom one could say anything in the world if one didn't think it of more importance to be sympathised with than to be understood. For a revolutionist he was strangely unexasperated, was indulgent even to contempt. The sight of all the things he wanted to change had seemingly no power to irritate him, and if he joked about questions that lay very near his heart his humour had no ferocity—the fault Hyacinth sometimes found with it rather was that it was innocent to puerility. Our hero envied his power of combining a care for the wide misery of mankind with the apparent state of mind of the cheerful and virtuous young workman who of a Sunday morning has put on a clean shirt and, not having taken the gilt off his wages the night before, weighs against each other, for a happy day, the respective attractions of Epping Forest and Gravesend. He never dragged in with the least snarl his personal lot and his daily life; it had not seemed to occur to him for instance that 'society' was really responsible for the condition of his sister's spinal column, though Eustache Poupin and his wife (who practically, however, were as patient as he) did everything they could to make him say so, believing evidently that it would relieve him. Apparently he cared nothing for women, talked of them rarely and always decently, and had never a sign of a sweetheart save in so far as Lady Aurora Langrish might pass for one. He never drank a drop of beer nor touched a pipe; he always had a clear tone, a fresh cheek and a merely, an imperturbably intelligent eye, and once excited on Hyacinth's part a kind of elder-brotherly indulgence by the open-mouthed glee and credulity with which, when the pair were present, in the sixpenny gallery, at Astley's, at an equestrian pantomime, he followed the tawdry spectacle. He once pronounced the young bookbinder a suggestive little beggar, and Hyacinth's opinion of him was by this time so exalted that the remark had almost the value of a patent of nobility. Our hero treated himself to a high unlimited faith in him; he had always dreamed of some grand friendship and this was the best opening he had yet encountered. No one could entertain a sentiment of that sort more nobly, more ingeniously than Hyacinth, or cultivate with more art the intimate personal relation. It disappointed him sometimes that this confidence was not more unreservedly repaid; that on certain important points of the socialistic programme Muniment would never commit himself and had not yet shown the *fond du sac*, as Eustache Poupin called it, to so ardent an admirer. He answered particular appeals freely enough, and answered them occasionally in a manner that made Hyacinth jump, as when in reply to a question about his attitude on capital punishment he said that so far from wishing it abolished he should go in for extending it much further—he should impose it on those who habitually lied or got drunk; but his friend had always a feeling that he kept back his best card and that even in the listening circle in Bloomsbury, when only the right men were present, there were unspoken conclusions in his mind which he didn't as yet think any one good enough to be favoured with. So far therefore from suspecting him of any real poverty of programme Hyacinth was sure he had extraordinary things in his head; that he was thinking them out to the logical end, wherever it might land him; and that the night he should produce them with the door of the club-room guarded and the company bound by a tremendous oath the others would look at each other, gasp and turn pale.

'She wants to see you; she asked me to bring you; she was very serious,' our young man meanwhile said, reporting his interview with the ladies in the box at the play; which, however, now that he looked back upon it, seemed as queer as a dream and not much more likely than that sort of experience to have a continuation in one's waking hours.

'To bring me—to bring me where?' asked Muniment. 'You talk as if I were a sample out of your shop or a little dog you had for sale. Has she ever seen me? Does she think I'm smaller than you? What does she know about me?'

'Well, principally that you're a friend of mine—that's enough for her.'

'Do you mean it ought to be enough for me that she's a friend of yours? I've a notion you'll have some queer ones before you've done; a good many more than I have time to talk to. And how can I go to see a delicate female with those paws?' Muniment said as he exhibited ten work-stained fingers.

'Buy a pair of gloves——' Hyacinth recognised the serious character of this obstacle. But after a moment he added: 'No, you oughtn't to do that. She wants to see dirty hands.'

'That's easy enough, good Lord! She needn't send for me for the purpose. But isn't she making game of you?'

'It's very possible, but I don't see what good it can do her.'

'You're not obliged to find excuses for the pampered classes. Their bloated luxury begets evil, impudent desires; they're capable of doing harm for the sake of harm. Besides, is she genuine?'

'If she isn't, what becomes of your explanation?' Hyacinth asked.

'Oh, it doesn't matter; at night all cats are grey. Whatever she is, she's an idle, bedizened trifler; perhaps even a real profligate female.'

'If you had seen her you wouldn't talk of her that way.'

'God forbid I should see her then, if she's going to corrupt me!'

'Do you suppose she'll corrupt *me*?' Hyacinth demanded with an expression of face and a tone of voice which produced on his friend's part an explosion of mirth.

'How can she, after all, when you're already such a little mass of corruption?'

'You don't think that——?' and Hyacinth looked very grave.

'Do you mean that if I did I wouldn't say it? Haven't you noticed that I say what I think?'

'No, you don't, not half of it: you're as dark as a fish.'

Paul Muniment glanced at his friend as if rather struck with the penetration of that remark; then he said: 'Well then, if I should give you the other half of my opinion of you do you think you'd fancy it?'

'I'll save you the trouble. I'm a very clever, conscientious, promising young chap, and any one would be proud to claim me as a friend.'

'Is that what your Princess told you? She must be a precious piece of goods!' Paul exclaimed. 'Did she pick your pocket meanwhile?'

'Oh yes; a few minutes later I missed a silver cigar-case engraved with the arms of the Robinsons. Seriously,'

Hyacinth continued, 'don't you consider it possible that a woman of that class should want to know what's going on among the like of us?'

'It depends on what class you mean.'

'Well, a woman with a lot of wonderful jewels and wonderful scents and the manners of an angel. I wonder if even the young ladies in the perfumery shops have such manners—they can't have such pearls. It's queer of course, that sort of interest, but it's conceivable; why not? There may be unselfish natures; there may be disinterested feelings.'

'And there may be fine ladies in an awful funk about their jewels and even about their manners. Seriously, as you say, it's perfectly conceivable. I'm not in the least surprised at the aristocracy being curious to know what we're up to and wanting very much to look into it. In their place I should be very uneasy, and if I were a woman with angelic manners very likely I too should be glad to get hold of a soft susceptible little bookbinder and pump him dry, bless his tender heart!'

'Are you afraid I'll tell her secrets?' cried Hyacinth, flushing with virtuous indignation.

'Secrets? What secrets could you tell her, my pretty lad?'

Hyacinth turned away. 'You don't trust me—you never have.'

'We will, some day—don't be afraid,' said Muniment, who evidently had no intention of harshness, at least in respect to Hyacinth, a thing that appeared impossible to him. 'And when we do you'll cry with disappointment.'

'Well, *you* won't,' Hyacinth returned. And then he asked if his friend thought the Princess Casamassima a spy of spies—the devil she'd have to be!—and why, if she were in that line, Sholto was not, since it must be supposed he was not when they had seen fit to let him walk in and out, at any rate, at the place in Bloomsbury. Muniment didn't even know whom he meant, not having had any relations with the gentleman; but he summoned a sufficient image

after his companion had described the Captain's appearance. He then remarked with his usual geniality that he
didn't take him for anything worse than a jackass; but even
if he had edged himself into the place with every intention
to betray them what handle could he possibly get—what
use against them could he make of anything he had seen or
heard? If he had a fancy to dip into working-men's clubs
(Paul remembered now the first night he came; he had been
brought by that German cabinet-maker who always had a
bandaged neck and smoked a pipe with a bowl as big as a
stove); if it amused him to put on a bad hat and inhale foul
tobacco and call his 'inferiors' 'my dear fellow'; if he
thought that in doing so he was getting an insight into the
people and going halfway to meet them and preparing for
what was coming—all this was his own affair and he was
very welcome, though a man must be a flat who would
spend his evening in a hole like that when he might enjoy
his comfort in one of those flaming big shops, full of arm-
chairs and flunkies, in Pall Mall. And what did he see after
all in Bloomsbury? Nothing but a remarkably stupid 'social
gathering' where there were clay pipes and a sanded floor
and not half enough gas and the principal papers; and
where the men, as any one would know, were advanced
radicals and mostly advanced idiots. He could pat as many
of them on the back as he liked and say the House of Lords
wouldn't last till midsummer; but what discoveries would
he make? He was simply on the same lay as Hyacinth's
Princess; he was nervous and scared and thought he would
see for himself.

'Oh, he isn't the same sort as the Princess. I'm sure he's
in a very different line!' Hyacinth objected.

'Different of course; she's a handsome woman, I suppose,
and he's an ugly man; but I don't think that either of them
will save us or spoil us. Their curiosity's natural, but I've
other things to do than to show them over: therefore you
can tell her Serene Highness that I'm much obliged.'

Hyacinth reflected a moment and then said: 'You show
Lady Aurora over; you seem to wish to give her the

information she desires; therefore what's the difference? If it's right for her to take an interest why isn't it right for my Princess?'

'If she's already yours what more can she want?' Muniment asked. 'All I know of Lady Aurora and all I look at is that she comes and sits with Rosy and brings her tea and waits on her. If the Princess will do as much I'll see what *I* can do; but apart from that I shall never take a grain of interest in her interest in the masses—or in this particular mass!' And Paul, with his discoloured thumb, designated his own substantial person. His tone was disappointing to Hyacinth, who was surprised at his not appearing to think the incident at the theatre more remarkable and romantic. He seemed to regard his mate's explanation of the passage as all-sufficient; but when a moment later he made use, in referring to the mysterious lady, of the expression that she was 'quaking' that critic broke out: 'Never in the world; she's not afraid of anything!'

'Ah, my lad, not afraid of you, evidently!'

Hyacinth paid no attention to this coarse sally, but resumed with a candour that was proof against further ridicule: 'Do you think she can do me a hurt of any kind if we follow up our acquaintance?'

'Yes, very likely, but you must hit her back and give it to her badly. That's your line, you know—to go in for what's going, to live your life, to gratify the "sex". I'm an ugly, grimy brute, I've got to watch the fires and mind the shop; but you're one of those taking little beggars who *must* run about and see the world. You ought to be an ornament to society, like a young man in an illustrated story-book. Only you know,' Muniment added in a moment, 'if she should hurt you very much I *would* have a go at her!'

Hyacinth had been intending for some time to take Pinnie to call on the prostrate damsel in Audley Court, to whom he had promised that his benefactress (he had told Rose Muniment she was his godmother—it sounded so right) should pay this civility; but the affair had been delayed by wan hesitations on the part of the dress-maker, the poor woman having hard work to imagine today that there were people in London forlorn enough for her countenance to be of value to them. Her social curiosity had quite died out and she knew she no longer made the same figure in public as when her command of the fashions enabled her to illustrate them in her own little person by the aid of a good deal of whalebone. Moreover she felt that Hyacinth had strange friends and still stranger opinions; she suspected him of taking an unnatural interest in politics and of being somehow not on the right side, little as she knew about parties or causes; and she had a vague convic-tion that this kind of perversity only multiplied the troubles of the poor, who, according to theories which Pinnie had never reasoned out but which in her breast were as deep as religion, ought always to be of the same way of thinking as the rich. They were unlike them enough in their poverty without trying to add other differences. When at last she accompanied Hyacinth to Camberwell one Saturday even-ing at midsummer it was in a sighing, sceptical, second-best manner; but if he had told her he wished it she would have gone with him to a soirée at a scavenger's. There was no more danger of Rose Muniment's being out than that one of the bronze couchant lions in Trafalgar Square should have walked down Whitehall; but he had let her know in advance and he perceived, as he opened her door in obedi-ence to a quick, shrill summons, that she had had the happy thought of inviting Lady Aurora to help her entertain Miss Pynsent. Such at least was the inference he drew from see-ing her ladyship's memorable figure rise before him for the first time since their meeting there. He presented his com-panion to their reclining hostess, and Rosy immediately repeated her name to the representative of Belgrave Square. Pinnie curtseyed down to the ground as Lady Aurora put out her hand to her, and then slipped noiselessly into a chair beside the bed. Lady Aurora laughed and fidgeted in a friendly, cheerful, yet at the same time rather pointless manner, and Hyacinth gathered that she had no recollection of having seen him. His attention, however, was mainly given to Pinnie: he watched her jealously, to see if on this important occasion she wouldn't put forth a certain stiff, quaint, polished politeness of which she possessed the secret and which made him liken her extraction of the sense of things to the nip of a pair of old-fashioned silver sugar-tongs. Not only for Pinnie's sake but for his own as well he wished her to figure as a superior little woman; so he hoped she wouldn't lose her head if Rosy should begin to talk about Inglefield. She was evidently much impressed by Rosy and kept repeating, 'Dear, dear!' under her breath while the small strange person in the bed rapidly explained to her that there was nothing in the world she would have liked so much as to follow *her* delightful profession, but that she couldn't sit up to it, and had never had a needle in her hand but once, when at the end of three minutes it had dropped into the sheets and got into the mattress, so that she had always been afraid it would work out again and stick into her: which it hadn't done yet and perhaps never would—she lay so quiet, pushing it about so little. 'Perhaps you'd think it's me that trimmed the little handkerchief I wear round my neck,' Miss Muniment said; 'perhaps you'd think I couldn't do less, lying here all day long with complete command of my time. Not a stitch of it. I'm the finest lady in London; I never lift my finger for myself. It's a present from her ladyship—it's her ladyship's own beautiful needlework. What do you think of that? Have you ever met any one so favoured before? And the work—just look at the work and tell me how it strikes you.' The girl pulled off the bit of muslin from her neck and thrust it at Pinnie, who looked at it confusedly and gasped 'Dear, dear, dear!' partly in sympathy, partly as if, in spite of the consideration she owed every one, those were very odd proceedings.

'It's very badly done; surely you see that,' said Lady Aurora. 'It was only a joke.'

'Oh yes, everything's a joke!' cried the irrepressible invalid—'everything except my state of health; that's admitted to be serious. When her ladyship sends me five shillings' worth of coals it's only a joke; and when she brings me a bottle of the finest port, that's another; and when she climbs up seventy-seven stairs (there are seventy-seven, I know perfectly, though I never go up or down) to spend the evening with me at the height of the London season, that's the best of all. I know all about the London season though I never go out, and I appreciate what her ladyship gives up. She's very jocular indeed, but fortunately I know how to take it. You can see it wouldn't do for me to be touchy, can't you, Miss Pynsent?'

'Dear, dear, I should be so glad to make you anything myself; it would be better—it would be better——!' poor Pinnie floundered.

'It would be better than my poor work. I don't know how to do that sort of thing in the least,' said Lady Aurora.

'I'm sure I didn't meant that, my lady—I only meant it would be more convenient. Anything in the world she might fancy,' the dressmaker went on as if it were a question of the invalid's appetite.

'Ah, you see I don't wear things—only a flannel jacket to be a bit tidy,' Miss Muniment returned. 'I go in only for smart counterpanes, as you can see for yourself'; and she spread her white hands complacently over her coverlet of brilliant patchwork. 'Now doesn't that look to you, Miss Pynsent, as if it might be one of her ladyship's jokes?'

'Oh my good friend, how can you? I never went so far as that!' Lady Aurora interposed with visible anxiety.

'Well, you've given me almost everything; I sometimes forget. This only cost me sixpence; so it comes to the same thing as if it had been a present. Yes, only sixpence in a raffle in a bazaar at Hackney, for the benefit of the Wesleyan Chapel three years ago. A young man who works with my brother and lives in that part offered him a couple of tickets; and he took one and I took one. When I say "I" of course I mean he took the two; for how should I find (by which I naturally mean how should *he* find) a sixpence in that little cup on the chimney-piece unless he had put it there first? Of course my ticket took a prize, and of course, as my bed's my dwelling-place, the prize was a beautiful counterpane of every colour of the rainbow. Oh there never was such luck as mine!' Rosy chattered, flashing her gay demented eyes at Hyacinth as if to irritate him with her contradictious optimism.

'It's very lovely, but if you'd like another for a change I've got a great many pieces,' Pinnie remarked with a generosity which made the young man feel she was acquitting herself finely.

Rose Muniment laid her little hand on the dressmaker's arm and responded straight: 'No, not a change, not a change. How can there be a change when there's already everything? There's everything here—every colour that was ever seen or invented or dreamed of since the world began.' And with her other hand she stroked affectionately her variegated quilt. 'You've a great many pieces, but you haven't as many as there are here; and the more you should patch them together the more the whole thing would resemble this dear dazzling old friend. I've another idea, very very charming, and perhaps her ladyship can guess what it is.' Rosy kept her fingers on Pinnie's arm and, smiling, turned her brilliant eyes from one of her female companions to the other as to associate and blend them as closely as possible in their interest in her. 'In connexion with what we were talking about a few minutes ago—couldn't your ladyship just go a little further in the same line?' Then as Lady Aurora looked troubled and embarrassed, blushing at being called upon to answer a conundrum, as it were, so publicly, her infirm friend came to her assistance. 'It will surprise you at first, but it won't when I've explained it: my idea is just simply a sweet pink dressing-gown!'

'A sweet pink dressing-gown!' Lady Aurora repeated.

'With a neat black trimming! Don't you see the connexion with what we were talking of before our good visitors came in?'

'That would be very pretty,' said Pinnie. 'I've made them like that in my time. Or a carefully-selected blue trimmed with white.'

'No, pink and black, pink and black—to suit my complexion. Perhaps you didn't know *I* have a complexion; but there are very few things I lack! Anything at all I should fancy, you were so good as to say. Well now, I fancy that! Your ladyship does see the connexion by this time, doesn't she?'

Lady Aurora looked distressed, as if she felt she certainly ought to see it but was not sure that even yet it didn't escape her, and as if at the same time she were struck with the fact that this sudden evocation might result in a strain on the small dressmaker's resources. 'A pink dressing-gown would certainly be very becoming and Miss Pynsent would be very kind,' she said; while Hyacinth made the mental comment that it was a largeish order, since Pinnie would have obviously to furnish the materials as well as the labour. The amiable coolness with which the invalid laid her under contribution was, however, to his sense, quite in character, and he reflected that after all when you were flat on your back like that you had the right to reach out your hands (it wasn't far you could reach at best) and grab what you could get. Pinnie declared she knew just the article Miss Muniment wanted and that she would undertake to make a perfect duck of it; and Rosy went on to say that she must explain of what use such an article would be, but for this purpose there must be another guess. She would give it to Miss Pynsent and Hyacinth—as many times as they liked: what *had* she and Lady Aurora been talking about before they came in? She clasped her hands and her eyes shone with her eagerness while she continued to turn them from Lady Aurora to the dressmaker. What would they imagine? What would they think natural, delightful, magnificent—if one could only end at last by making out the right place to put it? Hyacinth suggested successively a cage of Java sparrows, a music-box and a shower-bath—or perhaps even a full-length portrait of her ladyship; and Pinnie looked at him askance in a frightened way, as if perchance he were joking too broadly. Rosy at last relieved their suspense and announced: 'A sofa, just a sofa now! What do you say to that? Do you suppose that idea could have come from any one but her ladyship? She must have all the credit of it; she came out with it in the course of conversation. I believe we were talking of the peculiar feeling that comes just under the shoulder-blades if one never has a change. She mentioned it as she might have mentioned just the right sort of rub—there *are* such wrong sorts!—or another spoonful of that American stuff. We're thinking it over and one of these days, if we give plenty of time to the question, we shall find the place, the very nicest and snuggest of all and no other. I hope *you* see the connexion with the pink dressing-gown,' she pursued to Pinnie, 'and I hope you see the importance of the question "Shall anything go?" I should like you to look round a bit and tell me what you would answer if I were to say to you "*Can* anything go?"'

XV

'IM SURE there's nothing *I* should like to part with,' Pinnie returned; and while she surveyed the scene Lady Aurora, with discretion, to lighten Amanda's responsibility, got up and turned to the window, which was open to the summer evening and admitted still the last rays of the long day. Hyacinth, after a moment, placed himself beside her, looking out with her at the dusky multitude of chimney-pots and the small black houses roofed with grimy tiles. The thick warm air of a London July floated beneath them, suffused with the everlasting uproar of the town, which appeared to have sunk into quietness but again became a mighty voice as soon as one listened for it; here and there, in poor windows, glimmered a turbid light, and high above, in a clearer smokeless zone, a sky still fair and luminous, a faint silver star looked down. The sky was the same that bent far away in the country over golden fields and purple hills and gardens where nightingales sang; but from this point of view everything that covered the earth was ugly and sordid and seemed to express or to represent the weariness of toil. Presently, to Hyacinth's astonishment, Lady Aurora said to him: 'You never came after all to get the books.'

'Those you kindly offered to lend me? I didn't know it was an understanding.'

She gave an uneasy laugh. 'I've picked them out; they're quite ready.'

'It's awfully kind of you,' the young man hastened to say. 'I'll come and get them some day with pleasure.' He wasn't very sure he would, but it was the least he could profess.

'She'll tell you where I live, you know,' Lady Aurora went on with a movement of her head in the direction of the bed, as if she were too shy to mention it herself.

'Oh, I've no doubt she knows the way—she could tell me every street and every turn!' Hyacinth laughed.

'She has made me describe to her very often how I come and go,' his companion concurred. 'I think few people know more about London than she. She never forgets anything.'

'She's a wonderful little witch—she terrifies me!' he acknowledged.

Lady Aurora turned her modest eyes on him. 'Oh, she's so good, she's so patient!'

'Yes, and so preternaturally wise and so awfully all there.'

'Ah, she's immensely clever,' said her ladyship. 'Which do you think the cleverer?'

'The cleverer?'

'Of the girl or her brother.'

'Oh, I think he'll be some day prime minister of England.'

'Do you really? I'm so glad!' she cried with a flush of colour. 'I do rejoice if you think that will be possible. You know it ought to be if things were right.'

Hyacinth had not professed this high faith for the purpose of playing on her ladyship's feelings, but when he felt her intense agreement it was as if he had been making sport of her. Still he said no more than he believed when he observed in a moment that he had the greatest expectations of Paul Muniment's future: he was sure the world would hear of him, that England would need him, that the public some day would acclaim him. It was impossible to know him without feeling he was very strong and must play some important part.

'Yes, people wouldn't believe—they wouldn't believe.' She abounded in his sense and he could measure the good he did her. It was moreover a pleasure to himself to place on record his opinion of his friend; it seemed to make that opinion more clear, to give it the force of an invocation or a prophecy. This was especially the case when he asked why on earth nature had endowed Paul Muniment with such extraordinary powers of mind, and powers of body too—because he was as strong as a horse—if it hadn't been intended he should do something supreme for his fellow-men. Hyacinth confided to her ladyship that he thought the people in his own class generally very stupid—distinctly what he should call third-rate minds. He wished it hadn't been so, for heaven knew he felt kindly to them and only asked to cast his lot with theirs; but he was obliged to confess that centuries of poverty, of ill-paid toil, of bad insufficient food and wretched housing hadn't a favourable effect on the higher faculties. All the more reason that when there was a splendid exception like their friend it should count for a tremendous force—it had so much to make up for, so many to act for. And then Hyacinth repeated that in his own low walk of life people had really not the faculty of thought; their minds had been simplified—reduced to two or three elements. He saw that such judgements made his fellow-guest very uncomfortable; she turned about, she twisted herself vaguely as if she wished to protest, but she was far too considerate to interrupt him. He had no wish to worry her, but there were times when he couldn't withstand the perverse satisfaction of insisting on his lowliness of station, of turning the knife in the wound inflicted by such explicit reference, and of letting it be seen that if his place in the world was immeasurably small he at least had no illusions about either himself or his species. Lady Aurora replied as quickly as possibly that she knew a great deal about the poor —not the poor after the fashion of Rosy, but the terribly, hopelessly poor, with whom she was more familiar than Hyacinth would perhaps believe—and that she was often struck with their great talents and their quick wit, with their command of conversation really of much more interest to her than most of what one usually heard in drawing-rooms. She often found them immensely clever.

Hyacinth smiled at her and said: 'Ah when you get to the lowest depths of poverty they may become rich and rare again. But I'm afraid I haven't gone so far down. In spite of my opportunities I don't know many absolute paupers.'

'I know a great many.' Lady Aurora hesitated as if she didn't like to swagger, but she brought it out. 'I dare say I know more than any one.' There was something touching and beautiful to Hyacinth in this simple and diffident claim: it confirmed his impression that she was in some mysterious, incongruous and even slightly ludicrous manner a true heroine, a creature of a noble ideal. She perhaps guessed he was indulging in reflexions that might be favourable to her, for she said precipitately the next minute, as if there were nothing she dreaded so much as the danger of a compliment: 'I think your aunt's so very attractive—and I'm sure dear Rosy thinks so.' No sooner had she spoken than she blushed again; it appeared to have occurred to her that he might suppose she wished to contradict him by presenting this case of his aunt as a proof that the baser sort, even in a prosaic upper layer, were not without redeeming points. There was no reason why she should not have had this intention; so without sparing her he replied:

'You mean she's an exception to what I was saying?'

She stammered a little; then at last, as if, since he wouldn't spare her, she wouldn't spare him either: 'Yes, and you're an exception too; you'll not make me believe you're wanting in intelligence. The Muniments don't think so,' she added.

'No more do I myself; but that doesn't prove that exceptions are not frequent. I've blood in my veins that's not the blood of the people.'

'Oh, I see,' said Lady Aurora sympathetically. And with

a smile she went on: 'Then you're all the more of an exception—in the upper class!'

Her way of taking it was the kindest in the world, but it didn't blind Hyacinth to the fact that from his own point of view he had been extraordinarily indiscreet. He had believed a moment before that he would have been proof against the strongest temptation to refer to the mysteries of his lineage, inasmuch as if made in a boastful spirit (and he had not desire as yet to treat it as an exercise in humility) any such reference would inevitably contain an element of the grotesque. He had never opened his lips to any one about his birth since the dreadful days when the question was discussed with Mr Vetch's assistance in Lomax Place; never even to Paul Muniment, never to Millicent Henning nor to Eustache Poupin. He had his impression that people had ideas about him, and with some of Miss Henning's he had been made acquainted: these were of such a nature that he sometimes wondered if the tie uniting him to her were not on her own side a secret determination to satisfy her utmost curiosity before she had done with him. But he flattered himself he was impenetrable, and none the less he had begun to swagger idiotically the first time a temptation (really to call a temptation) presented itself. He turned crimson as soon as he had spoken, partly at the sudden image of what he had to swagger about and partly at the absurdity of a challenge from the model of civility before him. He hoped she didn't particularly regard what he had said—and indeed she gave no sign whatever of being startled by his claim to a pedigree, she had too much quick delicacy for that; she appeared to notice only the symptoms of confusion that followed. But as soon as possible he gave himself a lesson in humility by remarking: 'I gather you spend most of your time among the poor and I'm sure you carry blessings with you. But I frankly confess I don't understand a lady's giving herself up to people like us when there's no obligation. Wretched company we must be when there's so much better to be had.'

'I like it very much—you don't understand.'

'Precisely—that's what I say. Our little friend on the bed is perpetually talking about your house, your family, your splendours, your gardens and greenhouses. They must be magnificent of course——'

'Oh, I wish she wouldn't; really I wish she wouldn't. It makes one feel dreadfully!' Lady Aurora interposed with vehemence.

'Ah, you had better give her her way; it's such a pleasure to her.'

'Yes, more than to any of us!' sighed her ladyship helplessly.

'Well, how can you leave all those beautiful things to come and breathe this beastly air, surround yourself with hideous images and associate with people whose smallest fault is that they're ignorant, brutal and dirty? I don't speak of the ladies here present,' Hyacinth added with the manner which most made Millicent Henning (who at once admired and hated it) wonder where on earth he had got it.

'Oh, I wish I could make you understand!' cried Lady Aurora, looking at him with troubled, appealing eyes and as if he were unexpectedly discouraging.

'But when all's said I think I do understand! Charity exists in your nature as a kind of passion.'

'Yes, yes, it's a kind of passion!' her ladyship repeated eagerly, all thankful for the word. 'I don't know if it's charity—I don't mean that. But whatever it is it's a passion—it's my life—it's all I care for.' She faltered as if there might be something indecent in the confession or uncertain in the recipient; and then evidently was mastered by the comfort of being able to justify herself for an eccentricity that had excited notice, as well as by the luxury of discharging her soul of a long accumulation of intense things. 'Already when I was fifteen years old I wanted to sell all I had and give to the poor. And ever since I've wanted to do something: it has seemed as if my heart would break if I shouldn't be able!'

Hyacinth was struck with a great respect, which however didn't prevent his presently saying, though in words that sounded patronising even to himself: 'I suppose you're very religious.'

She looked away into the thickening dusk, at the smutty housetops, the blurred emanation of lamplight above the streets. 'I don't know. One has one's ideas. Some of them may be strange. I think a great many clergymen do good, but there are others I don't like at all. I dare say we had too many always at home; my father likes them so particularly. I think I've known too many bishops, I've had the church too much on my back. I dare say they wouldn't think at home, you know, that one was quite what one ought to be; but of course they consider me very odd in every way, as there's no doubt I am. I should tell you that I don't tell them everything; for what's the use when people don't understand? We're twelve at home and eight of us girls; and if you think it's so very splendid, and *she* thinks so, I should like you both to try it for a little! My father isn't rich and there's only one of us, Eva, married, and we're not at all handsome, and—oh there are all kinds of things,' the young woman went on, looking round at him an instant through her sense of being launched. 'I don't like society, and neither would you if you were to see the kind there is in London— at least in some parts,' Lady Aurora added considerately. 'I dare say you wouldn't believe all the humbuggery and the tiresomeness that one has to go through. But I've got out of it; I do as I like, though it has been rather a struggle. I have my liberty, and that's the greatest blessing in life except the reputation of being queer, and even a little mad, which is a greater advantage still. I'm a little mad, you know; you needn't be surprised if you hear it. That's because I stop in town when they go into the country; all the autumn, all the winter, when there's no one here (except three or four millions) and the rain drips, drips, drips from the trees in the big dull park where my people live. I dare say I oughtn't to say such things to you, but, as I tell you, I'm quite a proper lunatic and I might as well keep up the character. When one's one of eight daughters and there's very little money (for any of *us* at least) and nothing to do but to go out with three or four others in mackintoshes, one can easily go off one's head. Of course there's the village, and it's not at all a nice one, and there are the people to look after, and goodness knows they're in want of it; but one must work with the vicarage, and at the vicarage are four more daughters, all old maids, and it's dreary and dreadful and one has too much of it, for they don't understand what one thinks or feels or a single word one says to them. Besides, they *are* stupid, I admit, the country poor; they're very very dense. I like Camberwell better,' said Lady Aurora, smiling and taking breath at the end of her nervous, hurried, almost incoherent speech, of which she had delivered herself pantingly, with strange intonations and contortions, as if afraid that from one moment to the other she would repent, not of her confidence but of her egotism.

It placed her for Hyacinth in an unexpected light, making him feel that her awkward aristocratic spinsterhood was the cover of tumultuous passions. No one could have less the appearance of being animated by a vengeful irony; but he saw this timorous, scrupulous, though clearly all generous, creature to be evidently most a person not to spare, whereever she could prick them, the institutions among which she had been brought up and against which she had violently reacted. He had always supposed a reactionary to mean a backslider from the liberal faith, but Rosy's devotee gave a new value to the term; she appeared to have been driven to her present excesses by the squire and the parson and the conservative influences of that upper-class British home which our young man had always held the highest fruit of civilisation. It was clear that her ladyship was an original, and an original with force; but it gave Hyacinth a real pang to hear her make light of Inglefield (especially the park) and of the opportunities that must have abounded in Belgrave Square. It had been his belief that in a world of suffering and injustice these things were if not the most righteous at least the most fascinating. If they didn't give one the finest sensations where were such sensations to be had? He looked at Lady Aurora with a face that was a tribute to her sudden vividness while he said: 'I can easily understand your wanting to do some good in the world, because you're a kind of saint.'

'A very curious kind!' laughed her ladyship.

'But I don't understand your not liking what your position gives you.'

'I don't know anything about my position. I want to live!'

'And do you call *this* life?'

'I'll tell you what my position is if you want to know: it's the deadness of the grave!'

Hyacinth was startled by her tone, but he nevertheless laughed back at her: 'Ah, as I say, you're a regular saint!' She made no reply, for at that moment the door opened and Paul Muniment's tall figure emerged from the blackness of the staircase into the twilight, now very faint, of the room. Lady Aurora's eyes as they rested on him seemed to declare that such a vision as that at least was life. Another person as tall as himself appeared behind him, and Hyacinth recognised with astonishment their insinuating friend Captain Sholto. Paul had brought him up for Rosy's entertainment, being ready, and more than ready, always to introduce any one in the world, from the prime minister to the common hangman, who might give that young lady a sensation. They must have met at the 'Sun and Moon', and if the Captain, some accident smoothing the way, had made him half as many advances as he had made some other people, Hyacinth could see that it wouldn't take long for Paul to lay him under contribution. But what the mischief was the Captain up to? It can't be said that our young man arrived this evening at an answer to that question. The occasion proved highly festal and the hostess rose to it without lifting her head from the pillow. Her brother introduced Captain Sholto as a gentleman who had a great desire to know extraordinary people, and she made him take possession of the chair at her bedside, out of which Miss Pynsent quickly edged herself, and asked him who he was and where he came from and how Paul had made his acquaintance and whether he had many friends in Camberwell. Sholto had not the

same grand air that hovered about him at the theatre; he
was dressed with ingenious cheapness, to an effect coincid-
ing, however different the cause, with poor Hyacinth's own;
but his disguise prompted our young man to wonder what
made him so unmistakeably a gentleman in spite of it—in spite
too of his rather overdoing the manner of being appreciative
even to rapture and thinking everything and every one most
charming and curious. He stood out, in poor Rosy's tawdry
little room, among her hideous attempts at decoration, and
looked to Hyacinth a being from another sphere, playing
over the place and company a smile (one couldn't call it
false or unpleasant, yet it was distinctly not natural) of
which he had got the habit in camps and courts. It became
intense when it rested on our hero, whom he greeted as he
might have done a dear young friend from whom he had
been long and painfully separated. He was easy, he was
familiar, he was exquisitely benevolent and bland—he was
altogether a problem.

Rosy was a match for him, however; he evidently didn't
puzzle her in the least and she thought his visit the most
natural thing in the world. She expressed all the gratitude
decency required, but appeared to assume that people who
climbed her stairs would always find themselves repaid. She
remarked that her brother must have met him for the first
time that day, since the way he sealed a new acquaintance
was usually by bringing the person immediately to call on
her. And when the Captain said that if she didn't like them
he supposed the poor wretches were dropped on the spot
she admitted that this would be true if it ever happened
she disapproved: as yet, however, she had not been obliged
to draw the line. This was perhaps partly because he hadn't
brought up any of his awful firebrands, the people he knew
for unmentionable reasons. Of such in general she had a
very small opinion, and she wouldn't conceal from Captain
Sholto that she hoped he wasn't one of them. Rosy spoke as
if her brother represented the Camberwell district in the
House of Commons and she had discovered that a parlia-
mentary career lowered the moral tone. The Captain never-

theless entered quite into her views and told her that it was
as common friends of Mr Hyacinth Robinson Mr Muniment
and he had come together; they were both so fond of him
that this had immediately constituted a kind of tie. On hearing himself commemorated in such a brilliant way Mr Hyacinth Robinson averted his head; he saw Captain Sholto
might be trusted to make as great an effort for Rosy's entertainment as he gathered he had made for Milly Henning's
that evening at the theatre. There were not chairs enough to
go round, and Paul fetched a three-legged stool from his
own apartment, after which he undertook to make tea for
the company with the aid of a tin kettle and a spirit-lamp—
these implements having been set out, flanked by half a
dozen cups, in honour, presumably, of the little dressmaker,
who had come such a distance. The little dressmaker, Hyacinth observed with pleasure, fell into earnest conversation
with Lady Aurora, who bent over her, flushed, smiling,
stammering and apparently so nervous that Pinnie, in comparison, was majestic and serene. They communicated presently to Hyacinth a plan they had arrived at as by a quick
freemasonry, the idea that Miss Pynsent should go home
to Belgrave Square with her ladyship and settle certain
preliminaries in regard to the pink dressing-gown, toward
which, if Miss Pynsent assented, her ladyship hoped to be
able to contribute sundry brown 'breadths' that had proved
their quality in honourable service and might be dyed to the
proper hue. Pinnie, Hyacinth could see, was in a state of
religious exaltation; the visit to Belgrave Square and the
idea of co-operating in such a manner with the nobility were
privileges she couldn't take solemnly enough. The latter
luxury indeed she began to enjoy without delay, Lady
Aurora suggesting that Mr Muniment might be rather awkward about making tea and that they should take the business off his hands. Paul gave it up to them with a pretence
of compassion for their conceit and the observation that at
any rate it took two women to supplant one man; and Hyacinth drew him to the window to ask where he had encountered Sholto and how he liked him.

They had met in Bloomsbury, as Hyacinth supposed, and
Sholto had made up to him very much as a country curate
might make up to an archbishop. He wanted to know what
he thought of this and that: of the state of the labour market
at the East End, of the terrible case of the old woman who
had starved to death at Walham Green, of the practicability
of more systematic out-of-door agitation and of the prospect
of their getting one of their own men—one of the Bloomsbury lot—into the House. 'He was mighty civil,' Muniment
said, 'and I don't find that he has yet picked my pocket. He
looked as if he would like me to suggest that *he* should stand
as one of our own men, one of the Bloomsbury lot. He asks
too many questions, but makes up for it by not paying any
attention to the answers. He told me he'd give the world
to see a really superior working-man's "interior". I didn't
know at first just where he proposed to cut me open: he
wanted a favourable specimen, one of the best; he had seen
one or two that he didn't believe to be up to the average.
I suppose he meant Schinkel's, the cabinetmaker's, neat
home, and he wanted to compare. I told him I didn't know
what sort of a specimen my place would be, but that he was
welcome to look in and that it contained at any rate one or
two original features. I expect he has found that's the case
—with Rosy and the noble lady. I wanted to show him off
to Rosy; he's good for that if he isn't good for anything else.
I told him we expected a little company this evening, so it
might be a good time; and he assured me that to mingle in
such an occasion as that was the dream of his existence. He
seemed in a rare hurry, as if I were going to show him a
hidden treasure, and insisted on driving me over in a hansom. Perhaps his idea is to introduce the use of cabs among
the working classes; certainly I'll work to return him if that's
to be his platform. On our way over he talked to me about
you; told me you were an intimate friend of his.'

'What did he say about me?' Hyacinth asked with prompt-
ness.

'Vain little beggar!'

'Did he call me that?' said Hyacinth ingenuously.

'He said you were simply astonishing.'

'Simply astonishing?' Hyacinth repeated.

'For a person of your low extraction.'

'Well, I may be rum, but he is certainly rummer. Don't you think so now you know him?'

Paul eyed his young friend. 'Do you want to know what he is? He's a tout.'

'A tout? What do you mean?'

'Well, a cat's paw, if you like better.'

Hyacinth stared. 'For whom, pray?'

'Or a deep-sea fisherman, if you like better still. I give you your choice of comparisons. I made them up as we came along in the hansom. He throws his nets and hauls in the little fishes—the pretty little shining, wriggling fishes. They are all for *her*; she swallows 'em down.'

'For her? Do you mean the Princess?'

'Who else should I mean? Take care, my tadpole!'

'Why should I take care? The other day you told me not to.'

'Yes, I remember. But now I see more.'

'Did he speak of her? What did he say?' Hyacinth eagerly asked.

'I can't tell you now what he said, but I'll tell you what I guessed.'

'And what's that?'

They had been talking of course in a very low tone, and their voices were covered by Rosy's chatter in the corner, by the liberal laughter with which Captain Sholto accompanied it, and by the much more discreet, though earnest, intermingled accents of Lady Aurora and Miss Pynsent. But Muniment spoke more softly still—Hyacinth felt a kind of suspense—as he replied in a moment: 'Why, she's a monster!'

'A monster?' repeated our young man, from whom, this evening, his friend was destined to draw ejaculations and echoes.

Paul glanced towards the Captain, who was apparently

more and more engaged by Rosy. 'In him I think there's no great harm. He's only a patient angler.'

It must be admitted that Captain Sholto justified to a certain extent this definition by the manner in which he baited his hook for such little facts as might help him to a more intimate knowledge of his host and hostess. When the tea was made Rosy asked Miss Pynsent to be so good as to hand it about. They must let her poor ladyship rest a little, mustn't they?—and Hyacinth could see that in her innocent but inveterate self-complacency she wished to reward and encourage the dressmaker, draw her out and present her still more by offering her this graceful exercise. Sholto sprang up, however, and begged Pinnie to let him relieve her, taking a cup from her hand; and poor Pinnie, who noted in a moment that he was some kind of uncanny masquerader, who was bewildered by the strange mixture of elements that surrounded her and unused to being treated like a duchess (for the Captain's manner was a triumph of respectful gallantry), collapsed on the instant into a chair, appealing to Lady Aurora with a frightened smile and conscious that, deeply versed as she might be in the theory of decorum, she had no precedent that could meet such an occasion. 'Now how many families would there be in such a house as this, and what should you say about the sanitary arrangements? Would there be others on this floor—what is it, the third, the fourth?—besides yourselves, you know, and should you call it a fair example of a tenement of its class?' It was with such enquiries as this that the good gentleman beguiled their tea-drinking, while Hyacinth made the reflexion that, though he evidently meant them very well, they were characterised by a want of fine tact, by too patronising a curiosity. The Captain invited information as to the position in life, the avocations and habits of the other lodgers, the rent they paid, their relations with each other, both in and out of the family. 'Now would there be a good deal of close packing, do you suppose, and any perceptible want of —a—sobriety?'

Paul Muniment, who had swallowed his cup of tea at a

single gulp—there was no offer of a second—gazed out of the window into the dark, which had now come on, with his hands in his pockets, whistling, impolitely, no doubt, but with extreme animation. He had the manner of having made over their visitor altogether to Rosy and of thinking that whatever that personage said or did was all so much grist to her indefatigable little mill. Lady Aurora writhed in her pain, and it is a proof of the degree to which our slight hero had the instincts of a man of the world that he guessed exactly how vulgar she thought this new acquaintance. She was doubtless rather vexed also—Hyacinth had learned this evening that Lady Aurora could be vexed—at the alacrity of Rosy's responses: the little person in the bed gave the Captain every satisfaction, considered his questions as a proper tribute to humble respectability and supplied him, as regards the population of Audley Court, with statistics and anecdotes picked up by mysterious processes of her own. At last her ladyship, on whom Paul Muniment had not been at pains to bestow much conversation, took leave of her, signifying to Hyacinth that for the rest of the evening she would assume the care of Miss Pynsent. Pinnie might have been consciously laid bare for monstrous rites now that she was really about to be transported to Belgrave Square, but Hyacinth was sure she would acquit herself only the more honourably; and when he offered to call for her there later on she reminded him under her breath and with a small sad smile of the many years during which, after nightfall, she had carried her work, pinned up in a cloth, about London.

Paul Muniment, according to his habit, lighted Lady Aurora downstairs, and Captain Sholto and Hyacinth were alone for some minutes with Rosy; which gave the former, taking up his hat and stick, an opportunity to say to his young friend: 'Which way are you going? Not my way, by chance?' Hyacinth saw that he hoped for his company, and he became conscious that, strangely as Paul had indulged him and too promiscuously investigating as he had just shown himself, this ingratiating character was not more easy to resist than he had been the other night at the theatre. The Captain bent over Rosy's bed as if she had been a fine lady on a satin sofa, promising to come back very soon and very often, and the two men went downstairs. On their way they met their host coming up, and Hyacinth felt rather ashamed, he could scarce tell why, that his friend should see him marching off with the 'tout'. After all, if Paul had brought him to see his sister might not Paul's pupil and devotee at least walk with him? 'I'm coming again, you know, very often. I dare say you'll find me a great bore!' the Captain announced as he bade good-night to Muniment. 'Your sister's a most interesting creature, one of the most interesting creatures I've ever seen, and the whole thing, you know, exactly the type of place I wanted to get at, only much more—really much more—original and curious. It has been a jolly glimpse—a grand success!'

And the Captain felt his way down the dusky shaft, while Paul Muniment, above, gave him the benefit of rather a wavering candlestick and answered his civil speech with an 'Oh well, you take us as you find us, you know!' and an outburst of frank but not unfriendly laughter.

Half an hour later Hyacinth found himself in Captain Sholto's chambers, seated on a big divan covered with Persian rugs and cushions and smoking the most expensive cigar that had ever touched his lips. As they left Audley Court the Captain had taken his arm and they had walked along together in a desultory, colloquial manner, till on Westminster Bridge (they had followed the embankment beneath Saint Thomas's Hospital) Sholto brought out: 'By the way, why shouldn't you come home with me and see my little place? I've a few things that might amuse you—some pictures, some odds and ends I've picked up, and a few bindings; you might tell me what you think of them.' Hyacinth assented without demur; he had still in his ear the reverberation of the Captain's enquiries in Rosy's room, and he saw no reason why he on his side shouldn't embrace an occasion of ascertaining how, as his companion would have said, a man of fashion would live now.

This particular specimen lived in a large old-fashioned house in Queen Anne Street, of which he occupied the upper floors, where he had filled the high wainscoted rooms with the spoils of travel and the ingenuities of modern taste. There was not a country in the world he appeared not to have ransacked, and to Hyacinth his trophies represented a wonderfully long purse. The whole establishment, from the low-voiced inexpressive valet who, after he had poured brandy into tall tumblers, solemnised the very popping of soda-water corks, to the quaint little silver receptacle in which he was invited to deposit the ashes of his cigar, was such a revelation for our appreciative youth that he felt himself hushed and depressed, so poignant was the thought that it took thousands of things he then should never possess nor know to make a civilised being. He had often in evening walks wondered what was behind the walls of certain ample bright-windowed houses in the West End, and now he got an idea. The first effect of the idea was to lay him rather flat.

'Well now, tell me what you thought of our friend the Princess,' the Captain said, thrusting out the loose yellow slippers his servant had helped to exchange for his shoes. He spoke as if he had been waiting impatiently for the proper moment to ask that question, so much might depend on the answer.

'She's beautiful—beautiful,' Hyacinth answered almost dreamily while his eyes wandered all over the room.

'She was so interested in all you said to her; she'd like so much to see you again. She means to write to you—I suppose she can address to the "Sun and Moon"?—and I hope you'll go to her house if she proposes a day.'

'I don't know—I don't know. It seems so strange.'

'What seems strange, my dear chap?'

'Everything! My sitting here with you; my introduction to that lady; the idea of her wanting, as you say, to see me again and of her writing to me; and this whole place of yours, with all its dim rich curiosities hanging on the walls and glinting in the light of that rose-coloured lamp. You yourself too—you're strangest of all.'

The Captain looked at him so silently and so fixedly, through the fumes of their tobacco, after he had made this last charge that Hyacinth thought he was perhaps offended; but this impression was presently dissipated by further signs of sociability and hospitality, and Sholto took occasion later to let him know how important it was, in the days they were living in, not to have too small a measure of the usual, destined as they certainly were—'in the whole matter of the relations of class with class and all that sort of thing, you know'—to witness some very startling developments. The Captain spoke as if, for his part, he were a child of his age (so that he only wanted to see all it could show him) down to the points of his yellow slippers. Hyacinth felt that he himself had not been very satisfactory about the Princess; but as his nerves began to tremble a little more into tune with the situation he repeated to his host what Milly had said about her at the theatre—asked if this young lady had correctly understood him in believing she had been turned out of the house by her husband.

'Yes, he literally pushed her into the street—or into the garden; I believe the scene took place in the country. But perhaps Miss Henning didn't mention, or perhaps I didn't, that the Prince would at the present hour give everything he owns in the world to get her back. Fancy such an absurd scene!' said the Captain, laughing in a manner that struck Hyacinth as rather profane.

He stared with dilated eyes at this picture, which seemed to demand a comparison with the only incident of the sort that had come within his experience—the forcible ejection of intoxicated females from public-houses. 'That magnificent being—what had she done?'

'Oh, she had made him feel he was an ass!' the Captain answered promptly. He turned the conversation to Miss Henning; said he was so glad Hyacinth gave him an opportunity to speak of her. He got on with her famously;

perhaps she had told him. They became immense friends—
en tout bien tout honneur, s'entend. Now, *there* was another
London type, plebeian but brilliant; and how little justice
one usually did it, how magnificent it was! But she of
course was a wonderful specimen. 'My dear fellow, I've
seen many women, and the women of many countries,' the
Captain went on, 'and I've seen them as intimately as you
like, and I know what I'm talking about; and when I tell
you that that one—that one—!' Then he suddenly paused,
laughing in his democratic way. 'But perhaps I'm going too
far: you must always pull me up, you know, when I do. At
any rate I congratulate you; I do right heartily. Have
another cigar. Now what sort of—a—salary would she
receive at her big shop, you know? I know where it is; I
mean to go there and buy some pocket-handkerchiefs.'

Hyacinth knew neither how far Captain Sholto had been
going, nor exactly on what he congratulated him; and he
pretended at least an equal ignorance on the subject of
Millicent's pecuniary gains. He didn't want to talk about her
moreover, nor about his own life; he wanted to talk about
the Captain's and to elicit information that would be in
harmony with his romantic chambers, which reminded one
somehow of certain of Bulwer's novels. His host gratified
this pretention most liberally and told him twenty stories
of things of interest, often of amazement, that had happened
to him in Albania, in Madagascar and even in Paris. Hyacinth induced him easily to talk about Paris (from a different
point of view from M. Poupin's) and sat there drinking in
enchantments. The only thing that fell below the high level
of his entertainment was the bindings of his friend's books,
which he told him frankly, with the conscience of an artist,
were not up to the mark. After he left Queen Anne Street
he was quite too excited to go straight home; he walked
about with his mind full of images and strange speculations
till the grey London streets began to clear with the summer
dawn.

XVI

THE ASPECT of South Street, Mayfair, on a Sunday afternoon in August, is not enlivening, yet the Prince had stood
for ten minutes gazing out of the window at the genteel
vacancy of the scene; at the closed blinds of the opposite
houses, the lonely policeman on the corner, covering a
yawn with a white cotton hand, the low-pitched light itself,
which seemed conscious of an obligation to observe the
decency of the British Sabbath. Our personage, however,
had a talent for that kind of attitude; it was one of the
things by which he had exasperated his wife; he could
remain motionless, with the aid of some casual support for
his high, lean person, considering serenely and inexpres-
sively any object that might lie before him and presenting
his aristocratic head at a favourable angle, for periods of
extraordinary length. On first coming into the room he had
given some attention to its furniture and decorations, perceiving at a glance that they were rich and varied; some of
the things he recognised as old friends, odds and ends the
Princess was fond of, which had accompanied her in her
remarkable wanderings, while others were unfamiliar and
suggested vividly that she had not ceased to 'collect'. He
made two reflexions: one was that she was living as expen-
sively as ever; the other that, however this might be, no
one had such a feeling as she for the *mise-en-scène* of life,
such a talent for arranging a room. She had always, wherever she was, the most charming room in Europe.

It was his impression that she had taken the house in
South Street but for three months; yet, gracious heaven,
what had she not put into it? The Prince asked himself this
question without violence, for that was not to be his line
to-day. He could be angry to a point at which he himself
was often frightened, but he honestly believed this to be
only when he had been baited past endurance, so that as a

usual thing he was really as mild and accommodating as the extreme urbanity of his manner appeared to announce. There was indeed nothing to suggest to the world in general that he was an impracticable or vindictive nobleman: his features were not regular and his complexion had a bilious tone; but his dark brown eye, which was at once salient and dull, expressed benevolence and melancholy; his head drooped from his long neck in a considerate, attentive style; and his close-cropped black hair, combined with a short, fine, pointed beard, completed his resemblance to some old portrait of a personage of distinction under the Spanish dominion at Naples. To-day at any rate he had come in conciliation, almost in humility, and that is why he didn't permit himself even to murmur at the long delay he had to accept. He knew very well that if his wife should consent to take him back it would be only after a probation to which this little wait in her drawing-room was a trifle. It was a quarter of an hour before the door opened, and even then it was not the Princess who appeared, but only Madame Grandoni.

Their greeting was at first all a renouncement of words. She came to him with both hands outstretched, and took his own and held them a while, looking up at him with full benignity. She had elongated her florid, humorous face to a degree that was almost comical, and the pair might have passed, in their silent solemnity, for acquaintances meeting in a house in which last obsequies were about to take place. It was indeed a house on which death had descended, as he very soon learned from Madame Grandoni's expression; something had perished there for ever and he might proceed to bury it as soon as he liked. His wife's ancient German friend, however, was not a person to sustain that note very long, and when, after she had made him sit down on the sofa beside her, she shook her head slowly and definitely several times, it was with a brow on which a more genial appreciation of the facts had already begun to appear.

'Never—never—never?' said the Prince in a deep hoarse voice, a voice at variance with his attenuated capacity. He had much of the complexion which in late-coming members of long-descended races we qualify to-day as effete; but his tone might have served for the battle-cry of some deep-chested fighting ancestor.

'Surely you know your wife as well as I,' she replied in Italian, which she evidently spoke with facility, though with a strong guttural accent. 'I've been talking with her: that's what has made me keep you. I've urged her to see you. I've told her that this could do no harm and would pledge her to nothing. But you know your wife,' Madame Grandoni repeated with an intensity now much relaxed.

Prince Casamassima looked down at his boots. 'How can one ever know a person like that? I hoped she'd see me five little minutes.'

'For what purpose? Have you anything to propose?'

'For what purpose? To rest my eyes on her beautiful face.'

'Did you come to England for that?'

'For what else should I have come?' the Prince asked as he turned his blighted gaze to the opposite side of South Street.

'In London, such a day as this, *già*,' said the old lady sympathetically. 'I'm very sorry for you; but if I had known you were coming I'd have written to you that you might spare yourself the pain.'

He gave a deep interminable sigh. 'You ask me what I wish to propose. What I wish to propose is that my wife shouldn't kill me inch by inch.'

'She'd be much more likely to do that if you lived with her!' Madame Grandoni cried.

'*Cara amica*, she doesn't appear to have killed you,' the melancholy nobleman returned.

'Oh, me? I'm past killing. I'm as hard as a stone. I went through my miseries long ago; I suffered what you've not had to suffer; I wished for death many times and survived it all. Our troubles don't kill us, *Principe mio*; it's we who must try to kill them. I've buried not a few. Besides

Christina's fond of me, the devil knows why!' Madame Grandoni added.

'And you're so good to her,' said the Prince, who laid his hand on her fat wrinkled fist.

'*Che vuole?* I've known her so long. And she has some great qualities.'

'Ah, to whom do you say it?' And he gazed at his boots again, for some moments, in silence. Suddenly he resumed: 'How does she look to-day?'

'She always looks the same: like an angel who came down from heaven yesterday and has been rather disappointed in her first day on earth!'

The Prince was evidently a man of a simple nature, and Madame Grandoni's rather violent metaphor took his fancy. His face lighted up a little and he replied with eagerness: 'Ah, she's the only woman I've ever seen whose beauty never for a moment falls below itself. She has no bad days. She's so handsome when she's angry!'

'She's very handsome to-day, but she's not angry,' said the old lady.

'Not when my name was announced?'

'I was not with her then; but when she sent for me and asked me to see you it was quite without passion. And even when I argued with her and tried to persuade her (and she doesn't like that, you know) she was still perfectly quiet.'

'She hates me, she despises me too much, eh?'

'How can I tell, dear Prince, when she never mentions you?'

'Never, never?'

'That's much better than if she railed at you and abused you.'

'You mean it should give me more hope for the future?' the young man asked quickly.

His old friend had a pause. 'I mean it's better for *me*,' she answered with a laugh of which the friendly ring covered as much as possible her equivocation.

'Ah, you like me enough to care,' he murmured as he turned on her his sad grateful eyes.

'I'm very sorry for you. *Ma che vuole?*'

The Prince had apparently nothing to suggest and only exhaled in reply another gloomy groan. Then he enquired if his wife pleased herself in that country and if she intended to pass the summer in London. Would she remain long in England and—might he take the liberty to ask?—what were her plans? Madame Grandoni explained that the Princess had found the English capital much more to her taste than one might have expected, and that as for plans she had as many or as few as she had always had. Had he ever known her to carry out any arrangement or to do anything of any kind she had prepared or promised? She always at the last moment did the other thing, the one that had been out of the question; and it was for this Madame Grandoni herself privately made her preparations. Christina, now that everything was over, would leave London from one day to the other; but they shouldn't know where they were going till they arrived. The old lady concluded by asking if the Prince himself liked England. He thrust forward his full lips. 'How can I like anything? Besides, I've been here before; I've many friends.'

His companion saw he had more to say to her, to extract from her, but that he was hesitating nervously because he feared to incur some warning, some rebuff with which his dignity—in spite of his position of discomfiture, really very great—might find it difficult to square itself. He looked vaguely round the room and presently remarked: 'I wanted to see for myself how she's living.'

'Yes, that's very natural.'

'I've heard—I've heard——' And Prince Casamassima stopped.

'You've heard great rubbish, I've no doubt.' Madame Grandoni watched him as if she foresaw what was coming.

'She spends a terrible deal of money,' said the young man.

'Indeed she does.' The old lady knew that, careful as he was of his very considerable property, which at one time had required much nursing, his wife's prodigality was not

what lay heaviest on his mind. She also knew that expensive
and luxurious as Christina might be she had never yet
exceeded the income settled upon her by the Prince at the
time of their separation—an income determined wholly by
himself and his estimate of what was required to maintain
the social consequence of his name, for which he had a
boundless reverence. 'She thinks she's a model of thrift—
that she counts every shilling,' Madame Grandoni continued. 'If there's a virtue she prides herself upon it's her
economy. Indeed it's the only thing for which she takes
any credit.'

'I wonder if she knows that I'—he just hesitated, then
went on—'spend almost nothing at all. But I'd rather live
on dry bread than that in a country like this, in this great
English society, she shouldn't make a proper appearance.'

'Her appearance is all you could wish. How can it help
being proper with me to set her off?'

'You're the best thing she has, dear friend. So long as
you're with her I feel a certain degree of security; and one
of the things I came for was to extract from you a promise
that you won't leave her.'

'Ah, let us not tangle ourselves up with promises!'
Madame Grandoni exclaimed. 'You know the value of any
engagement one may take with regard to the Princess; it's
like promising you I'll stay in the bath when the hot water's
on. When I begin to be scalded I've to jump out—naked
as I may naturally be. I'll stay while I can, but I shouldn't
stay if she were to do certain things.' Madame Grandoni
uttered these last words with a clear emphasis, and for a
minute she and her companion looked deep into each other's
eyes.

'What things do you mean?'

'I can't say what things. It's utterly impossible to predict
on any occasion what Christina will do. She's capable of
giving us great surprises. The things I mean are things I
should recognise as soon as I saw them, and they would
make me leave the house on the spot.'

'So that if you've not left it yet——?' he asked with extreme eagerness.

'It's because I've thought I may do some good by staying.'

He seemed but half content with this answer; nevertheless he said in a moment: 'To me it makes all the difference. And if anything of the kind you speak of should happen, that would be only the greater reason for your staying.— You might interpose, you might arrest——' He stopped short before her large Germanic grimace.

'You must have been in Rome more than once when the Tiber had overflowed, *è vero*? What would you have thought then if you had heard people telling the poor wretches in the Ghetto, on the Ripetta, up to their knees in liquid mud, that they ought to interpose, to arrest?'

'*Capisco bene*,' said the Prince, dropping his eyes. He appeared to have closed them, for some moments, as if under a slow spasm of pain. 'I can't tell you what torments me most,' he presently went on—'the thought that sometimes makes my heart rise into my mouth. It's a haunting fear.' And his pale face and disturbed respiration might indeed have been those of a man before whom some horrible spectre had risen.

'You needn't tell me. I know what you mean, my poor friend.'

'Do you think then there *is* a danger—that she'll drag my name, do what no one has ever dared to do? That I'd never forgive,' he declared almost under his breath; and the hoarseness of his whisper lent it a great effect.

Madame Grandoni hastily wondered if she had not better tell him (as it would prepare him for the worst) that his wife cared about as much for his name as for any old label on her luggage; but after an instant's reflexion she reserved this information for another hour. Besides, as she said to herself, the Prince ought already to know perfectly to what extent Christina attached the idea of an obligation or an interdict to her ill-starred connexion with an ignorant and superstitious Italian race whom she despised for their provinciality, their parsimony and their futility (she thought their talk the climax of childishness) and whose fatuous conception of their importance in the great modern world she had on various public occasions sufficiently riddled with her derision. She finally contented herself with remarking: 'Dear Prince, your wife's a very proud woman.'

'Ah, how could my wife be anything else? But her pride's not my pride. And she has such ideas, such opinions! Some of them are monstrous.'

Madame Grandoni smiled. 'She doesn't think it so necessary to have them when you're not there.'

'Why then do you say that you enter into my fears—that you recognise the stories I've heard?'

I know not whether the good lady lost patience with his pressure; at all events she broke out with a certain sharpness. 'Understand this, understand this: Christina will never consider you—your name, your illustrious traditions—in any case in which she doesn't consider herself much more!'

The Prince appeared to study for a moment this somewhat ambiguous yet portentous phrase; then he slowly got up with his hat in his hand and walked about the room softly, solemnly, as if suffering from his long thin feet. He stopped before one of the windows and took another survey of South Street; then turning he suddenly asked in a voice into which he had evidently endeavoured to infuse a colder curiosity: 'Is she admired in this place? Does she see many people?'

'She's thought very strange of course. But she sees whom she likes. And they mostly bore her to death!' Madame Grandoni conscientiously added.

'Why then do you tell me this country pleases her?'

The old woman left her place. She had promised Christina, who detested the sense of being under the same roof with her husband, that the latter's visit should be kept within narrow limits; and this movement was intended to signify as kindly as possible that it had better terminate. 'It's the common people who please her,' she returned with her hands folded on her crumpled satin stomach and her ancient eyes, still keen for all comedy, raised to his face. 'It's the lower orders, the *basso popolo*.'

'The *basso popolo*?' The Prince stared at this fantastic announcement.

'The *povera gente*,' pursued his friend, amused at his dismay.

'The London mob—the most horrible, the most brutal——?'

'Oh, she wishes to raise them.'

'After all, something like that's no more than I had heard,' said the Prince gravely.

'*Che vuole?* Don't trouble yourself; it won't be for long!'

Madame Grandoni saw this comforting assurance lost upon him; his face was turned to the door of the room, which had been thrown open, and all his attention given to the person who crossed the threshold. She transferred her own to the same quarter and recognised the little artisan whom Christina had, in a manner so extraordinary and so profoundly characteristic, drawn into her box that night at the theatre—afterwards informing her old friend that she had sent for him to come and see her.

'Mr Robinson!' the butler, who had had a lesson, announced in a loud colourless tone.

'It won't be for long,' Madame Grandoni repeated for the Prince's benefit; but it was to Mr Robinson the words had the air of being addressed.

Hyacinth stood, while she signalled to the servant to leave the door open and wait, looking from the queer old lady, who was as queer as before, to the tall foreign gentleman (he recognised his foreignness at a glance) whose eyes seemed to challenge him, to devour him; wondering if he had made some mistake and needing to remind himself that he had the Princess's note in his pocket, with the day and hour as clear as her magnificent script could make them.

'Good-morning, good-morning. I hope you're well,' said Madame Grandoni with quick friendliness, but turning her back upon him at the same time in order to ask of their companion, in the other idiom, as she extended her hand: 'And don't you leave London soon—in a day or two?'

The Prince made no answer; he still scanned the little bookbinder from head to foot, as if wondering who the deuce he could be. His eyes seemed to Hyacinth to search for the small neat bundle he ought to have had under his arm and without which he was incomplete. To the reader, however, it may be confided that, dressed more carefully than he had ever been in his life before, stamped with that extraordinary transformation which the British Sunday often operates in the person of the wage-earning cockney, with his handsome head uncovered and the heat of wonder in his fine face, the young man from Lomax Place might have passed for anything rather than a carrier of parcels. 'The Princess wrote to me, madam, to come and see her,' he said as a prompt precaution; in case he should have incurred the reproach of undue precipitation.

'Oh yes, I dare say.' And Madame Grandoni guided the Prince to the door with an expression of the desire he might have a comfortable journey back to Italy.

But he stood stiff there; he appeared to have jumped to a dark conclusion about Mr Robinson. 'I must see you once more. I must. It's impossible——!'

'Ah well, not in this house, you know.'

'Will you do me the honour to meet me then?' And as the old lady hesitated he added with sudden intensity: 'Dearest friend, I beg you on my knees!' After she had agreed that if he would write to her proposing a day and place she would see him were it possible, he raised her ancient knuckles to his lips and, without further notice of Hyacinth, turned away. She bade the servant announce the other visitor to the Princess, and then approached Mr Robinson, rubbing her hands and smiling, her head very much to one side. He smiled back at her vaguely; he didn't know what she might be going to say. What she said was, to his surprise—

'My poor young man, may I take the liberty of asking your age?'

'Certainly, madam; I'm twenty-four.'

'And I hope you're industrious, and temperate in all ways and—what do you call it in English?—steady.'

'I don't think I'm very wild,' said Hyacinth without offence. He thought the old woman patronising, but he forgave her.

'I don't know how one speaks in this country to young men like you. Perhaps one's considered meddling or impertinent.'

'I like the way you speak,' Hyacinth hastened to profess.

She stared, and then with a comical affectation of dignity: 'You're very good. I'm glad it amuses you. You're evidently intelligent and clever,' she went on, 'and if you're disappointed it will be a pity.'

'How do you mean if I'm disappointed?'

'Well, I dare say you expect great things when you come into a house like this. You must tell me if I upset you. I'm very old-fashioned and I'm not of this country. I speak as one speaks to young men like you in other places.'

'I'm not so easily upset!' Hyacinth assured her with a flight of imagination. 'To expect anything one must know something, one must understand: isn't it so? And I'm here without knowing, without understanding. I've come only because a lady who seems to me very beautiful and very kind has done me the honour to send for me.'

Madame Grandoni examined him a moment as if struck by his good looks, by something delicate stamped on him everywhere. 'I can see you're very clever, very intelligent; no, you're not like the young men I mean. All the more reason——!' And she paused, giving a short sigh. Her case might have been all too difficult. 'I want to warn you a little, and I don't know how. If you were a young Roman it would be different.'

'A young Roman?'

'That's where I live properly, in the Eternal City. If I hurt you, you can explain it that way. No, you're not like them.'

'You don't hurt me—please believe that; you interest me

very much,' said Hyacinth, to whom it didn't occur that he himself might seem patronising. 'Of what do you want to warn me?'

'Well—only to advise you a little. Don't give up anything.'

'What can I give up?'

'Don't give up *yourself*. I say that to you in your interest. I think you've some honest little trade—I forget what. But whatever it may be remember that to do it well is the best thing; better than paying extraordinary visits, better even than being liked by Princesses!'

'Ah yes, I see what you mean!' Hyacinth returned, exaggerating a little. 'I'm very fond of my trade indeed, I assure you.'

'I'm delighted to hear it. Hold fast to it then and be quiet; be diligent and good and get on. I gathered the other night that you're one of the young men who want everything changed—I believe there are a great many in Italy and also in my own dear old Deutschland, and who even think it useful to throw bombs into innocent crowds and shoot pistols at their rulers or at any one. I won't go into that. I might seem to be speaking for myself, and the fact is that for myself I don't care; I'm so old that I may hope to spend the few days that are left me without receiving a bullet. But before you go any further please think a little whether you're right.'

'It isn't just that you should impute to me ideas which I may not have,' said Hyacinth, turning very red but taking more and more of a fancy, all the same, to Madame Grandoni. 'You talk at your ease about our ways and means, but if we were only to make use of those that you would like to see——!' And while he blushed, smiling, the young man shook his head two or three times with great significance.

'I shouldn't like to see any!' the old lady cried. 'I like people to bear their troubles as one has done one's self. And as for injustice, you see how kind I am to you when I say to you again Don't, don't, give anything up. I'll tell them to send you some tea,' she added as she took her way out of the room, presenting to him her round, low, aged back and dragging over the carpet a scanty and lustreless train.

XVII

HE HAD been warned by Mr Vetch as to what brilliant women might do with him—it was only a word on the old fiddler's lips, but the word had had a point; he had been warned by Paul Muniment, and now he was admonished by a person supremely well placed for knowing: a fact that couldn't fail to deepen the emotion which, any time these three days, had made him draw his breath more quickly. That emotion, nevertheless, didn't actually make him fear remote consequences; as he looked over the Princess Casamassima's drawing-room and inhaled an air that seemed to him inexpressibly delicate and sweet he hoped his adventure would throw him on his mettle only half as much as the old lady had wished to intimate. He considered, one after the other, the different chairs, couches and ottomans the room contained—he wished to treat himself to the most sumptuous—and then for reasons he knew best sank into a seat covered with rose-coloured brocade and of which the legs and frame appeared of pure gold. Here he sat perfectly still, only with his heart beating very sensibly and his eyes coursing again and again from one object to another. The splendours and suggestions of Captain Sholto's apartment were thrown completely into the shade by the scene before him, and as the Princess didn't scruple to keep him waiting twenty minutes (during which the butler came in and set out on a small table a glittering tea-service) Hyacinth had time to count over the innumerable *bibelots* (most of which he had never dreamed of) involved in the character of a woman of high fashion and to feel that their beauty and oddity revealed not only whole provinces of art, but refinements of choice on the part of their owner, complications of mind and—almost—terrible depths of temperament.

When at last the door opened and the servant, reappearing, threw it far back as to make a wide passage for a person of the importance of his mistress, Hyacinth's suspense became very acute; it was much the same feeling with which, at the theatre, he had sometimes awaited the entrance of a celebrated actress. In this case the actress was to perform for him alone. There was still a moment before she came on, and when she arrived she was so simply dressed—besides his seeing her now on her feet—that she looked quite a different figure. She approached him rapidly and a little stiffly and shyly, but in the prompt manner in which she shook hands was an evident desire to be very direct and perfectly easy. She might have been another person, but that person had a beauty even more radiant; the fairness of her face shone forth at our young man as if to dissipate any doubts assailing and bewildering him as to the reality of the vision bequeathed to him by his former interview. And in this peculiar high grace of her presence he couldn't have told you if she struck him as more proud or more kind.

'I've kept you a long time, but it's supposed not usually to be a bad place, my salon; there are various things to look at and perhaps you've noticed some of them. Over on that side for instance is rather a curious collection of miniatures.' She spoke abruptly, quickly, as if conscious that their communion might be awkward and she were trying to strike instantly (to conjure that element away) the sort of note that would make them both most comfortable. Quickly too she sat down before her tea-tray and poured him out a cup, which she handed him without asking if he would have it. He accepted it with a trembling hand, though he had no desire for it; he was too nervous to swallow the tea, but it wouldn't have appeared to him possible to decline. When he had murmured that he had indeed looked at all her things, but that it would take hours to do justice to such treasures, she asked if he were fond of works of art; immediately adding, however, that she was afraid he had not many opportunities of seeing them, though of course there were the public collections, open to all. He replied with perfect veracity that some of the happiest moments of his life had been spent at the British Museum and the National Gallery, and this fact appeared to interest her greatly, so that she straightway begged him to tell her what he thought of certain pictures and antiques. In this way it was that in an incredibly short time, as appeared to him, he found himself discussing the Bacchus and Ariadne and the Elgin Marbles with one of the most remarkable women in Europe. It was true that she herself talked most, passing precipitately from one point to another, putting questions and not waiting for answers, describing and qualifying things, expressing feelings, by the aid of phrases that he had never heard before but which seemed to him illuminating and happy— as when for instance she asked what art was, after all, but a synthesis made in the interest of pleasure, or said that she didn't like England in the least, but absurdly loved it. It didn't occur to him to think these discriminations pedantic. Suddenly she threw off, 'Madame Grandoni told me you saw my husband.'

'Ah, was the gentleman your husband?'

'Unfortunately! What do you think of him?'

'Oh, I can't think——!' Hyacinth decently pleaded.

'I wish I couldn't either! I haven't seen him for nearly three years. He wanted to see me to-day, but I refused.'

'Ah!'—and the young man stared, not knowing how he ought to receive so unexpected a confidence. Then as the suggestions of inexperience are sometimes the happiest of all he spoke simply what was in his mind and said gently: 'It has made you—naturally—nervous.' Later on, when he had left the house, he wondered how at that stage he could have ventured on such a familiar remark.

But she had taken it with a quick, surprised laugh. 'How do you know that?' Before he had time to tell she added: 'Your saying that—that way—shows me how right I was to ask you to come to see me. You know I hesitated. It shows me you've perceptions; I guessed as much the other night at the theatre. If I hadn't I wouldn't have asked you. I may be wrong, but I like people who understand what one says to them, and also what one doesn't say.'

'Don't think I understand too much. You might easily exaggerate that,' Hyacinth declared conscientiously.

'You confirm completely my first impression,' the Princess returned, smiling in a way that showed him he really amused her. 'We shall discover the limits of your comprehension! I *am* atrociously nervous. But it will pass. How's your cousin the dressmaker?' she enquired abruptly. And when Hyacinth had briefly given some account of poor Pinnie—described her as tolerably well for her, but old and tired and sad and not very successful—she exclaimed impatiently, 'Ah, well, she's not the only one!' and came back with irrelevance to the former question. 'It's not only my husband's visit—absolutely unexpected!—that has made me fidgety, but the idea that now you've been so kind as to come here you may wonder why, after all, I made such a point of it, and even think any explanation I might be able to give you entirely insufficient.'

'I don't want any explanation,' said Hyacinth with a sense of great presence of mind.

'It's charming of you to say that, and I shall take you at your word. Explanations usually make things worse. All the same I don't want you to think (as you might have done so easily the other evening) that I wish only to treat you as a curious animal.'

'I don't care how you treat me!' he smiled.

There was a considerable silence, after which she pursued: 'All I ask of my husband is to let me alone. But he won't. He won't return my indifference.'

Hyacinth wondered what reply he ought to make to such an announcement as that, and it seemed to him the least civility demanded was that he should say—as he could with such conviction—'It can't be easy to be indifferent to you.'

'Why not if I'm odious? I *can* be—oh there's no doubt of that! However, I can honestly say that with the Prince I've been exceedingly reasonable and that most of the wrongs—the big ones, those that settled the question—have

been on his side. You may tell me of course that that's the
pretension of every woman who has made a mess of her
marriage. But ask Madame Grandoni.'

'She'll tell me it's none of my business.'

'Very true—she might!' the Princess inconsequently
laughed. 'And I don't know either why I should bore you
with my domestic affairs; except that I've been wondering
what I could do to show you confidence in return for your
showing so much in me. As this matter of my separation
from my husband happens to have been turned uppermost
by his sudden descent on me I just mention it, though the
subject's tiresome enough. Moreover I ought to let you
know that I've very little respect for distinctions of class—
the sort of thing they make so much of in this country.
They're doubtless convenient in some ways, but when one
has a reason—a reason of feeling—for overstepping them,
and one allows one's self to be deterred by some dreary
superstition about one's place or some one else's place, then
I think it's ignoble. It always belongs to one's place not to
be a poor creature. I take it that if you're a socialist you
think about this as I do; but lest by chance, as the sense of
those differences is the English religion, it may have rubbed
off even on you (though I'm more and more impressed with
the fact that you're scarcely more British than I am): lest
you should in spite of your theoretic democracy be shocked
at some of the applications that I, who cherish the creed,
am capable of making of it, let me assure you without delay
that in that case we shouldn't get on together at all and had
better part company before we go further.' She paused
long enough for Hyacinth to declare with a great deal of
emphasis that he wasn't easily shocked; and then restlessly,
eagerly, as if it relieved her to talk and made their queer
conjunction less abnormal that she should talk most, she
arrived at the point that she wanted to know the *people*,
and know them intimately—the toilers and strugglers and
sufferers—because she was convinced they were the most
interesting portion of society, and at the question 'What
could really be in worse taste than for me to carry into

such an undertaking a pretension of greater delicacy and
finer manners? If I must do that,' she continued, 'it's
simpler to leave them alone. But I can't leave them alone;
they press on me, they haunt me, they fascinate me. There
it is—after all it's very simple: I want to know them and I
want you to help me.'

'I'll help you with pleasure to the best of my humble
ability. But you'll be awfully disappointed,' Hyacinth said.
Very strange it seemed to him that within so few days two
ladies of rank should have found occasion to express to him
the same mysterious longing. A breeze from a thoroughly
unexpected quarter was indeed blowing through the aristocracy. Nevertheless, though there was much of the same
accent of passion in the Princess Casamassima's communication that there had been in Lady Aurora's, and though he
felt bound to discourage his present interlocutress as he had
done the other, the force that drove her struck him as a
very different mixture from the shy, conscientious, anxious
heresies of Rose Muniment's friend. The temper varied in
the two women as much as the aspect and the address, and
that perhaps made their curiosity the more significant.

'I haven't the least doubt of it,' this investigator answered;
'there's nothing in life in which I've not been awfully disappointed. But disappointment for disappointment I shall
like it better than some others. You'll not persuade me either
that among the people I speak of characters and passions
and motives are not more natural, more complete, more
naïfs. The upper classes are so deadly *banals*. My husband
traces his descent from the fifth century, and he's the
greatest bore in Europe. That's the kind of people I was
condemned to by my marriage. Oh, if you knew what I've
been through you'd allow that intelligent mechanics (of
course I don't want to know idiots) would be a pleasant
change. I must begin with some one—mustn't I—so I began the other night with you!' As soon as she had uttered
these words the Princess added a correction with the consciousness of her mistake in her face. It made that face, to
Hyacinth, more nobly, tenderly beautiful. 'The only objec-

tion to you individually is that you've nothing of the people about you—to-day not even the dress.' Her eyes wandered over him from head to foot, and their recognitions made him ashamed. 'I wish you had come in the clothes you wear at your work.'

'You see you do regard me as a curious animal,' he returned.

It was perhaps to contradict this that, after a moment, she began to tell him more about her domestic affairs. He ought to know who she was, unless Captain Sholto had told him; and she mentioned her parentage—American on the mother's side, Italian on the father's—and how she had led from her youngest years a wandering Bohemian life in a thousand different places (always in Europe, she had never been in America and knew very little about it, though she wanted greatly to cross the Atlantic) and largely at one period in Rome. She had been married by her people, in a mercenary way, for the sake of a fortune and a great name, and it had turned out as badly as her worst enemy could have wished. Her parents were dead, luckily for them, and she had no one near her of her own except Madame Grandoni, who belonged to her only in the sense that she had known her as a girl; was an association of her—what should she call them?—her uneasy but innocent years. Not that she had ever been very innocent; she had had a horrible education. However, she had known a few good people—people she respected then; but Madame Grandoni was the only one who had stuck to her. She too was liable to leave her any day; the Princess appeared to intimate that her destiny might require her to take some step which would test severely the old woman's attachment. It would detain her too long to make him understand the stages by which she had arrived at her present state of mind: her disgust with a thousand social arrangements, her rebellion against the selfishness, the corruption, the iniquity, the cruelty, the imbecility of the people who all over Europe had the upper hand. If he could have seen her life, the *milieu* in which she had for several years been condemned to move, the evolution of her opinions (Hyacinth was delighted to hear her use that term) would strike him as perfectly logical. She had been humiliated, outraged, tortured; she considered that she too was one of the numerous class who could be put on a tolerable footing only by a revolution. At any rate she had some self-respect left, and there was still more that she wanted to recover; the only way to arrive at which was to throw herself into some effort that would make her forget her own affairs and comprehend the troubles and efforts of others. Hyacinth listened to her with a wonderment which, as she went on, was transformed into willing submission; she seemed so natural, so vivid, so exquisitely generous and sincere. By the time he had been with her half an hour she had made the situation itself easy and usual, and a third person who should have joined them at this moment would have noticed nothing to suggest that friendly social intercourse between little bookbinders and Neapolitan princesses was not in London a matter of daily occurrence.

Hyacinth had seen plenty of women who chattered about themselves and their affairs—a vulgar garrulity of confidence was indeed a leading characteristic of the sex as he had hitherto learned to know it—but he was quick to perceive that the great lady who now took the trouble to open herself to him was not of a gossiping habit; that she must be on the contrary, as a general thing, proudly, ironically reserved, even to the point of passing with many people for a model of the unsatisfactory. It was very possible she was capricious; yet the fact that her present sympathies and curiosities might be a caprice wore in her visitor's eyes no sinister aspect. Why was it not a noble and interesting whim, and why mightn't he stand for the hour at any rate in the silvery moonshine it cast on his path? It must be added that he was far from taking in everything she said, some of her allusions and implications being so difficult to seize that they mainly served to reveal to him the limits of his own acquaintance with life. Her words evoked all sorts of shadowy suggestions of things he was condemned not to know, touching him most when he had not the key to them.

This was especially the case with her reference to her career in Italy, on her husband's estates, and her relations with his family, who considered that they had done her a great honour in receiving her into their august circle (putting the best face on a bad business) after they had moved heaven and earth to keep her out of it. The position made for her among such people and what she had had to suffer from their family tone, their opinions and customs (though what these might be remained vague to her listener) had evidently planted in her soul a lasting resentment and contempt; and Hyacinth gathered that the force of reaction and revenge might carry her far, make her modern and democratic and heretical à outrance—lead her to swear by Darwin and Spencer and all the scientific iconoclasts as well as by the revolutionary spirit. He surely needn't have been so sensible of the weak spots in his comprehension of the Princess when he could already surmise that personal passion had counted for so much in the formation of her views. This induction, however, which had no harshness, didn't make her affect him any the less as a creature compounded of the finest elements; brilliant, delicate, complicated, but complicated with something divine.

It was not till after he had left her that he became conscious she had forced him to talk in spite of talking so much herself. He drew a long breath as he reflected that he hadn't made quite such an ass of himself as might very well have happened; he had been saved by the thrill of his interest and admiration, which had not gone to his head and prompted him to show that he too in his improbable little way was remarkable, but had kept him in a state of anxious, conscious tension, as if the occasion had been a great appointed solemnity, some initiation more formal than any he believed practised even in the grimmest subterranean circles. He had said indeed much more than he had warrant for when she questioned him on his 'radical' affiliations; he had spoken as if the movement were vast and mature, whereas in fact, so far at least as he was as yet concerned with it and could answer for it from personal knowledge, it was circumscribed by the hideously-papered walls of the little club-room at the 'Sun and Moon'. He reproached himself with this laxity, but it had not been engendered by pride. He was only afraid of disappointing his hostess too much, of making her say, 'Why in the world then did you come to see me if you've nothing more remarkable to put before me?'—a question to which of course he would have had an answer ready but for its being so impossible to say he had never asked to come and that his coming was her own affair. He wanted too much to come a second time to have the courage to make that speech. Nevertheless when she exclaimed, changing the subject abruptly, as she always did, from something else they had been talking about, 'I wonder if I shall ever see you again!' he replied with perfect sincerity that it was scarce possible for him to believe anything so delightful could be repeated. There were some kinds of happiness that to many people never came at all, and to others could come only once. He added: 'It's very true I had just that feeling after I left you the other night at the theatre. And yet here I am!'

'Yes, there you are,' said the Princess thoughtfully—as if this might be a still graver and more embarrassing fact than she had yet supposed it. 'I take it there's nothing essentially inconceivable in my seeing you again; but it may very well be that you'll never again find it so pleasant. Perhaps that's the happiness that comes but once. At any rate, you know, I'm going away.'

'Oh yes, of course; every one leaves town——!' Hyacinth rose to that occasion.

'Do *you*, Mr Robinson?' the Princess asked.

'Well, I don't as a general thing. Nevertheless it's possible that this year I may get three or four days at the seaside. I should like to take my old lady. I've done it before.'

'And except for that shall you be always at work?'

'Yes; but you must understand that I love my work. You must understand that it's a great blessing for a young fellow like me to have it.'

'And if you didn't have it what would you do? Should you starve?'

'Oh, I don't think I should starve,' our friend replied judicially.

She looked a little chagrined, but after a moment pursued: 'I wonder whether you'd come to see me in the country somewhere.'

'Oh cracky!' Hyacinth exclaimed, catching his breath. 'You're so kind I don't know what to do.'

'Don't be *banal*, please. That's what other people are. What's the use of my looking for something fresh in other walks of life if you're going to be *banal* too? I ask if you'd come.'

He couldn't have said at this moment whether he were plunging or soaring. 'Yes, I think I'd come. I don't know at all how I should do it—there would be several obstacles; but wherever you should call for me I'd come.'

'You mean you can't leave your work like that? You might lose it if you did, and then be in want of money and much embarrassed?'

'Yes, there would be little difficulties of that kind. You see that immediately, in practice, great obstacles and complications come up when it's a question of a person like you making friends with a person like me.'

'That's the way I like you to talk,' said the Princess with a pitying gentleness that struck her visitor as quite sacred. 'After all I don't know where I shall be. I've got to pay stupid visits myself, visits where the only comfort will be that I shall make the people jump. Every one here thinks me exceedingly odd—as there's no doubt I am! I might be ever so much more so if you'd only help me a little. Why shouldn't I have my bookbinder after all? In attendance, you know—it would be awfully *chic*. We might have immense fun, don't you think so? No doubt it will come. At any rate I shall return to London when I've got through that *corvée*; I shall be here next year. In the mean time don't forget me,' she went on as she rose to her feet. 'Remember on the contrary that I expect you to take me into the slums

—into very bad places.' Why the idea of these scenes of misery should have lighted up her face is more than may be explained; but she smiled down at Hyacinth—who even as he stood up was of slightly smaller stature—with all her strange high radiance. Then in a manner almost equally quaint she added a reference to what she had said a moment before. 'I recognise perfectly the obstacles in practice as you call them; but though I'm not by nature persevering, and am really very easily put off, I don't consider they'll prove insurmountable. They exist on my side as well, and if you'll help me to overcome mine I'll do the same for you with yours.'

These words, repeating themselves again and again in his consciousness, appeared to give him wings, to help him to float and soar as he turned that afternoon out of South Street. He had at home a copy of Tennyson's poems—a single comprehensive volume, with a double column on the page, in a tolerably neat condition despite much handling. He took it to pieces that same evening, and during the following week, in his hours of leisure, at home in his little room, with the tools he kept there for private use and a morsel of delicate, blue-tinted Russia leather of which he obtained possession at old Crook's, he devoted himself to the task of binding the book as perfectly as he knew how. He worked with passion, with religion, and produced a masterpiece of firmness and finish, of which his own appreciation was as high as that of M. Poupin when at the end of the week he exhibited to him the fruit of his toil, and much more freely expressed than that of old Crook himself, who grunted approbation but was always too long-headed to create precedents. Hyacinth carried the volume to South Street as an offering to the Princess, hoping she would not yet have left London; in which case he would ask the servant to deliver it to her along with a little note he had sat up all night to compose. But the majestic major-domo in charge of the house, opening the door yet looking down at him as if from a second-story window, took the life out of his vision and erected instead of it, by a touch, a high blank wall. The Princess had been absent for some days; her representative was so good as to inform the young man with the parcel that she was on a visit to a 'Juke' in a distant part of the country. He offered however to receive and even to forward anything Hyacinth might wish to leave; but our hero felt a sudden indisposition to launch his humble tribute into the vast, the possibly cold unknown of a 'jucal' circle. He decided to retain his little package for the present; he would offer it to her when he should see her again, and he retreated without giving it up. Later on it seemed to create a manner of material link between the Princess and himself, and at the end of three months it had almost come to appear not that the exquisite book was an intended present from his own hand, but that it had been placed in that hand by the most remarkable woman in Europe. Rare sensations and impressions, moments of acute happiness, almost always, with our young man, in retrospect, became rather mythic and legendary; and the superior piece of work he had done after seeing her last, in the immediate heat of his emotion, turned to a virtual proof and gage—as if a ghost in vanishing from sight had left a palpable relic.

XVIII

THE MATTER touched him but indirectly, yet it may concern the reader more closely to know that before the visit to the Duke took place Madame Grandoni granted to Prince Casamassima the private interview she had promised him on that sad Sunday afternoon. She crept out of South Street after breakfast—a repast which under the Princess's roof was served in the foreign fashion at twelve o'clock—crossed the sultry solitude into which at such a season that precinct resolves itself, and entered the Park, where the grass was already brown and a warm, smoky haze prevailed, a tepid and tasteless réchauffé, as it struck our old friend, of the typical London fog. The Prince met her by appointment at the gate and they went and sat down together under the trees beside the drive, amid a wilderness of empty chairs and with nothing to distract their attention from an equestrian or two left over from the cavalcades of a fort-night before and whose vain agitation in the saddle the desolate scene threw into high relief. They remained there nearly an hour, though Madame Grandoni, in spite of her leaning to friendly interpretations, couldn't have told her-self what comfort it was to her afflicted companion. She had nothing to say to him that could better his case as he bent his mournful gaze on a prospect not after all perceptibly improved by its not being Sunday, and could only feel that with her he must seem to himself to be nearer his wife— to be touching something she had touched. She wished he would resign himself more, but she was willing to minister to that thin illusion, little as she approved of the manner in which he had conducted himself at the time of the last sharp crisis in the remarkable history of his relations with Christina. He had conducted himself after the fashion of a spoiled child, a child with a bad little nature, in a rage; he had been fatally wanting in dignity and wisdom and had given the Princess an advantage which she took on the spot and would keep for ever. He had acted without manly judgement, had put his uncles upon her (as if she cared for his uncles, powerful prelate as one of them might be!), had been suspicious and jealous on exactly the wrong occasions— occasions as to which her resentment of it had been just and in particular had been showy. He had not been clever enough or strong enough to make good his valid rights, and had transferred the whole quarrel to ground where his wife was far too accomplished a combatant not to obtain the appearance of victory.

There was another reflexion for Madame Grandoni to make as her interview with her dejected friend prolonged itself. She could make it the more freely as, besides being naturally quick and appreciative, she had always, during her Roman career, in the dear old days (mixed with bitterness as they had been for her) lived with artists, archæologists,

ingenious strangers, people who abounded in good talk,
threw out ideas and played with them. It came over her that
really, even if things had not reached that particular crisis,
Christina's active, various, ironical mind, with all its audaci-
ties and impatiences, could not have tolerated long the
simple deadly dulness of the Prince's company. The old
lady had begun on meeting him: 'Of course what you want
to know at once is whether she has sent you a message. No,
my poor friend, I must tell you the truth. I asked her for
one, but she assures me she has nothing whatever, of any
kind, to say to you. She knew I was coming out to see you—
I haven't done so *en cachette*. She doesn't like it, but she
accepts the necessity for this once, since you've made the
mistake, as she considers it, of approaching her again. We
talked of you last night after your note came to me—for
five minutes; that is I talked in my independent way and
Christina was good enough to listen. At the end she spoke
briefly, with perfect calmness and the appearance of being
the most reasonable woman in the world. She didn't ask me
to repeat it to you, but I do so because it's the only substitute I can offer you for a message. "I try to occupy my life,
my mind, to create interests, in the odious position in which
I find myself; I endeavour to get out of myself, my small
personal disappointments and troubles, by the aid of such
poor faculties as I possess. There are things in the world
more interesting after all, and I hope to succeed in giving
my attention to them. It appears to me not too much to ask
that the Prince on his side should make the same conscientious effort—and leave me contentedly alone!" Those were
your wife's remarkable words; they're all I have to give you.'

After she had given them Madame Grandoni felt a pang
of regret; the Prince turned upon her a face so white, bewildered and wounded. It had seemed to her they might
form a wholesome admonition, but she now saw that, as
coming from his wife, they were cruel, and she herself felt
almost cruel for having repeated them. What they amounted
to was an exquisite taunt of his mediocrity—a mediocrity
after all neither a crime nor a design nor a preference. How

could the Prince occupy himself, what interests could he create and what faculties, gracious heaven, did he possess? He was as ignorant as one of the dingy London sheep browsing before them, and as contracted as his hat-band. His expression became pitiful; it was as if he dimly measured the insult, felt it more than saw it—felt he couldn't plead incapacity without putting his wife largely in the right. He gazed at Madame Grandoni, his face worked, and for a moment she thought he was going to cry right out. But he said nothing—perhaps because he was afraid of that—so that suffering silence, during which she gently laid her hand on his own, remained his sole answer. He might doubtless do so much he didn't that when Christina touched on this she was unanswerable. The old lady changed the subject: told him what a curious country England was in so many ways; offered information as to their possible movements during the summer and autumn, which within a day or two had taken more form. But at last, as if he had not heard her, he broke out on the identity of the young man who had come in the day he called, just as he was going.

Madame Grandoni risked the truth. 'He was the Princess's bookbinder.'

'Her bookbinder? Do you mean one of her lovers?'

'Prince, how can you dream she'll ever live with you again?' the old lady asked in reply to this.

'Why then does she have him in her drawing-room—announced like an ambassador, carrying a hat in his hand like mine? Where were his books, his bindings? I shouldn't say this to *her*,' he added as if the declaration justified him.

'I told you the other day that she's making studies of the people—the lower orders. The young man you saw is a study.' She couldn't help laughing out as she gave her explanation this turn; but her mirth elicited no echo.

'I've thought that over—over and over; but the more I think the less I understand. Would it be your idea that she's quite crazy? I must tell you I don't care if she is!'

'We're all quite crazy, I think,' said Madame Grandoni; 'but the Princess no more than the rest of us. No, she must try everything; at present she's trying democracy, she's going all lengths in radicalism.'

'*Santo Dio!*' murmured the young man. 'And what do they say here when they see the bookbinder?'

'They haven't seen him and perhaps they won't. But if they do it won't matter, because here everything's forgiven. That a person should be extraordinary in some way of his own—and a woman as much as a man—is all they want. A bookbinder will do as well as anything else.'

The Prince mused a while. 'How can she bear the dirt, the bad smell?'

'I don't know what you're talking about. If you mean the young man you saw at the house—I may tell you, by the way, that it was only the first time he had been there and that the Princess had only seen him once—if you mean the little bookbinder he isn't dirty, especially what *we* should call. The people of that kind here are not like our dear Romans. Every one has a sponge as big as your head; you can see them in the shops.'

'They're full of gin; their faces are awful, are purple,' said the Prince; after which he immediately asked: 'If she had only seen him once how could he have come into her drawing room that way?'

His friend looked at him a little sternly. 'Believe at least what *I* say, my poor friend! Never forget that this was how you spoiled your affairs most of all—by treating a person (and such a person!) as if, as a matter of course, she lied. Christina has many faults, but she hasn't that one; that's why I can live with her. She'll speak the truth always.'

It was plainly not agreeable to the Prince to be reminded so sharply of his greatest mistake, and he flushed a little as Madame Grandoni spoke. But he didn't admit his error and she doubted if he even saw it. At any rate he remarked rather grandly, like a man who has still a good deal to say for himself: 'There are things it's better to conceal.'

'It all depends on whether you're afraid. Christina never is. Oh, I grant you she's very perverse, and when the entertainment of watching her, to see how she'll carry out some of her inspirations, is not stronger than anything else I lose all patience with her. When she doesn't charm she can only exasperate. But, as regards yourself, since you're here and I mayn't see you again for a long time or perhaps ever (at my age—I'm a hundred and twenty!) I may as well give you the key of certain parts of your wife's conduct. It may make her seem to you a little less fantastic. At the bottom then of much that she does is the fact that she's ashamed of having married you.'

'Less fantastic?' the young man repeated, staring.

'You may say that there can be nothing more extravagant —as even more insane—than that. But you know—or if not it isn't for want of her having told you—how the Princess considers that in the darkest hour of her life she sold herself for a title and a fortune. She regards her doing so as such a horrible piece of frivolity that she can't for the rest of her days be serious enough to make up for it.'

'Yes, I know she pretends to have been forced. And does she think she's so serious now?'

'The young man you saw the other day thinks so,' the old woman smiled. 'Sometimes she calls it by another name: she says she has thrown herself with passion into being "modern". That sums up the greatest number of things that you and your family are not.'

'Yes, we're not anything of that low sort, thank God! *Dio mio, Mio mio!*' groaned the Prince. He seemed so exhausted by his reflexions that he remained sitting in his chair after his companion, lifting her crumpled corpulence out of her own, had proposed that they should walk about a little. She had no ill-nature, but she had already noticed that whenever she was with Christina's husband the current of conversation made her, as she phrased it, bump against him. After administering these small shocks she always steered away, and now, the Prince having at last got up and offered her his arm, she tried again to talk with him of things he could consider without bitterness. She asked him about the health and habits of his uncles, and he replied for the moment with the minuteness he had been taught that in such a case courtesy demanded; but by the time that at her request they had returned to the gate nearest South Street (she wished him to come no further) he had prepared a question to which she had not opened the way. 'And who and what then is this English captain? About him there's a great deal said.'

'This English captain?'

'Godfrey Gerald Cholto—you see I know a good deal about him,' said the Prince, articulating the English names with difficulty.

They had stopped near the gate, on the edge of Park Lane, and a couple of predatory hansoms dashed at them from opposite quarters. 'I thought that was coming, and at bottom it's he who has occupied you most!' Madame Grandoni exclaimed with a sigh. 'But in reality he's the last one you need trouble about. He doesn't count the least little bit.'

'Why doesn't he count?'

'I can't tell you—except that some people don't, you know. He doesn't even think he does.'

'Why not, when she receives him always—lets him go wherever she goes?'

'Perhaps that's just the reason. When people give her a chance to get tired of them she takes it rather easily. At any rate you needn't be any more jealous of him than you are of me. He's a convenience, a *factotum*, but he works without wages.'

'Isn't he then in love with her?'

'Naturally. He has however no hope.'

'Ah, poor gentleman!' said the Prince lugubriously.

'He accepts the situation better than you. He occupies himself—as she has strongly recommended him in my hearing to do—with other women!'

'Oh the brute!' the Prince exclaimed. 'At all events he sees her.'

'Yes, but she doesn't see *him*!' laughed Madame Grandoni as she turned away.

XIX

THE PINK dressing-gown that Pinnie had engaged to make for Rose Muniment became in Lomax Place a conspicuous object, supplying poor Amanda with a constant theme for reference to one of the great occasions of her life—her visit to Belgrave Square with Lady Aurora after their meeting at Rosy's bedside. She detailed this episode minutely to her companion, repeating a thousand times that her ladyship's affability was beyond anything she could have expected. The grandeur of the house in Belgrave Square figured in her recital as something oppressive and fabulous, tempered though it had been by shrouds of brown holland and the nudity of staircases and saloons of which the trappings had been put away. 'If it's so noble when they're out of town what can it be when they're all there together and everything's out?' she enquired suggestively; and she permitted herself to be restrictive only on two points, one of which was the state of Lady Aurora's gloves and bonnet-strings. If she hadn't been afraid to appear to notice the disrepair of these objects she should have been so happy to do any little mending. 'If she'd only come to me every week or two I'd keep up her rank for her,' said Pinnie, who had visions of a needle that positively flashed in the disinterested service of the aristocracy. She added that her ladyship got all dragged out with her long expeditions to Camberwell; she might be in tatters for all they could do to help her, at the top of those dreadful stairs, with that strange sick creature (she was too unnatural) thinking only of her own finery and talking about her complexion. If she wanted pink she should have pink; but to Pinnie there was something almost unholy in it, like decking out a corpse or dressing up the cat. This was the second perversity that left Miss Pynsent cold; it couldn't be other than difficult for her to enter into the importance her ladyship appeared to attach to those pushing people. The girl was unfortunate certainly, stuck up there like a puppy on a shelf, but in her ladyship's place she would have found some topic more in keeping while they walked about under those tremendous gilded ceilings. Lady Aurora, seeing how she was struck, showed her all over the house, carrying the lamp herself and telling an old woman who was there—a 'confidential' housekeeper, a person with ribbons in her cap who would have pushed Pinnie out if you could push with your eyes—that they would do very well without her. If the pink dressing-gown, in its successive stages of development, filled up the little brown parlour (it was terribly long on the stocks) making such a pervasive rose-coloured presence as had not been seen there for many a day, this was evidently because it was associated with Lady Aurora, not because it was dedicated to her humble friend.

One day when Hyacinth came home Pinnie at once announced to him that her ladyship had been there to look at it—to pass judgement before the last touches were conferred. The dressmaker intimated that in such a case as that her judgement was rather wild and she seemed to have embarrassing ideas about pockets. Whatever could poor Miss Muniment want of pockets and what had she to put in them? But Lady Aurora had evidently found the garment far beyond anything she expected, and she had been more affable than ever and had wanted to know about every one in the 'Plice': not in a meddling, prying way, either, like some of those condescending swells, but quite as if the poor people were the high ones and she was afraid her curiosity might be 'presumptious'. It was in the same discreet spirit that she had invited Amanda to relate her whole history and had expressed an interest in the career of her young friend.

'She said you had charming manners,' Miss Pynsent hastened to remark; 'but on my life, Hyacinth Robinson, I never mentioned a scrap that it could give you pain that any one should talk about.' There was an heroic explicitness in this, on Pinnie's part, for she knew in advance just how Hyacinth would look at her—fixedly, silently, hopelessly, as if she were still capable of tattling horribly (with the idea that her revelations would increase her importance) and putting forward this hollow theory of her supreme discretion to cover it up. His eyes seemed to say it all: 'How can I believe you, and yet how can I prove you're lying? I'm very helpless, for I can't prove that without applying to the person to whom your incorrigible folly has probably led you to brag, to throw out mysterious and tantalising hints. You know of course that I'd never condescend to that.' Pinnie suffered acutely from this imputation, yet exposed herself to it often, because she could never deny herself the pleasure, keener still than her pain, of letting Hyacinth know he was appreciated, admired and, for those 'charming manners' commended by Lady Aurora, even all but wondered at in so many words; and this kind of interest always appeared to imply a suspicion of his secret—something which, when he expressed to himself the sense of it, he called, resenting it at once and finding a certain softness in it, 'a beastly *attendrissement*'. When Pinnie went on to say to him that Lady Aurora appeared to feel a certain surprise at his never yet having come to Belgrave Square for the famous books he reflected that he must really wait upon her without more delay if he wished to keep up his reputation as a man of the world; and meanwhile he considered much the extreme oddity of this new phase of his life which had opened so suddenly from one day to the other: a phase in which his society should have become indispensable to ladies of high rank and the obscurity of his condition only an attraction the more. They were taking him up then one after the other and were even taking up poor Pinnie as a means of getting at him; so that he wondered with gaiety and irony if it meant that his destiny was really seeking him out —that the aristocracy, recognising a mysterious affinity (with that fineness of *flair* for which they were remarkable) were coming to him to save him the trouble of coming to them.

It was late in the day (the beginning of an October evening) and Lady Aurora was at home. Hyacinth had made a mental calculation of the time at which she would have risen from dinner; the operation of 'rising from dinner' having always been, in his imagination, for some reason or other, highly characteristic of the nobility. He was ignorant of the fact that Lady Aurora's principal meal consisted of a scrap of fish and a cup of tea served on a little stand in the dismantled breakfast-parlour. The door was opened for Hyacinth by the invidious old lady whom Pinnie had described and who listened to his appeal, conducted him through the house and ushered him into her ladyship's presence without the smallest relaxation of a pair of tightly-closed lips. His good hostess was seated in the little breakfast-parlour by the light of a couple of candles and apparently immersed in a collection of crumpled papers and account-books. She was ciphering, consulting memoranda, taking notes; she had had her head in her hands and the silky entanglement of her hair resisted the rapid effort she made to smooth herself down as she saw the little bookbinder come in. The impression of her fingers remained in little rosy streaks on her pink skin. She exclaimed instantly, 'Oh, you've come about the books—it's so very kind of you'; and she hurried him off to another room, to which, as she explained, she had had them brought down for him to choose from. The effect of this precipitation was to make him suppose at first that she might wish him to execute his errand as quickly as possible and take himself off; but he presently noted that her nervousness and her shyness were of an order that would always give false ideas. She wanted him to stay, she wanted to talk with him and she had rushed with him at the books in order to gain time and composure for exercising some subtler art. Hyacinth, staying half an hour, became more and more convinced that her ladyship was, as he had ventured to pronounce her on the occasion of their last meeting, a regular saint. He was privately a little disappointed in the books, though he selected three or four, as many as he could carry, and promised to come back for others: they denoted on Lady Aurora's part a limited acquaintance with French literature and even a certain puerility of taste. There were several volumes of Lamartine and a set of the spurious memoirs of the Marquise de Créqui; but for the rest the little library consisted mainly of Marmontel and Madame de Genlis, Le Récit d'une Sœur and the tales of M. J. T. de Saint-Germain. There were certain members of an intensely modern school, advanced and consistent realists of whom Hyacinth had heard and on whom he had long desired to put his hand; but evidently none of them had ever stumbled into Lady Aurora's candid collection, though she did possess a couple of Balzac's novels, which by ill luck happened to be just those our young man had read more than once.

There was nevertheless something very agreeable to him in the moments he passed in the big, dim, cool, empty house, where, at intervals, monumental pieces of furniture —not crowded and miscellaneous, as he had seen the appurtenances of the Princess—loomed and gleamed, and Lady Aurora's fantastic intonations awakened echoes which gave him a sense of privilege, of rioting, decently, in the absence of prohibitory presences. She spoke again of the poor people in the south of London and of the Muniments in particular; evidently the only fault she had to find with these latter was that they were not poor enough—not sufficiently exposed to dangers and privations against which she could step in. Hyacinth liked her for this, even though he wished she would talk of something else—he hardly knew what, unless it was that, like Rose Muniment, he wanted to hear more about Inglefield. He didn't mind, with the poor, going into questions of their state—it even gave him at times a strange savage satisfaction; but he saw that in discussing them with the rich the interest must inevitably be less: the rich couldn't consider poverty in the light of experience. Their mistakes and illusions, their thinking they had got hold of the sensations of want and dirt when they hadn't at all, would always be more or less irritating. It came over Hyacinth that if he found this deficient perspective in Lady Aurora's deep conscientiousness it would be a queer enough business when he should come to pretending to hold the candlestick for the Princess Casamassima.

His present hostess said no word to him about Pinnie, and he guessed she must have wished to place him on the

footing on which people don't express approbation or surprise at the decency or good-breeding of each other's rela-
tives. He saw how she would always treat him as a gentleman and that even if he should be basely ungrateful she
would never call his attention to the fact that she had done
so. He shouldn't have occasion to say to her, as he had said
to the Princess, that she regarded him as a curious animal;
and it gave him at once the sense of learning more about
life, a sense always delightful to him, to perceive there were
such different ways (which implied still a good many more)
of being a lady of rank. The manner in which Lady Aurora
appeared to wish to confer with him on the great problems
of pauperism and reform might have implied he was a
benevolent nobleman (of the type of Lord Shaftesbury) who
had endowed many charities and was noted, in philanthropic
schemes, for the breadth of his views. It was not less present
to him that Pinnie might have tattled, put forward his
claims to high consanguinity, than it had been when the
dressmaker herself decanted on her ladyship's condescen-
sions; but he remembered now that he too had only just
escaped being asinine when, the other day, he flashed out
an illusion to his accursed origin. At all events he was much
touched by the delicacy with which the earl's daughter
comported herself, simply assuming that he was 'one of
themselves'; and he reflected that if she did know his history
(he was sure he might pass twenty years in her society without discovering if she did) this shade of courtesy, this
natural tact, coexisting even with extreme awkwardness,
illustrated that 'best breeding' which he had seen alluded to
in novels portraying the aristocracy. The only remark on
Lady Aurora's part that savoured in the least of looking
down at him from a height was when she said cheerfully
and encouragingly: 'I suppose one of these days you'll be
setting up in business for yourself.' This was not so cruelly
patronising that he couldn't reply with a smile equally free
from any sort of impertinence: 'Oh dear, no, I shall never do
that. I should make a great mess of any attempt to carry on
a business. I've no turn at all for that sort of thing.'

Lady Aurora looked a little surprised. 'Oh, I see; you don't like—you don't like——!' She hesitated: he saw she was going to say he didn't like the idea of going in to that extent for a trade; but he stopped her in time from imputing to him a sentiment so foolish and declared what he meant to be simply that his one faculty was the faculty of doing his little piece of work, whatever it was, of liking to do it skilfully and prettily, and of liking still better to get his money for it when done. His conception of 'business' or of rising in the world did not go beyond that. 'Oh yes, I can fancy!' her ladyship exclaimed; but she looked at him a moment with eyes which showed that he puzzled her, that she didn't quite understand his tone. Before he left her she asked him abruptly (nothing had led up to it) what he thought of Captain Sholto, whom she had seen that other evening in Audley Court. Didn't he think him a very odd sort of person? Hyacinth confessed to this impression; whereupon Lady Aurora went on anxiously, eagerly: 'Don't you consider him decidedly vulgar?'

'How can I know?'

'You can know perfectly—as well as any one!' Then she added: 'I think it's a pity they should form relations with any one of that kind.'

'They' of course meant Paul Muniment and his sister. 'With a person who may be vulgar?'—Hyacinth regarded this solicitude as exquisite. 'But think of the people they know—think of those they're surrounded with—think of all Audley Court!'

'The poor, the unhappy, the labouring classes? Oh, I don't call *them* vulgar!' cried her ladyship with radiant eyes. The young man, lying awake a good deal that night, laughed to himself, on his pillow, not unkindly, at her fear that he and his friends would be contaminated by the familiar of a princess. He even wondered if she wouldn't find the Princess herself a bit vulgar.

XX

IT MUST not be supposed that his relations with Millicent
had remained unaffected by the remarkable incident that
had brushed her with its wing at the theatre. The whole
occurrence had made a great impression on the young lady
from Pimlico; he never saw her, for weeks afterwards, that
she had not an immense deal to say about it; and though it
suited her to cultivate the shocked state at the crudity of
such proceedings and to denounce the Princess for a bold-
faced foreigner, of a kind to which any one who knew anything of what could go on in London would give a wide
berth, it was easy to see she enjoyed having rubbed shoulders across the house with a person so splendid and having
found her own critical estimate of her friend confirmed in
such high quarters. She professed to draw her warrant for
her low opinion of the lady in the box from information
given her by Captain Sholto as he sat beside her—information of which at different moments she gave a different version; her notes of it having nothing in common save that
they were alike unflattering to the Princess. Hyacinth had
many doubts of the Captain's having talked indiscreetly; it
would be in such a case such a very unnatural thing for him
to do. He *was* unnatural—that was true—and he might have
told Millicent, who was capable of having plied him with
questions, that his distinguished friend was separated from
her husband; but, for the rest, it was more probable that
the girl had given the rein to a fine faculty of free invention
of which he had had frequent glimpses, under pressure of
her primitive half-childish, half plebeian impulse of destruction, the instinct of pulling down what was above her, the
reckless energy that would, precisely, make her so effective
in revolutionary scenes. Hyacinth (it has been mentioned)
didn't consider that Millicent was false, and it struck him
as a proof of positive candour that she should make up

absurd, abusive stories about a person as to whom she only knew that she disliked her and could hope for no esteem, and indeed for no recognition of any kind, in return. When people were fully false you didn't know where you stood with them, and on such a point as this Miss Henning could never be accused of leaving you in obscurity. She said little else about the Captain and didn't pretend to repeat the remainder of his conversation, taking on her air of grand indifference when Hyacinth amused himself with repaying her criticism of his new acquaintance by drawing a sufficiently derisive portrait of hers.

His line was that Sholto's admiration for the high-coloured beauty in the second balcony had been at the bottom of the whole episode: he had persuaded the Princess to pretend she was a revolutionist and should like therefore to confer with the little firebrand above in order that he might slip into the seat of this too easily deluded youth. At the same time it never occurred to our young man to conceal the fact that the lady in the box had followed him up; he contented himself with saying that this had been no part of the original plot, but a simple result—not unnatural after all—of his showing so much more charm than might have been expected. He described with sportive variations his visit in South Street, conscious that he would never feel the need, with his childhood's friend, of glossing over that sort of experience. She might make him a scene of jealousy and welcome—there were things that would have much more terror for him than that; her jealousy, with its violence, its energy, even a certain inconsequent, dare-devil humour that played through it, entertained him, emphasised the frankness, the passion and pluck he admired her for. He should never be on the footing of sparing Miss Henning's susceptibilities; how fond she might really be of him he couldn't take upon himself to say, but her affection would never assume the form of that sort of delicacy, and their intercourse was plainly foredoomed to be an exchange of thumps and concussions, of sarcastic shouts and mutual *défis*. He liked her, at bottom, strangely, absurdly; but after all it was

only well enough to torment her—she could bear so much
—not well enough to spare her. Of any actual ground for
the girl's jealousy of the Princess he never thought; it
couldn't occur to him to weigh against each other the sentiments he might excite in such opposed bosoms or those that
the spectacle of either emotion might have kindled in his
own. He had no doubt his share of fatuity, but he found
himself unable to associate mentally a great lady and a
bouncing shop-girl in a contest for a prize which should have
anything of *his* figure. How could they show the least common mark—even so small a one as a desire to possess themselves of Hyacinth Robinson? A fact he didn't impart to
Millicent and could have no wish to impart to her was the
different matter of his pilgrimage to Belgrave Square. He
might be in love with the Princess (how could he qualify
as yet the bewildered emotion she had produced in him?)
and he certainly never would conceive a passion for poor
Lady Aurora; yet it would have given him pain much
greater than any he felt in the other case to hear Milly make
free with the ministering angel of Audley Court. The distinction was perhaps somehow in her appearing really not
to touch or arrive at the Princess at all, whereas Lady Aurora
was within her range and compass.

After paying him that visit at his rooms Hyacinth lost
sight of Captain Sholto, who had not again reappeared at
the 'Sun and Moon', the little tavern which presented so
common and casual a face to the world, but offered in its
unsuspected rear a security still unimpugned to machinations going down to the very bottom of things. Nothing was
more natural than that the Captain should be engaged at
this season in the recreations of his class; and our young
man took for granted that if he were not hanging about the
Princess on that queer footing as to which one had a secret
hope one should some day command more light, he was
probably buffeting breezy northern seas on a yacht or creep-
ing after stags in the Highlands; our hero's acquaintance
with the light literature of his country being such as to
assure him that in one or other of these occupations people

of leisure, during the autumn, were necessarily immersed. If the Captain were giving his attention to neither he must have started for Albania, or at least for Paris. Happy Captain, Hyacinth mused, while his imagination followed him through vivid exotic episodes and his restless young feet continued to tread, through the stale flat weeks of September and October, the familiar pavements of Soho, Islington and Pentonville, and the shabby sinuous ways that unite these regions of labour. He had told the Princess he sometimes had a holiday at this period and that there was a chance of his escorting his respectable companion to the seaside; but as it turned out at present the spare cash for such an excursion was wanting. Hyacinth had indeed for the moment an exceptionally keen sense of the lack of this convenience and was forcibly reminded that the society of agreeable women was a direct and constant appeal to the pocket. He not only hadn't a penny, but was much in debt, owed pence and shillings, as he would have largely put it, all over the place, and the explanation of his pinched feeling was in a vague half-remorseful, half-resigned reference to the numerous occasions when he had had not to fail of funds under penalty of disappointing a young lady whose needs were positive, and especially to a certain high crisis (as it might prove to be) in his destiny when it had come over him that one couldn't call on a princess just as one was. So this year he didn't ask old Crook for the week which some of the other men took—Eustache Poupin, who had never quitted London since his arrival, launched himself precisely that summer, supported by his brave wife, into the British unknown on the strength of a return ticket to Worthing—simply because he shouldn't know what to do with it. The best way not to spend money, though no doubt not the best in the world to make it, was still to take one's daily course to the old familiar shabby shop where, as the days shortened and November thickened the air to a livid yellow, the uncovered flame of the gas, burning often from the morning on, lighted up the ugliness in which the hand of practice endeavoured to disengage a little beauty—the

ugliness of a dingy belittered interior, of battered dispapered
walls, of work-tables stained and hacked, of windows opening into a foul drizzling street, of the bared arms, the sordid
waistcoat-backs, the smeared aprons, the personal odour,
the patient obstinate irritating shoulders and vulgar narrow
inevitable faces of his fellow-labourers. Our young friend's
relations with his comrades would form a chapter by itself,
but all that may be said of the matter here is that the clever
little operator from Lomax Place had in a manner a double
identity and that much as he lived in Mr Crookenden's
establishment he lived out of it still more. In this busy,
pasty, sticky, leathery little world, where wages and beer
were the main objects of consideration, he played his part
in a way that marked him as a queer lot, but capable of
queerness in the line of equanimity too. He hadn't made
good his place there without discovering that the British
workman, when animated by the spirit of mirth, has rather
a heavy hand, and he tasted of the practical joke in every
degree of violence. During his first year he dreamed, with
secret passion and suppressed tears, of a day of bliss when
at last they would let him alone—a day which arrived in
time, for it is always an advantage to be clever if one be
only clever enough. Hyacinth was sufficiently so to have
invented a *modus vivendi* in respect to which M. Poupin
said to him '*Enfin vous voilà fermé!*' (the Frenchman himself, terribly *éprouvé* at the beginning, had always bristled
with firmness and opposed to insular grossness a refined
dignity) and under the influence of which the scenery of
Soho figured a daily dusky exhibition of projected shadows,
confined to the passive part of life and giving no hostages to
reality, or at least to ambition, save an insufficient number
of shillings on Saturday night and stray spasmodic reminiscences of delicate work that might have been more delicate
still, as well as of such applications of the tool as he flattered
himself unsurpassed unless by the supreme Eustache.
  One evening in November he had after discharging himself of a considerable indebtedness to Pinnie still a sovereign
in his pocket—a sovereign that seemed to spin there under

the equal breath of a dozen different uses. He had come out for a walk with a vague intention of pushing as far as Audley Court; and lurking within this nebulous design, on which the damp breath of the streets, making objects seem that night particularly dim and places particularly far, had blown a certain chill, was a sense of how nice it would be to take something to Rose Muniment, who delighted in a sixpenny present and to whom he hadn't for some time rendered any such homage. At last, after he had wandered a while, hesitating between the pilgrimage to Lambeth and the possibility of still associating the two or three hours with those perhaps in some lucky way or other at Millicent Henning's disposal, he reflected that if a sovereign was to be pulled to pieces it was a simplification to get it changed. He had struck through the region of Mayfair, partly with the preoccupation of a short cut and partly from an instinct of self-defence; if one was in danger of spending one's money with a rush it was so much gained to plunge into a quarter where, at that hour especially, there were no shops for little bookbinders. Hyacinth's victory, however, was imperfect when it occurred to him to turn into a public-house in order to convert his gold into convenient silver. When it was a question of entering these establishments he selected in preference the most decent; he never knew what unpleasant people he might find on the other side of the swinging door. Those which glitter at intervals amid the residential gloom of the large district abutting on Grosvenor Square partake of the general gentility of the neighbourhood, so that our friend was not surprised (he had passed into the compartment marked 'private bar') to see but a single drinker leaning against the counter on which, with his request very civilly enunciated, he put down his sovereign. He was surprised on the other hand when, glancing up again, he became aware that this lonely reveller was Captain Godfrey Sholto.

'Why, my dear boy, what a remarkable coincidence!' the Captain exclaimed. 'For once in five years that I come into a place like this!'

'I don't come in often myself. I thought you were in Madagascar,' Hyacinth said.

'Ah, because I've not been at the "Sun and Moon"? Well, I've been constantly out of town, you know. And then—don't you see what I mean?—I want to be tremendously careful. That's the way to get on, isn't it? But I dare say you don't believe in my discretion!' Sholto laughed. 'What shall I do to make you understand? I say, have a brandy and soda,' he continued as if this might assist Hyacinth's comprehension. He seemed a trifle flurried and, were it possible to imagine such a thing of so independent and whimsical a personage, the least bit abashed or uneasy at having been found in such a low place. Yet it was not any lower than the 'Sun and Moon'. He was dressed on this occasion according to his station, without the pot-hat and the shabby jacket, and Hyacinth looked at him with the pang of the felt charm that a good tailor would add to life. Our hero was struck more than ever before with his being the type of man whom, as he strolled about observing people, he had so often regarded with wonder and envy—the sort of man of whom one said to one's self that he was the 'finest white', feeling that he and his like had the world in their pocket. Sholto requested the barmaid to please not dawdle in preparing the brandy and soda Hyacinth had thought to ease the situation by accepting: this indeed was perhaps what the finest white would naturally do. And when the young man had taken the glass from the counter didn't he appear to encourage him not to linger as he drank it and to smile down at him very kindly and amusedly, as if the combination of so small a bookbinder and so big a tumbler were sufficiently droll? The Captain took time however to ask how he had spent his autumn and what was the news in Bloomsbury; he further enquired about those jolly people across the river. 'I can't tell you what an impression they made on me—that evening you know.' After this he went on suddenly and irrelevantly: 'And so you're just going to stay on for the winter quietly?' Our hero stared: he wondered what other high course could be imputed to him; he couldn't reflect immediately that this

was the sort of thing the finest whites said to each other
when they met after their fashionable dispersals, and that
his friend had only been guilty of a monetary inadvertence.
In point of fact the Captain recovered himself. 'Oh, of
course you've got your work, and that sort of thing'; and, as
Hyacinth didn't succeed in swallowing at a gulp the contents
of his big tumbler he asked him presently if he had heard
anything from the Princess. Our youth replied that he could
have no news except what the Captain might be good
enough to give him; but he added that he had been to see
her just before she left town.

'Ah, you did go? That was quite right—jolly right.'

'I went because she very kindly wrote me to come.'

'Ah, she wrote to you to come?' The Captain fixed him
a moment with his curious colourless eyes. 'Do you know
you're a devilish privileged mortal?'

'Certainly I know it.' Hyacinth blushed and felt foolish;
the barmaid, who had heard this odd couple talking of a
princess, was staring at him too with her elbows on the
counter.

'Do you know there are people who'd give their heads
that she should write them to come?'

'I've no doubt of it whatever!'—and he took refuge in
a laugh that sounded less natural than he would have liked,
and wondered if his interlocutor weren't precisely one of
these people. In this case the barmaid might well stare; for
deeply convinced as our young man might be that he was
the son of Lord Frederick Purvis, there was really no end to
the oddity of his being preferred—and by a princess—to
Captain Sholto. If anything could have re-enforced at that
moment his sense of this anomaly it would have been the
indescribably gentlemanly way, implying all sorts of common initiations, in which his companion went on.

'Ah well, I see you know how to take it! And if you're
in correspondence with her why do you say you can hear
from her only through me? My dear fellow, I'm not in correspondence with her. You might think I'd naturally be, but
I'm not.' He subjoined as Hyacinth had laughed again in a

manner that might have passed for ambiguous: 'So much the worse for me—is that what you mean?' Hyacinth replied that he himself had had the honour of hearing from the Princess but once, and mentioned her having told him how her letter-writing came on only in fits, when it was sometimes very profuse: there were months together that she didn't touch a pen. 'Oh, I can imagine what she told you!' the Captain knowingly returned. 'Look out for the next fit! She's visiting about, you know—at a lot of great houses. It's a great thing to be somewhere with her—an immense comedy.' He remarked that he had heard, now he remembered, that she either had taken or was thinking of taking a place in the country for a few months, and he added that if Hyacinth didn't propose to finish his brandy and soda they might as well turn out. Hyacinth's thirst had been very superficial, and as they turned out the Captain observed by way of explanation of his having been found in a public-house (it was the only attempt of this kind he made) that any friend of his would always know him by his love of rum out-of-the-way nooks. 'You must have noticed that,' he said —'my taste for exploration. If I hadn't explored I never should have known you, should I? That was rather a nice little girl in there; did you twig her good bust? It's a pity they always have such beastly hands.' Hyacinth had instinctively made a motion to go southward, but Sholto, passing a hand into his arm, led him the other way. The house they had quitted was near a corner, which they rounded, the Captain pushing forward as if there were some reason for haste. His haste was checked however by a prompt encounter with a young woman who, coming in the opposite direction, turned the angle as briskly as themselves. At this moment he gave his friend a great jerk, but not before Hyacinth had caught a glimpse of the young woman's face —it seemed to flash upon him out of the dusk—and given quick voice to his surprise.

'Hullo, Millicent!' This was the simple cry that escaped from his lips while the Captain, still going on, but threw off, 'What's the matter? Who's your pretty friend?' Hyacinth

declined to go on and repeated Miss Henning's baptismal
name so loudly that the young woman, who had passed
them without looking back, was obliged to stop. Then he
saw he was not mistaken, though Millicent gave no audible
response. She stood looking at him with her head very high,
and he approached her, disengaging himself from Sholto,
who however hung back only an instant before joining
them. Hyacinth's heart had suddenly begun to beat very
fast; there was a sharp shock in the girl's turning up just in
that place at that moment. Yet when she began to laugh,
and with violence, and to ask him why he should look at
her as if she were a kicking horse, he recognised that there
was nothing so very extraordinary, after all, in a casual
meeting between persons who were such frequenters of the
London streets. Millicent had never concealed the fact that
she 'trotted about' on various errands at night; and once
when he had said to her that the less a respectable young
woman took the evening air alone the better for her respectability she had asked how respectable he thought she
pretended to be and had remarked that if he would make
her a present of a brougham or even call for her three or
four times a week in a cab she would doubtless preserve
more of her social purity. She could turn the tables quickly
enough and she exclaimed now, professing on her own side
great astonishment:

'Whatever are you prowling about here for? You're after
no good, I'll be bound!'

'Good evening, Miss Henning; what a jolly meeting!' said
the Captain, removing his hat with a humorous flourish.

'Oh, how d'ye do?' Millicent returned as if not at once
placing him.

'Where were you going so fast? What are you doing?'
asked Hyacinth, who had looked from one to the other.

'Well, I never did see such a manner—from one that
knocks about like *you*!' cried Miss Henning. 'I'm going to
see a friend of mine—a lady's-maid in Curzon Street. Have
you anything to say to that?'

'Don't tell us—don't tell us!' Sholto interposed after she

had spoken—and she had not, however slightly, hesitated. 'I at least disavow the indiscretion. Where may not a charming woman be going when she trips with a light foot through the deepening dusk?'

'I say, what are you talking about?' the girl demanded with dignity of Hyacinth's companion. She spoke as if with a resentful suspicion that her foot had not really been felt to be light.

'On what errand of mercy, on what secret ministration?' the Captain laughed.

'Secret yourself!' cried Millicent. 'Do you two always hunt in couples?'

'All right, we'll turn round and go with you as far as your friend's,' Hyacinth said.

'All right,' Millicent replied.

'All right,' the Captain added; and the three took their way together in the direction of Curzon Street. They walked for a few minutes in silence, though the Captain whistled, and then Millicent suddenly turned to Hyacinth.

'You haven't told me where *you* were going yet, you know.'

'We met in that public-house,' the Captain said, 'and were each so ashamed of being found in such a place by the other that we tumbled out together without much thinking what we should do with ourselves.'

'When he's out with me he pretends he can't abide them houses,' Miss Henning declared. 'I wish I had looked in that one to see who was there.'

'Well, she's rather nice,' the Captain went on. 'She told me her name was Georgiana.'

'I went to get a piece of money changed,' Hyacinth said with the sense of a certain dishonesty in the air and glad he at least could afford to speak the truth.

'To get your grandmother's nightcap changed! I recommend you to keep your money together—you've none too much of it!' Millicent exclaimed.

'Is that the reason you're playing me false?' Hyacinth flashed out. He had been thinking with still intentness as

they walked; at once nursing and strangling a kindled suspicion. He was pale with the idea that he had been bamboozled, yet was able to say to himself that one must allow
in life, thank goodness, for the element of coincidence, and
that he might easily put himself immensely in the wrong by
making a groundless charge. It was only later that he pieced
his impressions together and saw them—as it appeared—
justify each other; at present, as soon as he had uttered it,
he was almost ashamed of his quick retort to Millicent's
taunt. He ought at least to have waited to see what Curzon
Street would bring forth.

The girl broke out on him immediately, repeating 'False,
false?' with high derision and wanting to know whether that
was the way to knock a lady about in public. She had
stopped short on the edge of a crossing and she went on with
a voice so uplifted that he was glad they were in a street
apt to be empty at such an hour: 'You're a pretty one to
talk about falsity when a woman has only to leer at you
out of an opera-box!'

'Don't say anything about *her*,' the young man interposed,
trembling.

'And pray why not about "her", I should like to know?
You don't pretend she's a decent woman, I suppose?' Millicent's laughter rang through the quiet neighbourhood.

'My dear fellow, you know you *have* been to her,' Captain
Sholto wonderfully smiled.

Hyacinth turned on him staring and at once provoked
and baffled by his ambiguous part in an incident it was
doubtless possible to magnify but not possible to treat as
perfectly simple. 'Certainly I've been to the Princess Casamassima, thanks to you. When you came and pressed me
to go, when you dragged me, do you make it a reproach?
Who the devil are you, anyway, and what do you want of
me?' our hero cried—his mind flooded in a moment with
everything in the Captain that had puzzled and worried and
escaped him. This swelling tide obliterated on the spot
everything that had beguiled.

'My dear fellow, whatever I am I'm not an ass,' this

gentleman replied with imperturbable good-humour. 'I don't reproach you with anything. I only wanted to put in a word as a peacemaker. My good friends—my good friends,' and he laid a hand in his practised way on Hyacinth's shoulder while with the other pressed to his heart he bent on the girl a face of gallantry which had something paternal in it: 'I'm determined this absurd misunderstanding shall end as lovers' quarrels ought always to end.'

Hyacinth withdrew himself from the Captain's touch and said to Millicent: 'You're not really jealous of—of any one. You pretend that only to throw dust in my eyes.'

To this sally Miss Henning returned him an answer which promised to be lively, but the Captain swept it away in the profusion of his protests. He declared them a dear delightful abominable pair; he pronounced it rarely interesting to see how in people of their sort the prime passions lay near the surface; he almost pushed them into each other's arms and then wound up with proposing that they should all terminate their little differences by proceeding together to the Pavilion music-hall, the nearest place of entertainment in that neighbourhood, leaving the lady's-maid in Curzon Street to dress her mistress's wig in peace. He has been presented to the reader as an accomplished man, and it will doubtless be felt that the picture is justified by his having eventually placed this idea in so attractive a light that his companions entered a hansom with him and rattled toward the haunt of pleasure, Hyacinth sandwiched, on the edge of the seat, between the others. Two or three times our young man's ears burned; he felt that if there was an understanding between them they had now, behind him, a rare opportunity for carrying it out. If this understanding flourished at his expense the whole evening constituted for them indeed an opportunity, and that thought rendered his diversion but scantly absorbing, though at the Pavilion the Captain engaged a big private box and ordered ices brought in. Hyacinth cared so little for his little pink pyramid that he suffered Millicent to consume it after she had disposed of her own. It was present to him, however, that if he should make a fool of himself the folly would be of a very gross kind, and this is why he withheld a question repeatedly on his lips—the impulse to demand of his entertainer why the mischief he had hurried him so out of the public-house if he had not been waiting there preconcertedly for Millicent. We know that in Hyacinth's eyes one of this young lady's compensatory merits had been that she was not deceitful, and he asked himself if a girl could change that way from one month to the other. This was optimistic, but, all the same, before leaving the Pavilion he decided with one of his highest flights of intelligence that he could quite well see what Lady Aurora had meant by calling Captain Sholto vulgar.

XXI

PAUL MUNIMENT had fits of silence while the others were talking; but on this occasion he had not opened his lips for half an hour. When he talked Hyacinth listened almost to the retention of breath, and when he said nothing watched him fixedly, listening to the others only through the medium of his candid countenance. At the 'Sun and Moon' Muniment paid very little attention to his young friend, doing nothing that should cause it to be perceived they were particular pals; and Hyacinth even divined him at moments bored or irritated by the serious manner in which his small worrying bookbinder couldn't conceal from the world that he regarded him. He wondered if this were a system, a calculated prudence, on Muniment's part, or only a manifestation of the superior brutality latent in his composition and which, without an intention of direct harshness, was naturally impatient of palaver. There was plenty of palaver at the 'Sun and Moon'; there were nights when a blast of imbecility seemed to blow over the place and one felt ashamed to be associated with so much crude fatuity and flat-faced vanity. Then every one, with two or three exceptions, made an ass of himself, thumping the table and repeating over some inane phrase which appeared for the hour to constitute the whole furniture of his mind. There were men who kept saying 'Them was my words in the month of February last, and what I say I stick to—what I say I stick to'; and others who perpetually enquired of the company 'And what the plague am I to do with seventeen bob—with seventeen bloody bob? What am I to do with them—will ye tell me that?' an interrogation which in truth usually ended by producing a ribald reply. There were still others who remarked to satiety that if it was not done to-day it would have to be done to-morrow, and several who constantly proclaimed their opinion that the only way was to pull up the Park rails again, just to haul 'em straight up. A little shoemaker with red eyes and a greyish face, whose appearance Hyacinth deplored, scarcely ever expressed himself but in the same form of words: 'Well, are we in earnest or ain't we in earnest?—that's the thing *I* want to know.' He was terribly in earnest himself, but this was almost the only way he had of showing it; and he had much in common (though they were always squabbling) with a large red-faced man, of uncertain attributes and stertorous breathing, who was understood to know a good deal about dogs, had fat hands and wore on his forefinger a big silver ring containing some one's hair—Hyacinth believed it to be that of a terrier snappish in life. He had always the same refrain: 'Well now are we just starving or ain't we just starving? I should like the v'ice of the company on that question.'

When the tone fell as low as this Paul Muniment held his peace save for whistling a little and leaning back with his hands in his pockets and his eyes on the table. Hyacinth often supposed him to be on the point of breaking out and letting the company know what he thought of them—he had a perfectly clear vision of what he must think: but Muniment never compromised his popularity to that degree; he judged it—this he once told his young comrade—too valuable a weapon, so that he cultivated the faculty of patience,

which had the advantage of showing one more and more
that one must do one's thinking for one's self. His popularity
indeed struck Hyacinth as rather an uncertain amount, and
the only mistake he had seen a symptom of on his friend's
part was a tendency to overestimate it. Muniment thought
many of their colleagues asinine, but it was Hyacinth's belief that he himself knew still better how asinine they were;
and this inadequate conception supported in some degree
on Paul's part his theory of his influence—an influence that
would be stronger than any other on the day he should
choose to exert it. Hyacinth only wished that day would
come; it wouldn't be till then, he was sure, that they would
all know where they were and that the good they were
striving for, blindly, obstructedly, in a kind of eternal dirty
intellectual fog, would pass from the stage of crude discussion and mere sore, sharp, tantalising desirableness into that
of solid, seated reality. Muniment was listened to unani-
mously when he spoke and much talked about, usually with
a knowing, implicit allusiveness, when he was absent; it
was generally admitted he could see further than most. But
it was suspected he wanted to see further than was necessary; as one of the most inveterate frequenters of the club
remarked one evening, if a man could see as far as he could
'eave a brick this was far enough. There was an idea he had
nothing particular to complain of personally, or perhaps
that if he had he didn't complain of it—an attitude which
could only contain the germs of a latent disaffection. Hyacinth was aware of being himself exposed to the same
imputation; but he couldn't help it—it would have been
impossible to him to keep up his character for sincerity
by revealing at the 'Sun and Moon' the condition of his
wardrobe or by announcing that he hadn't had a penn'orth
of bacon for six months. There were members of the club
who were apparently always in the enjoyment of involuntary
leisure—narrating the vainest peregrinations in search of a
job, the cruellest rebuffs, the most vivid anecdotes of the
insolence of office. They made Hyacinth uncomfortably
conscious at times that if *he* should be out of work it would

be wholly by his own fault; that he held in his hand a fine bread-winning tool on which he might absolutely count. He was also not unadvised however that his position in this little band of malcontents (it was small only if measured by the numbers gathered on any one occasion; he liked to think it large in its latent possibilities, its mysterious ramifications and affiliations) was peculiar and distinguished: it would be favourable if he should develop the kind of energy and assurance that would help him to make use of it. He had an intimate conviction—the proof of it was in the air, in the sensible facility of his footing at the 'Sun and Moon' —that Eustache Poupin had taken on himself to disseminate the anecdote of his origin, of his mother's disaster; in consequence of which, as the victim of social infamy, of heinous laws, it was conceded to him that he had a larger account to settle even than most. He was *ab ovo* a revolutionist, and that balanced against his smart neckties, a certain suspicious security that was perceived in him as to the *h* (he had had from his earliest years a natural command of it) and the fact that he possessed the sort of hand on which there is always a premium—an accident somehow to be guarded against in a thorough-going system of equality. He never challenged Poupin on the subject, for he owed the Frenchman too much to reproach him with any officious step that was meant in kindness; and moreover his fellow-labourer at old Crook's had said to him, as if to anticipate such an impugnment of his discretion: 'Remember, my child, that I'm incapable of drawing aside any veil that you may have preferred to drop over your lacerated personality. Your moral dignity will always be safe with me. But remember at the same time that among the disinherited there's a mystic language which dispenses with proofs—a freemasonry, a reciprocal divination: they understand each other at half a word.' It was at half a word then in Bloomsbury that Hyacinth had been understood; but there was a certain delicacy in him that forbade him to push his advantage, to treat implications of sympathy, none the less definite for being awkward and obscure, as steps in the ladder of success. He had no wish to be a leader because his mother had murdered her lover and died in penal servitude: these circumstances recommended intentness, but they also imposed modesty. When the gathering at the 'Sun and Moon' was at its best and its temper seemed really an earnest of what was the basis of all its calculations —that the people was only a sleeping lion, already breathing shorter and beginning to stretch its limbs and stiffen its claws—at these hours, some of them thrilling enough, Hyacinth waited for the voice that should allot him the particular part he was to play. His ambition was to play it with brilliancy, to offer an example—an example even that might survive him—of pure youthful, almost juvenile, consecration. He was conscious of no commission to give the promises, to assume the responsibilities, of a redeemer, and he had no envy of the man on whom this burden should rest. Muniment indeed might carry it, and it was the first article of his faith that to help him to carry it the better he himself was ready for any sacrifice. Then it was—on these nights of intenser vibration—that he waited for the sacred sign.

They came oftener this second winter, for the season was terribly hard; and as in that lower world one walked with one's ear nearer the ground the deep perpetual groan of London misery seemed to swell and swell and form the whole undertone of life. The filthy air reached the place in the damp coats of silent men and hung there till it was brewed to a nauseous warmth, and ugly serious faces squared themselves through it, and strong-smelling pipes contributed their element in a fierce dogged manner which appeared to say that it now had to stand for everything— for bread and meat and beer, for shoes and blankets and the poor things at the pawnbroker's and the smokeless chimney at home. Hyacinth's colleagues affected him as wiser then, as more richly permeated with intentions boding ill to the satisfied classes; and though the note of popularity was still most effectively struck by the man who could demand oftenest, unpractically, 'What the hell am I to do with half

a quid?' it was brought home to our hero on more than one
occasion that revolution was ripe at last. This was especially
the case on the evening I began by referring to, when
Eustache Poupin squeezed in and announced, as if it were
a great piece of news, that in the east of London that night
there were forty thousand men out of work. He looked
round the circle with his dilated foreign eye as he took his
place: he seemed to address the company individually as
well as collectively and to make each man responsible for
hearing him. He owed his position at the 'Sun and Moon' to
the brilliancy with which he represented the political exile,
the magnanimous immaculate citizen wrenched out of bed
at dead of night, torn from his hearthstone, his loved ones
and his profession and hurried across the frontier with only
the coat on his back. Poupin had performed in this character
now for many years, but had never lost the bloom of the
outraged proscript, and the passionate pictures he had often
drawn of the bitterness of exile were moving even to those
who knew with what success he had set up his household
gods in Lisson Grove. He was recognised as suffering
everything for his opinions; and his hearers in Bloomsbury,
who even in their most infuriated hours felt as Britons,
appeared never to have made the subtle reflexion, though
they made many others, that there was a want of tact in his
calling on them to sympathise with him for being one of
themselves. He imposed himself by the eloquence of his
assumption that if one were not in the beautiful supreme
France one was nowhere worth speaking of, and ended by
producing an impression that that country had a quite
supernatural charm. Muniment had once said to Hyacinth
that he was sure Poupin would be very sorry to be enabled
to go home again (as he really might from one week to the
other, the Republic being so indulgent and the amnesty
to the Communards constantly extended) for over there he
couldn't be a refugee; and however this might be he
certainly flourished a good deal in London on the basis of
this very fact that he so suffered from it.

'Why do you tell us that as if it was so very striking?

Don't we know it and haven't we known it always? But you're right; we behave as if we knew nothing at all,' said Mr Schinkel, the German cabinet-maker who had originally introduced Captain Sholto to the 'Sun and Moon'. He had a long, unhealthy, benevolent face and greasy hair, and constantly wore an untidy bandage round his neck, as if for a local ailment. 'You remind us—that's very well; but we shall forget it in half an hour. We're not serious.'

'*Pardon, pardon*; for myself I don't admit that!' Poupin replied, striking the table with his finger-tips several times, very fast. 'If I'm not serious I'm nothing.'

'Oh no, you're something,' said the German, smoking his monumental pipe with a contemplative air. 'We're all something, but I'm not sure it's anything very useful.'

'Well, things would be worse without us. I'd jolly rather be in here, in *this* kind of muck, than outside,' remarked the fat man who understood dogs.

'Certainly, it's very pleasant, especially if you've your beer; but not so pleasant over there at the Docks, where fifty thousand people starve. It's a very unpleasant night,' the cabinet-maker went on.

'How can it be worse?' Eustache Poupin asked while he looked at the German as to make him responsible for the fat man's reflexion. 'It's so bad that the imagination recoils, refuses——!'

'Oh, we don't care for the imagination!' the fat man declared. 'We want a compact body in marching order.'

'What do you call a compact body?' the little grey-faced shoemaker demanded. 'I dare say you don't mean your kind of body.'

'Well, I know what I mean,' said the fat man severely.

'That's a grand thing. Perhaps one of these days you'll tell us.'

'You'll see it for yourself perhaps, before that day comes,' the gentleman with the silver ring rejoined. 'Perhaps when you do you'll remember.'

'Well, you know, Schinkel says we don't,' said the shoemaker, nodding at the cloud-compelling German.

'I don't care a bloody rap what no man says!' the dog-fancier exclaimed, gazing straight before him.

'They say it's a bad year—the blockheads in the news-papers,' Mr Schinkel went on, addressing himself to the company at large. 'They say that on purpose—to convey the impression that there are such things as good years. I ask the company, has any gentleman present ever hap-pened to notice that article? The good year's yet to come: it might begin to-night, if we like: it all depends on our being able to be serious for a few hours. But that's too much to expect. Mr Muniment's very serious; he looks as if he was waiting for the signal, but he doesn't speak—he never speaks if I want particularly to hear him. He only deliberates very deeply—oh I'm sure. But it's almost as bad to think without speaking as to speak without thinking.'

Hyacinth always admired the cool, easy way in which Muniment comported himself when the attention of the public was directed at him. These manifestations of curiosity or of hostility would have put him out immensely himself. When a lot of people, especially the kind of people collected at the 'Sun and Moon', looked at him or listened to him all at once, he always blushed and stammered, feel-ing that if he couldn't have a million of spectators (which would have been inspiring) he should prefer to have but two or three; there was something rather awful in twenty.

Muniment smiled an instant good-humouredly; then after a moment's hesitation, looking across at the German and the German only, as if his remark were worth noticing but it didn't matter if the others didn't understand the reply, he said simply: 'Hoffendahl's in London.'

'Hoffendahl? *Gott in Himmel!*' the cabinet-maker exclaimed, taking the pipe out of his mouth. And the two men exchanged a longish glance. Then Mr Schinkel re-marked: 'That surprises me, *sehr*. Are you very sure?'

Muniment continued for a little to look at him. 'If I keep quiet half an hour, with so many valuable suggestions flying all round me, you think I say too little. Then if I open my head to give out three words you appear to think I say too much.'

'Ah no, on the contrary—I want you to say three more. If you tell me you've seen him I shall be perfectly satisfied.'

'Upon my word I should hope so! Do you think he's the kind of bloke a fellow says he has seen?'

'Yes, when he hasn't!' said Eustache Poupin, who had been listening. Every one was listening now.

'It depends on the fellow he says it to. Not even here?' the German asked.

'Oh here!' Paul Muniment exclaimed in a peculiar tone while he resumed his muffled whistle again.

'Take care—take care; you'll make me think you haven't!' cried Poupin with his excited expression.

'That's just what I want,' said Muniment.

'*Nun*, I understand,' the cabinet-maker remarked, restoring his pipe to his lips after an interval almost as momentous as the stoppage of a steamer in mid-ocean.

''*Ere*, 'ere?' repeated the small shoemaker indignantly. 'I dare say it's as good as the place he came from. He might look in and see what he thinks of it.'

'That's a place you might tell us a little about now,' the fat man suggested as if he had been waiting for his chance.

Before the shoemaker had time to notice this challenge some one enquired with a hoarse petulance who the bloody blazes they were talking about; and Mr Schinkel took upon himself to reply that they were talking about a man who hadn't done what he had done by simply exchanging abstract ideas, however valuable, with his friends in a respectable pot-house.

'What the devil has he done then?' some one else demanded; and Muniment replied quietly that he had spent twelve years in a Prussian prison and was consequently still an object of a good deal of interest to the police.

'Well, if you call that very useful I must say I prefer a pot-house!' cried the shoemaker, appealing to all the company and looking, as it appeared to Hyacinth, particularly hideous.

'*Doch, doch*, it's useful,' the German remarked philosophically among his yellow clouds.

'Do you mean to say you're not prepared for that yourself?' Muniment asked of the shoemaker.

'Prepared for that? I thought we were going to smash that sort of shop altogether; I thought that was the main part of the job.'

'They'll smash best who've been inside,' the German said; 'unless they've only gone bad, like fish too long caught. But Hoffendahl's all there yet.'

'Ah no; no smashing, no smashing of any valuable property,' Muniment went on. 'There are no wrong places —there are only wrong uses for them. We want to keep them standing and even to put up a few more; but the difference will be that we shall put the correct sort into them.'

'I take your idea—that Griffin's one of the correct sort,' the fat man remarked, indicating the shoemaker.

'I thought we was going to 'ave their 'eads—all that bloomin' lot!' Mr Griffin protested; while Eustache Poupin began to enlighten the company as to the great Hoffendahl, one of the purest martyrs of their cause, a man who had been through everything—who had been scarred and branded, tortured, almost flayed, and had never given his would-be butchers the names they wanted. Was it possible they didn't remember that great combined assault, early in the sixties, which took place in four Continental cities at once and which in spite of every effort to smother it up— there had been editors and journalists transported even for hinting at it—had done more for the social question than anything before or since? 'Through 'im being served in the manner you describe?' some one asked with plainness; to which Poupin replied that it was one of those failures that are more glorious than any success. Muniment said that the affair had been only a flash in the pan, but that the great value of it was this—that whereas some forty persons (and of both sexes) had been engaged in it, only one had been seized and had suffered. It had been Hoffendahl himself who was collared. Certainly he had suffered much, he had suffered for every one; but from that point of view—that of the economy of material—the thing had been a rare success.

'Do you know what I call the others? I call 'em bloody sneaks!' the fat man cried; and Eustache Poupin, turning to Muniment, expressed the hope that he didn't really approve of such a solution—didn't consider that an economy of heroism was an advantage to any cause. He himself esteemed Hoffendahl's attempt because it had shaken, more than anything—except of course the Commune—had shaken it since the French Revolution, the rotten fabric of the actual social order, and because that very fact of the impunity, the invisibility of the persons concerned in it had given the predatory classes, had given all Europe, a shudder that had not yet subsided; but for his part, he must regret that some of the associates of the devoted victim had not come forward and insisted on sharing with him his tortures and his captivity.

'Ç'aurait été d'un bel exemple!' said the Frenchman with an impressive moderation of statement which made even those who couldn't understand him see he was saying something fine; while the cabinet-maker observed that in Hoffendahl's place any of them would have stood out just the same. He didn't care if they set it down to self-love (Mr Schinkel called it 'loaf') but he might say that he himself would have done so if he had been trusted and had been bagged.

'I want to have it all drawn up clear first; then I'll go in,' said the fat man, who seemed to think it was expected of him to be reassuring.

'Well, who the dickens is to draw it up, eh? That's what we happen to be talking about,' returned his antagonist the shoemaker.

'A fine example, old man? Is that your idea of a fine example?' Muniment, with his amused face, asked of Poupin. 'A fine example of asininity! Are there capable people, in such plenty, about the place?'

'Capable of greatness of soul, I grant you not.'

'Your greatness of soul is usually greatness of blundering. A man's foremost duty is not to get collared. If you want to show you're capable, that's the way.'

At this Hyacinth suddenly felt himself moved to speak. 'But some one must be caught always, must he not? Hasn't some one always been?'

'Oh, I dare say you'll be if you like it!' Muniment replied without looking at him. 'If they succeed in potting you, do as Hoffendahl did, and do it as a matter of course; but if they don't, make it your supreme duty, make it your religion, to lie close and keep yourself for another go. The world's full of unclean beasts whom I shall be glad to see shovelled away by the thousand; but when it's a question of honest men and men of courage I protest against the idea that two should be sacrificed where one will serve.'

'*Trop d'arithmétique—trop d'arithmétique!*—That's fearfully English!' Poupin cried.

'No doubt, no doubt; what else should it be? You shall never share my fate if I have a fate and I can prevent it!' Muniment laughed.

Poupin stared at him and his coarse mirth, as if he thought the English frivolous as well as calculating; then he rejoined: 'If I suffer I trust it may be for suffering humanity, but I trust it may also be for France.'

'Oh, I hope you ain't going to suffer any more for France,' said Mr Griffin. 'Hasn't it done that insatiable old country of yours some good by this time, all you've had to put up with?'

'Well, I want to know what Hoffendahl has come over for; it's very kind of him, I'm sure. What's he going to do for *us*?—that's what *I* want to know,' brought out in a loud argumentative tone a personage at the end of the table most distant from Muniment's place. His name was Delancey and he gave himself out as holding a position in a manufactory of soda-water; but Hyacinth had a secret belief that he was really a hairdresser—a belief connected with a high lustrous curl or crest which he wore on the summit of his large head, as well as with the manner in which he thrust

over his ear, as if it were a barber's comb, the pencil
addressed to his careful note-taking on the discussions conducted at the 'Sun and Moon'. His opinions were distinct
and frequently expressed; he had a watery (Muniment had
once called it a soda-watery) eye and a personal aversion to
a lord. He desired to change everything except religion, of
which he approved.

Muniment answered that he was unable to say as yet
what the German revolutionist had come to England for,
but that he hoped to be able to give some information on
the matter the next time they should meet. It was very
certain Hoffendahl hadn't come for nothing, and he would
undertake to declare that they should all feel within a short
time that he had given a lift to the cause they had at heart.
He had had a great experience, which they might very well
find it useful to appeal to. If there was a way for them then
and there he would be sure to know the way. 'I quite agree
with the majority of you—as I take it to be,' Muniment
went on in his fresh, cheerful, reasonable manner—'I quite
agree with you that the time has come to settle upon it and
to follow it. I quite agree with you that the actual state of
things is'—he paused a moment and then went on in the
same pleasant tone—'is infamous and hellish.'

These remarks were received with a differing demonstration: some of the company declaring that if the Dutchman
cared to come round and smoke a pipe they'd be glad to see
him—perhaps he'd show where the thumbscrews had been
put on; others being strongly of the opinion that they didn't
want any more advice—they had already had advice enough
to turn a donkey's stomach. What they wanted was to put
forth their might without any more palaver; to do for
something or for some one; to go out somewhere and smash
something on the spot—why not?—smash it that very
night. While they sat still and talked there were about half
a million of people in London that didn't know where the
hell the morrow's meal was to come from; what they wanted
to do, unless they were just a collection of pettifogging old
women, was to show them where to get it, to take it to

them with heaped-up hands. Hyacinth listened, with a divided attention, to interlaced iterations, while the talk blew hot and cold; there was a genuine emotion, a quick pulse of high fever, to-night in the rear of the 'Sun and Moon', and he felt the contagion of excited purpose. But he was following a train of his own; he was wondering what Muniment had in reserve (for certainly Paul but played with the company) and his imagination, quickened by the sense of impending relations with the heroic Hoffendahl and the discussion as to the alternative duty of escaping or of facing one's fate, had launched itself into possible perils— into the idea of how he might in a given case settle for himself that question of paying for the lot. The loud, contradictory, vain, unpractical babble went on about him, but he was definitely conscious only that the project of breaking into the bakers' shops was well before the assembly and was receiving a vigorous treatment, and that there was likewise a good deal of reference to the butchers and grocers and even to the fishmongers. He was in a state of inward exaltation, possessed by an intense desire to stand face to face with the sublime Hoffendahl, to hear his voice and touch his mutilated hand. He was ready for anything: he knew he was himself safe to breakfast and dine, if poorly still sufficiently, and that his colleagues were perhaps even more crude and clumsy than usual; but a breath of popular passion had warmed his cheek and his heart, and he seemed to see, immensely magnified, the monstrosity of the great ulcers and sores of London—the sick, eternal misery crying out the darkness in vain, confronted with granaries and treasure-houses and places of delight where shameless satiety kept guard. In such a mood as this he felt there was no need to consider, to reason: the facts themselves were as imperative as the cry of the drowning, since while pedantry gained time didn't starvation and anguish gain it too? He knew Muniment disapproved of delay, that he held the day had come for a forcible rectification of horrible inequalities. In the last conversation they had had together his judicious friend had given him a more definite warrant than ever before for numbering him in the party of immediate action, though indeed he remarked on this occasion, once more, that that particular formula the little bookbinder appeared to have taken such a fancy to was mere gibberish. He hated this sort of pretentious label; it was fit only for politicians and amateurs. None the less he had been as plain as possible on the point that their game must be now to frighten society, and frighten it effectually; to make it believe that the swindled classes were at last fairly in league—had really grasped the idea that, closely combined, they would be irresistible. They were not in league and they hadn't in their totality grasped any idea at all—Muniment was not slow to make that equally plain. All the same society was scareable, and every great scare was a gain for the people. If Hyacinth had needed warrant to-night for a faith transcending logic he would have found it in his recall of this quiet profession; but his friend's words came back to him mainly to make him wonder what that friend had in his head just now. He took no part in any vociferation; he had called Schinkel to come round and sit beside him, and the two appeared to confer together in honest ease while the brown atmosphere grew denser, the passing to and fro of firebrands more lively and the flush of faces more portentous. What Hyacinth would have liked to know most of all was why Muniment had not mentioned to him first that Hoffendahl was in London and that he had seen him; for he *had* seen him, though he had dodged Schinkel's question—of that Hyacinth instantly felt sure. He would ask for more information later; and meanwhile he wished, without resentment, but with a patient conscious ache, that Muniment would treat him with a little more confidence. If there were a secret in regard to Hoffendahl—and there evidently was: Muniment, quite rightly, though he had dropped the announcement of his arrival for a certain effect, had no notion of sharing the rest of what he knew with that raw roomful—if there were something to be silent and devoted about Hyacinth ardently hoped that to him in particular would a chance be given to show how he could practise this superiority. He felt hot and nervous; he got up suddenly and, through the dark tortuous greasy passage communicating with the outer world, went forth into the street. The air was foul and sleety but refreshed him, and he stood in front of the public-house and smoked another pipe. Bedraggled figures passed in and out and a damp tattered wretched man with a spongy purple face, who had been thrust suddenly across the threshold, stood and whimpered in the brutal blaze of the row of lamps. The puddles glittered roundabout and the silent vista of the street, bordered with low black houses, stretched away in the wintry drizzle to right and left, losing itself in the huge tragic city where unmeasured misery lurked beneath the dirty night, ominously, monstrously still, only howling, for its pain, in the heated human cockpit behind him. Ah what could he do? What opportunity would rise? The blundering divided counsels he had been listening to but made the helplessness of every one concerned more abject. If he had a definite wish while he stood there it was that that exalted deluded company should pour itself forth with Muniment at its head and surge through the sleeping world and gather the myriad miserable out of their slums and burrows, should roll into the selfish squares and lift a tremendous hungry voice and awaken the gorged indifferent to a terror that would bring them down. He lingered a quarter of an hour, but this grand treat gave no sign of coming off, and he finally returned to the noisy club-room in a state of tormented wonder as to what better idea than this very bad one (which seemed to our young man to have at the least the merit that it *was* an idea) Muniment could be revolving in that too-comprehensive brain of his.

As he re-entered the place he saw the meeting was breaking up in disorder, or at all events in confusion, and that certainly no organised attempt at the rescue of any number of victims would take place that night. All the men were on their feet and were turning away amid a shuffle of benches and chairs, a hunch of shabby shoulders, a frugal abatement of flaring gas and a varied vivacity of disgust and

resignation. The moment after Hyacinth came in Mr
Delancey, the supposititious hairdresser, jumped upon a
chair at the far end of the room and shrieked out an accusation which made every one stop and stare at him.

'Well, I want you all to know what strikes me before we
part company. There isn't a man in the blessed lot of you
that isn't afraid of his bloody skin—afraid, afraid, afraid!
I'll go anywhere with any one, but there isn't another, by
G——, by what I can make out! There isn't a mother's son
of you that'll risk his precious bones!'

This little oration affected Hyacinth like a quick blow in
the face: it seemed to leap at him personally, as if a three-
legged stool or some hideous hob-nailed boot had been shied
at him. The room surged round, heaving up and down,
while he was conscious of a loud explosion of laughter and
scorn, of cries of 'Order, order!' of some clear word of
Muniment's, 'I say, Delancey, just step down'; of Eustache
Poupin shouting out '*Vous insultez le peuple—vous insultez
le peuple!*' of other retorts not remarkable for refinement.
The next moment he found he had himself sprung up on a
chair opposite the barber and that at the sight of so prompt
a display the commotion had suddenly turned to almost
amused suspense. It was the first time he had asked the ear
of the company, which was given on the spot. He was sure
he looked very white—it was even possible they could see
him tremble. He could only hope this didn't make him
ridiculous when he said: 'I don't think it's right of him to
say that. There are others besides him. At all events I want
to speak for myself: it may do some good; I can't help it.
I'm not afraid; I'm very sure I'm not. I'm ready to do anything that will do any good; anything, anything—I don't
care a damned rap. I don't consider my bones precious in
the least, compared with some other things. If one's sure
one isn't afraid, and one's accused, why shouldn't one say
so?'

It appeared to him he was talking a long time and when
it was over he scarcely knew what happened. He felt himself
in a moment down almost under the feet of the other men;

stamped upon with intentions of applause, of familiarity; laughed over and jeered over, hustled and poked in the ribs. He felt himself also pressed to the bosom of Eustache Poupin, who apparently was sobbing, while he heard some one say 'Did ye hear the little bloody beggar, as bold as a lion?' A trial of personal prowess between him and Mr Delancey was proposed, but somehow it didn't take place, and at the end of five minutes the club-room had emptied itself, yet clearly not to be reconstituted outside in a revolutionary procession. Paul Muniment had taken hold of him and said 'I'll trouble you to stay, you small desperado: I'll be blowed if I ever expected to see *you* on the stump!' Muniment remained and M. Poupin and Mr Schinkel lingered, donning overcoats, beneath a dim surviving gas-burner in the unventilated medium in which at each renewed gathering the Bloomsbury club seemed to recognise itself.

'Upon my life I believe you're game,' said Muniment, looking down at him with a serious face.

'Of course you think it's swagger, "self-loaf" as Schinkel says. But it isn't.' Then Hyacinth asked: 'In God's name why don't we do something?'

'Ah my child, to whom do you say it?' Eustache Poupin exclaimed, folding his arms despairingly.

'Who do you mean by "we"?' said Muniment.

'All the lot of us. There are plenty of them ready.'

'Ready for what? There's nothing to be done here.'

Hyacinth stared. 'Then why the deuce do you come?'

'I dare say I shan't come much more. It's a place in which you've always seen too much.'

'I wonder if I've seen too much in you,' Hyacinth risked, gazing at his friend.

'Don't say that—he's going to introduce us to Hoffendahl!' Schinkel exclaimed, putting away his pipe in a receptacle almost as large as a fiddle-case.

'Should you like to see the right man, Robinson, that is the real thing?' Muniment asked with the same rare grave sound.

'The real thing?' Hyacinth looked from one of his companions to the other.

'You've never seen it yet—though you think you have.'

'And why haven't you shown it me before?'

'Because I had never seen you on the stump.' This was more lightly said.

'Bother the stump! I was trusting you.'

'Exactly so. That gave me time.'

'Don't come unless your mind's made up, *mon petit*,' said Poupin.

'Are you going now—and to see Hoffendahl? Is *he* the right man?' Hyacinth cried.

'Don't shout it all over the place. He wants a perfect little gentleman, and if you're not one——!' Muniment went on.

'Is it true? Are we all going?' Hyacinth eagerly went on.

'Yes, these two are in it. They're not very wise, but they're decent,' said Muniment, looking at Poupin and Schinkel.

'Are *you* the real thing, Muniment?' asked Hyacinth, catching this look.

Muniment dropped his eyes on him. 'Yes, you're the lamb of sacrifice he wants. It's at the other end of London. We must have a growler.'

'Be calm, my child; *me voici!*' And Poupin led their young friend out.

They all walked away from the 'Sun and Moon', and it was not for some five minutes that they encountered the four-wheeled cab which so deepened and dignified their purpose. After they were seated in it Hyacinth learned that the 'right man' was in London but for three days, was liable to hurry away on the morrow, and was accustomed to receive visits at all kinds of queer hours. It was getting to be midnight; the drive seemed interminable to Hyacinth's impatience and curiosity. He sat next Muniment, who passed a strong arm round him, holding him all the way as if for a tacit sign of indebtedness. This gave Hyacinth pleasure till he began to wonder if it mightn't represent also the instinct to make sure of him as against possible weak afterthoughts. They all ended by sitting silent as the cab jogged along murky miles, and by the time it stopped our young man had wholly lost, in the drizzling gloom, a sense of their whereabouts.

BOOK THIRD

BOOK THIRD

XXII

HYACINTH GOT up early—an operation attended with very little effort, as he had scarce closed his eyes all night. What he saw from his window made him dress as quickly as a young man might who desired more than ever that his appearance shouldn't give strange ideas about him: an old garden with parterres in curious figures and little intervals of lawn that seemed to our hero's cockney vision fantastically green. At one end of the garden was a parapet of mossy brick which looked down on the other side into a canal, a moat, a quaint old pond (he hardly knew what to call it) and from the same standpoint showed a considerable part of the main body of the house—Hyacinth's room belonging to a wing that commanded the extensive irregular back—which was richly grey wherever clear of the ivy and the other dense creepers, and everywhere infinitely a picture: with a high-piled ancient russet roof broken by huge chimneys and queer peep-holes and all manner of odd gables and windows on different lines, with all manner of antique patches and protrusions and with a particularly fascinating architectural excrescence where a wonderful clock-face was lodged, a clock-face covered with gilding and blazonry but showing many traces of the years and the weather. He had never in his life been in the country—the real country, as he called it, the country which was not the mere ravelled fringe of London—and there entered through his open casement the breath of a world enchantingly new and after his recent feverish hours unspeakably refreshing; a sense of sweet sunny air and mingled odours, all strangely pure and agreeable, and of a musical silence that consisted for the greater part of the voices of many birds. There were tall quiet trees near by and afar off and everywhere; and the group of objects that greeted his eyes evidently formed only a corner of larger spaces and of a more complicated scene.

There was a world to be revealed to him: it lay waiting with the dew on it under his windows, and he must go down and take of it such possession as he might.

On his arrival at ten o'clock the night before he had only got the impression of a mile-long stretch of park, after turning in at a gate; of the cracking of gravel under the wheels of the fly and of the glow of several windows, suggesting indoor cheer, in a front that lifted a range of vague grand effects into the starlight. It was much of a relief to him then to be informed that the Princess, in consideration of the lateness of the hour, begged to be excused till the morrow: the delay would give him time to recover his balance and look about him. This latter opportunity was offered first as he sat at supper in a vast high hall with the butler, whose acquaintance he had made in South Street, behind his chair. He had not exactly wondered how he should be treated: too blank for that his conception of the way in which, at a country-house, invidious distinctions might be made and shades of importance marked; but it was plain the best had been ordered for him. He was at all events abundantly content with his reception and more and more excited by it. The repast was delicate—though his other senses were so awake that hunger dropped out and he ate, as it were, without eating—and the grave automatic servant filled his glass with a liquor that reminded him of some lines of Keats in the 'Ode to a Nightingale'. He wondered if he should hear a nightingale at Medley (he was vague about the seasons of this vocalist) and also if the butler would attempt to talk to him, had ideas about him, knew or suspected who he was and what: which after all there was no reason for his doing save perhaps the aspect of the scant luggage attending the visitor from Lomax Place. Mr Withers however (it was this name Hyacinth heard used by the driver of his fly) had given no further symptom of sociability than to ask him at what time he would be called in the morning; to which our young man replied that he preferred not to be called at all—he would get up by himself. The butler rejoined 'Very good, sir', while Hyacinth thought it probable he puzzled him a good deal and even considered the question of giving him a precautionary glimpse of an identity that might be later on less fortunately betrayed. The object of this diplomacy was that he should not be oppressed and embarrassed with attentions to which he was unused; but the idea came to nothing for the simple reason that before he spoke he found himself liking what he had feared. His impulse to deprecate services departed, he was already aware there were none he should care to miss or was not quite prepared for. He knew he had probably thanked Mr Withers too much, but he couldn't help this—it was an irrepressible tendency and an error he should doubtless always commit.

He had lain in a bed constituted in a manner so perfect to ensure rest that it was naturally responsible in some degree for his want of ease, and in a large high room where long dressing-glasses emitted ghostly glances even after the light was extinguished. Suspended on the walls were many prints, mezzotints and old engravings which he supposed, possibly without reason, to be of the finest and rarest. He got up several times in the night, lighted his candle and walked about looking at them. He looked at himself in one of the long glasses, and in a place where every-thing was on such a scale it seemed to him more than ever that Mademoiselle Vivier's son, lacking all the social dimensions, was scarce a perceptible person at all. As he came downstairs he encountered housemaids with dusters and brooms, or perceived them through open doors on their knees before fireplaces; and it was his belief that they regarded him more boldly than if he had been a guest of the usual kind. Such a reflexion as that, however, ceased to trouble him after he had passed out of doors and begun to roam through the park, into which he let himself loose at first, and then, in narrowing circles, through the nearer grounds. He rambled an hour in breathless ecstasy, brush-ing the dew from the deep fern and bracken and the rich borders of the garden, tasting the fragrant air and stopping everywhere, in murmuring rapture, at the touch of some

exquisite impression. His whole walk was peopled with
recognitions; he had been dreaming all his life of just such
a place and such objects, such a morning and such a chance.
It was the last of April and everything was fresh and vivid;
the great trees, in the early air, were a blur of tender shoots.
Round the admirable house he revolved repeatedly, catching
every aspect and feeling every value, feasting on the whole
expression and wondering if the Princess would observe his
proceedings from a window and if they would be offensive
to her. The house was not hers, but only hired for three
months, and it could flatter no princely pride that he should
be struck with it. There was something in the way the grey
walls rose from the green lawn that brought tears to his
eyes; the spectacle of long duration unassociated with some
sordid infirmity or poverty was new to him; he had lived
with people among whom old age meant for the most part
a grudged and degraded survival. In the favoured resistance
of Medley was a serenity of success, an accumulation of
dignity and honour.

A footman sought him out in the garden to tell him
breakfast was served. He had never thought of breakfast,
and as he walked back to the house attended by the inscrutable flunkey this offer appeared a free extravagant gift, unexpected and romantic. He found he was to breakfast alone
and asked no questions, but when he had finished the butler
came in to say that the Princess would see him after
luncheon but that in the mean while she wished him to
understand the library to be all at his service. 'After
luncheon'—that threw the hour he had come for very far
into the future, and it caused him some bewilderment that
she should think it worth while to invite him to stay with
her from Saturday evening to Monday morning only to let
so much of his visit elapse without their meeting. But he
felt neither slighted nor impatient; the impressions already
crowding on him were in themselves a sufficient reward,
and what could one do better precisely in such a house as
that than wait for a wonderful lady? Mr Withers conducted
him to the library and left him planted in the middle of it

and staring at the treasures he quickly and widely took in. It was an old brown room of great extent—even the ceiling was brown, though there were figures in it dimly gilt—where row upon row of finely-lettered backs consciously appealed for recognition. A fire of logs crackled in a great chimney, and there were alcoves with deep window-seats, and arm-chairs such as he had never seen, luxurious, leather-covered, with an adjustment for holding one's volume; and a vast writing-table before one of the windows, furnished with a perfect magazine of paper and pens, ink-stands and blotters, seals, stamps, candlesticks, reels of twine, paperweights, book-knives. He had never imagined so many aids to correspondence and before he turned away had written a note to Millicent in a hand even nobler than usual—his penmanship was very minute, but at the same time wonderfully free and fair—largely for the pleasure of seeing 'Medley Hall' stamped in heraldic-looking red characters at the top of his paper. In the course of an hour he had ravaged the collection, taken down almost every book, wishing he could keep it a week, and then put it back as quickly as his eye caught the next, which glowed with a sharper challenge. He came upon rare bindings and extracted precious hints—hints by which he felt himself perfectly capable of profiting. Altogether his vision of true happiness at this moment was that for a month or two he should be locked into the treasure-house of Medley. He forgot the outer world and the morning waned—the beautiful vernal Sunday—while he lingered there.

He was on the top of a ladder when he heard a voice remark, 'I'm afraid they're very dusty; in this house, you know, it's the dust of centuries,' and, looking down, saw Madame Grandoni posted in the middle of the room. He instantly prepared to descend and greet her, but she exclaimed: 'Stay, stay, if you're not giddy; we can talk from here! I only came in to show you we *are* in the house and to tell you to keep up your patience. The Princess will probably see you in a few hours.'

'I really hope so,' he returned from his perch, rather dismayed at the 'probably'.

'*Natürlich*,' said the old lady; 'but people have come sometimes and gone away without seeing her. It all depends on her mood.'

'Do you mean even when she has sent for them?'

'Oh who can tell whether she has sent for them or not?'

'But she sent for me, you know,' Hyacinth declared, staring down and struck with the odd effect of Madame Grandoni's wig in that bird's-eye view.

'Oh yes, she sent for you, poor young man!' The old lady looked up at him with a smile and they communicated a little in silence. Then she added: 'Captain Sholto has come like that more than once and has gone away no better off.'

'Captain Sholto?' Hyacinth repeated.

'Very true, if we talk at this distance I must shut the door.' She retraced her course while he watched her, and pushed it to, then advanced into the room again with her superannuated, shuffling step, walking as if her shoes were too big for her. Hyacinth moreover descended the ladder. 'There it is. She's a *capricciosa*.'

'I don't understand how you speak of her,' Hyacinth remarked gravely. 'You seem her friend, yet you say things not favourable to her.'

'Dear young man, I say much worse to her about herself than I should ever say to you. I'm rude, oh yes—even to you, to whom, no doubt, I ought to be particularly kind. But I'm not false. That's not our German nature. You'll hear me some day. I *am* the friend of the Princess; it would be well enough if she never had a worse one! But I should like to be yours too—what will you have? Perhaps it's of no use. At any rate here you are.'

'Yes, here I am decidedly!' Hyacinth uneasily laughed.

'And how long shall you stay? Pardon me if I ask that; it's part of my rudeness.'

'I shall stay till to-morrow morning. I must be at my work by noon.'

'That will do very well. Don't you remember, the other time, how I told you to remain faithful?'

'That was very good advice. But I think you exaggerate my danger.'

'So much the better,' said Madame Grandoni; 'though now that I look at you well I doubt it a little. I see you're one of those types that ladies like. I can be sure of that— I like you myself. At my age—a hundred and twenty— can't I say that? If the Princess were to do so it would be different; remember that—that any flattery she may ever offer you will be on her lips much less discreet. But perhaps she will never have the chance; you may never come again. There are people who have come only once. *Vedremo bene.* I must tell you that I'm not in the least against a young man's taking a holiday, a little quiet recreation, once in a while,' Madame Grandoni continued in her disconnected discursive confidential way. 'In Rome they take one every five days; that's no doubt too often. In Germany less often. In this country I can't understand if it's an increase of effort: the English Sunday's so difficult! This one will in any case have been beautiful for you. Be happy, make yourself comfortable; but go home to-morrow!' And with this injunction Madame Grandoni took her way again to the door while he went to open it for her. 'I can say that because it's not my house. I'm only here like you. And sometimes I think I also shall go to-morrow!'

'I imagine you've not, like me, your living to get every day. That's reason enough for me,' said Hyacinth.

She paused in the doorway with her expressive ugly kindly little eyes on his face. 'I believe I'm nearly as poor as you. And I've not, like you, the appearance of nobility. Yet I'm noble,' said the old lady, shaking her wig.

'And I'm not!' Hyacinth deeply smiled.

'It's better not to be lifted up high like our friend. It doesn't give happiness.'

'Not to one's self possibly; but to others!' From where they stood he looked out into the great panelled and decorated hall, lighted from above and roofed with a far-away dim fresco, and the reflexion of this grandeur came into his appreciative eyes.

'Do you admire everything here very much—do you receive great pleasure?' asked Madame Grandoni.

'Oh, so much—so much!'

She considered him a moment longer. '*Poverino!*' she murmured as she turned away.

A couple of hours later the Princess sent for him and he was conducted upstairs, through corridors carpeted with crimson and hung with pictures, and ushered into a large bright saloon which he afterwards learned that his hostess used as a boudoir. The sound of music had come to him outside the door, so that he was prepared to find her seated at the piano, if not to see her continue to play after he appeared. Her face was turned in the direction from which he entered, and she smiled at him without lifting her hands from the keys while the servant, as if he had just arrived, formally pronounced his name. The room, placed in an angle of the house and lighted from two sides, was large and sunny, upholstered in fresh gay chintz, furnished with all sorts of sofas and low familiar seats and convenient little tables, most of these holding great bowls of early flowers; littered over with books, newspapers, magazines, photographs of celebrities slashed across by signatures, and full of the marks of luxurious and rather indolent habitation. Hyacinth stood there, not advancing very far, and the Princess, still playing and smiling, nodded toward a seat near the piano. 'Put yourself there and listen to me.' He did so and she played a long time without glancing at him. This left him the more free to rest his eyes on her own face and person while she looked about the room, vaguely, absently, but with an expression of quiet happiness, as if lost in her music, soothed and pacified by it. A window near her was half-open and the soft clearness of the day and all the odour of the spring diffused themselves and made the place cheerful and pure. The Princess struck him as extraordinarily young and fair, and she seemed so slim and simple, and so friendly too, in spite of having neither abandoned her occupation nor offered him her hand, that he at last sank back in his seat with the sense that all his uneasiness, his nervous tension, was leaving him, and that he was safe in her kindness, in the free original way with which she evidently would always treat him. This peculiar manner, half consideration, half fellowship, seemed to him to have already so mild and wise an intention. She played ever so movingly, with different pieces succeeding each other; he had never listened to music nor to a talent of that order. Two or three times she turned her eyes on him, and then they shone with the wonderful expression which was the essence of her beauty; that profuse mingled light which seemed to belong to some everlasting summer and yet to suggest seasons that were past and gone, some experience that was only an exquisite memory. She asked him if he cared for music and then added, laughing, that she ought to have made sure of this before; while he answered—he had already told her so in South Street, but she appeared to have forgotten—that he was awfully fond of it.

The sense of the beauty of women had been given to our young man in a high degree; it was a faculty that made him conscious to adoration of all the forces of that power and depths of that mystery; of every element of loveliness, every delicacy of feature, every shade and tone that contributed to charm. Therefore even if he had appreciated less the strange harmonies the Princess drew from her instrument and her genius there would have been no lack of interest in his situation, in such an opportunity to watch her admirable outline and movement, the noble form of her head and face, the gathered-up glories of her hair, the living flower-like freshness which had no need to turn from the light. She was dressed in fair colours and as simply as a young girl. Before she ceased playing she asked him what he would like to do in the afternoon: would he have any objection to taking a drive with her? It was very possible he might enjoy the country. She seemed not to attend to his answer, which was covered by the sound of the piano; but if she had done so it would have left her very little doubt as to the reality of his inclination. She remained gazing at the cornice of the room while her hands wandered to and fro; then suddenly she stopped, got up and came toward him. 'It's probable that's the most I shall ever bore you. You know the worst. Would you very kindly close the piano?' He complied with her request and she went to another part of the room and sank into an arm-chair. When he approached her again she said: 'Is it really true that you've never seen a park nor a garden nor any of the beauties of nature and that sort of thing?' The allusion was to something gravely stated in his letter when he answered the note by which she proposed to him to run down to Medley, and after he had assured her it was perfectly true she exclaimed: 'I'm so glad—I'm so glad! I've never been able to show any one anything new and have always felt I should like it—especially with a fine sensitive mind. Then you *will* come and drive with me?' She spoke as if this would be a great favour.

That was the beginning of the communion—so strange considering their respective positions—which he had come to Medley to enjoy, and it passed into some singular phases. The Princess had an extraordinary way of taking things for granted, of ignoring difficulties, of assuming that her preferences might be translated into fact. After her guest had remained with her ten minutes longer—a period mainly occupied with her exclamations of delight at his having seen so little of the sort of thing of which Medley consisted (Where should he have seen it, gracious heaven? he asked himself); after she had rested thus briefly from her exertions at the piano she proposed that they should go out-of-doors together. She was an immense walker—she wanted her regular walk. She left him for a short time, giving him the last number of the *Revue des Deux Mondes* to entertain himself withal and calling his attention in particular to a story by M. Octave Feuillet (she should be so curious to know what he thought of it); to reappear later with dark hat and clear parasol, drawing on fresh loose gloves and offering herself to our young man at that moment as a sudden incarnation of the heroine of M. Feuillet's novel, in which

he had instantly become immersed. On their way downstairs
it occurred to her that he had not yet seen the house and
that it would be amusing for her to show it him; so she
turned aside and took him through it, up and down and
everywhere, even into the vast old-fashioned kitchen where
they found a small red-faced man in a white jacket and
apron and a white cap (he removed the latter ornament to
salute the little bookbinder) with whom his companion spoke
Italian, which Hyacinth understood sufficiently to perceive
that she addressed her cook in the second person singular,
as if he had been a feudal retainer. He remembered how it
was in the same way the three Musketeers spoke to their
lackeys. The Princess explained that the gentleman in the
white cap was a delightful creature (she couldn't endure
English servants, though she was obliged to have two or
three) who would make her plenty of risottos and polentas
—she had quite the palate of a contadina. She showed
Hyacinth everything: the queer transmogrified corner that
had once been a chapel; the secret stairway which had served
in the persecutions of the Catholics (the owners of Medley
were, like the Princess herself, of the old persuasion); the
musicians' gallery over the hall; the tapestried room which
people came from a distance to see; and the haunted chamber (the two, sometimes confounded, were quite distinct)
where a horrible figure at certain times made its appearance
—a dwarfish ghost with an enormous head, a dispossessed
eldest brother of long ago who had passed for an idiot, which
he wasn't, and had somehow been made away with. The
Princess offered her visitor the privilege of sleeping in this
apartment, declaring however that nothing would induce
her even to enter it alone, she being a benighted creature,
consumed with abject superstitions. 'I don't know if I'm
religious or whether if I were my religion would be superstitious, but my superstitions are what I'm faithful to.' She
made her young friend pass through the drawing-room very
cursorily, remarking that they should see it again: it was
rather stupid—drawing-rooms in English country-houses
were always stupid; indeed if it would amuse him they

would sit there after dinner. Madame Grandoni and she usually sat upstairs, but they would do anything he should find more comfortable.

At last they came out of the house together and while they went she explained, to justify herself against the imputation of extravagance, that, though the place doubtless struck him as absurdly large for a couple of quiet women and the whole thing was not in the least what she would have preferred, yet it was all far cheaper than he probably imagined; she would never have looked at it if it hadn't been cheap. It must appear to him so preposterous for a woman to associate herself with the great uprising of the poor and yet live in palatial halls—a place with forty or fifty rooms. This was one of her only two allusions as yet to her infatuation with the 'cause'; but it fell very happily, for Hyacinth had not been unconscious of the anomaly she mentioned. It had been present to him all day; it added much to the way of life practised on his sense of the tragi-comical to think of the Princess's having retired to a private paradise to think out the problem of the slums. He listened therefore with great attention while she made all conscientiously the point that she had taken the house only for three months in any case, because she wanted to rest after a winter of visiting and living in public (as the English spent their lives, with all their celebrated worship of the 'home') and yet didn't wish too soon to return to town; though she was obliged to confess that she had still the place in South Street on her hands, thanks to her deciding unexpectedly to go on with it rather than move out her things. One had to keep one's things somewhere, and why wasn't that as good a *dépôt* as another? Medley was not what she would have chosen if she had been left to herself; but she had not been left to herself—she never was; she had been bullied into taking it by the owners, whom she had met somewhere and who had made up to her immensely, persuading her that she might really have it for nothing, for no more than she would give for the little honeysuckle cottage, the old parsonage embowered in clematis, which were really what she had been looking for. Besides, it was one of those old musty mansions, ever so far from town, which it was alway difficult to let or to get a price for; and then it was a wretched house for any convenience. Hyacinth, for whom his three hours in the train had been a series of happy throbs, had not been struck with its geographic remoteness, and he asked the Princess what she meant in such a connexion by her use of the word 'wretched'. To this she replied that the place was tumbling to pieces, impossible in every respect, full of ghosts and bad smells. 'That's the only reason I come to have it. I don't want you to think me so sunk in luxury or that I throw away money. Never, never!' Hyacinth had no standard by which he could measure the importance his opinion would have for her, and he saw that though she judged him as a creature still open to every initiation, whose *naïveté* would entertain her, it was also her fancy to treat him as an old friend, a person to whom she might have had the habit of referring her difficulties. Her performance of the part she had undertaken to play was certainly complete, and everything lay before him but the reason she might have for playing it.

One of the gardens at Medley took the young man's heart beyond the others; it had high brick walls, on the sunny sides of which was a great training of apricots and plums; it had straight walks bordered with old-fashioned homely flowers and enclosing immense squares where other fruit-trees stood upright and mint and lavender floated in the air. In the southern quarter it overhung a small disused canal, and here a high embankment had been raised, which was also long and broad and covered with fine turf; so that the top of it, looking down at the canal, made a magnificent grassy terrace, than which on a summer's day there could be no more delightful place for strolling up and down with a companion—all the more that at either end was a curious pavilion, in the manner of a tea-house, which crowned the scene in an old-world sense and offered rest and privacy, a refuge from sun or shower. One of these pavilions was an asylum for gardeners' tools and superfluous flower-pots;

the other was covered inside with a queer chinese paper representing ever so many times over a group of people with faces like blind kittens, groups who drank tea while they sat on the floor. It also contained a straddling inlaid cabinet in which cups and saucers showed valuably through doors of greenish glass, together with a carved cocoanut and a pair of outlandish idols. On a shelf over a sofa which was not very comfortable, though it had cushions of faded tapestry that resembled samplers, stood a row of novels out of date and out of print—novels that one couldn't have found any more and that were only there. On the chimney-piece was a bowl of dried rose-leaves mixed with some aromatic spice, and the whole place suggested a certain dampness.

On the terrace Hyacinth paced to and fro with the Princess till she all ruefully remembered he had not had his luncheon. He protested that this was the last thing he wished to think of, but she declared she hadn't dragged him down to Medley to starve him and that he must go back and be fed. They went back, but by a very roundabout way, through the park, so that they really had half an hour's more talk. She explained to him that she herself breakfasted at twelve o'clock, in the foreign fashion, and had tea in the afternoon; as he too was so foreign he might like that better, and in this case on the morrow they would breakfast together. He could have coffee and anything else he wanted brought to his room at his waking. When he had sufficiently composed himself in the presence of this latter image—he thought he saw a footman arranging a silver service at his bedside—he mentioned that really, as regarded the morrow, he should have to be back in London. There was a train at nine o'clock—he hoped she didn't mind his taking it. She looked at him gravely and kindly, as if considering an abstract idea, and then said: 'Oh yes, I mind it very much. Not tomorrow—some other day.' He made no rejoinder and the Princess spoke of something else; that is his rejoinder was private and consisted of the reflexion that he *would* leave Medley in the morning, whatever she might say. He simply couldn't afford to stay; he couldn't be out of work.

And then Madame Grandoni thought it so important; for
though the old lady was obscure she was decidedly impressive. The Princess's protest however was to be reckoned
with; he felt it might take a form less cursory than the words
she had just uttered, a form that would make it embarrassing. She was less solemn, less explicit, than Madame Grandoni had been, but there was something in her light fine
pressure and the particular tone of her mentioned preference that seemed to tell him his liberty was going—the
liberty he had managed to keep (till the other day when he
gave Hoffendahl a mortgage on it) and the possession of
which had in some degree consoled him for other forms
of penury. This made him uneasy; what would become of
him if he should add another servitude to the one he had
undertaken at the end of that long, anxious cab-drive
through the rain, in the back bedroom of a house as to whose
whereabouts he was even now not clear, while Muniment
and Poupin and Schinkel, all visibly pale, listened and
accepted the vow? Muniment and Poupin and Schinkel—
how disconnected, all the same, he felt from them at the
present hour; how little he was the young man who had
made the pilgrimage in the cab; and how the two latter at
least, if they could have a glimpse of him now, would wonder what he was up to!

   As to this Hyacinth wondered sufficiently himself, while
the Princess touched upon the people and places she had
seen, the impressions and conclusions she had gathered since
their former meeting. It was to such matters as these she
directed the conversation; she seemed to wish to keep it off
his own concerns, and he was surprised at her continued
avoidance of the slums and the question of her intended
sacrifices. She mentioned none of her friends by name, but
she talked of their character, their houses, their manners,
taking for granted as before that Hyacinth would always
follow. So far as he followed he was edified, but he had to
admit to himself that half the time he didn't know what
she was talking about. He at all events, if *he* had been with
the dukes—she didn't call her associates dukes, but he was

sure they were of that order—would have got more satisfaction from them. She appeared on the whole to judge the
English world severely; to think poorly of its wit and even
worse of its morals. 'You know people oughtn't to be both
corrupt and dreary,' she said; and Hyacinth turned this
over, feeling he certainly had not yet caught the point of
view of a person for whom the aristocracy was a collection
of bores. He had sometimes taken great pleasure in hearing
it dubbed grossly profligate, but he was rather disappointed
in the bad account the Princess gave of it. She dropped the
remark that she herself had no sort of conventional morality
—she ought to have mentioned that before—yet had never
been accused of being stupid. Perhaps he wouldn't discover
it, but most of the people she had had to do with thought
her only too acute. The second allusion she made to their
ulterior designs (Hyacinth's and hers) was when she said,
'I determined to see it'—she was speaking still of English
society—'to learn for myself what it really is before we blow
it up. I've been here now a year and a half and, as I tell
you, I feel I've seen. It's the old régime again, the rotten-
ness and extravagance, bristling with every iniquity and
every abuse, over which the French Revolution passed like
a whirlwind; or perhaps even more a reproduction of the
Roman world in its decadence, gouty, apoplectic, depraved,
gorged and clogged with wealth and spoils, selfishness and
scepticism, and waiting for the onset of the barbarians. You
and I are the barbarians, you know.' The Princess was pretty
vague after all in her animadversions and regaled him with
no anecdotes—which indeed he rather missed—that would
have betrayed the hospitality she had enjoyed. She couldn't
treat him absolutely as if he had been an ambassador. By
way of defending the aristocracy he said to her that it
couldn't be true they were all a bad lot (he used that expression because she had let him know she liked him to speak
in the manner of the people) inasmuch as he had an acquaintance among them—a noble lady—who was one of the
purest, kindest, most conscientious human beings it was
possible to imagine. At this she stopped short and looked

at him; then she asked: 'Whom do you mean—a noble lady?'

'I suppose there's no harm saying. Lady Aurora Langrish.'

'I don't know her. Is she nice?'

'I like her ever so much.'

'Is she pretty, clever?'

'She isn't pretty, but she's very uncommon,' said Hyacinth.

'How did you make her acquaintance?' As he hesitated she went on: 'Did you bind some books for her?'

'No. I met her in a place called Audley Court.'

'Where's that?'

'In Camberwell.'

'And who lives there?'

'A young woman I was calling on, who's bed-ridden.'

'And the lady you speak of—what do you call her, Lady Lydia Languish?—goes to see her?'

'Yes, very often.'

The Princess, with her eyes on him, had a pause. 'Will you take me there?'

'With great pleasure. The young woman I speak of is the sister of the man—the one who works for a big firm of wholesale chemists—that you'll perhaps remember that I mentioned to you.'

'Yes, I remember. It must be one of the first places we go to. I'm sorry, you know,' the Princess added, walking on. Hyacinth asked what she might be sorry for, but she took no notice of his question, only soon saying: 'Perhaps she goes to see *him*.'

'Goes to see whom?'

'The young chemist—the brother.' She said this very seriously.

'Perhaps she does,' Hyacinth returned, laughing. 'But she's a fine sort of woman.'

The Princess repeated that she was sorry—and he again wanted to know for what—for Lady Aurora's being of that sort? To which she replied: 'No; I mean for my not being

the first—what is it you call them?—noble lady you've encountered.'

'I don't see what difference that makes. You needn't be
afraid you don't make an impression on me.'

'I wasn't thinking of that. I was thinking you might be
less fresh than I first thought.'

'Of course I don't know what you first thought,' Hyacinth
smiled.

'No; how should you?' The Princess strangely sighed.

XXIII

HE WAS in the library after luncheon when word was
brought him that the carriage was at the door for their
drive; and when he entered the hall he found Madame
Grandoni bonneted and cloaked and awaiting the descent of
their friend. 'You see I go with you. I'm always there,' she
remarked jovially. 'The Princess has me with her to take
care of her, and this is how I do it. Besides, I never miss my
drive.'

'You're different from me; this will be the first I've ever
had in my life.' He could establish that distinction without
bitterness, because he was too pleased with his prospect to
believe the old lady's presence could spoil it. He had nothing
to say to the Princess that she mightn't hear. He didn't dis-
like her for coming even after she had said to him in answer
to his own announcement, speaking rather more sententiously than her wont: 'It doesn't surprise me that you've
not spent your life in carriages. They've nothing to do with
your trade.'

'Fortunately not,' he answered. 'I should have made a
ridiculous coachman.'

The Princess appeared and they mounted into a great
square barouche, an old-fashioned, high-hung vehicle with
a green body, a faded hammer-cloth and a rumble where
the footman sat (their hostess mentioned that it had been let

with the house) which rolled ponderously and smoothly along the winding avenue and through the gilded park-gates that were surmounted with an immense escutcheon. The progress of this apparently mismatched trio had a high respectability, and that is one of the reasons why Hyacinth felt the occasion intensely memorable. There might still be greater joys in store for him—he was by this time quite at sea and could recognise no shores—but he should never again in his life be so respectable. The drive was long and comprehensive, but little was said while it lasted. 'I shall show you the whole country: it's exquisitely beautiful; it speaks to the heart.' Of so much as this his entertainer had informed him at the start; and she added with all her foreignness and with a light allusive nod at the rich human-ised landscape, *'Voilà ce que j'aime en Angleterre.'* For the rest she sat there fronting him in quiet fairness and under her softly-swaying lace-fringed parasol: moving her eyes to where she noticed his eyes rest; allowing them when the carriage passed anything particularly charming to meet his own; smiling as if she enjoyed the whole affair very nearly as much as he; and now and then calling his attention to some prospect, some picturesque detail, by three words of a cadence as soft as a hand-stroke. Madame Grandoni dozed most of the time, her chin resting on the rather mangy ermine tippet in which she had enveloped herself; expand-ing into consciousness at moments, however, to greet the scenery with comfortable confused ejaculations in the first language that came into her head. If Hyacinth was uplifted during these delightful hours he at least measured his verti-ginous eminence, and it kept him quite solemnly still, as with the fear that a wrong movement of any sort would break the charm, cause the curtain to fall on the play. This was especially the case when his sensibility swung back from the objects that sprang up by the way, every one of which was a rich image of something he had longed for, to the most beautiful woman in England, who sat there, well before him, as completely for his benefit as if he had been a painter engaged to paint her portrait. More than once he saw everything through a strange mist; his eyes were full of tears.

That evening they sat in the drawing-room after dinner, as the Princess had promised or, as he was inclined to consider it, threatened him. The force of the threat was in his prevision that the ladies would make themselves fine and that in contrast with the setting and company he should feel dingier than ever; having already on his back the one approach to a 'cut' coat he possessed and being unable to exchange it for a garment of the pattern that civilised people (so much he knew, if he couldn't emulate them) put on about eight o'clock. The ladies when they came to dinner looked festal indeed; but he was able to make the reflexion that he was more pleased to be dressed as he was dressed, meanly and unsuitably as it was, than he should have been to present such a figure as Madame Grandoni, in whose toggery there was something comical. He was coming more and more round to the sense that if the Princess didn't mind his poorness of every sort he had no call to mind it himself. His present position wasn't of his seeking—it had been forced on him; it wasn't the fruit of a disposition to push. How little the Princess minded—how much indeed she enjoyed the consciousness that in having him about her in that manner she was playing a trick on society, the false and conventional society she had sounded and she despised —was manifest from the way she had introduced him to the group they found awaiting them in the hall on the return from their drive, four ladies, a mother and three daughters, who had come over to call from Broome, a place some five miles off. Broome was also a great house, as he gathered, and Lady Marchant, the mother, was the wife of a county magnate. She explained that they had come in on the persuasion of the butler, who had represented the return of the Princess as imminent and had then administered tea without waiting for this event. The evening had drawn in chill; there was a fire in the hall and they all sat near it, round the tea-table, under the great roof that rose to the top of the house. Hyacinth conversed mainly with one of the daughters, a very fine girl with a straight back and long arms, whose neck was encircled so tightly with a fur boa that, to look a little to one side, she was obliged to move her whole body. She had a handsome inanimate face, over which the firelight played without making it more lively, a beautiful voice and the occasional command of a few short words. She asked Hyacinth with what pack he hunted and whether he went in for tennis, and she ate three muffins.

Our young man made out that Lady Marchant and her daughters had already been at Medley, and even guessed that their reception by the Princess, who probably thought them of a tiresome type, had not been enthusiastic; and his imagination projected itself, further still, into the motives which, in spite of this tepidity, must have led them, on consideration of the rarity of a princess in that country, to come a second time. The talk in the firelight, while our youth laboured rather recklessly (for the spirit of the occasion on his hostess's part was passing into his own blood) with his muffin-eating beauty—the conversation, accompanied with the light click of delicate tea-cups, was as well-bred as could be consistent with an odd evident *parti-pris* of the Princess's to put poor Lady Marchant, as the phrase might be, through her paces. With great urbanity of manner she appealed for the explanation of everything, and especially of her ladyship's own thin remarks and of the sense in which they had been meant; so that Hyacinth was scarce able to follow her, wondering what interest she could have in trying to appear dense. It was only afterwards he learned that the Marchant family produced a very peculiar and at moments almost maddening effect on her nerves. He asked himself what would happen to that member of it with whom he was engaged if it should be revealed to her that she was conversing (how little soever) with a beggarly London artisan; and though he was rather pleased at her not having discovered his station (for he didn't attribute her brevity to this idea) he entertained a little the question of its being perhaps his duty not to keep it hidden from her, not to flourish in a cowardly disguise. What did she take him for

—or rather what didn't she take him for—when she asked
him if he hunted and 'went in'? Perhaps that was because it
was rather dark; if there had been more light in the great
vague hall she would have seen he was not one of themselves. He felt that by this time he had associated a good
deal with swells, but they had always known what he was
and had been able to choose how to treat him. This was the
first time a young gentlewoman hadn't been warned, and
as a consequence he appeared to pass muster. He determined
not to unmask himself, on the simple ground that he should
by the same stroke betray the Princess. It was quite open
to *her* to lean over and say to Miss Marchant: 'You know
he's a wretched little bookbinder who earns a few shillings
a week in a horrid street in Soho. There are all kinds of low
things—and I suspect even something very horrible—connected with his birth. It seems to me I ought to mention it.'
He almost wished she would mention it for the sake of the
strange violent sensation of the thing, a curious quivering
within him to know what Miss Marchant would do at such
a pinch and what chorus of ejaculations—or what appalled
irremediable silence—would rise to the painted roof. The
responsibility, however, was not his; he had entered a dim
passage of his fate where responsibilities had dropped.
Madame Grandoni's tea had waked her up; she came at
every crisis to the rescue of the conversation and talked to
the visitors about Rome, where they had once spent a
winter, describing with much drollery the manner in which
the English families she had seen there for nearly half a
century (and had met of an evening in the Roman world)
inspected the ruins and monuments and squeezed into the
great ceremonies of the Church. Clearly the four ladies
didn't know what to make of the Princess; but, though they
perhaps wondered if she were a paid companion, they were
on firm ground in the fact that the queer familiar fat person
had been acquainted with the Millingtons, the Bunburys
and the Tripps.

After dinner (during which the Princess allowed herself
a considerable licence of pleasantry on the subject of her

recent visitors, declaring that Hyacinth must positively go
with her to return their call and must see their interior,
their manner at home) Madame Grandoni sat down to the
piano at Christina's request and played to her companions
for an hour. The spaces were large in the big drawing-room,
and our friends had placed themselves at a distance from
each other. The old lady's music trickled forth discreetly
into the multiplied mild candlelight; she knew dozens of
Italian local airs, which sounded like the forgotten tunes of
a people, and she followed them by a series of tender plaintive German *Lieder*, rousing without violence the echoes of
the high pompous apartment. It was the music of an old
woman and seemed to quaver a little as her lifted voice might
have done. The Princess, buried in a deep chair, listened
behind her fan. Hyacinth at least supposed she listened, for
she never moved. At last Madame Grandoni left the piano
and came to the young man. She had taken up on the way
a French book in a pink cover which she nursed in the
hollow of her arm as she stood looking at him.

'My poor little friend, I must bid you good-night. I shall
not see you again for the present, as, to take your early
train, you'll have left the house before I put on my wig—
and I never show myself to gentlemen without it. I've looked
after the Princess pretty well, all day, to keep her from
harm, and now I give her up to you for a little. Take the
same care, I earnestly beg you. I must put myself in my
dressing-gown; at my age, at this hour, it's the only thing.
What will you have? I hate to be tight,' pursued Madame
Grandoni, who appeared even in her ceremonial garment to
have evaded this discomfort successfully enough. 'Don't sit
up late,' she added, 'and don't keep him, Christina. Remember that for an active young man like Mr Robinson, going
every day to his work, there's nothing more exhausting than
such an unoccupied life as ours. For what do we do after
all? His eyes are very heavy. *Basta!*'

During this little address the Princess, who made no rejoinder to that part of it which concerned herself, remained
hidden behind her fan; but after Madame Grandoni had

wandered away she lowered this emblazoned shield and rested her eyes a while on Hyacinth. At last she said: 'Don't sit half a mile off. Come nearer to me. I want to say something to you that I can't shout across the room.' He immediately got up, but at the same moment she also rose; so that, approaching each other, they met half-way and before the great marble chimney-piece. She stood opening and closing her fan, then she began: 'You must be surprised at my not having yet spoken to you about our great interest.'

'No indeed: I'm not now surprised at anything.'

'When you take that tone I feel as if we should never after all become friends,' said the Princess.

'I hoped we were already. Certainly after the kindness you've shown me there's no service of friendship you might ask of me——!'

'That you wouldn't gladly perform? I know what you're going to say, and have no doubt you speak truly. But what good would your service do me if all the while you think of me as a hollow-headed, hollow-hearted trifler, behaving in the worst possible taste and oppressing you with clumsy attentions? Perhaps you believe me a bad bold ravening flirt.'

'Capable of wanting to flirt with *me*?' Hyacinth demurred. 'I should be very conceited.'

'Surely you've the right to be as conceited as you please after the advances I've made you! Pray who has a better one? But you persist in remaining humble, and that's very provoking.'

'It's not I who am provoking; it's life and society and all the difficulties that surround us.'

'I'm precisely of that opinion—that they're exasperating; that when I appeal to you frankly, candidly, disinterestedly —simply because I like you, for no other reason in the world—to help me to disregard and surmount these conventions and absurdities, to treat them with the contempt they deserve, you drop your eyes, you even blush a little and make yourself small and try to edge out of the situation by pleading general devotion and insignificance. Please remem-

ber this: you cease to be insignificant from the moment I've
anything to do with you. My dear fellow,' the Princess went
on in her free audacious fraternising way, to which her
beauty and simplicity gave nobleness, 'there are people who
would be very glad to enjoy, in your place, that form of
obscurity.'

'What do you wish me then to do?' Hyacinth asked as
quietly as he could.

If he had had an idea that this question, to which, as
coming from his lips and even as being uttered with perceptible impatience, a certain unexpectedness might attach,
would cause her a momentary embarrassment, he was completely out in his calculation. She answered on the instant:
'I want you to give me time! That's all I ask of my friends in
general—all I ever asked of the best I've ever had. But
none of them ever did it; none of them, that is, save the
excellent creature who has just left us. She understood me
long ago.'

'That's all I on my side ask of you,' said Hyacinth with
a smile, as to attest presence of mind, that might have come
from some flushed young captive under cross-examination for
his life. 'Give *me* time, give *me* time,' he murmured, looking
up at her splendour.

'Dear Mr Hyacinth, I've given you months!—months
since our first meeting. And at present haven't I given you
the whole day? It has been intentional, my not speaking to
you of our plans. Yes, our plans—I know what I'm saying.
Don't try to look stupid; with your beautiful intelligent face
you'll never succeed. I wished to leave you free to amuse
yourself.'

'Oh, I've amused myself,' said Hyacinth.

'You'd have been very fastidious if you hadn't. However,
that's precisely in the first place what I wished you to come
here for. To observe the impression made by such a house
as this on such a nature as yours introduced to it for the
first time, has been, I assure you, quite worth my while.
I've already given you a hint of how extraordinary I think it
that you should be what you are without having seen—what

shall I call them?—beautiful delightful old things. I've been watching you; I'm frank enough to tell you that. I want you to see more—more—more!' the Princess exclaimed with a sudden emphasis that, had he heard her use it to another, he would have taken for a passion of tenderness. 'And I want to talk with you about this matter as well as others. That will be for to-morrow.'

'To-morrow?'

'I noticed Madame Grandoni took for granted just now that you're going. But that has nothing to do with the business. She has so little imagination!'

He shook his head with a pale grin and had an idea his mind was made up. 'I can't stay.'

She returned his smile, but there was something strangely touching—it was so sad, yet as a rebuke so gentle—in the tone in which she replied: 'You oughtn't make me too abject. It isn't nice.'

He had reckoned without that tone; all his reasons suddenly seemed to fall from under him and crumble. He remained a moment looking on the ground. 'Princess,' he then said, 'you've no idea—how should you have?—into the midst of what abject pitiful preoccupations you thrust yourself. I've no money—I've no clothes.'

'What do you want of money? This isn't an hotel.'

'Every day I stay here I lose a day's wages. I live on my wages from day to day.'

'Let me then give you wages. You'll work for me.'

'What do you mean—work for you?'

'You'll bind all my books. I've ever so many foreign ones in paper.'

'You speak as if I had brought my tools!'

'No, I don't imagine that. I'll give you the wages now, and you can do the work, at your leisure and convenience, afterwards. Then if you want anything you can go over to Bonchester and buy it. There are very good shops; I've used them.' Hyacinth thought of a great many things at this juncture; she had that quickening effect on him. Among others he thought of these two: first that it was indelicate (though such an opinion was not very strongly held either in Pentonville or Soho) to accept money from a woman; and second that it was still more indelicate to make such a woman as that go down on her knees to him. But it took more than a minute for one of these convictions to prevail over the other, and before that he had heard his friend continue in the tone of mild disinterested argument: 'If we believe in the coming democracy, if it seems to us right and just and we hold that in sweeping over the world the great wave will wash away a myriad iniquities and cruelties, why not make some attempt with our own poor means—for one must begin somewhere—to carry out the spirit of it in our lives and our manners? I want to do that. I try to do it— in my relations with you for instance. But you hang ridiculously back. You're really not a bit democratic!'

Her accusing him of a patrician offishness was a very fine stroke; nevertheless it left him lucidity (though he still hesitated an instant, wondering if the words wouldn't offend her) to say straightforwardly enough: 'I've been strongly warned against you.'

The offence seemed not to touch her. 'I can easily understand that. Of course my proceedings—though after all I've done little enough as yet—must appear most unnatural. *Che vuole?* as Madame Grandoni says.'

A certain knot of light blue ribbon which formed part of the trimming of her dress hung down at her side in the folds of it. On these glossy loops Hyacinth's eyes happened for a moment to have rested, and he now took up one of them and carried it to his lips. 'I'll do all the work for you that you'll give me. If you give it on purpose and by way of munificence that's your own affair. I myself will estimate the price. What decides me is that I shall do the job so well; certainly it shall be better than any one else can do—so that if you employ me there will have been at least that reason. I've brought you a book—so you can see. I did it for you last year and went to South Street to give it to you, but you had already gone.'

'Give it to me to-morrow.' These words appeared to express

so exclusively the calmness of relief at finding he could be reasonable, as well as a friendly desire to see the proof of his talent, that he was surprised when in the next breath she said irrelevantly: 'Who was it warned you against me?'

He feared she might suppose he meant Madame Grandoni, so he made the plainest answer, having no desire to betray the old lady and reflecting how, as the likelihood was small that his friend in Camberwell would ever consent to meet the Princess (in spite of her plan of going there) no one would be hurt by it. 'A friend of mine in London—Paul Muniment.'

'Paul Muniment?'

'I think I mentioned him to you the first time we met.'

'The person who said something good? I forget what it was.'

'It was sure to be something good if he said it. He's awfully wise.'

'That makes his warning very flattering to me! What does he know about me?'

'Oh nothing of course but the little I could tell him. He only spoke on general grounds.'

'I like his odd name—Paul Muniment,' the Princess said. 'If he resembles it I think I should like him.'

'You'd like him much better than me.'

'How do you know how much—or how little—I like you? I'm determined to keep hold of you simply for what you can show me.' She paused a moment with her beautiful deep eyes lighted as by possibilities that half dazzled and half defied him; then again her wondrous words took it up. 'On general grounds, *bien entendu*, your friend was quite right to warn you. Now those general grounds are just what I've undertaken to make as small as possible. It's to reduce them to nothing that I talk to you, that I conduct myself with regard to you as I've done. What in the world is it I'm trying to do but by every clever trick I can think of fill up the inconvenient gulf that yawns between my position and yours? You know what I make of "positions"—I told you in London. For heaven's sake let me feel that I've—a little—

succeeded!' He satisfied her sufficiently to enable her five minutes later apparently to entertain no further doubt on the question of his staying over. On the contrary she burst into a sudden explosion of laughter, replacing her argumentative pressure by one of her singular sallies. 'You must absolutely go with me to call on the Marchants. It will be lovely to see you there!'

As he walked up and down the empty drawing-room after she had a trifle abruptly and, as struck him, almost unceremoniously and inconsequently left him, it occurred to him to wonder if that was mainly what she was keeping him for—so that he might help her to play one of her tricks on the good people at Broome. He paced there in the still candle-light for a longer time than he measured; until the butler came and stood in the doorway, looking at him silently and fixedly as to let him know that he interfered with the custom of the house. He had told the Princess that what determined him was the thought of the manner in which he might exercise his craft in her service; but this was only half the influence that pressed him into forgetfulness of what he had most said to himself when, in Lomax Place, in an hour of unprecedented introspection, he wrote the letter by which he accepted the invitation to Medley. He would go there, he reasoned, because a man must be gallant, especially if he be a poor little bookbinder; but after he should be there he would insist at every step on knowing what he was in for. The change that had taken place in him now, from one moment to another, was that he had simply ceased to wonder what that mystery might be. All warnings, reflexions, considerations of verisimilitude, of the delicate, the natural and the possible, of the value of his independence, had become as nothing to him. The cup of an exquisite experience—a week in that enchanted palace, a week of such immunity from Lomax Place and old Crook as he had never dreamed of —was at his lips; it was purple with the wine of romance, of reality, of civilisation, and he couldn't push it aside without drinking. He might go home ashamed, but he would have for evermore in his mouth the taste of nectar. He went upstairs under the eye of the butler and on his way to his room, at the turning of a corridor, found himself face to face with Madame Grandoni. She had apparently just issued from her own apartment, the door of which stood open near her; she might have been hovering there at watch for his footstep. She had donned her dressing-gown, which seemed to give her all respiratory and other ease, but had not yet parted from her wig. She still had her pink French book under her arm, and her fat little hands, tightly locked together in front of her, formed the clasp of her generous girdle.

'Do tell me it's positive, Mr Robinson!' she said as she stopped short.

'What's positive, Madame Grandoni?'

'That you take the train in the morning.'

'I can't tell you that, because it wouldn't be true. On the contrary it has been settled I shall stay over. I'm very sorry if it distresses you—but *che vuole?*' he heard himself almost 'cheekily' risk.

Madame Grandoni was a humorous woman, but she gave him no smile in return; she only looked at him hard a moment and then, shrugging her shoulders silently but expressively, shuffled back to her room.

XXIV

'I CAN give you your friend's name—in a single guess. He's Diedrich Hoffendahl!' They had been strolling more and more slowly the next morning, and as she made this announcement the Princess stopped altogether, standing there under a great beech with her eyes on Hyacinth's and her hands full of primroses. He had breakfasted at noon with his hostess and Madame Grandoni, but the old lady had fortunately not joined them when the Princess afterwards proposed he should accompany her on her walk in the park. She told him how her venerable friend had, while the day was still very young, pronounced it in the worst possible taste that she shouldn't let their companion yet depart in peace; to which she had replied that about tastes there was no disputing and that they had disagreed on such matters before without any one's being the worse. Hyacinth expressed the hope that they wouldn't dispute about *him*—of all thankless subjects in the world; and the Princess assured him that she never disputed about anything. She held that there were other ways than this of arranging one's relations with people; and he guessed how thoroughly she meant that when a difference became sharp she broke off altogether. On her side then there was as little possibility as on his that they should ever quarrel: their acquaintance would be a grand friendship or would be nothing at all. The Princess gave it from hour to hour more of this quality, and it may be figured how safe her guest felt by the time he began to tell her that something had happened to him in London three months before, one night, or rather in the small hours of the morning, that had altered his life altogether—had indeed as he might say changed the terms on which he held it. He was aware that he didn't know exactly what he meant by this last phrase; but it expressed sufficiently well the new feeling that had come over him since that interminable, tantalising cab-drive in the rain.

The Princess had led to this almost as soon as they left the house; making up for her avoidance of such topics the day before by saying suddenly: 'Now tell me what's going on among your friends. I don't mean your worldly acquaintances, but your colleagues, your brothers. *Où en êtes-vous* at the present time? Is there anything new, is anything going to be done? I'm afraid you're always simply dawdling and muddling.' Hyacinth felt as if of late he had by no means either dawdled or muddled; but before he had committed himself so far as to refute the imputation she broke out with a different effect: 'How annoying it is that I can't ask you anything without giving you the right to say to yourself "After all what do I know? Mayn't she be in the pay of the police——?"'

'Oh that doesn't occur to me,' Hyacinth gallantly protested.

'It might at all events; by which I mean it may at any moment. Indeed I think it ought.'

'If you were in the pay of the police you wouldn't trouble your head about me.'

'I should make you think that certainly! That would be my first care. However, if you've no tiresome suspicions so much the better,' said the Princess; and she pressed him again for some news from behind the scenes.

In spite of his absence of doubt on the subject of her honesty—he was sure he should never again entertain any such trumpery idea as that she might be an agent on the wrong side—he didn't open himself immediately; but at the end of half an hour he let her know that the most important event of his life had taken place, scarcely more than the other day, in the most unexpected manner. And to explain in what it had consisted he said: 'I pledged myself by everything that's sacred.'

'To what did you pledge yourself?'

'I took a vow—a tremendous solemn vow—in the presence of four witnesses,' Hyacinth went on.

'And what was it about, your vow?'

'I gave my life away,' he consciously smiled.

She looked at him askance as if to see how he would indeed carry off such a statement as that; but she betrayed no levity of criticism—her face was politely grave. They moved together a moment, exchanging a glance in silence, and then she said: 'Ah well then I'm all the more glad you stayed!'

'That was one of the reasons.'

'I wish you had waited—till after you had been here,' it occurred to her, however, to remark.

'Why till after I had been here?'

'Perhaps then you wouldn't have given away your life. You might have seen reasons for keeping it.' With which, like Hyacinth, she sacrificed to the brighter bravery. He replied that he had not the least doubt that on the whole her influence was relaxing; but without heeding this she went on: 'Be so good as to tell me what you're talking about.'

'I'm not afraid of you, but I'll give you no names,' said Hyacinth; and he related what had happened at the place known to him in Bloomsbury and during that night of which I have given some account. The Princess listened intently while they strolled under the budding trees with a more interrupted step. Never had the old oaks and beeches, renewing themselves in the sunshine as they did to-day or naked in some grey November, witnessed such an extraordinary series of confidences since the first pair that sought isolation wandered over the grassy slopes and ferny dells beneath them. Among other things our young man mentioned that he didn't go to the 'Sun and Moon' any more; he now perceived, what he ought to have perceived long before, that this particular temple of their faith, with everything that pretended to get hatched there, was a hopeless sham. He had been a rare muff from the first to take it seriously. He had done so mainly because a friend of his in whom he had confidence appeared to set him the example; but now it turned out that this friend (it was Paul Muniment again by the way) had always thought the men who went there a pack of shufflers and was trying them only to try everything. There was nobody you could begin to call a first-rate man, putting aside another friend of his, a Frenchman named Poupin—and Poupin was magnificent but wasn't first-rate. Hyacinth had a standard now that he had seen a man who was the very incarnation of a strong plan. You felt *him* a big chap the very moment you came into his presence.

'Into whose presence, Mr Robinson?' the Princess demanded.

'I don't know that I ought to tell you, much as I believe in you! I'm speaking of the extraordinary man with whom I entered into that engagement.'

'To give away your life?'

'To do something that in a certain contingency he'll require of me. He'll require my poor little carcass.'

'Those "strong" plans have a way of failing—unfortunately,' the Princess murmured, adding the last word more quickly.

'Is that a consolation or a regret?' Hyacinth asked. 'This one shan't fail—so far as depends on me. They wanted an obliging young man. Well, the place was vacant and I stepped in.'

'I've no doubt you're right. We must pay for all we do.' She noted this hard law calmly and coldly and then said: 'I think I know the person in whose power you've placed yourself.'

'Possibly, but I doubt it.'

'You can't believe I've already gone so far? Why not? I've given you a certain amount of proof that I don't hang back.'

'Well, if you know my friend you've gone very far indeed.'

The Princess appeared on the point of pronouncing a name; but she checked herself and said instead, suddenly eager: 'Don't they also want by chance an obliging young woman?'

'I happen to know he doesn't think much of women, my first-rate man. He doesn't trust them.'

'Is that why you call him first-rate? You've very nearly betrayed him to me.'

'Do you imagine there's only one of that opinion?' Hyacinth returned.

'Only one who, having it, still remains a superior man. That's a very difficult opinion to reconcile with others it's important to have.'

'Schopenhauer did so, successfully,' said Hyacinth.

'How delightful you should know old Schopenhauer!' the Princess exclaimed. 'The gentleman I have in my eye is also German.' Hyacinth let this pass, not challenging her, because he wished not to be challenged in return, and she went on: 'Of course such an engagement as you speak of must make a tremendous difference in everything.'

'It has made this difference, that I've now a far other sense from any I had before of the reality, the solidity, of what's being prepared. I was hanging about outside, on the steps of the temple, among the loafers and the gossips, but now I've been in the innermost sanctuary. Yes, I've seen the holy of holies.'

'And it's very dazzling?'

'Ah Princess!' the young man strangely sighed.

'Then it *is* real, it *is* solid?' she pursued. 'That's exactly what I've been trying to make up my mind about so long.'

'It's beyond anything I can say. Nothing of it appears above the surface; but there's an immense underworld peopled with a thousand forms of revolutionary passion and devotion. The manner in which it's organised is what astonished me. I knew that, or thought I knew it, in a general way, but the reality was a revelation. And on top of it all society lives! People go and come, and buy and sell, and drink and dance, and make money and make love, and seem to know nothing and suspect nothing and think of nothing; and iniquities flourish, and the misery of half the world is prated about as a "necessary evil", and generations rot away and starve in the midst of it, and day follows day, and everything is for the best in the best of possible worlds. All that's one half of it; the other half is that everything's doomed! In silence, in darkness, but under the feet of each one of us, the revolution lives and works. It's a wonderful, immeasurable trap, on the lid of which society performs its antics. When once the machinery is complete there will be a great rehearsal. That rehearsal is what they want me for. The invisible impalpable wires are everywhere, passing through everything, attaching themselves to objects in which one would never think of looking for them. What could be more strange and incredible for instance than that they should exist just here?'

'You make me believe it,' said the Princess thoughtfully.

'It matters little whether one believes it or not!'

'You've had a vision,' she continued.

'*Pardieu*, I've had a vision! So would you, if you had been there.'

'I wish I had!' she declared in a tone charged with such ambiguous implications that Hyacinth, catching them a moment after she had spoken, rejoined with a quick, incongruous laugh—

'No, you'd have spoiled everything. He made me see, he made me feel, he made me do, everything he wanted.'

'And why should he have wanted you in particular?'

'Simply because I struck him as the right person. That's his affair: I can't tell you. When he meets the right person he chalks him. I sat on the bed. There were only two chairs in the dirty little room and by way of curtain his overcoat was hung up before the window. He himself didn't sit; he leaned against the wall straight in front of me, his hands behind him. He told me certain things and his manner was extraordinarily quiet. So was mine, I think I may say; and indeed it was only poor Poupin who made a row. It was for my sake somehow: he didn't think we were all conscious enough; he wanted to call attention to my sublimity. There was no sublimity about it—I simply couldn't help myself. He and the other German had the two chairs and Muniment sat on a queer old battered hair-covered trunk, a most foreign-looking article.' Hyacinth had taken no notice of the little ejaculation with which his companion greeted in this last sentence the word 'other'.

'And what did Mr Muniment say?' she presently asked.

'Oh he said it was all right. Of course he thought so from the moment he determined to bring me. He knew what the other fellow was looking for.'

'I see.' Then the Princess added: 'We've a curious way of being fond of you.'

'Whom do you mean by "we"?'

'Your friends. Mr Muniment and I for instance.'

'I like it as well as any other. But you don't feel alike. I've an idea you yourself are sorry.'

'Sorry for what?'

'That I've put my head into a noose.'

'Ah you're rather snubby—I thought I concealed it so well!' the Princess cried. He recognised that his discrimination had been invidious, as there might have been for an instant a hint of tears in her voice. She looked away from him, and it was after this that, stopping short, she remarked as I have related: 'Your man's Diedrich Hoffendahl.'

Hyacinth took it with a stare and parted lips. 'Well, you *are* in it—more than I supposed!'

'You know he doesn't trust women,' his companion smiled.

'Why in the world should you have cared for any light *I* can throw if you've ever been in relation with him?'

She hesitated a little. 'Oh you're very different. I like you better,' she added.

'Ah if it's for that!' murmured Hyacinth.

The Princess coloured as he had seen her colour before, and in this liability on her part there was even after repetition an unexpectedness, something all too touching. 'Don't try to fix my inconsistencies on me,' she said with an humility that matched her blush. 'Of course there are plenty of them, but it will always be kinder of you to let them pass. Besides, in this case they're not so serious as they seem. As a product of the "people" and of that strange fermenting underworld (what you say of it's so true!) you interest me more and have more to say to me even than Hoffendahl—wonderful creature as he assuredly is.'

'Would you object to telling me how and where you came to know him?' her visitor asked.

'Through a couple of friends of mine in Vienna, two of the affiliated, both passionate revolutionists and clever men. They're Neapolitans, originally *poveretti* like yourself, who emigrated years ago to seek their fortune. One of them's a teacher of singing, the wisest, most accomplished person in his line I've ever known. The other, if you please, is a confectioner! He makes the most delicious *pâtisserie fine*. It would take long to tell you how I made *their* acquaintance and how they put me into relation with the Maestro, as they called him, of whom they spoke with bated breath. It's not from yesterday—though you don't seem able to believe it—that I've had a care for these interests. I wrote to Hoffendahl and had several letters from him; the singing-master and the pastry-cook went bail for my sincerity. The next year I had an interview with him at Wiesbaden; but I can't tell you the circumstances of our meeting in that place without implicating another person to whom just now at least I've no right to give you a clue. Of course Hoffendahl made an immense impression on me; he struck me as the Master indeed, the very genius of a new social order, and I fully understand the manner in which you were affected by him. When he was in London three months ago I knew it and knew where to write to him. I did so and asked him if he wouldn't see me somewhere. I said I'd meet him anywhere, in any darkness, if it should have to be, that he might designate. He answered by a charming letter which I'll show you—it has nothing in the least compromising—but declined my offer, pleading his short stay and a press of engagements. He'll write to me but won't trust me. However, he shall some day!'

Hyacinth was thrown quite off his balance by this representation of the ground the Princess had already traversed, and the explanation was still but half restorative when, on his asking her why she hadn't exhibited her titles before, she replied: 'Well, I thought my being quiet was the better way to draw you out.' There was but little difficulty in drawing him out now, and before their walk was over he had told her more definitely what Hoffendahl demanded. This was simply that he should hold himself ready for the next five years to do at a given moment an act which would in all probability cost him his life. The act was as yet indefinite, but one might get an idea of it from the penalty involved, which would certainly be capital. The only thing settled was that it was to be done instantly and absolutely, without a question, a condition or a scruple, in the manner that should be prescribed at the moment from headquarters. Very likely it would be to shoot some one—some blatant humbug in a high place; but whether the individual should deserve it or shouldn't deserve it was not to be one's affair. If he recognised generally Hoffendahl's wisdom—and the other night it had seemed to shine like a great cold splendid northern aurora—it was not in order that he might challenge

it in the particular case. He had taken a vow of blind
obedience, the vow as of the Jesuit fathers to the head of
their order. It was because the Jesuits had carried out their
vows (having in the first place great administrators) that
their organisation had been mighty, and this sort of mighti-
ness was what people who felt as Hyacinth and the Princess
felt should go in for. It was not certain sure he should be
bagged after his *coup* any more than it was certain sure he
should bring down his man; but it was much to be looked
for and was what he counted on and indeed preferred. He
should probably take little trouble to save his skin, and he
should never enjoy the idea of dodging or hiding or dis-
avowing. If it were a question of really placing his bullet he
himself should naturally deserve what would come to him.
If one did that sort of thing there was an indelicacy in not
being ready to pay for it, and he at least was perfectly willing. He shouldn't judge, he should simply execute. He
didn't pretend to say what good his little job might do or
what *portée* it might have; he hadn't the data for appreciating it and simply took upon himself to believe that at headquarters they knew what they were about. The thing was to
be part of a very large plan, of which he couldn't measure
the scope—something that was to be done simultaneously in
a dozen different countries. The impression was to be very
much in this immense coincidence. It was to be hoped it
wouldn't be spoiled by any muffing. At all events *he*
wouldn't hang fire, whatever the other fellows might do. He
didn't say it because Hoffendahl had done him the honour
of giving him the business to do, but he believed the Master
knew how to pick out his men. To be sure they had known
nothing about him in advance; he had only been suggested
from one day to the other by those who were always looking
out. The fact remained, however, that when Hyacinth stood
before him he recognised him as the sort of little chap he
had in his eye—one who could pass through a very small
opening. Humanity, in his scheme, was classified and sub-
divided with a truly German thoroughness and altogether
of course from the point of view of the revolution—as it

might forward or obstruct that cause. Hyacinth's little job was a very small part of what Hoffendahl had come to England for; he had in his hand innumerable other threads. Hyacinth knew nothing of these and didn't much want to know, except for the portentous wonder of the way Hoffendahl kept them apart. He had exactly the same mastery of them that a great musician—that the Princess herself—had of the keyboard of the piano; he treated all things, persons, institutions, ideas, as so many notes in his great symphonic massacre. The day would come when—far down in the treble—one would feel one's self touched by the little finger of the composer, would grow generally audible (with a small sharp crack) for a second.

It was impossible that our young man shouldn't become aware at the end of ten minutes that he had charmed the Princess into the deepest, most genuine attention: she was listening to him as she had never listened before. He enjoyed that high effect on her, and his sense of the tenuity of the thread by which his future hung, renewed by his hearing himself talk about it, made him reflect that at present anything in the line of enjoyment, any scrap filched from the feast of life, was so much gained for eager young experience. The reader may judge if he had held his breath and felt his heart-beats after placing himself on his new footing of utility in the world; but that emotion had finally spent itself, through a hundred forms of restlessness, of vain conjecture —through an exaltation which alternated with despair and which, equally with the despair, he concealed more successfully than he supposed. He would have detested the idea that his companion might have heard his voice tremble while he told his story; but though to-day he had really grown used to his danger and resigned, as it were, to his consecration, and though it couldn't fail to be agreeable to him to perceive that, like some famous novel, he was thrilling, he still couldn't guess how very remarkable, in such a connexion, the Princess thought his composure, his lucidity, his good humour. It is true she tried to hide her wonder, for she owed it to her self-respect to let it still appear that even such a one as she was prepared for a personal sacrifice as complete. She had the air—or she endeavoured to have it—of accepting for him everything that he accepted for himself; nevertheless there was something rather forced in the smile (lovely as it might be) with which she covered him while she said after a little: 'It's very serious—it's very serious indeed, isn't it?' He replied that the serious part was to come—there was no particular grimness for him (comparatively) in strolling in that fine park and gossiping with her about the matter; and it occurred to her presently to suggest to him that perhaps Hoffendahl would never give him any sign at all, so that he might wait, all the while *sur les dents*, in a false suspense. He admitted that this would be a sell, but declared that either way he should be sold, though differently; and that at any rate he would have conformed to the great religious rule—to live each hour as if it were to be one's last.

'In holiness, you mean—in great *recueillement*?' the Princess asked.

'Oh dear no; simply in extreme thankfulness for every good minute that's added.'

'Ah well, there will probably be a great many good minutes,' she returned.

'The more the better—if they're as good as this one.'

'That won't be the case with many of them in Lomax Place.'

'I assure you that since that night Lomax Place has improved.' Hyacinth stood there smiling, his hands in his pockets and his hat pushed back.

The Princess appeared to consider this quaint truth, as well as the charming facts of his appearance and attitude, with an extreme intellectual curiosity. 'If after all then you're not called you'll have been positively happy.'

'I shall have had some fine moments. Perhaps Hoffendahl's plot is simply for that: Muniment may have put him up to it!'

'Who knows? However, with me you must go on as if nothing were changed.'

'Changed from what?'

'From the time of our first meeting at the theatre.'

'I'll go on in any way you like,' said Hyacinth. 'Only the real difference will be there, you know.'

'The real difference?'

'That I shall have ceased to care for what you care for.'

'I don't understand,' she confessed with all the candour of her beauty.

'Isn't it enough now to give my life to the beastly cause,' the young man broke out, 'without giving my sympathy?'

'The beastly cause?' the Princess murmured, opening her deep eyes.

'Of course it's really just as holy as ever; only the people I find myself pitying now are the rich, the happy.'

'I see. You're very remarkable. You're splendid. Perhaps you pity my husband,' she added in a moment.

'Do you call him one of the happy?' Hyacinth enquired as they walked on again.

But she only repeated: 'You're very remarkable. Yes, you're splendid.'

To which he made answer: 'Well, it's what I want to be!'

I have related the whole of this conversation because it supplies a highly important chapter of Hyacinth's history, but we may not take time to trace all the stages and reproduce all the passages through which the friendship of the Princess Casamassima with the young man she had constituted her bookbinder was confirmed. By the end of a week the standard of fitness she had set up in the place of exploded proprieties appeared the model of justice and convenience; and during this period, a season of strange revelations for our young man, many other things happened. One of them was that he drove over to Broome with his hostess and called on Lady Marchant and her daughters; an episode that appeared to minister in the Princess to a thorough ironic glee. When they came away he asked her why she hadn't told the ladies who he was. Otherwise where was the point? And she replied: 'Simply because they wouldn't have believed me. That's your fault!' This was the same note she had struck when the third day of his stay (the weather had changed for the worse and a rainy afternoon kept them indoors) she remarked to him irrelevantly and abruptly: 'It *is* most extraordinary, your knowing poor dear old "Schop"!' He answered that she really seemed quite unable to accustom herself to his little talents; and this led to a long talk, longer than the one I have already narrated, in which he took her still further into his confidence. Never had the pleasure of conversation, the greatest he knew, been so largely opened to him. The Princess admitted frankly that he would to her sense take a great deal of accounting for; she observed that he was, no doubt, pretty well used to himself, but must give stupider persons time. 'I've watched you constantly since you came—in every detail of your behaviour—and I'm more and more *intriguée*. You haven't a vulgar intonation, you haven't a common gesture, you never make a mistake, you do and say everything exactly in the right way. You come out of the poor cramped hole you've described to me, and yet you might have stayed in country-houses all your life. You're much better than if you had! *Jugez donc*, from the way I talk to you! I've to make no allowances—not one little allowance. I've seen Italians with that sort of natural tact and ease, but I didn't know it was ever to be found in any Anglo-Saxon in whom it hadn't been cultivated at a vast expense; unless perhaps in certain horribly "refined" little American women.'

'Do you mean I'm a gentleman?' asked Hyacinth in a peculiar tone while he looked out into the wet garden.

She faltered and then said: 'It's I who make the mistakes!' Five minutes later she broke into an exclamation which touched him almost more than anything she had ever done, giving him the highest opinion of her delicacy and sympathy, putting him before himself as vividly as if the words were a little portrait. 'Fancy the strange, the bitter fate: to be constituted as you're constituted, to be conscious of the capacity you must feel, and yet to look at the good things of life only through the glass of the pastry-cook's window!'

'Every class has its pleasures,' he made answer with perverse sententiousness in spite of his emotion; but the remark didn't darken their mutual intelligence, which was to expand to still greater wonders, and before they separated that evening he told her the things that had never yet passed his lips—the things to which he had awaked when he made Pinnie explain to him the visit to the prison. He told her in short what he was.

XXV

HE TOOK several long walks by himself beyond the gates of the park and through the neighbouring country—walks during which, committed as he was to reflexion on the general 'rumness' of his destiny, he had still a delighted attention to spare for the green dimness of leafy lanes, the attraction of meadow-paths that led from stile to stile and seemed a clue to some pastoral happiness, some secret of the fields; the hedges thick with flowers, bewilderingly common, for which he knew no names, the picture-making power of thatched cottages, the mystery and sweetness of blue distances, the bloom of rural complexions, the quaintness of little girls bobbing curtsies by waysides (a sort of homage he had never prefigured); the soft sense of the turf under feet that had never ached but from paving-stones. One morning as he had his face turned homeward after a long stroll he heard behind him the sound of a horse's hoofs and, looking back, perceived a gentleman who would presently pass him advancing up the road which led to the lodge-gates of Medley. He went his way and as the horse overtook him noticed that the rider slackened pace. Then he turned again and recognised in this personage his occasional florid friend Captain Sholto. The Captain pulled up alongside of him, saluting him with a smile and a movement of the whip-handle. Hyacinth stared with surprise, not having heard from the Princess that she was expecting him. He gathered however in a moment that she was not; and meanwhile he received the impression on Sholto's part of riding-gear that was 'knowing'—of gaiters and spurs and a hunting-crop and a curious waistcoat; perceiving this to be a phase of the Captain's varied nature that he had not yet had occasion to observe. He struck him as very high in the air, perched on his big lean chestnut, and Hyacinth noticed that if the horse was heated the rider was cool.

'Good-morning, my dear fellow. I thought I should find you here!' the Captain exclaimed. 'It's a good job I've met you this way without having to go to the house.'

'Who gave you reason to think I was here?' Hyacinth asked; partly occupied with the appositeness of this enquiry and partly thinking, as his eyes wandered over his handsome friend bestriding so handsome a beast, what a jolly thing it would be to know how to ride. He had already, during the few days he had been at Medley, had time to observe that the knowledge of luxury and the wider range of sensation begot in him a taste for still bolder pleasures.

'Why, I knew the Princess was capable of asking you,' Sholto said; 'and I learned at the "Sun and Moon" that you had not been there for a long time. I knew furthermore that as a general thing you go there a good deal, don't you? So I put this and that together and judged you were out of town.'

This was very clear and straightforward and might have satisfied just exactions save for that irritating reference to the Princess's being 'capable of asking him'. He knew as well as the Captain that it had been tremendously eccentric in her to do so, but somehow a transformation had lately taken place in him which made it unpleasant he should receive that view from another, and particularly from a gentleman of whom at a certain juncture several months before he had had strong grounds for thinking unfavourably. He had not seen Sholto since the evening when a queer combination of circumstances caused him to sit more queerly still and listen to comic songs in the company of Millicent Henning and this admirer. The Captain had not concealed his admiration; Hyacinth had his own ideas about his taking that line in order to look more innocent. When he accompanied Millicent that evening to her lodgings (they parted with Sholto on coming out of the Pavilion) the situation was tense between the young lady and her childhood's friend. She let him have it as she said; she gave him a dressing which she evidently intended should be memorable for having suspected her, for having insulted her before one of the military. The tone she took and the magnificent audacity with which she took it reduced him to an odd gratified helplessness; he watched her at last with something of the excitement with which he would have watched a clever but uncultivated actress while she worked herself into a passion that he believed to be fictitious. He gave more credence to his jealousy and to the whole air of the case than to her loud rebuttals, enlivened though these were by tremendous head-tossings and skirt-shakings. But he felt baffled and outfaced, and had recourse to sarcasms which after all proved no more than her high gibes; seeking a final solution in one of those beastly little French shrugs, as Millicent called them, with which she had already denounced him for interlarding his conversation.

The air was never cleared, though the subject of their dispute was afterwards dropped. Hyacinth promising himself to watch his playmate as he had never done before. She let him know, as may well be supposed, that she had her eye on *him*, and it must be confessed that as regards the exercise of a right of supervision he had felt himself at a disadvantage ever since the night at the theatre. It scantly mattered that she had pushed him into the Princess's box (for she herself had not been jealous beforehand; she had wanted too much to know what such a person could be 'up to', desiring perhaps to borrow a hint) and it signified as little also that his relations with the great lady were all for the sake of suffering humanity. The atmosphere, however these things might be, was full of thunder for many weeks, and of what importance was the quarter from which the flash and the explosion should proceed? Hyacinth was a good deal surprised to find he could care whether Millicent

deceived him or not, and even tried to persuade himself
that he didn't; but it was as if he yet felt between them a
personal affinity deeper than any difference, so that it would
torment him more never to see her at all than to see her go
into tantrums in order to cover her tracks. An inner sense
told him that her mingled beauty and grossness, her vulgar
vitality, the spirit of contradiction yet at the same time of
attachment that was in her, had ended by making her indispensable to him. She bored as much as she irritated; but
if she was full of excruciating taste she was also full of life,
and her rustlings and chatterings, her wonderful stories,
her bad grammar and good health, her insatiable thirst, her
shrewd perceptions and grotesque opinions, her blunders
and her felicities, were now all part of the familiar human
sound of his little world. He could say to himself that she
made up to him far more than he to her, and it helped him
a little to believe, though the logic was but lame, that she
was not 'larking' at his expense. If she were really in with
a swell he didn't see why she wished to retain a bookbinder.
Of late, it must be added, he had ceased to devote much
consideration to Millicent's ambiguities; for although he was
lingering on at Medley for the sake of suffering humanity
he was quite aware that to say so (should she ask him for a
reason) would have almost as low a value as some of the
girl's own speeches. As regards Sholto he was in the awkward position of having let him off, as it were, by accepting
his hospitality, his bounty; thus he couldn't quarrel with
him save on a fresh pretext. This pretext the Captain had
apparently been careful not to give, and Millicent had told
him after the triple encounter in the street that he had
driven him out of England, the poor gentleman he insulted
by his vulgar insinuations even more (why "even more"
Hyacinth hardly could think) than he outraged herself.
When he asked her what she knew about the Captain's
movements she made no scruple to announce to him that
the latter had come to her great shop to make a little purchase (it was a pair of silk braces, if she remembered rightly,
and she acknowledged unreservedly the thinness of the pre-

text) and had asked her with much concern whether his gifted young friend (that's what he called him—Hyacinth could see he meant well) was still in a huff. Millicent had replied that she was afraid he was—the more shame to him; and then the Captain had declared it didn't matter, as he himself was on the point of leaving England for several weeks (Hyacinth—he called him Hyacinth this time— couldn't have ideas about a man in a foreign country, could he?) and hoped that by the time he returned the little cloud would have blown over. Sholto had added that she had better tell him frankly—recommending her at the same time to be gentle with their morbid friend—about his visit to the shop. Their candour, their humane precautions, were all very well; but after this, two or three evenings, Hyacinth passed and repassed the Captain's chambers in Queen Anne Street to see if there were signs at the window of his being in London. Darkness in fact prevailed and he was forced to comfort himself a little when, at last making up his mind to ring at the door and enquire, as a test, for the occupant, he was informed by the superior valet whose acquaintance he had already made and whose air of wearing a jacket left behind by his master confirmed the state- ment, that the gentleman in question was at Monte Carlo.

'Have you still got your back up a little?' the Captain now demanded without rancour; and in a moment he had swung a long leg over the saddle and dismounted, walking beside his young friend and leading his horse by the bridle. Hyacinth pretended not to know what he meant, for it came over him that after all, even if he had not condoned at the time the Captain's suspected treachery, he was in no position, sitting at the feet of the Princess, to sound the note of jealousy in relation to another woman. He reflected that the Princess had originally been in a manner Sholto's property, and if he did *en fin de compte* wish to quarrel with him about Millicent he would have to cease to appear to poach on the Captain's preserves. It now occurred to him for the first time that the latter might have intended a prac- tical exchange; though it must be added that the Princess, who on a couple of occasions had alluded slightingly to her military friend, had given him no sign of recognising this gentleman's claim. Sholto let him know at present that he was staying at Bonchester, seven miles off; he had come down from London and put up at the inn. That morning he had ridden over on a hired horse (Hyacinth had supposed this steed to be a very fine animal, but Sholto spoke of it as an infernal screw); he had felt a sudden prompting to see how his young friend was coming on.

'I'm coming on very well, thank you,' said Hyacinth with some shortness, not knowing exactly what business it was of the Captain's.

'Of course you understand my interest in you, don't you? I'm responsible for you—I put you forward.'

'There are a great many things in the world I don't understand, but I think the thing I understand least is your interest in me. Why the devil——?' And Hyacinth paused, breathless with the force of his enquiry. Then he went on: 'If I were you I shouldn't care tuppence for the sort of person I happen to be.'

'That proves how different my nature is from yours! But I don't believe it, my dear boy; you're too generous for that.' Sholto's imperturbability always appeared to grow with the irritation it produced, and it was proof even against the just resentment excited by his deficiency of tact. That deficiency was marked when he went on to say: 'I wanted to see you here with my own eyes. I wanted to see how it looked, your domesticated state—and it *is* a rum sight! Of course you know what I mean, though you're always trying to make a fellow explain. I don't explain well in any sense, and that's why I go in only for clever people who can do without it. It's very grand, her having brought you down.'

'Grand, no doubt, but hardly surprising, considering that, as you say, I was put forward by you.'

'Oh that's a great thing for me, but it doesn't make any difference to her!' Sholto returned. 'She may care for certain things for themselves, but it will never signify a jot to her what I may have thought about them. One good turn deserves another. I wish you'd put *me* forward!'

'I don't understand you and I don't think I want to,' said Hyacinth as his companion strolled beside him.

The latter put a hand on his arm, stopping him, and they stood face to face a moment. 'I say, my dear Robinson, you're not spoiled already, at the end of a week—how long is it? It isn't possible you're jealous!'

'Jealous of whom?' asked Hyacinth, whose measure of the allusion was, amid the strangeness of everything, imperfect.

Sholto looked at him a moment; then with a laugh: 'I don't mean Miss Henning.' Hyacinth turned away and the Captain resumed his walk, now taking the young man's arm and passing his own through the bridle of the horse. 'The courage of it, the insolence, the *crânerie*! There isn't another woman in Europe who could carry it off.'

Hyacinth was silent a little; after which he remarked: 'This is nothing, here. You should have seen me the other day over at Broome, at Lady Marchant's.'

'Gad, did she take you there? I'd have given ten pounds to see it. There's no one like her!' cried the Captain gaily, enthusiastically.

'There's no one like me, I think—for going.'

'Why, didn't you enjoy it?'

'Too much—too much. Such excesses are dangerous.'

'Oh I'll back you,' said the Captain; then checking their pace, 'Is there any chance of our meeting her?' he asked. 'I won't go into the park.'

'You won't go to the house?' Hyacinth demanded in wonder.

'Oh dear no, not while you're there.'

'Well, I shall ask the Princess about you, and so have done with it once for all.'

'Lucky little beggar, with your fireside talks!' the Captain lamented. 'Where does she sit now in the evening? She won't tell you anything except that I'm a beastly nuisance; but even if she were willing to take the trouble to throw some light on me it wouldn't be of much use, because she doesn't understand me herself.'

'You're the only thing in the world then of which that can be said,' Hyacinth returned.

'I dare say I am, and I'm rather proud of it. So far as the head's concerned the Princess is all there. I told you when I presented you that she was the cleverest woman in Europe, and that's still my opinion. But there are some mysteries you can't see into unless you happen to have a little decent human feeling, what's commonly called a bit of heart. The Princess isn't troubled with that sort of thing, though doubtless just now you may think it her strong point. One of these days you'll see. I don't care a rap myself about her quantity of heart. She has hurt me already so much that she can't hurt me any more, and my interest in her is quite independent of it. To watch her, to adore her, to see her lead her life and act out her extraordinary nature, all the while she pays me no more attention than if I were the postman's knock several doors on, that's absolutely the only thing that appeals to me. It doesn't do me a scrap of good, but all the same it's my principal occupation. You may believe me or not—it doesn't in the least matter; but I'm the most disinterested human being alive. She'll tell you one's the biggest kind of donkey, and so of course one is. But that isn't all.'

It was Hyacinth who stopped this time, arrested by something new and natural in the tone of his companion, a simplicity of emotion he had not hitherto associated with him. He stood there a moment looking up at him and thinking again what improbable confidences it decidedly appeared to be his lot to receive from gentlefolk. To what quality in himself were they a tribute? The honour was one he could easily dispense with; though as he scrutinised Sholto he found something in his odd light eyes—a sort of wasted flatness of fidelity—which made of an accepted relation with him a less fantastic adventure. 'Please go on,' he said in a moment.

'Well, what I mentioned just now is my real and only

motive in anything. The rest's the mere gabble of the juggler to cover up his trick and help himself do it.'

'What do you mean by the rest?' asked Hyacinth, thinking of Millicent Henning.

'Oh all the straw one chews to cheat one's appetite; all the rot one dabbles in because it may lead to something which it never does lead to; all the beastly buncombe (you know) that you and I have heard together in Bloomsbury and that I myself have poured out, damme, with an assurance worthy of a better cause. Don't you remember what I've said to you—all as my own opinion—about the impending change of the relations of class with class? Impending collapse of the crust of the earth! I believe those on top of the heap are better than those under it, that they mean to stay there, and that if they're not a pack of poltroons they will.'

'You don't care for the social question then?' Hyacinth enquired with an aspect of the blankness of which he was conscious.

'I only took it up because she did. It hasn't helped me,' Sholto smiled. 'My dear Robinson,' he went on, 'there's only one thing I care for in life: to have a look at that woman when I can—and when I can't to approach her in the sort of way I'm doing now.'

'It's a very funny sort of way.'

'Indeed it is; but if it's good enough for me it ought to be good enough for you. What I want you to do is this—to induce her to ask me over to dine.'

'To induce her——?' Hyacinth echoed.

'Tell her I'm staying at Bonchester and it would be an act of common humanity.'

They proceeded till they reached the gates and in a moment Hyacinth said: 'You took up the social question then because she did. But do you happen to know why *she* took it up?'

'Ah my dear fellow, you must worry that out for yourself. I found you the place, but I can't do your work for you!'

'I see—I see. But perhaps you'll tell me this: if you had

free access to her a year ago, taking her to the theatre and that sort of thing, why shouldn't you have it now?'

This time Sholto's yellow eyes were strange again. '*You* have it now, my dear chap, but I'm afraid it doesn't follow that you'll have it a year hence. She was tired of me then, and of course she's still more tired of me now, for the simple reason that I'm more tiresome. She has sent me to Coventry and I want to come out for a few hours. See how awfully decent I am—I won't pass the gates.'

'I'll tell her I met you,' said Hyacinth. Then, irrelevantly, he added: 'Is that what you mean by her having no heart?'

'Her treating me as she treats me? Oh dear no. Her treating *you!*'

This had a portentous sound, but it didn't prevent Hyacinth from turning round with his visitor—for it was the greatest part of the oddity of the present meeting that the hope of a little conversation with him, if accident were favourable, had been the motive not only of Sholto's riding over to Medley but of his coming down to stay, in the neighbourhood, at a musty inn in a dull market-town—it didn't prevent him, I say, from bearing the Captain company for a mile on his backward way. Our young man pursued this particular topic little further, but he discovered still another reason or two for admiring the light free action with which his companion had unmasked himself, as well as the nature of his interest in the revolutionary idea, after he had asked him abruptly what he had had in his head when he travelled over that evening, the summer before—and he didn't appear to have come back as often as he promised—to Paul Muniment's place in Camberwell. What was he looking for, whom was he looking for there?

'I was looking for anything that would turn up, that might take her fancy. Don't you understand that I'm always looking? There was a time when I went in immensely for illuminated missals, and another when I collected horrible ghost-stories (she wanted to cultivate a belief in ghosts) all for her. The day I saw she was turning her attention to the rising democracy I began to collect little democrats. That's how I collected you.'

'Muniment made you out exactly then. And what did you find to your purpose in Audley Court?'

'Well, I think the little woman with the popping eyes—she reminded me of a bedridden grasshopper—will do. And I made a note of the other one, the old virgin with the high nose, the aristocratic sister of mercy. I'm keeping them in reserve for my next propitiatory offering.'

Hyacinth had a pause. 'And Muniment himself—can't you do anything with him?'

'Oh my dear fellow, after you he's poor!'

'That's the first stupid thing you've said. But it doesn't matter, for he dislikes the Princess—what he knows of her —too much ever to consent to see her.'

'That's his line, is it? Then he'll do!' Sholto cried.

XXVI

'OF COURSE he may come, and may stay as long as he likes!' the Princess exclaimed when Hyacinth, that afternoon, told her of his encounter: she spoke with the sweet bright surprise her face always wore when people went through the form (supererogatory she apparently meant to declare it) of asking her leave. From the manner in which she granted Sholto's petition—with a facility that made light of it, as if the question were not worth talking of one way or the other—the account he had given Hyacinth of their relations might have passed for an elaborate but none the less foolish hoax. She sent a messenger with a note over to Bonchester, and the Captain arrived just in time to dress for dinner. The Princess was always late, and Hyacinth's toilet on these occasions occupied him considerably (he was acutely conscious of its deficiencies, and yet tried to persuade himself that they were positively honourable and that the only garb of dignity for him was the costume, as it were, of his profession); therefore when the fourth member of the little party descended to the drawing-room Madame Grandoni was the only person he found there.

'*Santissima Vergine!* I'm glad to see you! What good wind has sent you?' she exclaimed as soon as Sholto came into the room.

'Didn't you know I was coming?' he asked. 'Has the idea of my arrival produced so little agitation?'

'I know nothing of the affairs of this house. I've given them up at last, and it was time. I remain in my room.' There was nothing at present in the old lady's countenance of her usual spirit of cheer; it expressed anxiety and even a certain sternness, and the excellent woman had perhaps at this moment more than she had ever had in her life of the air of a duenna who took her duties seriously. She looked almost august. 'From the moment you come it's a little better. But it's very bad.'

'Very bad, dear madam?'

'Perhaps you'll be able to tell me where Christina *veut en venir.* I've always been faithful to her—I've always been loyal. But to-day I've lost patience. It has no sense.'

'I'm not sure I know what you're talking about,' Sholto said; 'but if I understand you I must tell you I think it all magnificent.'

'Yes, I know your tone; you're worse than she, because you're cynical. It passes all bounds. It's very serious. I've been thinking what I should do.'

'Precisely. I know what you'll probably do.'

'Oh this time I shouldn't come back!' the old lady declared. 'The scandal's too great. It's intolerable. But my danger's of making it worse.'

'Dear Madame Grandoni, you can't make it worse and you can't make it better,' Sholto returned as he seated himself on the sofa beside her. 'In point of fact no idea of scandal can possibly attach itself to our friend. She's above and outside all such considerations, such dangers. She carries everything off; she heeds so little, she cares so little. Besides, she has one great strength—she does no wrong.'

'Pray what do you call it when a lady sends for a book-binder to come and live with her?'

'Why not for a bookbinder as well as for a bishop? It all depends upon who the lady is and what she is.'

'She had better take care of one thing first,' cried Madame Grandoni—'that she shall not have been separated, with a hundred stories, from her husband!'

'The Princess can carry off even that. It's unusual, it's eccentric, it's fantastic if you will, but it isn't necessarily wicked. From her own point of view our friend goes straight. Besides, she has her opinions.'

'Her opinions are perversity itself.'

'What does it matter,' asked Sholto, 'if they keep her quiet?'

'Quiet! Do you call this quiet?'

'Surely, if you'll only be so yourself. Putting the case at the worst, moreover, who's to know he's her bookbinder? It's the last thing you'd take him for.'

'Yes, for that she chose him carefully,' the old woman murmured, still with a ruffled eyebrow.

'*She* chose him? It was I who chose him, dear lady!' the Captain cried with a laugh that showed how little he shared her solicitude.

'Yes, I had forgotten. At the theatre,' said Madame Grandoni, gazing at him as if her ideas were confused, yet as if a certain repulsion from her interlocutor nevertheless disengaged itself. 'It was a fine turn you did him there, poor young man!'

'Certainly he'll have to be sacrificed. But why was I bound to consider him so much? Haven't I been sacrificed myself?'

'Oh if he bears it like you!'—and she almost snorted with derision.

'How do you know how I bear it? One does what one can,' said the Captain while he settled his shirtfront. 'At any rate remember this: she won't tell people who he is for his own sake, and he won't tell them for hers. So, as he looks much more like a poet or a pianist or a painter, there won't be that sensation you fear.'

'Even so it's bad enough,' said Madame Grandoni. 'And he's capable of bringing it out suddenly himself.'

'Ah if he doesn't mind it *she* won't! But that's his affair.'

'It's too terrible to spoil him for his station,' the old lady went on. 'How can he ever go back?'

'If you want him kept then indefinitely you're inconsistent. Besides, if he pays for it he deserves to pay. He's an abominable little conspirator against society.'

Madame Grandoni was silent a time; then she looked at the Captain with a gravity which might have been impressive to him had not his accomplished jauntiness suggested an insensibility to that sort of influence. 'What then does Christina deserve?' she asked with solemnity.

'Whatever she may get; whatever in the future may make her suffer. But it won't be the loss of her reputation. She's too distinguished.'

'You English are strange. Is it because she's a princess?' Madame Grandoni reflected audibly.

'Oh dear no, her princedom's nothing here. We can easily beat that. But we can't beat——!' And he had a pause.

'What then?' his companion asked.

'Well, the perfection of her indifference to public opinion and the unaffectedness of her originality; the sort of thing by which she has bedevilled me.'

'Oh *you!*' Madame Grandoni tossed off.

'If you think so poorly of me why did you say just now that you were glad to see me?' Sholto demanded in a moment.

'Because you make another person in the house, and that's more regular; the situation is by so much less—what did you call it?—eccentric. *Nun,*' she presently went on, 'so long as you're here I won't go off.'

'Depend upon it I shall hang on tight till I'm turned out.'

She rested her small troubled eyes on him, but they betrayed no particular enthusiasm at this announcement. 'I don't understand how for yourself on such an occasion you should like it.'

'Dear Madame Grandoni, the heart of man, without

being such a hopeless labyrinth as the heart of woman, is still sufficiently complicated. Don't I know what will become of the little beggar?'

'You're very horrible,' said the old woman. Then she added in a different tone: 'He's much too good for his fate.'

'And pray wasn't I for mine?' the Captain asked.

'By no manner of means!' Madame Grandoni returned as she rose and moved away from him.

The Princess had come into the room accompanied by Hyacinth. As it was now considerably past the dinner-hour the old lady judged that this couple, on their side, had met in the hall and had prolonged their conversation there. Hyacinth watched with extreme interest the way the Princess greeted the Captain—taking it for very simple, easy and friendly. At dinner she made no stranger of him, including him in everything as if he had been a useful familiar like Madame Grandoni, only a little less venerable, yet not giving him any attention that might cause their eyes to meet. She had told Hyacinth she didn't like his eyes, nor indeed very much any part of him. Of course any admiration from almost any source couldn't fail to be in some degree grateful to an amiable woman, but of any unintended effect one might ever have produced the impression made on Godfrey Sholto in an evil hour ministered least to her vanity. He had been useful undoubtedly at times, but at others had been as a droning in her ears. He was so uninteresting in himself, so shallow, so unoccupied and futile, and really so frivolous in spite of his pretension (of which she was unspeakably weary) of being all wrapped up in a single idea. It had never by itself been sufficient to interest her in any man, the fact that he was in love with her; but indeed she could honestly say that most of the people who had liked her had had on their own side something, something in their character or conditions, that she could trouble her head about. Not so far as would do any harm save perhaps in one or two cases; but still some personal mark.

Sholto was a curious and not particularly edifying English type, as the Princess further described him; one of those odd figures produced by old societies that have run to seed, corrupt and exhausted civilisations. He was a cumberer of the earth—purely selfish for all his devoted disinterested airs. He was nothing whatever in himself and had no character or merit save by tradition, reflexion, imitation, superstition. He had a longish pedigree—he came of some musty mouldy 'county family', people with a local reputation and an immense lack of general importance; he had taken the greatest care of his little fortune. He had travelled all over the globe several times, 'for the shooting', in that murdering ravaging way of the English, the destruction, the extirpation of creatures more beautiful, more soaring and more nimble than themselves. He had a little taste, a little cleverness, a little reading, a little good furniture, a little French and Italian (he exaggerated these latter quantities), an immense deal of assurance and unmitigated leisure. That, at bottom, was all he represented—idle, trifling, luxurious, yet at the same time pretentious leisure, the sort of thing that led people to invent false humbugging duties because they had no real ones. Sholto's great idea of himself, after his profession of being her slave, was that he was a cosmopolite and exempt from every prejudice. About the prejudices the Princess couldn't say and didn't care; but she had seen him in foreign countries, she had seen him in Italy, and she was bound to say he understood nothing of those people. It was several years before, shortly after her marriage, that she had first encountered him. He had not begun immediately to go in for adoring her—it had come little by little. It was only after she had separated from her husband that he had taken so to hanging about her—since when she had suffered much from him. She would do him one justice, however: he had never, so far as she knew, had the impudence to represent himself as anything but hopeless and helpless. It was on this he took his stand—he wanted to pass for the great model of unrewarded constancy. She couldn't imagine what he was waiting for—perhaps it was for the death of the Prince. But the Prince would never

die, nor had she the least desire he should. She had no wish
to be harsh, for of course that sort of thing was from any
one very flattering; but really, whatever feeling poor Sholto
might have, four fifths of it were purely theatrical. He was
not in the least a natural quiet person, and had only a
hundred affectations and attitudes, the result of never having
been obliged to put his hand to anything, of having no
serious tastes and yet being born to a little position. The
Princess remarked that she was so glad Hyacinth had no
position, had been forced to do something else in life but
amuse himself; that was the way she liked her friends now.
She had said to Sholto again and again, 'There are plenty of
others who will be much more pleased with you; why not
go to *them*? It's such a waste of time.' She was sure indeed
he had in some degree taken her advice, was by no means,
as regards herself, the absorbed annihilated creature he endeavoured to pass for. He had told her once he was trying
to take an interest in other women—though indeed he had
added that it was of no use. Of what use did he expect anything he could possibly do to be? Hyacinth, at this, didn't
tell the Princess he had reason to believe the Captain's
effort in that direction had not been absolutely vain; but he
made the reflexion privately and with increased confidence.
He recognised a further truth even when his companion said
at the end that with all she had touched upon poor Sholto
was a queer combination. Trifler as he was there was something sinister in him too; and she confessed she had had
a vague feeling at times that some day he might do her a
hurt. It was a remark that caused our young man to stop
short on the threshold of the drawing-room and ask in a
low voice: 'Are you afraid of him?'

The Princess smiled as he had not yet seen her. '*Dio mio*,
how you say that! Should you like to kill him for me?'

'I shall have to kill some one, you know. Why not him
while I'm about it if he troubles you?'

'Ah my friend, if you should begin to kill every one who
has troubled me!' she wonderfully wailed as they went into
the room.

XXVII

HE KNEW there was something out of the way as soon as
he saw Lady Aurora's face look forth at him in answer to
his tap while she held the door ajar. What was she doing in
Pinnie's bedroom?—a very poor place, into which the dressmaker, with her reverence, would never have admitted a
person of that quality unless things had got pretty bad. She
was solemn too and without her usual incoherent laugh;
she had removed her large hat, with its limp old-fashioned
veil, and she raised her finger to her lips. Hyacinth's first
alarm had been immediately after he let himself into the
house with his latch-key, as he always did, and found the
little room on the right of the passage, in which Pinnie had
lived ever since he remembered, fireless and untenanted. As
soon as he had paid the cabman who put down his port-
manteau for him in the hall—he was not used to paying
cabmen and was conscious he gave too much, but was too
impatient in his sudden anxiety to care—he had hurried
up the vile staircase that seemed viler, even through his
preoccupation, than ever, and given the knock, accompanied
by a call the least bit tremulous, precipitately answered by
Lady Aurora. She had drawn back into the room a moment
while he stared in his dismay; then she emerged again, closing the door behind her—all with the air of enjoining him
to be terribly quiet. He felt suddenly so sick at the idea of
having lingered at Medley while there was distress in the
wretched little house to which he owed so much that he
scarcely found strength for an articulate question and obeyed
mechanically the mute urgent gesture by which their noble
visitor appealed to him to go downstairs with her. It was
only when they stood together in the deserted parlour—
where he noted as for the first time what an inelegant odour
prevailed—that he asked, 'Is she dying—is she dead?' That
was the least the strained sadness looking out of Lady
Aurora's face appeared to announce.

'Dear Mr Robinson, I'm so sorry for you. I wanted to write, but I promised her I wouldn't. She's very ill, poor dear—we're very anxious. It began ten days ago and I suppose I *must* tell you how much she has gone down.' Lady Aurora spoke with more than all her usual embarrassments and precautions—eagerly, yet as if it cost her much pain: pausing a little after everything to see how he would take it, then going on with a small propitiatory rush. He learned presently what was the matter, what doctor she had sent for, and that if he would wait a little before going into the room it would be so much better; the invalid having sunk within half an hour into a doze of a less agitated kind than she had had for some time, from which it would be an immense pity to run the risk of waking her. The doctor gave her the right things, as it seemed to her ladyship, but he admitted that she had very little power of resistance. He was of course not a very large practitioner, Mr Buffery from round the corner, yet he seemed really clever; and she herself had taken the liberty (as she confessed to this she threw off one of her odd laughs and her colour rose) of sending an elderly, respectable person—a decent nursing body known to many doctors. She was out just then, she had to go once a day for the air—'only when I come of course,' Lady Aurora hastened to note. Dear Miss Pynsent had had a cold hanging about her and had not taken care of it. Hyacinth would know how plucky she was about that sort of thing; she took so little interest in herself. 'Of course a cold's a cold, whoever has it; isn't it?' his friend asked as if superior to the old discrimination against the power of the lowly to do justice to such visitations. Ten days previous she had taken an additional chill through falling asleep in her chair, at night, down there, and letting the fire go out. 'It would have been nothing if she had been like you or me, you know,' his benefactress went on; 'but as she was then it made the difference. The day was horribly damp—the chill had struck into the lungs and inflammation come on. Mr Buffery says she was impoverished, you know—so weak and low she had nothing to *go* on.' The next morning she had

bad pains and a good deal of fever, yet had got up. Poor
Pinnie's gracious ministrant didn't make clear to Hyacinth
what time had elapsed before she came to the rescue, nor
by what means she had been notified, and he saw that she
slurred this over from the admirable motive of wishing him
not to feel that their patient had suffered by his absence or
called for him in vain. This indeed appeared not to have
been the case if Pinnie had opposed successfully his being
written to. 'I came in very soon,' Lady Aurora only said—
'it was such a delightful chance. Since then she has had
everything—if it wasn't so sad to see a person *need* so little.
She did want you to stay where you were: she has clung to
that idea. I speak the simple truth, Mr Robinson.'

'I don't know what to say to you—you're so extraordinarily
good, so angelic,' Hyacinth replied, bewildered and sickened
by a strange, unexpected shame. The episode he had just
traversed, the splendour he had been living in and drinking
so deep of, the unnatural alliance to which he had given
himself up while his wretched little foster-mother struggled
alone with her death-stroke—he could see it was that; the
presentiment of it, the last stiff horror, was in all the place
—this whole contrast cut him like a knife and made the
ugly accident of his absence a perversity of his own. 'I can
never blame you when you're so kind, but I wish to God
I had known!' he broke out.

Lady Aurora clasped her hands, begging him to judge her
fairly. 'Of course it was a great responsibility for us, but we
thought it right to consider what she urged upon us. She
went back to it constantly, that your visit should *not* be cut
short. When you should come of yourself it would be time
enough. I don't know exactly where you've been, but she
said it was such a pleasant house. She kept repeating that it
would do you so much good.'

Hyacinth felt his eyes fill with tears. 'She's dying—she's
dying! How can she live when she's like that?'

He sank upon the old yellow sofa, the sofa of his lifetime
and of so many years before, and buried his head on the
shabby, tattered arm. A succession of sobs broke from his

lips—sobs in which the accumulated emotion of months and the strange acute conflict of feeling that had possessed him for the three weeks just past found relief and a kind of solution. Lady Aurora sat down beside him and laid her finger-tips gently on his hand. So for a minute, while his tears flowed and she said nothing, he felt her timid touch of consolation. At the end of the minute he raised his head; it came back to him that she had said 'we' just before, and he asked her whom she meant.

'Oh Mr Vetch, don't you know? I've made his charming acquaintance; it's impossible to be more kind.' Then while for a space Hyacinth was silent, wincing, pricked with the thought that Pinnie had been beholden to the fiddler while *he* was masquerading in high life, Lady Aurora added: 'He's a charming musician. She asked him once at first to bring his violin; she thought it would soothe her.'

'I'm much obliged to him, but now that I'm here we needn't trouble him,' said Hyacinth.

Apparently there had been a certain dryness in his tone, which was the cause of her ladyship's venturing to reply after an hesitation: 'Do let him come, Mr Robinson; let him be near you! I wonder if you know that—that he has a great affection for you.'

'The more fool he; I've always treated him like a brute!' Hyacinth declared, colouring.

The way Lady Aurora spoke proved to him later that she now definitely did know his secret, or one of those mysteries rather; for at the rate things had been going for the last few months he was making a regular collection. She knew the smaller secret—not of course the greater; she had decidedly been illuminated by Pinnie's divagations. At the moment he made that reflexion, however, he was almost startled to perceive how completely he had ceased to resent such betrayals and how little it suddenly seemed to signify that the innocent source of them was about to be quenched. The sense of his larger treasure of experience swallowed up that particular anxiety, making him ask himself what it mattered, for the little time now left him, that people should exchange allusions, below their breath, to the hidden mark he now bore. The day came quickly when he believed, and yet didn't care, that it had been in that manner immensely talked about.

After Lady Aurora left him, promising she would call him the first moment it should seem prudent, he walked up and down the cold stale parlour sunk in his meditations. The shock of the danger of losing Pinnie had already passed away; he had achieved so much of late in the line of accepting the idea of death that the little dressmaker, in taking her departure, seemed already to benefit by this curious discipline. What was most vivid to him in the deserted field of her unsuccessful industry was the changed vision with which he had come back to objects familiar for twenty years. The picture was the same, and all its horrid elements, wearing a kind of greasy gloss in the impure air of Lomax Place, made, through the mean window-panes, a dismal *chiaroscuro*— showed, in their polished misery, the friction of his own little life; yet the eyes with which he looked at it had new terms of comparison. He had known the scene for hideous and sordid, but its aspect to-day was pitiful to the verge of the sickening; he couldn't believe that for years he had accepted and even a little revered it. He was frightened at the sort of service his experience of grandeur had rendered him. It was all very well to have assimilated that element with a rapidity which had surprises even for himself; but with sensibilities now so improved what fresh arrangement could one come to with the very humble, which was in its nature uncompromising? Though the spring was far advanced the day was a dark drizzle and the room had the clamminess of a finished use, an ooze of dampness from the muddy street where the shallow defensive areas were a narrow slit. No wonder Pinnie had felt it at last, no wonder her small underfed organism had grown numb and ceased to act. At the thought of her limited stinted life, the patient humdrum effort of her needle and scissors, which had ended only in a show-room where there was nothing to show and a pensive reference to the cut of sleeves no longer worn, the tears again rose to his eyes; but he brushed them aside when he heard a cautious tinkle at the house-door, which was presently opened by the little besmirched slavey retained for the service of the solitary lodger—a domestic easily bewildered, who had a particularly lamentable conscious squint and distressed Hyacinth by wearing shoes that didn't match, though of an equal antiquity and intimately emulous in the facility with which they dropped off. He had not heard Mr Vetch's voice in the hall, apparently because he spoke in a whisper; but the young man was not surprised when, taking every precaution not to make the door creak, their neighbour came into the parlour. The fiddler said nothing to him at first; they only looked at each other for a long minute. Hyacinth saw what he most wanted to know— whether *he* knew the worst about Pinnie; but what was further in his eyes, which had an expression considerably different from any hitherto seen in them, defined itself to our hero only little by little.

'Don't you think you might have written me a word?' said Hyacinth at last. His anger at having been left in ignorance had quitted him, but he thought the question fair. None the less he expected a sarcastic answer, and was surprised at the mild reasonableness with which Mr Vetch replied—

'I assure you that no responsibility, in the course of my life, ever did more to distress me. There were obvious reasons for calling you back, and yet I couldn't help wishing you might finish your visit. I balanced one thing against the other. It was very difficult.'

'I can imagine nothing more simple. When people's nearest and dearest are dying they're usually sent for.'

The visitor gave a strange argumentative smile. If Lomax Place and Miss Pynsent's select lodging-house wore a new face of vulgarity to Hyacinth it may be imagined whether the renunciation of the niceties of the toilet, the resigned seediness, which marked Mr Vetch's old age was unlikely to lend itself to comparison. The glossy butler at Medley had had a hundred more of the signs of success in life. 'My dear boy, this case was exceptional,' the fiddler returned. 'Your visit had a character of importance.'

'I don't know what you know about it. I don't remember that I told you anything.'

'No certainly, you've never told me much. But if, as is probable, you've seen that kind lady who's now upstairs you'll have learned that Pinnie made a tremendous point of your not being disturbed. She threatened us with her displeasure if we should hurry you back. You know what Pinnie's displeasure is!' As at this Hyacinth turned away with a gesture of irritation Mr Vetch went one: 'No doubt she's absurdly fanciful, poor dear thing; but don't now cast any disrespect on it. I assure you that if she had been here alone, suffering, sinking, without a creature to tend her and nothing before her but to die in a corner like a starved cat, she would still have faced that fate rather than cut short by a single hour your experience of novel scenes.'

Hyacinth turned it miserably over. 'Of course I know what you mean. But she spun her delusion—she always did all of them—out of nothing. I can't imagine what she knows about my "experience" of any kind of scenes. I told her when I went out of town very little more than I told you.'

'What she guessed, what she gathered, has been at any rate enough. She has made up her mind that you've formed a connexion by means of which you'll come somehow or other into your own. She has done nothing but talk about your grand kindred. To her mind, you know, it's all one, the aristocracy, and nothing's simpler than that the person —very exalted, as she believes—with whom you've been to stay should undertake your business with her friends.'

'Oh well,' said Hyacinth, 'I'm very glad not to have deprived you of that entertainment.'

'I assure you the spectacle was exquisite.' Then the fiddler added: 'My dear fellow, please leave her the idea.'

'Leave it? I'll do much more!' Hyacinth returned. 'I'll tell her my great relations have adopted me and that I've come back in the character of Lord Robinson.'

'She'll need nothing more to die happy,' said Mr Vetch.

Five minutes later, after Hyacinth had obtained from his old friend a confirmation of Lady Aurora's account of Miss Pynsent's condition, this worthy explaining that he came over like that to see how she was half a dozen times a day—five minutes later a silence had descended upon the pair while our youth awaited some sign from Lady Aurora that he might come upstairs. The fiddler, who had lighted a pipe, looked out of the window as if the view were a chart of all the grey past; and Hyacinth, making his tread discreet, walked about the room with his hands in his pockets. At last Mr Vetch observed without taking his pipe out of his lips or looking round: 'I think you might be a little more frank with me at this time of day and at such a crisis.'

Hyacinth stopped in his walk, wondering for a moment all sincerely what his companion meant, for he had no consciousness at present of an effort to conceal anything he could possibly tell—there were some things of course he couldn't: on the contrary his life seemed to him particularly open to the public view and exposed to invidious comment. It was at this moment he first noticed a certain difference; there was a tone in Mr Vetch's voice he seemed never to have felt before—an absence of that note which had made him say in other days that the impenetrable old man was diverting himself at his expense. It was as if his attitude had changed, become more explicitly considerate, in consequence of some alteration or promotion on Hyacinth's part, his having grown older or more important, or even grown simply more surpassingly odd. If the first impression made upon him by Pinnie's old neighbour, as to whose place in the list of the sacrificial (his being a gentleman or one of the sovereign people) he formerly was so perplexed; if the sentiment excited by Mr Vetch in a mind familiar now for nearly a month with forms of indubitable gentility was not favourable to the idea of fraternisation, this secret impatience in Hyacinth's breast was soon corrected by one of the sudden reactions or quick conversions of which the young man was so often the victim. In the light of the fiddler's appeal, which evidently meant more than it said, his musty antiquity, his typical look of having had for years a small definite use and taken all the creases and contractions of it, even his visible expression of ultimate parsimony and of having ceased to care for the shape of his trousers because he cared more for something else—these things became so many reasons for turning round, going over to him, touching marks of an invincible fidelity, the humble continuous single-minded practice of daily duties and an art after all very charming; pursued moreover while persons of the species our restored prodigal had lately been consorting with fidgeted from one selfish sensation to another and couldn't even live in the same place for three months together.

'What should you like me to do, to say, to tell you? Do you want to know what I've been doing in the country? I should have first to know myself,' Hyacinth decently pleaded.

'Have you enjoyed it very much?'

'Yes certainly, very much—not knowing anything about Pinnie. I've been in a beautiful house with a beautiful woman.'

Mr Vetch had turned round; he looked very impartial through the smoke of his pipe. 'Is she really a princess?'

'I don't know what you mean by "really": I suppose all titles are great rot. But every one seems agreed to call her so.'

'You know I've always liked to enter into your life, and to-day the wish is stronger than ever,' the old man presently said, while he fixed his eyes steadily on his companion's.

Hyacinth returned his gaze a moment. 'What makes you say that just now?'

The fiddler appeared to deliberate and at last replied: 'Because you're in danger of losing the best friend you've ever had.'

'Be sure I feel it. But if I've got *you*——!' his companion added.

'Oh me! I'm very old and very tired of life.'

'I suppose that that's what one arrives at. Well, if I can

help you in any way you must lean on me, you must make use of me.'

'That's precisely what I was going to say to you,' said Mr Vetch. 'Should you like any money?'

'Of course I should! But why should you offer it to me?'

'Because in saving it up little by little I've had you in mind.'

'Dear Mr Vetch,' our young man returned, 'you have me too much in mind. I'm not worth it, please believe that; and for all sorts of reasons. I should make money enough for any uses I have for it, or have any right to have, if I stayed quietly in London and attended to my work. As you know, I can earn a decent living.'

'Yes, I can see that. But if you stayed quietly in London what would become of your princess?'

'Oh they can always manage, ladies in that position.'

'Hanged if I understand her position!' cried Mr Vetch, but without laughing. 'You've been for three weeks without work and yet you look uncommonly smart.'

'Well, my living, you see, has cost me nothing. When you stay with great people you don't pay your score,' Hyacinth explained with great gentleness. 'Moreover the lady whose hospitality I've been enjoying has made me a very handsome offer of work.'

'What kind of work?'

'The only kind I know. She's going to send me a lot of books to do up for her.'

'And to pay you fancy prices?'

'Oh no; I'm to fix the prices myself.'

'Are not transactions of that kind rather disagreeable— with a lady whose hospitality one has been enjoying?' Mr Vetch enquired.

'Exceedingly! That's exactly why I shall do the books and then take no money.'

'Your princess is rather clever!' the fiddler coldly laughed.

'Well, she can't force me to take it if I won't,' said Hyacinth.

'No; you must only let *me* do that.'

'You've curious ideas about me,' the young man declared.

Mr Vetch turned about to the window again, remarking that he had curious ideas about everything. Then he added after an interval: 'And have you been making love to your great lady?'

He had expected a flash of impatience in reply to this appeal and was rather surprised at the manner in which Hyacinth began: 'How shall I explain? It's not a question of that sort.'

'Has she been making love to you then?'

'If you should ever see her you'd understand how absurd that supposition is.'

'How shall I ever see her?' returned Mr Vetch. 'In the absence of that privilege I think there's something in my idea.'

'She looks quite over my head,' said Hyacinth simply. 'It's by no means impossible you may see her. She wants to know my friends, to know the people who live in the Place. And she would take a particular interest in you on account of your opinions.'

'Ah I've no opinions now—none any more!' the old man broke out sadly. 'I only had them to frighten Pinnie.'

'She was easily frightened,' said Hyacinth.

'Yes, and easily reassured. Well, I like to know about your life,' his neighbour sighed irrelevantly. 'But take care the great lady doesn't lead you too far.'

'How do you mean, too far?'

'Isn't she a conspiring socialist, a dabbler in plots and treasons? Doesn't she go in for a general rectification, as Eustache calls it?'

Hyacinth had a pause. 'You should see the place—you should see what she wears, what she eats and drinks.'

'Ah you mean that she's inconsistent with her theories? My dear boy, she'd be a droll woman if she weren't. At any rate I'm glad of it.'

'Glad of it?' Hyacinth repeated.

'For you, I mean, when you stay with her; it's more luxurious!' Mr Vetch exclaimed, turning round and smiling.

At this moment a little rap on the floor above, given by Lady Aurora, announced that Hyacinth might at last come up and see Pinnie. Mr Vetch listened and recognised it, and it led him to say with considerable force: 'There's a woman whose theories and conduct do square!'

Hyacinth, on the threshold, leaving the room, stopped long enough to meet it. 'Well, when the day comes for my friend to give up—you'll see.'

'Yes, I've no doubt there are things she'll bring herself to sacrifice,' the old man retorted. But Hyacinth was already out of hearing.

XXVIII

MR VETCH waited below till Lady Aurora should come down and give him the news he was in suspense for. His mind was pretty well made up about Pinnie. It had seemed to him the night before that death was written in her face, and he judged it on the whole a very good moment for her to lay down her earthly burden. He had reasons for believing that the future couldn't be sweet to her. As regards Hyacinth his mind was far from being at ease; for though aware in a general way that he had taken up with strange company, and though having flattered himself of old that he should be pleased to act out his life and solve the problem of his queer inheritance, he was worried by the absence of full knowledge. He put out his pipe in anticipation of Lady Aurora's reappearance and without this consoler was more accessible still to certain fears that had come to him in consequence of a recent talk, or rather an attempt at a talk, with Eustache Poupin. It was through the Frenchman that he had gathered the little he knew about the occasion of Hyacinth's strange and high 'social' adventure. His vision of the matter had been wholly inferential; for Hyacinth had made a mystery of his absence to Pinnie, merely letting her know that there was a lady in the case and that the best luggage he could muster and the best way his shirts could be done up would still be far from good enough. Poupin had seen Godfrey Sholto at the 'Sun and Moon', and it had come to him, through Hyacinth, that a remarkable feminine influence in the Captain's life was conducive in some way to his presence in Bloomsbury—an influence moreover by which Hyacinth himself, for good or for evil, was in peril of being touched. Sholto was the young man's visible link with a society for which Lisson Grove could have no importance in the scheme of the universe save as a short cut (too disagreeable to be frequently used) out of Bayswater; therefore if Hyacinth left town with a new hat and a pair of kid gloves it must have been to move in the direction of that superior circle and in some degree at the solicitation of the before-mentioned feminine influence. So much as this the Frenchman suggested explicitly enough, as his manner was, to the old fiddler; but his talk had a strain of other and rarer reference which excited Mr Vetch's curiosity rather than satisfied it. They were obscure, these deeper implications; they were evidently painful to the speaker; they were confused and embarrassed and totally wanting in that effect of high hand-polish which usually characterised the lightest allusions of M. Poupin. It was the fiddler's fancy that his friend had something on his mind which he was not at liberty to impart, and that it related to Hyacinth and might, for those who took an interest in the singular lad, give ground for no small anxiety. Mr Vetch, on his own part, nursed this anxiety into a tolerably definite shape: he persuaded himself that the Frenchman had been leading the boy too far in the line of social criticism, had given him a push on some crooked path where a slip would be a likely accident. When on a subsequent occasion, with Poupin, he indulged in a hint of this suspicion, the bookbinder flushed a good deal and declared that his conscience was pure. It was one of his peculiarities that when his colour rose he looked angry, and Mr Vetch held that his displeasure was a proof that in spite of his repudiations he had been unwise; though before they parted Eustache gave this sign of softness that he shed tears of emotion of which the source was not clear to the fiddler and which appeared in a general way to be dedicated to Hyacinth. The interview had taken place in Lisson Grove, where Madame Poupin, however, had not shown herself.

Altogether the old man was a prey to suppositions which led him to feel how much he himself had outlived the democratic glow of his prime. He had ended by accepting everything—though indeed he couldn't swallow the idea that a trick should be played upon Hyacinth; and even by taking an interest in current politics, as to which of old he had held the opinion—the opinion deep-based in the Poupins to-day —that they had been invented on purpose to throw dust in the eyes of disinterested reformers and to circumvent the social solution. He had renounced that problem some time ago; there was no way to clear it up that didn't seem to make a bigger mess than the actual muddle of human affairs, which by the time one had reached sixty-five might mostly cease to exasperate. Mr Vetch could still feel a certain sharpness on the subject of the prayer-book and the bishops, and if at moments he was a little ashamed of having accepted this world could reflect that at all events he continued to repudiate every other. The idea of great changes, however, took its place among the dreams of his youth; for what was any possible change in the relations of men and women but a new combination of the same elements? If the elements could be made different the thing would be worth thinking of; but it was not only impossible to introduce any new ones—no means had yet been discovered for getting rid of the old. The figures on the chessboard were still the passions and jealousies and superstitions and stupidities of man, and their position with regard to each other at any given moment could be of interest only to the grim invisible fates who played the game—who sat, through the ages, bow-backed over the table. This laxity had come upon our fiddling friend with the increase of his measurement round the waist and with that of the little heap of half-crowns and half-sovereigns that had accumulated in a tin box very stiffly padlocked which he kept under his bed and the interwoven threads of sentiment and custom uniting him to the dressmaker and her foster-son. If he was no longer pressing about the demands he felt he should have a right to make of society, as he had been in the days when his conversation scandalised Pinnie, so he was now not pressing for Hyacinth either; reflecting that though indeed the constituted powers might have to 'count' with him it would be in better taste for him not to be importunate about a settlement. What he had come to fear for the interesting youth was that he should be precipitated by crude agencies into depths where the deplorable might not exclude the ridiculous. It may even be said that Mr Vetch had a secret project of settling a little on his behalf.

Lady Aurora peeped into the room, very noiselessly, nearly half an hour after Hyacinth had left it, and let the fiddler know that she was called to other duties but that the nurse had come back and the doctor had promised to look in at five o'clock. She herself would return in the evening, and meanwhile Hyacinth was with his aunt, who had recognised him without a protest; indeed seemed intensely happy that he should be near her again and lay there with closed eyes, very weak and speechless, holding his hand. Her restlessness had passed and her fever abated, but she had no pulse to speak of and Lady Aurora didn't disguise the fact that by any good judgement she was rapidly sinking. Mr Vetch had already accepted it and after her ladyship had quitted him he lighted another philosophic pipe upon it, lingering on, till the doctor came, in the dressmaker's dismal forsaken bower, where in past years he had indulged in so many sociable droppings-in and hot tumblers. The echo of all her little simple surprises and pointless contradictions, her gasping reception of contemplative paradox, seemed still to float in the air; but the place felt as relinquished and bereft as if she were already beneath the sod. Pinnie had always been a wonderful hand at 'putting away'; the litter that testified to her most elaborate efforts was often immense, but the reaction in favour of an unspeckled carpet was greater still; and on the present occasion, before taking to her bed, she had found strength to sweep and set in order

as tidily as if she had been sure the room would never again
know her care. Even to the old fiddler, who had not Hyacinth's sensibility to the scenery of life, it had the cold
propriety of a place arranged for internment. After the
doctor had seen Pinnie that afternoon there was no doubt
left as to its soon being the stage of dismal preliminaries.

Miss Pynsent, however, resisted her malady for nearly a
fortnight more, during which Hyacinth was constantly in
her room. He never went back to old Crook's, with whose
establishment, through violent causes, his relations seemed
indefinitely suspended; and in fact for the rest of the time
that Pinnie demanded his care absented himself but twice
from Lomax Place during more than a few minutes. On
one of these occasions he travelled over to Audley Court
and spent an hour there; on the other he met Millicent
Henning by previous understanding and took a walk with
her on the Embankment. He tried to find an hour to go and
thank Madame Poupin for a sympathetic offering, many
times repeated, of *tisane* concocted after a receipt thought
supreme by the couple in Lisson Grove (though little appreciated in the neighbourhood generally); but he was obliged
to acknowledge her kindness only by a respectful letter,
which he composed with some trouble, though much elation, in the French tongue, peculiarly favourable, as he
believed, to little courtesies of this kind. Lady Aurora came
again and again to the darkened house, where she diffused
her beneficent influence in nightly watches, in the most
modern sanative suggestions, in conversations with Hyacinth
more ingeniously addressed than her fluttered embarrassments might have betrayed to the purpose of diverting his
mind, and in tea-makings (there was a great deal of this
liquid consumed on the premises during Pinnie's illness)
after a system more enlightened than the usual fashion of
Pentonville. She was the bearer of several messages and of
a good deal of medical advice from Rose Muniment, whose
interest in the dressmaker's case irritated Hyacinth by its
fine courage, which even at second-hand was still extrava-

gant: she appeared very nearly as resigned to the troubles of others as she was to her own.

Hyacinth had been seized the day after his return from Medley with a sharp desire to do something enterprising and superior on Pinnie's behalf. He felt the pressure of an angry sense that she was dying of her poor career, of her uneffaced remorse for the trick she had played him in his boyhood—as if he hadn't long ago and indeed at the time forgiven it, judging it to have been the highest wisdom!—of something basely helpless in the attitude of her acquaintance. He wanted to do something that should prove to himself he had got the very best opinion about the invalid it was possible to have: so he insisted that Mr Buffery should consult with a West End doctor if the West End doctor would consent to meet Mr Buffery. An oracle not averse to this condescension was discovered through Lady Aurora's agency—she had not brought him of her own movement because on the one hand she hesitated to impose on the little household in Lomax Place the expense of such a visit, and on the other, with all her narrow personal economies for the sake of her charities, had not the means to meet it herself; and in prevision of the great man's fee Hyacinth applied to Mr Vetch, as he had applied before, for a loan. The great man came and was wonderfully civil to Mr Buffery, whose conduct of the case he pronounced judicious; he remained several minutes in the house, gazing at Hyacinth over his spectacles—he seemed rather more concerned about him than about the patient—and with almost the whole of the Place turning out to stare at his chariot. After all he consented to accept no fee. He put the question aside with a gesture full of urbanity—a course disappointing and displeasing to Hyacinth, who felt in a manner cheated of the full effect of the fine thing he had wished to do for Pinnie; though when he said as much or something like it to Mr Vetch the caustic fiddler greeted the observation with a face of amusement which, considering the situation, verged on the unseemly.

Hyacinth at any rate had done the best he could, and the

fashionable doctor had left directions which foreshadowed commerce with an expensive chemist in Bond Street—a prospect by which our young man was to some extent consoled. Poor Pinnie's decline, however, was not arrested, and one evening more than a week after his return from Medley, as he sat with her alone, it struck him that her mild spirit must already have passed. The respectable nurse had moved away to supper, and by the aid of the staircase a perceptible odour of fizzling bacon indicated that a more cheerful state of things prevailed in the lower regions. Hyacinth couldn't make out if his old friend were asleep or awake; he believed she had not lost consciousness, yet for more than an hour she had given no sign of life. At last she put out her hand as if aware he was near her and wished to feel for him, and murmured, 'Why did she come? I don't want to see her.' In a moment, as she went on, he perceived to whom she was alluding: her mind had travelled back through all the years to the dreadful day—she had described every incident of it to him—when Mrs Bowerbank had invaded her quiet life and startled her sensitive conscience with a message from the prison. 'She sat there so long—so long. She was so very large and I was so frightened. She moaned and moaned and cried—too dreadful. I couldn't help it—I couldn't help it!' Her thought wandered from Mrs Bowerbank in the discomposed show-room, enthroned on the yellow sofa, to the tragic creature at Milbank, whose accents again, for the hour, lived in her ears; and mixed with this mingled vision was still the haunting sense that she herself might have acted differently. That had been cleared up in the past, so far as Hyacinth's intention was concerned; but what was most alive in Pinnie at the present hour was the passion of repentance, of still further expiation. It sickened him that she should believe these things were still necessary, and he leaned over her and talked tenderly, said everything he could think of to soothe her. He told her not to think of that dismal far-off time, which had ceased long ago to have any consequences for either of them; to consider only the future, when she should be quite strong again and he would look after her and keep her all to himself and take care of her better, far better than he had ever done before. He had thought of many things while he sat with Pinnie watching the shadows made by the night-lamp—high imposing shadows of objects low and mean—and among them he had followed with an imagination that went further in that direction than ever before the probable consequences of his not having been adopted in his babyhood by the dressmaker. The workhouse and the gutter, ignorance and cold, filth and tatters, nights of huddling under bridges and in doorways, vermin, starvation and blows, possibly even the vigorous efflorescence of an inherited disposition to crime—these things, which he saw with unprecedented vividness, suggested themselves as his natural portion. Intimacies with a princess, visits to fine old country-houses, intelligent consideration, even, of the best means of inflicting a scare on the classes of privilege, would in that case not have been within his compass; and that Pinnie should have rescued him from such a destiny and put these luxuries within his reach represented almost a grand position as opposed to a foul, if he could only have the magnanimity to take it so.

Her eyes were open and fixed on him, but the sharp ray the little dressmaker used to direct into Lomax Place as she plied her needle at the window had completely left them. 'Not there—what should I do there?' she enquired very softly. 'Not with the great—the great——' and her voice failed.

'The great what? What do you mean?'

'You know—you know,' she went on, making another effort. 'Haven't you been with them? Haven't they received you?'

'Ah they won't separate us, Pinnie; they won't come between us as much as that,' said Hyacinth; and he sank to his knees by her bed.

'*You* must be separate—that makes me happier. I knew they'd find you at last.'

'Poor Pinnie, poor Pinnie,' murmured the young man.

'It was only for that—now I'm going,' she sighed.

'If you'll stay with me you needn't fear,' he smiled at her.

'Oh what would *they* think?' she quavered.

'I like you best,' he insisted.

'You've had me always. Now it's their turn; they've waited.'

'Yes indeed they've waited!' Hyacinth said.

'But they'll make it up; they'll make up everything!' the poor woman panted. Then she added: 'I couldn't, couldn't help it!'—which was the last flicker of her strength. She gave no further sign of consciousness and four days later ceased to breathe. Hyacinth was with her and Lady Aurora, but neither could recognise the moment.

Hyacinth and Mr Vetch carried her bier with the help of Eustache Poupin and Paul Muniment. Lady Aurora was at the funeral and Madame Poupin as well and twenty neighbours from Lomax Place; but the most distinguished member—in appearance at least—of the group of mourners was Millicent Henning, the grave yet brilliant beauty of whose countenance, the high propriety of whose demeanour and the fine taste and general style of whose rich black 'costume' excited no little attention. Mr Vetch had his idea; he had been nursing it ever since Hyacinth's return from Medley, and three days after Pinnie had been consigned to the earth he broached it to his young friend. The funeral had been on a Friday and Hyacinth had mentioned that he should return to old Crook's on Monday morning. This was Sunday night and he had been out for a walk neither with Millicent Henning nor with Paul Muniment, but alone, after the manner of old days. When he came in he found the fiddler waiting for him and snuffing a tallow candle in the blighted show-room. He had three or four little papers in his hand, which exhibited some jottings of his pencil, and Hyacinth guessed, what was the truth but not all the truth, that he had come to speak to him about business. Pinnie had left a little will, of which she had appointed her old friend executor; this fact had already become known to our hero, who thought such an arrangement highly natural. Mr Vetch informed him of the purport of this simple and judicious document and mentioned that he had been looking into the dressmaker's 'affairs'. They consisted, poor Pinnie's affairs, of the furniture of the house in Lomax Place, of the obligation to pay the remainder of a quarter's rent and of a sum of money in the savings-bank. Hyacinth was surprised to learn that Pinnie's economies had produced fruit at this late day (things had gone so ill with her in recent years, and there had been often such a want of money in the house) until Mr Vetch explained to him with eager clearness that he himself had watched over the little hoard, accumulated during the period of her comparative prosperity, with the stiff determination that it should be sacrificed only in case of desperate stress. Work had become scarce with her but she could still do it when it came, and the money was to be kept for the very possible event of her turning helpless. Mercifully enough she had not lived to see that day, and the sum in the bank had survived her, though diminished by more than half. She had left no debts but the matter of the house and those incurred during her illness. Of course the fiddler had known—he hastened to give his young friend this assurance—that Pinnie, had she become infirm, would have been able to count absolutely upon *him* for the equivalent, in her old age, of the protection she had given him in his youth. But what if an accident had overtaken Hyacinth? What if he had incurred some horrid penalty for his revolutionary dabblings, which, little dangerous as they might be to society, were quite capable, in a country where authority, though good-natured, liked occasionally making an example, to put him on the wrong side of a prison-wall? At any rate, for better or worse, by pinching and scraping, she had saved a little, and of that little after everything was paid off a fraction would still be left. Everything was bequeathed to Hyacinth—everything but a couple of plated candlesticks and the old 'cheffonier' which had been so handsome in its day; these Pinnie begged Mr Vetch to accept in recognition of services beyond all price. The furniture, everything he didn't want for his own use, Hyacinth could sell in a lump, and with the proceeds he could wipe out old scores. The sum of money would remain to him; it amounted to about thirty-seven pounds. In mentioning this figure Mr Vetch appeared to imply that Hyacinth would be master of a very pretty little fortune. Even to the young man himself, in spite of his recent initiations, such a windfall seemed far from contemptible; it represented sudden possibilities of still not returning to old Crook's. It represented them, that is, till he presently remembered the various advances made him by the fiddler, and till he reflected that by the time these had been repaid there would hardly be twenty pounds left. That, however, was a far larger sum than he had ever had in his pocket at once. He thanked the old man for his information and remarked—and there was no hypocrisy in the speech—that he was too sorry Pinnie had not given herself the benefit of the whole of the little fund in her lifetime. To this her executor replied that it had yielded her an interest far beyond any other investment, for he was persuaded she had believed she should never live to enjoy it, and that this faith had been rich to her in pictures, visions of the effect, for her brilliant boy, of his 'coming into' something handsome.

'What effect did she mean—do you mean?' Hyacinth asked. As soon as he had spoken he felt he knew what the old man would say—it would be a reference to Pinnie's belief in his reunion with his 'relations' and to the facilities thirty-seven pounds would afford him for cutting a figure among them; and for a moment Mr Vetch looked at him as if exactly that response were on his lips. At the end of the moment, however, he replied quite differently.

'She hoped you'd go abroad and see the world.' The fiddler watched his young friend and then added: 'She had a particular wish you should go to Paris.'

Hyacinth had turned pale at this suggestion and for a moment said nothing. 'Ah Paris!' he almost wailed at last.

'She would have liked you even to take a little run down to Italy.'

'Doubtless that would be jolly. But there's a limit to what one can do with twenty pounds.'

'How do you mean, with twenty pounds?' the old man asked, lifting his eyebrows while the wrinkles in his forehead made deep shadows in the candle-light.

'That's about what will remain after I have settled my account with you.'

'How do you mean, your account with me? I shan't take any of your money.'

Hyacinth's eyes wandered over his interlocutor's suggestive shabbiness. 'I don't want to be beastly ungracious, but suppose *you* should lose your powers.'

'My dear boy, I shall have one of the resources that was open to Pinnie. I shall look to you to be the support of my old age.'

'You may do so with perfect safety, except for that danger you just mentioned—of my being imprisoned or hanged.'

'It's precisely because I think the danger will be less if you go abroad that I urge you to take this chance. You'll see the world and you'll like it better. You'll think society, even as it is, has some good points,' said Mr Vetch.

'I've never liked it better than the last few months.'

'Ah well, wait till you see Paris!'

'Oh, Paris, Paris,' Hyacinth repeated vaguely—and he stared into the turbid flame of the candle as if making out the most brilliant scenes there: an attitude, accent and expression which the fiddler interpreted both as the vibration of a latent hereditary chord and a symptom of the acute sense of opportunity.

BOOK FOURTH

XXIX

THE BOULEVARD was all alive, brilliant with illumina-
tions, with the variety and gaiety of the crowd, the dazzle
of shops and cafés seen through uncovered fronts or immense lucid plates, the flamboyant porches of theatres and
the flashing lamps of carriages, the far-spreading murmur
of talkers and strollers, the uproar of pleasure and prosperity, the general magnificence of Paris on a perfect evening
in June. Hyacinth had been walking about all day—he had
walked from rising till bedtime every day of the week spent
since his arrival—and now an extraordinary fatigue, a
tremendous lassitude had fallen upon him, which, however, was not without its delight of sweet satiety, and he
settled himself in a chair beside a little table in front of
Tortoni's not so much to rest from it as to enjoy it. He had
seen so much, felt so much, learnt so much, thrilled and
throbbed and laughed and sighed so much during the past
several days that he was conscious at last of the danger of
becoming incoherent to himself and of the need of balancing his accounts.

To-night he came to a full stop; he simply sat at the
door of the most dandified café in Paris and felt his pulse
and took stock of his impressions. He had been intending
to visit the Variétés Theatre, which blazed through intermediate lights and through the thin foliage of trees not
favoured by the asphalt, on the other side of the great
avenue. But the impression of Chaumont—he relinquished
that for the present; it added to the luxury of his situation
to reflect that he should still have plenty of time to see the
succès du jour. The same effect proceeded from his determination to order a *marquise* when the waiter, whose
superior shirt-front and whisker emerged from the long
white cylinder of an apron, came to take his commands.
He knew the decoction was expensive—he had learnt as

much at the moment he happened to overhear for the first time a mention of it; which had been the night before as he sat in his stall during an *entr'acte* of the Comédie Française. A gentleman beside him, a young man in evening-dress, conversing with an acquaintance in the row behind, recommended the latter to refresh himself with the luxury in question after the play: there was nothing like it, the speaker remarked, of a hot evening in the open air when one was thirsty. The waiter brought Hyacinth a tall glass of champagne in which a pineapple ice was in solution, and our hero felt he had hoped for a sensation no less intense in looking for an empty table on Tortoni's terrace. Very few tables were empty, and it was his belief that the others were occupied by high celebrities; at any rate they were just the types he had had a prevision of and had wanted to meet when the extraordinary opportunity to come abroad with his pockets full of money (it was more extraordinary even than his original meeting with the Princess) turned real to him in Lomax Place. He knew about Tortoni's from his study of the French novel, and as he sat there he had a vague sense of fraternising with Balzac and Alfred de Musset: there were echoes and reminiscences of their works in the air, all confounded with the indefinable exhalations, the strange composite odour, half agreeable, half impure, of the Boulevard. 'Splendid Paris, charming Paris'—that refrain, the fragment of an invocation, a beginning without an end, hummed itself perpetually in Hyacinth's ears; the only articulate words that got themselves uttered in the hymn of praise his imagination had been addressing to the French capital from the first hour of his stay. He recognised, he greeted with a thousand palpitations, the seat of his maternal ancestors—was proud to be associated with so much of the superb, so many proofs of a civilisation that had no visible rough spots. He had his perplexities and even now and then a revulsion for which he had made no allowance, as when it came over him that the most brilliant city in the world was also the most bloodstained; but the great sense that he understood and sympathised was preponderant, and his comprehension gave him wings—appeared to transport him to still wider fields of knowledge, still higher sensations.

In other days, in London, he had thought again and again of his mother's father, the revolutionary watchmaker who had known the ecstasy of the barricade and had paid for it with his life, and his reveries had not been sensibly chilled by the fact that he knew next to nothing about him. He figured him in his mind, this mystic ancestor, had a conviction that he was very short like himself and had curly hair, an immense talent for his work and an extraordinary natural eloquence, together with many of the most attractive qualities of the French character. But he was reckless and a little cracked, also probably immoral; he had difficulties and debts and irrepressible passions; his life had been an incurable fever and its tragic termination was a matter of course. None the less it would have been a charm to hear him talk, to feel the influence of a gaiety which even political madness could never quench; for his grandson had a theory that he spoke the French tongue of an earlier time, delightful and sociable in accent and phrase, exempt from the baseness of modern slang. This vague yet vivid personage became our young friend's constant companion from the day of his arrival; he roamed about with Florentine's boy hand in hand, sat opposite him at dinner, by the small table in the restaurant, finished the bottle with him, made the bill a little longer—treating him furthermore to innumerable revelations and counsels. He knew the lad's secret without being told and looked at him across the diminutive tablecloth where the great cube of bread, pushed aside a little, left room for his elbows—it puzzled Hyacinth that the people of Paris should ever have had the fierceness of hunger when the loaves were so big; gazed at him with eyes of deep kind glowing comprehension and with lips which seemed to murmur that when one was to die to-morrow one must eat and drink, one must gratify all one's poor senses all one could to-day. There was nothing venerable, no constraint of importance or disapproval, in this edifying and impalpable presence; the young man considered that Hyacinthe Vivier was of his own time of life and could enter into his pleasures as well as his pains. Wondering repeatedly where the barricade on which his grandfather must have fallen had been erected he at last satisfied himself—though I am unable to trace the course of the induction—that it had bristled across the Rue Saint-Honoré very near to the Church of Saint-Roch. The pair had now roamed together through all the museums and gardens, through the principal churches—the republican martyr was very good-natured about this; through the passages and arcades, up and down the great avenues, across all the bridges and above all again and again along the river, where the quays were an endless entertainment to Hyacinth, who lingered by the half-hour beside the boxes of old books on the parapets, stuffing his pockets with five-penny volumes while the bright industries of the Seine flashed and glittered beneath him and on the other bank the glorious Louvre stretched either way for a league. Our young man took the same satisfaction in the Louvre as if he had been invited there, as he had been to poor obliterated Medley; he haunted the museum during all the first days, couldn't look enough at certain pictures nor sufficiently admire the high polish of the great floors in which the golden frescoed ceilings repeated themselves. All Paris struck him as tremendously artistic and decorative; he felt as if hitherto he had lived in a dusky frowsy Philistine world, a world in which the taste was the taste of Little Peddlington and the idea of beautiful arrangement had never had an influence. In his ancestral city it had been active from the first, and that was why his quick sensibility responded and why he murmured his constant refrain whenever the fairness of the great monuments arrested him in the pearly silvery light or he saw them take grey-blue delicate tones at the end of stately vistas. It seemed to him the place expressed herself, and did it in the grand style, while London remained vague and blurred, inarticulate, blunt and dim. Splendid Paris, charming Paris indeed!

Eustache Poupin had given him letters to three or four democratic friends, ardent votaries of the social question, who had by a miracle either escaped the cruelty of exile or suffered the outrage of pardon and, in spite of republican *mouchards* no less infamous than the imperial and the periodical swoops of a despotism which had only changed its buttons and postage-stamps, kept alive the sacred spark which would some day become a consuming flame. Hyacinth, however, had not had the thought of delivering these introductions; he had accepted them because Poupin had had such a solemn glee in writing them, and also because he had not the courage to let the couple in Lisson Grove know how since that terrible night at Hoffendahl's a change had come over the spirit of his dream. He had not grown more concentrated, he had grown more relaxed, and it was inconsistent with relaxation that he should rummage out Poupin's friends—one of them lived in the Batignolles and the others in the Faubourg Saint Antoine— and make believe he cared for what they cared for in the same way as they cared for it. What was supreme in his mind to-day was not the idea of how the society that surrounded him should be destroyed; it was much more the sense of the wonderful precious things it had produced, of the fabric of beauty and power it had raised. That destruction was waiting for it there was forcible evidence, known to himself and others, to show; but since this truth had risen before him in its magnitude he had become conscious of a transfer, partial if not complete, of his sympathies; the same revulsion of which he had given a sign to the Princess in saying that now he pitied the rich, those who were regarded as happy. While the evening passed therefore, as he kept his place at Tortoni's, the emotion that was last to visit him was compunction for not having put himself in relation with poor Poupin's friends, for having neglected to make the acquaintance of earnest people.

Who in the world, if one should come to that, was as earnest as he himself or had given such signal even though secret proofs of it? He could lay that unction to his soul in spite of his having amused himself cynically, spent all his time in theatres, galleries, walks of pleasure. The feeling had not failed him with which he accepted Mr Vetch's furtherance—the sense that since he was destined to perish in his flower he was right to make a dash at the beautiful horrible world. That reflexion had been natural enough, but what was strange was the fiddler's own impulse, his desire to do something pleasant for him, to beguile him and ship him off. What had been most odd in this was the way Mr Vetch appeared to overlook the fact that his young friend had already had that year such a turn of dissipation as was surely rare in the experience of London artisans. This was one of the many things Hyacinth thought of; he thought of others in turn and out of turn; it was almost the first time he had sat still long enough to collect himself. A hundred confused reverberations of the recent past crowded on him and he saw that he had lived more intensely in the previous six months than in all the rest of his time. The succession of events finally straightened itself and he tasted over some of those rarest, strangest moments. His last week at Medley in especial had already become a far-off fable, the echo of a song; he could read it over as a romance bound in vellum and gold, gaze at it as he would have gazed at some exquisite picture. His visit there had been perfect to the end, and even the three days compromised by Sholto's sojourn had not broken the spell, for the three more that had elapsed before his own departure—when the Princess herself had given him the signal—were the most important of all. It was then she had made it clear to him that she was in earnest, was prepared for the last sacrifice. He felt her his standard of comparison, his authority, his measure, his perpetual reference; and in taking possession of his mind to this extent she had completely renewed it. She was altogether a new term, and now that he was in a foreign country he observed how much her conversation, itself so foreign, had prepared him to understand it. In Paris he saw of course a great many women and noticed almost all of them, especially the

actresses; inwardly confronting their movement, their
speech, their manner of dressing, with that of his extraordinary friend. He judged her to be beyond them in every
respect, though there were one or two actresses who had
the air of trying to copy her.

The recollection of the last days he had spent with her
affected him now like the touch of a tear-washed cheek.
She had in the last intimacy, strangest and richest of revelations, shed tears for him, and it was his suspicion that her
secret idea was to frustrate the redemption of his vow to
Hoffendahl, to the immeasurable body that Hoffendahl represented. She pretended to have accepted it, and what she
said was simply that when he should have played his part
she would engage to save him—to fling a cloud about him
as the goddess-mother of the Trojan hero used in Virgil's
poem to *escamoter* Æneas. What she meant was in his view
to prevent him from playing his part at all. She was in
earnest for herself, not for him. The main result of his
closest commerce with her, in which somehow, all without
herself stooping, she had only raised him higher and
higher and absolutely highest, had been to make him feel
that he was good enough for anything. When he had asked
her the last day if he might write to her she said Yes, after
two or three weeks. He had written about Pinnie's death,
and again just before coming abroad, and in doing so had
taken account of something else she had said in regard to
their correspondence—that she didn't wish vague phrases,
protestations or compliments; she wanted the realities of
his life, the smallest, the 'dearest', the most personal details.
Therefore he had treated her to the whole business of the
break-up in Lomax Place, including the sale of the rickety
furniture and similar sordid items. He had told her what
that transaction brought—a beggarly sum, but sufficient to
help a little to pay debts, and had informed her further
that one of the ways Mr Vetch had taken to hurry him off
to Paris was to press upon him thirty pounds out of his
quaint little hoard, crowning the sum already inherited
from Pinnie—which, in a manner that none of Hyacinth's

friends of course could possibly regard as frugal or even as respectable, now was consecrated to a mere excursion. He even mentioned that he had ended by accepting the thirty pounds, adding that he feared his peculiar situation —she would know what he meant by that—made for a failure of proper dignity: it disposed one to grab all one could get, kept one at least very tolerant of whims that took the form of offered comforts.

What he didn't mention to his shining friend was the manner in which he had been received by Paul Muniment and by Millicent Henning on his return from Medley. Millicent's reception had been of the queerest; it had been quite unexpectedly mild. She had made him no scene of violence and appeared to have given up the line of throwing a blur of recrimination over her own equivocal doings. She treated him as if she liked him for having got in with the swells; she had an appreciation of success which would lead her to handle him more tenderly now that he was really successful. She tried to make him describe the style of life that was led in a house where people were invited to stay like that without having to pay, and she surprised almost as much as she gratified him by not indulging in any of her former digs at the Princess. She was lavish of ejaculations when he answered certain of her questions— ejaculations that savoured of Pimlico, 'Oh I say!' and 'Oh my stars!'—and he was more than ever struck with her detestable habit of saying 'Aye, that's where it is' when he had made some remark to which she wished to give an intelligent and sympathetic assent. But she didn't jeer at the Princess's private character; she stayed her satire in a case where there was such an opening for it. Hyacinth reflected that this was lucky for her: he couldn't have stood it (nervous and anxious as he was about Pinnie) if she had had at such a time the bad taste to be low and abusive. Under that stress he would have broken with her completely—would have been too disgusted. She displeased him enough as it was by her vulgar tricks of speech. There were two or three little recurrent thumb-marks of the common that smutched her more blackly for him than their size warranted—as when she said 'full up' for full, 'sold out' for sold, or remarked to him that she supposed he was now going to 'chuck up' his work at old Crook's. It was as if he were fairly requiring of her to speak *better* than women of fashion. These phrases at any rate had fallen upon his ear many a time before, but now they seemed almost unpardonable enough to quarrel about. Not that he had any wish to quarrel, for if the question had been pushed he would have admitted that to-day his intimacy with the Princess had caused any claims he might have had upon Millicent to lapse. Millicent was all discretion, however; she only, it was evident, wished to convey to him that it was better for both parties they should respect each other's liberty. A genial understanding on this subject was what Miss Henning desired, and Hyacinth forbade himself to enquire what use she proposed to make of her freedom. During the month that elapsed between Pinnie's death and his visit to Paris he had seen her several times, since the respect for each other's freedom had somehow not implied cessation of intercourse and it was only natural she should have been soft to him in his bereaved condition. Hyacinth's sentiment about Pinnie was deep, and Millicent was clever enough to guess it; the consequence of which was that on these occasions she was very soft indeed. She talked to him almost as if she had been his mother and he a convalescent child; called him her dearest dear and a precious young rascal and her own old boy; moralised a good deal, abstained from beer (till she learnt he had inherited a fortune) and when he remarked once (moralising a little too) that after the death of a person we have loved we are haunted by the memory of our failures of kindness, of generosity, rejoined with a dignity that made the words almost a contribution to the philosophic view, 'Yes, that's where it is!'

Something in her behaviour at this period had even made Hyacinth wonder if there were not some mystical sign in his appearance, some final betrayal in the very expression

of his face, of the predicament in which he had been
placed by Diedrich Hoffendahl; he began to suspect anew
the operation of that 'beastly *attendrissement*' he had de-
tected of old in people who had the benefit of Miss Pynsent's innuendoes. The compassion Millicent felt for him
had never been one of the reasons why he liked her; it had
fortunately been corrected moreover by his power to make
her furious. This evening, on the Boulevard, as he watched
the endless facial successions, one of the ideas that came
to him was that it was odd he should like her even yet; for
heaven knew he liked the Princess better, and he had
hitherto supposed that when a sentiment of this kind had
the energy of a possession it made a clean sweep of all
minor predilections. But it was clear to him that she still
existed for him as a loud-breathing feminine fact, that he
couldn't feel he had quite done with her or she with him,
and that in spite of his having now so many other things
to admire there was still a comfort in the recollection of
her robust beauty and her primitive passions. Hyacinth
thought of her as some clever young barbarian who in
ancient days should have made a pilgrimage to Rome might
have thought of a Dacian or Iberian mistress awaiting his
return on the rough provincial shore. If Millicent judged
his visit at a 'hall' a proof of the sort of success that was
to attend him—how he reconciled this with the supposition
that she perceived as a ghostly crown intermingled with
his curly hair the lurid light of destiny, the aureola of
martyrdom, he would have had some difficulty in explaining—if Miss Henning considered, on his return from
Medley, that he had taken his place on the winning side it
was only consistent of her to borrow a grandeur from the
fact of his course of travel; and indeed by the time he was
ready to start she spoke of his participation in this privilege
of the upper classes as if she had invented it herself and
had even contributed materially to the funds required. It
had been her theory from the first that she only liked
people of spirit; and Hyacinth certainly had never had so
much spirit as when he went 'abroad', after the fashion of

Mr Vetch of old, with a hatbox. He could say to himself
quite without bitterness that of course she would profit by
his absence to put her relations with Sholto on a comfortable footing; yet somehow, after all, at this moment, as her
distant English face out-blossomed the nearer, the livid
Parisian, it had not that gentleman's romantic shadow
across it. It was the general brightness of Paris perhaps that
made him see things sharp; at any rate he remembered
with kindness something she had said to him the last time
he saw her and that it touched him exceedingly at the
moment. He had happened to observe to her in a friendly
way that now Miss Pynsent had gone she was, with the
exception of Mr Vetch, the person in his whole circle who
had known him longest. To this Millicent had replied that
Mr Vetch wouldn't live for ever and that she should then
have the satisfaction of being his very oldest friend. 'Oh
well, I shan't live for ever either,' said Hyacinth; which led
her to ask if by chance he had a weakness of the chest.
'Not that I know of, but I might get smashed in a row';
and when she broke out into scorn of his silly notion of
turning everything up—as if any one wanted to know what
a costermonger would like, or any of that low sort at the
East End!—he amused himself with enquiring if she were
satisfied with the condition of society and thought nothing
ought to be done for people who at the end of a lifetime of
starvation-wages had only the reward of the hideous workhouse and a pauper's grave.

'I shouldn't be satisfied with anything if ever _you_ was
to slip up,' she had answered simply, looking at him with
her beautiful boldness. Then she had added: 'There's one
thing I can tell you, Mr Robinson: that if ever any one
was to do you a turn——!' And she had paused again, toss-
ing back the head she carried as if it were surmounted by
the plumes of a chieftainess, while Hyacinth asked what
would occur in that contingency. 'Well, there'd be _one_ left
behind who would take it up!' she had announced; and in
the tone of the declaration there had been something clear
and brave. It struck Hyacinth as a strange fate—though

not stranger after all than his native circumstances—that one's memory should come to be represented by a shop-girl overladen with bracelets of imitation silver; but he was reminded that Millicent was a fine specimen of a woman of a type opposed to the whining, and that in her large free temperament many disparities were reconciled.

XXX

ON THE other hand the intensity of Paris had not much power to transfigure the impression made upon him by such intercourse with Paul Muniment as he had enjoyed during the weeks that followed Pinnie's death—an impression considerably more severe than any idea of renunciation or oblivion that could connect itself with Millicent. Why it should have had the taste of sadness was not altogether clear, for Muniment's voice was as distinct as any in the chorus of approbation excited by the news that the youth was about to cultivate the most characteristic of the pleasures of gentility—an applausive unanimity the effect of which was to place his journey to Paris in a light almost ridiculous. What had got into them all—did they think he was good for nothing but to amuse himself? Mr Vetch had been the most zealous, but the others clapped him on the back almost exactly in the same manner he had seen his mates in Soho bring their palms down on one of their number when it was disclosed to them that his 'missus' had made him yet once again a father. That had been Poupin's tone, and his wife's as well; and even poor Schinkel, with his everlasting bandage, whom he had met in Lisson Grove, appeared to feel it necessary to remark that a little run across the Rhine while he was about it would open his eyes to a great many wonders. The Poupins shed tears of joy, and the letters which have already been mentioned and which lay day after day on the mantel-shelf of the little room our hero occupied at an *hôtel garni* tremendously tall and somewhat lopsided in the Rue Jacob (that recommendation proceeded also from Lisson Grove, the garni being kept by a second cousin of Madame Eustache)—these valuable documents had been prepared by the obliging exile many days before his young friend was ready to start. It was almost refreshing to Hyacinth when old Crook, the sole outspoken dissentient, told him he was a blockhead to waste his money on the bloody French. This worthy employer of labour was evidently disgusted at such an innovation; if he wanted a little recreation why couldn't he take it as it had been taken in Soho from the beginning of time, in the shape of a trip to Brighton or two or three days of alcoholic torpor? Old Crook was right. Hyacinth conceded freely that he was a blockhead, and was only a little uncomfortable that he couldn't explain why he didn't pretend not to be and had a kind of right to that compensatory ease.

Paul guessed why, of course, and smiled approval with a candour which gave Hyacinth a strange inexpressible heartache. He already knew his friend's view of him as mainly ornamental, as adapted only to the softer forms of the subversive energy, as constituted in short to show that the revolution was not necessarily brutal and illiterate; but in the light of the cheerful stoicism with which Muniment faced the sacrifice our hero was committed to the latter had found it necessary to remodel a good deal his original conception of his sturdy friend's character. The result of this process was not that he admired it less but that he felt almost awe-stricken in presence of it. There had been an element of that sort in his appreciation of Muniment from the first, but the weight now to carry was the sense of such a sublime consistency. Hyacinth felt that he himself could never have risen so high. He was competent to take the stiff engagement to Hoffendahl and was equally competent to keep it; but he couldn't have had the same fortitude for another, couldn't have detached himself from personal prejudice so effectually as to put forward in that manner for the terrible 'job' a little chap he to all appearance really liked. That Muniment did like him it never occurred to the little chap to doubt. He had quite all the air of it to-day; he had never been more good-humoured, more placidly talkative; he was like an elder brother who knew that the 'youngster' was clever and felt rather proud of it even when there was no one there to see. That temporary look of suspending their partnership which had usually marked him at the 'Sun and Moon' was never visible in other places; in Audley Court he only chaffed his young friend occasionally for taking him too seriously. To-day that devotee hardly knew just how to take him; the episode of which Hoffendahl was the central figure had, as far as one could see, made so little change in his attitude. For a loyal servant, an effective agent, he was so extraordinarily candid—bitterness and denunciation so rarely sat on his lips. The criticism of everything—since everything *was* wrong—took so little of his time. It was as if he had been ashamed to complain; and indeed for himself as the months went on he had nothing particular to complain of. He had had a rise at the chemical works and a plan of getting a bigger room for Rosy was under serious consideration. On behalf of others he never sounded the pathetic note—he thought that sort of thing unbusiness-like; and the most that he did in the way of expatiation on the woes of humanity was occasionally to allude to certain statistics, certain 'returns', in regard to the remuneration of industries, applications for employment and the discharge of hands. In such matters as these he was deeply versed, moving ever in a dry statistical and scientific air in which it cost Hyacinth an effort of respiration to accompany him. Simple and kindly as he was, and thoughtful of the sufferings of beasts, attentive and merciful to small insects and addicted even to kissing dirty babies in Audley Court, he sometimes emitted a short satiric gleam which showed that his esteem for the poor was small and that if he had no illusions about the people who had got everything into their hands he had as few about those who had egregiously failed to do so. He was tremendously reasonable, which was largely why Hyacinth admired him, having a desire to be so himself but finding it terribly difficult.

Muniment's absence of passion, his fresh-coloured coolness, his easy exact knowledge, the way he kept himself clean (save for fine chemical stains on his hands) in circumstances of foul contact, constituted a group of qualities that had always appeared to his admirer singularly enviable. Most enviable of all was the force that enabled him to sink personal sentiment where a great public good was to be attempted and yet keep up the form of caring for that minor interest. It seemed to our friend that if *he* had introduced a young fellow to Hoffendahl for his purposes, and Hoffendahl had accepted him on such a recommendation and everything had been settled, he would have preferred never to look at the young fellow again. That was his weakness and Paul carried it off far otherwise. It must be added that he had never made an allusion to their visit to the great taskmaster; so that Hyacinth also, out of pride, held his tongue on the subject. If his friend didn't propose expressly to yearn over him he wasn't going to beg for it (especially as he didn't want it) by restless references. It had originally been a surprise to him that Muniment should be willing to countenance a possible assassination; but after all none of his ideas were narrow (one had such a sense that they ripened all the while) and if a pistol-shot would do any good he was not the man to raise pedantic objections. It is true that as regards his quiet acceptance of the predicament in which Hyacinth might be placed by it our young man had given him the benefit of a certain amount of doubt; it had occurred to him that perhaps Muniment had his own good grounds for believing that imperative sign would never really arrive, so that he might only be treating himself to the entertainment of judging of a little bookbinder's nerve. But in this case why did he take an interest in the little bookbinder's going to Paris? That was a thing he wouldn't have cared for had he held that in fact there was nothing to fear. He despised the sight of idleness, and in spite of the indulgence he had more than once been good enough to express on the subject of his young friend's sneaking love of ease what he would have been most likely to say at present was, 'Go to Paris? Go to the dickens! Haven't you been out at grass long enough for one while, didn't you lark enough in the country there with the noble lady, and hadn't you better take up your tools again before you forget how to handle them?' Rosy had said something of that sort in her free familiar way—whatever her intention she had been in effect only a little less caustic than old Crook: that Mr Robinson was going in for a life of leisure, a life of luxury, like herself; she must congratulate him on having the means and the time. Oh the time—that was the great thing! She could speak with knowledge, having always enjoyed these advantages herself. And she intimated—or was she mistaken?— that this good fortune emulated hers also in the matter of his having a high-born and beneficent friend (such a blessing now he had lost dear Miss Pynsent) who covered him with little attentions. Rose Muniment in short had been more exasperating than ever.

The Boulevard became even more brilliant as the evening went on and Hyacinth wondered whether he had a right to occupy the same table for so many hours. The theatre on the other side discharged its multitude; the crowd thickened on the wide asphalt, on the terrace of the café; gentlemen accompanied by ladies of whom he knew already how to characterise the type—*des femmes très-chic* —passed into the portals of Tortoni. The nightly emanation of Paris seemed to rise more richly, to float and hang in the air, to mingle with the universal light and the many-voiced sound, to resolve itself into a thousand solicitations and opportunities, addressed, however, mainly to those in whose pockets the chink of a little loose gold might respond. Hyacinth's retrospections had not made him drowsy, but quite the reverse; he grew restless and excited and a kind of pleasant terror of the place and hour entered into his blood. But it was nearly midnight and he got up to walk home, taking the line of the Boulevard toward the

Madeleine. He passed down the Rue Royale, where comparative stillness reigned; and when he reached the Place de la Concorde, to cross the bridge which faces the Corps Législatif, he found himself almost isolated. He had left the human swarm and the obstructed pavements behind, and the wide spaces of the splendid square lay quiet under the summer stars. The plash of the great fountains was audible and he could almost hear the wind-stirred murmur of the little wood of the Tuileries on one side and of the vague expanse of the Champs Elysées on the other. The place itself—the Place Louis Quinze, the Place de la Révolution—had given him a sensible emotion from the day of his arrival; he had recognised so quickly its tremendous historic character. He had seen in a rapid vision the guillotine in the middle, on the site of the inscrutable obelisk, and the tumbrils, with waiting victims, were stationed round the circle now made majestic by the monuments of the cities of France. The great legend of the French Revolution, a sunrise out of a sea of blood, was more real to him here than anywhere else; and, strangely, what was most present was not its turpitude and horror, but its magnificent energy, the spirit of creation that had been in it, not the spirit of destruction. That shadow was effaced by the modern fairness of fountain and statue, the stately perspective and composition; and as he lingered before crossing the Seine a sudden sense overtook him, making his heart falter to anguish—a sense of everything that might hold one to the world, of the sweetness of not dying, the fascination of great cities, the charm of travel and discovery, the generosity of admiration. The tears rose to his eyes as they had done more than once in the past six months, and a question, low but poignant, broke from his lips to end in nothing. 'How could he—how *could* he——?' It may be explained that 'he' was a reference to Paul Muniment; for Hyacinth had dreamed of the religion of friendship.

Three weeks after this he found himself in Venice,

whence he addressed to the Princess Casamassima a letter of which I reproduce the principal passages.

'This is probably the last time I shall write you before I return to London. Of course you've been in this place and you'll easily understand why here, especially here, the spirit should move me. Dear Princess, what an enchanted city, what ineffable impressions, what a revelation of the exquisite! I have a room in a little campo opposite a small old church which has cracked marble slabs let into the front; and in the cracks grow little wild delicate flowers of which I don't know the name. Over the door of the church hangs an old battered leather curtain, polished and tawny, as thick as a mattress and with buttons in it like a sofa; and it flops to and fro laboriously as women and girls, with shawls on their heads and their feet in little wooden shoes which have nothing but toes, pass in and out. In the middle of the campo is a fountain that looks still older than the church; it has a primitive barbaric air, and I've an idea it was put there by the first settlers—those who came to Venice from the mainland, from Aquileia. Observe how much historical information I've already absorbed; it won't surprise you, however, for you never wondered at anything after you discovered I knew something of Schopenhauer. I assure you I don't think of that musty misogynist in the least to-day, for I bend a genial eye on the women and girls I just spoke of as they glide with a small clatter and with their old copper water-jars to the fountain. The Venetian girl-face is wonderfully sweet and the effect is charming when its pale sad oval (they all look underfed) is framed in the old faded shawl. They have also the most engaging hair, which never has done curling, and they slip along together, in couples or threes, interlinked by the arms and never meeting one's eye—so that its geniality doesn't matter—dressed in thin cheap cotton gowns whose limp folds make the same delightful line that everything else in Italy makes. The weather is splendid and I roast—but I like it; apparently I was made to be spitted and "done", and I discover that I've been cold all my life even

when I thought I was warm. I've seen none of the beautiful
patricians who sat for the great painters—the gorgeous
beings whose golden hair was intertwined with pearls; but
I'm studying Italian in order to talk with the shuffling
clicking maidens who work in the bead-factories—I'm determined to make one or two of them look at me. When
they've filled their old water-pots at the fountain it's jolly
to see them perch them on their heads and patter away
over the polished Venetian stones. It's a charm to be in a
country where the women don't wear the hideous British
bonnet. Even in my own class—forgive the expression, I
remember it used to offend you—I've never known a young
female in London to put her nose out of the door without
it; and if you had frequented such young females as much
as I have you would have learnt of what degradation that
dreary imposition is the source. The floor of my room is
composed of little brick tiles, and to freshen the air in this
temperature one sprinkles it, as you no doubt know, with
water. Before long if I keep on sprinkling I shall be able
to swim about; the green shutters are closed and the place
makes a very good tank. Through the chinks the hot light
of the campo comes in. I smoke cigarettes and in the pauses
of this composition recline on a faded magenta divan in
the corner. Convenient to my hand in that attitude are the
works of Leopardi and a second-hand dictionary. I'm very
happy—happier than I have ever been in my life save at
Medley—and I don't care for anything but the present
hour. It won't last long, for I'm spending all my money.
When I've finished this I shall go forth and wander about
in the splendid Venetian afternoon; and I shall spend the
evening in that enchanted square of Saint Mark's which
resembles an immense open-air drawing-room, listening to
music and feeling the sea-breeze blow in between those
two strange old columns of the piazzetta which seem to
make a doorway for it. I can scarcely believe that it's of
myself I'm telling you these fine things; I say to myself a
dozen times a day that Hyacinth Robinson isn't in it—I
pinch my leg to see if I'm not dreaming. But a short time

hence, when I've resumed the exercise of my profession in sweet Soho, I shall have proof enough that it has been my very self: I shall know this by the terrible grind of the life and the penance to come.

'That will mean, no doubt, that I'm deeply demoralised. It won't be for you, however, in this case to cast the stone at me; for my demoralisation began from the moment I first approached you. Dear Princess, I may have done you good, but you haven't done me much. I trust you'll understand what I mean by that speech and not think it flippant or impertinent. I may have helped you to understand and enter into the misery of the people—though I protest I don't know much about it; but you've led my imagination into quite another train. Nevertheless I'm not wholly pretending it's all your fault if I've lost sight of the sacred cause almost altogether in my recent adventures. It's not that it hasn't been there to see, for that perhaps is the clearest result of extending one's horizon—the sense, increasing as we go, that want and toil and suffering are the constant lot of the immense majority of the human race. I've found them everywhere but haven't minded them. Forgive the cynical confession. What has struck me is the great achievements of which man has been capable in spite of them—the splendid accumulations of the happier few, to which doubtless the miserable many have also in their degree contributed. The face of Europe appears to be covered with them and they've had much the greater part of my attention. They seem to me inestimably precious and beautiful and I've become conscious more than ever before of how little I understand what in the great rectification you and Poupin propose to do with them. Dear Princess, there are things I shall be too sorry to see you touch, even you with your hands divine; and—shall I tell you *le fond de ma pensée*, as you used to say?—I feel myself capable of fighting for them. You can't call me a traitor, for you know the obligation I supremely, I immutably recognise. The monuments and treasures of art, the great palaces and properties, the conquests of learning and taste, the general fabric of civilisation as we know it, based if you will upon all the despotisms, the cruelties, the exclusions, the monopolies and the rapacities of the past, but thanks to which, all the same, the world is less of a "bloody sell" and life more of a lark—our friend Hoffendahl seems to me to hold them too cheap and to wish to substitute for them something in which I can't somehow believe as I do in things with which the yearnings and the tears of generations have been mixed. You know how extraordinary I think our Hoffendahl—to speak only of him; but if there's one thing that's more clear about him than another, it's that he wouldn't have the least feeling for this incomparable abominable old Venice. He would cut up the ceilings of the Veronese into strips, so that every one might have a little piece. I don't want every one to have a little piece of anything and I've a great horror of that kind of invidious jealousy which is at the bottom of the idea of a redistribution. You'll say I talk of it all at my ease while in a delicious capital I smoke cigarettes on a magenta divan; and I give you leave to scoff at me if it turns out that when I come back to London without a penny in my pocket I don't hold the same language. I don't know what it comes from, but during the last three months there has crept over me a deep distrust of that same grudging attitude—the intolerance of positions and fortunes that are higher and brighter than one's own; a fear moreover that I may in the past have been actuated by such motives, and a devout hope that if I'm to pass away while I'm yet young it may not be with that odious stain upon my soul.'

XXXI

HE SPENT the first days after his return to London in a process supposed by him to be the quest of a lodging; but in reality he was pulling himself together for the business of his livelihood, an effort he found by no means easy or agreeable. As he had told the Princess, he was demoralised, and the perspective of old Crook's dirty staircase had never seemed so steep. He lingered on the brink before he plunged again into Soho: he wished not to go back to the shop till he should be settled and delayed to get settled in order not to go back to the shop. He saw no one during this interval, not even Mr Vetch; he waited to call on the fiddler till he should have the appearance of not coming as a beggar or a borrower—have recovered his employment and be able to give an address, as he had heard Captain Sholto say. He went to South Street—not meaning to go in at once but wishing to look at the house—and there he had the surprise of seeing the advertisement of an auctioneer in the window of the Princess's late residence. He had not expected to find her in town—having heard from her the last time three weeks before, when she had said nothing about her prospects; but he was puzzled by this indication that she had moved away altogether. There was something in it all, however, that he felt he had at bottom been expecting; it appeared to prove the justice of a suspicion attached to all the steps of any intercourse with the Princess—a vague apprehension that one might suddenly stretch out one's hand and miss her altogether from one's side. He decided to ring at the door and ask for news of her; but there was no response to his summons: the stillness of an August afternoon—the year had come round again from his first visit—hung over the place, the blinds were down and the caretaker appeared to be absent. Before these facts he was much at a loss; unless indeed he should address a letter to his wonderful friend at Medley. It would doubtless be forwarded, though her short lease of the country-house had terminated, as he knew, several weeks before. Captain Sholto was of course a possible agent, a probable source of light; but nothing would have induced Hyacinth to ask such a service of him.

He turned away from South Street with a strange sinking of the heart; his state of ignorance struck inward, as it were—had the force of a deeply disquieting portent. He went to old Crook's only when he had arrived at his last penny. This, however, was very promptly the case. He had disembarked at London Bridge with only seventeen pence in his pocket and had lived on that sum for three days. The old fiddler in Lomax Place was having a chop before he went to the theatre, and he invited Hyacinth to share his repast, sending out at the same time for another pot of beer. He took the youth with him to the play, where, as at that season there were very few spectators, he had no difficulty in finding him a place. He seemed to wish to keep hold of him and peered strangely over his spectacles—Mr Vetch wore the homely double glass in these latter years—when he learned that Hyacinth had found a retreat not in their old familiar quarter but in the unexplored purlieus of Westminster. What had determined our young man was the fact that from this part of the town the journey was comparatively a short one to Camberwell; he had suffered so much, before Pinnie's death, from being separated by such a distance from his best friends. There was a pang in his heart connected with the image of Paul Muniment, but none the less the prospect of an evening hour from time to time in Audley Court struck him as one of the few nameable beguilements of his odd future. He could have gone straight to Camberwell to live, but that would carry him too far from the scene of his profession, and in Westminster he was nearer to old Crook's than he had been in Lomax Place. He said to Mr Vetch that if it would give *him* pleasure he would abandon his lodging and take another in Pentonville. But the old man replied after a moment that he should be sorry to put that constraint upon him; if he were to make such an exaction Hyacinth would think he wanted to watch him.

'How do you mean, to watch me?'

Mr Vetch had begun to tune his fiddle, and he scraped it a little before answering. 'I mean it as I've always meant it. Surely you know that in Lomax Place I had my eyes on you. I watched you as a child on the edge of a pond watches the little boat he has constructed and set afloat.'

'You couldn't discover much. You saw, after all, very little of me,' Hyacinth said.

'I made what I could of that little. It was better than nothing.'

Hyacinth laid his hand gently on the old man's arm; he had never felt so acute a kindness for him, not even when accepting his thirty pounds before going abroad. 'Certainly I'll come to see you.'

'I was much obliged to you for your letters,' Mr Vetch observed without heeding these words but continuing to scrape. He had always, even into the shabbiness of his old age, kept that mark of English good-breeding (which is composed of some such odd elements) that there was a shyness, an aversion to possible phrase-making, in his manner of expressing gratitude for favours, and that in spite of this cursory tone his acknowledgement had ever the accent of sincerity.

Hyacinth took little interest in the piece, which was an inanimate revival; he had been at the Théâtre Français and the tradition of that house was still sufficiently present to him to make any other style of interpretation of comedy appear at the best but a confident form of horseplay. He sat in one of the front stalls, close to the orchestra; and while the thing went forward—or backward, ever backward, as it seemed to him—his thoughts wandered far from the shabby scene and the dusty boards, revolving round a question which had come up immensely during the last few hours. The Princess was a *capricciosa*—this at least had been Madame Grandoni's account of her; and was that blank expressionless house in South Street a sign that an end had come to the particular caprice in which he had happened to be involved? On his return to London the desire to be with her again on the same terms as at Medley had begun to ache in him like a sorrow or a dreaded wrong —so sharp was his sense that if he mightn't absolutely count upon her she had been all cruelly, all abominably dishonest. Yet the wonder of the other time remained, in the great silence that had come, altogether a wonder. Circum-

stances had favoured in an extraordinary degree his visit to
her, and it was by no means clear that they would again
be so accommodating or that what had been possible for a
few days should be possible with continuity and in the
midst of the ceremonies and complications of London.
Hyacinth felt poorer than he had ever felt before, inasmuch
as he had had money and spent it, whereas in previous
times he had never had it to spend. He never for an instant regretted his squandered wealth, for he said to himself
that he had made a good bargain and become master of a
precious equivalent. The equivalent was a rich experience
—an experience that would grow richer still as he should
talk it over, in the right conditions that *she* would find
again, with the one person in the world to whom he was
now interesting. His poverty would be no obstacle to their
friendship so long as he should have a pair of legs to carry
him to her door; for she liked him better shabby than fur-
bished up, and she had given him too many pledges, they
had taken together too many appointments, worked out too
many ideas, to be disconcerted on either side by obstacles
that were merely a part of the general conventionality. He
was to go with her into the slums, to introduce her to the
worst that London contained—he should have precisely to
make acquaintance with it first—to show her the reality
of the horrors of which she dreamed the world might be
purged. He had ceased himself to care for the slums and
had reasons for not wishing to spend his remnant in the
study of foul things; but he would go through with his
part of the engagement. He might be detached and mechanical, but any dreariness would have a gilding that should
involve an association with her. What indeed if she should
have changed, have availed herself of that great right of un-
apologetic inconsequence which he believed to be, at least
in their relation with nobodies, the highest luxury of the
happy? What if, from a high insolence which he thought
of as lurking somewhere in the side-scenes of her nature,
though he had really not once seen it step to the front,
she should toss back her perfect head with a movement

signifying that he was too basely literal and that she knew him no more? His imagination represented her this evening in places where a barrier of dazzling light shut her out from access or even from any appeal. He saw her with other people, in splendid rooms where 'the dukes' had possession of her, smiling, satisfied, surrounded, covered with jewels. When this vision grew intense he found a reassurance in reflecting that after all she would be unlikely to throw him personally over so long as she should remain as deeply compromised, subterraneously speaking, as she had —successfully it seemed—tried to become, and that it would not be easy for her to liberate herself from that entanglement. She had of course told him more, at Medley, of the manner in which she had already committed herself, and he remembered with a strange perverse elation that she had gone very far indeed.

In the intervals of the foolish play Mr Vetch, who lingered in his place in the orchestra while his mates descended into the little hole under the stage, leaned over the rail and asked his young friend occasional questions, carrying his eyes at the same time about the dingy house at whose smoky ceiling and tarnished galleries he had been staring for so many a year. He came back to Hyacinth's letters and said: 'Of course you know they were clever; they entertained me immensely. But as I read them I thought of poor Pinnie: I wished she could have listened to them; they would have made her so happy.'

'Yes, poor Pinnie,' Hyacinth murmured while his friend went on:

'I was in Paris in 1846; I stayed at a small hotel in the Rue Mogador. I judge from your letters that everything's changed. Does the Rue Mogador still exist? Yes, everything's changed. I dare say it's all much finer, but I liked it very much as it was then. At all events I'm right in supposing—am I not?—that it cheered you up considerably, making you really happy.'

'Why should I have wanted any cheering? I was happy enough,' Hyacinth replied.

The fiddler projected his old white conscious face; it had the stale smoothness that betrays a sedentary occupation, thirty years spent in a close crowd, amid the smoke of lamps and the odour of stage-paint. 'I thought you were sad about Pinnie.'

'When I jumped with that avidity at your proposing I should take a tour? Poor old Pinnie!' Hyacinth added.

'Well, I hope you think a little better of the world. We mustn't make up our minds too early in life.'

'Oh I've made up mine: the world's an awfully jolly place.'

'Awfully jolly, no; but I like it as I like an old pair of shoes—I like so much less the idea of putting on the new ones.'

'Why should I complain?' Hyacinth asked. 'What have I known but kindness? People have done such a lot for me.'

'Oh well, of course they've liked you. But that's all right,' murmured Mr Vetch, beginning to scrape again. What remained in Hyacinth's mind from their colloquy was the fact that this veteran, whom he regarded distinctly as cultivated, had thought his letters clever. He only wished he had made them cleverer still; he had no doubt of his ability to have done so.

It may be imagined whether the first hours he spent at old Crook's after he took up work again were altogether to his taste, and what was the nature of the reception given him by his former comrades, whom he found exactly in the same attitudes and the same clothes (he knew and hated every article they wore) and with the same primitive pleasantries on their lips. Our young man's feelings were mingled; the place and the people affected him as loathsome, but there was something delightful in handling his tools. He gave a little private groan of relief when he discovered that he still liked his work and that the shining swarm of his ideas in the matter of sides and backs returned to him. They came in still brighter, more suggestive form, and he had the satisfaction of feeling that his taste had improved, that it had been purified by experience, and that the covers of a book might be made to express an astonishing number of high conceptions. Strange enough it was, and a proof surely of our little hero's being a true artist, that the impressions he had accumulated during the last few months appeared to mingle and confound themselves with the very sources of his craft and to lie open to technical 'rendering'. He had quite determined by this time to carry on his life as if nothing were hanging over him and he had no intention of remaining a little bookbinder to the end of his days; for that medium would after all translate only some of his conceptions. Yet his trade was a resource, an undiminished resource, for the present, and he had a particular as well as a general motive in attempting new flights—the prevision of the exquisite work he was to do during the coming year for the Princess, work it was so definite to him he owed her. When that debt should have been paid and his other arrears made up he proposed to himself to write something. He was far from having decided as yet what it should be; the only point settled was that it should be very remarkable and should not, at least on the face of it, have anything to do with a fresh deal of the social pack. That was to be his transition—into literature: to bind the book, charming as the process might be, was after all much less fundamental than to write it. It had occurred to Hyacinth more than once that it would be a fine thing to produce a rare death-song.

It is not surprising that among such reveries as this he should have been conscious of a narrow range in the tone of his old workfellows. They had only one idea: that he had come into a thousand pounds and had gone to spend them in France with a regular high one. He was aware in advance of the diffusion of this legend and did his best to allow for it, taking the simplest course, which was to gainsay nothing, but to catch the ball as it came and toss it still further, enlarging and embroidering humorously until Grugan and Roker and Hotchkin and all the rest, who struck him as not having washed since he left them, seemed really to begin to understand how it was he could have spent such a rare sum in so short a time. The impressiveness of this achievement helped him greatly to slip into his place; he could see that, though the treatment it received was superficially irreverent, the sense that he was very sharp and that the springs of his sharpness were somehow secret gained a good deal of strength from it. Hyacinth was not incapable of being rather pleased that it *should* be supposed, even by Grugan, Roker and Hotchkin, that he could get rid of a thousand pounds in less than five months, especially as to his own conscience the fact had altogether yet to be proved. He got off on the whole easily enough to feel a little ashamed, and he reflected that the men at old Crook's showed at any rate no symptoms of the social jealousy lying at the bottom of the desire for a fresh deal. This was doubtless an accident and not inherent in the fact that they were highly skilled workmen—old Crook had no others—and therefore sure of constant employment; for it was impossible to be more skilled in a special line than Paul Muniment, who yet—though not out of jealousy of course—went in for the great grim restitution. What struck him most, after he had got used again to the sense of his apron and bent his back a while over his battered table, was the simple synthetic patience of the others who had bent *their* backs and felt the rub of that dirty drapery all the while he was lounging in the halls of Medley, dawdling through boulevards and museums and admiring the purity of the Venetian girl-face. With Poupin, to be sure, his relations were all particular; but the explanations he owed the sensitive Frenchman were not such as could make him very unhappy, once he had determined to resist as much as possible the friction of a consciousness as galling at times as a misfitting harness. There was moreover more sorrow than anger in Poupin's face when he learned that his young friend and pupil had failed to cultivate the rich opportunities he had offered him. 'You're cooling off, my child; there's something about you! Have you the weakness to flatter yourself that anything has been done or that humanity suffers a particle less? *Enfin* it's between you and your conscience.'

'Do you think I want to get out of it?' Hyacinth grimaced; this expositor's phrases about humanity, which used to thrill him so, having grown of late strangely hollow and rococo.

'You owe me no explanations; the conscience of the individual is absolute, except of course in those classes in which, from the very nature of the infamies on which they're founded, no conscience can exist. Speak to me, however, of my City; *she* is always divine,' Poupin went on, though showing signs of irritation when Hyacinth began to praise to him the magnificent creations of the arch-fiend of December. In the presence of this picture he was in a terrible dilemma—gratified as a Parisian and a patriot but all disconcerted as a lover of liberty: it cost him a pang to admit that anything amid the *seuils sacrés* was defective, yet he saw still less his way to concede that it could owe any charm to the perjured monster of the Second Empire or even to the hypocritical mendacious republicanism of the régime before which the inspired Commune had gone down in blood and fire. 'Ah yes, it's very fine, no doubt,' he remarked at last, 'but it will be finer still when it's ours!'— a speech which caused Hyacinth to turn back to his work with a feeling of sickness. Everywhere, everywhere he saw the ulcer of envy—the greed of a party hanging together only that it might despoil another to its advantage. In old Eustache, one of the 'pure', this was especially disenchanting.

XXXII

THE LANDING at the top of the stairs in Audley Court was always dark; but it seemed darker than ever to Hyacinth while he fumbled for the door-latch after he had heard Rose Muniment's penetrating voice bid him to come in. During that instant his ear caught the sound, if it could

trust itself, of another voice, which prepared him a little
for the spectacle fully presented as soon as the door—his
attempt to reach the handle in his sudden agitation proving
fruitless—was opened to him by Paul. His friend stood
there tall and hospitable, saying something loud and jovial
that he didn't distinguish. His eyes had crossed the
threshold in a flash, but his step faltered, only to obey,
however, the vigour of Muniment's outstretched hand.
Hyacinth's glance had gone straight, and though with four
persons in it Rosy's little apartment looked crowded he
saw no one but the object of his quick preconception—no
one but the Princess Casamassima seated beside the low
sofa, the grand feature introduced during his absence from
London, on which, arrayed in the famous pink dressing-
gown, Miss Muniment now received her visitors. He wondered afterwards why he should have been so startled; for
he had said often enough both to himself and to his wonderful lady that so far as she was concerned he was proof
against astonishment: it was so evident that the note of
her conduct would always be a sort of splendour of freedom. In fact now that he perceived she had made her way
to Camberwell without his assistance the feeling in possession of him was a refined embarrassment; he blushed a
little as he entered the circle, the fourth member of which
was inevitably Lady Aurora Langrish. Was it that his intimacy with the Princess gave him a certain sense of responsibility for her course in respect to people who knew
her as yet so scantly, and that there was something too
little explained in the confidence with which she had practised a descent upon them? It indeed came over our young
man that by this time perhaps they knew her a good deal;
and moreover a woman's behaviour spoke for itself when
she could sit looking in that fashion like a radiant angel
dressed in a simple bonnet and mantle and immensely interested in an appealing corner of the earth. It took Hyacinth but an instant to infer that her character was in a
different phase from any yet exhibited to him. There had
been a glory of gentleness about her the night he made

her acquaintance, and she had never ceased at any moment since to strike him as full of the imagination of sympathy and pity, unless perforce in relation to her husband, against whom—for reasons after all doubtless very sufficient—her heart appeared absolutely steeled. Now at any rate this high mildness had deepened to a rapture of active ministering charity. She had put off her splendour, but her beauty was unquenchably bright; she had made herself humble for her pious excursion; she had, beside Rosy (who in the pink dressing-gown looked much the more luxurious of the two) almost the attitude of an hospital nurse; and it was easy to see from the meagre line of her garments that she was tremendously in earnest. If Hyacinth was flurried her own countenance expressed no confusion; for her evidently this queer little bower of poverty and pain was a place in which it was perfectly natural that *he* should turn up. The sweet still greeting her eyes offered him might exquisitely have conveyed that she had been waiting for him, that she knew he would come and that there had been a tacit appointment for that very moment. They said other things besides in their beautiful friendliness; they said: 'Don't notice me too much or make any kind of scene. I've an immense deal to say to you, but remember that I've the rest of our life before me to say it in. Consider only what will be easiest and kindest to these people, these delightful people, whom I find enchanting (why didn't you ever tell me more—I mean really more—about them?). It won't be particularly complimentary to them if you've the air of seeing a miracle in my presence here. I'm very glad of your return. The quavering fidgety "ladyship" is as striking as the others.'

Hyacinth's reception at the hands of his old friends was cordial enough quite to obliterate the element of irony that had lurked, fifteen weeks before, in their godspeed; their welcome was not boisterous, but it seemed to express the idea that the occasion, already so rare and agreeable, needed but his arrival to make it perfect. By the time he had been three minutes in the room he was able to measure the impression produced by the Princess, who, it was clear, had cast the charm of the worshipful over the little company. This was in the air, in the face of each, in their smiling, their excited eyes and heightened colour; even Rosy's wan grimace, at all times screwed up to ecstasy, had the supreme glitter of great occasions. Lady Aurora looked more than ever dishevelled with interest and wonder; the long strands of her silky hair floated like gossamer while, in her extraordinary religious attention, with her hands raised and clasped to her bosom as if she were praying, her respiration rose and fell. She had never seen any one like the Princess, but Hyacinth's apprehension of some months before had been groundless—she evidently didn't think her 'flashy'. She thought her divine and a revelation of beauty and benignity; and the illuminated amplified room could contain no dissentient opinion. It was her beauty primarily that 'fetched' them, Hyacinth could easily see, and it was not hidden from him that the impression had been made as much on Paul Muniment as on his companions. It was not in Paul's nature to be jerkily demonstrative and he had not lost his head on the present occasion; but he had already appreciated the difference between a plain suspicious man's preconception of a meretricious factitious fine lady and the actual influence of such a personage. She was gentler, fairer, wiser than even a chemical expert could have guessed in advance. In short she held the trio in her hand, having reduced Lady Aurora to exactly the same simplicity as the others, and she performed admirably and artistically for their benefit. Almost before Hyacinth had had time to wonder how she had found the Muniments out —he had no recollection of giving her specific directions— she mentioned that Captain Sholto had been so good as to introduce her; doing so as if she owed him that explanation and were a woman who would be scrupulous in such a case. It was rather a blow to him to learn she had been accepting the Captain's mediation, and this was not softened by her saying she was too impatient to wait for his own return: he was apparently so pleased with the roving life that one couldn't be sure it would ever take place. The Princess might at least have been sure that to see her again very soon was still more necessary to his happiness than anything the roving life could offer. No adventure was so prodigious as sticking as fast as possible to *her*.

It came out in the conversation he had with her, to which the others listened with respectful curiosity, that Captain Sholto had brought her a week before, but that she had then seen only Miss Muniment. 'I took the liberty of coming again by myself to-day, because I wanted to see the whole family,' she developed, looking from Paul to Lady Aurora with a bright blandness which purified the statement (as regarded her ladyship) of impertinence. The Princess added frankly that she had now been careful to arrive at an hour when she thought Mr Muniment might be at home. 'When I come to see gentlemen I like at least to find them,' she continued, and she was so great a lady that there was no dowdy diffidence in her attitude: it was a simple matter for her to call on a young man employed at large chemical works if she had a reason. Hyacinth could see that the reason had already been brought forward—her immense interest in problems that Mr Muniment had completely mastered and in particular their common acquaintance with the extraordinary man whose mission it was to solve them. He learned later that she had pronounced the name of the great patient powerful Hoffendahl. A part of the lustre in Rosy's eye came no doubt from the declaration she had inevitably been moved to make in respect to any sympathy with wicked theories that might be imputed to *her*; and of course the effect of this intensely individual little protest—such was always its effect —emanating from the sofa and the pink dressing-gown was to render the home of the Muniments still more quaint and original. In that spot Paul always gave the pleasantest go-by to any attempt to draw out his views; so you would have thought, to hear him, that he allowed himself the reputation of having them only in order to get a 'rise' out of his sister and let their visitors see with what wit and spirit she could repudiate them. This, however, would only be a reason the more for the Princess's following up her scent. She would doubtless not expect to get at the bottom of his ideas in Audley Court: the opportunity would occur rather in case of his having the civility—on which surely she might count—to come and talk them over with her in her own house.

Hyacinth mentioned to her the disappointment he had had in South Street and she replied: 'Oh, I've given up that house and taken quite a different one.' But she didn't say where it was, and in spite of her having given him so much the right to expect she would communicate to him a matter so nearly touching them both as a change of address he felt a great shyness about asking.

Their companions watched them as if they considered that something rather witty and showy now would be likely to come off between them; but Hyacinth was too full of regard for his beautiful friend's tacit notification to him that they must not appear too thick, which was after all more flattering than the most pressing enquiries or the most liberal announcements about herself could have been. She never asked him when he had come back; and indeed it was not long before Rose Muniment took that business on herself. Hyacinth, however, ventured to assure himself if Madame Grandoni were still at her post and even to remark—when his fellow visitor had replied, 'Oh yes, still, still. The great refusal, as Dante calls it, has not yet come off'—'You ought to bring her to see Miss Rosy. She's a person Miss Rosy would particularly appreciate.'

'I'm sure I should be most happy to receive any friend of the Princess Casamassima,' said this young lady from the sofa; and when the Princess answered that she certainly would not fail to produce Madame Grandoni some day Hyacinth—though he doubted if the presentation would really take place—guessed how much she wished her old friend might have heard the strange bedizened little invalid make that speech.

There were only three other seats, for the introduction

of the sofa—the question profoundly studied in advance—
had rendered necessary the elimination of certain articles;
so that Muniment, on his feet, hovered round the little
circle with his hands in his pockets, laughing freely and
sociably but not looking at the Princess; even if, as Hyacinth was sure, none the less agitated by her presence.

'You ought to tell us about foreign parts and the grand
things you've seen; except that our distinguished visitor
must know all about them,' Muniment threw out to him.
Then he added: 'Surely, at any rate, you've seen nothing
more worthy of your respect than Camberwell.'

'Is this the worst part?' the Princess asked, looking up
with her noble interested face.

'The worst, madam? What grand ideas you must have!
We admire Camberwell immensely.'

'It's my brother's ideas that are grand!' cried Rose
Muniment, betraying him conscientiously. 'He does want
everything changed, no less than you, Princess; though he's
more cunning than you and won't give one a handle where
one can take him up. He thinks all this part most objec-
tionable—as if dirty people won't always make everything
dirty where they live! I dare say he thinks there ought to
be no dirty people, and it may be so; only if every one
was clean where would be the merit? You'd get no credit
for keeping yourself tidy. If it's a question of soap and
water, at any rate, every one can begin by himself. My
brother thinks the whole place ought to be as handsome
as Brompton.'

'Ah yes, that's where the artists and literary people live,
isn't it?' the Princess asked attentively.

'I've never seen it, but it's very well laid out,' Rosy returned with her competent manner.

'Oh I like Camberwell better than that,' Muniment said
with due amusement.

The Princess turned to Lady Aurora and, with the air
of appealing to her for her opinion, gave her a glance that
travelled in a flash from the topmost bow of her large misfitting hat to the crumpled points of her substantial shoes.

'I must get *you* to tell me the truth,' she breathed. 'I want so much to know London—the real London. It seems so difficult!'

Lady Aurora looked a little frightened, but at the same time gratified, and after a moment responded: 'I believe a great many artists live in Saint John's Wood.'

'I don't care about the artists!' said the Princess, shaking her head slowly and with the sad smile that sometimes made her beauty so inexpressibly touching.

'Not when they've painted you such beautiful pictures?' Rosy demanded. 'We know about your pictures—we've admired them so much. Mr Hyacinth has described to us your precious possessions.'

The Princess transferred her smile to Rosy and rested it on that young lady's shrunken countenance with the same ineffable head-shake. 'You do me too much honour. I've no possessions.'

'Gracious, was it all a make-believe?' Rosy cried, flashing at Hyacinth an eye that was never so eloquent as when it demanded an explanation.

'I've nothing in the world—nothing but the clothes on my back!' the Princess repeated very gravely and without looking at their indiscreet friend.

The words struck Hyacinth as an admonition, so that, though much puzzled, he made no attempt for the moment to reconcile the contradiction. He only replied: 'I meant the things in the house. Of course I didn't know to whom they belonged.'

'There are no things in my house now,' the Princess went on; and there was a touch of pure high resignation in the words.

'Laws, I shouldn't like that!' Rose Muniment declared, glancing with complacency over her own decorated walls. 'Everything here belongs to me.'

'I shall bring Madame Grandoni to see you,' said the Princess irrelevantly but kindly.

'Do you think it's not right to have a lot of things about?' Lady Aurora, with sudden courage, enquired of her distinguished companion, pointing a vague chin at her but looking into one of the upper angles of the room.

'I suppose one must always settle that for one's self. I don't like to be surrounded with objects I don't care for, and I can care only for one thing—that is for one class of things—at a time. Dear lady,' the Princess pursued, 'I fear I must confess to you that my heart's not in bibelots. When thousands and tens of thousands haven't bread to put in their mouths I can dispense with tapestry and old china.' And her fair face, bent charmingly, conciliatingly, on Lady Aurora, appeared to argue that if she was narrow at least she was honest.

Hyacinth wondered, rather vulgarly, what strange turn she had taken and whether this singular picture of her denuded personality were not one of her famous caprices, a whimsical joke, a nervous perversity. Meanwhile he heard Lady Aurora urge anxiously: 'But don't you think we ought to make the world more beautiful?'

'Doesn't the Princess make it so by the mere fact of her existence?' Hyacinth interposed, his perplexity escaping in a harmless manner through this graceful hyperbole. He had observed that though the lady in question could dispense with old china and tapestry she couldn't dispense with a pair of immaculate gloves which fitted her to a charm.

'My people have a mass of things, you know, but I've really nothing myself,' said Lady Aurora, as if she owed this assurance to such a representative of suffering humanity.

'The world will be beautiful enough when it becomes good enough,' the Princess resumed. 'Is there anything so ugly as unjust distinctions, as the privileges of the few contrasted with the degradation of the many? When we want to beautify we must begin at the right end.'

'Surely there are none of us but what have our privileges!' Rose Muniment exclaimed with eagerness. 'What do you say to mine, lying here between two members of the aristocracy and with Mr Hyacinth thrown in?'

'You're certainly lucky—with Lady Aurora Langrish. I

wish she would come and see *me*,' the Princess genially sighed as she rose.

'Do go, my lady, and tell me if it's so poor!' Rose went on gaily.

'I think there can't be too many pictures and statues and works of art,' Hyacinth broke out. 'The more the better, whether people are hungry or not. In the way of ameliorating influences are not those the most definite?'

'A piece of bread and butter's more to the purpose if your stomach's empty,' the Princess declared.

'Robinson has been corrupted by foreign influences,' Paul Muniment suggested. 'He doesn't care for bread and butter now; he likes French cookery.'

'Yes, but I don't get it. And have you sent away the little man, the Italian, with the white cap and apron?' Hyacinth asked of the Princess.

She hesitated a moment but presently replied laughing and not in the least offended at his question, though it was an attempt to put her in the wrong from which Hyacinth had not been able to refrain in his astonishment at these ascetic pretensions: 'I've sent him away many times!'

Lady Aurora had also got up; she stood there gazing at her beautiful fellow visitor with a timidity that made her wonder only more apparent. 'Your servants must be awfully fond of you.'

'Oh my servants!' said the Princess as if it were only by a stretch of the meaning of the word that she could be said to enjoy the ministrations of menials. Her manner seemed to imply that she had a charwoman for an hour a day. Hyacinth caught the tone and determined that since she was going, as it appeared, he would break off his own visit and accompany her. He had flattered himself at the end of three weeks of Medley that he knew her in every phase, but here was a field of freshness. She turned to Paul Muniment and put out her hand to him, and while he took it in his own his face was visited by the most beautiful eyes that had ever rested there. 'Will you come and see me one of these days?' she asked with a voice as pure as her glance.

Hyacinth waited for Paul's answer with an emotion that could only be accounted for by his affectionate sympathy, the manner in which he had spoken of him to the Princess and which he wished to justify, the interest he had in his appearing completely the fine fellow he believed him. Muniment neither stammered nor blushed; he held himself straight and looked back at his interlocutress with eyes at least as open as her own to everything that concerned him. Then by way of answer: 'Well madam, pray what good will it do me?' And the tone of the words was so humorous and kindly, and so instinct with a plain manly sense, that though they were not gallant Hyacinth was not ashamed for him. At the same moment he observed that Lady Aurora was watching their friend as if she had at least an equal stake in what he might say.

'Ah none; only me perhaps a little.' With this rejoinder and with a wonderful sweet indulgent dignity in which there was none of the stiffness of pride or resentment the Princess quitted him and approached Lady Aurora. She asked if *she* wouldn't do her the kindness to come. She should like so much to know her and had an idea there was a great deal they might talk about. Lady Aurora said she should be delighted, and the Princess took one of her cards out of her pocket and gave it to the noble spinster. After she had done so she stood a moment holding her hand and brought out: 'It has really been such a happiness to me to meet you. Please don't think it's very clumsy if I say I *do* like you so!' Lady Aurora was evidently exceedingly moved and impressed; but Rosy, when the Princess took leave of her and the irrepressible invalid had assured her of the pleasure with which she should receive her again, uttered the further truth that in spite of this she herself could never conscientiously enter into such theories.

'If every one was equal,' Rosy asked, 'where would be the gratification I feel in getting a visit from a grandee? That's what I have often said to her ladyship, and I consider that I've kept her in her place a little. No, no; no equality while *I*'m about the place!'

The company appeared to comprehend that there was a natural fitness in Hyacinth's seeing the great lady on her way, and accordingly no effort was made to detain him. He guided her, with the help of an attendant illumination from Muniment, down the dusky staircase, and at the door of the house there was a renewed brief leave-taking with their host, who, however, showed no signs of relenting or re-canting in respect to the Princess's invitation. The warm evening had by this time grown thick and the population of Audley Court appeared to be passing it for the most part in the open air. As Hyacinth assisted his companion to thread her way through groups of sprawling chattering children, gossiping women with bare heads and babies at the breast and heavily-planted men smoking very bad pipes, it seemed to him that their project of exploring the slums was already in the way of execution. He said nothing till they gained the outer street, but then, pausing a moment, enquired how she would be conveyed. Had she a carriage somewhere or should he try and get a cab?

'A carriage, my dear fellow? For what do you take me! I won't trouble you about a cab: I walk everywhere now.'

'But if I had not been here?'

'I should have gone alone'; and she smiled at him through the turbid twilight of Camberwell.

'And where, please, gracious heaven? I may at least have the honour of accompanying you.'

'Certainly, if you can walk so far.'

'So far as what, dear Princess?'

'As Madeira Crescent, Paddington.'

'Madeira Crescent, Paddington?' Hyacinth stared.

'That's what I call it when I'm with people with whom I wish to be fine, as with you. I've taken a small house there.'

'Then it's really true that you've given up your beautiful things?'

'I've sold everything to give to the poor.'

'Ah, Princess——!' the young man almost moaned; for the memory of some of her treasures was vivid to him.

She became very grave, even stern, and with an accent of reproach that seemed to show she had been wounded where she was most sensitive demanded: 'When I said I was willing to make the last sacrifice did you then believe I was lying?'

'Haven't you kept *anything*?' he went on without heeding her challenge.

She looked at him a moment. 'I've kept *you!*' Then she passed her hand into his arm and they moved forward. He saw what she had done; she was living in a little ugly bare middle-class house and wearing simple gowns; and the energy and good faith of her behaviour, with the abruptness of the transformation, took away his breath. 'I thought I should please you so much,' she added after they had gone a few steps. And before he had time to reply, as they came to a part of the street where there were small shops, those of butchers, greengrocers and pork-pie men, with open fronts, flaring lamps and humble purchasers, she broke out joyously: 'Ah, this is the way I like to see London!'

XXXIII

THE HOUSE in Madeira Crescent was a low stucco-fronted edifice in a shabby, shallow semicircle, and Hyacinth could see as they approached it that the window-place in the parlour, on a level with the street-door, was ornamented by a glass case containing stuffed birds and surmounted by an alabaster Cupid. He was sufficiently versed in his London to know that the descent in the scale of the gentility was almost immeasurable for a person who should have moved into that quarter from the neighbourhood of Park Lane. The street was not squalid and was strictly residential; but it was mean and meagre and fourth-rate and had in the highest degree that petty parochial air, that absence of style and elevation, which is the stamp of whole districts of London and which Hyacinth had already more than once mentally compared with the high-piled important look of the Parisian perspective. It was marked by the union of every quality which should have made it detestable to the Princess; it was almost as bad as Lomax Place. As they stopped before the narrow ill-painted door, on which the number of the house appeared on a piece of common porcelain cut in a fanciful shape, it struck him that he had felt in their long walk the touch of the passion persuading his companion to divest herself of her superfluities, but that it would take the romantic out of one's heroism to settle one's self in such a paltry Philistine row. However, if the Princess had wished to mortify the flesh she had chosen an effective means of doing so, and of mortifying the spirit as well. The long light of the grey summer evening was still in the air and Madeira Crescent wore a soiled dusty expression. A hand-organ droned in front of a neighbouring house and the cart of the local washerwoman, to which a donkey was harnessed, was drawn up opposite. The local children as well were dancing on the pavement to the music of the organ, and the scene was surveyed from one of the windows by a gentleman in a dirty dressing-gown, smoking a pipe, who made Hyacinth think of Mr Micawber. The young man gave the Princess a deep look before they went into the house, and she smiled as if she guessed every comment he hadn't uttered.

The long, circuitous walk with her from the faraway south of London had been strange and delightful; it reminded him more queerly than he could have expressed of some of the rambles he had taken on summer evenings with Millicent Henning. It was impossible to resemble this young lady less than the Princess resembled her, but in her enjoyment of her unwonted situation (she had never before, on a summer's evening—to the best of Hyacinth's belief at least—lost herself in the unfashionable districts on the arm of a seedy artisan) the distinguished personage exhibited certain coincidences with the shop-girl. She stopped as Millicent had done to look into the windows of vulgar establishments and amused herself with picking out the abominable objects she should like to possess; selecting them from a new point of view, that of a reduced fortune and the domestic arrangements of the 'lower middle class', and deriving extreme diversion from the idea that she now belonged to that aggrieved body. She was in a state of light fresh sociable exhilaration which Hyacinth had hitherto not in the same degree seen in her, and before they reached Madeira Crescent it had become clear to him that her present phase was little more than a brilliant *tour de force*—which he could yet not imagine her keeping up long, for the simple reason that after the novelty and strangeness of the affair had passed away she wouldn't be able to endure the contact of so much that was common and ugly. For the moment, none the less, her discoveries in this line diverted her as all discoveries did, and she pretended to be sounding in a scientific spirit—that of the social philosopher, the student and critic of manners—the depths of the British Philistia. Hyacinth was struck more than ever with the fund of life that was in her, the energy of feeling, the high free reckless spirit. These things expressed themselves, as the couple proceeded, in a hundred sallies and droll proposals, kindling the young man's pulses and making him conscious of the joy with which, in any extravagance, he would bear her company to the death. She affected him at this moment as playing with life so audaciously and defiantly that the end of it all would inevitably be some violent catastrophe.

She desired exceedingly that Hyacinth should take her to a music-hall or a coffee-tavern; she even professed a curiosity to see the inside of a public-house. Since she still had self-control enough to remember that if she stayed out beyond a certain hour Madame Grandoni would begin to worry about her they were obliged to content themselves with the minor 'lark', as the Princess was careful to designate their peep into an establishment, glittering with polished pewter and brass, which bore the name of the 'Happy Land'. He had feared she would turn nervous after the narrow befingered door had swung behind her, or that at all events she would be disgusted at what she might see and hear in such a place and would immediately wish to retreat. By good luck, however, there were only two or three convivial spirits in occupancy and the presence of the softer sex was apparently not so rare as to excite surprise. The softer sex furthermore was embodied in a big hard red woman, the publican's wife, who looked as if she were in the habit of dealing with all sorts and mainly interested in seeing whether even the finest put down their money before they were served. The Princess pretended to 'have something' and to admire the ornamentation of the bar; and when Hyacinth asked her in a low tone what disposal they should make, when the great changes came, of such an embarrassing type as that, replied off-hand, 'Oh, drown her in a barrel of beer!' She professed when they came out to have been immensely interested in the 'Happy Land' and was not content until Hyacinth had fixed an evening on which they might visit a music-hall together. She talked with him largely, by fits and starts, of his adventures abroad and his impressions of France and Italy; breaking off suddenly with some irrelevant but almost extravagantly appreciative allusion to Rose Muniment and Lady Aurora and then returning with a question as to what he had seen and done—the answer to which, however, in many cases, she was not at pains to wait for. Yet it implied her having paid considerable attention to what he told her that she should be able to say toward the end, with that fraternising frankness which was always touching because it appeared to place her at one's mercy, to show how she counted on one's having an equal loyalty: 'Well, my dear friend, you've not wasted your time; you know everything, you've missed nothing; there are lots of things you can tell me—so that we shall have some famous talks in the winter evenings.' This last reference was apparently to the coming season, and there was something in the tone of quiet friendship with which it was uttered and which seemed to involve so many delightful things, something that for Hyacinth bound them still closer together. To live out of

the world with her that way, lost among the London millions in a queer little cockneyfied retreat, was a refinement
of intimacy—with revelations perhaps even beyond those
that had left him wonder-struck at Medley.

They found Madame Grandoni sitting alone in the twilight, very patient and peaceful and having after all, it was
clear, accepted the situation too completely to fidget at such
a trifle as her companion's not coming home at a ladylike
hour. She had placed herself in the back part of the tawdry
little drawing-room, which looked into a small smutty garden whence by the open front window the sound of the
hurdy-gurdy and the voices of the children romping to its
music came to her through the summer dusk. The influence
of London was present in a mitigated far-away hum, and
for some reason or other at that moment the place took on
to our young friend the semblance of the home of an exile
—a spot and an hour to be remembered with a throb of
fondness in some danger or sorrow of after years. The old
lady never moved from her chair as she saw the Princess
come in with the little bookbinder, and her observation
rested on that member of their circle as familiarly as if she
had seen him go out with her in the afternoon. The Princess
stood smiling a moment before her mild monitress. 'I've
done a great thing. What do you think I've done?' she
asked as she drew off her gloves.

'God knows! I've ceased to think!'—and Madame
Grandoni stared up with her fat empty hands on the arms
of her chair.

'I've come on foot from the far south of London—how
many miles? four or five—and I'm not a particle tired.'

'*Che forza, che forza!*' the old woman sighed. 'She'll
knock you up completely,' she added, turning to Hyacinth
with her customary compassion.

'Poor darling, *she* misses the carriage,' Christina remarked, passing out of the room.

Madame Grandoni's eyes followed her and Hyacinth
made out in them a considerable lassitude, a plaintive bewilderment and surrender. 'Don't you like to use cabs—I

mean hansoms?' he asked, wishing to be of comfort and suggestion.

'It's not true I miss anything; my life's only too full,' she replied. 'I lived worse than this—in my bad days.' In a moment she went on: 'It's because you're here—she doesn't like Assunta to come.'

'Assunta—because I'm here?' Hyacinth didn't immediately catch her meaning.

'You must have seen her Italian maid at Medley. She has kept her and is ashamed of it. When we're alone Assunta comes for her hat and things. But she likes you to think she waits on herself.'

'That's a weakness—when she's so strong! And what does Assunta think of it?' Hyacinth asked, looking at the stuffed birds in the window, the alabaster Cupid, the wax flowers on the chimney-piece, the florid antimacassars on the chairs, the sentimental engravings on the walls—in frames of papier-mâché and 'composition', some of them enveloped in pink tissue paper—and the prismatic glass pendants attached to everything.

'She says "What on earth will it matter to-morrow?"'

'Does she mean that to-morrow the Princess will have her luxury back again? Hasn't she sold all her beautiful things?'

Madame Grandoni made up a face. 'She has kept a few. They're put away.'

'*A la bonne heure!*' Hyacinth cried with a laugh. He sat down with the ironical old woman; he spent nearly half an hour in desultory conversation with her before candles were brought in and while their friend was in Assunta's hands. He noticed how resolutely the Princess had withheld herself from any attempt to sweeten the dose she had taken it into her head to swallow, to mitigate the ugliness of her vulgar little house. She had respected its horrible signs and token, had left rigidly in their places the gimcracks finding favour in Madeira Crescent. She had flung no draperies over the pretentious furniture and disposed no rugs upon the staring carpet; and it was plainly her theory that the right way to acquaint one's self with the sensations of the wretched was to suffer the anguish of exasperated taste. Presently a female servant came in—not the sceptical Assunta, but a stunted young woman of the maid-of-all-work type, the same who had opened the door to the pair a short time before—and let him know of the Princess's wishing him to understand that he was expected to remain to tea. He learned from Madame Grandoni that the custom of an early dinner followed in the evening by the frugal repast of the lower orders was another of Christina's mortifications; and when shortly afterwards he saw the table laid in the back parlour, which was also the dining-room, and observed the nature of the crockery with which it was decorated, he noted that whether or no her earnestness were durable it was at any rate for the time intense. Madame Grandoni put before him definitely, as the Princess had done only in scraps, the career of the two ladies since his departure from Medley, their relinquishment of that fine house and the sudden arrangements Christina had made to change her mode of life after they had been only ten days in South Street. At the climax of the London season, in a society which only desired to treat her as one of its brightest ornaments, she had retired to Madeira Crescent, concealing her address—with only partial success of course—from every one, and inviting a celebrated curiosity-monger to come and look at her bibelots and tell her what he would give for the lot. In this manner she had parted with them at a fearful sacrifice. She had wished to avoid the nine days' wonder of a public sale; for, to do her justice, though she liked to be original she didn't like to be notorious, an occasion of stupid chatter. What had precipitated this violent step was a remonstrance received from her husband just after she had left Medley on the subject of her excessive expenditure: he had written her that it was past a joke—as she had appeared to consider it—and that she must really pull up. Nothing could gall her more than an interference on that head—since she maintained that she knew the exact figure of the Prince's income, of

which her allowance was an insignificant part—and she
had pulled up with a vengeance, as Hyacinth might perceive. The young man divined on this occasion one of the
eminent lady's high anxieties, of which he had never
thought before—the danger of the Prince's absolutely putting on the screw, of his attempting to make her come back
and live with him by withholding supplies altogether. In
this case she would find herself in a very tight place,
though she had a theory that if she should go to law about
the matter the courts would allow her a separate maintenance. This course, however, it would scarce be in her character to adopt; she would be more likely to waive her right
and support herself by lessons in music and the foreign
tongues supplemented by the remnant of property that had
come to her from her mother. That she was capable of returning to the Prince some day as an effect of her not daring
to face the loss of luxury was an idea that couldn't occur
to our youth in the midst of her assurances, uttered at
various times, that she positively yearned for a sacrifice;
and such an apprehension was less present to him than
ever while he listened to Madame Grandoni's account of
the manner in which their friend's rupture with the fashionable world had been enacted. It must be added that the old
lady devoted a deep groan to her not knowing how it would
all end, as some of Christina's economies were most expensive; and when Hyacinth pressed her a little she proceeded
to say that it was not at present the question of complications arising from the Prince that troubled her most, but
the fear that his wife was seriously compromised by her
reckless, her wicked correspondences: letters arriving from
foreign countries, from God knew whom (Christina never
told her, nor did she desire it), all about uprisings and
manifestations and liberations—of so much one could be
sure—and other matters that were no concern of honest
folk. Hyacinth but half knew what Madame Grandoni
meant by this allusion, which seemed to show that during
the last few months their hostess had considerably extended her revolutionary connexion; he only thought of

Hoffendahl, whose name, however, he was careful not to pronounce, and wondered whether his friend had been writing to the Master to intercede for *him*, to beg that he might be let off. His cheeks burned at the thought, but he contented himself with remarking to his entertainer that their extraordinary companion enjoyed the sense of danger. The old lady wished to know how she would enjoy the hangman's rope—with which, *du train dont elle allait*, she might easily make acquaintance; and when he expressed the hope that she didn't regard him as a counsellor of imprudence replied: 'You, my poor child? Oh I saw into you at Medley. You're a simple *codino!*'

The Princess came back to tea in a very dull gown and with a bunch of keys at her girdle; and nothing could have suggested the thrifty housewife better than the manner in which she superintended the laying of the cloth and the placing on it of a little austere refreshment—a pile of bread and butter flanked by a pot of marmalade and a morsel of bacon. She filled the teapot from a shiny tin canister locked up in a cupboard, of which the key worked with difficulty, and made the tea with her own superb hands; taking pains, however, to explain to Hyacinth that she was far from imposing that régime on Madame Grandoni, who understood that the grocer had a standing order to supply her, for her private consumption, with any delicacy she might desire. For herself she had never been so well as since following a homely diet. On Sundays they had muffins and sometimes for a change a smoked haddock or even a fried sole. Hyacinth lost himself in worship of the Princess's housewifely ways and of the exquisite figure she made as a small bourgeoise; judging that if her attempt to combine plain living with high thinking were all a burlesque it was at least the most finished entertainment she had yet offered him. She talked to Madame Grandoni of Lady Aurora; described her with much drollery, even to the details of her dress; declared that she was a delightful creature and one of the most interesting persons she had seen for an age; expressed to Hyacinth the conviction that she should like her exceed-

ingly if the poor dear would only believe a little in *her*.
'But I shall like her whether she does or not,' the Princess
all the same declared. 'I always know when that's going to
happen; it isn't so common. She'll begin very well with me
and be "fascinated"—isn't that the way people begin with
me?—but she won't understand me at all nor make out in
the least what kind of a queer fish I am, try as I may to
show her. When she thinks she does at last she'll give me
up in disgust and never know she has understood me quite
wrong. That has been the way with most of the people I've
liked; they've run away from me *à toutes jambes*. Oh I've
inspired aversions!' she mirthfully wailed as she handed
Hyacinth his cup of tea. He recognised it by the aroma as
a mixture not inferior to that of which he had partaken at
Medley. 'I've never succeeded in knowing any one who
would do me good, for by the time I began to improve
under their influence they could put up with me no longer.'

'You told me you were going to visit the poor. I don't
understand what your Gräfin was doing there,' said
Madame Grandoni.

'She had come out of charity—in the same way as I. She
evidently goes about immensely over there; I shall insist
on her taking me with her.'

'I thought you had promised to let *me* be your guide in
those explorations,' Hyacinth promptly pleaded.

The Princess looked at him a moment. 'Dear Mr Robinson, Lady Aurora knows more than you.'

'There have been times surely when you've compli-
mented me on my knowledge.'

'Oh I mean more about the lower classes!' she returned;
and oddly enough there was a sense in which he was unable to deny the claim made for her ladyship. He presently
came back to something said by his hostess a moment before, declaring that it had not been the way with Madame
Grandoni and him to take to their heels, and to this she
replied: 'Oh you'll run away yet! Don't be afraid.'

'I think that if I had been capable of quitting you I
should have done it by this time: I've neglected such

opportunities,' the old woman sighed. Hyacinth now made out that her eye had quite lost or intermitted its fine old pleasantry: she was troubled about many things.

'It's true that if you didn't leave me when I was rich it wouldn't look well for you to leave me at present,' the Princess suggested; and before Madame Grandoni could meet this speech she said to Hyacinth: 'I liked that odd man, your friend Muniment, so much for saying he wouldn't come to see me. "What good would it do him," poor fellow? What good would it do him indeed? You were not so difficult: you held off a little and pleaded obstacles, but one easily saw you'd come down,' she continued while she covered her guest with her mystifying smile. 'Besides I was smarter then, more splendid; I had on gewgaws and suggested worldly lures. I must have been more attractive. But I liked him for refusing,' she repeated; and of the many words she uttered that evening it was these that made most impression on our hero. He remained an hour after tea, for on rising from the table she had gone to the piano—not depriving herself of this resource she had a humble instrument of the so-called 'cottage' kind— and begun to play in a manner that reminded him of her commemorative outburst, as he might have fancied it, the day of his arrival at Medley. The night had grown close and as the piano was in the front room he opened at her request the window that looked into Madeira Crescent. Beneath it assembled the youth of both sexes, the dingy loiterers, who had clustered an hour before round the hurdy-gurdy. But on this occasion they didn't caper about; they leaned in silence against the area-rails and listened to the wondrous music. When Hyacinth told the player of the spell she had thrown on them she declared that it made her singularly happy; she added that she was really glad, almost proud, of her day; she felt as if she had begun to do something for the people. Just before he took leave she encountered some occasion for saying that she was certain the odd man in Audley Court wouldn't come; and he forebore to contradict her because he believed in fact he wouldn't.

XXXIV

HOW RIGHT had been her prevision that Lady Aurora
would be fascinated at first was proved as soon as Hyacinth
went to Belgrave Square—a visit he was promptly led to
pay by a deep sense of the obligations under which her
ladyship had placed him at the time of Pinnie's death.
The conditions in which he found her were quite the same
as those of his visit the year before; she was spending the
unfashionable season in her father's empty house and amid
a desert of brown holland and the dormant echoes of heavy
conversation. He had seen so much of her during Pinnie's
illness that he felt—or had felt then—that he knew her
almost intimately, that they had become real friends, almost comrades, and might meet henceforth without reserves
or ceremonies. She was in spite of this as fluttered and awkward as she had been on the other occasion: not distant, but
entangled in new coils of shyness and apparently unmindful of what had happened to draw them closer. Hyacinth,
however, always liked extremely to be with her, for she
was the person in the world who quietly, delicately and as
a matter of course treated him most as a gentleman and
appeared most naturally to take him for one. She had never
addressed him the handsome flattering freedoms that had
fallen from the lips of the Princess, and never explained
at all her view of him; but her timid cursory receptive
manner, which took all sorts of equalities and communities
for granted, was a homage to the idea of his fine essence.
It was in this manner that she now conversed with him on
the subject of his foreign travels; he found himself discussing the political indications of Paris and the Ruskinian
theories of Venice in Belgravia after the fashion of the
cosmopolites bred by those wastes. It took him none the
less but a few minutes to be sure Lady Aurora's heart was
not in these considerations; the deferential smile she bent

upon him while she sat with her head thrust forward and her long hands clasped in her lap was slightly mechanical, her attitude all perfunctory. When he gave her his views of some of the *arrière-pensées* of M. Gambetta—for he had views not altogether, as he thought, deficient in originality —she didn't interrupt, for she never interrupted; but she took advantage of his first pause to say quickly and irrelevantly: 'Will the Princess Casamassima come again to Audley Court?'

'I've no doubt she'd come again if they'd particularly like her to.'

'I do hope she will. She's very wonderful,' Lady Aurora richly breathed.

'Oh yes, she's very wonderful. I think she gave Rosy pleasure.'

'Rosy can talk of nothing else. It would really do her great good to have such an experience again. Don't you think her quite different from anybody one has ever seen?' But her ladyship added before waiting for an answer to this: 'I liked her quite extraordinarily.'

'She liked you just as much. I know it would give her great pleasure if you could go to see her,' Hyacinth said.

'Fancy that!' his companion gasped; and she instantly obtained the Princess's address from him and made a note of it in a small shabby pocketbook. She mentioned that the card the Princess had given her in Camberwell exhibited in fact no address, and he recognised that vagary—the Princess was so offhand. Then she said, hesitating a little: 'Does she really care for the poor?'

'If she doesn't,' the young man replied, 'I can't imagine what interest she has in pretending to.'

'If she does she's very remarkable—she deserves great honour.'

'You really care—so why is she more remarkable than you?' Hyacinth demanded.

'Oh it's very different—she's so wonderfully attractive!' Lady Aurora replied, making recklessly the one allusion to the oddity of her own appearance in which he was destined to hear her indulge. She became conscious of it the moment she had spoken, and said quickly, to turn it off, 'I should like to talk with her, but I'm rather afraid. She's tremendously clever.'

'Ah what she is—"tremendously"—you'll find out when you know her!' he could but all portentously sigh.

His hostess looked at him a little and then vaguely returned: 'How very interesting!' The next moment she continued: 'She might do so many other things. She might charm the world.'

'She does that, whatever she does,' Hyacinth smiled. 'It's all by the way; it needn't interfere.'

'That's what I mean, that most other people would be content—beautiful as she is. There's great merit when you give up something.'

'She has known a great many bad people and she wants to know some good,' he explained. 'Therefore be sure to go to see her soon.'

'She looks as if she had known nothing bad since she was born,' said Lady Aurora rapturously. 'I can't imagine her going into all the dreadful places she'd have to.'

'You've gone into them, and it hasn't hurt you,' he suggested.

'How do you know that? My family think it has.'

'You make me glad then that I haven't a family,' said the young man.

'And the Princess—has she no one?'

'Ah yes, she has a husband. But she doesn't live with him.'

'Is he one of the bad persons?' asked Lady Aurora as earnestly as a child listening to a tale.

'Well, I don't like to abuse him—he's down.'

'If I were a man I should be in love with her,' said Lady Aurora. Then she added: 'I wonder if we might work together.'

'That's exactly what she hopes.'

'I won't show her the worst places,' her ladyship maliciously protested.

To which her visitor returned: 'I expect you'll do what every one else has done—which is exactly what she wants!' Before he took leave he said to her: 'Do you know if Paul Muniment also liked the Princess?'

She meditated a moment, apparently with some intensity. 'I think she struck him as extraordinarily beautiful—as the most beautiful person he had ever seen.'

'Does he still believe her a humbug?'

'Still——?' asked Lady Aurora as if she didn't understand.

'I mean that that was the impression apparently made upon him last winter by my description of her.'

'Oh I'm sure he thinks her tremendously plucky!' Which was all the satisfaction Hyacinth got just then as to Muniment's estimate of the Princess.

A few days later he returned to Madeira Crescent in the evening, the only time he was free, the Princess having given him a general invitation to take tea with her. He felt he ought to be discreet in acting on it, though he was not without reasons that would have warranted him in going early and often. He had a peculiar dread of her growing used to him and tired of him—boring herself in his society; yet at the same time he had rather a sharp vision of her boring herself without him during the dull summer evenings when even Paddington was out of town. He wondered what she did, what visitors dropped in, what pastimes she cultivated, what saved her from the sudden vagary of throwing up the whole of her present game. He remembered that there was a complete side of her life with which he was almost unacquainted—Lady Marchant and her daughters, at Medley, and three or four other persons who had called while he was there being, in his experience, the only illustrations of it—and didn't know, by the same token, to what extent she had in spite of her transformation preserved relations with her old friends; but he made out as looming the day she would discover that what she found in Madeira Crescent was less striking than what she missed. Going thither a second time he noted, for all this, that he

had done her great injustice: she was full of resources, she
had never been so happy, she found time to read, to write,
to commune with her piano and above all to think—a delightful detachment from the invasive vulgar gossiping dis-
tracting world she had known hitherto. The only interruption to her felicity was that she received quantities of notes
from her former acquaintance, endless appeals to give some
account of herself, to say what had become of her, to come
and stay with them in the country. With these survivals of
her past she took a very short way, she simply burned
them without answering. She told Hyacinth immediately
that Lady Aurora had called two days before, at an hour
when she was not in, and that she had straightway addressed
her in return an invitation to come to tea any evening at
eight o'clock. That was the way the people in Madeira
Crescent entertained each other—the Princess knew everything about them now and was eager to impart her knowledge; and the evening, she was sure, would be much more
convenient to Lady Aurora, whose days were filled with
good works, with peregrinations of charity. Her ladyship
arrived ten minutes after Hyacinth; she assured the Princess her invitation had been expressed in a manner so flattering that she was unwilling to wait more than a day to
respond. She was introduced to Madame Grandoni and
tea all bustlingly served; Hyacinth being gratefully conscious the while of the "considerate" way in which Lady
Aurora forbore to appear bewildered at meeting him in
such society. She knew he frequented it, having been witness of his encounter with their high personage in Audley
Court; but it might have startled her to have ocular evidence of the footing on which he stood. Everything the
Princess did or said at this time had for effect, whatever its
purpose, to make her seem more rare and fine; and she had
seldom given him greater pleasure than by the exquisite
art she put forth to win Lady Aurora's confidence, to place
herself under the pure and elevating influence of the noble
spinster. She made herself small and simple; she spoke of
her own little aspirations and efforts; she appealed and

persuaded; she laid her white hand on her gentle guest's, gazing at her with an interest all visibly sincere but which yet derived half its effect from the contrast between the quality of her beauty, the whole air of her person, and the hard dreary problems of misery and crime. It was touching and Lady Aurora was touched; that was quite clear as they sat together on the sofa after tea and the Princess protested that she only wanted to know what her friend was doing—what she had done for years—in order that she might go and do likewise. She asked personal questions with a directness that was sometimes embarrassing to the subject—he had seen that habit in her from the first—and her yearning guest, though charmed and excited, was not quite comfortable at being so publicly probed and sounded. The public was formed of Madame Grandoni and Hyacinth; but the old lady—whose intercourse with the visitor had consisted almost wholly of watching her with a deep speculative anxiety—presently shuffled away and was heard, through the thin partitions that prevailed in Madeira Crescent, to ascend to her own apartment. It seemed to Hyacinth that he ought also in delicacy to retire, and this was his intention from one moment to the other; to him certainly—and the very second time she met him—Lady Aurora had made as much of her confession as he had a right to look for. After that one little flash of egotism he had never again heard her refer to her own feelings or conditions.

'Do you stay in town like this, at such a season, on purpose to attend to your work?' the Princess asked; and there was something archly rueful in the tone in which she made this enquiry—as if it cost her just a pang to find that in taking such a line she herself had not been so original as she hoped. 'Mr Robinson has told me about your big house in Belgrave Square—you must let me come and see you there. Nothing would make me so happy as that you should allow me to help you a little—how little soever. Do you like to be helped or do you like to go quite alone? Are you very independent or do you need to look up, to cling, to lean on some one? Pardon me if I ask impertinent questions; we speak that way—rather, you know—in Rome, where I've spent a large part of my life. That idea of your being there by yourself, in your great dull home, with all your charities and devotions, makes a kind of picture in my mind; it's quaint and touching, it's like something in some English novel. Englishwomen are so awfully accomplished, are they not? I'm really a foreigner, you know, and though I've lived here a while it takes one some time to find those things out *au juste*. Is your work for the people therefore only one of your occupations or is it everything, does it absorb your whole life? That's what I should like it to be for me. Do your family like you to throw yourself into all this or have you had to brave a certain amount of ridicule? I dare say you have; that's where you English are strong, in braving ridicule. They have to do it so often, haven't they? I don't know whether I could do it. I never tried—but with you I think I would brave anything. Are your family clever and sympathetic? No? the kind of thing that one's family generally is? Ah well, dear lady, we must make a little family together. Are you encouraged or disgusted? Do you go on doggedly or have you some faith, some great idea, that lifts you up? Are you actively religious now, *par exemple*? Do you do your work in connexion with any pious foundation or earnest movement, any missions or priests or sisters? I'm a Catholic, you know—but so little by my own doing! I shouldn't mind in the least joining hands with any one who's really producing results. I express myself awkwardly, but perhaps you know what I mean. Possibly you don't know that I'm one of those who believe that a great new deal is destined to take place and that it can't make things worse than they are already. I believe, in a word, in the action of the people for themselves—the others will never act for them; and I'm all ready to act *with* them—in any intelligent or intelligible way. If that shocks you I shall be immensely disappointed, because there's something in the impression you make on me that seems to suggest you haven't the usual prejudices, so that if certain things were to happen you wouldn't be afraid. You're beautifully shy, are you not?—but you're not craven. I suppose that if you thought the inequalities and oppressions and miseries now universal were a necessary part of life and were going on for ever you wouldn't be interested in those people over the river (the bedridden girl and her brother, I mean); because Mr Robinson tells me they're advanced socialists— or at least the brother is. Perhaps you'll say you don't care for him—the sister, to your mind, being the remarkable one. She's indeed a perfect little *femme du monde*—she talks so much better than most of the people in society. I hope you don't mind my saying that, because I've an idea you're not in society. You can imagine whether I am! Haven't you judged it like me, condemned it and given it up? Aren't you sick of the egotism, the snobbery, the meanness, the frivolity, the immorality, the hypocrisy? Isn't there a great resemblance in our situations? I don't mean in our natures, for you're far better than I shall ever be. Aren't you quite divinely good? When I see a woman of your sort—not that I often do—I try to be a little less bad. You've helped hundreds, thousands of people: you must help *me!*'

These remarks, which I have strung together, didn't of course fall from the Princess's lips in an uninterrupted stream; they were arrested and interspersed by frequent inarticulate responses and embarrassed protests. Lady Aurora shrank from them even while they gratified her, blinking and fidgeting in the dazzling direct light of her hostess's sympathy. I needn't repeat her answers, the more so as they none of them arrived at completion but passed away into nervous laughter and averted looks, the latter directed at the ceiling, the floor, the windows, and appearing to project a form of entreaty to some occult or supernatural power that the conversation should become more impersonal. In reply to the Princess's allusion to the convictions prevailing in the Muniment family she said that the brother and sister thought differently about public ques-

tions but were of the same mind with regard to the interest taken by persons of the upper class in the working
people, the attempt on the part of their so-called superiors
to enter into their life: they pronounced it a great mistake.
At this information the Princess looked much disappointed;
she wished to know if the Muniments deemed it so impossible to do them any good. 'Oh I mean a mistake from *our*
point of view,' said Lady Aurora. 'They wouldn't do it in
our place; they think we had much better occupy ourselves
with our own pleasures.' And as her new friend stared, not
comprehending, she went on: 'Rosy thinks we've a right
to our own pleasures under all circumstances, no matter
how badly off the poor may be; and her brother takes the
ground that we're not likely to have them much longer and
that in view of what may happen we're great fools not to
make the most of them.'

'I see, I see. That's very strong,' the Princess murmured
in a tone of high appreciation.

'I dare say. But, all the same, whatever's going to come
one *must* do something.'

'You do think then that something's going to come?'
said the Princess.

'Oh immense changes, I dare say. But I don't belong to
anything, you know.'

The Princess thought this over. 'No more do I. But many
people do. Mr Robinson for instance.' And she turned her
golden light on Hyacinth.

'Oh if the changes depend on *me*——!' Mr Robinson
exclaimed with a blush.

'They won't set the Thames on fire—I quite agree to
that!'

Lady Aurora had the manner of not considering she had
a warrant for going into the question of Hyacinth's affiliations; so she stared abstractedly at the piano and in a
moment remarked to her hostess: 'I'm sure you play awfully well. I should like so much to hear you.'

Hyacinth could see their friend thought this *banal*. She
had not asked Lady Aurora to spend the evening with her

simply that they should fall back on the resources of the vulgar. Nevertheless she replied with perfect good nature that she should be delighted to play; only there was a thing she should like much better—which was that Lady Aurora should narrate her life.

'Oh don't talk about mine; yours, yours!' her ladyship cried, colouring with eagerness and for the first time since her arrival indulging in the free gesture of laying her hand on that of the Princess.

'With so many grand confidences in the air I certainly had better take myself off,' said Hyacinth; and the Princess offered no opposition to his departure. She and Lady Aurora were evidently on the point of striking up a tremendous intimacy, and as he turned this idea over walking away it made him sad for strange vague reasons that he couldn't have expressed.

XXXV

THE SUNDAY following this occasion he spent almost entirely with the Muniments, with whom, since his return to his work, he had been able to have no long fraternising talk of the kind that had marked their earlier relations. The present, however, was a happy day; it added its large measure to the esteem in which he now held the inscrutable Paul. The warm bright September weather enriched even the dinginess of Audley Court, and while in the morning Rosy's brother and their visitor sat beside her sofa the trio amused themselves with discussing a dozen different plans for giving a festive turn to the day. There had been moments in the last six months when Hyacinth had the conviction he should never again be able to enter into such ideas as that, and these moments had been connected with the strange conversion taking place in his mental image of the man whose hardness—of course he was obliged to be hard—he had never expected to see turned upon a pas-

sionate admirer. At present, for the hour at least, the darkness had cleared away and Paul's company become a
sustaining influence. He had never been kinder, jollier,
safer, as it were; it had never appeared more desirable to
hold fast to him and trust him. Less than ever would an
observer have guessed at a good reason why the two young
men might have winced as they looked at each other. Rosy
naturally took part in the question debated between her
companions—the question whether they should limit their
excursion to a walk in Hyde Park; should embark at Lambeth Pier on the penny steamer which would convey them
to Greenwich; or should start presently for Waterloo
Station and go thence by train to Hampton Court. Miss
Muniment had visited none of these scenes, but she contributed largely to the discussion, for which she seemed
perfectly qualified; talked about the crowd on the steamer
and the inconvenience arising from drunken persons on the
return quite as if she had suffered from such drawbacks;
reminded the others that the view from the hill at Greenwich was terribly smoky and at that season the fashionable
world—half the attraction of course—altogether absent
from Hyde Park; and expressed strong views in favour of
Wolsey's old palace, with whose history she appeared intimately acquainted. She threw herself into her brother's
holiday with eagerness and glee, and Hyacinth marvelled
again at the stoicism of the hard bright creature, polished,
as it were, by pain, whose imagination appeared never to
concern itself with her own privations, so that she could
lie in her close little room the whole golden afternoon
without bursting into sobs as she saw the western sunbeams
slant upon the shabby ugly familiar paper of her wall and
thought of the far-off fields and gardens she should never
see. She talked immensely of the Princess, for whose
beauty, grace and benevolence she could find no sufficient
praise; declaring that of all the fair faces that had ever
hung over her couch—and Rosy spoke as from immense
opportunities for comparison—she had far the noblest and
most refreshing. She seemed to make a kind of light in the

room and to leave it behind after she had gone. Rosy could call up her image as she could hum a tune she had heard, and she expressed in her quaint particular way how, as she lay there in the quiet hours, she repeated over to herself the beautiful air. The Princess might be anything, she might be royal or imperial, and Rosy was well aware how little *she* should complain of the dulness of a life in which such apparitions as that could pop in any day. She made a difference in the place—it gave it a regular finish for her to have come there; if it was good enough for a princess it was good enough for the likes of *her*, and she hoped she shouldn't hear again of Paul's wishing her to move out of a room with which she should have henceforth such delightful associations. The Princess had found her way to Audley Court and perhaps wouldn't find it to another lodging, for they couldn't expect her to follow them about London at their pleasure; and at any rate she had evidently been altogether struck with the little room, so that if they were quiet and canny who could say but the fancy would take her to send them a bit of carpet or a picture, or even a mirror with a gilt frame, to make it a bit more tasteful? Rosy's transitions from pure enthusiasm to the imaginative calculation of benefits were performed with a serenity peculiar to herself. Her chatter had so much spirit and point that it always commanded attention, but to-day Hyacinth was less tolerant of it than usual, because so long as it lasted Muniment held his tongue, and what he had been anxious about was much more Paul's impression of the Princess. Rosy made no remark to him on the monopoly he had so long enjoyed of this wonderful lady: she had always had the manner of an indulgent incredulity about Hyacinth's social adventures, and he saw the hour might easily come when she would begin to talk of their grand acquaintance as if she herself had been the first to discover her. She had much to say, however, about the nature of the connexion Lady Aurora had formed with her, and she was mainly occupied with the glory she had drawn upon herself by bringing two such exalted persons together. She fancied them alluding, in the great world, to the occasion on which 'we first met—at Miss Muniment's, you know'; and she related how Lady Aurora, who had been in Audley Court the day before, had declared she owed her a debt she could never repay. The two ladies had liked each other more, almost, than they liked any one; and wasn't it a rare picture to think of them moving hand in hand, like great twin lilies, through the bright upper air? Muniment enquired in rather a coarse unsympathetic way what the mischief she ever wanted of *her*; which led Hyacinth to demand in return: 'What do you mean? What does who want of whom?'

'What does the beauty of beauties want of *our* poor plain lady? She has a totally different stamp. I don't know much about women, but I can see that.'

'Where do you see a different stamp? They both have the stamp of their rank!' cried Rosy.

'Who can ever tell what women want, at any time?' Hyacinth asked with the off-handedness of a man of the world.

'Well, my boy, if you don't know any more than I you disappoint me! Perhaps if we wait long enough she'll tell us some day herself.'

'Tell you what she wants of Lady Aurora?'

'I don't mind about Lady Aurora so much; but what in the name of long journeys she wants with *us*!'

'Don't you think you're worth a long journey?' Rosy cried gaily. 'If you weren't my brother, which is handy for seeing you, and I weren't confined to my sofa, I'd go from one end of England to the other to make your acquaintance! He's in love with the Princess,' she went on to Hyacinth, 'and he asks those senseless questions to cover it up. What does any one want of anything?'

It was decided at last that the two young men should go down to Greenwich, and after they had partaken of bread and cheese with Rosy they embarked on a penny-steamer. The boat was densely crowded, and they leaned, rather squeezed together, in the fore part of it, against the rail

of the deck, and watched the big black fringe of the yellow
stream. The river had always for Hyacinth a deep beguile-
ment. The ambiguous appeal he had felt as a child in all
the aspects of London came back to him from the dark
detail of its banks and the sordid agitation of its bosom:
the great arches and pillars of the bridges, where the water
rushed and the funnels tipped and sounds made an echo
and there seemed an overhanging of interminable proces-
sions; the miles of ugly wharves and warehouses; the
lean protrusions of chimney, mast and crane; the painted
signs of grimy industries staring from shore to shore; the
strange flat obstructive barges, straining and bumping on
some business as to which everything was vague but that
it was remarkably dirty; the clumsy coasters and colliers
which thickened as one went down; the small loafing boats
whose occupants, somehow, looking up from their oars at
the steamer, as they rocked in the oily undulations of its
wake, appeared profane and sarcastic; in short all the
grinding, puffing, smoking, splashing activity of the turbid
flood. In the good-natured crowd, amid the fumes of vile
tobacco, beneath the shower of sooty particles and to the
accompaniment of the bagpipe of a dingy Highlander who
sketched occasionally an unconvincing reel, Hyacinth forbore to speak to his companion of what he had most at
heart; but later, as they lay in the brown crushed grass on
one of the slopes of the Greenwich Park and saw the river
stretch away and shine beyond the pompous colonnades
of the Hospital, he asked him if there were any truth in
what Rosy had said about his being sweet on their friend
the Princess. He said 'their friend' on purpose, speaking as
if, now that she had been twice to Audley Court, Muniment might be regarded as knowing her almost as well as
he himself did. He wished to conjure away the idea that
he was jealous of Paul, and if he desired information on
the point I have mentioned this was because it still made
him almost as uncomfortable as it had done at first that
his comrade should take the scoffing view. He didn't easily
see such a fellow as Muniment wheel about from one day

to the other, but he had been present at the most exquisite
exhibition he had ever observed the Princess make of that
divine power of conciliation which was not perhaps in
social intercourse the art she chiefly exercised but was certainly the most wonderful of her secrets, and it would be
remarkable indeed that a sane young man shouldn't have
been affected by it. It was familiar to Hyacinth that Muniment wasn't easily reached or rubbed up by women, but
this might perfectly have been the case without detriment
to the Princess's ability to work a miracle. The companions had wandered through the great halls and courts
of the Hospital; had gazed up at the glories of the famous
painted chamber and admired the long and lurid series of
the naval victories of England—Muniment remarking to
his friend that he supposed he had seen the match to all
that in foreign parts, offensive little travelled beggar that
he was. They had not ordered a fish-dinner either at the
'Trafalgar' or the 'Ship'—having a frugal vision of tea and
shrimps with Rosy on their return—but they had laboured
up and down the steep undulations of the shabby, charming park; made advances to the tame deer and seen them
amble foolishly away; watched the young of both sexes,
hilarious and red in the face, roll in promiscuous accouple-
ment over the slopes; gazed at the little brick observatory,
perched on one of the knolls, which sets the time to English history and in which Hyacinth could see that his
companion took an expert, a technical interest; wandered
out of one of the upper gates and admired the trimness of
the little villas at Blackheath, where Muniment declared it
his conception of supreme social success to be able to live.
He pointed out two or three small semi-detached houses,
faced with stucco and with 'Mortimer Lodge' or 'The
Sycamores' inscribed on the gate-posts, and Hyacinth
guessed these to be the sort of place where he would like
to end his days—in high pure air, with a genteel window
for Rosy's couch and a cheerful view of suburban excursions. It was when they came back into the Park that,

being rather hot and a little sated, they stretched themselves under a tree and Hyacinth yielded to his curiosity.

'Sweet on her—sweet on her, my boy!' said Muniment.
'I might as well be sweet on the dome of Saint Paul's,
which I just make out off there.'

'The dome of Saint Paul's doesn't come to see you and
doesn't ask you to return the visit.'

'Oh I don't return visits—I've got plenty of jobs of my
own to attend to. If I don't put myself out for the Princess
isn't that a sufficient answer to your question?'

'I'm by no means sure,' said Hyacinth. 'If you went to
see her, simply and civilly, because she asked you, I
shouldn't regard it as a proof you had taken a fancy to her.
Your hanging off is more suspicious; it may mean that
you don't trust yourself—that you're in danger of falling
in love if you go in for a more intimate acquaintance.'

'It's a rum go, your wanting me to make up to her. I
shouldn't think it would suit your book,' Muniment returned while he stared at the sky with his hands clasped
under his head.

'Do you suppose I'm afraid of you?' his comrade asked.
'Besides,' Hyacinth added in a moment, 'why the devil
should I care now?'

Paul made for a little no rejoinder; he turned over on
his side and, with his arm resting on the ground, leaned his
head on his hand. Hyacinth felt his eyes on his own face,
but he also felt himself colouring and didn't meet them.
He had taken a private vow never to indulge, to this companion, in certain inauspicious references, and the words
just spoken had slipped out of his mouth too easily. 'What
do you mean by that?' Paul demanded at last; and when
Hyacinth looked at him, he saw nothing but the strong
fresh irresponsible, the all so manly and sturdy face. Its
owner had had time before speaking to prefigure a meaning.

Suddenly an impulse he had never known before, or
rather that he had always resisted, took possession of our
young man. There was a mystery which it concerned his
happiness to clear up, and he became unconscious of his

scruples, of his pride, of the strength he had ever believed to be in him—the strength for going through his work and passing away without a look behind. He sat forward on the grass with his arms round his knees and offered his friend a presence quickened by his difficulties. For a minute the two pairs of eyes met with extreme clearness, and then Hyacinth brought out: 'What an extraordinary chap you are!'

'You've hit it there!' Paul smiled.

'I don't want to make a scene or work on your feelings, but how will you like it when I'm strung up on the gallows?'

'You mean for Hoffendahl's job? That's what you were alluding to just now?' Muniment lay there in the same position, chewing a long blade of dry grass which he held to his lips with his free hand.

'I didn't mean to speak of it; but after all why shouldn't it come up? Naturally I've thought of it a good deal.'

'What good does that do?' Muniment returned. 'I hoped you didn't—I noticed you never spoke of it. You don't like it. You'd rather chuck it up,' he added.

There was not in his voice the faintest note of irony or contempt, no sign whatever that he passed judgement on such an attitude. He spoke in a quiet human memorising manner, as if it had originally quite entered into his thought to allow for weak regrets. Nevertheless the complete reasonableness of his tone itself cast a chill on Hyacinth's spirit; it was like the touch of a hand at once very firm and very soft, yet strangely cold. 'I don't want in the least to repudiate business, but did you suppose I liked it?' our hero asked with rather a forced laugh.

'My dear fellow, how could I tell? You like a lot of things I don't. You like excitement and emotion and change, you like remarkable sensations—whereas I go in for a holy calm, for sweet repose.'

'If you object, for yourself, to change, and are so fond of still waters, why have you associated yourself with a revolutionary movement?' Hyacinth demanded with a little air of making rather a good point.

'Just for that reason!' Paul blandly said. 'Isn't our revolutionary movement as quiet as the grave? Who knows, who suspects anything like the full extent of it?'

'I see. You take only the quiet parts!'

In speaking these words Hyacinth had had no derisive intention, but a moment later he flushed with the sense that they had a sufficiently low sound. Paul, however, appeared to see no offence in them, and it was in the gentlest, most suggestive way, as if he had been thinking over what might comfort his little mate, that he replied: 'There's one thing you ought to remember—that it's quite on the cards the beastly call may never be made.'

'I don't desire that reminder,' Hyacinth said; 'and moreover you must let me tell you I somehow don't easily fancy *you* mixed up with things that don't come off. Anything you have to do with will come off, I think.'

Muniment reflected a moment, as if his little mate were charmingly ingenious. 'Surely I've nothing to do with the particular job——!'

'With the execution, perhaps not; but how about the idea of it? You seemed to me to have a great deal to do with it the night you took me to see him.'

Paul changed his posture, raising himself, and in a moment was seated Turk-fashion beside his friend. He put his arm over his shoulder and drew him, studying his face; and then in the kindest manner in the world he brought out: 'There are three or four definite chances in your favour.'

'I don't want second-rate comfort, you know,' said Hyacinth, with his eyes on the distant atmospheric mixture that represented London.

'What the devil *do* you want?' Paul asked, still holding him and with perfect good humour.

'Well, to get inside of *you* a little; to know how a chap feels when he's going to part with his particular pal.'

'To part with him?' this character repeated.

'I mean putting it at the worst.'

'I should think you'd know by yourself—if you're going to part with *me*.'

At this Hyacinth prostrated himself, tumbled over to the grass on his face, which he buried in his hands. He remained in this attitude, saying nothing, a long time; and while he lay there he thought, with a sudden quick flood of association, of many strange things. Most of all he had the sense of the brilliant charming day; the warm stillness, touched with cries of amusement; the sweetness of loafing there in an interval of work with a chum who was a tremendously fine fellow even if he didn't understand the inexpressible. Paul also kept the peace, and Hyacinth felt him all unaffectedly puzzled. He wanted now to relieve him, so that he pulled himself together again and turned round, saying the first thing he could think of, in relation to the general subject of their talk, that would carry them away from the personal question. 'I've asked you before, and you've told me, but somehow I've never grasped it—so I just touch on the matter again—exactly what good you think it will do.'

'The stroke of work, eh——? Well, you must remember that as yet we know only very vaguely what it is. It's difficult therefore to measure closely the importance it may have, and I don't think I've ever, in talking with you, pretended to fix that importance. I don't suppose it will matter immensely whether your own engagement's carried out or not; but if it is it will have been a detail in a scheme of which the general effect will be decidedly useful. I believe, and you pretend to believe, though I'm not sure you do, in the advent of the democracy. It will help the democracy to get possession that the classes that keep them down shall be admonished from time to time that they've a very definite and very determined intention of doing so. An immense deal will depend upon that. Hoffendahl's a jolly admonisher.'

Hyacinth listened to this explanation with an expression of interest that was not feigned; and after a moment he returned: 'When you say you believe in the democracy I take for granted you mean you positively wish for their coming into power, as I've always supposed. Now what I really have never understood is this—why should you desire to put forward a lot of people whom you regard almost without exception as rather dismal donkeys.'

'Ah, my dear lad,' Paul laughed, 'when one undertakes to meddle in human affairs one must deal with human material. The upper classes have the longest ears.'

'I've heard you say you were working for an equality in human conditions—to abolish the immemorial inequality. What you want then for all mankind is the selfsame shade of asininity.'

'That's very neat; did you pick it up in France? Damn the too-neat, you know; it's as bad as the too-rotten. The low tone of our fellow mortals is a result of bad conditions; it's the conditions I want to alter. When those who have no start to speak of have a good one it's but fair to infer they'll go further. I want to try them, you know.'

'But why equality?' Hyacinth asked. 'Somehow that word doesn't say so much to me as it used to. Inequality—inequality! I don't know whether it's by dint of repeating it over to myself, but *that* doesn't shock me as it used.'

'They didn't put you up to that in France, I'm sure!' Paul exclaimed. 'Your point of view's changed. You've risen in the world.'

'Risen? Good God, what have I risen to?'

'True enough; you were always a bloated little swell!' And the so useful man at the great chemical works gave his young friend a sociable slap on the back. There was a momentary bitterness in its being imputed to such a one as Hyacinth, even in joke, that he had taken sides with the lucky beggars as a class, and he had it on his tongue's end to ask his friend if he had never guessed what his proud titles were—the bastard of a murderess, spawned in a gutter out of which he had been picked by a poor sewing-girl. But his lifelong reserve on this point was a habit not easily broken, and before such a challenge could burn

through it Paul had gone on. 'If you've ceased to believe
we can do anything it will be rather awkward, you know.'

'I don't know what I believe, God help me!' Hyacinth
remarked in a tone of an effect so lugubrious that his mate
indulged in prompt hilarity of attenuation. But our young
man added: 'I don't want you to think I've ceased to care
for the people. What am I but one of the poorest and
meanest of them?'

'You, my boy? You're a duke in disguise, and so I
thought the first time I ever saw you. That night I took
you to our precious "exchange of ideas"—I liked the beggar's name for it—you had a little way with you that made
me forget it; I mean that your disguise happened to be
better than usual. As regards caring for the people there's
surely no obligation at all,' Muniment continued. 'I
wouldn't if I could help it—you can bet your life on that.
It all depends on what you see. The way *I've* used my eyes
in that sink of iniquity off there has led to my seeing that
present arrangements won't do. They won't do,' he repeated
placidly.

'Yes, I see that too,' said Hyacinth, with the same dole-
fulness that had marked his tone a moment before—a dole-
fulness begotten of the rather helpless sense that, whatever
he saw, he saw—and this was always the case—so many
other things besides. He saw the immeasurable misery of
the people, and yet he saw all that had been, as it were,
rescued and redeemed from it: the treasures, the felicities,
the splendours, the successes of the world. This quantity
took the form sometimes, to his imagination, of a vast
vague dazzling presence, an irradiation of light from objects
undefined, mixed with the atmosphere of Paris and of
Venice. He presently added that a hundred things Muniment had told him about the four horrors of the worst districts of London, pictures of incredible shame and suffering that he had put before him, came back to him now
with the memory of the passion they had kindled at the
time.

'Oh I don't want you to go by what I've told you; I

want you to go by what you've seen yourself. I remember there were things you told *me* that weren't bad in their way.' And at this Paul Muniment sprang to his feet, as if their conversation had drawn to an end or they must at all events be thinking of their homeward way. Hyacinth got up too while his companion stood there. Paul was looking off toward London with a face that expressed all the healthy singleness of his vision. Suddenly he remarked, as if it occurred to him to complete, or at any rate confirm, the declaration he had made a short time before: 'Yes, I don't believe in the millennium, but I do believe in the democracy with a *chance*.'

He struck Hyacinth while he spoke these words as such a fine embodiment of the spirit of the people; he stood there in his powerful sturdy newness with such an air of having learnt what he had learnt and of good nature that had purposes in it, that our hero felt the simple inrush of his old frequent pride at having a person of that promise, a nature of that capacity, for a friend. He passed his hand into the arm that was so much stronger and longer than his own and said with an imperceptible tremor of voice: 'It's no use your saying I'm not to go by what you tell me. I'd go by what you tell me anywhere. There's no awkwardness to speak of. I don't know that I believe exactly what you believe, but I believe in *you*, and doesn't that come to the same thing?'

Paul evidently appreciated the cordiality and candour of this little tribute, and the way he showed it was by a motion of his elbow, to check his companion, before they started to leave the spot, and by looking down at him with a certain anxiety of friendliness. 'I should never have taken you to that shop that night if I hadn't thought you'd jump at the job. It was that flaring little oration of yours, at the club, when you floored Delancey for saying you were afraid, that put me up to it.'

'I did jump at it—upon my word I did; and it was just what I was looking for. That's all correct!' said Hyacinth cheerfully as they went forward. There was a strain of heroism in these words—of heroism of which the sense was not conveyed to Muniment by a vibration in their interlocked arms. Hyacinth didn't make the reflexion that he was infernally literal; he dismissed the sentimental problem that had worried him; he condoned, excused, admired—he merged himself, resting happy for the time, in the consciousness that Paul was a grand person, that friendship was a purer feeling than love and that there was an immense deal of affection between them. He didn't even observe at that moment that it was preponderantly on his own side.

XXXVI

A CERTAIN Sunday in November, more than three months after she had gone to live in Madeira Crescent, was so important an occasion for the Princess as to require reporting with a certain fulness. Early in the afternoon a loud peal from her door-knocker came to her ear; it had a sound of resolution, almost of defiance, which made her look up from her book and listen. She was sitting alone by the fire, over a heavy volume on Labour and Capital. It was not yet four o'clock, but she had had candles this hour; a dense brown fog made the daylight impure without suggesting an answer to the question of whether the scheme of nature had been to veil or to deepen the sabbatical dreariness. She was not tired of Madeira Crescent, such an idea she would indignantly have repudiated; but the prospect of a visitor had a happy application—the possibility even of his being an ambassador or a cabinet minister or another of the eminent personages with whom she had conversed before embracing the ascetic life. They had not knocked at her present door hitherto in any great numbers, for more reasons than one; they were out of town and she had taken pains to diffuse the belief that she had left England. If the impression prevailed it was exactly the impression she had desired; she forgot this fact whenever she felt a certain surprise—even, it may be, a certain irritation—in perceiving that people were not taking the way to Madeira Crescent. She was making the discovery, in which she had had many predecessors, that to hide in London is only too easy a game. It was very much in that fashion that Godfrey Sholto was in the habit of announcing himself when he reappeared after the intervals she explicitly imposed on him; there was a witless grace, for so world-worn a personage, in the point he made of showing that he knocked with confidence, that he had as good a right as any other. This afternoon she would have accepted his visit; she was perfectly detached from the shallow frivolous world in which he lived, but there was still a freshness in her renunciation which coveted reminders and enjoyed comparisons—he would prove to her how right she had been to do exactly what she was doing. It didn't occur to her that Hyacinth Robinson might be at her door, for it had been understood between them that save by special appointment he was to come to her only in the evening. She heard in the hall, when the servant arrived, a voice she failed to recognise; but in a moment the door of the room was thrown open and the name of Mr Muniment pronounced. It may be noted at once that she took pleasure in the sound, for she had both wished to see more of Hyacinth's extraordinary friend and had given him up—so little likely had it begun to appear that he would put himself out for her. She had been glad he wouldn't come, as she had told Hyacinth three months before; but now that he had come she was still more glad.

Presently he was sitting before her on the other side of the fire, his big foot crossed over his big knee, his large gloved hands fumbling with each other, drawing and smoothing in places the gloves of very red new-looking dogskin that appeared to hurt him. So far as the size of his extremities and even his attitude and movement went he might have belonged to her former circle. With the details of his dress remaining vague in the lamplight, which threw into relief mainly his powerful important head, he might

have been one of the most considerable men she had ever
known. The first thing she said to him was that she wondered extremely what had brought him at last to present
himself: the idea, when she proposed it, had clearly so
little attracted him. She had only seen him once since then
—the day she met him coming into Audley Court when
she was leaving it after a visit to his sister—and, as he
probably remembered, she had not on that occasion repeated her invitation.

'It wouldn't have done any good, at the time, if you
had,' Muniment returned with his natural laugh.

'Oh I felt that; my silence wasn't accidental!' the Princess declared with due gaiety.

'I've only come now—since you've asked me the reason
—because my sister has hammered at me, week after week,
dinning it into me that I ought to. Oh I've been under the
lash! If she had left me alone I wouldn't have come.'

The Princess blushed on hearing these words, but neither
with shame nor with pain; rather with the happy excitement of being spoken to in a manner so fresh and original.
She had never before had a visitor who practised so racy
a frankness or who indeed had so curious a story to tell.
She had never before so completely failed, and her failure
greatly interested her, especially as it seemed now to be
turning a little to success. She had succeeded promptly
with everyone, and the sign of it was that every one had
rendered her a monotony of homage. Even poor little Hyacinth had tried, in the beginning, to say grand things to
her. This very different type of man appeared to have his
thoughts fixed on anything but flowers of speech; she felt
the liveliest hope that he would move further and further
from that delusion. 'I remember what you asked me—what
good it would do you. I couldn't tell you then; and though
I now have had a long time to turn it over I haven't
thought of it yet.'

'Oh but I hope it will do me some,' the young man said.
'A fellow wants a reward when he has made a great effort.'

'It does *me* some,' the Princess freely answered.

'Naturally the awkward things I say amuse you. But I don't say them for that, but just to give you an idea.'

'You give me a great many ideas. Besides, I know you already a good deal.'

'From little Robinson, I suppose,' said Muniment.

She had a pause. 'More particularly from Lady Aurora.'

'Oh she doesn't know much about me!' he protested.

'It's a pity you say that, because she likes you.'

'Yes, she likes me,' he serenely admitted.

Again his hostess hesitated. 'And I hope you like her.'

'Aye, she's a dear old girl!'

The Princess reflected that her visitor was not a gentleman, like Hyacinth; but this made no difference in her present attitude. The expectation that he would be a gentleman had had nothing to do with her interest in him; that had in fact rested largely on his probably finding felicity in a deep indifference to the character. 'I don't know that there's any one in the world I envy so much,' she observed; a statement that her visitor received in silence. 'Better than any one I've ever met she has solved the problem—which if we are wise we all try to solve, don't we?—of getting out of herself. She has got out of herself more perfectly than any one I've ever known. She has merged herself in the passion of doing something for others. That's why I envy her,' she concluded with an explanatory smile, as if perhaps he didn't understand her.

'It's an amusement like any other,' said Paul Muniment.

'Ah not like any other! It carries light into dark places; it makes a great many wretched people considerably less wretched.'

'How many, eh?' asked the young man, not exactly as if he wished to dispute but as if it were always in him to enjoy discussing.

The Princess wondered why he should wish to argue at Lady Aurora's expense. 'Well, one who's very near to you, to begin with.'

'Oh she's kind, most kind; it's altogether wonderful. But

Rosy makes *her* considerably less wretched,' Muniment added.

'Very likely, of course; and so she does me.'

'May I enquire what you're wretched about?' he went on.

'About nothing at all. That's the worst of it. But I'm much happier now than I've ever been.'

'Is that also about nothing?'

'No, about a sort of change that has taken place in my life. I've been able to do some little things.'

'For the poor, I suppose you mean. Do you refer to the presents you've made to Rosy?' the young man asked.

'The presents?' She appeared not to remember. 'Oh those are trifles. It isn't anything one has been able to give. It's some talks one has had, some convictions one has arrived at.'

'Convictions are a source of very innocent pleasure,' said the young man, smiling at his interlocutress with his bold pleasant eyes, which seemed to project their glance further and drive it harder than any she had seen.

'Having them's nothing. It's the acting on them,' the Princess replied.

'Yes; that doubtless too is good.' He continued to look at her patiently, as if he liked to consider that this might be what she had asked him to come for. He said nothing more, and she went on:

'It's far better of course when one's a man.'

'I don't know. Women do pretty well what they like. My sister and you have managed, between you, to bring me to this.'

'It's more your sister, I suspect, than I. But why, after all, should you have disliked so much to come?'

'Well, since you ask me,' said Paul Muniment, 'I'll tell you frankly, though I don't mean it uncivilly, that I don't know what to make of you.'

'Most people don't,' returned the Princess. 'But they usually take the risk.'

'Ah well, I'm the most prudent of men.'

'I was sure of it; that's one of the reasons I wanted to

know you. I know what some of your ideas are—Hyacinth
Robinson has told me; and the source of my interest in
them is partly the fact that you consider very carefully
what you attempt.'

'That I do—I do,' he agreed.

The tone in which he said this would have been almost
ignoble, as regards a kind of northern canniness latent in
it, had it not been corrected by the character of his face,
his youth and strength, his almost military eyes. The Princess recognised both the shrewdness and the natural ease
as she rejoined: 'To do anything in association with you
would be very safe. It would be sure to succeed.'

'That's what poor Hyacinth thinks,' he said.

She wondered a little that he could allude in that light
tone to the faith their young friend had placed in him, considering the consequences such a trustfulness might yet
have; but this curious mixture of qualities could only
make her visitor, as a tribune of the people, more interesting to her. She abstained for the moment from touching
on the subject of Hyacinth's peculiar position and only
pursued: 'Hasn't he told you about me? Hasn't he explained me a little?'

'Oh his explanations are grand!' Muniment laughed.
'He's fine sport when he talks about you.'

'Don't betray him,' she said gently.

'There's nothing to betray. You'd be the first to admire
it if you were there. Besides, I don't betray,' he added.

'I love him very much,' said the Princess; and it would
have been impossible for the most impudent cynic to smile
at the manner in which she made the declaration.

Her guest accepted it respectfully. 'He's a sweet little
lad and, putting her ladyship aside, quite the light of our
humble home.'

There was a short pause after this exchange of amenities,
which the Princess terminated by enquiring: 'Wouldn't
some one else do his work quite as well?'

'His work? Why, I'm told he's a master-hand.'

'Oh I don't mean his bookbinding.' Then she added: 'I

don't know if you know it, but I'm in correspondence with
a certain person. If you understand me at all you'll know
whom I mean. I'm acquainted with many of our most important men.'

'Yes, I know. Hyacinth has told me. Do you mention it
as a guarantee, so that I may know you're sound?'

'Not exactly; that would be weak, wouldn't it?' the
Princess asked. 'My soundness must be in myself—a matter
for you to appreciate as you know me better; not in my
references and vouchers.'

'I shall never know you better. What business is it of
mine?'

'I want to help you,' she said; and as she made this
earnest appeal her face became transfigured: it wore an
expression of the most passionate yet the purest longing.
'I want to do something for the cause you represent; for
the millions who are rotting under our feet—the millions
whose whole life is passed on the brink of starvation, so
that the smallest accident pushes them over. Try me, test
me; ask me to put my hand to something, to prove that
I'm as deeply in earnest as those who have already given
proof. I know what I'm talking about—what one must meet
and face and count with, the nature and the immensity of
your organisation. I'm not trifling. No, I'm not trifling.'

Paul Muniment watched her with his steady smile until
this sudden outbreak had spent itself. 'I was afraid you'd
be like this—that you'd turn on the fountains and let off
the fireworks.'

'Permit me to believe you thought nothing about it.
There's no reason my fireworks should disturb you.'

'I have always had a fear of clever women.'

'I see—that's a part of your prudence,' said the Princess
reflectively. 'But you're the sort of man who ought to know
how to use them.'

He made no immediate answer to this; the way he appeared to regard her suggested that he was not following
closely what she said so much as losing himself in certain
matters which were beside that question—her beauty, for

instance, her grace, her fragrance, the spectacle of a manner and quality so new to him. After a little, however, he
brought out irrelevantly: 'I'm afraid I'm awfully rude.'

'Of course you are, but it doesn't signify. What I mainly
object to is that you don't meet my questions. Wouldn't
some one else do Hyacinth Robinson's work quite as well?
Is it necessary to take a nature so delicate, so intellectual?
Oughtn't we to keep him for something finer?'

'Finer than what?'

'Than what he'll be called upon to do.'

'And pray what's that?' the young man demanded. 'You
know nothing about it; no more do I,' he added in a
moment. 'It will require whatever it will. Besides, if some
one else might have done it no one else volunteered. It
happened that Robinson did.'

'Yes, and you nipped him up!' the Princess returned.

This expression made Muniment laugh. 'I've no doubt
you can easily keep him if you want him.'

'I should like to do it in his place—that's what I should
like,' said the Princess.

'As I say, you don't even know what it is.'

'It may be nothing,' she went on with her grave eyes
fixed on her visitor. 'I dare say you think that what I
wanted to see you for was to beg you to let him off. But it
wasn't. Of course it's his own affair and you can do nothing. But oughtn't it to make some difference if his opinions
have changed?'

'His opinions? He never had any opinions,' Muniment
replied. 'He's not like you and me.'

'Well then, his feelings, his attachments. He hasn't the
passion for the popular triumph that he had when I first
knew him. He's much more tepid.'

'Ah well, he's quite right.'

The Princess stared. 'Do you mean that *you* are giving
up——?'

'A fine stiff conservative's a thing I perfectly understand,' said Paul Muniment. 'If I were on the top I'd stick.'

'I see, you're not narrow,' she breathed appreciatively.

'I beg your pardon, I am. I don't call that wide. One must be narrow to penetrate.'

'Whatever you are you'll succeed,' said the Princess. 'Hyacinth won't, but you will.'

'It depends upon what you call success!' the young man returned. And in a moment, before she could take it up, he added as he looked about the room: 'You've got a lovely home.'

'Lovely? My dear sir, it's hideous. That's what I like it for,' she hastened to explain.

'Well, I like it, but perhaps I don't know the reason. I thought you had given up everything—pitched your goods out of window for a grand scramble.'

'It's what I *have* done. You should have seen me before.'

'I should have liked that,' he quite shamelessly smiled. 'I like to see solid wealth.'

'Ah you're as bad as Hyacinth. I'm the only consistent one!' the Princess sighed.

'You've a great deal left, for a person who has given everything away.'

'These are not mine—these abominations—or I would give them too!' Paul's hostess returned artlessly.

He got up from his chair, still looking over the scene. 'I'd give my nose for such a place as this. At any rate, you're not yet reduced to poverty.'

'I've a little left—to help you.'

'I'd lay a wager you've a great deal,' he declared with his north-country accent.

'I could get money—I could get money,' she continued gravely. She had also risen and was standing before him.

These two remarkable persons faced each other, their eyes met again, and they exchanged a long deep glance of mutual scrutiny. Each seemed to drop a plummet into the other's mind. Then a strange and, to the Princess, unexpected expression passed over the countenance of her guest; his lips compressed themselves as in the strain of a strong effort, his colour rose and in a moment he stood there blushing like a boy. He dropped his eyes and stared at the carpet while he repeated: 'I don't trust women—I don't trust clever women!'

'I'm sorry, but after all I can understand it,' she said; 'therefore I won't insist on the question of your allowing me to work with you. But this appeal I *will* make: help me a little yourself—help me!'

'How do you mean, help you?' he asked as he raised his eyes, which had a new conscious look.

'Advise me; you'll know how. I'm in trouble—I've gone very far.'

'I've no doubt of that!' Paul laughed.

'I mean with some of those people abroad. I'm not frightened, but I'm worried. I want to know what to do.'

'No, you're not frightened,' Muniment returned after a moment.

'I'm, however, in a sad entanglement. I think you can straighten it out. I'll give you the facts, but not now, for we shall be interrupted—I hear my old lady on the stairs. For this you must come back to me.'

As she spoke the door opened, and Madame Grandoni appeared cautiously, creepingly, as if she didn't know what might be going on in the parlour. 'Yes, I'll come back,' said Paul quietly but clearly enough; with which he walked away, passing Madame Grandoni on the threshold and overlooking the handshake of farewell. In the hall he paused an instant, feeling his hostess behind him; whereby he learned that she had not come to extract from him this omitted observance, but to say once more, dropping her voice so that her companion, through the open door, might not catch: 'I *could* get money—I could!'

He passed his hand through his hair and, as if he had not heard, observed: 'I've not after all given you half Rosy's messages.'

'Oh that doesn't matter!' she answered as she turned back into the parlour.

Madame Grandoni was in the middle of the room, wrapped in her old shawl, looking vaguely round her, and the two ladies heard the house-door close. 'And pray who may that be? Isn't it a new face?' the elder one enquired.

'He's the brother of the little person I took you to see over the river—the chattering cripple with the wonderful manners.'

'Ah she had a brother! That then was why you went?'

It was striking, the good humour with which the Princess received this rather coarse thrust, which could have been drawn from Madame Grandoni only by the petulance and weariness of increasing age and the antipathy she now felt to Madeira Crescent and everything it produced. Christina bent a calm charitable smile on her ancient support and replied: 'There could have been no question of our seeing him. He was of course at his work.'

'Ah how do I know, my dear? And is he a successor?'

'A successor?'

'To the little bookbinder.'

'*Mia cara,*' said the Princess, 'you'll see how absurd that question is when I tell you he's his greatest friend!'

XXXVII

HALF AN hour after the departure of the young chemical expert she heard another rat-tat-tat at her door; but this was a briefer, discreeter peal and was accompanied by a faint tintinnabulation. The person who had produced it was presently ushered in, without, however, causing Madame Grandoni to look round, or rather to look up, from an armchair as low as a sitz-bath and of very much the shape of such a receptacle, in which, near the fire, she had been immersed. She left this care to the Princess, who rose on hearing the name of the visitor pronounced inadequately by her maid. 'Mr Fetch,' Assunta called it; but that functionary's mistress recognised without difficulty the little fat 'reduced' fiddler of whom Hyacinth had talked to her, who, as Pinnie's most intimate friend, had been so mixed up with his existence, and whom she herself had always had a curiosity to see. Hyacinth had not told her he was coming, and the unexpectedness of the apparition added to its interest. Much as she liked seeing queer types and exploring out-of-the-way social corners, she never engaged in a fresh encounter nor formed a new relation of this kind without a fit of nervousness, a fear she might herself be wanting, might fail to hit the right tone. She perceived in a moment however that Mr Vetch would take her as she was and require no special adjustments; he was a gentleman and a man of experience and she should only have to leave the tone to him. He stood there with his large polished hat in his two hands, a hat of the fashion of ten years before, with a rusty sheen and an undulating brim—stood there without a salutation or a speech, but with a small fixed, acute, tentative smile which seemed half to interrogate and half to explain. What he explained, at all events, was that he was clever enough to be trusted and that if he had called this way, without ceremony and without invitation, he had a reason which she would be sure to think good enough when she should hear it. There was even a certain jauntiness in his confidence—an insinuation that he knew how to present himself to a lady; and though it quickly appeared that he really did, this was the only thing about him that was inferior. It suggested a long experience of actresses at rehearsal, with whom he had formed habits of advice and compliment.

'I know who you are—I know who you are,' said the Princess, though she could easily see he knew she did.

'I wonder if you also know why I've come to see you,' Mr Vetch replied, presenting the top of his hat to her as if it were a looking-glass.

'No, but it doesn't matter. I'm very glad. You might even have come before.' Then she added with her characteristic honesty: 'Aren't you aware of the great interest I've taken in your nephew?'

'In my nephew? Yes, my young friend Robinson. It's for his sake I've ventured to intrude on you.'

She had been on the point of pushing a chair toward him, but she stopped in the act, staring with a smile. 'Ah I hope you haven't come to ask me to give him up!'

'On the contrary—on the contrary!' the old man returned, lifting his hand expressively and with his head on one side as if he were holding his fiddle.

'How do you mean, on the contrary?' she asked after he had seated himself and she had sunk into her former place. As if that might sound contradictious she went on: 'Surely he hasn't any fear that I shall cease to be a good friend to him?'

'I don't know what he fears; I don't know what he hopes,' said Mr Vetch, looking at her now with a face in which she could see there was something more tonic than old-fashioned politeness. 'It will be difficult to tell you, but at least I must try. Properly speaking, I suppose, it's no business of mine, as I'm not a blood-relation to the boy; but I've known him since he was a mite—he's not much more even now—and I can't help saying that I thank you for your great kindness to him.'

'All the same I don't think you like it,' the Princess declared. 'To me it oughtn't to be difficult to say anything.'

'He has told me very little about you; he doesn't know I've taken this step,' the fiddler said, turning his eyes about the room and letting them rest on Madame Grandoni.

'Why do you speak of it as a "step"? That's what people say when they've to do something disagreeable.'

'I call very seldom on ladies. It's a long time since I've been in the house of a person like the Princess Casamassima. I remember the last time,' said the old man. 'It was to get my money from a lady at whose party I had been playing—for a dance.'

'You must bring your fiddle some time and play to us. Of course I don't mean for money,' the Princess added.

'I'll do it with pleasure, or anything else that will gratify you. But my ability's very small. I only know vulgar music—things that are played at theatres.'

'I don't believe that. There must be things you play for yourself—in your room alone.'

Mr Vetch had a pause. 'Now that I see you, that I hear you, it helps me to understand.'

'I don't think you do see me!' his hostess freely laughed; on which he desired to know if there were danger of Hyacinth's coming in while he was there. She replied that he only came, unless by prearrangement, in the evening, and her visitor made a request that she wouldn't let their young friend imagine he himself had been with her. 'It doesn't matter; he'll guess it, he'll know it by instinct, as soon as he comes in. He's terribly subtle,' she said; and she added that she had never been able to hide anything from him. Perhaps this served her right—for attempting to make a mystery of things not worth it.

'How well you know him!' the fiddler commented while his eyes wandered again to Madame Grandoni, who paid no attention to him as she sat staring at the fire. He delayed visibly to say what he had come for, and his hesitation could only be connected with the presence of the old lady. He considered that the Princess might have divined this from his manner; he had an idea he could trust himself to convey such an intimation with clearness and yet with delicacy. But the most she appeared to apprehend was that he desired to be presented to her companion. 'You must know the most delightful of women. She also takes a particular interest in Mr Robinson: of a different kind from mine—much more sentimental!' And then she explained to her friend, who seemed absorbed in other ideas, that Mr Vetch was a distinguished musician, a person whom she, who had known so many in her day and was so fond of that kind of thing, would like to talk with. The Princess spoke of 'that kind of thing' quite as if she herself had given it up, though Madame Grandoni often heard her by the hour together improvising at the piano revolutionary battle-songs and pæans.

'I think you're laughing at me,' Mr Vetch said to her while the other figure twisted itself slowly round in its chair and regarded him. It looked at him conveniently, up and down, and then sighed out:

'Strange people—strange people!'

'It's indeed a strange world, madam,' the fiddler replied; after which he enquired of the Princess if he might have a little conversation with her in private.

She looked about her, embarrassed and smiling. 'My dear sir, I've only this one room to receive in. We live in a very small way.'

'Yes, your excellency *is* laughing at me. Your ideas are very large too. However, I'd gladly come at any other time that might suit you.'

'You impute to me higher spirits than I possess. Why should I be so gay?' the Princess asked. 'I should be delighted to see you again. I'm extremely curious as to what you may have to say to me. I'd even meet you anywhere— in Kensington Gardens or the British Museum.'

He took her deeply in before replying, and then, his white old face flushing a little, exclaimed: 'Poor dear little Hyacinth!'

Madame Grandoni made an effort to rise from her chair, but she had sunk so low that at first it was not successful. Mr Vetch gave her a hand of help, and she slowly erected herself, keeping hold of him for a moment after she stood there. 'What did she tell me? That you're a great musician? Isn't that enough for any man? You ought to be content, my dear gentleman. It has sufficed for people whom I don't believe you surpass.'

'I don't surpass any one,' said poor Mr Vetch. 'I don't know what you take me for.'

'You're not a wicked revolutionary then? You're not a conspirator nor an assassin? It surprises me, but so much the better. In this house one can never know. It's not a good house, and if you're a respectable person it's a pity you should come here. Yes, she's very gay and I'm very sad. I don't know how it will end. After me, I hope. The world's not good, certainly; but God alone can make it better.' And as the fiddler expressed the hope that he was not the cause of her leaving the room she went on: '*Doch, doch*, you're the cause; but why not you as well as another? I'm always leaving it for some one or for something, and I'd sooner do so for an honest man, if you *are* one—but, as I say, who can tell?—than for a destroyer. I wander about. I've no rest. I have however a very nice room, the best in the house. Me at least she doesn't treat ill. It looks to-day like the end of all things. If you'd turn your climate the other side up the rest would do well enough. Good-night to you, whoever you are.'

The old lady shuffled away in spite of Mr Vetch's renewed apologies, and the subject of her criticism stood before the fire watching the pair while he opened the door. 'She goes away, she comes back; it doesn't matter. She thinks it a bad house, but she knows it would be worse without her. I remember about you now,' the Princess added. 'Mr Robinson told me you had been a great democrat in old days, but that at present you'd ceased to care for the people.'

'The people—the people? That's a silly term. Whom do you mean?'

She hesitated. 'Those you used to care for, to plead for; those who are underneath every one, underneath everything, and have the whole social mass crushing them.'

'I see you think I'm a renegade. The way certain classes arrogate to themselves the title of the people has never pleased me. Why are some human beings the people, the people only, and others not? I'm of the people myself, I've worked all my days like a knife-grinder and I've really never changed.'

'You mustn't let me make you angry,' she laughed as she sat down again. 'I'm sometimes very provoking, but you must stop me off. You wouldn't think it perhaps, but no one takes a snub better than I.'

Mr Vetch dropped his eyes a minute; he appeared to wish to show that he regarded such a speech as that as one of this great perverse lady's characteristic humours and knew he should be wanting in respect to her if he took it seriously or made a personal application of it. 'What I want is this,' he began after a moment: 'that you'll, that you'll——' But he stopped before he had got further. She was watching him, listening to him; she waited while he paused. It was a long pause and she said nothing. 'Princess,' the old man broke out at last, 'I'd give my own life many times for that boy's!'

'I always told him you must have been fond of him!' she cried with bright exultation.

'Fond of him? Pray who can doubt it? I made him, I invented him!'

'He knows it moreover,' the Princess smiled. 'It's an exquisite organisation.' And as the old man gazed at her, not knowing apparently what to make of her tone, she kept it up: 'It's a very interesting opportunity for me to learn certain things. Speak to me of his early years. How was he as a child? When I like people I like them altogether and want to know everything about them.'

'I shouldn't have supposed there was much left for you to learn about our young friend. You've taken possession of his life,' Mr Vetch added gravely.

'Yes, but as I understand you, you don't complain of it? Sometimes one does so much more than one has intended. One must use one's influence for good,' she went on with the noble, gentle air of accessibility to reason that sometimes lighted up her face. And then irrelevantly: 'I know the terrible story of his mother. He told it me himself when he was staying with me. In the course of my life I think I've never been more affected.'

'That was my fault—that he ever learnt it. I suppose he also told you that.'

'Yes, but I think he understood your idea. If you had the question to determine again would you judge differently?'

'I thought it would do him good,' said the old man simply and rather wearily.

'Well, I dare say it has,' she returned with the manner of wishing to encourage him.

'I don't know what was in my head. I wanted him to quarrel with society. Now I want him to be reconciled to it,' Mr Vetch remarked earnestly. He appeared to desire her to understand how great a point he made of this.

'Ah, but he is!' she immediately said. 'We often talk about that; he's not like me, who see all kinds of abominations. He's a bloated little aristocrat. What more would you have!'

'Those are not the opinions he expresses to *me*'—and Mr Vetch shook his head sadly. 'I'm greatly distressed and I don't make out——! I've not come here with the presumptuous wish to cross-examine you, but I should like very much to know if I *am* wrong in believing that he has gone about with you in the bad quarters—in Saint Giles's and Whitechapel.'

'We've certainly enquired and explored together,' the Princess admitted, 'and in the depths of this huge luxurious wanton wasteful city we've seen sights of unspeakable misery and horror. But we've been not only in the slums; we've been to a music hall and a penny-reading.'

The fiddler received this information at first in silence, so that his hostess went on to mention some of the phases of life they had observed; describing with great vividness, but at the same time with a kind of argumentative moderation, several scenes which did little honour to 'our boasted civilisation'. 'What wonder is it then that he should tell me things can't go on any longer as they are?' he asked when she had finished. 'He said only the other day that he should regard himself as one of the most contemptuous of human beings if he should do nothing to alter them, to better them.'

'What wonder indeed? But if he said that he was in one of his bad days,' the Princess replied. 'He changes constantly and his impressions change. The misery of the people is by no means always on his heart. You tell me what he has told you; well, he has told me that the people may perish over and over rather than the conquests of civilisation shall be sacrificed to them. He declares at such moments that they'll be sacrificed—sacrificed utterly—if the ignorant masses get the upper hand.'

'He needn't be afraid. That will never happen.'

'I don't know. We can at least try,' she said.

'Try what you like, madam, but for God's sake get the boy out of his muddle!'

The Princess had suddenly grown excited in speaking of the cause she believed in, and she gave for the moment no heed to this appeal, which broke from Mr Vetch's lips with a sudden passion of anxiety. Her beautiful head raised itself higher and the constant light of her fine eyes became an extraordinary radiance. 'Do you know what I say to Mr Robinson when he makes such remarks as that to me? I ask him what he means by civilisation. Let civilisation come a little, first, and then we'll talk about it. For the present, face to face with those horrors, I scorn it, I deny it!' And she laughed ineffable things, she might have been some splendid siren of the Revolution.

'The world's very sad and very hideous, and I'm happy to say that I soon shall have done with it. But before I go I want to save Hyacinth,' Mr Vetch insisted. 'If he's a bloated little aristocrat, as you say, there's so much the less fitness in his being ground in your mill. If he doesn't even believe in what he pretends to do, that's a pretty situation! What's he in for, madam? What devilish folly has he undertaken?'

'He's a strange mixture of contradictory impulses,' said the Princess musingly. Then as if calling herself back to the old man's question she pursued: 'How can I enter into his affairs with you? How can I tell you his secrets? In the first place I don't know them, and if I did—well, fancy me!'

Her visitor gave a long low sigh, almost a moan, of discouragement and perplexity. He had told her that now he saw her he understood how their young friend should have become her slave, but he wouldn't have been able to tell her that he understood her own motives and mysteries, that he embraced the immense anomaly of her behaviour.

It came over him that she was fine and perverse, a more complicated form of the feminine mixture than any he had hitherto dealt with, and he felt helpless and baffled, fore-doomed to failure. He had come prepared to flatter her without scruple, thinking this would be the expert and effective way of dealing with her; but he now recognised that these primitive arts had, though it was strange, no application to such a nature, while his embarrassment was increased rather than diminished by the fact that the lady at least made the effort to be accommodating. He had put down his hat on the floor beside him and his two hands were clasped on the knob of an umbrella which had long since renounced pretensions to compactness; he collapsed a little and his chin rested on his folded hands. 'Why do you take such a line? Why do you believe such things?' he asked; and he was conscious that his tone was weak and his challenge beside the question.

'My dear sir, how do you know what I believe? How-ever, I have my reasons, which it would take too long to tell you and which after all would not particularly interest you. One must see life as one can; it comes no doubt to each of us in different ways. You think me affected of course and my behaviour a fearful *pose*; but I'm only try-ing to be natural. Are you not yourself a little inconse-quent?' she went on with the bright hard mildness which assured Mr Vetch, while it chilled him, that he should ex-tract no pledge of relief from her. 'You don't want our young friend to pry into the wretchedness of London, be-cause that excites his sense of justice. It's a strange thing to wish, for a person of whom one is fond and whom one esteems, that his sense of justice shall not be excited.'

'I don't care a fig for his sense of justice—I don't care a fig for the wretchedness of London; and if I were young and beautiful and clever and brilliant and of a noble posi-tion, like you, I should care still less. In that case I should have very little to say to a poor mechanic—a youngster who earns his living with a glue-pot and scraps of old leather.'

'Don't misrepresent him; don't make him out what you know he's not!' the Princess retorted with her baffling smile. 'You know he's one of the most civilised of little men.'

The fiddler sat breathing unhappily. 'I only want to keep him—to get him free.' Then he added: 'I don't understand you very well. If you like him because he's one of the lower orders, how can you like him because he's a swell?'

She turned her eyes on the fire as if this little problem might be worth considering, and presently she answered: 'Dear Mr Vetch, I'm very sure you don't mean to be impertinent, but some things you say have that effect. Nothing's more annoying than when one's sincerity is doubted. I'm not bound to explain myself to you. I ask of my friends to trust me and of the others to leave me alone. Moreover anything not very nice you may have said to me—out of inevitable awkwardness—is nothing to the insults I'm perfectly prepared to see showered upon me before long. I shall do things which will produce a fine crop of them— oh I shall do things, my dear sir! But I'm determined not to mind them. Come therefore, pull yourself together. We both take such an interest in young Robinson that I can't see why in the world we should quarrel about him.'

'My dear lady,' the old man pleaded, 'I've indeed not the least intention of failing in respect or patience, and you must excuse me if I don't look after my manners. How can I when I'm so worried, so haunted? God knows I don't want to quarrel. As I tell you, I only want to get Hyacinth free.'

'Free from what?' the Princess asked.

'From some abominable secret brotherhood or international league that he belongs to, the thought of which keeps me awake at night. He's just the sort of youngster to be made a catspaw.'

'Your fears seem very vague.'

'I hoped you would give me chapter and verse.'

'On what do your suspicions rest? What grounds have you?' she insisted.

'Well, a great many; none of them very definite, but all contributing something—his appearance, his manner, the way he strikes me. Dear lady, one feels those things, one guesses. Do you know that poor infatuated phrasemonger Eustache Poupin, who works at the same place as Hyacinth? He's a very old friend of mine and he's an honest man, as phrasemongers go. But he's always conspiring and corresponding and pulling strings that make a tinkle which he takes for the death-knell of society. He has nothing in life to complain of and drives a roaring trade. But he wants folk to be equal, heaven help him; and when he has made them so I suppose he's going to start a society for making the stars in the sky all of the same size. He isn't serious, though he imagines he's the only human being who never trifles; and his machinations, which I believe are for the most part very innocent, are a matter of habit and tradition with him, like his theory that Christopher Columbus, who discovered America, was a Frenchman, and his hot foot-bath on Saturday nights. He has *not* confessed to me that Hyacinth has taken some intensely private engagement to do something for the cause which may have nasty consequences, but the way he turns off the idea makes me almost as uncomfortable as if he had. He and his wife are very sweet on their young friend, but they can't make up their minds to interfere; perhaps for them indeed, as for me, there's no way in which interference can be effective. Only *I* didn't put him up to those devil's tricks—or rather I did originally! The finer the work, I suppose, the higher the privilege of doing it; yet the Poupins heave socialistic sighs over the boy, and their peace of mind evidently isn't all that it ought to be if they've given him a noble opportunity. I've appealed to them in good round terms, and they've assured me every hair of his head is as precious to them as if he were their own child. That doesn't comfort me much, however, for the simple reason that I believe the old woman (whose grandmother, in Paris, in the Revolution, must certainly have carried bloody heads on a pike) would be quite capable of chopping up her own child if it would do any harm to proprietors. Besides, they say, what influence have they on Hyacinth any more? He's a deplorable little backslider; he worships false gods. In short they'll give me no information, and I dare say they themselves are tied up by some unholy vow. They may be afraid of a vengeance if they tell tales. It's all sad rubbish, but rubbish may be a strong motive.'

The Princess listened attentively, following her visitor with patience. 'Don't speak to me of the French; I've never cared for them.'

'That's awkward if you're a socialist. You're likely to meet them.'

'Why do you call me a socialist? I hate tenth-rate labels and flags,' she declared. Then she added: 'What is it you suppose on Mr Robinson's part?—for you must suppose something.'

'Well, that he may have drawn some accursed lot to do some idiotic thing—something in which even he himself doesn't believe.'

'I haven't an idea of what sort of thing you mean. But if he doesn't believe in it he can easily let it alone.'

'Do you think he's a customer who will back out of a real vow?' the fiddler asked.

The Princess freely wondered. 'One can never judge of people in that way till they're tested.' And the next thing: 'Haven't you even taken the trouble to question him?'

'What would be the use? He'd tell me nothing. It would be like a man giving notice when he's going to fight a duel.'

She sat for some seconds in thought; she looked up at Mr Vetch with a pitying indulgent smile. 'I'm sure you're worrying about a mere shadow; but that never prevents, does it? I still don't see exactly how I can help you.'

'Do you want him to commit some atrocity, some mad infamy?' the old man appealed.

'My dear sir, I don't want him to do anything in all the

wide world. I've not had the smallest connexion with any engagement of any kind that he may have entered into. Do me the honour to trust me,' the Princess went on with a certain high dryness of tone. 'I don't know what I've done to deprive myself of your confidence. Trust the young man a little too. He's a gentleman and will behave as a gentleman.'

The fiddler rose from his chair, smoothing his hat silently with the cuff of his coat. He stood there, whimsical and piteous, as if the sense he had still something to urge mingled with that of his having his dismissal and as if indeed both were tinged with the oddity of another idea. 'That's exactly what I'm afraid of!' he returned. Then he added, continuing to look at her: 'But he *must* be very fond of life.'

The Princess took no notice of the insinuation contained in these words. 'Leave him to me—leave him to me. I'm sorry for your anxiety, but it was very good of you to come to see me. That has been interesting, because you've been one of our friend's influences.'

'Unfortunately yes! If it hadn't been for me he wouldn't have known Poupin, and if he hadn't known Poupin he wouldn't have known his chemical friend—what's his name?—Muniment.'

'And has that done him harm, do you think?' the Princess asked. She had risen to her feet.

'Surely: that deep fellow has been the main source of his infection.'

'I lose patience with you!' she made answer, turning away.

And indeed her visitor's persistence was irritating. He went on, lingering, his head thrust forward and his short arms, out at his sides, terminating in his hat and umbrella, which he held grotesquely and as if intended for emphasis or illustration: 'I've supposed for a long time that it was either Muniment or you who had got him into his scrape. It was you I suspected most—much most; but if it isn't you it must be he.'

'You had better go to him then!'

'Of course I'll go to him. I scarcely know him—I've seen him but once—but I'll speak my mind.'

The Princess rang for her maid to usher Mr Vetch out, but at the moment he laid his hand on the door of the room she checked him with a quick gesture. 'Now that I think of it don't go, please, to Mr Muniment. It will be better to leave him quiet. Leave him to me,' she added with a softer smile.

'Why not, why not?' he pleaded. And as she couldn't tell him on the instant why not he asked: 'Doesn't he know?'

'No, he doesn't know; he has nothing to do with it.' She suddenly found herself desiring to protect Paul Muniment from the imputation that was in Mr Vetch's mind— the imputation of an ugly responsibility; and though she was not a person who took the trouble to tell fibs this repudiation on his behalf issued from her lips before she could stay it. It was a result of the same desire, though also an inconsequence, that she added: 'Don't do that— you'll spoil everything!' She went to him suddenly eager, she herself opened the door for him. 'Leave him to me— leave him to me,' she continued persuasively, while the fiddler, gazing at her, dazzled and submissive, allowed himself to be wafted away. A thought that excited her had come to her with a bound, and after she had heard the house-door close behind Mr Vetch she walked up and down the room half an hour, all restlessly, under possession of it.

BOOK FIFTH

XXXVIII

HYACINTH FOUND, that winter, considerable occupation
for his odd hours, his evenings and holidays and scraps of
leisure, in putting in hand the books he had promised himself at Medley to enclose in covers worthy of the high
station and splendour of the lady of his life—these brilliant
attributes had not then been shuffled out of sight—and of
the confidence and generosity she showed him. He had
determined she should receive from him something of
value, and took pleasure in thinking that after he was gone
they would be passed from hand to hand as specimens of
rare work, connoisseurs bending charmed heads over them,
smiling and murmuring, handling them delicately. His invention stirred itself and he had a hundred admirable ideas,
many of which he sat up late at night to execute. He used
all his skill, and by this time his skill was of a very high
order. Old Crook recognised it by raising the rates at
which he was paid; and though it was not among the traditions of the proprietor of the establishment in Soho, who
to the end wore the apron with his workmen, to scatter
sweet speeches, our young man learned accidentally that
several books he had given him to do had been carried off
and placed on a shelf of treasures at the villa, where they
were exhibited to the members of the Crookenden circle
who came to tea on Sundays. Hyacinth himself indeed was
included in this company on a great occasion—invited to
a musical party where he made the acquaintance of half a
dozen Miss Crookendens, an acquaintance which consisted
in his standing in a corner behind several broad-backed
old ladies and watching the rotation, at the piano and the
harp, of three or four of his employer's thick-fingered
daughters. 'You know it's a tremendously musical house,'
said one of the old ladies to another (she called it
' 'ouse'); but the principal impression made upon him by

the performance of the Miss Crookendens was that it was wonderfully different from the Princess's playing.

He knew he was the only young man from the shop who had been invited, not counting the foreman, who was sixty years old and wore a wig which constituted in itself a kind of social position, besides being accompanied by a little frightened furtive wife who closed her eyes, as if in the presence of a blinding splendour, when Mrs Crookenden spoke to her. The Poupins were not there; which, however, was not a surprise to Hyacinth, who knew that—even if they had been asked, which they were not—they had objections of principle to putting their feet *chez les bourgeois*. They were not asked because, in spite of the place Eustache had made for himself in the prosperity of the business, it had come to be known that his wife was somehow not his wife—though she was certainly no one's else; and the evidence of this irregularity was conceived to reside vaguely in the fact that she had never been seen save in the laxity of a camisole. There had doubtless been an apprehension that if she had come to the villa she would not have come with the proper number of hooks and eyes—albeit Hyacinth, on two or three occasions, notably the night he took the pair to Mr Vetch's theatre, had been witness of the proportions to which she could reduce her figure when wishing to give the impression of a lawful tie.

It was not clear to him how the distinction conferred on him became known in Soho, where, however, it excited no sharpness of jealousy—Grugan, Roker and Hotchkin being hardly more likely to envy a person condemned to spend a genteel evening than they were to envy a monkey performing antics on a barrel-organ: both forms of effort indicated an urbanity painfully acquired. But Roker took his young comrade's breath half away with his elbow while remarking that he supposed he saw the old man had spotted him for one of the darlings at home—and while enquiring furthermore what would become in that case of the little thing he took to France, the one to whom he had stood champagne and lobster. This was the first allusion Hyacinth had heard made to the idea that he might some day marry his master's daughter, like the virtuous apprentice of tradition; but the suggestion somehow was not inspiring even when he had thought of an incident or two which gave colour to it. None of the Miss Crookendens spoke to him —they all had large faces and short legs and a comical resemblance to that elderly male with wide nostrils their father, and, unlike the Miss Marchants at Medley, they knew who he was; but their mother, who had on her head the plumage of a cockatoo mingled with a structure of glass beads, looked at him with an almost awful fixedness of charity and asked him three distinct times if he would have a glass of negus.

He had much difficulty in getting his books from the Princess; for when he reminded her of the promise she had given at Medley to make over to him as many volumes as he should require she answered that everything was changed since then, that she was completely *dépouillée*, that she had now no pretension to have a library, and that in fine he had much better leave the matter alone. He was welcome to any books in the house, but, as he could see for himself, these were cheap editions, on which it would be foolish to expend such work as his. He asked Madame Grandoni to help him—to tell him at least if there were not some good volumes among the things the Princess had sent to be warehoused; it being known to him, through casual admissions of her own, that she had allowed her maid to save certain articles from the wreck and pack them away at the Pantechnicon. This had all been Assunta's work—the woman had begged so hard for a few reservations, a loaf of bread for their old days; but the Princess herself had washed her hands of the job. '*Chè, chè*, there are boxes, I'm sure, in that place, with a little of everything,' the old lady had said in answer to his enquiry; and Hyacinth had conferred with Assunta, who took a sympathetic talkative Italian interest in his undertaking and promised to fish out for him any block of printed matter that should remain. She arrived at his lodging one evening, in a cab, with an armful of pretty books, and when he asked her where they had come from waved her forefinger in front of her nose after a fashion at once evasive and expressive. He brought each volume to the Princess as it was finished, but her manner of receiving it was to shake her head over it with a kind sad smile. 'It's beautiful, I'm sure, but I've lost my sense for such things. Besides, you must always remember what you once told me, that a woman, even the most culti-vated, is incapable of feeling the difference between a bad binding and a good. I remember your once saying that fine ladies had brought cobbled leather to your shop and wished it imitated. Certainly those are not the differences I most feel. My dear fellow, such things have ceased to speak to me; they're doubtless charming, but they leave me cold. What will you have? One can't serve God and Mammon.' Her thoughts were fixed on far other things than the delight of dainty covers, and she evidently considered that in caring so much for them Hyacinth resembled the mad em-peror who fiddled in the flames of Rome. European society, to her mind, was in flames, and no frivolous occupation could give the measure of the emotion with which she watched them. It produced occasionally demonstrations of hilarity, of joy and hope, but these always took some form connected with the life of the people. It was the people she had gone to see when she accompanied Hyacinth to a music-hall in the Edgware Road, and all her excursions and pastimes this winter were prompted by her interest in the classes on whose behalf the fundamental change was to be wrought.

To ask himself if she were in earnest was now an old story to him, and indeed the conviction he might arrive at on this head had ceased to have any high importance. It was just as she was, superficial or profound, that she held him, and she was at any rate sufficiently animated by a purpose for her doings to have consequences actual and possible. Some of these might be serious even if she her-self were shallow, and there were times when she was much visited by the apprehension of them. On the Sundays when she had gone with him into the darkest places, the most fetid holes in London, she had always taken money with her in considerable quantities and had always left it behind. She said very naturally that one couldn't go and stare at people for an impression without paying them, and she gave alms right and left, indiscriminately, without enquiry or judgement, as simply as the abbess of some beggar-haunted convent or a lady-bountiful of the superstitious unscientific ages who should have hoped to be assisted to heaven by her doles. Hyacinth never said to her, though he sometimes thought it, that since she was so full of the modern spirit her charity should be administered according to the modern lights, the principles of economic science: partly because she wasn't a woman to be directed and regulated—she could take other peoples' meanings but could never take their forms. Besides, what did it matter? To himself what did it matter to-day whether he were drawn into right methods or into wrong ones, his time being too short for regret or for cheer? The Princess was an embodied passion—she was not a system: and her behaviour, after all, was more addressed to relieving herself than to relieving others. And then misery was sown so thick in her path that wherever her money was dropped it fell into some clutching palm. He wondered she should still have so much cash to dispose of till she explained that she came by it through putting her personal expenditure on a rigid footing. What she gave away was her savings, the margin she had succeeded in creating; and now that she had tasted of the satisfaction of making little hoards for such a purpose she regarded her other years, with their idleness and waste, their merely personal motives, as a long, stupid sleep of the conscience. To do something for others was not only so much more human—it was so much more amusing!

She made strange acquaintances under Hyacinth's conduct; she listened to extraordinary stories and formed theories about them, and about the persons who narrated them to her, which were often still more extraordinary. She took romantic fancies to vagabonds of either sex, attempted to establish social relations with them and was the cause of infinite agitation to the gentleman who lived near her in the Crescent, who was always smoking at the window and who reminded our hero of Mr Micawber. She received visits that were a scandal to the Crescent, and Hyacinth neglected his affairs, whatever they were, to see what tatterdemalion would next turn up at her door. This intercourse, it is true, took a more fruitful form as her intimacy with Lady Aurora deepened; her ladyship practised discriminations which she brought the Princess to recognise, and before the winter was over Mr Robinson's services in the slums were found unnecessary. He gave way with relief, with delight, to Lady Aurora, for he had himself not in the least grasped the principle of his behaviour for the previous four months nor taken himself seriously as a *cicerone*. He had plunged into a sea of barbarism without having any civilising energy to put forth. He was aware the people were direfully wretched—more aware, it often seemed to him, than they themselves were; so frequently was he struck with their brutal insensibility, a grossness proof against the taste of better things and against any desire for them. He knew it so well that the repetition of contact could add no vividness to the conviction; it rather smothered and befogged his impression, peopled it with contradictions and difficulties, a violence of reaction, a sense of the inevitable and insurmountable. In these hours the poverty and ignorance of the multitude seemed so vast and preponderant, and so much the law of life, that those who had managed to escape from the black gulf were only the happy few, spirits of resource as well as children of luck: they inspired in some degree the interest and sympathy that one should feel for survivors and victors, those who have come safely out of a shipwreck or a battle. What was most in Hyacinth's mind was the idea, of which every pulsation of the general life of his time was a syllable, that the flood of democracy was rising over the world; that it would sweep all the traditions of the past before it; that, whatever it might fail to bring, it would at least carry in its bosom a magnificent energy; and that it might be trusted to look after its own. When this high healing uplifting tide should cover the world and float in the new era, it would be its own fault (whose else?) if want and suffering and crime should continue to be ingredients of the human lot. With his mixed, divided nature, his conflicting sympathies, his eternal habit of swinging from one view to another, he regarded the prospect in different moods with different intensities. In spite of the example Eustache Poupin gave him of the reconcilement of disparities, he was afraid the democracy wouldn't care for perfect bindings or for the finer sorts of conversation. The Princess gave up these things in proportion as she advanced in the direction she had so audaciously chosen; and if the Princess could give them up it would take very transcendent natures to stick to them. At the same time there was joy and exultation in the thought of surrendering one's self to the wash of the wave, of being carried higher on the sun-touched crests of wild billows than one could ever be by a dry lonely effort of one's own. That vision could deepen to ecstasy; make it indifferent if one's ultimate fate, in such a heaving sea, were not almost certainly to be submerged in bottomless depths or dashed to pieces on immoveable rocks. Hyacinth felt that, whether his personal sympathy should rest finally with the victors or the vanquished, the victorious force was potentially infinite and would require no testimony from the irresolute.

The reader will doubtless smile at his mental debates and oscillations, and not understand why a little bastard bookbinder should attach importance to his conclusions. They were not important for either cause, but they were important for himself—if only because they would rescue him from the torment of his present life, the perpetual sore shock of the rebound. There was no peace for him between the two currents that flowed in his nature, the blood of his passionate plebeian mother and that of his long-descended supercivilised sire. They continued to toss him from one side to the other; they arrayed him in intolerable defiances and revenges against himself. He had a high ambition: he wanted neither more nor less than to get hold of the truth and wear it in his heart. He believed with the candour of youth that it is brilliant and clear-cut, like a royal diamond; but to whatever quarter he turned in the effort to find it he seemed to know that behind him, bent on him in reproach, was a tragic wounded face. The thought of his mother had filled him with the vague clumsy fermentation of his first impulses toward social criticism; but since the problem had become more complex by the fact that many things in the world as it was constituted were to grow intensely dear to him he had tried more and more to construct some conceivable and human countenance for his father—some expression of honour, of tenderness and recognition, of unmerited suffering, or at least of adequate expiation. To desert one of these presences for the other—that idea was the source of shame, as an act of treachery would have been; for he could almost hear the voice of his father ask him if it were the conduct of a gentleman to take up the opinions and emulate the crudities of fanatics and cads. He had quite got over holding that it would not have become his father to talk of what was proper to gentlemen, got over making the mental reflexion that from such a worthy's son at least the biggest cad in London could not have deserved less consideration. He had worked himself round to allowances, to interpretations, to such hypotheses as the evidence in the *Times*, read in the British Museum on that never-to-be-forgotten afternoon, did not exclude. Though they had been frequent enough, and too frequent, his hours of hot resentment against the man who had attached to him the stigma he was to carry for ever, he threw himself, in other conditions and with a certain success, into the effort to find filial condonations and excuses. It was comparatively easy for him to accept himself as the son of a terribly light Frenchwoman; there seemed a deeper obloquy even than that in his having for his other parent a nobleman altogether wanting in nobleness. He was absolutely too poor to afford it. Sometimes, in imagina-

tion, he sacrificed one of the authors of his being to the
other, throwing over Lord Frederick much the oftener;
sometimes, when the theory failed that his father would
have done great things for him if he had lived, or the assumption broke down that he had been Florentine Vivier's
only lover, he cursed and disowned them alike; sometimes
he arrived at conceptions which presented them side by
side, looking at him with eyes infinitely sad but quite un-
ashamed—eyes that seemed to tell him they had been surpassingly unfortunate but had not been base. Of course his
worst moments now, as they had always been the worst,
were those in which his grounds for holding that Lord
Frederick had really been his father viciously fell away
from him. It must be added that they always passed off,
since the mixture in his tormenting, his incorrigible pulses
could be accounted for by no other dream.

I mention these dim broodings not because they belong
in an especial degree to the history of our young man during the winter of the Princess's residence in Madeira Crescent, but because they were a constant element in his
moral life and need to be remembered in any view of him
at a given time. There were nights of November and December, as he trod the greasy pavements that lay between
Westminster and Paddington, groping his way through the
baffled lamplight and tasting the smoke-seasoned fog, when
there was more happiness in his heart than he had ever
known. The influence of his permeating London had closed
over him again; Paris and Milan and Venice had shim-
mered away into reminiscence and picture; and as the great
city which was most his own lay round him under her pall
like an immeasurable breathing monster he felt with a
vague excitement, as he had felt before, only now with
more knowledge, that it was the richest expression of the
life of man. His horizon had been immensely widened, but
it was filled again by the expanse that sent dim night-
gleams and strange blurred reflexions and emanations into
a sky without stars. He suspended, so to say, his small
sensibility in the midst of it, to quiver there with joy and

hope and ambition as well as with the effort of renunciation. The Princess's quiet fireside glowed with deeper assurances, with associations of intimacy, through the dusk
and the immensity; the thought of it was with him always,
and his relations with its mistress were more organised than
they had been in his first vision of her. Whether or no it
was better for the cause she cherished that she should have
been reduced to her present simplicity, it was better at
least for poor Mr Robinson. It made her more near and
him more free; and if there had been a danger of her
nature's seeming really to take the tone of the vulgar things
about her he would only have had to remember her as she
was at Medley to restore the perspective. Her beauty
always appeared in truth to have the setting that best became it; her fairness made the element in which she lived
and, among the meanest accessories, constituted a kind of
splendour. Nature had emphasised the difficult, the deter-
rent, for her establishing properties in common with the
horrible populace of London. Hyacinth used to smile at
this pretension in his night-walks to Paddington or homeward; the populace of London were scattered upon his
path, and he asked himself by what wizardry they could
ever be raised to high participations. There were nights
when every one he met appeared to reek with gin and filth
and he found himself elbowed by figures as foul as lepers.
Some of the women and girls in particular were appalling
—saturated with alcohol and vice, brutal, bedraggled, ob-
scene. 'What remedy but another deluge, what alchemy but
annihilation?' he asked himself as he went his way; and he
wondered what fate there could be in the great scheme of
things for a planet overgrown with such vermin, what redemption but to be hurled against a ball of consuming fire.
If it was the fault of the rich, as Paul Muniment held, the
selfish congested rich who allowed such abominations to
flourish, that made no difference and only shifted the
shame; since the terrestrial globe, a visible failure, produced
the cause as well as the effect.

It didn't occur to our young man that the Princess had

withdrawn her confidence from him because, for the work
of investigating still further the condition of the poor, she
had placed herself in the hands of Lady Aurora. He could
have no jealousy of the noble spinster; he had too much
respect for her philanthropy, the thoroughness of her knowledge and her capacity to answer any question it could
come into the Princess's extemporising head to ask, and
too acute a consciousness of his own desultory and superficial view of the great question. It was enough for him
that the little parlour in Madeira Crescent was a spot
round which his thoughts could revolve and toward which
his steps could direct themselves with an unalloyed sense
of security and privilege. The picture of it hung before
him half the time in colours to which the feeling of the
place gave a rarity that doubtless didn't literally characterise the scene. His relations with the Princess had long
since ceased to appear to him to belong to the world of
fable; they were as natural as anything else—everything in
life was queer enough; he had by this time assimilated
them, as it were, and they were an indispensable part of
the happiness of each. 'Of each'—Hyacinth risked that, for
there was no particular vanity now involved in his perceiving that the most remarkable woman in Europe was simply
quite fond of him. The quiet familiar fraternal welcome he
found on the nasty winter nights was proof enough of that.
They sat together like very old friends whom long pauses,
during which they merely looked at each other with kind
acquainted eyes, couldn't make uncomfortable. Not that
the element of silence was the principal part of their conversation, for it interposed only when they had talked a
great deal. Hyacinth, on the opposite side of the fire, felt
at times almost as if he were married to his hostess, so
many things were taken for granted between them. For intercourse of that sort, intimate, easy, humorous, circumscribed by drawn curtains and shaded lamplight, interfused
with domestic embarrassments and confidences that all
turned to the jocular, the Princess was incomparable. It
was her theory of her present existence that she was pic-

nicking, but all the accidents of the business were happy accidents. There was a household quietude in her steps and gestures, in the way she sat, in the way she listened, in the way she played with the cat or looked after the fire or folded Madame Grandoni's ubiquitous shawl; above all in the inveteracy with which she spent her evenings at home, never dining out nor going to parties, ignorant of the dissipations of the town. There was something in the isolation of the room when the kettle was on the hob and he had given his wet umbrella to the maid and his friend had made him sit in a certain place near the fire, the better to dry his shoes—there was something that evoked the idea of the *vie de province* he had read about in French fiction. The French term came to him because it represented more the especial note of the Princess's company, the cultivation, the facility, of talk. She expressed herself often in the French tongue itself; she could borrow that convenience for certain shades of meaning, though she had told Hyacinth she had her own intenser Latin view of the people to whom it was native. Certainly the strain of her discourse was not provincial; her talk was singularly free and unabashed; there was nothing one mightn't say to her or that she was not liable to say herself. She had cast off prejudices and gave no heed to conventional danger-posts. Hyacinth admired the movement—his eyes seemed to see it—with which in any direction, intellectually, she could fling open her windows. There was an extraordinary charm in this mixture of liberty and humility—in seeing a creature capable socially of immeasurable flights sit dove-like and with folded wings.

The young man met Lady Aurora several times in Madeira Crescent—her days, like his own, were filled with work, so that she came in the evening—and he knew that her friendship with the Princess had arrived at a rich maturity. The two ladies were a source of almost rapturous interest to each other, each rejoicing that the other was not a bit different. The Princess prophesied freely that her visitor would give her up—all nice people did very soon;

but to the acuteness of our hero's observation the end of
her ladyship's almost breathless enthusiasm was not yet in
view. She was bewildered but was fascinated; she thought
her foreign friend not only the most distinguished, the most
startling, the most edifying and the most original person in
the world, but the most amusing and the most delightful
to have tea with. As for that personage herself her sentiment about Lady Aurora was the same Hyacinth's had
been: she held her a saint, the first she had ever seen, and
the purest specimen conceivable; as good in her way as
Saint Francis of Assisi, as tender and quaint and trans-
parent, of a spirit of charity as sublime. She felt that when
one met a human flower as fresh as that in the dusty ways
of the world one should pluck it and wear it; and she was
always inhaling Lady Aurora's fragrance, always kissing her
and holding her hand. The spinster was frightened at her
generosity, at the way her imagination embroidered; she
wanted to convince her—as the Princess did on her own side
—that such exaggerations destroyed their unfortunate subject. The Princess delighted in her clothes, in the way she
put them on and wore them, in the economies she practised
in order to have money for charity and the ingenuity with
which these slender resources were made to go far—in the
very manner in which she spoke, a kind of startled simplicity. She wished to emulate her in all these particulars;
to learn how to economise still more cunningly, to get her
bonnets at the same shop, to care as little for the fit of her
gloves, to ask in the same tone, 'Isn't it a bore Susan Crotty's
husband has got a ticket-of-leave?' She said Lady Aurora
made her feel like a French milliner and that if there was
anything in the world she loathed it was a French milliner. Each of these persons was powerfully affected by the
other's idiosyncrasies, and each wanted the other to remain
as she was while she herself should be transformed into
the image of her friend.

One night, going to Madeira Crescent a little later than
usual, Hyacinth met the pilgrim from Belgrave Square just
leaving the house. She had a different air from any he had

seen in her before; appeared flushed and even a little agitated, as if she had been learning a piece of bad news. She said, 'Oh how do you do?' with her customary quick vague laugh, but she went her way without stopping to talk. Three minutes later he mentioned to the Princess that he had encountered her, and this lady replied: 'It's a pity you didn't come a little sooner. You'd have assisted at a scene.'

'At a scene?' he repeated, not understanding what violence could have taken place between mutual adorers.

'She made me a scene of tears, of earnest remonstrance—perfectly well meant, I needn't tell you. She thinks I'm going too far.'

'I imagine you tell her things you don't tell me,' Hyacinth said.

'Oh you, my dear fellow!' his hostess murmured. She spoke absent-mindedly, as if she were thinking of what had passed with Lady Aurora and as if the futility of telling things to Mr Robinson had become a commonplace.

There was no annoyance for him in this, his pretension to keep pace with her 'views' being quite extinct. The tone they now for the most part took with each other was one of mutual derision, of shrugging commiseration for lunacy on the one hand and pusillanimity on the other. In discussing with her he exaggerated deliberately, went fantastic lengths in the way of reaction, a point where it was their habit and their amusement to hurl all manner of denunciation at each other's head. They had given up serious discussion altogether, and when not engaged in bandying, in the spirit of burlesque, the amenities I have mentioned, talked for a compromise of matters as to which it couldn't occur to them to differ. There were evenings when she did nothing but relate her life and all she had seen of humanity, from her earliest years, in a variety of countries. If evil appearances seemed mainly to have been presented to her view this didn't diminish the interest and vividness of her reminiscences, nor her power, the greatest Hyacinth had ever encountered, of light mimetic, dramatic evocation. She was irreverent and invidious, but she made him hang on her lips; and when she regaled him with anecdotes of foreign courts—he delighted to know how monarchs lived and conversed—there was often for hours together nothing to indicate that she would have liked to get into a conspiracy and he would have liked to get out of one. Nevertheless his mind was by no means exempt from wonder as to what she was really doing in such holes and in what queer penalties she might find herself landed. When he questioned her she wished to know by what title, with his sentiments, he pretended to enquire. He did so but little, not being himself altogether convinced of the validity of his warrant; but on an occasion when she had challenged him he replied, smiling and hesitating: 'Well, I must say it seems to me that from what I've told you it ought to strike you I've rather a title.'

'You mean your famous pledge to "act" on demand? Oh that will never come to anything.'

'Why won't it come to anything?'

'It's too absurd, it's too vague. It's like some silly humbug in a novel.'

'*Vous me rendez la vie!*' Hyacinth said theatrically.

'You won't have to do it,' she went on.

'I think you mean I won't do it. I've offered at least. Isn't that a title?'

'Well, then you won't do it,' said the Princess; after which they looked at each other a couple of minutes in silence.

'You will, I think, at the pace you're going,' the young man resumed.

'What do you know about the pace? You're not worthy to know!'

He did know, however; that is he knew her to be in communication with strange birds of passage, to have, or to believe she had, irons on the fire, to hold in her hand some of the strings that are pulled in great movements. She received letters that made Madame Grandoni watch her askance, of which, though she knew nothing of their contents and had only her general suspicions and her scent for disaster, now dismally acute, the old woman had spoken more than once to Hyacinth. Madame Grandoni had begun to have sombre visions of the interference of the police: she was haunted with the idea of a search for compromising papers; of being dragged herself, as an accomplice in direful plots, into a court of justice, possibly into a prison. 'If she would only burn—if she would only burn! But she keeps—I know she keeps!' she groaned to Hyacinth in her helpless gloom. He could only guess what it might be she kept; asking himself if she were seriously entangled, were being really exploited by plausible outlaws, predatory adventurers who counted on her getting frightened at a given moment and offering hush-money to be allowed to slip out —out of a complicity which they themselves of course would never have taken seriously; or were merely coquetting with paper schemes, giving herself cheap sensations, discussing preliminaries that could have no second stage. It would have been easy for him to smile at her impression that she was 'in it', and to conclude that even the cleverest women fail to know when they are futile, had not the vibration remained which had been imparted to his nerves two years before and of which he had spoken to his hostess at Medley—the sense, vividly kindled and never quenched, that the forces secretly arrayed against the present social order were pervasive and universal, in the air one breathed, in the ground one trod, in the hand of an acquaintance that one might touch or the eye of a stranger that might rest a moment on one's own. They were above, below, within, without, in every contact and combination of life; and it was no disproof of them to say it was too odd they should lurk in a particular improbable form. To lurk in improbable forms was precisely their strength, and they would doubtless have still queerer features to show than this of the Princess's being a genuine participant even when she most flattered herself she was.

'You do go too far,' he none the less said to her the evening Lady Aurora had passed him at the door.

To which she answered: 'Of course I do—that's exactly

what I mean. How else does one know one has gone far enough? That poor dear woman's an angel, yet isn't in the least in it,' she added in a moment. She would give him no further satisfaction on the subject; when he pressed her she asked if he had brought the copy of Browning he had promised the last time. If he had he was to sit down and read it to her. In such a case as this Hyacinth had no disposition to insist; he was glad enough not to talk about the everlasting nightmare. He took *Men and Women* from his pocket and read aloud for twenty minutes; but on his making some remark on one of the poems at the end of this time he noted that his companion had paid no attention. When he charged her with this levity she only replied, looking at him musingly: 'How *can* one, after all, go too far? That's the word of cowards.'

'Do you mean her ladyship's a coward?'

'Yes, in not having the courage of her opinions, of her conclusions. The way the English can go halfway to a thing and then stick in the middle!' the Princess exclaimed impatiently.

'That's not your fault, certainly!' said Hyacinth. 'But it seems to me Lady Aurora, for herself, goes pretty far.'

'We're all afraid of some things and brave about others,' his friend pursued.

'The thing Lady Aurora's most afraid of is the Princess Casamassima,' Hyacinth returned.

His companion looked at him but wouldn't take this up. 'There's one particular in which she would be very brave. She'd marry her friend—your friend—Mr Muniment.'

'Marry him, do you think?'

'What else pray?' the Princess asked. 'She adores the ground he walks on.'

'And what would Belgrave Square and Inglefield and all the rest of it say?'

'What do they say already and how much does it make her swerve? She'd do it in a moment, and it would be fine to see it, it would be magnificent,' said the Princess, kind-

ling, as she was apt to kindle, at the idea of any great free
stroke.

'That certainly wouldn't be a case of what you call
sticking in the middle,' Hyacinth declared.

'Ah it wouldn't be a matter of logic; it would be a
matter of passion. When it's a question of that the English,
to do them justice, don't stick!'

This speculation of the Princess's was by no means new
to Hyacinth, and he had not thought it heroic, after all,
that their high-strung associate should feel herself capable
of sacrificing her family, her name, and the few habits of
gentility that survived in her life, of making herself a
scandal, a fable and a nine days' wonder, for Muniment's
sake: the young chemical expert being, to his mind, as we
know, exactly the type of man who produced convulsions,
made ruptures and renunciations easy. But it was less clear
to him what opinions Muniment himself might hold on
the subject of a union with a young woman who should
have come out of her class for him. He would marry some
day, evidently, because he would do all the natural human
productive things; but for the present he had business on
hand which would be likely to pass first. Besides—Hyacinth had seen him give evidence of this—he didn't think
people could really come out of their class; he believed the
stamp of one's origin ineffaceable and that the best thing
one can do is to wear it and fight for it. Hyacinth could
easily imagine how it would put him out to be mixed up
closely with a person who, like Lady Aurora, was fighting
on the wrong side. 'She can't marry him unless he asks her,
I suppose—and perhaps he won't,' he reflected.

'Yes, perhaps he won't,' said the Princess thoughtfully.

XXXIX

ON SATURDAY afternoons Paul Muniment was able to
leave his work at four o'clock, and on one of these occa-

sions, some time after his visit to Madeira Crescent, he
came into Rosy's room at about five, carefully dressed and
brushed and ruddy with the freshness of an abundant washing. He stood at the foot of her sofa with a conscious
smile, knowing how she chaffed him when his necktie was
new; and after a moment, during which she ceased singing
to herself as she twisted the strands of her long black hair
together and let her eyes travel over his whole person, inspecting every detail, she said to him: 'My dear Mr Muniment, you're going to see the Princess.'

'Well, have you anything to say against it?' Mr Muniment asked.

'Not a word; you know I like princesses. But *you* have.'

'Well, my girl, I'll not speak it to you,' the young man
returned. 'There's something to be said against everything
if you give yourself trouble enough.'

'I should be very sorry if ever anything was said against
my big brother.'

'The man's a sneak who's only and always praised,' Paul
lucidly remarked. 'If you didn't hope to be finely abused
where would be the encouragement?'

'Ay, but not with reason,' said Rosy, who always brightened to an argument.

'The better the reason the greater the incentive to expose one's self. However, you won't hear of it—if people
do heave bricks at me.'

'I won't hear of it? Pray don't I hear of everything? I
should like any one to keep anything from *me!*' And Miss
Muniment gave a toss of her recumbent head.

'There's a good deal I keep from you, my dear,' said
Paul rather dryly.

'You mean there are things I don't want, I don't take
any trouble, to know. Indeed and indeed there are: things
I wouldn't hear of for the world—that no amount of persuasion would induce me, not if you was to go down on
your knees. But if I did, if I did, I promise you that just
as I lie here I should have them all in my pocket. Now
there are others,' the young woman went on, 'there are

special points on which you'll just be so good as to enlighten me. When the Princess asked you to come and see
her you refused and wanted to know what good it would
do. I hoped you'd go then; I should have liked you to go,
because I wanted to know how she lived and whether she
really had things handsome or only in the poor way she
said. But I didn't push you, because I couldn't have told
you what good it would do you: that was only the good it
would have done me. At present I've heard everything from
Lady Aurora and that it's all quite decent and tidy—
though not really like a princess a bit—and that she knows
how to turn everything about and put it best end foremost,
just as I do, though I oughn't to say it, no doubt. Well,
you've been, and more than once, and I've had nothing to
do with it; of which I'm very glad now, for reasons you
perfectly know—you're too honest a man to pretend you
don't. Therefore when I see you going again I just enquire
of you, as you enquired of her, what good *does* it do you?'

'I like it—I like it, my dear,' said Paul with his fresh
unembarrassed smile.

'I dare say you do. So should I in your place. But it's
the first time I have heard you express the idea that we
ought to do everything we like.'

'Why not, when it doesn't hurt any one else?'

'Oh Mr Muniment, Mr Muniment!' Rosy exclaimed
with exaggerated solemnity, holding up at him a straight
attenuated forefinger. Then she added: 'No, she doesn't do
you good, that beautiful, brilliant woman.'

'Give her time, my dear—give her time,' said Paul,
looking at his watch.

'Of course you're impatient, but you *must* hear me. I've
no doubt she'll wait for you—you won't lose your turn.
But what would you do, please, if any one was to break
down altogether?'

'My bonny lassie,' the young man returned, 'if *you* only
keep going I don't care who fails.'

'Oh I shall keep going, if it's only to look after my
friends and get justice for them,' said Miss Muniment—

'the delicate, sensitive creatures who require support and protection. Have you really forgotten that we've such a one as that?'

The young man walked to the window with his hands in his pockets and looked out at the fading light. 'Why does she go herself then, if she doesn't like her?'

Rose Muniment hesitated a moment. 'Well, I'm glad I'm not a man!' she broke out. 'I think a woman on her back's sharper than a man on his two legs. And you such a wonderful one too!'

'You're all too sharp for me, my dear. If she goes—and twenty times a week too—why shouldn't I go once in ever so long? Especially as I like her and Lady Aurora doesn't.'

'Lady Aurora doesn't? Do you think she'd be guilty of hypocrisy? Lady Aurora delights in her; she won't let me say that she's fit to dust the Princess's shoes. I needn't tell *you* how she goes down before them she likes. And I don't believe you care a button; you've something in your head, some wicked game or other, that you think she can hatch for you.'

At this he turned round and looked at her a moment, smiling still and whistling just audibly. 'Why shouldn't I care? Ain't I soft, ain't I susceptible?'

'I never thought I should hear you ask that—after what I've seen these four years. For four years she has come, and it's all for you—as well it might be; yet with your never showing any more sense of what she'd be willing to do for you than if you had been that woollen cat on the hearthrug!'

'What would you like me to do? Would you like me to hang round her neck and hold her hand the same as you do?' Muniment asked.

'Yes, it would do me good, I can tell you. It's better than what I see—the poor lady getting spotted and dim like a mirror that wants rubbing.'

'How the devil am I to rub her?' Muniment quaintly asked. 'You know a good deal, Rosy, but you don't know everything,' he pursued with a face that gave no sign of seeing a reason in what she said. 'Your mind's too poetical —as full of sounding strings and silver chords as some old elegant harp. There's nothing in the world I should care for that her ladyship would be willing to do for me.'

'She'd marry you at a day's notice—she'd do that for you.'

'I shouldn't care a hang for that. Besides, if I was to lay it before her she'd never come into the place again. And I shouldn't care for that—for you.'

'Never mind me; I'll take the risk!' cried Rosy with high cheer.

'But what's to be gained if I can have her for you without any risk!'

'You won't have her for me or for any one when she's dead of a broken heart.'

'Dead of a broken tea-cup!' said the young man. 'And pray what should we live on when you had got us set up? —the three of us without counting the kids.'

He evidently was arguing from pure good nature and not in the least from curiosity; but his sister replied as eagerly as if he would be floored by her answer: 'Hasn't she got a hundred a year of her own? Don't I know every penny of her affairs?'

Paul gave no sign of any inward judgement passed on Rosy's conception of the delicate course or of a superior policy; perhaps indeed, for it is perfectly possible, her question didn't strike him as having a mixture of motives. He only said with a small pleasant patient sigh: 'I don't want the dear old girl's money.'

His sister, in spite of her eagerness, waited twenty seconds; then she flashed at him: 'Pray do you like the Princess's better?'

'If I did there'd be much more of it,' he quietly returned.

'How can she marry you? Hasn't she got a husband?' Rosy cried.

'Lord, how you give me away!' laughed her brother. 'Daughters of earls, wives of princes—I've only to pick.'

'I don't speak of the Princess so long as there's a Prince. But if you haven't seen that Lady Aurora's a beautiful wonderful exception and quite unlike any one else in all the wide world—well, all I can say is that *I* have.'

'I thought it was your opinion,' Paul objected, 'that the swells should remain swells and the high ones keep their place.'

'And pray would she lose hers if she were to marry you?'

'Her place at Inglefield certainly,' he answered as lucidly as if his sister could never tire him with any insistence or any minuteness.

'Hasn't she lost that already? Does she ever go there?'

'Surely you appear to think so from the way you always question her about it.'

'Well, they think her so mad already that they can't think her any madder,' Rosy continued. 'They've given her up, and if she were to marry you——'

'If she were to marry me they wouldn't touch her with a ten-foot pole,' Paul broke in.

She flinched a moment, then said serenely: 'Oh I don't care for that!'

'You ought to, to be consistent, though possibly she shouldn't, admitting that she wouldn't. You've more imagination than logic—which of course for a woman is quite right. That's what makes you say that her ladyship's in affliction because I go to a place she herself goes to without the least compulsion.'

'She goes to keep you off,' said Rosy with decision.

'To keep me off?'

'To interpose with the Princess—and in a sense to interfere against her. To be nice to her and conciliate her, so she mayn't take you.'

'Has she told you any such rigmarole as that?' Paul enquired, this time staring a little.

'Do I need to be told things to know them? I'm not a fine strong superior male; therefore I can discover them for myself,' Rosy answered with a dauntless little laugh and a

light in her eyes which might indeed have made it appear
she was capable of wizardry.

'You make her out at once too passionate and too calculating,' the young man returned. 'She has no personal
feelings, she wants nothing for herself. She only wants one
thing in the world—to make the poor a little less poor.'

'Precisely; and she regards you, a helpless blundering
bachelor, as one of them.'

'She knows I'm not helpless so long as you're about the
place, and that my blunders don't matter so long as you
correct them.'

'She wants to assist me to assist you then!' the girl exclaimed with the levity with which her earnestness was
always interfused: it was a spirit that seemed of a sudden,
in argument, to mock at her own contention. 'Besides, isn't
that the very thing you want to bring about?' she went on.
'Isn't that what you're plotting and working and waiting
for? She wants to throw herself into it—to work with you.'

'My dear girl, she doesn't understand a pennyworth of
what I think. She couldn't if she would.'

'And no more do I, I suppose you mean.'

'No more do you; but with you it's different. If you
would you could. However, it matters little who understands and who doesn't, for all there happens to be of it.
I'm not doing much, you know.'

Rosy lay there looking up at him. 'It must be pretty
thick when you talk that way. However, I don't care what
you bring on, for I know I shall be looked after.'

'Nothing's going to happen—nothing's going to happen,'
Paul remarked simply.

Her rejoinder to this was to say in a moment: 'You've a
different tone since you've taken up the Princess.'

She spoke with a certain severity, but he broke out as
if he hadn't heard her: 'I like your idea of the female
aristocracy quarrelling over a dirty brute like me.'

'I don't know how dirty you are, but I know you smell
of soap,' said his sister inexorably. 'They won't quarrel;

that's not the way they do it. Yes, you're taking a different tone for some purpose I can't discover just yet.'

'What do you mean by that? When did I ever take a tone?' Paul demanded.

'Why then do you speak as if you weren't remarkable, immensely remarkable—more remarkable than anything any one, male or female, good or bad, of the aristocracy or of the vulgar sort, can ever do for you?'

'What on earth have I ever done to show it?' he asked as with amusement.

'Oh I don't know your secrets, and that's one of them. But we're out of the common beyond any one, you and I, and between ourselves, with the door fastened, we might as well admit it.'

'I admit it for you with all my heart!' the young man promptly laughed.

'Well then if I admit it for you that's all that's required.'

The pair considered themselves a while in silence, as if each were tasting agreeably the distinction the other conferred; then Muniment said: 'If I'm such an awfully superior chap why shouldn't I behave in keeping?'

'Oh you do, you do!'

'For all that you don't like it.'

'It isn't so much what you do. It's what *she* does.'

'How do you mean, what she does?'

'She makes Lady Aurora suffer.'

'Oh I can't go into that,' said Paul. 'A man feels such a muff, talking about the women who "suffer" for him.'

'Well, if they do it I think a man might bear it!' Rosy retorted. 'That's what a man *is*. When it comes to being sorry, oh that's too ridiculous!'

'There are plenty of things in the world I'm sorry for,' he patiently conceded. 'One of them is that you should keep me gossiping here when I want to go out.'

'Oh I don't care if I worry her a little. Does she do it on purpose?' Rosy continued.

'You ladies must settle all that together'—and he rubbed his hat with the cuff of his coat. It was a new one, the bravest he had ever possessed, and in a moment he put it on his head as if to re-enforce his reminder to his sister that it was time she should release him.

'Well, you do look genteel,' she said with high complacency. 'No wonder she has lost her head! I mean the Princess,' she explained. 'You never went to any such expense for her ladyship.'

'My dear, the Princess is worth it, she's worth it.' Which appeared at last on his part all seriously spoken.

'Will she help you very much?' Rosy demanded, as at the touch of it, with a strange sudden transition to eagerness.

'Well,' said Paul, 'that's rather what I look for.'

She threw herself forward on her sofa with a movement that was rare with her and, shaking her clasped hands, exclaimed: 'Then go off, go off quickly!'

He came round and kissed her as if he were not more struck than usual with her freakish inconsistency. 'It's not bad to have a little person at home who wants a fellow to succeed.'

'Oh I know they'll look after me.' And she sank back on her pillow with an air of agreeable security.

He was aware that whenever she said 'they', without further elucidation, she meant the populace surging up in his rear, and he met it with his usual ease. 'I don't think we'll leave it much to "them".'

'No it's not much you'll leave to them, I'll be bound.'

He gave a louder laugh at this and said: 'You're the deepest of the lot, Miss Muniment.'

Her eyes kindled at his praise and as she rested them on his own she brought out: 'Ah I pity the poor Princess too, you know!'

'Well now, I'm not conceited, but I don't,' Paul returned, passing in front of the little mirror on the mantel-shelf.

'Yes, you'll succeed, and so shall I—but *she* won't,' Rosy went on.

He stopped a moment with his hand on the latch of the door and said gravely, almost sententiously: 'She's not only

handsome, handsome as a picture, but she's uncommon
sharp and has taking ways beyond anything ever known.'

'I know her ways,' his sister replied. Then as he left the
room she called after him: 'But I don't care for anything so
long as you become prime minister of England!'

Three quarters of an hour after this he knocked at the
door in Madeira Crescent, and was immediately ushered
into the parlour, where the Princess, in her bonnet and
mantle, sat alone. She made no movement as he came in;
she only looked up at him with a smile.

'You're braver than I gave you credit for,' she said in
her rich voice.

'I shall learn to be brave if I associate a while longer
with you. But I shall never cease to be shy,' Muniment
added, standing there and looking tall in the middle of the
small room. He cast his eyes about him for a place to sit
down, but she gave him no help to choose; she only
watched him in silence from her own place, her hands
quietly folded in her lap. At last, when without remonstrance from her he had selected the most uncomfortable
chair in the room, she replied:

'That's only another name for desperate courage. I put
on my things on the chance, but I didn't expect you.'

'Well, here I am—that's the great thing,' he said good-
humouredly.

'Yes, no doubt it's a very great thing. But it will be a
still greater thing when you're there.'

'I'm afraid you hope too much,' the young man observed. 'Where is it? I don't think you told me.'

The Princess drew a small folded letter from her pocket
and, without saying anything, held it out to him. He got
up to take it from her, opened it and as he read it remained
standing in front of her. Then he went straight to the fire
and thrust the paper into it. At this act she rose quickly, as
to save the document, but the expression of his face while
he turned round to her made her stop. The smile that came
into her own was a little forced. 'What are you afraid of?'

she asked. 'I take it the house is known. If we go I suppose we may admit that we go.'

Paul's face showed he had been annoyed, but he answered quietly enough: 'No writing—no writing.'

'You're terribly careful,' said the Princess.

'Careful of you——yes.'

She sank upon her sofa again, asking her companion to ring for tea; they would do much better to have it before going out. When the order had been given she went on: 'I see I shall have much less keen emotion than when I acted by myself.'

'Is that what you go in for—keen emotion?'

'Surely, Mr Muniment. Don't you?'

'God forbid! I hope to have as little of any sort as possible.'

'Of course one doesn't want any vague rodomontade, one wants to do something. But it would be hard if one couldn't have a little pleasure by the way.'

'My pleasure's in keeping very cool,' Muniment said.

'So is mine. But it depends on how you understand it. I like quietness in the midst of a tumult.'

'You've rare ideas about tumults. They're not good in themselves.'

The Princess considered this a moment. 'I wonder if you're too prudent. I shouldn't like that. If it's made an accusation against you that you've been—where we're going—shall you deny it?'

'With that prospect it would be simpler not to go at all, wouldn't it?' he lucidly asked.

'Which prospect do you mean? That of being found out or that of having to lie?'

'I suppose that if you lie well enough you're not found out.' And he spoke again as for amusement.

'You won't take me seriously,' said the Princess—and without irritation, without resentment, with accepted, intelligent sadness. Yet there was a fineness of reproach in the tone in which she added: 'I don't believe you want to go at all.'

'Why else should I have come—especially if I don't take you seriously?'

'That has never been a reason for a man's not going to see a woman,' said the Princess. 'It's usually a reason in favour of it.'

Paul turned his steady eyes over the room, looking from one article of furniture to another: this was a way he had when engaged in a discussion, and it suggested not so much his reflecting on what his interlocutor said as that his thoughts were pursuing a bravely independent course. Presently he took up her remark. 'I don't know that I quite understand what you mean by that question of taking a woman seriously.'

'Ah you're very perfect!' she lightly wailed. 'Don't you consider that the changes you look for will be also for our benefit?'

'I don't think they'll alter your position.'

'If I didn't hope for that I wouldn't do anything,' said the Princess.

'Oh I've no doubt you'll do a great deal.'

The young man's companion was silent for some minutes, during which he also was content to say nothing. 'I wonder you can find it in your conscience to work with me,' she observed at last.

'It isn't in my conscience I find it,' he laughed.

The maid-servant brought in the tea, and while his hostess made a place for it on a table beside her she returned: 'Well, I don't care, for I think I have you in my power.'

'You've every one in your power,' Paul declared.

'Every one's no one,' she answered rather dryly; and a moment later she said to him: 'That extraordinary little sister of yours—surely you take *her* seriously?'

'I'm particularly fond of her, if that's what you mean. But I don't think her position will ever be altered.'

'Are you alluding to her position in bed? If you consider that she'll never recover her health,' the Princess said, 'I'm very sorry to hear it.'

'Oh her health will do. I mean that she'll continue to be, like all the most amiable women, just a kind of ornament to life.'

She had already noted that he pronounced amiable 'emiable'; but she had accepted this peculiarity of her visitor in the spirit of imaginative transfiguration in which she had accepted several others. 'To *your* life of course. She can hardly be said to be an ornament to her own.'

'Her life and mine are all one.'

'She's a prodigious person'—the Princess dismissed her. But while he drank his tea she remarked that for a revolutionist he was certainly prodigious as well; and he wanted to know in answer if it weren't rather in keeping for revolutionists to be revolutionary. He drank three cups, declaring his hostess's decoction rare; it was better even than Lady Aurora's. This led him to observe as he put down his third cup, looking round the room again lovingly, almost covetously: 'You've got everything so handy I don't see what interest you can have.'

'How do you mean, what interest?'

'In getting in so uncommon deep.'

The light in her face flashed on the instant into pure passion. 'Do you consider that I'm in—really far?'

'Up to your neck, ma'am.'

'And do you think that *il y va* of my neck—I mean that it's in danger?' she translated eagerly.

'Oh I understand your French. Well, I'll look after you,' Muniment said.

'Remember then definitely that I expect not to lie.'

'Not even for me?' Then he added in the same familiar tone, which was not rough nor wanting in respect, but only homely and direct, suggestive of growing acquaintance: 'If I was your husband I'd come and take you away.'

'Please don't speak of my husband,' she returned gravely. 'You've no qualification for doing so. You know nothing whatever about him.'

'I know what Hyacinth has told me.'

'Oh Hyacinth!' she sighed impatiently. There was another silence for some minutes, not disconnected apparently from this reference to the little bookbinder; but when Muniment spoke after the interval it was not to carry on the allusion.

'Of course you think me very plain and coarse.'

'Certainly you've not such a nice address as Hyacinth'— the Princess had no wish, on her side, to evade the topic. 'But that's given to very few,' she added; 'and I don't know that pretty manners are exactly what we're working for.'

'Ay, it won't be very endearing when we cut down a few allowances,' her visitor concurred. 'But I want to please you; I want to be as much as possible like Hyacinth,' he went on.

'That's not the way to please me. I don't forgive him—he's very foolish.'

'Ah don't say that; he's a fine little flute!' Paul protested.

'He's a delightful nature, with extraordinary qualities. But he's deplorably conventional.'

'Yes, if you talk about taking things seriously—*he* takes them so,' Muniment again agreed.

'Has he ever told you his life?' the Princess asked.

'He hasn't required to tell me. I've seen a good bit of it.'

'Yes, but I mean before you knew him.'

Paul thought. 'His birth and his poor mother? I think it was Rosy told me all that.'

'And pray how did *she* know?'

'Ah when you come to the way Rosy knows——!' He gave that up. 'She doesn't like people in such a box at all. She thinks we ought all to be grandly born.'

'Then they agree, for so does poor Hyacinth.' The Princess had a pause, after which, as with a deep effort: 'I want to ask you something. Have you had a visit from Mr Vetch?'

'The old gentleman who fiddles? No, he has never done me that honour.'

'It was because I prevented him then. I told him to leave it to me.'

'To leave what now?' And Paul looked out in placid perplexity.

'He's in great distress about Hyacinth—about the danger he runs. You know what I mean.'

'Yes, I know what you mean,' Muniment answered slowly. 'But where does *he* come in? I thought it was supposed to be a grand secret.'

'So it is. He doesn't know anything; he only suspects.'

'How do *you* know then?'

She had another wait. 'Oh I'm like Rosy—I find out. Mr Vetch, as I suppose you're aware, has been near Hyacinth all his life; he takes a most affectionate interest in him. He believes there's something hanging over him and wants it to be made impossible.' She paused afresh, but her visitor made no response and she continued: 'He was going to see you, to beg you to do something, to interfere; he seemed to suppose your power in such a matter would be very great. But as I tell you, I requested him—a particular favour to me—to let you alone.'

'What favour would it be to you?' Muniment asked.

'It would give me the satisfaction of feeling you not worried.'

He appeared struck with the curious inadequacy of this explanation, considering what was at stake; so that he confessed to almost rude amusement. 'That was considerate of you beyond anything.'

'It was not meant as consideration for you; it was a piece of calculation.' Having made this statement the Princess gathered up her gloves and turned away, walking to the chimney-piece, where she stood arranging her bonnet-ribbons in the mirror with which it was decorated. Paul watched her with clear curiosity; in spite both of his inaccessibility to nervous agitation and of the general scepticism he had cultivated about her he was not proof against her faculty of creating a feeling of suspense, a tension of interest, on the part of those involved with her. He fol-

lowed her movements, but plainly didn't follow her calculations, so that he could only listen more attentively when
she brought out suddenly: 'Do you know why I asked you
to come and see me? Do you know why I went to see your
sister? It was all a plan,' said the Princess.

'We hoped it was just an ordinary humane social impulse,' the young man returned.

'It was humane, it was even social, but it was not ordinary. I wanted to save Hyacinth.'

'To save him?'

'I wanted to be able to talk with you just as I'm talking
now.'

'That was a fine idea!' Paul candidly cried.

'I've an exceeding, a quite inexpressible regard for him.
I've no patience with some of his opinions, and that's why
I permitted myself to say just now that he's silly. But after
all the opinions of our friends are not what we love them
for—so I don't see why they should be a ground of aversion. Robinson's nature is singularly generous and his intelligence very fine, though there *are* things he muddles
up. You just now expressed strongly your own interest in
him; therefore we ought to be perfectly agreed. Agreed I
mean about getting him out of his scrape.'

Muniment had the air of a man feeling he must consider a little before assenting to these successive proposi-
tions; it being a limitation of his intellect that he couldn't
respond without understanding. After a moment he answered, referring to his hostess's last remark, in which the
others appeared to culminate, and at the same time shaking
his head with a rise of his strong eyebrows: 'His scrape
isn't important.'

'You thought it was when you got him into it.'

'I thought it would give him pleasure.'

'That's not a reason for letting people do what isn't
good for them.'

'I wasn't thinking so much about what would be good
for him as about what would be bad for some others. He
can do as he likes.'

'That's easy to say. They must be persuaded not to call him.'

'Persuade them then, dear madam.'

'How can I persuade them?' she cried. 'If I could do that I wouldn't have approached you. I've no influence, and even if I had it my motives would be suspected. You're the one to come in.'

'Shall I tell them he funks it?' Muniment asked.

'He doesn't—he doesn't!' she declared.

'On what ground then shall I put it?'

'Tell them he has changed his opinions.'

'Wouldn't that be rather like denouncing him as a traitor —and doing it hypocritically?'

'Tell them then it's simply my wish.'

'That won't do *you* much good,' Paul said with his natural laugh.

'Will it put me in danger? That's exactly what I want.'

'Yes; but as I understand you, you want to suffer *for* the people, not by them. You're very fond of Robinson; it couldn't be otherwise,' the young man argued. 'But you ought to remember that in the line you've chosen our affections, our natural ties, our timidities, our shrink-ings——' His voice had become low and grave, and he paused a little while the Princess's deep and lovely eyes, attaching themselves to his face, showed how quickly she had been affected by this unwonted adjuration. He spoke now as if he were taking her seriously. 'All those things are as nothing, they must never weigh a feather, beside our service.'

She began to draw on her gloves. 'You're a most extra-ordinary man.'

'That's what Rosy tells me.'

'Why don't you do it yourself?'

'Do Hyacinth's job? Because it's better to do my own.'

'And pray what *is* your own?'

'I don't know,' said Paul Muniment with perfect equa-nimity. 'I expect to be instructed.'

'Have you taken an oath like Hyacinth?'

'Ah madam, the oaths *I* take I don't tell,' he gravely returned.

'Oh *you*——!' she breathed with a deep ambiguous cadence. She appeared to dismiss the question, but to suggest at the same time that he was very abnormal. This imputation was further conveyed by the next words she uttered. 'And can you see a dear friend whirled away like that?'

At this, for the first time, her visitor showed impatience. 'You had better leave my dear friend to me.'

The Princess, her eyes still fixed on him, gave a long soft sigh. 'Well then, shall we go?'

He took up his hat again, but made no movement toward the door. 'If you did me the honour to seek my acquaintance, to ask me to come and see you, only in order to say what you've just said about Hyacinth, perhaps we needn't carry out the form of going to the place you proposed. Wasn't this only your pretext?'

'I believe you *are* afraid!' she frankly returned; but in spite of her exclamation the pair presently went out of the house. They quitted the door together, after having stood on the step a little to look up and down, apparently for a cab. So far as the darkness, which was now complete, permitted the prospect to be scanned, there was no such vehicle within hail. They turned to the left and after a walk of several minutes, during which they were engaged in small dull by-streets, emerged on a more populous way, where they found lighted shops and omnibuses and the evident chance of a hansom. Here they stayed afresh and very soon an empty hansom passed and, at a sign, pulled up near them. Meanwhile, it should be recorded, they had been followed, at an interval, by a cautious figure, a person who, in Madeira Crescent, when they came out of the house, was stationed on the other side of the street, at a considerable distance. On their appearing he had retreated a little, still however keeping them in sight. When they moved away he had moved in the same direction, watching them but maintaining his distance. He had drawn nearer, seemingly because he couldn't control his eagerness, as they passed into Westbourne Grove, and during the minute they stood there had been exposed to recognition by the Princess should she have happened to turn her head. In the event of her having felt such an impulse she would have discovered, in the lamplight, that her noble husband was hovering in her rear. But she was otherwise occupied; she failed to see that at one moment he came so close as to suggest an intention of breaking out on her from behind. The reader scarce need be informed, nevertheless, that his design was but to satisfy himself as to the kind of person his wife was walking with. The time allowed him for this research was brief, especially as he had perceived, more rapidly than he sometimes perceived things, that they were looking for a vehicle and that with its assistance they would pass out of his range —a reflexion which caused him to give half his attention to the business of hailing any second cab that should come that way. There are parts of London in which you may never see a cab at all, but there are none in which you may see only one; in accordance with which fortunate truth Prince Casamassima was able to wave his stick to good purpose as soon as the two objects of his pursuit had rattled away. Behind them now, in the gloom, he had no fear of being seen. In little more than an instant he had jumped into another hansom, the driver of which accompanied the usual exclamation of 'All right, sir!' with a small, amused grunt, regarded by the Prince as eminently British, after he had hissed at him, over the hood, expressively and in a manner by no means indicative of that nationality, the injunction 'Follow, follow, follow!'

XL

AN HOUR after her companion had left the house with Paul Muniment Madame Grandoni came down to supper, a meal for which she made use, in gloomy solitude, of the little back parlour. She had pushed away her plate and sat motionless, staring at the crumpled cloth with her hands folded on the edge of the table, when she became aware that a gentleman had been ushered into the drawing-room and was standing before the fire in discreet suspense. At the same moment the maid-servant approached the old lady, remarking with bated breath: 'The Prince, the Prince, mum! It's you he 'ave asked for, mum!' Upon this Madame Grandoni called out to the visitor from her place, addressed him as her poor dear distinguished friend and bade him come and give her his arm. He obeyed with solemn alacrity, conducting her to the front room and the fire. He helped her to arrange herself in her chair and gather her shawl about her; then he seated himself at hand and remained with his dismal eyes bent on her. After a moment she said: 'Tell me something about Rome. The grass in Villa Borghese must already be thick with flowers.'

'I would have brought you some if I had thought,' he answered. Then he turned his gaze about the room. 'Yes, you may well ask in such a black little hole as this. My wife shouldn't live here,' he added.

'Ah my dear friend, for all she's your wife——!' the old woman exclaimed.

The Prince sprang up in sudden sharp agitation, and then she saw that the stiff propriety with which he had come into the room and greeted her was only an effort of his good manners. He was really trembling with excitement. 'It's true—it's true! She *has* lovers—she *has* lovers!' he broke out. 'I've seen it with my eyes and I've come here to know!'

'I don't know what you've seen, but your coming here to know won't have helped you much. Besides, if you've seen you know for yourself. At any rate I've ceased to be able to tell you.'

'You're afraid,—you're afraid!' cried the visitor with a wild accusatory gesture.

The old woman looked up at him with slow speculation. 'Sit down and be quiet, very quiet. I've ceased to pay attention—I take no heed.'

'Well, I do then,' said the Prince, subsiding a little. 'Don't you know she has gone out to a house in a horrible quarter with a man?'

'I think it highly probable, dear Prince.'

'And who is he? That's what I want to discover.'

'How can I tell you? I haven't seen him.'

He looked at her with eyes of anguish. 'Dear lady, is that kind to me when I've counted on you?'

'Oh I'm not kind any more; it's not a question of that. I'm angry—as angry almost as you.'

'Then why don't you watch her, eh?'

'It's not with her I'm angry. It's with myself,' said Madame Grandoni, all in thought.

'For becoming so indifferent, do you mean?'

'On the contrary, for staying in the house.'

'Thank God you're still here, or I couldn't have come. But what a lodging for the Princess!' the visitor exclaimed. 'She might at least live in a manner befitting.'

'Eh, the last time you were in London you thought it too expensive!' she cried.

He cast about him. 'Whatever she does is wrong. Is it because it's so bad that you must go?' he went on.

'It's foolish—foolish—foolish,' said his friend, slowly and impressively.

'Foolish, *chè, chè!* He was in the house nearly an hour, this one.'

'In the house? In what house?'

'Here where you sit. I saw him go in, and when he came out it was after a long time, and she with him.'

'And where were you meanwhile?'

Again the Prince faltered. 'I was on the other side of the street. When they came out I followed them. It was more than an hour ago.'

'Was it for that you came to London?'

'Ah what I came for——! To put myself in hell!'

'You had better go back to Rome,' said Madame Grandoni.

'Of course I'll go back, but only if you'll tell me who this one is! How can you be ignorant, dear friend, when he comes freely in and out of the place?—where I have to watch at the door for a moment I can snatch. He wasn't the same as the other.'

'As the other?'

'Doubtless there are fifty! I mean the little one I met in the house that Sunday afternoon.'

'I sit in my room almost always now,' said the old woman. 'I only come down to eat.'

'Dear lady, it would be better if you would sit here,' the Prince returned.

'Better for whom?'

'I mean that if you didn't withdraw yourself you could at least answer my questions.'

'Ah but I haven't the slightest desire to answer them,' Madame Grandoni replied. 'You must remember that I'm not here as your spy.'

'No,' said the Prince in a tone of extreme and simple melancholy. 'If you had given me more information I shouldn't have been obliged to come here myself. I arrived in London ony this morning, and this evening I spent two hours walking up and down opposite there, like a groom waiting for his master to come back from a ride. I wanted a personal impression. It was so I saw him come in. He's not a gentleman—not even one of the strange ones of this country.'

'I think he's Scotch or Welsh,' Madame Grandoni explained.

'Ah then you *have* seen him?'

'No, but I've heard him. He speaks straight out (the floors of this house are not built as we build in Italy) and his voice is the same I've noticed in the people of the wild parts, where they "shoot". Besides, she has told me—some few things. He's a chemist's assistant.'

'A chemist's assistant? *Santo Dio!* And the other one, a year ago—more than a year ago—was a bookbinder.'

'Oh the bookbinder——!' the old woman wailed.

'And does she associate with no people of good? Has she no other society?'

'For me to tell you more, Prince, you must wait till I'm free,' she pleaded.

'How do you mean, free?'

'I must choose. I must either go away—and then I can tell you what I've seen—or if I stay here I must hold my tongue.'

'But if you go away you'll have seen nothing,' the Prince objected.

'Ah plenty as it is—more than I ever expected to!'

He clasped his hands as in strenuous suppliance, but at the same time smiled as to conciliate, to corrupt. 'Dearest friend, you torment my curiosity. If you'll tell me this I'll never ask you anything more. Where did they go? For the love of God, what is that house?'

'I know nothing of their houses,' she returned with an impatient shrug.

'Then there are others? there are many?' She made no answer but to sit intent, her chin in her bulging kerchief. Her visitor presently continued with his pressure of pain and his beautiful Italian distinctness, as if his lips cut and carved the sound, while his fine fingers quivered into quick emphasising gestures: 'The street's small and black, but it's like all the dreadful streets. It has no importance; it's at the end of a long imbroglio. They drove for twenty minutes, then stopped their cab and got out. They went together on foot some minutes more. There were many turns; they seemed to know them well. For me it was very difficult—of course I also got out; I had to stay so far behind—close against the houses. Chiffinch Street, N.E.—that was the name,' the Prince continued, pronouncing the word with difficulty; 'and the house is number 32—I looked at that after they went in. It's a very bad house—worse than this; but it has no sign of a chemist and there are no shops in the street. They rang the bell—only once, though they waited a long time; it seemed to me at least that they didn't touch it again. It was several minutes before the door was opened,

and that was a bad time for me, because as they stood there
they looked up and down. Fortunately you know the air of
this place! I saw no light in the house—not even after they
went in. Who opened to them I couldn't tell. I waited nearly
half an hour, to see how long they might stay and what they
would do on coming out; then at last my impatience brought
me here, for to know she was absent made me hope I might
see you. While I was there two persons went in: two men
together, both smoking, who looked like *artisti*—I saw them
badly—but no one came out. I could see they took their
cigars—and you can fancy what tobacco!—into the presence
of the Princess. Formerly,' pursued Madame Grandoni's
visitor with a touching attempt at pleasantry on this point,
'she never tolerated smoking—never mine at least. The
street's very quiet—very few people pass. Now what's the
house? Is it where that man lives?' he almost panted.

He had been encouraged by her consenting, in spite of
her first protests, to listen to him—he could see she *was*
listening; and he was still more encouraged when after a
moment she answered his question by a question of her
own. 'Did you cross the river to go there? I know he lives
over the water!'

'Ah no, it was not in that part. I tried to ask the cabman
who brought me back to explain to me what it's called; but
I couldn't make him understand. They've heavy minds,'
the Prince declared. Then he pursued, drawing a little closer
to his hostess: 'But what were they doing there? Why did
she go with him?'

'They think they're conspiring. *Ecco*!' said Madame
Grandoni.

'You mean they've joined a secret society, a band of
revolutionists and murderers? *Capisco bene*—that's not new
to me. But perhaps they only pretend it's for that,' added
the Prince.

'Only pretend? Why should they pretend? That's not
Christina's way.'

'There are other possibilities,' he portentously observed.

'Oh of course when your wife goes off with strange low

men in the dark, goes off to *des maisons louches*, you can think anything you like and I've nothing to say to your thoughts. I've my own, but they're my affair, and I shall not undertake to defend Christina, who's indefensible. When she commits these follies she provokes, she invites, the worst construction; there let it rest save for this one remark which I will content myself with making. That is if she were a real wretch, capable of *all*, she wouldn't behave as she does now, she wouldn't expose herself to *the* supposition; the appearance of everything would be good and proper. I simply tell you what I believe. If I believed that what she's doing concerned you alone I should say nothing about it—at least sitting here. But it concerns others, it concerns every one, so I open my mouth at last. She has gone to that house to break up society.'

'To break it up, yes, as she has wanted before?'

'Oh more than ever before! She's very much entangled. She has relations with people who are watched by the police. She hasn't told me, but I've grown sure of it by simply living with her.'

The poor Prince stared. 'And is *she* watched by the police?'

'I can't tell you; it's very possible—except that the police here isn't like that of other countries.'

'It's more stupid.' He gazed at his cold comforter with a flush of shame on his face. 'Will she bring us to *that* scandal? It would be the worst of all.'

'There's one chance—the chance she'll get tired of it,' the old lady remarked. 'Only the scandal may come before that.'

'Dear friend, she's the Devil in person,' said the Prince woefully.

'No, she's not the Devil, because she wishes to do good.'

'What good did she ever wish to do to me?' he asked with glowing eyes.

She shook her head with a gloom that matched his own. 'You can do no good of any kind to each other. Each on your own side you must be quiet.'

'How can I be quiet when I hear of such infamies?' He got up in his violence and, after a fashion that caused his companion to burst into a short incongruous laugh as soon as she heard the words, pronounced: 'She shall *not* break up society!'

'No, she'll bore herself to death before the *coup* is ripe. Make up your mind to that.'

'That's what I expected to find—that the caprice was over. She has passed through so many madnesses.'

'Give her time—give her time,' replied Madame Grandoni.

'Time to drag my name into an assize-court? Those people are robbers, incendiaries, murderers!'

'You can say nothing to me about them that I haven't said to her.'

'And how does she defend herself!'

'Defend herself? Did you ever hear Christina do that?' the old woman asked. 'The only thing she says to me is: "Don't be afraid; I promise you by all that's sacred you personally shan't suffer." She speaks as if she had it all in her hands. That's very well. No doubt I'm a selfish old pig, but after all one has a heart for others.'

'And so have I, I think I may pretend,' said the Prince. 'You tell me to give her time, and it's certain she'll take it whether I give it or no. But I can at least stop giving her money. By heaven it's my duty as an honest man.'

'She tells me that as it is you don't give her much.'

'Much, dear lady? It depends on what you call so. It's enough to make all these scoundrels flock round her.'

'They're not all scoundrels any more than she's all one. That's the tiresome part of it!' she wearily sighed.

'But this fellow, the chemist—to-night—what do you call *him*?'

'She has spoken to me of him as a fine young man.'

'But she thinks it fine to blow us all up,' the Prince returned. 'Doesn't *he* take her money?'

'I don't know what he takes. But there are some things—

heaven forbid one should forget them! The misery of London's fearful.'

'*Che vuole?* There's misery everywhere,' our personage opined. 'It's the will of God. *Ci vuol' pazienza!* And in this country does no one give alms?'

'Every one, I believe. But it appears that that's not enough.'

He said nothing for a moment; this statement of Madame Grandoni's seemed to present difficulties. The solution, however, soon suggested itself; it was expressed in the enquiry: 'What will you have in a country that hasn't the true faith?'

'Ah the true faith's a great thing, but there's suffering even in countries that have it.'

'*Evidentemente.* But it helps suffering to be borne and, later, makes it up; whereas here——!' said the visitor with a sad if inconclusive smile. 'If I may speak of myself it's to me, in any circumstances, a support.'

'That's good,' she returned a little curtly.

He stood before her, resting his eyes for a moment on the floor. 'And the famous Cholto—Godfrey Gerald—does he come no more?'

'I haven't seen him for months. I know nothing about him.'

'He doesn't like the chemists and the bookbinders, eh?' asked the Prince.

'Ah it was he who first brought them—to gratify your wife.'

'If they've turned him out then that's very well. Now if only some one could turn *them* out!'

'*Aspetta, aspetta!*' said the old woman.

'That's very good advice, but to follow it isn't amusing.' Then the Prince added: 'You alluded, just now, as to something particular, to *quel' giovane*, the young artisan whom I met in the other house. Is he also still proposed to our admiration, or has he paid the penalty of his crimes?'

'He has paid the penalty, but I don't know of what. I've

nothing bad to tell you of him except that I think his star's on the wane.'

'*Poverino!*' the Prince exclaimed.

'That's exactly the manner in which I addressed him the first time I saw him. I didn't know how it would happen, but I felt it would happen somehow. It has happened through his changing his opinions. He has now the same idea as you—*ci vuol' pazienza.*'

Her friend listened with the same expression of wounded eagerness, the same parted lips and excited eyes, to every fact that dropped from Madame Grandoni's lips. 'That at least is more honest. Then *he* doesn't go to Chiffinch Street?'

'I don't know about Chiffinch Street, though it would be my impression that he doesn't go to any place visited by Christina and the other one, by the Scotchman, together. But these are delicate matters,' the old woman pursued.

They seemed much to impress her interlocutor. 'Do you mean that the Scotchman is—what shall I call it?—his successor?'

For a time she made no reply. 'I imagine this case different. But I don't understand; it was the other, the little one, who helped her to know the Scotchman.'

'And now they've quarrelled—about my wife? It's all tremendously edifying!' the Prince wailed.

'I can't tell you, and shouldn't have attempted it, only that Assunta talks to me.'

'I wish she would talk to me,' he said wistfully.

'Ah my friend, if Christina were to find you getting at her servants——!'

'How could it be worse for me than it is now? However, I don't know why I speak as if I cared, for I don't care any more. I've given her up. It's finished.'

'I'm glad to hear it,' said Madame Grandoni gravely.

'You yourself made the distinction perfectly. So long as she endeavoured only to injure *me*, and in my private capacity, I could condone, I could wait, I could hope. But since she has so shamelessly thrown herself into criminal undertakings, since she lifts her hand with a determined purpose, as you tell me, against the most sacred institutions —it's too much; ah yes, it's too much! She may go her way; she's no wife of mine. Not another penny of mine shall go into her pocket and into that of the wretches who prey upon her, who have corrupted her.'

'Dear Prince, I think you're right. And yet I'm sorry!' sighed his hostess, extending her hand for assistance to rise from her chair. 'If she becomes really poor it will be much more difficult for me to leave her. *This* is not poverty, and not even a good imitation of it, as she would like it to be. But what will be said of me if, having remained with her through so much of her splendour, I turn away from her the moment she begins to want?'

'Dear lady, do you ask that to make me relent?' the Prince uneasily quavered.

'Not in the least; for whatever's said and whatever you do there's nothing for me in decency at present but to pack my trunk. Judge by the way I've tattled.'

'If you'll stay on she shall have everything.' He spoke in a very low tone, with a manner that betrayed the shame he felt for his attempt at bribery.

Madame Grandoni gave him an astonished glance and moved away from him. 'What does that mean? I thought you didn't care.'

I know not what explanation of his inconsequence her guest would have given her if at that moment the door of the room hadn't been pushed open to permit the entrance of Hyacinth Robinson. He stopped short on finding a stranger in the field, but before he had time to say anything the old lady addressed him rather shortly. 'Ah you don't fall well; the Princess isn't at home.'

'That was mentioned to me, but I ventured to come in to see you as I've done before,' our young man replied. Then he added as to accommodate: 'I beg many pardons. I was not told you were not alone.'

'My visitor's going, but I'm going too,' said Madame

Grandoni. 'I must take myself to my room—I'm all falling to pieces. Therefore kindly excuse me.'

Hyacinth had had time to recognise the Prince, and this nobleman paid him the same compliment, as was proved by his asking of their companion in a rapid Italian aside: 'Isn't it the bookbinder?'

'*Sicuro*,' said the old lady; while Hyacinth, murmuring a regret that he should find her indisposed, turned back to the door.

'One moment—one moment, I pray!' the Prince interposed, raising his hand persuasively and looking at Mr Robinson with an unexpected exaggerated smile. 'Please introduce me to the gentleman,' he added in English to Madame Grandoni.

She manifested no surprise at the request—she had none left for anything—but pronounced the name of Prince Casamassima and then added for Hyacinth's benefit: 'He knows who you are.'

'Will you permit me to keep you a very little minute?' The Prince appealed to his fellow visitor, after which he remarked to Madame Grandoni: 'I'll talk with him a little. It's perhaps not necessary we should incommode you if you don't wish to stay.'

She had for an instant, as she tossed off a small satirical laugh, a return of her ancient drollery. 'Remember that if you talk long she may come back! Yes, yes, I'll go upstairs. *Felicissima notte, signori!*' She took her way to the door, which Hyacinth, considerably bewildered, held open for her.

The reasons for which Prince Casamassima wished to converse with him were mysterious; nevertheless he was about to close the door behind their friend as a sign that he was at the service of the greater personage. At this moment the latter raised again a courteous remonstrant hand. 'After all, as my visit is finished and as yours comes to nothing, might we not go out?'

'Certainly I'll go with you,' said Hyacinth. He spoke with an instinctive stiffness in spite of the Prince's queer affability, and in spite also of the fact that he felt sorry for the nobleman to whose countenance Madame Grandoni's last injunction, uttered in English, could bring a deep and painful blush. It is forbidden us to try the question of what Hyacinth, face to face with an aggrieved husband, may have had on his conscience, but he assumed, naturally enough, that the situation might be grave, though indeed the Prince's manner was for the moment incongruously bland. He invited his new, his grand acquaintance to pass, and in a minute they were in the street together.

'Do you go here—do you go there?' the Prince enquired as they stood a moment before the house. 'If you permit I'll take the same direction.' On Hyacinth's answering that it was indifferent to him he said, turning to the right: 'Well then here, but *adagio*, if that pleases you, and only a little way.' His English was far from perfect, but his errors were like artificial flowers of accent: Hyacinth was struck with his effort to express himself very distinctly, so that in intercourse with a small untutored Briton his foreignness should not put him at a disadvantage. Quick to perceive and appreciate, our hero noted how the quality of breeding in him just enabled him to compass that coolness, and he mentally applauded the success of a difficult feat. Difficult he judged it because it seemed to him that the purpose for which the Prince wished to speak to him was one requiring an immensity of explanation, and it was a sign of training to explain adequately, in a strange tongue, especially if one were agitated, to a person in a social position very different from one's own. Hyacinth knew what the Prince's estimate of *his* importance must be—he could have no illusions as to the character of the people his wife received; but while he heard him carefully put one word after the other he was able to smile to himself at his needless precautions. Our young man reflected that at a pinch he could have encountered him in his own tongue: during his stay at Venice he had picked up an Italian vocabulary. 'With Madame Grandoni I spoke of you,' the Prince announced dispassionately as they walked along. 'She told me a thing that interested me,' he added; 'that's why I walk with you.' Hyacinth said nothing, deeming that better by silence than in any other fashion he held himself at the disposal of his interlocutor. 'She told me you've changed—you've no more the same opinions.'

'The same opinions?'

'About the arrangement of society. You desire no more the assassination of the rich.'

'I never desired any such thing!' said Hyacinth indignantly.

'Oh if you've changed you can confess,' his friend declared in an encouraging tone. 'It's very good for some people to be rich. It wouldn't be right for all to be poor.'

'It would be pleasant if all could be rich,' Hyacinth more mildly suggested.

'Yes, but not by stealing and shooting.'

'No, not by stealing and shooting. I never desired that.'

'Ah no doubt she was mistaken. But to-day you think we must have patience?' the Prince went on as if greatly hoping Hyacinth would allow this valuable conviction to be attributed to him. 'That's also my view.'

'Oh yes, we must have patience,' said his companion, who was now smiling to himself in the dark.

They had by this time reached the end of the little Crescent, where the Prince paused under the street-lamp. He considered the small bookbinder's countenance for a moment by its help and then pronounced: 'If I'm not mistaken you know very well the Princess.'

Hyacinth hung back: 'She has been very kind to me.'

'She's my wife—perhaps you know.'

Again Mr Robinson faltered, but after a moment he replied: 'She has told me that she's married.' As soon as he had spoken these words he thought them idiotic.

'You mean you wouldn't know if she hadn't told you, I suppose. Evidently there's nothing to show it. You can think if that's agreeable to me.'

'Oh I can't think, I can't judge.'

'You're right—that's impossible.' The Prince stood before his companion, and in the pale gaslight the latter saw more of his face. It had an unnatural expression, a look of wasted anxiety; the eyes seemed to glitter, and our fond observer conceived the unfortunate nobleman to be feverish and ill. He pursued in a moment: 'Of course you think it strange—my conversation. I want you to tell me something.'

'I'm afraid you're very unwell,' said Hyacinth.

'Yes, I'm very unwell; but I shall be better if you'll tell me. It's because you've come back to good ideas—that's why I ask you.'

A sense that the situation of the Princess's husband was really pitiful, that at any rate he suffered and was helpless, that he was a gentleman and even a person who would never have done any great harm—a perception of these appealing truths came into Hyacinth's heart and stirred there a desire to be kind to him, to render him any service that in reason he might ask. It struck him he must be pretty sick to ask any at all, but that was his own affair. 'If you'd like me to see you safely home I'll do that,' our young friend brought out; and even while he spoke he was struck with the oddity of his being already on such friendly terms with a person whom he had hitherto supposed to be the worst enemy of the rarest of women. He found himself unable to consider the Prince with resentment.

This personage acknowledged the civility of the offer with a slight inclination of his high slimness. 'I'm very much obliged to you, but I don't go home. I don't go home till I know this—to what house she has gone. Will you tell me that?'

'To what house?' Hyacinth repeated.

'She has gone with a person whom you know. Madame Grandoni told me that. He's a Scotch chemist.'

'A Scotch chemist?' Hyacinth stared.

'I saw them myself—an hour, two hours, ago. Listen, listen; I'll be very clear,' said the Prince, laying his forefinger on the other hand with a pleading emphasis. 'He came to that house—this one, where we've been, I mean—and stayed there a long time. I was here in the street—I've

passed my day in the street! They came out together and
I watched them—I followed them.'

Hyacinth had listened with wonder and even with suspense; the Prince's manner gave an air of such importance
and such mystery to what he had to relate. But at this he
broke out: 'This's not my business—I can't hear it! *I* don't
watch, *I* don't follow.'

His friend stared in surprise, but then rejoined, more
quickly than he had spoken yet: 'Do you understand that
they went to a house where they conspire, where they prepare horrible acts? How can you like that?'

'How do you know it, sir?' Hyacinth gravely asked.

'It's Madame Grandoni who has told me.'

'Why then do you question me?'

'Because I'm not sure, I don't think she knows. I want to
know more, to be sure of what's the truth. Does she go to
such a place only for the revolution, or does she go to be
alone with him?'

'With *him?*' The Prince's tone and his excited eyes had
somehow made the suggestion live.

'With the tall man—the chemist. They got into a hansom
together; the house is far away, in the lost quarters.'

Hyacinth drew himself together. 'I know nothing about
the matter and I don't care. If that's all you wish to ask
me we had better separate.'

The Prince's high face grew long; it seemed to grow
paler. 'Then it's not true that you hate those abominations!'

Hyacinth frankly wondered. 'How can you know about
my opinions? How can they interest you?'

The Prince looked at him with sick eyes; he raised his
arms a certain distance and then let them drop at his sides.
'I hoped you'd help me.'

'When we're in trouble we can't help each other much!'
our young man exclaimed. But this austere reflexion was
lost on the Prince, who at the moment it was uttered had
already turned to look in the direction from which they had
moved, the other end of the Crescent, his attention suddenly
jerked round by the sound of a rapid hansom. The place was

still and empty and the wheels of this vehicle reverberated. He glowered at it through the darkness and in an instant cried, under his breath, excitedly: 'They've come back—they've come back! Now you can see—yes, the two!' The hansom had slackened pace and pulled up; the house before which it stopped was clearly the house the two men had lately quitted. Hyacinth felt his arm seized by his strange confidant, who hastily, with a strong effort, drew him forward several yards. At this moment a part of the agitation that possessed the Princess's unhappy husband seemed to pass into his own blood; a wave of anxiety rushed through him—anxiety as to the relations of the two persons who had descended from the cab: he had in short for several instants a very exact revelation of the state of feeling of those who love in the rage of jealousy. If he had been told half an hour before that he was capable of surreptitious peepings in the interest of that passion he would have resented the insult; yet he allowed himself to be checked by his companion just at the nearest point at which they might safely consider the proceedings of the couple who alighted. It was in fact the Princess accompanied by Paul Muniment. Hyacinth noticed that the latter paid the cabman, who immediately drove away, from his own pocket. He stood with the Princess for some minutes at the door of the house—minutes during which Mr Robinson felt his heart beat insanely, ignobly. He couldn't tell why.

'What does he say? what does *she* say?' hissed the Prince; and when he went on the next moment, 'Will he go in again or will he go away?' our stricken youth felt a voice given to his own sharpest thought. The pair were talking together with rapid sequences, and as the door had not yet been opened it was clear that, to prolong the conversation on the steps, the Princess delayed to ring. 'It will make three, four, hours he has been with her,' moaned the Prince.

'He may be with her fifty hours!' Hyacinth laughed as he turned away ashamed of himself.

'He has gone in—*sangue di Dio!*' cried the Prince, catching his companion again by the arm and making him look. All our friend saw was the door just closing; Paul and the Princess were on the other side of it. 'Is *that* for the revolution?' the trembling nobleman panted. But Mr Robinson made no answer; he only gazed at the closed door an instant and then, disengaging himself, walked straight away, leaving the victim of the wrong he could even then feel as deeper than his own to shake, in the dark, a helpless foolish gold-headed stick at the indifferent house where Madame Grandoni's bedroom light glimmered aloft.

XLI

HYACINTH WAITED a long time, but when at last Millicent came to the door the splendour of her appearance did much to justify her delay. He heard an immense rustling on the staircase, accompanied by a creaking of that inexpensive structure, and then she brushed forward into the narrow dusky passage where he had been standing a quarter of an hour. Highly flushed, she exhaled a strong cheap perfume, and she instantly thrust her muff, a tight fat beribboned receptacle, at him to be held while she adjusted her gloves to her large vulgar hands. He opened the door—it was so natural an assumption that they shouldn't be able to talk properly in the passage—and they came out to the low steps, lingering there in the yellow Sunday sunshine. A loud ejaculation on the beauty of the day broke from Millicent, though, as we know, she was not addicted to facile admirations. Winter was not over but spring had begun, and the smoky London air allowed the baffled vision, by way of a change, to pierce it almost through. The town could refresh its recollections of the sky and the sky could ascertain the geographical position of the town. The essential dimness of the low perspectives had by no means disappeared, but it had loosened its folds; it lingered as a blur of mist inter-woven with pretty sun-tints and faint transparencies. There was warmth and iridescence and a view of the shutters of shops, and the church-bells were ringing. Miss Henning remarked that it was a 'shime' she couldn't have a place to ask a gentleman to sit down; but what were you to do when you had such a grind for your living and a room, to keep yourself tidy, no bigger than a pill-box? She couldn't herself abide waiting outside; she knew something about it when she took things home to ladies to choose—the time they spent was long enough to choose a husband!—and it always made her feel quite wicked. It was something 'croo'l'. If she could have what she liked she knew what she'd have; and she hinted at a mystic bower where a visitor could sit and enjoy himself—with the morning paper or a nice view out of the window or even a glass of sherry—so that, close at hand but perfectly private, she could dress without getting in a fidget, which always made her red in the face.

'I don't know how I *'ave* pitched on my things,' she remarked as she offered her magnificence to Hyacinth, who became aware she had put a small plump book into her muff. He explained that, the day being so fine, he had come to propose to her a walk in the manner of ancient times. They might spend an hour or two in the Park and stroll beside the Serpentine, or even paddle about on it if she liked; they might watch the lambkins or feed the ducks if she would put a crust in her pocket. The privilege of paddling Millicent entirely declined; she had no idea of wetting her flounces and she left those rough pleasures, especially of a Sunday, to a lower class of young woman. But she didn't mind if she did go a turn, though he didn't deserve any such favour after the way he hadn't been near her, not if she had died in her garret. She wasn't one that was to be dropped and taken up at any man's convenience—she didn't keep one of those offices for servants out of place. Her conviction was strong that if the day hadn't been so grand she would have sent her friend about his business; it was lucky for him she was always forgiving—such was her sensitive generous nature—when the sun was out. Only there was one thing—she couldn't abide making no difference for Sunday; it was her personal habit to go to church and she

should have it on her conscience if she gave that up for a
lark. Hyacinth had already been impressed, more than once,
by the manner in which his old playmate stickled for the
religious observance: of all the queer disparities of her
nature her devotional turn struck him as perhaps the
queerest. She held her head erect through the longest and
dullest sermon and quitted the sacred edifice with her fine
face embellished by the publicity of her virtue. She was
exasperated by the general secularity of Hyacinth's behaviour, especially taken in conjunction with his general
straightness, and was only consoled a little by the fact that if
he didn't drink or fight or steal he at least dabbled in unlimited wickedness of opinion—theories as bad as anything
people often got ten years for. He had not yet revealed to
her that his theories had somehow lately come to be held
with less of a clutch; an instinct of kindness had forbidden
him to deprive her of a grievance doing so much for
sociability. He had not reflected that she would have been
more aggrieved, and consequently more delightful, if her
condemnation of his godlessness had missed corroborative
signs.

On the present occasion she let him know he might have
his pleasure if he would first accompany her to church; and
it was in vain he represented to her that this proceeding
would deprive them of their morning, inasmuch as after
church she would have to dine and in the interval there
would be no time left. She replied with a toss of her head
that she dined when she liked; besides, on Sundays she had
cold fare—it was left out for her: an argument to which
Hyacinth had to assent, his ignorance of her domestic
economy being complete, thanks to the maidenly mystery,
the vagueness of reference and explanation in which, despite
great freedom of complaint, perpetual announcements of
intended change, of impending promotion and of high bids
for her services in other quarters, she had always en-
shrouded her private affairs. He walked by her side to the
place of worship she preferred—her choice was made apparently from a large experience; and as they went he observed

that it was a good job he wasn't married to her. Lord, how she would bully him, how she would 'squeeze' him, in such a case! The worst of it would be that—such was his amiable peace-loving nature—he should obey like a showman's poodle. And pray who *was* a man to obey, asked Millicent, if he wasn't to obey his own wife? She sat up in her pew with a majesty that carried out this idea; she seemed to answer in her proper person for creeds and communions and sacraments; she was more than devotional, she was individually almost pontifical. Hyacinth had never felt himself under such distinguished protection; the Princess Casamassima came back to him in comparison as a loose Bohemian, a shabby adventuress. He had sought her out to-day not for the sake of her austerity—he had had too gloomy a week for that—but for that of her genial side; yet now that she treated him to the severer spectacle it struck him for the moment as really grand sport, a kind of magnification of her rich vitality. She had her phases and caprices like the Princess herself, and if they were not the same as those of the lady of Madeira Crescent they proved at least that she was as brave a woman. No one but a really big creature could give herself such airs; she would have a consciousness of the large reserve of pliancy required to make up for them. The Princess wanted to destroy society and Millicent to uphold it; and as Hyacinth, by the side of his childhood's friend, listened to practised intonings and felt the brush of a rich unction, he was obliged to recognise the liberality of a fate that had sometimes appeared invidious. He had been provided with the best opportunities for choosing between the beauty of the original and the beauty of the conventional.

On this particular Sunday there was by luck no sermon—by the luck, I mean, of his heretical impatience—so that after the congregation dispersed there was still plenty of time for a walk in the Park. Our friends traversed that barely-interrupted expanse of irrepressible herbage which stretches from the Birdcage Walk to Hyde Park Corner and took their way to Kensington Gardens beside the

Serpentine. Once her religious exercises were over for the day—she as rigidly forbore to repeat them in the afternoon as she made a point of the first service—once she had lifted her voice in prayer and praise Millicent changed her carriage; moving to a different measure, uttering her sentiments in a high free manner and not minding if it was noticed she had on her very best gown and was out if need be for the day. She was mainly engaged at first in overhauling Hyacinth for his long absence and demanding as usual some account of what he had been up to. He listened at his ease, liking and enjoying her chaff, which seemed to him, oddly enough, wholesome and refreshing, and amusedly and absolutely declining to satisfy her. He alleged, as he had had occasion to do before, that if he asked no explanations of her the least he had a right to expect in return was that she should let him off as easily; and even the indignation with which she received this plea didn't make him feel that a clearing-up between them could be a serious thing. There was nothing to clear up and nothing to forgive; they were a pair of very fallible creatures, united much more by their weaknesses than by any consistency or fidelity they might pretend to practise toward each other. It was an old acquaintance—the oldest thing to-day, except Mr Vetch's friendship, in Hyacinth's life; and, oddly enough, it inspired our young man with a positive indulgent piety. The probability that the girl 'kept company' with other men had quite ceased to torment his imagination; it was no longer necessary to his happiness to be so certain about it that he might dismiss her from his mind. He could be as happy without it as with it, and he felt a new modesty over prying into her affairs. He was so little in a position to be stern with her that her assumption of his recognising a right in her to pull him to pieces seemed but a part of her perpetual clumsiness—a clumsiness that was not soothing, yet was nevertheless, in its rich spontaneity, one of the things he liked her for.

'If you've come to see me only to make low jokes at my expense you had better have stayed away altogether,' she said with dignity as they came out of the Green Park. 'In the first place it's rude, in the second place it's silly, and in the third place I see through you.'

'My dear Milly, the motions you go through, the resentment you profess, are all a kicking up of dust which I blow away with a breath,' her companion replied. 'But it doesn't matter; go on—say anything you like. I came to see you for recreation, to enjoy myself without effort of my own. I scarcely ventured to hope, however, that you'd make me laugh—I've been so dismal for a long time. In fact I'm dismal still. I wish I had your disposition. My mirth, as you see, is a bit feverish.'

'The first thing I require of any friend is that he should respect me,' Miss Henning announced. 'You lead a bad life. I know what to think about that,' she continued irrelevantly.

'And is it through respect for *you* that you wish me to lead a better one? To-day then is so much saved out of my wickedness. Let us get on the grass,' Hyacinth pursued; 'it's innocent and pastoral to feel it under one's feet. It's jolly to be with you. You understand everything.'

'I don't understand everything you say, but I understand everything you hide,' the young woman returned as the great central expanse of the Park, looking intensely green and browsable, stretched away before them.

'Then I shall soon become a mystery to you, for I mean from this time forth to cease to seek safety in concealment. You'll know nothing about me then—for it will be all under your nose.'

'Well, there's nothing so pretty as nature,' Millicent observed at a venture, surveying the smutty sheep who find pasturage in the fields that extend from Knightsbridge to the Bayswater Road. 'What will you do when you're so bad you can't go to the shop?' she added with a sudden transition. And when he asked why he should ever be so bad as that she said she could see he *was* in a fever: she hadn't noticed it at first because he never had had any more complexion than a cheese. Was it something he had caught in some of those back slums where he went prying about with his mad ideas? It served him right for taking as little good into such places as ever came out of them. Would his fine friends—a precious lot *they* were, that put it off on him to do all the nasty part!—would they find the doctor and the port wine and the money and all the rest when he was laid up, perhaps for months, through their putting such rot into his head and his putting it into others that could carry it even less? She stopped on the grass in the watery sunshine and bent on her companion a pair of eyes in which he noted afresh a stirred curiosity, a friendly reckless ray, a possibility of ardour, a pledge of really closer comradeship. Suddenly she brought out, quitting the tone of exaggerated derision she had employed a moment before: 'You precious little rascal, you've got something on your heart! Has your Princess given you the sack?'

'My poor girl, your talk's a queer mixture,' he resignedly sighed. 'But it may well be. It's not queerer than my life.'

'Well, I'm glad you admit that!' Milly cried as she walked on with a flutter of ribbons.

'Your ideas about my ideas!' Hyacinth wailed. 'Yes, you should see me in the back slums. I'm a bigger Philistine than you, Miss Henning.'

'You've got more ridiculous names, if that's what you mean. I don't believe you half the time know what you do mean yourself. I don't believe you even know with all your thinking what you do think. That's your disease.'

'It's astonishing how you sometimes put your finger on the place,' he now returned with interest. 'I mean to think no more—I mean to give it up. Avoid it yourself, dear friend—avoid it as you would a baleful vice. It confers no true happiness. Let us live in the world of irreflective contemplation—let us live in the present hour.'

'I don't care how I live nor where I live,' she cried, 'so long as I can do as I like. It's them that are over you—it's them that cut it fine! But you never were really satisfactory to me—not as one friend should be to another,' she pursued, reverting irresistibly to the concrete and turning still upon her companion that fine fairness which had no cause to shrink from a daylight exhibition. 'Do you remember that day I came back to the Plice, ever so long ago, and called on poor dear Miss Pynsent—she couldn't abide me, she never understood my form—and waited till you came in, and then went a walk with you and had tea at a coffee-shop? Well, I don't mind telling you that you weren't satisfactory to me even that night, and that I consider myself remarkably good-natured, ever since, to have kept you so little up to the mark. You always tried to carry it off as if you were telling one everything, and you never told me nothing at all.'

'What is it you want me to tell, my dear child?' Hyacinth freely fluted, putting his hand into her arm. 'I'll tell you anything in life you like.'

'I dare say you'll tell me no end of rot. Certainly I tried kindness on you,' Miss Henning declared.

'Try it again; don't give it up,' said her friend while he moved with her in close association.

She stopped short, detaching herself, though not with intention. 'Well then, *has* she clean chucked you?'

Hyacinth's eyes turned away; he looked at the green expanse, misty and sunny, dotted with Sunday-keeping figures which made it seem larger; at the wooded boundary of the Park, beyond the grassy moat of the Gardens; at a shining reach of the Serpentine on the one side and the far façades of Bayswater, brightened by the fine weather and the privilege of their view, on the other. 'Well, you know, I rather fancy it,' he replied in a moment.

'Ah the vile brute!' she rang out as they resumed their walk.

Upwards of an hour later they were sitting under the great trees of Kensington, those scattered, in the Gardens, over the slope which rises gently from the side of the water most distant from the old red palace. They had taken possession of a couple of the chairs placed there to the convenience of that superior part of the public for which a penny is not prohibitive, and Millicent, of whom such speculations were highly characteristic, had devoted considerable conjecture to the question of whether the functionary charged with collecting the penny would omit to come and demand his fee. Miss Henning liked to enjoy her pleasures *gratis* as well as to see others do so, and even that of sitting in a penny chair could touch her more deeply in proportion as she might feel she was 'doing' some vested interest by it. The man came round, however, and after that her pleasure could only take the form of sitting as long as possible, to recover her money. This issue had been met, and two or three others of a much weightier kind had come up. At the moment we again participate in them she was leaning forward, earnest and attentive, her hands clasped in her lap and her multitudinous silver bracelets tumbled forward on her thick wrists. Her face, with its parted lips and eyes clouded to gentleness, wore an expression Hyacinth had never seen there before and which caused him to say to her: 'After all, dear Milly, you're a sweet old boy!'

'Why did you never tell me before—years ago?' she asked.

'It's always soon enough to make a fool of one's self! I don't know why I've slobbered over to-day—sitting here in a charming place, in balmy air, amid pleasing suggestions and without any reason or practical end. The story's hideous and I've kept it down so long! It would have been an effort to me, an impossible effort at any time, to do otherwise. Somehow, just now it hasn't been an effort; and indeed I've spoken just *because* the air's sweet and the place ornamental and the day a holiday and your person so lovely and your presence so moving. All this has had the effect an object has if you plunge it into a cup of water—the water overflows. Only in my case it's not water, but a very foul liquid indeed. Pardon the bad odour!'

There had been a flush of excitement in Millicent's face while she listened to what had gone before; it lingered, and as a fine colour still further refined by an access of sensibility is never unbecoming to a handsome woman it enriched her unwonted expression. 'I wouldn't have been so rough with you,' she presently remarked.

'My dear lass, *this* isn't rough!' Hyacinth protested.

'You're all of a tremble.' She put out her hand and laid it on his own as if she had been a nurse feeling his pulse.

'Very likely. I'm a nervous little beast,' he said.

'Any one would be nervous to think of anything so awful. And when it's yourself!' The girl's manner represented the dreadfulness of such a contingency. 'You require sympathy,' she added in a tone that made him perversely grin; the words sounded like a medical prescription.

'A tablespoonful every half-hour.' And he kept her hand, which she was about to draw away.

'You'd have been nicer too,' Millicent went on.

'How do you mean, I'd have been nicer?'

'Well, I like you now,' said Miss Henning. And this time she drew away her hand as if, after such a speech, to recover her dignity.

'It's a pity I've always been so terribly under the influence of women,' Hyacinth sighed again as he folded his arms.

He was surprised at the delicacy with which she replied. 'You must remember they've a great deal to make up to you.'

'Do you mean for my mother? Ah *she*'d have made it up if they had let her! But the sex in general have been very nice to me,' he declared. 'It's wonderful the kindness they've shown me and the amount of pleasure I've derived from their society.'

It would perhaps be enquiring too closely to consider whether this reference to sources of consolation other than those that sprang from her own bosom had an irritating effect on Milly; she at all events answered it by presently saying: 'Does *she* know—your trumpery Princess?'

'Yes, but she doesn't mind it.'

'That's most uncommonly kind of her!' cried the girl with a scornful laugh.

'It annoys me very much,' he interposed—though still with detachment—'to hear you apply invidious epithets to her. You know nothing about her.'

'How do you know what I know, please?' She asked this

question with the habit of her natural pugnacity, but the next instant she dropped her voice as in remembrance of the appeal made by a great misfortune. 'Hasn't she treated you most shamefully, and you such a regular dear?'

'Not in the least. It is I who, as you may say, have rounded on her. She made my acquaintance because I was interested in the same things as herself. Her interest has continued, has increased, but mine, for some reason or other, has declined. She has been consistent and I've been beastly fickle.'

'Your interest in the Princess has declined?' Millicent questioned, following imperfectly this somewhat complicated statement.

'Oh dear, no. I mean only in some opinions I used to hold.' And he might have been speaking of 'shaky' shares, to a considerable amount, of which he had at a given moment shrewdly directed his broker to relieve him.

'Ay, when you thought everything should go to the lowest! That's a good job!'—and Miss Henning's laugh suggested that, after all, Hyacinth's views and the changes in his views were not what was most important. 'And your grand lady still goes in for the costermongers?'

'She wants to take hold of the great question of material misery; she wants to do something to make that misery less. I don't care for her means, I don't like her processes. But when I think of what there is to be done, and of the courage and devotion of those who set themselves to do it, it seems to me sometimes that with my reserves and scruples I'm a very poor creature.'

'You *are* a poor creature—to sit there and put such accusations on yourself!' the girl flashed out. 'If you haven't a spirit for yourself I promise I've got one for you! If she hasn't kicked you out why in the name of common sense did you say just now she has? And why is your dear old face as white as my stocking?'

Hyacinth looked at her a while without answering and as if he took a placid pleasure in her violence. 'I don't know —I don't understand.'

She put out her own hand now and took possession of his; for a minute she held it as wishing to check herself, as finding some influence in his touch that would help her. They sat in silence, looking at the ornamental water and the landscape-gardening reflected in it, till Milly turned her eyes again and brought out: 'Well, that's the way I'd have served him too!'

It took him a moment to perceive she was alluding to the vengeance wrought on Lord Frederick. 'Don't speak of that; you'll never again hear a word about it on my lips. It's all darkness.'

'I always knew you were a gentleman,' the girl went on with assurance.

'A queer variety, *cara mia*,' her companion rejoined—not very candidly, as we know the theories he himself had cultivated on this point. 'Of course you had heard poor Pinnie's wild maunderings. They used to exasperate me when she was alive, but I forgive her now. It's time I should, when I begin to talk myself. I think I'm breaking up.'

'Oh it wasn't Miss Pynsent; it was just yourself.'

'Pray what did I ever say—in those days?'

'It wasn't what you said,' she answered with refinement. 'I guessed the whole business—except of course what she got her time for and you being taken to that death-bed—the very day I came back to the Plice. Couldn't you see I was turning it over? And did I ever throw it up at you, whatever high words we might have had? Therefore what I say now is no more than I thought then. It only makes you nicer.'

She was crude, she was common, she even had the vice of pointless exaggeration, for he himself honestly couldn't understand how the situation he had described could make him nicer. But when the faculty of affection that was in her rose to the surface it diffused a glow of rest, almost of protection, deepening at any rate the luxury of their small cheap pastoral, the interlude in the grind of the week's work; so that though neither of them had dined he would have been delighted to sit with her there the whole after-

noon. It seemed a pause in something harsh that was hap-
pening to him, making it all easier, pushing it off to a distance. His thoughts hovered about that with a pertinacity
of which they themselves wearied, but they hung there now
with an ache of indifference. It would be too much, no
doubt, to say that Millicent's society appeared a compensation, yet he felt it at least a resource. For her too, evidently,
the time had a taste; she made no proposal to retrace their
steps. She questioned him about his father's family and as
to their letting him go on like that without ever holding out
so much as a little finger; and she declared in a manner that
was meant to gratify him by the indignation it conveyed,
though the awkwardness of the turn made him smile, that
if she had been one of such a bloated crew she should never
have been able to 'abear' the thought of a relation in such
a poor way. Hyacinth already knew what Miss Henning
thought of his business at old Crook's and of the feeble
show of a young man of his parts contented with a career
that was after all a mere getting of one's living by one's
'ands. He had to do with books, but so had any shop-boy
who should carry such articles to the residence of purchasers; and plainly Millicent had never discovered wherein
the art he practised differed from that of a plumber or a
saddler. He had not forgotten the shock once administered
to her by his letting her know he wore an apron; she looked
down on such conditions from her own so much higher
range, since *she* wore mantles and jackets and shawls and
the long trains of robes exhibited behind plate glass on
dummies of wire and drawn forth to be transferred to her
own undulating person, and had moreover never a scrap to
do with making them up, but just with talking about them
and showing them off and persuading people—people too
quite gaping with the impression—of their beauty and
cheapness. It had been a source of endless comfort to her,
in her arduous evolution, that she herself never worked with
her 'ands. Hyacinth answered her enquiries, as she had
answered his own of old, by asking her what 'his family'
owed to the son of a person who had brought murder and

mourning into their bright sublimities, and whether she thought he was very highly recommended to them. His question pulled her up a moment; after which she returned with the finest spirit: 'Well, if your position was so low ain't that all the more reason they should give you a lift? Oh it's something cruel!' she cried; and she added that in his place she would have found a way to bring herself under their notice. *She* wouldn't have drudged out her life in Soho if she had had the blood of half the Peerage in her veins! 'If they had noticed you they'd have liked you,' she was so good as to observe; but she immediately remembered also that in that case he would have been carried away quite over her head. She wasn't prepared to say that she would have given him up, little good as she had ever got of him. In that case he would have been thick with real swells, and she emphasised the 'real' by way of a thrust at the fine lady of Madeira Crescent—an artifice wasted, however, inasmuch as Hyacinth was sure she had extracted from Sholto a tolerably detailed history of the Princess. Millicent was tender and tenderly sportive, and he was struck with the fact that his base birth really made little impression on her: she accounted it an accident much less grave than he had been in the habit of doing. She was touched and moved, but what moved her was his story of his mother's dreadful revenge, her long imprisonment and his childish visit to the jail, with his later discovery of his peculiar footing in the world. These things produced in her a generous agitation—something the same in kind as the emotion she had occasionally owed to the perusal of the *Family Herald*. What affected her most and what she came back to was the whole element of Lord Frederick and the mystery of Hyacinth's having got so little good out of his affiliation to that nobleman. She couldn't get over his friends' not having done something, though her imagination was still vague as to what they might have done. It was the queerest thing in the world to find her apparently assuming that if he hadn't been so inefficient he might have 'worked' the whole dark episode as a source of distinction, of glory, of profit. *She* wouldn't have been a nobleman's daughter for nothing! Oh the left hand was as good as the right; her respectability, for the moment, made nothing of that! His long silence was what most astonished her; it put her out of patience, and there was a strange candour in her wonderment at his not having bragged about his ancestry. The generations representing it were vivid and concrete to her now in comparison with the timid shadows Pinnie had set into spasmodic circulation. Millicent bumped about in his hushed past with the oddest mixture of enthusiasm and criticism, and with good intentions which had the effect of profane voices bawling for sacred echoes.

'Me only—me and her? Certainly I ought to be obliged, even though it's late in the day. The first time you saw her I suppose you told her—that night you went into her box at the theatre, eh? She'd have worse to tell you, I'm sure, if she could ever bring herself to speak the proper truth. And do you mean to say you never broke it to your big friend in the chemical line?'

'No, we've never talked about it.'

'Men are rare creatures!' Millicent cried. 'You never so much as mentioned it?'

'It wasn't necessary. He knew it otherwise—he knew it through his sister.'

'How do you know that if he never spoke?'

'Oh because he was jolly good to me,' said Hyacinth.

'Well, I don't suppose that ruined him,' Miss Henning rejoined. 'And how did his sister know it?'

'Oh I don't know. She guessed it.'

The girl stared, then fairly snorted. 'It was none of her business.' Then she added: 'He *was* jolly good to you? Ain't he good to you now?' She asked this question in her loud free voice, which rang through the bright stillness of the place.

Hyacinth delayed for a minute to meet it, and when at last he did so it was without looking at her. 'I don't know. I can't make it out.'

'Well, I can then!' And she jerked him round toward her

and inspected him with her big bright eyes. 'You silly baby, has *he* been serving you?' She pressed her curiosity upon him; she asked if that was what disagreed with him. His lips gave her no answer, but apparently after an instant she found one in his face. 'Has he been making up to her Serene Highness—is that his game?' she broke out. 'Do you mean to say she'd look at the likes of him?'

'The likes of him? He's as fine a man as stands!' said Hyacinth. 'They've the same views, they're doing the same work.'

'Oh, he hasn't changed *his* opinions then—not like you?'

'No, he knows what he wants; he knows what he thinks.'

'Very much the "same work", I'll be bound!' cried Millicent in large derision. 'He knows what he wants, and I dare say he'll get it.'

He was now on his feet, turning away from her; but she also rose and passed her hand into his arm. 'It's their own business; they can do as they please.'

'Oh don't try to be a blamed saint; you put me out of patience!' the girl responded with characteristic energy. 'They're a precious pair, and it would do me good to hear you say so.'

'A man shouldn't turn against his friends,' he went on with desperate sententiousness.

'That's for them to remember; there's no danger of *your* forgetting it.' They had begun to walk but she stopped him; she was suddenly smiling at him and her face was radiant. She went on with caressing inconsequence: 'All you've terribly told me—it *has* made you nicer.'

'I don't see that, but it has certainly made *you* so. My dear girl, you're a comfort,' Hyacinth added as they moved further. Soon after which, the protection offered by the bole of a great tree being sufficiently convenient, he had, on a large look about them, passed his arm round her and drawn her closer and closer—so close that as they again paused together he felt her yield with a fine firmness, as it were, and with the full mass of her interest.

XLII

HE HAD no intention of going later on to Madeira Crescent, and that is why he asked her before they separated if he mightn't see her again after tea. The evenings were bitter to him now and he feared them in advance. The darkness had become a haunted element; it had visions for him that passed even before his closed eyes—sharp doubts and fears and suspicions, suggestions of evil, revelations of pain. He wanted company to lighten up his gloom, and this had driven him back to Millicent in a manner not altogether consistent with the respect which it was still his theory that he owed to his nobler part. He felt no longer free to drop in at the Crescent and tried to persuade himself, in case his mistrust should be overdone, that his reasons were reasons of magnanimity. If Paul were seriously occupied with the Princess, if they had work in hand for which their most earnest attention was required (and Sunday was all likely to be the day they would take: they had spent so much of the previous Sunday together) his absence would have the superior, the marked motive of his leaving his friend a clear field. There was something inexpressibly representative to him in the way that friend had abruptly decided to re-enter the house, after pausing outside with its mistress, at the moment he himself stood glaring through the fog with the Prince. The movement repeated itself innumerable times to his inward sense, suggesting to him things he couldn't bear to learn. Hyacinth was afraid of being jealous even after he had become so, and to prove to himself he was not he had gone to see the Princess one evening in the middle of the week. Hadn't he wanted Paul to know her months and months before, and was he now to entertain a vile feeling at the first manifestation of an intimacy which rested, in each party to it, on aspirations that he respected? The Princess had not been at home, and he had turned away from the door without asking for Madame Grandoni: he had not forgotten that on the occasion of his previous visit she had excused herself from staying below. After the little maid in the Crescent had told him her mistress was out he walked away with a quick curiosity—a curiosity which, if he had listened to it, would have led him to mount the first omnibus that travelled in the direction of Camberwell. Was Paul Muniment, he such a rare one in general for stopping at home of an evening, was he also out, and would Rosy in this case be in the humour to mention—for of course she would know—where he had gone? Hyacinth let the omnibus pass, for he suddenly became aware with a rueful pang that he was in danger of playing the spy. He had not been near Muniment since, on purpose to leave his curiosity unsatisfied. He allowed himself however to notice that the Princess had now not written him a word of consolation, as she had been kind enough to do in the old days when he had knocked at her door without finding her. At present he had missed her twice in succession, and yet she had given no sign of regret—regret even on his own behalf. This determined him to stay away a bit longer; it was such a proof that she was absorbingly occupied. Hyacinth's glimpse of her in earnest talk with her friend—or rather with his—as they returned from the excursion described by the Prince, his memory of Paul's beguiled figure crossing the threshold once more, could leave him no doubt as to the degree of that absorption.

Milly meanwhile hung back a little when he proposed to her that they should finish the day together. She smiled indeed and her splendid eyes rested on his with an air of indulgent wonder; they seemed to ask if it were worth her pains, in face of his probable incredulity, to mention the *real* reason why she couldn't have the pleasure of acceding to his delightful pressure. Since he would be sure to deride her explanation wouldn't some trumped-up excuse do as well, something he could knock about without hurting her? We are not to know exactly in what sense Miss Henning decided; but she confessed at last that there *was* an odious

obstacle to their meeting again later—a promise she had
made to go and see a young lady, the forewoman of her
department, who was kept indoors with a bad face and
nothing in life to help her pass the time. She was under a
pledge to spend the evening with her, and it was not in her
nature to fail of such a charity. Hyacinth made no comment
on this speech; he received it in silence, looking at the girl
gloomily.

'I know what's passing in your mind!' Millicent suddenly
broke out. 'Why don't you say it at once and give me a
chance to contradict it? I oughtn't to care, but I do care!'

'Stop, stop—don't let us fight!' He spoke in a tone of
pleading weariness; she had never heard just that accent
before.

Millicent just considered: 'I've a mind to play her false.
She's a real lady, highly connected, and the best friend I
have—I don't count men,' she sarcastically sniffed—'and
there isn't one in the world I'd do such a thing for but you.'

'No, keep your promise; don't play any one false,' said
Hyacinth.

'Well, you *are* a gentleman!' she returned with a sweetness
her voice occasionally took.

'Especially——'Hyacinth began; but he suddenly stopped.

'Especially what? Something impudent, I'll engage! Especially as you don't believe me?'

'Oh no! Don't let's fight!' he repeated.

'Fight, my darling? I'd fight *for* you!' Miss Henning
declared.

He offered himself after tea the choice between a visit to
Lady Aurora and a pilgrimage to Lisson Grove. He was a
little in doubt about the former experiment, having an
idea her ladyship's family might be reinstalled in Belgrave
Square. He reflected, however, that he couldn't recognise
this as a reason for not going to see her; his relations with
her had nothing of the underhand, and she had given him
the kindest general invitation. If her haughty parents were
at home she was probably at dinner with them: he would
take that risk. He had taken it before without disastrous

results. He was determined not to spend the evening alone, and he would keep the Poupins as a more substantial alternative in case Lady Aurora shouldn't be able to receive him.

As soon as the great portal in Belgrave Square was drawn open before him he saw the house was occupied and animated—if animation might be talked about in a place which had hitherto mainly answered to his idea of a magnificent mausoleum. It was pervaded by subdued light and tall domestics; he found himself looking down a kind of colonnade of colossal footmen, an array more imposing even than the retinue of the Princess at Medley. His enquiry died away on his lips and he stood there struggling with dumbness. It was manifest to him that some high festival was taking place, a scene on which his presence could only be a blot; and when a large official, out of livery, bending over him for a voice that didn't issue, suggested, not unencouragingly, that it might be Lady Aurora he wished to see, he replied with detachment and despair: 'Yes, yes, but it can't be possible!' The butler took no pains to controvert this proposition verbally; he merely turned round with a majestic air of leading the way, and as at the same moment two of the footmen closed the wings of the door behind the visitor Hyacinth judged it his cue to follow. In this manner, after crossing a passage where, in the perfect silence of the servants, he heard the shorter click of his plebeian shoes upon a marble floor, he found himself ushered into a small room, lighted by a veiled lamp, which, when he had been left there alone, without further remark on the part of his conductor, he recognised as the place—only now more amply decorated—of one of his former interviews. Lady Aurora kept him waiting a little, but finally fluttered in with an anxious incoherent apology. The same transformation had taken place in her own aspect as in that of her parental halls: she had on a light-coloured, crumpled-looking, faintly-rustling dress; her head was adorned with a languid plume that flushed into little pink tips, and in her hand she carried a pair of white gloves. All her repressed eagerness was in her face, and she smiled as if wishing to anticipate any scruples or embarrassments on the part of her visitor; frankly admitting herself disguised and bedizened and the shock the fact might convey. Hyacinth said to her that, no doubt, on inferring the return of her family to town, he ought to have backed out; he knew this must make a difference in her life. But he had been marched in, for all his protest, and now it was clear he had interrupted her at dinner. She answered that no one who asked for her at any hour was ever turned away; she had managed to arrange that and was very happy in her success. She didn't usually dine—there were so many of them and it took so long. Most of her friends couldn't come at visiting-hours and it wouldn't be right she shouldn't ever receive them. On that occasion she *had* been dining, but it was all over; she was only sitting there because she was going to a party. Her parents were dining out and she was just in the drawing-room with some of her sisters. When they were alone it wasn't so long, though it was rather long afterwards, when they went up again. It wasn't time yet: the carriage wouldn't come for nearly half an hour. She hadn't been to an evening thing for months and months, but—didn't he know?—one sometimes had to do it. Lady Aurora expressed the idea that one ought to be fair all round and that one's duties were not all of the same species; some of them would come up from time to time that were quite different from the others. Of course it wasn't just unless one did all, and that was why she was in for something to-night. It was nothing of consequence; only the family meeting the family, as they might do of a Sunday, at one of their houses. It was there that papa and mamma were dining. Since they had given her that room for any hour she wanted—it was really tremendously convenient— she had resolved to do a party now and then, like a respectable young woman, because it pleased them: though why it should create even that thrill to see *her* at a place was more than she could imagine. She supposed it was because it would perhaps keep some people, a little, from thinking she was mad and not safe to be at large—which was of course a sort of thing that people didn't like to have thought of their belongings. Lady Aurora explained and expatiated with a kind of yearning superabundance; she talked more continuously than Hyacinth had ever heard her do before, and the young man made out that she was not, so to speak, in equilibrium. He thought it scarcely probable she was excited by the simple prospect of again dipping into the great world she had forsworn, and he soon became aware of his having himself in a manner upset her. His senses were fine enough to hint to him that there were associations and wounds he revived and quickened. She suddenly stopped talking and the two sat there looking at each other in an odd, an occult community of suffering. He made mechanical remarks, explaining insufficiently why he had come, and in the course of a very few moments, quite independently of these observations, it seemed to him there was a deeper, a measurelessly deep, confidence between them. A tacit confession passed and repassed, and each understood the situation of the other. They wouldn't speak of it—it was very definite they would never do that; for there was something in their common consciousness that was inconsistent with the grossness of accusation. Besides, the grievance of each was an apprehension, an instinct of the soul—not a sharp definite wrong supported by proof. It was in the air and in their restless pulses, and not in anything they could exhibit or complain of for comfort. Strange enough it seemed to him that the history of each should be the counterpart of that of the other. What had each done but lose that which he or she had never so much as had? Things had gone ill with them; but even if they had gone well, even if the Princess had not combined with his friend in that manner which made his heart sink and produced an effect exactly corresponding on Lady Aurora's—even in this case what would felicity, what would success, have amounted to? They would have been very barren. He was sure the singular creature before him would never have had a chance to take the unprecedented social step for the sake of which she was ready to go forth from Belgrave Square for ever; Hyacinth had judged the smallness of Paul Muniment's appetite for that complication sufficiently to have begun really to pity her ladyship long ago. And now, even when he most felt the sweetness of her sympathy, he might wonder what she could have imagined for him in the event of his not having been supplanted— what security, what completer promotion, what honourable, satisfying sequel. They were unhappy because they were unhappy, and they were right not to rail about that.

'Oh I like to see you—I like to talk with you,' she said simply. They talked for a quarter of an hour, and he made her such a visit as any clever gentleman might have made any gentle lady. They exchanged remarks about the lateness of the spring, about the loan-exhibition at Burlington House —which Hyacinth had paid his shilling to see—about the question of opening the museums on Sunday, about the danger of too much coddling legislation on behalf of the working classes. He declared that it gave him great pleasure to catch any sign of her amusing herself; it was unnatural never to do that, and he hoped that now she had taken a turn she would keep it up. At this she looked down, smiling, at her frugal finery and then she said: 'I dare say I shall begin to go to balls—who knows?'

'That's what our friends in Audley Court think, you know—that it's the worst mistake you can make not to drink deep of the cup while you have it.'

'Oh I'll do it then—I'll do it for *them*!' Lady Aurora exclaimed. 'I dare say that, as regards all that, I haven't listened to them enough.' This was the only allusion that passed on the subject of the Muniments.

Hyacinth got up, he had stayed long enough, since she was going out; and as he put forth his hand to her she seemed to him a heroine. She would try to cultivate the pleasures of her class if the brother and sister in Camberwell thought it right—try even to be a woman of fashion in order to console herself. Paul Muniment didn't care for her, but she was capable of considering that it might be her duty to regulate her life by the very advice that made an abyss be- tween them. Hyacinth didn't believe in the success of this attempt; there passed before his imagination a picture of the poor lady coming home and pulling off her feathers for evermore after an evening spent watching the agitation of a ballroom from the outer edge of the circle and with a white, irresponsive face. 'Let us eat and drink, for to-morrow we die,' he said, laughing.

'Oh I don't mind dying.'

'I think I do,' Hyacinth declared as he turned away. There had been no mention whatever of the Princess.

It was early enough in the evening for him to risk a visit to Lisson Grove; he calculated that the Poupins would still be sitting up. When he reached their house he found this calculation justified; the brilliancy of the light in the window appeared to announce that Madame was holding a salon. He ascended to this apartment without delay—it was free to a visitor to open the house-door himself—and, having knocked, he obeyed the hostess's invitation to enter. Poupin and his wife were seated, with a third person, at a table in the middle of the room, round a staring kerosene lamp adorned with a globe of clear glass, of which the transparency was mitigated only by a circular pattern of bunches of grapes. The third person was his friend Schinkel, who had been a member of the little party that had waited that wet black night upon Hoffendahl. No one said anything as he came in; but in their silence the three others got up, looking at him, he thought, as he had on occasion imagined his being looked at before, only never quite so unmistakeably.

BOOK SIXTH

XLIII

'My child, you're always welcome,' said Eustache Poupin, taking Hyacinth's hand in both his own and holding it for some moments. An impression had come to our young man, immediately, that they were talking about him before he appeared and that they would rather have been left to talk at their ease. He even thought he saw in Poupin's face the kind of consciousness that comes from detection, or at least interruption, in a nefarious act. With Poupin, however, it was difficult to tell; he always looked so heated and exalted, so like a conspirator defying the approach of justice. Hyacinth took in the others: they were standing as if they had shuffled something on the table out of sight, as if they had been engaged in the manufacture of counterfeit coin. Poupin kept hold of his hand; the Frenchman's ardent eyes, fixed, unwinking, always expressive of the greatness of the occasion, whatever the occasion was, had never seemed to him to protrude so far from the head. 'Ah my dear friend, *nous causions justement de vous*,' Eustache remarked as if this were a very extraordinary fact.

'Oh *nous causions, nous causions*——!' his wife exclaimed as if to deprecate a loose overstatement. 'One may mention a friend, I suppose, in the way of conversation, without taking such a liberty.'

'A cat may look at a king, as your English proverb says,' added Schinkel jocosely. He smiled so hard at his own pleasantry that his eyes closed up and vanished—an effect which Hyacinth, who had observed it before, thought particularly unbecoming to him, appearing as it did to administer the last perfection to his ugliness. He would have consulted his facial interests by cultivating blankness.

'Oh a king, a king——!' Poupin demurred, shaking his head up and down. 'That's what it's not good to be, *au point où nous en sommes*.'

567

'I just came in to wish you good-night,' said Hyacinth. 'I'm afraid it's rather late for a call, though Schinkel doesn't seem to think so.'

'It's always too late, *mon très-cher*, when you come,' the Frenchman returned. 'You know if you've a place at our fireside.'

'I esteem it too much to disturb it,' said Hyacinth smiling and looking round at the three.

'We can easily sit down again; we're a comfortable party. Put yourself beside me.' And the Frenchman drew a chair close to the one, at the table, that he had just quitted.

'He has had a long walk, he's tired—he'll certainly accept a little glass,' Madame Poupin pronounced with decision as she moved toward the tray containing the small gilded service of liqueurs.

'We'll each accept one, *ma bonne*; it's a very good occasion for a drop of *fine*,' her husband interposed while Hyacinth seated himself in the chair marked by his host. Schinkel resumed his place, which was opposite; he looked across at the new visitor without speaking, but his long face continued to flatten itself into a representation of mirth. He had on a green coat which Hyacinth had seen before; this was a garment of ceremony, such as our young man judged it would have been impossible to procure in London or in any modern time. It was eminently German and of high antiquity, and had a tall stiff clumsy collar which came up to the wearer's ears and almost concealed his perpetual bandage. When Hyacinth had sat down Eustache Poupin remained out of his own chair and stood beside him resting a hand on his head. At this touch something came over Hyacinth that brought his heart into his throat. The possibility that occurred to him, conveyed in Poupin's whole manner as well as in the reassuring intention of his caress and in his wife's instant uneasy offer of refreshment, explained the confusion of the circle and reminded our hero of the engagement he had taken with himself to live up to a grand conception of the quiet when a certain crisis in his fate should have arrived. It struck him this crisis was in the air, very near—that he should touch it if he made another movement: the pressure of the Frenchman's hand, which was meant as an attenuation, only worked as a warning. As he looked across at Schinkel he felt dizzy and a little sick; for a moment, to his senses, the room whirled round. His resolution to be quiet appeared only too easy to keep; he couldn't break it even to the extent of speaking. He knew his voice would tremble, and this was why he made no answer to Schinkel's rather honeyed words, uttered after an hesitation. '*Also*, my dear Robinson, have you passed your Sunday well—have you had an 'appy day?' Why was every one so treacherously mild? His eyes questioned the table, but encountered only its well-wiped surface, polished for so many years by the gustatory elbows of the Frenchman and his wife, and the lady's dirty pack of cards for 'patience'—she had apparently been engaged in this little exercise when Schinkel came in—which indeed gave a little the impression of startled gamblers who might have shuffled away the stakes. Madame Poupin, diving into a cupboard, came back with a bottle of green chartreuse, an apparition which led the German to exclaim: '*Lieber Gott*, you Vrench, you Vrench, how well you always arrange! What on earth would you have more?'

The hostess distributed the liquor, but our youth could take none of it down, leaving it to the high appreciation of his friends. His indifference to this luxury excited discussion and conjecture, the others bandying theories and contradictions and even ineffectual jokes about him over his head—all with a volubility that seemed to him unnatural. For Poupin and Schinkel there was something all wrong with a man who couldn't smack his lips over a drop of that tap; he must either be in love or have some still more insidious complaint. It was true Hyacinth *was* always in love—that was no secret to his friends; but it had never been observed to stop his thirst. The Frenchwoman poured scorn on this view of the case, declaring that the effect of the tender passion was to make one enjoy one's victual—when everything went straight, *bien entendu*; and how could an ear be deaf to the wily words of a person so taking?—in proof of which she deposed that she had never eaten and drunk with such relish as at the time (oh far away now) when she had a soft spot in her heart for her rascal of a husband. For Madame Poupin to allude to the companion of her trials as a rascal indicated a high degree of conviviality. Hyacinth sat staring at the empty table with the feeling that he was somehow a detached irresponsible witness of the evolution of his doom. Finally he looked up and said to his mates collectively: 'What's up and what the deuce is the matter with you all?' He followed this enquiry by a request they would tell him what it was they had been saying about him, since they admitted he had been the subject of their talk. Madame Poupin answered for them that they had simply been saying how much they loved him, but that they wouldn't love him any more if he became suspicious and *grincheux*. She had been telling Mr Schinkel's fortune on the cards and she would tell Hyacinth's if he liked. There was nothing much for Mr Schinkel, only that he would find something some day that he had lost, but would probably lose it again, and serve him right if he did! He had objected that he had never had anything to lose and never expected to have; but that was a vain remark, inasmuch as the time was fast coming when every one would have something—though indeed it was to be hoped Schinkel would keep it when he had got it. Eustache rebuked his wife for her levity, reminded her that their young friend cared nothing for old women's tricks, and said he was sure Hyacinth had come to talk over a very different matter: the question—he was so good as to take an interest in it, as he had done in everything that related to them—of the terms which M. Poupin might owe it to himself, to his dignity, to a just though not exaggerated sentiment of his value, to make in accepting Mr 'Crook's' offer of the foremanship of the establishment in Soho; an offer not yet formally enunciated but visibly in the air and destined—it would seem at least—to arrive within a day or two. The actual old titulary was going, late in the day, to set up for himself. The Frenchman intimated that before

accepting any such proposal he must have the most substantial guarantees. '*Il me faudrait des conditions très-parti-
culières.*' It was strange to Hyacinth to hear M. Poupin talk
so comfortably about these high contingencies, the chasm
by which he himself was divided from the future having
suddenly doubled its width. His host and hostess sat down
on either side of him, and Poupin gave a sketch, in somewhat sombre tints, of the situation in Soho, enumerating
certain elements of decomposition which he perceived to be
at work there and which he would not undertake to deal
with unless he should be given a completely free hand. Did
Schinkel understand—and if so what was he grinning at?
Did Schinkel understand that poor Eustache was the victim
of an absurd hallucination and that there was not the
smallest chance of his being invited to assume a lieutenancy?
He had less capacity for tackling the British workman to-day
than on originally beginning to rub shoulders with him, and
old Crook had never in his life made a mistake, at least in
the use of his tools. Hyacinth's responses were few and
mechanical, and he presently ceased to try and look as if
he were entering into his host's ideas.

'You've some news—you've some news about me,' he
brought out abruptly to Schinkel. 'You don't like it, you
don't like to have to give it to me, and you came to ask our
friends here if they wouldn't help you out with it. But I
don't think they'll assist you particularly, poor dears! Why
do you mind? You oughtn't to mind more than I do. That
isn't the way.'

'*Qu'est-ce qu'il dit—qu'est-ce qu'il dit, le pauvre chéri?*'
Madame Poupin demanded eagerly; while Schinkel looked
very hard at her husband and as to ask for wise direction.

'My dear child, *vous vous faites des idées!*' the latter
exclaimed, again laying his hand on his young friend all
soothingly.

But Hyacinth pushed away his chair and got up. 'If you've
anything to tell me it's cruel of you to let me see it as you've
done and yet not satisfy me.'

'Why should I have anything to tell you?' Schinkel almost whined.

'I don't know that—yet I believe you have. I make out things, I guess things quickly. That's my nature at all times, and I do it much more now.'

'You do it indeed; it's very wonderful,' Schinkel feebly conceded.

'Mr Schinkel, will you do me the pleasure to go away— I don't care where: out of this house?' Madame Poupin broke out in French.

'Yes, that will be the best thing, and I'll go with you,' said Hyacinth.

'If you'd retire, my child, I think it would be a service that you'd render us,' Poupin returned appealing to him as with indulgence for his temper. 'Won't you do us the justice to believe you may leave your interests in our hands?'

Hyacinth earnestly debated; it was now perfectly clear to him that Schinkel had some sort of message for him, and his curiosity as to what it might be had become nearly intolerable. 'I'm surprised at your weakness,' he observed as sternly as he could manage it to Poupin.

The Frenchman stared at him and then fell on his neck. 'You're sublime, my young friend—you're truly sublime!'

'Will you be so good as to tell me what you're going to do with that young man?' demanded Madame Poupin with a glare at Schinkel.

'It's none of your business, my poor lady,' Hyacinth replied, disengaging himself from her husband. 'Schinkel, I wish you'd just walk away with me.'

'*Calmons-nous, entendons-nous, expliquons-nous!* The situation's very simple,' Poupin went on.

'I'll go with you if it will give you pleasure,' said Schinkel very obligingly to Hyacinth.

'Then you'll give me that letter, the sealed one, first!' Madame Poupin, erecting herself, declared to the German.

'My wife, you're *bien sotte*!' Poupin groaned, lifting his hands and shoulders and turning away.

'I may be anything you like, but I won't be a party—no,

God help me, not to that!' the good woman protested, planted before Schinkel as to prevent his moving.

'If you've a letter for me you ought to give it to me, hang you!' said Hyacinth to Schinkel. 'You've no right to give it to any one else.'

'I'll bring it to you in your house, my good friend,' Schinkel replied with a vain public wink which seemed to urge how Madame Poupin must be considered.

'Oh in his house—*I*'ll go to his house!' this lady cried. 'I regard you, I've always regarded you, as my child,' she continued to Hyacinth, 'and if this isn't an occasion for a mother——!'

'It's you who are making it an occasion. I don't know what you're talking about,' said Hyacinth. He had been questioning Schinkel's face and believed he found in it a queer convulsed but honest appeal to depend on him. 'I've disturbed you and I think I had better go away.'

Poupin had turned round again; he seized the young man's arm eagerly, as to prevent his retiring without taking in his false position. 'How can you care when you know everything's changed?'

'What do you mean—everything's changed?'

'Your opinions, your sympathies, your whole attitude. I don't approve of it—*je le constate*. You've withdrawn your confidence from the people; you've said things on this spot, where you stand now, that have given pain to my wife and me.'

'If we didn't love you we should say you had madly betrayed us!'—she quickly took her husband's idea.

'Oh I shall never madly betray you,' Hyacinth rather languidly smiled.

'You'll never hand us over—of course you think so. But you've no right to act for the people when you've ceased to believe in the people. *Il faut être conséquent, nom de Dieu!*' Poupin went on.

'You'll give up all thoughts of acting for me—*je ne permets pas ça!*' grandly added his wife.

'The thing's probably not of importance—only a little word of consideration,' Schinkel suggested soothingly.

'We repudiate you, we deny you, we denounce you!' shouted Poupin with magnificent heat.

'My poor friends, it's you who have broken down, not I,' said Hyacinth. 'I'm much obliged to you for your solicitude, but the inconsequence is yours. At all events good-night.'

He turned away from them and was leaving the room when Madame Poupin threw herself upon him as her husband had done a moment before, but in silence and with an extraordinary force of passion and distress. Being stout and powerful she quickly got the better of him and pressed him to her ample bosom in a long, dumb embrace.

'I don't know what you want me to do,' he said as soon as he could speak. 'It's for me to judge of my convictions.'

'We want you to do nothing, because we *know* you've changed,' Poupin insisted. 'Doesn't it stick out of you, in every glance of your eye and every breath of your lips? It's only for that, because that alters everything.'

'Does it alter my sacred vow? There are some things in which one can't change. I didn't promise to believe; I promised to obey.'

'We want you to be sincere—that's the great thing,' Poupin edifyingly urged. 'I'll go to see them—I'll make them understand.'

'Ah you should have done that before!' his poor wife flashed.

'I don't know who you're talking about, but I'll allow no one to meddle in my affairs.' Hyacinth spoke now with vehemence; the scene was cruel to his nerves, which were not in a condition to bear it.

'When it's a case of Hoffendahl it's no good to meddle,' Schinkel gravely contributed.

'And pray who's Hoffendahl and what authority has *he* got?' demanded Madame Poupin, who had caught his meaning. 'Who has put him over us all, and is there nothing to do but to lie down in the dust before him? Let him attend to his little affairs himself and not put them off on innocent children, no matter whether the poor dears are with us or against us.'

This protest went so far that Poupin clearly felt bound to recover a dignity. 'He has no authority but what we give him; but you know how we respect him and that he's one of the pure, *ma bonne*. Hyacinth can do exactly as he likes; he knows that as well as we do. He knows there's not a feather's weight of compulsion; he knows that for my part I long ago ceased to expect anything of him.'

'Certainly there's no compulsion,' said Schinkel. 'It's to take or to leave. Only *they* keep the books.'

Hyacinth stood there before the three with his eyes on the floor. 'Of course I can do as I like, and what I like is what I *shall* do. Besides, what are we talking about with such passion?' he asked, looking up. 'I've no summons, I've no sign, I've no order. When the call reaches me it will be time to discuss it. Let it come or not come: it's not my affair.'

'*Ganz gewiss*, it's not your affair,' said Schinkel.

'I can't think why M. Paul has never done anything, all this time, knowing that everything's different now!' Madame Poupin threw in.

'Yes, my dear boy, I don't understand our friend,' her husband remarked, watching Hyacinth with suspicious contentious eyes.

'It's none of his business any more than ours; it's none of any one's business!' Schinkel earnestly opined.

'Muniment walks straight; the best thing you can do is to imitate him,' said Hyacinth, trying to pass Poupin, who had placed himself before the door.

'Promise me only this—not to do anything till I've seen you first,' the Frenchman almost piteously begged.

'My poor old friend, you're very weak.' And Hyacinth opened the door in spite of him and passed out.

'Ah well, if you *are* with us that's all I want to know!' the young man heard him call from the top of the stairs in a different voice, a tone of sudden extravagant fortitude.

XLIV

HYACINTH HAD hurried down and got out of the house, but without the least intention of losing sight of Schinkel. The odd behaviour of the Poupins was a surprise and annoyance, and he had wished to shake himself free from it. He was candidly astonished at the alarm they were so good as to feel for him, since he had never taken in their having really gone round to the faith that the note he had signed to Hoffendahl would fail to be presented. What had he said, what had he done, after all, to give them the right to fasten on him the charge of apostasy? He had always been a free critic of everything, and it was natural that on certain occasions in the little parlour at Lisson Grove he should have spoken in accordance with that freedom; but it was with the Princess alone that he had permitted himself really to rail at their grimy 'inferiors' and give the full measure of his scepticism. He would have thought it indelicate to express contempt for the opinions of his old foreign friends, to whom associations that made them venerable were attached; and moreover for Hyacinth a change of heart was in the nature of things much more an occasion for a hush of publicity and a kind of retrospective reserve: it couldn't prompt one to aggression or jubilation. When one had but lately discovered what could be said on the opposite side one didn't want to boast of one's sharpness—not even when one's new convictions cast shadows that looked like the ghosts of the old.

He lingered in the street a certain distance from the house, watching for Schinkel's exit and prepared to remain there if necessary till the dawn of another day. He had said to the agitated trio just before that the manner in which the communication they looked so askance at should reach him was none of his business—it might reach him as it either smoothly or clumsily could. This was true enough in theory, but in fact his desire was overwhelming to know what Madame Poupin had meant by her allusion to a sealed letter, destined for him, in Schinkel's possession—an allusion confirmed by Schinkel's own virtual acknowledgement. It was indeed this eagerness that had driven him out of the house, for he had reason to believe the German wouldn't fail him, and it galled his suspense to see the foolish Poupins try to interpose, to divert the missive from its course. He waited and waited in the faith that Schinkel was dealing with them in his slow categorical Germanic way, and only reprehended him for having in the first place paltered with his sacred trust. Why hadn't he come straight to him—whatever the mysterious document was—instead of talking it over with French featherheads? Passers were rare at this hour in Lisson Grove and lights mainly extinguished; there was nothing to look at but the vista of the low black houses, the dim interspaced street-lamps, the prowling cats who darted occasionally across the road and the terrible mysterious far-off stars, which appeared to him more than ever to see everything of our helplessness and tell nothing of help. A policeman creaked along on the opposite side of the way, looking across at him as he passed, and stood for some minutes on the corner as to keep an eye on him. Hyacinth had leisure to reflect that the day was perhaps not far off when a policeman might have an eye on him for a very good reason—might walk up and down, pass and repass as he mounted guard on him.

It seemed horribly long before Schinkel came out of the house, but it was probably only half an hour. In the stillness of the street he heard Poupin let his visitor out, and at the sound he stepped back into the recess of a doorway on the same side, so that in looking out the Frenchman shouldn't see him waiting. There was another delay, for the two stood talking together interminably and without seizable sounds on the doorstep. At last however Poupin went in again, and then Schinkel came down the street toward Hyacinth, who had felt sure he would proceed to that quarter, it being, as our young friend happened to know, that of his habitation.

After he had heard Poupin go in he stopped and looked up and down; it was evidently his idea that Hyacinth would be awaiting him. Our hero stepped out of the shallow recess in which he had flattened himself, and came straight to him, and the two men stood there face to face in the dusky empty sordid street.

'You didn't let them have the letter?'

'Oh no, I retained it,' said Schinkel with his eyes more than ever like invisible points.

'Then hadn't you better give it to me?'

'We'll talk of that—we'll talk.' Schinkel made no motion to satisfy him; having his hands in the pockets of his trousers and an appearance marked by the exasperating assumption that they had the whole night before them. As one of the 'dangerous' he was too intolerably for order.

'Why should we talk? Haven't you talked enough with those people all the evening? What have they to say about it? What right have you to detain a letter that belongs to me?'

'*Erlauben Sie:* I'll light my pipe,' the German simply returned. And he proceeded to this business methodically, while Hyacinth's pale excited face showed in the glow of the match that ignited on the rusty railing beside them. 'It isn't yours unless I've given it you,' Schinkel went on as they walked along. 'Be patient and I'll tell you,' he added, passing his hand into his comrade's arm. 'Your way, not so? We'll go down toward the Park.' Hyacinth tried to be patient and listened with interest when Schinkel added: 'She tried to take it; she atacked me with her hands. But that wasn't what I went for, to give it up.'

'Is she mad? I don't recognise them'—and Hyacinth spoke as one scandalised.

'No, but they lofe you.'

'Why then do they try to disgrace me?'

'They think it no disgrace if you've changed.'

'That's very well for her; but it's pitiful for him, and I declare it surprises me.'

'Oh *he* came round—he helped me to resist. He pulled his wife off. It was the first shock,' said Schinkel.

'You oughtn't to have shocked them, my dear fellow,' Hyacinth pronounced.

'I was shocked myself—I couldn't help it.'

'Lord, how shaky you all are!' He was more and more aware now of the superiority still left him to cling to.

'You take it well. I'm very sorry. But it is a fine chance,' Schinkel went on, smoking away.

His pipe seemed for the moment to absorb him, so that after a silence Hyacinth resumed:

'Be so good as to remember that all this while I don't in the least understand what you're talking about.'

'Well, it was this morning, early,' said the German. 'You know in my country we don't lie in bett late, and what they do in my country I try to do everywhere. I think it's good enough. In winter I get up of course long before the sun, and in summer I get up almost at the same time. I should see the fine picture of the sunrise if in London you *could* see. The first thing I do of a Sunday is to smoke a pipe at my window, which is at the front, you remember, and looks into a little dirty street. At that hour there's nothing to see there—you English are so slow to leave the bett. Not much, however, at any time; it's not important, my bad little street. But my first pipe's the one I enjoy most. I want nothing else when I have that pleasure. I look out at the new fresh light—though in London it's not very fresh—and I think it's the beginning of another day. I wonder what such a day will bring—if it will bring anything good to us poor devils. But I've seen a great many pass and nothing has come. This morning, *doch*, brought something—something at least to you. On the other side of the way I saw a young man who stood just opposite my house and looking up at my window. He looked at me straight, without any ceremony, and I smoked my pipe and looked at him. I wondered what he wanted, but he made no sign and spoke no word. He was a very neat young man; he had an umbrella and he wore spectacles. We remained that way, face to face, perhaps for a quarter of an hour, and at last he took out his watch—he had a watch too—and held it in his hand, just glancing at it every few minutes, as if to let me know that he would rather not give me the whole day. Then it came over me that he wanted to speak to me! You would have guessed that before, but we good Germans are slow. When we understand, however, we act; so I nodded at him to let him know I'd come down. I put on my coat and my shoes, for I was only in my shirt and stockings—though of course I had on my trousers—and I went down into the street. When he saw me come he walked slowly away, but at the end of a little distance he waited for me. When I came near him I saw him to be a very neat young man indeed— very young and with a very nice friendly face. He was also very clean and he had gloves, and his umbrella was of silk. I liked him very much. He said I should come round the corner, so we went round the corner together. I thought there would be someone there waiting for us; but there was nothing—only the closed shops and the early light and a little spring mist that told that the day would be fine. I didn't know what he wanted; perhaps it was some of our business—that's what I first thought—and perhaps it was only a little game. So I was very careful; I didn't ask him to come into the house. Yet I told him that he must excuse me for not understanding more quickly that he wished to speak with me; and when I said this he said it was not of consequence—he would have waited there, for the chance to see me, all day. I told him I was glad I had spared him that at least, and we had some very polite conversation. He *was* a very pleasant young man. But what he wanted was simply to put a letter in my hand; as he said himself he was only a good private postman. He gave me the letter—it was not addressed; and when I had taken it I asked him how he knew and if he wouldn't be sorry if it should turn out that I was not the man for whom the letter was meant. But I didn't give him a start; he told me he knew all it was necessary for him to know—he knew exactly what to do and how to do it. I think he's a valuable member. I asked

him if the letter required an answer, and he told me he had
nothing to do with that; he was only to put it in my hand.
He recommended me to wait till I had gone into the house
again to read it. We had a little more talk—always very
polite; and he mentioned that he had come so early because
he thought I might go out if he delayed, and because also
he had a great deal to do and had to take his time when he
could. It's true he looked as if he had plenty to do—as if he
was in some very good occupation. I should tell you he
spoke to me always in English, but he was not English; he
sounded his words only as if he had learnt them very well.
I could see he has learnt everything very well. I suppose he's
not German—so he'd have spoken to me in German. But
there are so many, of all countries! I said if he had so much
to do I wouldn't keep him; I would go to my room and open
my letter. He said it wasn't important; and then I asked
him if he wouldn't come into my room also and rest. I told
him it wasn't very handsome, my room—because he looked
like a young man who would have for himself a very neat
lodging. Then I found he meant it wasn't important that we
should talk any more, and he went away without even offering to shake hands. I don't know if he had other letters to
give, but he went away, as I have said, like a good postman
on his rounds, without giving me any more information.'

It took Schinkel a long time to tell this story—his calm
and conscientious thoroughness made no allowance for any
painful acuteness of curiosity his auditor might feel. He
went from step to step, treating all his points with lucidity
and as if each would have exactly the same interest for his
companion. The latter made no attempt to hurry him, and
indeed listened now with a rare intensity of patience; for he
was interested and it was moreover clear to him that he was
safe with Schinkel, who would satisfy him in time—wouldn't
worry him with attaching conditions to their business in
spite of the mistake, creditable after all to his conscience, he
had made in going for discussion to Lisson Grove. Hyacinth
learned in due course that on returning to his apartment and
opening the little packet of which he had been put into

possession, Mr Schinkel had found himself confronted with two separate articles: one a sealed letter superscribed with our young man's name, the other a sheet of paper containing in three lines a request that within two days of receiving it he would hand the letter to the 'young Robinson'. The three lines in question were signed D.H., and the letter was addressed in the same hand. Schinkel professed that he already knew the writing; it was the neat fist—neatest in its very flourishes—of Diedrich Hoffendahl. 'Good, good,' he said, bearing as to soothe on Hyacinth's arm. 'I'll walk with you to your door and I'll give it to you there; unless you like better I should keep it till to-morrow morning, so that you may have a quiet sleep—I mean in case it might contain anything that will be unpleasant to you. But it's probably nothing; it's probably only a word to say you need think no more about your undertaking.'

'Why should it be that?' Hyacinth asked.

'Probably he has heard that you've cooled off.'

'That I've cooled off?' Our hero stopped him short; they had just reached the top of Park Lane. 'To whom have I given a right to say that?'

'Ah well, if you haven't so much the better. It may be then for some other reason.'

'Don't be an idiot, Schinkel,' Hyacinth returned as they walked along. And in a moment he went on: 'What the devil did you go and tattle to the Poupins for?'

'Because I thought they'd like to know. Besides, I felt my responsibility; I thought I should carry it better if they knew it. And then I'm like them—I lofe you.'

Hyacinth made no answer to this profession; he only said the next instant: 'Why didn't your young man bring the letter directly to me?'

'Ah I didn't ask him that! The reason was probably not complicated, but simple—that those who wrote it knew my address and didn't know yours. And wasn't I one of your backers?'

'Yes, but not the principal one. The principal one was Paul Muniment. Why wasn't any communication made me through Paul Muniment?' And this now struck him as a question that would reverberate the more one thought of it.

'My dear Robinson, you want to know too many things. Depend on it there are always good reasons. I should have preferred—yes—it had been Muniment. But if they didn't send to him——!' With which Schinkel's lucidity dropped and lost itself in a thick cloud of smoke.

'Well, if they didn't send to him——?' Hyacinth persisted.

'You're a great friend of his—how can I tell you?'

At this Hyacinth looked up at him askance and caught an ambiguous, an evasive roll in his companion's small mild eye. 'If it's anything against him my being his friend makes me just the man to hear it. I can defend him.'

'Well, it's a possibility they're not satisfied.'

'How do you mean it—not satisfied?'

'How shall I say it?—that they don't trust him.'

'Don't trust him? And yet they trust me!'

'Ah my boy, depend on it there are reasons,' Schinkel replied; and in a moment he added: 'They know everything—everything. They're like the great God of the believers: they're searchers of hearts; and not only of hearts, but of all a man's life—his days, his nights, his spoken, his unspoken words. Oh they go deep and they go straight!'

The pair pursued the rest of their course for the most part in silence, Hyacinth being considerably struck with something that dropped from his companion in answer to a question he asked as to what Eustache Poupin had said when Schinkel, this evening, first told him what he had come to see him about. '*Il vaut du galme—il vaut du galme*': that was the German's version of the Frenchman's words; and Hyacinth repeated them over to himself several times and almost with the same accent. They had a certain soothing effect. In fact the good Schinkel was somehow salutary altogether, as our hero felt when they stopped at last at the door of his lodging in Westminster and stood there face to face while Hyacinth waited—just waited. The sharpness of his impatience had passed away and he watched without irritation the loving manner in which his mate shook the ashes out of the big smoked-out—so vehemently smoked-out —pipe and laid it to rest in its coffin. It was only after he had gone through this business with his usual attention to every detail of it that he said, '*Also*, now for the letter' and, putting his hand inside his old waistcoat, drew forth the portentous missive. It passed instantly into Hyacinth's grasp, and our young man transferred it to his own pocket without looking at it. He thought he saw disappointment in Schin- kel's ugly kindly face at this indication that he himself should have no knowledge—present and relieving at least— of its contents; but he liked that better than his pretending to attribute to it again some silly comfortable sense. Schinkel had now the shrewdness or the good taste not to repeat that remark, and as the letter pressed against his heart Hyacinth felt it still more distinctly not as a vain balm to apprehen- sion, but as the very penetration of a fatal knife. What his friend did say in a moment was: 'Now you've got it I'm very glad. It's easier for me.' And he effected a poor strained grin.

'I should think so!' Hyacinth exclaimed. 'If you hadn't done your job you'd have paid for it.'

Schinkel mumbled as for accommodation while he lin- gered, and then as Hyacinth turned away, putting in his door-key, brought out: 'And if you don't do yours so will you.'

'Yes, as you say, they themselves go straight! Good- night.' And our young man let himself in.

The passage and staircase were never lighted and the lodgers either groped their way bedward with the infalli- bility of practice or scraped the wall with a casual match the effect of which, in the milder gloom of day, was a rude immensity of laceration. Hyacinth's room was a second floor back, and as he approached it he was startled by seeing a light proceed from the crevice under the door, the imperfect fitting of which figured to him thus as quite squalid. He stopped and considered this new note of his crisis, his first impulse being to connect it with the case just presented by

Schinkel—since what could anything that touched him now be but a part of the same business? It was doubtless all in order that some second portent should now await him there. Yet it occurred to him that when he went out to call on Lady Aurora after tea he must simply have left a tallow candle burning, and that it showed a cynical spirit on the part of his landlady, who could be so closefisted for herself, not to have gone in and put it out. Lastly it came over him that he had had a visitor in his absence and that the visitor had taken possession of his apartment till his return, seeking such poor sources of comfort as were perfectly just. When he opened the door this last prevision proved the correct one, though the figure in occupation was not one of the possible presences that had loomed. Mr Vetch sat beside the little table at which Hyacinth did his writing; he showed a weary head on a supporting hand and eyes apparently closed. But he looked up when his young man appeared. 'Oh I didn't hear you; you're very quiet.'

'I come in softly when I'm late, for the sake of the house —though I'm bound to say I'm the only lodger who has that refinement. Besides, you've been asleep,' Hyacinth said.

'No, I've not been asleep,' the old man returned. 'I don't sleep much nowadays.'

'Then you've been plunged in meditation.'

'Yes, I've been thinking.' With which Mr Vetch explained that the woman of the house had begun by refusing him admittance without proper assurances that his intentions were pure and that he was moreover the oldest friend Mr Robinson had in the world. He had been there an hour; he had thought he might find him by coming late.

Mr Robinson was very glad he had waited and was delighted to see him and expressed regret that he hadn't known in advance of his visit, so that he might have something to offer him. He sat down on the bed, vaguely expectant; he wondered what special purpose had brought the fiddler so far at that unnatural hour. Yet he spoke but the truth in saying he was glad to see him. Hyacinth had come upstairs in such pain of desire to be alone with the revelation carried in his pocket that the sight of a guest had given him positive relief by postponing solitude. The place where he had put his letter seemed to throb against his side, yet he was thankful to his old friend for forcing him still to leave it so. 'I've been looking at your books,' the fiddler said; 'you've two or three exquisite specimens of your own. Oh yes, I recognise your work when I see it; there are always certain little finer touches. You've a manner, as who would say, like one of the masters. With such a hand and such feeling your future's assured. You'll make a fortune and become famous.'

Mr Vetch sat forward to sketch this vision; he rested his hands on his knees and looked very hard at his young host, as if to challenge him to dispute a statement so cheering and above all so authoritative. The effect of what Hyacinth saw in his face was to produce immediately the idea that the fiddler knew something, though there was no guessing how he could know it. The Poupins for instance had had no time to communicate with him, even granting them capable of that baseness—all inconceivable in spite of Hyacinth's having seen them, less than an hour before, fall so much below their own standard. With this suspicion there rushed into his mind an intense determination to dissemble before his visitor to the last: he might imagine what he liked, but he should have no grain of satisfaction—or rather should have only that of being led to believe if possible that his suspicions were 'rot'. Hyacinth glanced over the books he had taken down from the shelf and admitted that they were pleasing efforts and that so long as one didn't become blind or maimed the ability to produce that sort of thing was a legitimate source of confidence. Then suddenly, as they continued simply to look at each other, the pressure of the old man's curiosity, the expression of his probing beseeching eyes, which had become strange and tragic in these latter times and completely changed their character, grew so intolerable that to defend himself our hero took the aggressive and asked him boldly if it were simply to look at his work, of which he had half a dozen specimens in Lomax Place, that he had made a nocturnal pilgrimage. 'My dear old friend, you've something on your mind—some fantastic fear, some extremely erroneous *idée fixe*. Why has it taken you to-night in particular? Whatever it is it has brought you here at an unnatural hour under some impulse you don't or can't name. I ought of course to be thankful to anything that brings you here; and so I am in so far as that it makes me happy. But I can't like it if it makes *you* miserable. You're like a nervous mother whose baby's in bed upstairs; she goes up every five minutes to see if he's all right—if he isn't uncovered or hasn't tumbled out of bed. Dear Mr Vetch, don't, don't worry; the blanket's up to my chin and I haven't tumbled yet.'

He heard himself say these things as if he were listening to another person; the impudence of them in the grim conditions seemed to him somehow so rare. But he believed himself to be on the edge of a form of action in which impudence evidently must play a considerable part, and he might as well try his hand at it without delay. The way the old man looked out might have indicated that he too was able to take the measure of his perversity—judged him false to sit there declaring there was nothing the matter while a brand-new revolutionary commission burned in his pocket. But in a moment Mr Vetch said very mildly and as if he had really been reassured: 'It's wonderful how you read my thoughts. I don't trust you; I think there are beastly possibilities. It's not true at any rate that I come to look at you every five minutes. You don't know how often I've resisted my fears—how I've forced myself to let you alone.'

'You had better let me come and live with you as I proposed after Pinnie's death. Then you'll have me always under your eyes,' Hyacinth smiled.

The old man got up eagerly and, as Hyacinth did the same, laid firm hands on his shoulders, holding him close. 'Will you now really, my boy? Will you come to-night?'

'To-night, Mr Vetch?'

'To-night has worried me more than any other, I don't know why. After my tea I had my pipe and a glass, but I couldn't keep quiet; I was very, very bad. I got to thinking of Pinnie—she seemed to be in the room. I felt as if I could put out my hand and touch her. If I believed in ghosts, in signs or messages from the dead, I should believe I had seen her. She wasn't there for nothing; she was there to add her fears to mine—to talk to me about you. I tried to hush her up, but it was no use—she drove me out of the house. About ten o'clock I took my hat and stick and came down here. You may judge if I thought it important—I took a cab.'

'Ah why do you spend your money so foolishly?' Hyacinth asked in a tone of the most affectionate remonstrance.

'Will you come to-night?' said his companion for rejoinder, holding him still.

'Surely it would be simpler for you to stay here. I see perfectly you're ill and nervous. You can take the bed and I'll spend the night in the chair.'

The fiddler thought a moment. 'No, you'll hate me if I subject you to such discomfort as that; and that's just what I don't want.'

'It won't be a bit different in your room. There as here I shall have to sleep in a chair.'

'I'll get another room. We shall be close together,' the fiddler went on.

'Do you mean you'll get another room at this hour of the night, with your little house stuffed full and your people all in bed? My poor Anastasius, you're very bad; your reason totters on its throne,' said Hyacinth with excellent gaiety.

'Very good, we'll get a room to-morrow. I'll move into another house where there are two side by side.' His 'boy's' tone was evidently soothing to him.

'*Comme vous y allez!*' the young man continued. 'Excuse me if I remind you that in case of my leaving this place I've to give a fortnight's notice.'

'Ah you're backing out!' Mr Vetch lamented, dropping his hands.

'Pinnie wouldn't have said that,' Hyacinth returned. 'If you're acting, if you're speaking, at the behest of her pure spirit, you had better act and speak exactly as she'd have done. She'd have believed me.'

'Believed you? Believed what? What's there to believe? If you'll make me a promise I'll believe that.'

'I'll make you any promise you like,' said Hyacinth.

'Oh any promise I like—that isn't what I want! I want just one very particular little proof—and that's really what I came here for to-night. It came over me that I've been an ass all this time never to have got it out of you before. Give it to me now and I'll go home quietly and leave you in peace.' Hyacinth, assenting in advance, requested again that he would formulate his demand, and then Mr Vetch said: 'Well, make me a promise—on your honour and as from the man you are, God help you, to the man I am—that you'll never, under any circumstances whatever, "do" anything.'

' "Do" anything——?'

'Anything those people expect of you.'

'Those people?' Hyacinth repeated.

'Ah don't torment me—worried as I already am—with pretending not to understand!' the old man wailed. 'You know the people I mean. I can't call them by their names, because I don't know their names. But you do, and they know *you.*'

Hyacinth had no desire to torment him, but he was capable of reflecting that to enter into his thought too easily would be tantamount to betraying himself. 'I suppose I know the people you've in mind,' he said in a moment; 'but I'm afraid I don't grasp the need of such solemnities.'

'Don't they want to make use of you?'

'I see what you mean,' said Hyacinth. 'You think they want me to touch off some train for them. Well, if that's what troubles you, you may sleep sound. I shall never do any of their work.'

A radiant light came into the fiddler's face; he stared as if this assurance were too fair for nature. 'Do you take your oath to that? Never anything, anything, anything?'

'Never anything at all.'

'Will you swear it to me by the memory of that good

woman of whom we've been speaking and whom we both loved?'

'My dear old Pinnie's memory? Willingly.'

Mr Vetch sank down in his chair and buried his face in his hands; the next moment his companion heard him sobbing. Ten minutes later he was content to take his departure and Hyacinth went out with him to look for another cab. They found an ancient four-wheeler stationed languidly at a crossing of the ways, and before he got into it he asked his young friend to kiss him. The young friend did so with a fine accolade and in the frank foreign manner, on both cheeks, and then watched the vehicle get itself into motion and rattle away. He saw it turn a neighbouring corner and then approached the nearest gas-lamp to draw from his breast-pocket the sealed letter Schinkel had given him.

XLV

'AND Madame Grandoni then?' he asked, all loth to turn away. He felt pretty sure he should never knock at that door again, and the desire was strong in him to see once more, for the last time, the ancient afflicted titular 'companion' of the Princess, whom he had always liked. She had struck him as ever in the slightly ridiculous position of a confidant of tragedy in whom the heroine, stricken with reserves unfavourable to the dramatic progression, should have ceased to confide.

'*È andata via, caro signorino,*' said Assunta, smiling at him as she held the door open.

'She has gone away? Bless me! when did she go?'

'It's now five days, dear young sir. She has returned to *our* fine country.'

'Is it possible?' He felt it somehow as a personal loss.

'*È possibilissimo!*' Then Assunta added: 'There were many times when she almost went; but this time, *capisce——*!' And without finishing her sentence this most exiled of Romans and expertest of tire-women indulged in a subtle suggestive indefinable play of expression to which hands and shoulders contributed as well as lips and eyebrows.

Hyacinth looked at her long enough to catch any meaning she might have wished to convey, but gave no sign of apprehending it. He only remarked gravely: 'In short she's off!'

'Eh, and the worst is she'll probably never come back. She didn't move, as she kept threatening, for a long time; but when at last she decided——!' And Assunta's flattened hand, sweeping the air sidewise, figured the straightness of the old lady's course. *'Peccato!'* she ended with a sigh.

'I should have liked to see her again—I should have liked to bid her good-bye.' He lingered, suddenly helpless, though, informed of the Princess's own more temporary absence, he had no reason for remaining save the possibility she might reappear before he turned away. This possibility however was small, since it was only nine o'clock, the middle of the evening—too early an hour for her return if, as Assunta said, she had gone out after tea. He looked up and down the Crescent, gently swinging his stick, and became aware in a moment of some tender interest on the part of his humbler friend.

'You should have come back sooner; then perhaps Madama wouldn't have gone, *povera vecchia,*' she rejoined in a moment. 'It's too many days since you've been here. She liked you—I know that.'

'She liked me, but she didn't like me to come,' said Hyacinth. 'Wasn't that why she went—because we keep coming?'

'Ah that other one—with the long legs—yes. But you're better.'

'The Princess doesn't think so, and she's the right judge,' Hyacinth smiled.

'Eh, who knows what she thinks? It's not for me to say. But you had better come in and wait. I dare say she won't be long, and she'll be content to find you.'

Hyacinth wondered. 'I'm not sure of that.' Then he asked: 'Did she go out alone?'

'*Sola, sola*. Oh don't be afraid; you were the first!' And Assunta, delightfully, frankly insidious, flung open the door of the little drawing-room.

He sat there nearly an hour, in the chair the Princess habitually used, under her shaded lamp, with a dozen objects round him which seemed as much a part of herself as if they had been folds of her dress or even tones of her voice. His thoughts rattled like the broken ice of a drink he had once wistfully seen mixed at an 'American Bar', but he was too tired for unrest; he had not been to work and had walked about all day to fill the time; so that he simply lay back there with his head on one of the Princess's cushions, his feet on one of her little stools—one of the ugly ones that belonged to the house—and his respiration coming as quick as that of a man in sharp suspense. He was agitated beneath his fatigue, yet not because he was waiting for the Princess; a deeper source of emotion had been opened to him and he had not on the present occasion more mere 'nervous' intensity than he had known at other moments of the past twenty hours. He had not closed his eyes the night before, and the day had not made up for that torment. A fever of reflexion had descended on him and the range of his imagination had been wide. It whirled him through circles of immeasurable compass; and this is the reason for which, thinking of many things while he sat in the Princess's place, he wondered why, after all, he had come to Madeira Crescent and what interest he could have in seeing the lady of the house. Wasn't everything over between them and the link snapped which had for its brief hour bound them so closely together? And this not simply because for a long time now he had received no sign nor communication from her, no invitation to come back, no enquiry as to why his visits had stopped; not even because he had seen her go in and out with Paul Muniment and it had suited Prince Casamassima to point to him the moral of her doing so; nor still because, quite independently of the Prince, he believed her to be more deeply absorbed in her acquaintance with that superior young man than she had ever been in her relations with himself. The ground of his approach, so far as he became conscious of it in his fitful meditations, could only be a strange detached curiosity—strange and detached because everything else of his past had been engulfed in the abyss that opened before him when, after his separation from Mr Vetch, he stood under the lamp in the paltry Westminster street. That had swallowed up all familiar feelings, and yet out of the ruin had sprung the impulse of which this vigil was the result.

The solution of his difficulty—he flattered himself he had arrived at it—involved a winding-up of his affairs; and though, even had no solution been required, he would have felt clearly that he had been dropped, yet since even in that case it would have been sweet to him to bid her good-bye, so at present the desire for some last vision of her own hurrying fate could still appeal to him. If things had not gone well for him he was still capable of wondering if they looked better for her. There rose in his mind all perversely, yet all humanly, a yearning need to pity her. These were odd feelings enough, and by the time half an hour had elapsed they had throbbed themselves into the stupor of exhaustion. While it came to him in how different a frame he was waiting now from that of his first visit in South Street he closed his eyes and lost himself. His unconsciousness lasted, he afterwards supposed, nearly half an hour; it ended in his feeling the lady of the house stand there before him. Assunta was behind and as he opened his eyes took from her the bonnet and mantle of which she divested herself. 'It's charming of you to have waited,' the Princess said, smiling down at him with all her old kindness. 'You're very tired—don't get up; that's the best chair and you must keep it.' She made him remain where he was; she placed herself near him on a smaller seat; she declared she wasn't tired herself, that she didn't know what was the matter with her —nothing tired her now; she exclaimed on the time that had elapsed since he had last called, as if she were reminded of it simply by seeing him again; and she insisted that he should have some tea—he looked so much as if he needed it. She considered him with deeper attention and wished to know where he ailed—what he had done to use himself up; adding that she must begin to look after him again, since while she had had the care of him that kind of thing didn't happen. In response to this Hyacinth made a great confession; he admitted he had stayed away from work and simply amused himself—amused himself by loafing about London all day. This didn't pay—he had arrived at that wisdom as he grew older; it was doubtless a sign of increasing years when one felt one's self finding wanton pleasures hollow and that to stick to one's tools was not only more profitable but more refreshing. However, he did stick to them as a general thing: that was no doubt partly why, from the absence of the habit of it, a day off turned out rather a sell. Meanwhile, when he hadn't seen her for some time he always on meeting the Princess again had a renewed formidable sense of her beauty, and he had it to-night in an extraordinary degree. Splendid as that beauty had ever been it shone on this occasion, like a trimmed lamp, clearer and further, so that—if what was already supremely fine could be capable of greater refinement—it might have worked itself free of all earthly grossness and been purified and consecrated by her new life. Her gentleness, when she turned it on, was quite divine—it had always the irresistible charm that it was the humility of a high spirit—and on this occasion she gave herself up to it. Whether it was because he had the consciousness of resting his eyes on her for the last time, or because she wished to be particularly pleasant to him in order to make up for having amid other pre-occupations rather dropped him of late—it was probable the effect sprang from both causes—at all events the sight of each great easy natural, yet all so coercive, fact of her seemed no poorer a privilege than when, the other year, he had gone into her box at the play. She affected him as raising and upholding the weight that rested on him very much after the form of some high bland caryatid crowned with a crushing cornice. He suffered himself to be coddled and absently, even if radiantly, smiled at, and his state of mind was such that it could produce no alteration of his pain to see that these were on the Princess's part inexpensive gifts. She had sent Assunta to bring them tea, and when the tray arrived she gave him cup after cup with every grace of hospitality; but he had not sat with her a quarter of an hour before he was sure she scarcely measured a word he said to her or a word she herself uttered. If she had the best intention of being 'balmy' by way of making up, she was still rather vague about what she was to make up *for*. Two points became perfectly clear; first that she was thinking of something quite other than her present, her past, or her future relations with Hyacinth Robinson; second that he was superseded indeed. This was so completely the case that it didn't even occur to her, evidently, how cruel the sense of supersession might be to one who was sick and sore. If she was charming to such weakness wasn't it because she was good-natured and he had been hanging off, and not because she had done him an injury? Perhaps after all she hadn't, for he got the impression it might be no great loss of comfort to any shuffler not to constitute part of her intimate life to-day. It was manifest from things in her face, from her every movement and tone, and indeed from all the irradiation of her beauty, that this life was involving intimacies and efforts arduous all round. If he had called from curiosity about her success it was sufficiently implied for him that her success was good: she was living more than ever on high hopes and bold plans and far-reaching combinations. These things, from his own point of view, were not now so quite the secret of joy, and to be mixed up with them was perhaps not so much greater a sign that one hadn't lived for nothing than the grim understanding he had in the interest of peace just arrived at with himself. She asked why he hadn't been to her for so long, much as if this failure were only a vulgar form of social neglect; and she scarce seemed to note it either as a good or as a poor excuse when he said he had stayed away because he knew

her to be deep in business. But she didn't deny the impeach-
ment; she admitted she had been busier than ever in her
life before. She looked at him as if he would know what that
meant, and he said he was very sorry for her.

'Because you think it's all a mistake? Yes, I know that.
Perhaps it is, but if so it's a magnificent one. If you were
scared about me three or four months ago I don't know
what you'd think to-day—if you knew! I've risked,' she yet
all portentously simply stated, 'everything.'

'Fortunately I don't know anything,' he said.

'No indeed. How should you?'

'And to tell the truth,' he went on, 'that's really the reason
I haven't been back here till to-night. I haven't wanted to
know—I've feared and hated to know.'

'Then why did you come at last?'

'Well, out of the most illogical of curiosities.'

'I suppose then you'd like me to tell you where I've been
to-night, eh?' she asked.

'No, my curiosity's satisfied. I've learnt something—what
I mainly wanted to know—without your telling me.'

She stared an instant. 'Ah you mean whether Madame
Grandoni had gone? I suppose Assunta told you.'

'Yes, Assunta told me, and I was sorry to hear it.'

The Princess looked grave, as if her old friend's departure
had been indeed a very awkward affair. 'You may imagine
how I feel it! It leaves me completely alone; it makes, in the
eyes of the world, an immense difference in my position.
However, I don't consider the eyes of the world. At any rate
she couldn't put up with me any more; it appears I'm more
and more of a scandal—and it was written!' On Hyacinth's
asking what the old lady would do she said: 'I suppose she'll
go and live with my husband. Funny, isn't it? that it should
have always to be with one of us and that it should matter
so little which.' Five minutes later she enquired of him if
the same reason he had mentioned just before was the
explanation of his absence from Audley Court. Mr Muniment had told her he hadn't been near him and the sister
for more than a month.

'No, it isn't the fear of learning something that would make me uneasy: because somehow, in the first place, it isn't natural to feel uneasy about Paul, and because in the second, if it were, he never lets one see anything—of any effect or impression on him. It's simply the general sense of real divergence of view. When that divergence becomes sharp there are forms and lame pretences——'

'It's best not to try to keep up? I see what you mean—when you're grimly sincere. But you might go and see the sister.'

'I don't like the sister,' Hyacinth frankly averred.

'Ah neither do I!' the Princess said; while her visitor remained conscious of the perfect composure, the absence of false shame, with which she had named their common friend. But she was silent after this, and he judged he had stayed long enough and sufficiently taxed a preoccupied attention. He got up and was bidding her good-night when she suddenly brought out: 'By the way, your not going to see so good a friend as Mr Muniment because you disapprove to-day of his work suggests to me that you'll be in an awkward fix, with your disapprovals, the hour you're called upon to serve the cause according to your vow.'

'Oh of course I've thought of that,' Hyacinth smiled.

'And would it be indiscreet to ask what you've thought?'

'Ah so many things, Princess! It would take me a long time to say.'

'I've never talked to you of this, because it seemed to me indelicate and the whole thing too much a secret of your own breast for even so intimate a friend as I've been to have a right to meddle with it. But I've wondered much, seeing you take all the while less and less interest—in the real business, I mean, less and less—how you'd reconcile your change of heart with your meeting your engagement. I pity you, my poor friend,' she went on with a noble benignity, 'for I can imagine nothing more terrible than to find yourself face to face with your obligation and to feel at the same time the spirit originally prompting it dead within you.'

'Terrible, terrible, most terrible.' And he looked at her gravely.

'But I pray God it may never be your fate!' The Princess had a pause, after which she added: 'I see you feel it. Heaven help us all! Why shouldn't I tell you when I worry?' she went on. 'A short time ago I had a visit from Mr Vetch.'

'It was kind of you to see him,' Hyacinth said.

'He was delightful, I assure you. But do you know what he came for? To beg me on his knees to snatch you away?'

'Away from what?'

'From the danger that hangs over you. He was most touching.'

'Oh yes, he has talked to me about it,' our young man said. 'He has picked up the idea, but is utterly at sea. And how did he expect you'd be able to snatch me?'

'He left that to me; he had only a general—and such a flattering—belief in my possible effect on you.'

'And he thought you'd set it in motion to make me back out? He does you injustice. You wouldn't!' Hyacinth finely laughed. 'In that case, taking one false position with another, yours would be no better than mine.'

'Oh, speaking seriously, I'm perfectly quiet about you and about myself. I know you won't be called,' the Princess returned.

'May I be told how you know it?'

She waited but an instant. 'Mr Muniment keeps me informed.'

'And how does *he* know?'

'We've information. My poor dear friend,' the Princess went on, 'you're so much out of it now that if I were to tell you I fear you wouldn't understand.'

'Yes, no doubt I'm out of it; but I still have a right to say, all the same, in contradiction to your charge of a moment ago, that I take interest in the "real business" exactly as much as I ever did.'

'My poor Hyacinth, my dear infatuated little aristocrat, was that ever very much?' she asked.

'It was enough, and it's still enough, to make me willing to lay down my life for anything that will clearly help.'

'Yes, and of course you must decide for yourself what that is—or rather what it's not.'

'I didn't decide when I gave my promise. I agreed to abide by the decision of others,' Hyacinth answered.

'Well you said just now that in relation to this business of yours you had thought of many things,' his friend pursued. 'Have you ever by chance thought of anything that *will* do their work?'

'Their work?'

'The people's.'

'Ah you call me fantastic names, but I'm one of them myself!' he cried.

'I know what you're going to say,' the Princess broke in. 'You're going to say it will help them to do what you do—to do their work themselves and earn their wages. That's beautiful so far as it goes. But what do you propose for the thousands and hundreds of thousands for whom no work —on the overcrowded earth, under the pitiless heaven—is to be found? There's less and less work in the world, and there are more and more people to do the little there is. The old ferocious selfishness *must* come down. They won't come down gracefully, so they must just be assisted.'

The tone in which she spoke made his heart beat fast, and there was something so inspiring in the great union of her beauty, her sincerity and her energy that the image of a heroism not less great flashed up again before him in all the splendour it had lost—the idea of a tremendous risk and an unregarded sacrifice. Such a woman as that, at such an hour, one who could shine like silver and ring like crystal, made every scruple a poor prudence and every compunction a cowardice. 'I wish to God I could see it as you see it!' he wailed after he had looked at her some seconds in silent admiration.

'I see simply this: that what we're doing is at least worth trying, and that as none of those who have the power, the place, the means, will bethink themselves of anything else, on *their* head be the responsibility, on *their* head be the blood!'

'Princess,' said Hyacinth, clasping his hands and feeling that he trembled, 'dearest Princess, if anything should happen to *you*——!' But his voice fell; the horror of it, a dozen hideous images of her possible perversity and her possible punishment were again before him, as he had already seen them in sinister musings: they seemed to him worse than anything he had imagined for himself.

She threw back her head, looking at him almost in anger. 'To me! And pray why not to me? What title have I to exemption, to security, more than any one else? Why am I so sacrosanct and so precious?'

'Simply because there's no one in the world and has never been any one in the world like you.'

'Oh thank you!' said the Princess impatiently. And she turned from him as with a beat of great white wings that raised her straight out of the bad air of the personal. It took her up too high, it put an end to their talk; expressing an indifference to what it might interest him to think of her to-day, and even a contempt for it, which brought tears to his eyes. His tears, however, were concealed by the fact that he bent his head low over the hand he had taken to kiss; after which he left the room without looking at her.

XLVI

'I'VE RECEIVED a letter from your husband,' Paul Muniment said to her the next evening as soon as he came into the room. He announced this truth with an unadorned directness as well as with a freedom of manner that showed his visit to be one of a closely-connected series. The Princess was evidently not a little surprised and immediately asked how in the world the Prince could know his address. 'Couldn't it have been by your old lady?' Muniment returned. 'He must have met her in Paris. It's from Paris he writes.'

'What an incorrigible cad!' she exclaimed.

'I don't see that—for writing to me. I've his letter in my pocket and I'll show it to you if you like.'

'Thank you, nothing would induce me to touch anything he has touched.'

'You touch his money, my dear lady,' Muniment remarked with one of the easy sequences of a man who sees things as they are.

The Princess considered. 'Yes, I make an exception for that, because it hurts him, it makes him suffer.'

'I should think on the contrary it would gratify him by showing you in a state of weakness and dependence.'

'Not when he knows I don't use it for myself. What exasperates him is that it's devoted to ends which he hates almost as much as he hates me and yet which he can't call selfish.'

'He doesn't hate you,' said Muniment with the same pleasant reasonableness—that of a man who has mastered not two or three but all the possible aspects of a question. 'His letter satisfies me of that.' The Princess stared at this and asked what he was coming to—if he were leading up to the hint that she should go back and live with her husband. 'I don't know that I'd go so far as to advise it,' he replied; 'when I've so much benefit from seeing you here on your present footing, that wouldn't sound well. But I'll just make bold to prophesy you'll go before very long.'

'And on what does that extraordinary prediction rest?'

'On this plain fact—that you'll have nothing to live upon. You decline to read the Prince's letter, but if you were to look at it it would give you evidence of what I mean. He informs me that I need count on no more supplies from your hands, since you yourself will receive no more.'

'He addresses you in those plain terms?'

'I can't call them very plain, because the letter's in French and I naturally have had a certain difficulty in making it out, in spite of my persevering study of the tongue and the fine example set me by poor Robinson. But that appears to be the gist of the matter.'

'And you can repeat such an insult to me without the smallest apparent discomposure? You're indeed the most extraordinary of men!' the Princess broke out.

'Why is it an insult? It's the simple truth. I do take your money,' Muniment said.

'You take it for a sacred cause. You don't take it for yourself.'

'The Prince isn't obliged to look at that,' he answered amusedly.

His companion had a pause. 'I didn't know you were on his side.'

'Oh you know on what side I am!'

'What does *he* know? What business has he to address you so?'

'I suppose, as I tell you, that he knows from Madame Grandoni. She has told him I've great influence with you.'

'Ah she was welcome to tell him that!' the Princess tossed off.

'His reasoning therefore has been that when I find you've nothing more to give to the cause I'll let you go.'

'Nothing more? And does he count *me* myself, and every pulse of my being, every capacity of my nature, as nothing?' the Princess cried with shining eyes.

'Apparently he thinks *I* do.'

'Oh as for that, after all, I've known you care far more for my money than for me. But it has made no difference to me,' she finely said.

'Then you see by your own calculation the Prince is right.'

'My dear sir,' Muniment's hostess replied, 'my interest in you never depended on your interest in me. It depended wholly on a sense of your great destinies. I suppose that what you began to tell me,' she went on, 'is that he stops my allowance.'

'From the first of next month. He has taken legal advice. It's now clear—so he tells me—that you forfeit your settlements.'

'Can't I take legal advice too?' she demanded. 'I can fight that to the last inch of ground. I can forfeit my settlements only by an act of my own. The act that led to our separation was *his* act; he turned me out of his house by physical violence.'

'Certainly,' said her visitor, displaying even in this simple discussion his easy aptitude for argument; 'but since then there *have* been acts of your own——!' He stopped for a moment, smiling; then went on: 'Your whole connexion with a league working for as great ends as you like, but for ends and by courses necessarily averse to the eye of day and the observation of the police—this constitutes an act; and so does your exercise of the pleasure, which you appreciate so highly, of feeding it with money extorted from an old Catholic and princely family. You know how little it's to be desired that these matters should come to light.'

'Why in the world need they come to light? Allegations in plenty of course he'd have, but not a particle of proof. Even if Madame Grandoni were to testify against me, which is inconceivable, she wouldn't be able to produce a definite fact.'

'She'd be able to produce the fact that you had a little bookbinder staying for a month in your house.'

'What has that to do with it?' she promptly asked. 'If you mean that that's a circumstance which would put me in the wrong as against the Prince, is there not on the other side this marked detail that while our young friend was staying with me Madame Grandoni herself, a person of the highest and most conspicuous respectability, never saw fit to withdraw from me her countenance and protection? Besides, why shouldn't I have my bookbinder just as I might have—and the Prince should surely appreciate my consideration in not having—my physician and my chaplain?'

'Am I not your chaplain?' Muniment again amusedly enquired. 'And does the bookbinder usually dine at the Princess's table?'

'Why not—when he's an artist? In the old times, I know, artists dined with the servants; but not to-day.'

'That would be for the court to appreciate,' he said. And in a moment he added: 'Allow me to call your attention to the fact that Madame Grandoni *has* left you—*has* withdrawn her countenance and protection.'

'Ah but not for Hyacinth!' the Princess returned in a tone which would have made the fortune of an actress if an actress could have caught it.

'For the bookbinder or for the chaplain, it doesn't matter. But that's only a detail. In any case,' he noted, 'I shouldn't in the least care for your going to law.'

The Princess rested her eyes on him a while in silence and at last replied: 'I was speaking just now of your great future, but every now and then you do something, you say something, that makes me really doubt you. It's when you seem afraid. That's terribly against your being a first-rate man.'

'Ah I know you've thought me little better than a smooth sneak from the first of your knowing me. But what does it matter? I haven't the smallest pretension to being a first-rate man.'

'Oh you're deep and you're provoking!' she said with sombre eyes.

'Don't you remember,' he went on without heeding this rich comment, 'Don't you remember how the other day you accused me of being not only a coward but a traitor; of playing false, of wanting, as you said, to back out?'

'Most distinctly. How can I help its coming over me at times that you've incalculable ulterior views and are but consummately using me—but consummately using us all? Well, I don't care!'

'No, no; I'm genuine,' said Muniment simply, yet in a tone which might have implied that their discussion was idle. And he made a transition doubtless too abrupt for perfect civility. 'The best reason in the world for your not going to law with your husband is this: that when you haven't a penny left you'll be obliged to go back and live with him.'

'How do you mean, when I haven't a penny left? Haven't I my own property?' the Princess demanded.

'The Prince assures me you've drawn on your own property at such a rate that the income to be derived from it amounts, to his positive knowledge, to no more than a thousand francs—forty pounds—a year. Surely with your habits and tastes you can't live on forty pounds. I should add that your husband implies that your property originally was rather a small affair.'

'You've the most extraordinary tone,' she answered gravely. 'What you appear to wish to express is simply this: that from the moment I've no more money to give you I'm of no more value than the washed-out tea-leaves in that pot.'

Muniment looked down a while at his substantial boot. His companion's words had brought a flush to his cheek; he appeared to admit to himself and to her that at the point their conversation had reached there was a natural difficulty in his delivering himself. But presently he raised his head, showing a face slightly embarrassed, but more for her than for himself. 'I've no intention whatever of saying anything harsh or offensive to you, but since you challenge me perhaps it's well that I should let you know how inevitably I *do* consider that in giving your money—or rather your husband's—to our business you gave the most valuable thing you had to contribute.'

'This is the day of plain truths!' she rang out with a high mildness. 'You don't count then any devotion, any intelligence that I may have placed at your service—even rating my faculties modestly?'

'I count your intelligence, but I don't count your devotion, and one's nothing without the other. You're not trusted—well, where it makes the difference.'

'Not trusted!' the Princess repeated with her splendid stare. 'Why I thought I could be hanged to-morrow!'

'They may let you hang, perfectly, without letting you act. You're liable to be weary of us,' he went on; 'and indeed I think you're weary even now.'

'Ah you *must* be a first-rate man—you're such a brute!'

she replied, noticing, as she had noticed before, that he pronounced 'weary' *weery*.

'I didn't say you were weary of *me*,' he said with a certain awkwardness. 'But you can never live poor—you don't begin to know the meaning of it.'

'Oh no, I'm not tired of you,' she declared as if she wished she were. 'In a moment you'll make me cry with rage, and no man has done that for years. I was very poor when I was a girl,' she added in a different manner. 'You yourself recognised it just now in speaking of the insignificant character of my fortune.'

'It had to be a fortune to be insignificant,' Muniment smiled. 'You'll go back to your husband!'

To this she made no answer, only looking at him with a high gradual clearance of her heat. 'I don't see after all why they trust you more than they trust me,' she said at last.

'I am not sure they do. I've heard something this evening that suggests that.'

'And may one know what it is?'

'A communication which I should have expected to be made through me has been made through another person.'

'A communication——?'

'To Hyacinth Robinson.'

'To Hyacinth——?' The Princess sprang up; she had turned pale in a moment.

'He has got his billet, but they didn't send it through me.'

'Do you mean his "call"? He was here last night,' the Princess said.

'A fellow, a worker, named Schinkel, a German—whom you don't know, I think, but who was originally a witness, with me and another, of his undertaking—came to see me this evening. It was through him the call came, and he put Hyacinth up to it on Sunday night.'

'On Sunday night?' The Princess stared. 'Why he was here yesterday, and he talked of it and told me nothing.'

'That was quite right of him, bless his pluck!' Muniment returned.

She closed her eyes a moment and when she opened them

again he had risen and was standing before her. 'What do they want him to do?' she asked.

'I'm like Hyacinth; I think I had better not tell you—at least till it's over.'

'And when will it be over?'

'They give him several days and, I believe, minute instructions—with, however,' Paul went on, 'considerable discretion in respect to seizing his chance. The thing's made remarkably easy for him. All this I know from Schinkel, who himself knew nothing on Sunday, being merely the fellow to see he got the thing, and who saw him in fact yesterday morning.'

'Schinkel trusts you then?' the Princess remarked.

Muniment looked at her steadily. 'Yes, but he won't trust you. Hyacinth's to receive a card of invitation to a certain big house,' he explained, 'a card with the name left in blank, so that he may fill it out himself. It's to be good for each of two grand parties which are to be given at a few days' interval. That's why they give him the job—because at a grand party he'll look in his place.'

'He'll like that,' she said musingly—'repaying hospitality with a pistol-shot.'

'If he doesn't like it he needn't do it.'

She made no return to this, but in a moment said: 'I can easily find out the place you mean—the big house where two parties are to be given at a few days' interval and where the master—or is it to be the principal guest?—is worth your powder.'

'Easily, no doubt. And do you want to warn him?'

'No, I want to do the business myself first, so that it won't be left for another. If Hyacinth will look in his place at a grand party shall not I look still more in mine? And as I know the individual I should be able to approach him without exciting the smallest suspicion.'

Muniment appeared for a little to consider her suggestion as if it were practical and interesting; but presently he answered quietly enough: 'To fall by your hand would be too good for him.'

'However he falls, will it be useful, valuable?' the Princess asked.

'It's worth trying. He's a very bad institution.'

'And don't you mean to go near Hyacinth?'

'No, I wish to leave him free.'

'Ah, Paul Muniment,' she said, 'you *are* a first-rate man!' She sank down on the sofa and sat looking up at him. 'In God's name, why have you told me this?'

'So that you shall not be able to throw it up at me later that I haven't.'

She flung herself over, burying her face in the cushions, and remained so for some minutes in silence. He watched her a while without speaking, then at last brought out: 'I don't want to aggravate you, but you *will* go back!' The words failed to cause her even to raise her head, and after a moment he—as for the best attenuation of any rudeness—stepped out of the room.

XLVII

THAT SHE had done with him, done with him for ever, was to remain the most vivid impression Hyacinth had carried away from Madeira Crescent the night before. He went home and threw himself on his narrow bed, where the consolation of sleep again descended on him. But he woke up with the earliest dawn, and the beginning of a new day was a quick revival of pain. He was overpast, he had become vague, he was extinct. Things Sholto had said came back to him, and the compassion of foreknowledge Madame Grandoni had shown him from the first. Of Paul Muniment he only thought to wonder if this great fellow worker knew. An insurmountable desire to do more than justice to him for the very reason that there might be a temptation to do less forbade him to challenge his friend even in imagination. He vaguely asked himself if *he* would ever be superseded; but this possibility faded away in a stronger light—a dazz-

ling vision of some great tribuneship which swept before
him now and again and in which the figure of the Princess
herself seemed merged and blurred. When full morning
came at last and he got up it brought with it in the restlessness making it impossible he should remain in his room a
return of that beginning of an answerless question, 'After
all, after all——?' which the Princess had planted there the
night before when she spoke so bravely in the name of the
Revolution. 'After all, after all, since nothing else was tried or
would apparently ever be tried——!' He had a sense that
his mind, made up as he believed, would fall to pieces
again; but that sense in turn lost itself in a shudder which
was already familiar—the horror of the public reappearance, in his person, of the imbrued hands of his mother.
This loathing of the idea of a *repetition* had not been sharp,
strangely enough, till he felt the great hard hand on his
shoulder; in all his previous meditations the growth of his
reluctance to act for the 'party of action' had not been the
fear of a personal stain, but the simple growth of yearning
observation. Yet now the idea of the personal stain made
him horribly sick; it seemed by itself to make service impossible. It passed before him, or rather it stayed, like a
blow dealt back at his mother, already so hideously disfigured; to suffer it to start out in the life of her son was in
a manner to place her own forgotten pollution again in the
eye of the world. The thought that was most of all with him
was that he had time, he had time; he was grateful for that
and saw a delicacy, a mercy, in their having given him a
margin, not condemned him to be pressed by the hours.
He had another day, he had two days, he might take three,
he might take several. He knew he should be terribly weary
of them before they were over; but for that matter they
would be over whenever he liked.

Anyhow he went forth again into the streets, into the
squares, into the parks, solicited by an aimless desire to
steep himself yet once again in the great indifferent city he
so knew and so loved and which had had so many of his
smiles and tears and confidences. The day was grey and

damp, though no rain fell, and London had never appeared to him to wear more proudly and publicly the stamp of her imperial history. He passed slowly to and fro over Westminster bridge and watched the black barges drift on the great brown river; looked up at the huge fretted palace that rose there as a fortress of the social order which he, like the young David, had been commissioned to attack with a sling and pebble. At last he made his way to Saint James's Park and wandered and pointlessly sat. He watched the swans as from fascination and followed the thoroughfare that communicates with Pimlico. He stopped here presently and came back again; then, over the same pavement, he retraced his steps westward. He looked in the windows of shops— looked especially into the long, glazed expanse of that establishment in which at that hour of the day Millicent Henning discharged superior functions. Her image had descended on him after he came out, and now it moved before him as he went, it clung to him, it refused to quit him. He made in truth no effort to drive it away; he held fast to it in return, and it murmured strange things in his ear. She had been so jolly to him on Sunday; she was such a strong obvious simple nature, with such a generous breast and such a freedom from the sophistries of civilisation. All he had ever liked in her came back to him now with a finer air, and there was a moment, during which he again made time on the bridge that spans the lake in the Park, seemingly absorbed in the pranks of a young ass in a boat, when he asked himself if at bottom he hadn't liked her better almost than any one. He tried to think he had, he wanted to think he had, and he seemed to see the look her eyes would have if he should swear to her he had. Something of that sort had really passed between them on Sunday, only the business coming up since had brushed it away. Now the taste of the vague primitive comfort his Sunday had given him revived, and he asked himself if he mightn't have a second and even a deeper draught of it. After he had thought he couldn't again wish for anything he found himself wishing he might believe there was something Millicent could do for him. Mightn't she help him—mightn't she even extricate him? He was looking into a window—not that of her own shop—when a vision rose before him of a quick flight with her, for an undefined purpose, to an undefined spot; and he was glad at that moment to have his back turned to the people in the street, because his face suddenly grew red to the tips of his ears. Again and again, all the same, he indulged in the reflexion that spontaneous uncultivated minds often have inventions, inspirations. Moreover, whether Millicent should have any or not, he might at least feel the firm roundness of her arms about him. He didn't exactly know what good this would do him or what door it would open, but he should like it. The sensation was not one he could afford to defer, but the nearest moment at which he should be able to enjoy it would be that evening. He had thrown over everything, but she herself would be busy all day; nevertheless it would be a gain, it would be a kind of foretaste, to see her earlier, to have three words with her. He wrestled with the temptation to go into her haberdasher's, because he knew she didn't like it—he had tried it once of old; as the visits of gentlemen even when ostensible purchasers (there were people watching about who could tell who was who) compromised her in the eyes of her employers. This was not an ordinary case, however; and though he hovered a long time, undecided, embarrassed, half-ashamed, at last he went in as by the force of the one, the last, sore personal need left him. He would just make an appointment with her, and a glance of the eye and a single word would suffice.

He remembered his way through the labyrinth of the shop; he knew her department was on the upper floor. He walked through the place, which was crowded, as if he had as good a right as any one else; and as he had entertained himself on rising with putting on his holiday garments, in which he made such a tidy figure, he was not suspected of any purpose more nefarious than that of looking for some nice thing to give a lady. He ascended the stairs and found himself in a large room where made-up articles were ranged and where, though there were twenty people in it, a glance told him he shouldn't find Millicent. She was perhaps in the next one, into which he passed by a wide opening. Here also were numerous purchasers, most of them ladies; the men were but three or four and the disposal of the wares all committed to neat young women attired in black dresses with long trains. It struck him at first that the young woman he sought was even here not within sight, and he was turning away to look elsewhere when he suddenly noted a tall gentleman who stood in the middle of the room and who was none other than Captain Sholto. It next became plain to him that the person standing upright before the Captain, as still as a lay-figure and with her back turned to himself, was the object of his own quest. In spite of her averted face he instantly 'spotted' Millicent; he knew her shop-attitude, the dressing of her hair behind and the long grand lines of her figure draped in the last new thing. She was showing off this treasure to the Captain, who was lost in contemplation. He had been beforehand with Hyacinth as a false purchaser, but he imitated a real one better than our young man, as, with his eyes travelling up and down the front of their beautiful friend's person, he frowned consider-ingly and rubbed his lower lip slowly with his walking-stick. Millicent stood admirably still—the back view of the gar-ment she displayed was magnificent. Hyacinth stood for a minute as still as she. By the end of that minute he was convinced Sholto saw him, and for an instant he thought him about to make Milly do as much. But Sholto only looked at him very hard a few seconds, not telling her he was there; to enjoy that satisfaction he would wait until the interloper had gone. Hyazinth gazed back at him for the same length of time—what these two pairs of eyes said to each other requires perhaps no definite mention—and then turned away.

That evening about nine o'clock the Princess Casamassima drove in a hansom to Hyacinth's lodgings in Westminster. The door of the house was a little open and a man stood on the step, smoking his big pipe and looking up and down.

The Princess, seeing him while she was still at some distance, had hoped he was Hyacinth, but he proved a different figure indeed from her devoted young friend. He had not a forbidding countenance, but he faced her very directly as she descended from her hansom and approached the door. She was used to the last vulgarity of stare and didn't mind it; she supposed him one of the lodgers in the house. He edged away to let her pass and watched her while she tried to twist life into the limp bell-pull beside the door. It gave no audible response, so that she said to him: 'I wish to ask for Mr Hyacinth Robinson. Perhaps you can tell me——'

'Yes, I too,' the man strangely smirked. 'I've come also for that.'

She seemed to wonder about him. 'I think you must be Mr Schinkel. I've heard of you.'

'You know me by my bad English,' her interlocutor said with a shade of benevolent coquetry.

'Your English is remarkably good—I wish I spoke German as well. Only just a hint of an accent, and evidently an excellent vocabulary.'

'I think I've heard also of you,' Schinkel returned with freedom.

'Yes, we know each other in our circle, don't we? We're all brothers and sisters.' The Princess was anxious, was in a fever; but she could still relish the romance of standing in a species of back slum and fraternising with a personage so like a very tame horse whose collar galled him. 'Then he's at home, I hope; he's coming down to you?' she went on.

'That's what I don't know. I'm waiting.'

'Have they gone to call him?'

Schinkel looked at her while he puffed his pipe. 'I've galled him myself, but he won't zay.'

'How do you mean he won't say?'

'His door's locked. I've knocked many times.'

'I suppose he is out,' said the Princess.

'Yes, he may be out,' Schinkel remarked judicially.

They stood a moment face to face, after which she asked: 'Have you any doubt of it?'

'Oh *es kann sein*. Only the woman of the house told me five minutes ago that he came in.'

'Well then he probably went out again.'

'Yes, but she didn't hear him.'

The Princess reflected and was conscious she was flushing. She knew what Schinkel knew about their young friend's actual situation and she wished to be very clear with him and to induce him to be the same with her. She was rather baffled, however, by the sense that he was cautious—justly cautious He was polite and inscrutable, quite like some of the high personages—ambassadors and cabinet-ministers—whom she used to meet in the great world. 'Has the woman been here in the house ever since?' she asked in a moment.

'No, she went out for ten minutes half an hour ago.'

'Surely then he may have gone out again in that time,' the Princess argued.

'That's what I've thought. It's also why I've waited here,' said Schinkel. 'I've nothing to do,' he added serenely.

'Neither have I,' she returned. 'We can wait together.'

'It's a pity you haven't some nice room,' the German suggested with sympathy.

'No indeed; this will do very well. We shall see him the sooner when he comes back.'

'Yes, but perhaps it won't be for long.'

'I don't care for that; I'll wait. I hope you don't object to my company,' she smiled.

'It's good, it's good,' Schinkel responded through his smoke.

'Then I'll send away my cab.' She returned to the vehicle and paid the driver, who said with expression, 'Thank you, my lady' and drove off.

'You gave him too much,' observed Schinkel when she came back.

'Oh he looked like a nice man. I'm sure he deserved it.'

'It's very expensive,' Schinkel went on sociably.

'Yes, and I've no money—but it's done. Was there no one

else in the house while the woman was away?' the Princess resumed.

'No, the people are out; she only has single men. I asked her that. She has a daughter, but the daughter has gone to see her cousin. The mother went only a hundred yards, round the corner there, to buy a pennyworth of milk. She locked this door and put the key in her pocket; she stayed at the grocer's, where she got the milk, to have a little conversation with a friend she met there. You know ladies always stop like that—*nicht wahr?* It was half an hour later that I came. She told me he was at home, and I went up to his room. I got no sound, as I have told you. I came down and spoke to her again, and she told me what I say.'

'Then you determined to wait, as I've done,' said the Princess.

'Oh yes, I want to see him.'

'So do I, very much.' She said nothing more for a minute, but then added: 'I think we want to see him for the same reason.'

'*Dass kann sein—das kann sein.*'

The two continued to stand there in the brown evening, and they had some further conversation of a desultory and irrelevant kind. At the end of ten minutes the Princess broke out in a low tone, laying her hand on her companion's arm: 'Mr Schinkel, this won't do. I'm intolerably worried.'

'Yes, that's the nature of ladies,' the German sagely answered.

'I want to go up to his room,' the Princess said. 'You'll be so good as to show me where it is.'

'It will do you no good if he's not there.'

'I'm not sure he's not there.'

'Well, if he won't speak it shows he likes better not to have visitors.'

'Oh he may like to have me better than he does you!' she frankly suggested.

'*Das kann sein—das kann sein.*' But Schinkel made no movement to introduce her into the house.

'There's nothing to-night—you know what I mean,' she remarked with a deep look at him.

'Nothing to-night?'

'At the Duke's. The first party's on Thursday, the other next Tuesday.'

'*Schön.* I never go to parties,' said Schinkel.

'Neither do I.'

'Except that *this* is a kind of party—you and me,' he dreadfully grinned.

'Yes, and the woman of the house doesn't approve of it.' The footstep of a jealous landlady had become audible in the passage, through the open door, which was presently closed from within with a little reprehensive bang. Something in this touch appeared to quicken exceedingly the Princess's impatience and fear; the danger of being warned off made her wish still more uncontrollably to arrive at the satisfaction she had come for. 'For God's sake, Mr Schinkel, take me up there. If you won't I'll go alone,' she pleaded.

Her face was white now and, it need hardly be added, all beautiful with anxiety. The German took in this impression and then, with no further word, turned and reopened the door and went forward, followed closely by his companion.

There was a light in the lower region which tempered the gloom of the staircase—as high, that is, as the first floor; the ascent the rest of the way was so dark that the pair went slowly and Schinkel led his companion by the hand. She gave a suppressed exclamation as she rounded a sharp turn in the second flight. 'Good God, is that his door—with the light?'

'Yes, you can see under it. There was a light before,' he said without confusion.

'And why in heaven's name didn't you tell me?'

'Because I thought it would worry you.'

'And it doesn't worry *you*?'

'A little, but I don't mind,' Schinkel professed. 'Very likely he may have left it.'

'He doesn't leave candles!' she returned with vehemence. She hurried up the few remaining steps to the door and paused there with her ear against it. Her hand grasped the handle and turned it, but the door resisted. Then she panted to her companion: 'We must go in—we must go in!'

'But what will you do when it's locked?' he contended.

'You must break it down.'

'It's very expensive,' said Schinkel.

'Don't be abject!' cried the Princess. 'In a house like this the fastenings are worth nothing; they'll easily yield.'

'And if he's not there—if he comes back and finds what we've done?'

She looked at him a moment through the darkness, which was mitigated only by the small glow proceeding from the chink. 'He *is* there! Before God he's there!'

'*Schön, schön,*' said her friend as if he felt the contagion of her own dread but was deliberating and meant to remain calm. She assured him that one or two vigorous thrusts with his shoulder would burst the bolt—certain to be some wretched morsel of tin—and she made way for him to come close. He did so, he even leaned against the door, but he gave no violent push, and the Princess waited with her hand against her heart. Schinkel apparently was still deliberating. At last he gave a low sigh. 'I know they find him the pistol, it's only for that,' he mumbled; and the next moment she saw him sway sharply to and fro in the gloom. She heard a crack and saw the lock had yielded. The door collapsed: they were in the light; they were in a small room which looked full of things. The light was that of a single candle on the mantel; it was so poor that for a moment she made out nothing definite. Before that moment was over, however, her eyes had attached themselves to the small bed. There was something on it—something black, something ambiguous, something outstretched. Schinkel held her back, but only an instant; she saw everything and with the very vision flung herself, beside the bed, upon her knees. Hyacinth lay there as if asleep, but there was a horrible thing, a mess of blood, on the counterpane, in his side, in his heart. His arm hung limp beside him, downwards, off the narrow couch; his face was white and his eyes were closed.

So much Schinkel saw, but only for an instant; a convulsive movement of the Princess, bending over the body while a strange low cry came from her lips, covered it up. He looked about him for the weapon, for the pistol, but in her rush at the bed she had pushed it out of sight with her knees. 'It's a pity they found it—if he hadn't had it here!' he wailed to her under his breath. He had determined to remain calm, so that, on turning round at the quick advent of the little woman of the house, who had hurried up, white, staring, scared by the sound of the smashed door, he was able to say very quietly and gravely: 'Mr Robinson has shot himself through the heart. He must have done it while you were fetching the milk.' The Princess rose, hearing another person in the room, and then Schinkel caught sight of the small revolver lying just under the bed. He picked it up and carefully placed it on the mantel-shelf—keeping all to himself, with an equal prudence, the reflexion that it would certainly have served much better for the Duke.